THE ROBOT COLLECTION

THE ROBOT NOVELS

The Caves of Steel
The Naked Sun

◎

THE COMPLETE ROBOT

Isaac Asimov

THE ROBOT COLLECTION

THE ROBOT NOVELS

The Caves of Steel
The Naked Sun

◎

THE COMPLETE ROBOT

DOUBLEDAY & COMPANY, INC.
GARDEN CITY, NEW YORK

Library of Congress Cataloging in Publication Data

Asimov, Isaac, 1920—
The robot collection.

Contents: The caves of steel — The naked sun —
The complete robot.
1. Science fiction, American. 2. Automata — Fiction.
I. Title.
PS3551.S5A6 1983   813'.54   83-14093
ISBN 0-385-19152-9

Printed in the United States of America

The Caves of Steel

To my wife, Gertrude,
and my son, David

Contents

1

Conversation With a Commissioner

LIJE BALEY had just reached his desk when he became aware of R. Sammy watching him expectantly.

The dour lines of his long face hardened. "What do you want?"

"The boss wants you, Lije. Right away. Soon as you come in."

"All right."

R. Sammy stood there blankly.

Baley said, "I said, all right. Go away!"

R. Sammy turned on his heel and left to go about his duties. Baley wondered irritably why those same duties couldn't be done by a man.

He paused to examine the contents of his tobacco pouch and make a mental calculation. At two pipefuls a day, he could stretch it to next quota day.

Then he stepped out from behind his railing (he'd rated a railed corner two years ago) and walked the length of the common room.

Simpson looked up from a merc-pool file as he passed. "Boss wants you, Lije."

"I know. R. Sammy told me."

A closely coded tape reeled out of the merc-pool's vitals as the small instrument searched and analyzed its "memory" for the desired information stored in the tiny vibration patterns of the gleaming mercury surface within.

"I'd kick R. Sammy's behind if I weren't afraid I'd break a leg," said Simpson. "I saw Vince Barrett the other day."

"Oh?"

"He was looking for his job back. Or any job in the Department. The poor kid's desperate, but what could I tell him. R. Sammy's doing his job and that's all. The kid has to work a delivery tread on the yeast farms now. He was a bright boy, too. Everyone liked him."

Baley shrugged and said in a manner stiffer than he intended or felt, "It's a thing we're all living through."

The boss rated a private office. It said JULIUS ENDERBY on the clouded glass. Nice letters. Carefully etched into the fabric of the glass. Underneath, it said COMMISSIONER OF POLICE, CITY OF NEW YORK.

Baley stepped in and said, "You want to see me, Commissioner?"

Enderby looked up. He wore spectacles because his eyes were sensitive and couldn't take the usual contact lenses. It was only after one got used to the sight of them that one could take in the rest of the face, which was quite undistinguished. Baley had a strong notion that the Commissioner valued his glasses for the personality they lent him and suspected that his eyeballs weren't as sensitive as all that.

The Commissioner looked definitely nervous. He straightened his cuffs, leaned back, and said, too heartily, "Sit down, Lije. Sit down."

Baley sat down stiffly and waited.

Enderby said, "How's Jessie? And the boy?"

"Fine," said Baley, hollowly. "Just fine. And your family?"

"Fine," echoed Enderby. "Just fine."

It had been a false start.

Baley thought: Something's wrong with his face.

Aloud, he said, "Commissioner, I wish you wouldn't send R. Sammy out after me."

"Well, you know how I feel about those things, Lije. But he's been put here and I've got to use him for something."

"It's uncomfortable, Commissioner. He tells me you want me and then he stands there. You know what I mean. I have to tell him to go or he just keeps on standing there."

"Oh, that's my fault, Lije. I gave him the message to deliver and forgot to tell him specifically to get back to his job when he was through."

Baley sighed. The fine wrinkles about his intensely brown eyes grew more pronounced. "Anyway, you wanted to see me."

"Yes, Lije," said the Commissioner, "but not for anything easy."

He stood up, turned away, and walked to the wall behind his desk. He touched an inconspicuous contact switch and a section of the wall grew transparent.

Baley blinked at the unexpected insurge of grayish light.

The Commissioner smiled. "I had this arranged specially last year, Lije. I don't think I've showed it to you before. Come over here and take a look. In the old days, all rooms had things like this. They were called 'windows.' Did you know that?"

Baley knew that very well, having viewed many historical novels.

"I've heard of them," he said.

"Come here."

Baley squirmed a bit, but did as he was told. There was something indecent about the exposure of the privacy of a room to the outside world. Sometimes the Commissioner carried his affectation of Medievalism to a rather foolish extreme.

Like his glasses, Baley thought.

That was it! That was what made him look wrong!

Baley said, "Pardon me, Commissioner, but you're wearing new glasses, aren't you?"

The Commissioner stared at him in mild surprise, took off his glasses, looked at them and then at Baley. Without his glasses, his round face seemed rounder and his chin a trifle more pronounced. He looked vaguer, too, as his eyes failed to focus properly.

He said, "Yes."

He put his glasses back on his nose, then added with real anger, "I broke my old ones three days ago. What with one thing or another I wasn't able to replace them till this morning. Lije, those three days were hell."

"On account of the glasses?"

"And other things, too. I'm getting to that."

He turned to the window and so did Baley. With mild shock, Baley realized it was raining. For a minute, he was lost in the spectacle of water dropping from the sky, while the Commissioner exuded a kind of pride as though the phenomenon were a matter of his own arranging.

"This is the third time this month I've watched it rain. Quite a sight, don't you think?"

Against his will, Baley had to admit to himself that it was impressive. In his forty-two years he had rarely seen rain, or any of the phenomena of nature, for that matter.

He said, "It always seems a waste for all that water to come down on the city. It should restrict itself to the reservoirs."

"Lije," said the Commissioner, "you're a modernist. That's your trouble. In Medieval times, people lived in the open. I don't mean on the farms only. I mean in the cities, too. Even in New York. When it rained, they didn't think of it as waste. They gloried in it. They lived close to nature. It's healthier, better. The troubles of modern life come from being divorced from nature. Read up on the Coal Century, sometimes."

Baley had. He had heard many people moaning about the invention of the atomic pile. He moaned about it himself when things went wrong, or when he got tired. Moaning like that was a built-in facet of human nature. Back in the Coal Century, people moaned about the invention of the steam engine. In one of Shakespeare's plays, a character moaned about the invention of gunpowder. A thousand years in the future, they'd be moaning about the invention of the positronic brain.

The hell with it.

He said, grimly, "Look, Julius." (It wasn't his habit to get friendly with the Commissioner during office hours, however many 'Lijes' the Commissioner threw at him, but something special seemed called for here.) "Look, Julius, you're talking about everything except what I came in here for, and it's worrying me. What is it?"

The Commissioner said, "I'll get to it, Lije. Let me do it my way. It's—it's trouble."

"Sure. What isn't on this planet? More trouble with the R's?"

"In a way, yes, Lije. I stand here and wonder how much more trouble the old world can take. When I put in this window, I wasn't just letting in the sky once in a while. I let in the City. I look at it and I wonder what will become of it in another century."

Baley felt repelled by the other's sentimentality, but he found himself staring outward in fascination. Even dimmed by the weather, the City was a tremendous thing to see. The Police Department was in the upper levels of City Hall, and City Hall reached high. From the Commissioner's window, the neighboring towers fell short and the tops were visible. They were so many fingers, groping upward. Their walls were blank, featureless. They were the outer shells of human hives.

"In a way," said the Commissioner, "I'm sorry it's raining. We can't see Spacetown."

Baley looked westward, but it was as the Commissioner said. The horizon closed down. New York's towers grew misty and came to an end against blank whiteness.

"I know what Spacetown is like," said Baley.

"I like the picture from here," said the Commissioner. "It can just be made out in the gap between the two Brunswick Sectors. Low domes spread out. It's the difference between us and the Spacers. We reach high and crowd close. With them, each family has a dome for itself. One family: one house. And land between each dome. Have you ever spoken to any of the Spacers, Lije?"

"A few times. About a month ago, I spoke to one right here on your intercom," Baley said, patiently.

"Yes, I remember. But then, I'm just getting philosophical. We and they. Different ways of life."

Baley's stomach was beginning to constrict a little. The more devious the Commissioner's approach, the deadlier he thought might be the conclusion.

He said, "All right. But what's so surprising about it? You can't spread eight billion people over Earth in little domes. They've got space on their worlds, so let them live their way."

The Commissioner walked to his chair and sat down. His eyes looked unblinkingly at Baley, shrunken a bit by the concave lenses in his spectacles. He said, "Not everyone is that tolerant about differences in culture. Either among us or among the Spacers."

"All right. So what?"

"So three days ago, a Spacer died."

Now it was coming. The corners of Baley's thin lips raised a trifle, but the effect upon his long, sad face was unnoticeable. He said, "Too bad. Something contagious, I hope. A virus. A cold, perhaps."

The Commissioner looked startled, "What are you talking about?"

Baley didn't care to explain. The precision with which the Spacers had bred disease out of their societies was well known. The care with which they avoided, as far as possible, contact with disease-riddled Earthmen was even better known. But then, sarcasm was lost on the Commissioner.

Baley said, "I'm just talking. What did he die of?" He turned back to the window.

The Commissioner said, "He died of a missing chest. Someone had used a blaster on him."

Baley's back grew rigid. He said, without turning, "What are *you* talking about?"

"I'm talking about murder," said the Commissioner, softly. "You're a plain-clothes man. You know what murder is."

And now Baley turned. "But a Spacer! Three days ago?"

"Yes."

"But who did it? How?"

"The Spacers say it was an Earthman."

"It can't be."

"Why not? You don't like the Spacers. I don't. Who on Earth does? Someone didn't like them a little too much, that's all."

"Sure, but——"

"There was the fire at the Los Angeles factories. There was the Berlin R-smashing. There were the riots in Shanghai."

"All right."

"It all points to rising discontent. Maybe to some sort of organization."

Baley said, "Commissioner, I don't get this. Are you testing me for some reason?"

"What?" The Commissioner looked honestly bewildered.

Baley watched him. "Three days ago a Spacer was murdered and the Spacers think the murderer is an Earthman. Till now," his finger tapped the desk, "nothing's come out. Is that right? Commissioner, that's unbelievable. Jehoshaphat, Commissioner, a thing like this would blow New York off the face of the planet if it really happened."

The Commissioner shook his head. "It's not as simple as that. Look, Lije, I've been out three days. I've been in conference with the Mayor. I've been out to Spacetown. I've been down in Washington, talking to the Terrestrial Bureau of Investigation."

"Oh? And what do the Terries have to say?"

"They say it's our baby. It's inside city limits. Spacetown is under New York jurisdiction."

"But *with* extraterritorial rights."

"I know. I'm coming to that." The Commissioner's eyes fell away from Baley's flinty stare. He seemed to regard himself as having been suddenly demoted to the position of Baley's underling, and Baley behaved as though he accepted the fact.

"The Spacers can run the show," said Baley.

"Wait a minute, Lije," pleaded the Commissioner. "Don't rush me. I'm trying to talk this over, friend to friend. I want you to know my position. I was there when the news broke. I had an appointment with him—with Roj Nemennuh Sarton."

"The victim?"

"The victim." The Commissioner groaned. "Five minutes more and I, myself, would have discovered the body. What a shock that would have been. As it was, it was brutal, brutal. They met me and told me. It started a three-day nightmare, Lije. That on top of having everything blur on me and having no time to replace my glasses for days. *That* won't happen again, at least. I've ordered three pairs."

Baley considered the picture he conjured up of the event. He could see the tall, fair figures of the Spacers approaching the Commissioner with the news and breaking it to him in their unvarnished emotionless way. Julius would remove his glasses and polish them. Inevitably, under the impact of the event, he would drop them, then look down at the broken remnants with a quiver of his soft, full lips. Baley was quite certain that, for five minutes anyway, the Commissioner was much more disturbed over his glasses than over the murder.

The Commissioner was saying, "It's a devil of a position. As you say, the Spacers have extraterritorial rights. They *can* insist on their own investigation, make whatever report they wish to their home governments. The Outer Worlds could use this as an excuse to pile on indemnity charges. You know how *that* would sit with the population."

"It would be political suicide for the White House to agree to pay."

"And another kind of suicide not to pay."

"You don't have to draw me a picture," said Baley. He had been a small boy when the gleaming cruisers from outer space last sent down their soldiers into Washington, New York, and Moscow to collect what they claimed was theirs.

"Then you see. Pay or not pay, it's trouble. The only way out is to find the murderer on our own and hand him over to the Spacers. It's up to us."

"Why not give it to the TBI? Even if it is our jurisdiction from a legalistic viewpoint, there's the question of interstellar relations——"

"The TBI won't touch it. This is *hot* and it's in our lap." For a moment, he lifted his head and gazed keenly at his subordinate.

"And it's not good, Lije. Every one of us stands the chance of being out of a job."

Baley said, "Replace us all? Nuts. The trained men to do it with don't exist."

"R's," said the Commissioner. "*They* exist."

"What?"

"R. Sammy is just a beginning. He runs errands. Others can patrol the expressways. Damn it, man, I know the Spacers better than you do, and I know what they're doing. There are R's that can do your work and mine. We can be declassified. Don't think differently. And at our age, to hit the labor pool . . ."

Baley said, gruffly, "All right."

The Commissioner looked abashed. "Sorry, Lije."

Baley nodded and tried not to think of his father. The Commissioner knew the story, of course.

Baley said, "When did all this replacement business come up?"

"Look, you're being naïve, Lije. It's been happening all along. It's been happening for twenty-five years, ever since the Spacers came. You know that. It's just beginning to reach higher, that's all. If we muff this case, it's a big, long step toward the point where we can stop looking forward to collecting our pension-tab booklets. On the other hand, Lije, if we handle the matter well, it can shove that point far into the future. And it would be a particular break for you."

"For me?" said Baley.

"You'll be the operative in charge, Lije."

"I don't rate it, Commissioner. I'm a C-5, that's all."

"You want a C-6 rating, don't you?"

Did he? Baley knew the privileges a C-6 rating carried. A seat on the expressway in the rush hour, not just from ten to four. Higher up on the list-of-choice at the Section kitchens. Maybe even a chance at a better apartment and a quota ticket to the Solarium levels for Jessie.

"I want it," he said. "Sure. Why wouldn't I? But what would I get if I couldn't break the case?"

"Why wouldn't you break it, Lije?" the Commissioner wheedled. "You're a good man. You're one of the best we have."

"But there are half a dozen men with higher ratings in my department section. Why should they be passed over?"

Baley did not say out loud, though his bearing implied it strongly, that the Commissioner did not move outside protocol in this fashion except in cases of wild emergency.

The Commissioner folded his hands. "Two reasons. You're not just another detective to me, Lije. We're friends, too. I'm not forgetting we were in college together. Sometimes it may look as though I have forgotten, but that's the fault of rating. I'm Commissioner, and you know what that means. But I'm still your friend and this is a tremendous chance for the right person. I want you to have it."

"That's one reason," said Baley, without warmth.

"The second reason is that I think you're my friend. I need a favor."

"What sort of favor?"

"I want you to take on a Spacer partner in this deal. That was the condition the Spacers made. They've agreed not to report the murder; they've agreed to leave the investigation in our hands. In return, they insist one of their own agents be in on the deal, the whole deal."

"It sounds like they don't trust us altogether."

"Surely you see their point. If this is mishandled, a number of them will be in trouble with their own governments. I'll give them the benefit of the doubt, Lije. I'm willing to believe they mean well."

"I'm sure they do, Commissioner. That's the trouble with them."

The Commissioner looked blank at that, but went on. "Are you willing to take on a Spacer partner, Lije?"

"You're asking that as a favor?"

"Yes, I'm asking you to take the job with all the conditions the Spacers have set up."

"I'll take a Spacer partner, Commissioner."

"Thanks, Lije. He'll have to live with you."

"Oh, now, hold on."

"I know. I know. But you've got a large apartment, Lije. Three rooms. Only one child. You can put him up. He'll be no trouble. No trouble at all. And it's necessary."

"Jessie won't like it. I know that."

"You tell Jessie," the Commissioner was earnest, so earnest that his eyes seemed to bore holes through the glass discs blocking his stare, "that if you do this for me, I'll do what I can when this is all over to jump you a grade. C-7, Lije. C-7!"

"All right, Commissioner, it's a deal."

Baley half rose from his chair, caught the look on Enderby's face, and sat down again.

"There's something else?"

Slowly, the Commissioner nodded. "One more item."

"Which is?"

"The name of your partner."

"What difference does that make?"

"The Spacers," said the Commissioner, "have peculiar ways. The partner they're supplying isn't—isn't . . ."

Baley's eyes opened wide. "Just a minute!"

"You've got to, Lije. You've *got* to. There's no way out."

"Stay at my apartment? A thing like that?"

"As a friend, please!"

"No. *No!*"

"Lije, I can't trust anyone else in this. Do I have to spell it out for you? We've *got* to work with the Spacers. We've got to succeed, if we're to keep the indemnity ships away from Earth. But we can't succeed just any old way. You'll be partnered with one of their R's. If *he* breaks the case, if he can report that we're incompetent, we're ruined, anyway. We, as a department. You see that, don't you? So you've got a delicate job on your hands. You've got to work with him, but see to it that *you* solve the case and not he. Understand?"

"You mean co-operate with him 100 per cent, except that I cut his throat? Pat him on the back with a knife in my hand?"

"What else can we do? There's no other way out."

Lije Baley stood irresolute. "I don't know what Jessie will say."

"I'll talk to her, if you want me to."

"No, Commissioner." He drew a deep, sighing breath. "What's my partner's name?"

"R. Daneel Olivaw."

Baley said, sadly, "This isn't a time for euphemism, Commissioner. I'm taking the job, so let's use his full name. *Robot* Daneel Olivaw."

2

Round Trip on an Expressway

THERE WAS the usual, entirely normal crowd on the expressway: the standees on the lower level and those with seat privileges above. A continuous trickle of humanity filtered off the expressway, across the decelerating strips to localways or into the stationaries that led under arches or over bridges into the endless mazes of the City Sections. Another trickle, just as continuous, worked inward from the other side, across the accelerating strips and onto the expressway.

There were the infinite lights: the luminous walls and ceilings that seemed to drip cool, even phosphorescence; the flashing advertisements screaming for attention; the harsh, steady gleam of the "lightworms" that directed THIS WAY TO JERSEY SECTIONS, FOLLOW ARROWS TO EAST RIVER SHUTTLE, UPPER LEVEL FOR ALL WAYS TO LONG ISLAND SECTIONS.

Most of all there was the noise that was inseparable from life: the sound of millions talking, laughing, coughing, calling, humming, breathing.

No directions anywhere to Spacetown, thought Baley.

He stepped from strip to strip with the ease of a lifetime's practice. Children learned to "hop the strips" as soon as they learned to walk. Baley scarcely felt the jerk of acceleration as his velocity increased with each step. He was not even aware that he leaned forward against the force. In thirty seconds he had reached the final sixty-mile-an-hour strip and could step aboard the railed and glassed-in moving platform that was the expressway.

No directions to Spacetown, he thought.

No need for directions. If you've business there, you know the

way. If you don't know the way, you've no business there. When
Spacetown was first established some twenty-five years earlier, there
was a strong tendency to make a showplace out of it. The hordes
of the City herded in that direction.

The Spacers put a stop to that. Politely (they were always polite),
but without any compromise with tact, they put up a force barrier
between themselves and the City. They established a combination
Immigration Service and Customs Inspection. If you had business,
you identified yourself, allowed yourself to be searched, and submitted to a medical examination and a routine disinfection.

It gave rise to dissatisfaction. Naturally. More dissatisfaction than
it deserved. Enough dissatisfaction to put a serious spoke in the program of modernization. Baley remembered the Barrier Riots. He
had been part of the mob that had suspended itself from the rails
of the expressways, crowded onto the seats in disregard of rating
privileges, run recklessly along and across the strips at the risk of a
broken body, and remained just outside the Spacetown barrier for
two days, shouting slogans and destroying City property out of sheer
frustration.

Baley could still sing the chants of the time if he put his mind to
it. There was "Man Was Born on Mother Earth, Do You Hear?" to
an old folk tune with the gibberish refrain, "Hinky-dinky-parley-
voo."

"Man was born on Mother Earth, do you hear?
Earth's the world that gave him birth. do you hear?
Spacer, get you off the face
Of Mother Earth and into space.
Dirty Spacer, do you hear?"

There were hundreds of verses. A few were witty, most were stupid, many were obscene. Every one, however, ended with "Dirty
Spacer, do you hear?" Dirty, dirty. It was the futile throwing back
in the face of the Spacers their most keenly felt insult: their insistence on considering the natives of Earth as disgustingly diseased.

The Spacers didn't leave, of course. It wasn't even necessary for
them to bring any of their offensive weapons into play. Earth's outmoded fleet had long since learned that it was suicide to venture near
any Outer World ship. Earth planes that had ventured over the
Spacetown area in the very early days of its establishment had sim-

ply disappeared. At the most, a shredded wing tip might tumble down to Earth.

And no mob could be so maddened as to forget the effect of the subetheric hand disruptors used on Earthmen in the wars of a century ago.

So the Spacers sat behind their barrier, which itself was the product of their own advanced science, and that no method existed on Earth of breaking. They just waited stolidly on the other side of the barrier until the City quieted the mob with somno vapor and retch gas. The below-level penitentiaries rattled afterward with ringleaders, malcontents, and people who had been picked up simply because they were nearest at hand. After a while they were all set free.

After a proper interval, the Spacers eased their restrictions. The barrier was removed and the City Police entrusted with the protection of Spacetown's isolation. Most important of all, the medical examination was more unobtrusive.

Now, thought Baley, things might take a reverse trend. If the Spacers seriously thought that an Earthman had entered Spacetown and committed murder, the barrier might go up again. It would be bad.

He lifted himself onto the expressway platform, made his way through the standees to the tight spiral ramp that led to the upper level, and there sat down. He didn't put his rating ticket in his hatband till they passed the last of the Hudson Sections. A C-5 had no seat rights east of the Hudson and west of Long Island, and although there was ample seating available at the moment, one of the way guards would have automatically ousted him. People were increasingly petty about rating privileges and, in all honesty, Baley lumped himself in with "people."

The air made the characteristic whistling noise as it frictioned off the curved windshields set up above the back of every seat. It made talking a chore, but it was no bar to thinking when you were used to it.

Most Earthmen were Medievalists in one way or another. It was an easy thing to be when it meant looking back to a time when Earth was *the* world and not just one of fifty. The misfit one of fifty at that.

Baley's head snapped to the right at the sound of a female shriek.

A woman had dropped her handbag; he saw it for an instant, a pastel pink blob against the dull gray of the strips. A passenger hurrying from the expressway must inadvertently have kicked it in the direction of deceleration and now the owner was whirling away from her property.

A corner of Baley's mouth quirked. She might catch up with it, if she were clever enough to hurry to a strip that moved slower still and if other feet did not kick it this way or that. He would never know whether she would or not. The scene was half a mile to the rear, already.

Chances were she wouldn't. It had been calculated that, on the average, something was dropped on the strips every three minutes somewhere in the City and not recovered. The Lost and Found Department was a huge proposition. It was just one more complication of modern life.

Baley thought: It was simpler once. Everything was simpler. That's what makes Medievalists.

Medievalism took different forms. To the unimaginative Julius Enderby, it meant the adoption of archaisms. Spectacles! Windows!

To Baley, it was a study of history. Particularly the history of folkways.

The City now! New York City in which he lived and had his being. Larger than any City but Los Angeles. More populous than any but Shanghai. It was only three centuries old.

To be sure, something had existed in the same geographic area before then that had been *called* New York City. That primitive gathering of population had existed for three thousand years, not three hundred, but it hadn't been a *City*.

There were no Cities then. There were just huddles of dwelling places large and small, open to the air. They were something like the Spacer's Domes, only much different, of course. These huddles (the largest barely reached ten million in population and most never reached one million) were scattered all over Earth by the thousands. By modern standards, they had been completely inefficient, economically.

Efficiency had been forced on Earth with increasing population. Two billion people, three billion, even five billion could be supported by the planet by progressive lowering of the standard of living. When the population reaches eight billion, however, semistarvation becomes too much like the real thing. A radical change had to take place in man's culture, particularly when it turned out that the Outer Worlds (which had merely been Earth's colonies a thousand years before) were tremendously serious in their immigration restrictions.

The radical change had been the gradual formation of the Cities over a thousand years of Earth's history. Efficiency implied bigness. Even in Medieval times that had been realized, perhaps unconsciously. Home industry gave way to factories and factories to continental industries.

Think of the inefficiency of a hundred thousand houses for a hundred thousand families as compared with a hundred-thousand-unit Section; a book-film collection in each house as compared with a Section film concentrate; independent video for each family as compared with video-piping systems.

For that matter, take the simple folly of endless duplication of kitchens and bathrooms as compared with the thoroughly efficient diners and shower rooms made possible by City culture.

More and more the villages, towns, and "cities" of Earth died and were swallowed by the Cities. Even the early prospects of atomic war only slowed the trend. With the invention of the force shield, the trend became a headlong race.

City culture meant optimum distribution of food, increasing utilization of yeasts and hydroponics. New York City spread over two thousand square miles and at the last census its population was well over twenty million. There were some eight hundred Cities on Earth, average population, ten million.

Each City became a semiautonomous unit, economically all but self-sufficient. It could roof itself in, gird itself about, burrow itself under. It became a steel cave, a tremendous, self-contained cave of steel and concrete.

It could lay itself out scientifically. At the center was the enormous complex of administrative offices. In careful orientation to one another and to the whole were the large residential Sections connected and interlaced by the expressway and the localways. Toward the outskirts were the factories, the hydroponic plants, the yeast-culture vats, the power plants. Through all the melee were the water pipes and sewage ducts, schools, prisons and shops, power lines and communication beams.

There was no doubt about it: the City was the culmination of man's mastery over the environment. Not space travel, not the fifty colonized worlds that were now so haughtily independent, but the City.

Practically none of Earth's population lived outside the Cities. Outside was the wilderness, the open sky that few men could face with anything like equanimity. To be sure, the open space was necessary. It held the water that men must have, the coal and the wood that were the ultimate raw materials for plastics and for the eternally growing yeast. (Petroleum had long since gone, but oil-rich strains of yeast were an adequate substitute.) The land between the Cities still held the mines, and was still used to a larger extent than most men realized for growing food and grazing stock. It was inefficient, but beef, pork, and grain always found a luxury market and could be used for export purposes.

But few humans were required to run the mines and ranches, to exploit the farms and pipe the water, and these supervised at long distance. Robots did the work better and required less.

Robots! That was the one huge irony. It was on Earth that the positronic brain was invented and on Earth that robots had first been put to productive use.

Not on the Outer Worlds. Of course, the Outer Worlds always acted as though robots had been born of their culture.

In a way, of course, the culmination of robot economy had taken place on the Outer Worlds. Here on Earth, robots had always been restricted to the mines and farmlands. Only in the last quarter century, under the urgings of the Spacers, had robots filtered their slow way into the Cities.

The Cities were good. Everyone but the Medievalists knew that there was no substitute, no reasonable substitute. The only trouble was that they wouldn't stay good. Earth's population was still rising. Some day, with all that the Cities could do, the available calories per person would simply fall below basic subsistence level.

It was all the worse because of the existence of the Spacers, the descendants of the early emigrants from Earth, living in luxury on their underpopulated robot-ridden worlds out in space. They were coolly determined to keep the comfort that grew out of the emptiness of their worlds and for that purpose they kept their birth rate down and immigrants from teeming Earth out. And this——

Spacetown coming up!

A nudge at Baley's unconscious warned him that he was approaching the Newark Section. If he stayed where he was much longer, he'd find himself speeding southwestward to the Trenton Section turning of the way, through the heart of the warm and musty-odored yeast country.

It was a matter of timing. It took so long to shinny down the ramp, so long to squirm through the grunting standees, so long to slip along the railing and out an opening, so long to hop across the decelerating strips.

When he was done, he was precisely at the off-shooting of the proper stationary. At no time did he time his steps consciously. If he had, he would probably have missed.

Baley found himself in unusual semi-isolation. Only a policeman was with him inside the stationary and, except for the whirring of the expressway, there was an almost uncomfortable silence.

The policeman approached, and Baley flashed his badge impatiently. The policeman lifted his hand in permission to pass on.

The passage narrowed and curved sharply three or four times. That was obviously purposeful. Mobs of Earthmen couldn't gather in it with any degree of comfort and direct charges were impossible.

Baley was thankful that the arrangements were for him to meet his partner this side of Spacetown. He didn't like the thought of a medical examination any better for its reputed politeness.

A Spacer was standing at the point where a series of doors marked the openings to the open air and the domes of Spacetown. He was dressed in the Earth fashion, trousers tight at the waist, loose at the ankle, and color-striped down the seam of each leg. He wore an ordinary Textron shirt, open collar, seam-zipped, and ruffled at the wrist, but he was a Spacer. There was something about the way he stood, the way he held his head, the calm and unemotional lines of his broad, high-cheekboned face, the careful set of his short, bronze hair lying flatly backward and without a part, that marked him off from the native Earthman.

Baley approached woodenly and said in a monotone, "I am Plainclothes Man Elijah Baley, Police Department, City of New York, Rating C-5."

He showed his credentials and went on, "I have been instructed to meet R. Daneel Olivaw at Spacetown Approachway." He looked

2

at his watch. "I am a little early. May I request the announcement of my presence?"

He felt more than a little cold inside. He was used, after a fashion, to the Earth-model robots. The Spacer models would be different. He had never met one, but there was nothing more common on Earth than the horrid whispered stories about the tremendous and formidable robots that worked in superhuman fashion on the far-off, glittering Outer Worlds. He found himself gritting his teeth.

The Spacer, who had listened politely, said, "It will not be necessary. I have been waiting for you."

Baley's hand went up automatically, then dropped. So did his long chin, looking longer in the process. He didn't quite manage to say anything. The words froze.

The Spacer said, "I shall introduce myself. I am R. Daneel Olivaw."

"Yes? Am I making a mistake? I thought the first initial——"

"Quite so. I am a robot. Were you not told?"

"I was told." Baley put a damp hand to his hair and smoothed it back unnecessarily. Then he held it out. "I'm sorry, Mr. Olivaw. I don't know what I was thinking of. Good day. I am Elijah Baley, your partner."

"Good." The robot's hand closed on his with a smoothly increasing pressure that reached a comfortably friendly peak, then declined. "Yet I seem to detect disturbance. May I ask that you be frank with me? It is best to have as many relevant facts as possible in a relationship such as ours. And it is customary on my world for partners to call one another by the familiar name. I trust that that is not counter to your own customs."

"It's just, you see, that you don't look like a robot," said Baley, desperately.

"And that disturbs you?"

"It shouldn't, I suppose, Da-Daneel. Are they all like you on your world?"

"There are individual differences, Elijah, as with men."

"Our own robots . . . Well, you can tell they're robots, you understand. You look like a Spacer."

"Oh, I see. You expected a rather crude model and were surprised. Yet it is only logical that our people use a robot of pronounced humanoid characteristics in this case if we expected to avoid unpleasantness. Is that not so?"

It was certainly so. An obvious robot roaming the City would be in quick trouble.

Baley said, "Yes."

"Then let us leave now, Elijah."

They made their way back to the expressway. R. Daneel caught the purpose of the accelerating strips and maneuvered along them with a quick proficiency. Baley, who had begun by moderating his speed, ended by hastening it in annoyance.

The robot kept pace. He showed no awareness of any difficulty. Baley wondered if R. Daneel were not deliberately moving slower than he might. He reached the endless cars of expressway and scrambled aboard with what amounted to outright recklessness. The robot followed easily.

Baley was red. He swallowed twice and said, "I'll stay down here with you."

"Down here?" The robot, apparently oblivious to both the noise and the rhythmic swaying of the platform said, "Is my information wrong? I was told that a rating of C-5 entitled one to a seat on the upper level under certain conditions."

"You're right. I can go up there, but you can't."

"Why can I not go up with you?"

"It takes a C-5, Daneel."

"I am aware of that."

"You're not a C-5." Talking was difficult. The hiss of frictioning air was louder on the less shielded lower level and Baley was understandably anxious to keep his voice low.

R. Daneel said, "Why should I not be a C-5? I am your partner and, consequently, of equal rank. I was given this."

From an inner shirt pocket he produced a rectangular credential card, quite genuine. The name given was Daneel Olivaw, without the all-important initial. The rating was C-5.

"Come on up," said Baley, woodenly.

Baley looked straight ahead, once seated, angry with himself, very conscious of the robot sitting next to him. He had been caught twice. First he had not recognized R. Daneel as a robot; secondly, he had not guessed the logic that demanded R. Daneel be given C-5 rating.

The trouble was, of course, that he was not the plain-clothes man of popular myth. He was not incapable of surprise, imperturbable of appearance, infinite of adaptability, and lightning of mental grasp. He had never supposed he was, but he had never regretted the lack before.

What made him regret it was that, to all appearances, R. Daneel Olivaw *was* that very myth, embodied.

He had to be. He was a robot.

Baley began to find excuses for himself. He was accustomed to the robots like R. Sammy at the office. He had expected a creature with a skin of a hard and glossy plastic, nearly dead white in color. He had expected an expression fixed at an unreal level of inane good humor. He had expected jerky, faintly uncertain motions.

R. Daneel was none of it.

Baley risked a quick side glance at the robot. R. Daneel turned simultaneously to meet his eye and nod gravely. His lips had moved naturally when he had spoken and did not simply remain parted as those of Earth robots did. There had been glimpses of an articulating tongue.

Baley thought: Why does he have to sit there so calmly? This must be something completely new to him. Noise, lights, crowds!

Baley got up, brushed past R. Daneel, and said, "Follow me!"

Off the expressway, down the decelerating strips.

Baley thought: Good Lord, what do I tell Jessie, anyway?

The coming of the robot had rattled that thought out of his head, but it was coming back with sickening urgency now that they were heading down the localway that led into the very jaws of the Lower Bronx Section.

He said, "This is all one building, you know, Daneel; everything you see, the whole City. Twenty million people live in it. The expressways go continuously, night and day, at sixty miles an hour. There are two hundred and fifty miles of it altogether and hundreds of miles of localways."

Any minute now, Baley thought, I'll be figuring out how many tons of yeast product New York eats per day and how many cubic feet of water we drink and how many megawatts of power the atomic piles deliver per hour.

Daneel said, "I was informed of this and other similar data in my briefing."

Baley thought: Well, that covers the food, drink, and power situation, too, I suppose. Why try to impress a robot?

They were at East 182nd Street and in not more than two hundred yards they would be at the elevator banks that fed those steel and concrete layers of apartments that included his own.

He was on the point of saying, "This way," when he was stopped by a knot of people gathering outside the brilliantly lighted force door of one of the many retail departments that lined the ground levels solidly in this Section.

He asked of the nearest person in an automatic tone of authority, "What's going on?"

The man he addressed, who was standing on tiptoe, said, "Damned if I know. I just got here."

Someone else said, excitedly, "They got those lousy R's in there. I think maybe they'll throw them out here. Boy, I'd like to take them apart."

Baley looked nervously at Daneel, but, if the latter caught the significance of the words or even heard them, he did not show it by any outward sign.

Baley plunged into the crowd. "Let me through. Let me through. Police!"

They made way. Baley caught words behind him.

". . . take them apart. Nut by nut. Split them down the seams slowlike . . ." And someone else laughed.

Baley turned a little cold. The City was the acme of efficiency, but it made demands of its inhabitants. It asked them to live in a tight routine and order their lives under a strict and scientific control. Occasionally, built-up inhibitions exploded.

He remembered the Barrier Riots.

Reasons for anti-robot rioting certainly existed. Men who found themselves faced with the prospect of the desperate minimum involved in declassification, after half a lifetime of effort, could not decide cold-bloodedly that individual robots were not to blame. Individual robots could at least be struck at.

One could not strike at something called "governmental policy" or at a slogan like "Higher production with robot labor."

The government called it growing pains. It shook its collective head sorrowfully and assured everyone that after a necessary period of adjustment, a new and better life would exist for all.

But the Medievalist movement expanded along with the declassification process. Men grew desperate and the border between bitter frustration and wild destruction is sometimes easily crossed.

At this moment, minutes could be separating the pent-up hostility of the crowd from a flashing orgy of blood and smash.

Baley writhed his way desperately to the force door.

3

Incident at a Shoe Counter

THE INTERIOR of the store was emptier than the street outside. The manager, with commendable foresight, had thrown the force door early in the game, preventing potential troublemakers from entering. It also kept the principals in the argument from leaving, but that was minor.

Baley got through the force door by using his officer's neutralizer. Unexpectedly, he found R. Daneel still behind him. The robot was pocketing a neutralizer of his own, a slim one, smaller and neater than the standard police model.

The manager ran to them instantly, talking loudly. "Officers, my clerks have been assigned me by the City. I am perfectly within my rights."

There were three robots standing rodlike at the rear of the department. Six humans were standing near the force door. They were all women.

"All right, now," said Baley, crisply. "What's going on? What's all the fuss about?"

One of the women said, shrilly, "I came in for shoes. Why can't I have a decent clerk? Ain't I respectable?" Her clothing, especially her hat, were just sufficiently extreme to make it more than a rhetorical question. The angry flush that covered her face masked imperfectly her overdone makeup.

The manager said, "I'll wait on her myself if I have to, but I can't wait on all of them, Officer. There's nothing wrong with my men. They're registered clerks. I have their spec charts and guarantee slips——"

"Spec charts," screamed the woman. She laughed shrilly, turning to the rest. "Listen to him. He calls them men! What's the matter with you anyway? They ain't men. They're ro-bots!" She stretched out the syllables. "And I tell you what they do, in case you don't know. They steal jobs from men. That's why the government always protects them. They work for nothin' and, on account o' that, families gotta live out in the barracks and eat raw yeast mush. Decent hard-working families. We'd smash up all the ro-bots, if *I* was boss. I tell you that!"

The others talked confusedly and there was always the growing rumble from the crowd just beyond the force door.

Baley was conscious, brutally conscious, of R. Daneel Olivaw standing at his elbow. He looked at the clerks. They were Earthmade, and even on that scale, relatively inexpensive models. They were just robots made to know a few simple things. They would know all the style numbers, their prices, the sizes available in each. They could keep track of stock fluctuations, probably better than humans could, since they would have no outside interests. They could compute the proper orders for the next week. They could measure the customer's foot.

In themselves, harmless. As a group, incredibly dangerous.

Baley could sympathize with the woman more deeply than he would have believed possible the day before. No, two hours before. He could feel R. Daneel's nearness and he wondered if R. Daneel could not replace an ordinary plain-clothes man C-5. He could see the barracks, as he thought that. He could taste the yeast mush. He could remember his father.

His father had been a nuclear physicist, with a rating that had put him in the top percentile of the City. There had been an accident at the power plant and his father had borne the blame. He had been declassified. Baley did not know the details; it had happened when he was a year old.

But he remembered the barracks of his childhood; the grinding communal existence just this side of the edge of bearability. He remembered his mother not at all; she had not survived long. His father he recalled well, a sodden man, morose and lost, speaking sometimes of the past in hoarse, broken sentences.

His father died, still declassified, when Lije was eight. Young Baley and his two older sisters moved into the Section orphanage.

Children's Level, they called it. His mother's brother, Uncle Boris, was himself too poor to prevent that.

So it continued hard. And it was hard going through school, with no father-derived status privileges to smooth the way.

And now he had to stand in the middle of a growing riot and beat down men and women who, after all, only feared declassification for themselves and those they loved, as he himself did.

Tonelessly, he said to the woman who had already spoken, "Let's not have any trouble, lady. The clerks aren't doing you any harm."

"Sure they ain't done me no harm," sopranoed the woman. "They ain't gonna, either. Think I'll let their cold, greasy fingers touch me? I came in here expecting to get treated like a human being. I'm a citizen. I got a right to have human beings wait on me. And listen, I got two kids waiting for supper. They can't go to the Section kitchen without me, like they was orphans. I gotta get out of here."

"Well, now," said Baley, feeling his temper slipping, "if you had let yourself be waited on, you'd have been out of here by now. You're just making trouble for nothing. Come on now."

"Well!" The woman registered shock. "Maybe you think you can talk to me like I was dirt. Maybe it's time the guv'min' reelized robots ain't the only things on Earth. I'm a hard-working woman and I've got rights." She went on and on and on.

Baley felt harassed and caught. The situation was out of hand. Even if the woman would consent to be waited on, the waiting crowd was ugly enough for anything.

There must be a hundred crammed outside the display window now. In the few minutes since the plain-clothes men had entered the store, the crowd had doubled.

"What is the usual procedure in such a case?" asked R. Daneel Olivaw, suddenly.

Baley nearly jumped. He said, "This is an unusual case in the first place."

"What is the law?"

"The R's have been duly assigned here. They're registered clerks. There's nothing illegal about that."

They were speaking in whispers. Baley tried to look official and threatening. Olivaw's expression, as always, meant nothing at all.

"In that case," said R. Daneel, "order the woman to let herself be waited on or to leave."

Baley lifted a corner of his lip briefly. "It's a mob we have to deal with, not a woman. There's nothing to do but call a riot squad."

"It should not be necessary for citizens to require more than one officer of the law to direct what should be done," said Daneel.

He turned his broad face to the store manager. "Open the force door, sir."

Baley's arm shot forward to seize R. Daneel's shoulder, swing him about. He arrested the motion. If, at this moment, two law men quarreled openly, it would mean the end of all chance for a peaceful solution.

The manager protested, looked at Baley. Baley did not meet his eye.

R. Daneel said, unmoved, "I order you with the authority of the law."

The manager bleated, "I'll hold the City responsible for any damage to the goods or fixtures. I serve notice that I'm doing this under orders."

The barrier went down; men and women crowded in. There was a happy roar from them. They sensed victory.

Baley had heard of similar riots. He had even witnessed one. He had seen robots being lifted by a dozen hands, their heavy unresisting bodies carried backward from straining arm to straining arm. Men yanked and twisted at the metal mimicry of men. They used hammers, force knives, needle guns. They finally reduced the miserable objects to shredded metal and wire. Expensive positronic brains, the most intricate creation of the human mind, were thrown from hand to hand like footballs and mashed to uselessness in a trifle of time.

Then, with the genius of destruction so merrily let loose, the mobs turned on anything else that could be taken apart.

The robot clerks could have no knowledge of any of this, but they squealed as the crowd flooded inward and lifted their arms before their faces as though in a primitive effort at hiding. The woman who had started the fuss, frightened at seeing it grow suddenly so far beyond what she had expected, gasped, "Here, now. Here, now."

Her hat was shoved down over her face and her voice became only a meaningless shrillness.

The manager was shrieking, "Stop them, Officer. Stop them!"

R. Daneel spoke. Without apparent effort, his voice was suddenly decibels higher than a human's voice had a right to be. Of course, thought Baley for the tenth time, he's not——

R. Daneel said, "The next man who moves will be shot."

Someone well in the back yelled, "Get him!"

But for a moment, no one moved.

R. Daneel stepped nimbly upon a chair and from that to the top of a Transtex display case. The colored fluorescence gleaming through the slits of polarized molecular film turned his cool, smooth face into something unearthly.

Unearthly, thought Baley.

The tableau held as R. Daneel waited, a quietly formidable person.

R. Daneel said crisply, "You are saying, This man is holding a neuronic whip, or a tickler. If we all rush forward, we will bear him down and at most one or two of us will be hurt and even they will recover. Meanwhile, we will do just as we wish and to space with law and order."

His voice was neither harsh nor angry, but it carried authority. It had the tone of confident command. He went on, "You are mistaken. What I hold is not a neuronic whip, nor is it a tickler. It is a blaster and very deadly. I will use it and I will not aim over your heads. I will kill many of you before you seize me, perhaps most of you. I am serious. I look serious, do I not?"

There was motion at the outskirts, but the crowd no longer grew. If newcomers still stopped out of curiosity, others were hurrying away. Those nearest R. Daneel were holding their breath, trying desperately not to sway forward in response to the mass pressure of the bodies behind them.

The woman with the hat broke the spell. In a sudden whirlpool of sobbing, she yelled, "He's gonna kill us. I ain't done nothing. Oh, lemme outta here."

She turned, but faced an immovable wall of crammed men and women. She sank to her knees. The backward motion in the silent crowd grew more pronounced.

R. Daneel jumped down from the display counter and said, "I will now walk to the door. I will shoot the man or woman who touches me. When I reach the door, I will shoot any man or woman who is not moving about his business. This woman here——"

"No, no," yelled the woman with the hat, "I tell ya I didn't do nothing. I didn't mean no harm. I don't want no shoes. I just wanta go home."

"This woman here," went on Daneel, "will remain. She will be waited on."

He stepped forward.

The mob faced him dumbly. Baley closed his eyes. It wasn't his fault, he thought desperately. There'll be murder done and the worst mess in the world, but *they* forced a robot on me as partner. *They* gave him equal status.

It wouldn't do. He didn't believe himself. He might have stopped R. Daneel at the start. He might at any moment have put in the call for a squad car. He had let R. Daneel take responsibility, instead, and had felt a cowardly relief. When he tried to tell himself that R. Daneel's personality simply dominated the situation, he was filled with a sudden self-loathing. A *robot* dominating . . .

There was no unusual noise, no shouting and cursing, no groans, no yells. He opened his eyes.

They were dispersing.

The manager of the store was cooling down, adjusting his twisted jacket, smoothing his hair, muttering angry threats at the vanishing crowd.

The smooth, fading whistle of a squad car came to a halt just outside. Baley thought: Sure, when it's all over.

The manager plucked his sleeve. "Let's have no more trouble, Officer."

Baley said, "There won't be any trouble."

It was easy to get rid of the squad-car police. They had come in response to reports of a crowd in the street. They knew no details and could see for themselves that the street was clear. R. Daneel stepped aside and showed no sign of interest as Baley explained to the men in the squad car, minimizing the event and completely burying R. Daneel's part in it.

Afterward, he pulled R. Daneel to one side, against the steel and concrete of one of the building shafts.

"Listen," he said, "I'm not trying to steal your show, you understand."

"Steal my show? Is it one of your Earth idioms?"

"I didn't report your part in this."

"I do not know all your customs. On my world, a complete report is usual, but perhaps it is not so on your world. In any case, civil rebellion was averted. That is the important thing, is it not?"

"Is it? Now you look here." Baley tried to sound as forceful as possible under the necessity of speaking in an angry whisper. "Don't you ever do it again."

"Never again insist on the observance of law? If I am not to do that, what then is my purpose?"

"Don't ever threaten a human being with a blaster again."

"I would not have fired under any circumstances, Elijah, as you know very well. I am incapable of hurting a human. But, as you see, I did not have to fire. I did not expect to have to."

"That was the purest luck, your not having to fire. Don't take that kind of chance again. I could have pulled the grandstand stunt you did——"

"Grandstand stunt? What is that?"

"Never mind. Get the sense from what I'm saying. I could have pulled a blaster on the crowd myself. I had the blaster to do it with. But it isn't the kind of gamble I am justified in taking, or you, either. It was safer to call squad cars to the scene than to try one-man heroics."

R. Daneel considered. He shook his head. "I think you are wrong, partner Elijah. My briefing on human characteristics here among the people of Earth includes the information that, unlike the men of the Outer Worlds, they are trained from birth to accept authority. Apparently this is the result of your way of living. One man, representing authority firmly enough, was quite sufficient, as I proved. Your own desire for a squad car was only an expression, really, of your almost instinctive wish for superior authority to take responsibility out of your hands. On my own world, I admit that what I did would have been most unjustified."

Baley's long face was red with anger. "If they had recognized you as a robot——"

"I was sure they wouldn't."

"In any case, remember that you *are* a robot. Nothing more than a robot. Just a robot. Like those clerks in the shoe store."

"But this is obvious."

"And you're *not* human." Baley felt himself being driven into cruelty against his will.

R. Daneel seemed to consider that. He said, "The division between human and robot is perhaps not as significant as that between intelligence and nonintelligence."

"Maybe on your world," said Baley, "but not on Earth."

He looked at his watch and could scarcely make out that he was an hour and a quarter late. His throat was dry and raw with the thought that R. Daneel had won the first round, had won when he himself had stood by helpless.

He thought of the youngster, Vince Barrett, the teen-ager whom R. Sammy had replaced. And of himself, Elijah Baley, whom R. Daneel *could* replace. Jehoshaphat, at least his father had been thrown out because of an accident that had done damage, that had killed people. Maybe it *was* his fault; Baley didn't know. Suppose he had been eased out to make room for a mechanical physicist. Just for that. For no other reason. Nothing he could do about it.

He said, curtly, "Let's go now. I've got to get you home."

R. Daneel said, "You see, it is not proper to make any distinction of lesser meaning than the fact of intel——"

Baley's voice rose. "All *right*. The subject is closed. Jessie is waiting for us." He walked in the direction of the nearest intrasection communo-tube. "I'd better call and tell her we're on our way up."

"Jessie?"

"My wife."

Jehoshaphat, thought Baley, I'm in a fine mood to face Jessie.

4

Introduction to a Family

IT HAD BEEN her name that had first made Elijah Baley really conscious of Jessie. He had met her at the Section Christmas party back in '02, over a bowl of punch. He had just finished his schooling, just taken his first job with the City, just moved into the Section. He was living in one of the bachelor alcoves of Common Room 122A. Not bad for a bachelor alcove.

She was handing out the punch. "I'm Jessie," she said. "Jessie Navodny. I don't know you."

"Baley," he said, "Lije Baley. I've just moved into the Section."

He took his glass of punch and smiled mechanically. She impressed him as a cheerful and friendly person, so he stayed near her. He was new and it is a lonely feeling to be at a party where you find yourself watching people standing about in cliques of which you aren't a part. Later, when enough alcohol had trickled down throats, it might be better.

Meanwhile, he remained at the punch bowl, watching the folks come and go and sipping thoughtfully.

"I helped make the punch." The girl's voice broke in upon him. "I can guarantee it. Do you want more?"

Baley realized his little glass was empty. He smiled and said, "Yes."

The girl's face was oval and not precisely pretty, mostly because of a slightly overlarge nose. Her dress was demure and she wore her light brown hair in a series of ringlets over her forehead.

She joined him in the next punch and he felt better.

"Jessie," he said, feeling the name with his tongue. "It's nice. Do you mind if I use it when I'm talking to you?"

"Certainly. If you want to. Do you know what it's short for?"

"Jessica?"

"You'll never guess."

"I can't think of anything else."

She laughed and said archly, "My full name is Jezebel."

That was when his interest flared. He put his punch glass down and said, intently, "No, really?"

"Honestly. I'm not kidding. Jezebel. It's my real-for-true name on all my records. My parents liked the sound of it."

She was quite proud of it, even though there was never a less likely Jezebel in the world.

Baley said, seriously, "My name is Elijah, you know. My full name, I mean."

It didn't register with her.

He said, "Elijah was Jezebel's great enemy."

"He was?"

"Why, sure. In the Bible."

"Oh? I didn't know that. Now isn't that *funny?* I hope that doesn't mean you'll have to be my enemy in real life."

From the very beginning there was no question of that. It was the coincidence of names at first that made her more than just a pleasant girl at the punch bowl. But afterward he had grown to find her cheerful, tender-hearted, and, finally, even pretty. He appreciated her cheerfulness particularly. His own sardonic view of life needed the antidote.

But Jessie never seemed to mind his long grave face.

"Oh, goodness," she said, "what if you do look like an awful lemon? I know you're not really, and I guess if you were always grinning away like clockwork, the way I do, we'd just explode when we got together. You stay the way you are, Lije, and keep me from floating away."

And she kept Lije Baley from sinking down. He applied for a small Couples apartment and got a contingent admission pending marriage. He showed it to her and said, "Will you fix it so I can get out of Bachelor's, Jessie? I don't like it there."

Maybe it wasn't the most romantic proposal in the world, but Jessie liked it.

Baley could only remember one occasion on which Jessie's habitual cheer deserted her completely and that, too, had involved her name.

It was in their first year of marriage, and their baby had not yet come. In fact, it had been the very month in which Bentley was conceived. (Their I.Q. rating, Genetic Values status, and his position in the Department entitled him to two children, of which the first might be conceived during the first year.) Maybe, as Baley thought back upon it, Bentley's beginnings might explain part of her unusual skittishness.

Jessie had been drooping a bit because of Baley's consistent overtime.

She said, "It's embarrassing to eat alone at the kitchen every night."

Baley was tired and out of sorts. He said, "Why should it be? You can meet some nice single fellows there."

And of course she promptly fired up. "Do you think I can't make an impression on them, Lije Baley?"

Maybe it was just because he was tired; maybe because Julius Enderby, a classmate of his, had moved up another notch on the C-scale rating while he himself had not. Maybe it was simply because he was a little tired of having her try to act up to the name she bore when she was nothing of the sort and never could be anything of the sort.

In any case, he said bitingly, "I suppose you can, but I don't think you'll try. I wish you'd forget your name and be yourself."

"I'll be just what I please."

"Trying to be Jezebel won't get you anywhere. If you must know the truth, the name doesn't mean what you think, anyway. The Jezebel of the Bible was a faithful wife and a good one according to her lights. She had no lovers that we know of, cut no high jinks, and took no moral liberties at all."

Jessie stared angrily at him. "That isn't so. I've heard the phrase, 'a painted Jezebel.' I know what that means."

"Maybe you think you do, but listen. After Jezebel's husband, King Ahab died, her son, Jehoram, became king. One of the captains of his army, Jehu, rebelled against him and assassinated him. Jehu then rode to Jezreel where the old queen-mother, Jezebel, was residing. Jezebel heard of his coming and knew that he could only mean to kill her. In her pride and courage, she painted her face and dressed herself in her best clothes so that she could meet him as a haughty and defiant queen. He had her thrown from the window of the palace and killed, but she made a good end, according to my notions. And that's what people refer to when they speak of 'a painted Jezebel,' whether they know it or not."

The next evening Jessie said in a small voice, "I've been reading the Bible, Lije."

"What?" For a moment, Baley was honestly bewildered.

"The parts about Jezebel."

"Oh! Jessie, I'm sorry if I hurt your feelings. I was being childish."

"No. No." She pushed his hand from her waist and sat on the couch, cool and upright, with a definite space between them. "It's good to know the truth. I don't want to be fooled by not knowing. So I read about her. She *was* a wicked woman, Lije."

"Well, her enemies wrote those chapters. We don't know her side."

"She killed all the prophets of the Lord she could lay her hands on."

"So they say she did." Baley felt about in his pocket for a stick of chewing gum. (In later years he abandoned that habit because Jessie said that with his long face and sad, brown eyes, it made him look like an old cow stuck with an unpleasant wad of grass it couldn't swallow and wouldn't spit out.) He said, "If you want her side, I could think of some arguments for you. She valued the religion of her ancestors who had been in the land long before the Hebrews came. The Hebrews had their own God, and, what's more, it was an exclusive God. They weren't content to worship Him themselves; they wanted everyone in reach to worship Him as well.

"Jezebel was a conservative, sticking to the old beliefs against the new ones. After all, if the new beliefs had a higher moral content, the old ones were more emotionally satisfying. The fact that she killed priests just marks her as a child of her times. It was the usual method of proselytization in those days. If you read I Kings, you must remember that Elijah (*my* namesake this time) had a contest with 850 prophets of Baal to see which could bring down fire from heaven. Elijah won and promptly ordered the crowd of onlookers to kill the 850 Baalites. And they did."

Jessie bit her lip. "What about Naboth's vineyard, Lije. Here was this Naboth not bothering anybody, except that he refused to sell the King his vineyard. So Jezebel arranged to have people perjure themselves and say that Naboth had committed blasphemy or something."

"He was supposed to have 'blasphemed God and the king,'" said Baley.

"Yes. So they confiscated his property after they executed him."

"That was wrong. Of course, in modern times, Naboth would have been handled quite easily. If the City wanted his property or even if one of the Medieval nations had wanted his property, the courts would have ordered him off, had him removed by force if necessary, and paid him whatever they considered a fair price. King Ahab didn't have that way out. Still, Jezebel's solution was wrong. The only excuse for her is that Ahab was sick and unhappy over the situation and she felt that her love for her husband came ahead of Naboth's welfare. I keep telling you, she was the model of a faithful wi——"

Jessie flung herself away from him, red-faced and angry. "I think you're mean and spiteful."

He looked at her with complete dismay. "What have I done? What's the matter with you?"

She left the apartment without answering and spent the evening and half the night at the subetheric video levels, traveling petulantly from showing to showing and using up a two-month supply of her quota allowance (and her husband's, to boot).

When she came back to a still wakeful Lije Baley, she had nothing further to say to him.

It occurred to Baley later, much later, that he had utterly smashed an important part of Jessie's life. Her name had signified something intriguingly wicked to her. It was a delightful makeweight for her prim, overrespectable past. It gave her an aroma of licentiousness, and she adored that.

But it was gone. She never mentioned her full name again, not to Lije, not to her friends, and maybe, for all Baley knew, not even to herself. She was Jessie and took to signing her name so.

As the days passed she began speaking to him again, and after a week or so their relationship was on the old footing and, with all subsequent quarrels, nothing ever reached that one bad spot of intensity.

Only once was there even an indirect reference to the matter. It was in her eighth month of pregnancy. She had left her own position as dietitian's assistant in Section Kitchen A-23 and with unaccustomed time on her hands was amusing herself in speculation and preparation for the baby's birth.

She said, one evening, "What about Bentley?"

"Pardon me, dear?" said Baley, looking up from a sheaf of work he had brought home with him. (With an additional mouth soon to feed and Jessie's pay stopped and his own promotions to the nonclerical levels as far off, seemingly, as ever, extra work was necessary.)

"I mean if the baby's a boy. What about Bentley as a name?"

Baley pulled down the corners of his mouth. "Bentley Baley? Don't you think the names are too similar?"

"I don't know. It has a swing, I think. Besides, the child can always pick out a middle name to suit himself when he gets older."

"Well, it's all right with me."

"Are you sure? I mean . . . Maybe you wanted him to be named Elijah?"

"And be called Junior? I don't think that's a good idea. He can name his son Elijah, if he wants to."

Then Jessie said, "There's just one thing," and stopped.

After an interval, he looked up. "What one thing?"

She did not quite meet his eye, but she said, forcefully enough, "Bentley isn't a Bible name, is it?"

"No," said Baley, "I'm quite sure it isn't."

"All right, then. I don't want any Bible names."

And that was the only harking back that took place from that time to the day when Elijah Baley was coming home with Robot Daneel Olivaw, when he had been married for more than eighteen years and when his son Bentley Baley (middle name still unchosen) was past sixteen.

Baley paused before the large double door on which there glowed in large letters PERSONAL—MEN. In smaller letters were written SUBSECTIONS 1A—1E. In still smaller letters, just above the key slit, it stated: "In case of loss of key, communicate at once with 27-101-51."

A man inched past them, inserted an aluminum sliver into the key slit, and walked in. He closed the door behind him, making no attempt to hold it open for Baley. Had he done so, Baley would have been seriously offended. By strong custom men disregarded one another's presence entirely either within or just outside the Personals. Baley remembered one of the more interesting marital confidences to have been Jessie's telling him that the situation was quite different at Women's Personals.

She was always saying, "I met Josephine Greely at Personal and she said . . ."

It was one of the penalties of civic advancement that when the Baleys were granted permission for the activation of the small washbowl in their bedroom, Jessie's social life suffered.

Baley said, without completely masking his embarrassment, "Please wait out here, Daneel."

"Do you intend washing?" asked R. Daneel.

Baley squirmed and thought: Damned robot! If they were briefing him on everything under steel, why didn't they teach him manners? I'll be responsible if he ever says anything like this to anyone else.

He said, "I'll shower. It gets crowded evenings. I'll lose time then. If I get it done now we'll have the whole evening before us."

R. Daneel's face maintained its repose. "Is it part of the social custom that I wait outside?"

Baley's embarrassment deepened. "Why need you go in for—for no purpose."

"Oh, I understand you. Yes, of course. Nevertheless, Elijah, my hands grow dirty, too, and I will wash them."

He indicated his palms, holding them out before him. They were pink and plump, with the proper creases. They bore every mark of excellent and meticulous workmanship and were as clean as need be.

Baley said, "We have a washbasin in the apartment, you know." He said it casually. Snobbery would be lost on a robot.

"Thank you for your kindness. On the whole, however, I think it would be preferable to make use of this place. If I am to live with you men of Earth, it is best that I adopt as many of your customs and attitudes as I can."

"Come on in, then."

The bright cheerfulness of the interior was a sharp contrast to the busy utilitarianism of most of the rest of the City, but this time the effect was lost on Baley's consciousness.

He whispered to Daneel, "I may take up to half an hour or so.

Wait for me." He started away, then returned to add, "And listen, don't talk to anybody and don't look at anybody. Not a word, not a glance! It's a custom."

He looked hurriedly about to make certain that his own small conversation had not been noted, was not being met by shocked glances. Nobody, fortunately, was in the antecorridor, and after all it *was* only the antecorridor.

He hurried down it, feeling vaguely dirty, past the common chambers to the private stalls. It had been five years now since he had been awarded one—large enough to contain a shower, a small laundry, and other necessities. It even had a small projector that could be keyed in for the news films.

"A home away from home," he had joked when it was first made available to him. But now, he often wondered how he would bear the adjustment back to the more Spartan existence of the common chambers if his stall privileges were ever canceled.

He pressed the button that activated the laundry and the smooth face of the meter lighted.

R. Daneel was waiting patiently when Baley returned with a scrubbed body, clean underwear, a freshened shirt, and, generally, a feeling of greater comfort.

"No trouble?" Baley asked, when they were well outside the door and able to talk.

"None at all, Elijah," said R. Daneel.

Jessie was at the door, smiling nervously. Baley kissed her.

"Jessie," he mumbled, "this is my new partner, Daneel Olivaw."

Jessie held out a hand, which R. Daneel took and released. She turned to her husband, then looked timidly at R. Daneel.

She said, "Won't you sit down, Mr. Olivaw? I must talk to my husband on family matters. It'll take just a minute. I hope you won't mind."

Her hand was on Baley's sleeve. He followed her into the next room.

She said, in a hurried whisper, "You aren't hurt, are you? I've been so worried ever since the broadcast?"

"What broadcast?"

"It came through nearly an hour ago. About the riot at the shoe counter. They said two plain-clothes men stopped it. I knew you

were coming home with a partner and this was right in our sub-
section and right when you were coming home and I thought they
were making it better than it was and you were——"

"*Please*, Jessie. You see I'm perfectly all right."

Jessie caught hold of herself with an effort. She said, shakily,
"Your partner isn't from your division, is he?"

"No," replied Baley miserably. "He's—a complete stranger."

"How do I treat him?"

"Like anybody else. He's just my partner, that's all."

He said it so unconvincingly, that Jessie's quick eyes narrowed.
"What's wrong?"

"Nothing. Come, let's go back into the living room. It'll begin to
look queer."

Lije Baley felt a little uncertain about the apartment now. Until
this very moment, he had felt no qualms. In fact, he had always
been proud of it. It had three large rooms; the living room, for instance, was an ample fifteen feet by eighteen. There was a closet
in each room. One of the main ventilation ducts passed directly by.
It meant a little rumbling noise on rare occasions, but, on the other
hand, assured first-rate temperature control and well-conditioned air.
Nor was it too far from either Personal, which was a prime convenience.

But with the creature from worlds beyond space sitting in the
midst of it, Baley was suddenly uncertain. The apartment seemed
mean and cramped.

Jessie said, with a gaiety that was slightly synthetic, "Have you
and Mr. Olivaw eaten, Lije?"

"As a matter of fact," said Baley, quickly, "Daneel will not be
eating with us. I'll eat, though."

Jessie accepted the situation without trouble. With food supplies
so narrowly controlled and rationing tighter than ever, it was good
form to refuse another's hospitality.

She said, "I hope you won't mind our eating, Mr. Olivaw. Lije,
Bentley, and I generally eat at the Community kitchen. It's much
more convenient and there's more variety, you see, and just between
you and me, bigger helpings, too. But then, Lije and I *do* have permission to eat in our apartment three times a week if we want to—
Lije is quite successful at the Bureau and we have very nice status—

and I thought that just for this occasion, if you wanted to join us, we would have a little private feast of our own, though I do think that people who overdo their privacy privileges are just a bit anti-social, you know."

R. Daneel listened politely.

Baley said, with an undercover "shushing" wiggle of his fingers, "Jessie, I'm hungry."

R. Daneel said, "Would I be breaking a custom, Mrs. Baley, if I addressed you by your given name?"

"Why, no, of course not." Jessie folded a table out of the wall and plugged the plate warmer into the central depression on the table top. "You just go right ahead and call me Jessie all you feel like—uh —Daneel." She giggled.

Baley felt savage. The situation was getting rapidly more uncomfortable. Jessie thought R. Daneel a man. The thing would be someone to boast of and talk about in Women's Personal. He was good-looking in a wooden way, too, and Jessie was pleased with his deference. Anyone could see that.

Baley wondered about R. Daneel's impression of Jessie. She hadn't changed much in eighteen years, or at least not to Lije Baley. She was heavier, of course, and her figure had lost much of its youthful vigor. There were lines at the angles of the mouth and a trace of heaviness about her cheeks. Her hair was more conservatively styled and a dimmer brown than it had once been.

But that's all beside the point, thought Baley, somberly. On the Outer Worlds the women were tall and as slim and regal as the men. Or, at least, the book-films had them so and that must be the kind of women R. Daneel was used to.

But R. Daneel seemed quite unperturbed by Jessie's conversation, her appearance, or her appropriation of his name. He said, "Are you sure that is proper? The name, Jessie, seems to be a diminutive. Perhaps its use is restricted to members of your immediate circle and I would be more proper if I used your full given name."

Jessie, who was breaking open the insulating wrapper surrounding the dinner ration, bent her head over the task in sudden concentration.

"Just Jessie," she said, tightly. "Everyone calls me that. There's nothing else."

"Very well, Jessie."

The door opened and a youngster entered cautiously. His eyes found R. Daneel almost at once.

"Dad?" said the boy, uncertainly.

"My son, Bentley," said Baley, in a low voice. "This is Mr. Olivaw, Ben."

"He's your partner, huh, Dad? How d'ya do, Mr. Olivaw." Ben's eyes grew large and luminous. "Say, Dad, what happened down in the shoe place? The newscast said——"

"Don't ask any questions now, Ben," interposed Baley sharply.

Bentley's face fell and he looked toward his mother, who motioned him to a seat.

"Did you do what I told you, Bentley?" she asked, when he sat down. Her hands moved caressingly over his hair. It was as dark as his father's and he was going to have his father's height, but all the rest of him was hers. He had Jessie's oval face, her hazel eyes, her light-hearted way of looking at life.

"Sure, Mom," said Bentley, hitching himself forward a bit to look into the double dish from which savory vapors were already rising. "What we got to eat? Not zymoveal again, Mom? Huh, Mom?"

"There's nothing wrong with zymoveal," said Jessie, her lips pressing together. "Now, you just eat what's put before you and let's not have any comments."

It was quite obvious they *were* having zymoveal.

Baley took his own seat. He himself would have preferred something other than zymoveal, with its sharp flavor and definite aftertaste, but Jessie had explained her problem before this.

"Well, I just can't, Lije," she had said. "I live right here on these levels all day and I can't make enemies or life wouldn't be bearable. They know I used to be assistant dietitian and if I just walked off with steak or chicken every other week when there's hardly anyone else on the floor that has private eating privileges even on Sunday, they'd say it was pull or friends in the prep room. It would be talk, talk, talk, and I wouldn't be able to put my nose out the door or visit Personal in peace. As it is, zymoveal and protoveg are very good. They're well-balanced nourishment with no waste and, as a matter of fact, they're full of vitamins and minerals and everything anyone needs and we can have all the chicken we want when we eat in Community on the chicken Tuesdays."

Baley gave in easily. It was as Jessie said; the first problem of living is to minimize friction with the crowds that surround you on all sides. Bentley was a little harder to convince.

On this occasion, he said, "Gee, Mom, why can't I use Dad's ticket and eat in Community myself? I'd just as soon."

Jessie shook her head in annoyance and said, "I'm surprised at you, Bentley. What would people say if they saw you eating by yourself as though your own family weren't good enough for you or had thrown you out of the apartment?"

"Well, gosh, it's none of people's business."

Baley said, with a nervous edge in his voice, "Do as your mother tells you, Bentley."

Bentley shrugged, unhappily.

R. Daneel said, suddenly, from the other side of the room, "Have I the family's permission to view these book-films during your meal?"

"Oh, sure," said Bentley, slipping away from the table, a look of instant interest upon his face. "They're mine. I got them from the library on special school permit. I'll get you my viewer. It's a pretty good one. Dad gave it to me for my last birthday."

He brought it to R. Daneel and said, "Are you interested in robots, Mr. Olivaw?"

Baley dropped his spoon and bent to pick it up.

R. Daneel said, "Yes, Bentley. I am quite interested."

"Then you'll like these. They're all about robots. I've got to write an essay on them for school, so I'm doing research. It's quite a complicated subject," he said importantly. "I'm against them myself."

"Sit down, Bentley," said Baley, desperately, "and don't bother Mr. Olivaw."

"He's not bothering me, Elijah. I'd like to talk to you about the problem, Bentley, another time. Your father and I will be very busy tonight."

"Thanks, Mr. Olivaw." Bentley took his seat and, with a look of distaste in his mother's direction, broke off a portion of the crumbly pink zymoveal with his fork.

Baley thought: Busy tonight?

Then, with a resounding shock, he remembered his job. He thought of a Spacer lying dead in Spacetown and realized that for hours he had been so involved with his own dilemma that he had forgotten the cold fact of murder.

5

Analysis of a Murder

JESSIE SAID good-by to them. She was wearing a formal hat and a little jacket of keratofiber as she said, "I hope you'll excuse me, Mr. Olivaw. I know you have a great deal to discuss with Lije."

She pushed her son ahead of her as she opened the door.

"When will you be back, Jessie?" asked Baley.

She paused. "When do you want me to be back?"

"Well . . . No use staying out all night. Why don't you come back your usual time? Midnight or so." He looked doubtfully at R. Daneel.

R. Daneel nodded. "I regret having to drive you from your home."

"Don't worry about *that*, Mr. Olivaw. You're not driving me out at all. This is my usual evening out with the girls anyway. Come on, Ben."

The youngster was rebellious. "Aw, why the dickens do I have to go, anyway. I'm not going to bother them. Nuts!"

"Now, do as I say."

"Well, why can't I go to the etherics along with you?" .

"Because I'm going with some friends and you've got other things——" The door closed behind them.

And now the moment had come. Baley had put it off in his mind. He had thought: First let's meet the robot and see what he's like. Then it was: Let's get him home. And then: Let's eat.

But now it was all over and there was no room for further delay. It was down at last to the question of murder, of interstellar complications, of possible raises in ratings, of possible disgrace. And he had no way of even beginning except to turn to the robot for help.

His fingernails moved aimlessly on the table, which had not been returned to its wall recess.

R. Daneel said, "How secure are we against being overheard?"

Baley looked up, surprised. "No one would listen to what's proceeding in another man's apartment."

"It is not your custom to eavesdrop?"

"It just isn't done, Daneel. You might as well suppose they'd—I don't know—that they'd look in your plate while you're eating."

"Or that they would commit murder?"

"What?"

"It is against your customs to kill, is it not, Elijah?"

Baley felt anger rising. "See here, if we're going to be partners, don't try to imitate Spacer arrogance. There's no room for it in you, R. Daneel." He could not resist emphasizing the "R."

"I am sorry if I have hurt your feelings, Elijah. My intention was only to indicate that, since human beings are occasionally capable of murder in defiance of custom, they may be able to violate custom for the smaller impropriety of eavesdropping."

"The apartment is adequately insulated," said Baley, still frowning. "You haven't heard anything from the apartments on any side of us, have you? Well, they won't hear us, either. Besides, why should anyone think anything of importance is going on here?"

"Let us not underestimate the enemy."

Baley shrugged. "Let's get started. My information is sketchy, so I can spread out my hand without much trouble. I know that a man named Roj Nemennuh Sarton, a citizen of the planet Aurora, and a resident of Spacetown, has been murdered by person or persons unknown. I understand that it is the opinion of the Spacers that this is not an isolated event. Am I right?"

"You are quite right, Elijah."

"They tie it up with recent attempts to sabotage the Spacer-sponsored project of converting us to an integrated human/robot society on the model of the Outer Worlds, and assume the murder was the product of a well-organized terrorist group."

"Yes."

"All right. Then to begin with, is this Spacer assumption necessarily true? Why can't the murder have been the work of an isolated fanatic? There is strong anti-robot sentiment on Earth, but there are no organized parties advocating violence of this sort."

"Not openly, perhaps. No."

"Even a secret organization dedicated to the destruction of robots and robot factories would have the common sense to realize that the worst thing they could do would be to murder a Spacer. It seems much more likely to have been the work of an unbalanced mind."

R. Daneel listened carefully, then said, "I think the weight of probability is against the 'fanatic' theory. The person killed was too well chosen and the time of the murder too appropriate for anything but deliberate planning on the part of an organized group."

"Well, then, you've got more information than I have. Spill it!"

"Your phraseology is obscure, but I think I understand. I will have to explain some of the background to you. As seen from Spacetown, Elijah, relations with Earth are unsatisfactory."

"Tough," muttered Baley.

"I have been told that when Spacetown was first established, it was taken for granted by most of our people that Earth would be willing to adopt the integrated society that has worked so well on the Outer Worlds. Even after the first riots, we thought that it was only a matter of your people getting over the first shock of novelty.

"That has not proven to be the case. Even with the co-operation of the Terrestrial government and of most of the various City governments, resistance has been continuous and progress has been very slow. Naturally, this has been a matter of great concern to our people."

"Out of altruism, I suppose," said Baley.

"Not entirely," said R. Daneel, "although it is good of you to attribute worthy motives to them. It is our common belief that a healthy and modernized Earth would be of great benefit to the whole Galaxy. At least, it is the common belief among our people at Spacetown. I must admit that there are strong elements opposed to them on the Outer Worlds."

"What? Disagreement among the Spacers?"

"Certainly. There are some who think that a modernized Earth will be a dangerous and an imperialistic Earth. This is particularly true among the populations of those older worlds which are closer to Earth and have greater reason to remember the first few centuries of interstellar travel when their worlds were controlled, politically and economically, by Earth."

Baley sighed. "Ancient history. Are they really worried? Are they still kicking at us for things that happened a thousand years ago?"

"Humans," said R. Daneel, "have their own peculiar makeup. They are not as reasonable, in many ways, as we robots, since their circuits are not as preplanned. I am told that this, too, has its advantages."

"Perhaps it may," said Baley, dryly.

"You are in a better position to know," said R. Daneel. "In any case, continuing failure on Earth has strengthened the Nationalist parties on the Outer Worlds. They say that it is obvious that Earthmen are different from Spacers and cannot be fitted into the same traditions. They say that if we imposed robots on Earth by superior force, we would be loosing destruction on the Galaxy. One thing they never forget, you see, is that Earth's population is eight billions, while the total population of the fifty Outer Worlds combined is scarcely more than five and a half billions. Our people here, particularly Dr. Sarton——"

"He was a doctor?"

"A Doctor of Sociology, specializing in robotics, and a very brilliant man."

"I see. Go on."

"As I said, Dr. Sarton and the others realized that Spacetown and all it meant would not exist much longer if such sentiments on the Outer Worlds were allowed to grow by feeding on our continued failure. Dr. Sarton felt that the time had come to make a supreme effort to understand the psychology of the Earthman. It is easy to say that the Earth people are innately conservative and to speak tritely of 'the unchanging Earth' and 'the inscrutable Terrestrial mind,' but that is only evading the problem.

"Dr. Sarton said it was ignorance speaking and that we could not dismiss the Earthman with a proverb or a bromide. He said the Spacers who were trying to remake Earth must abandon the isolation of Spacetown and mingle with Earthmen. They must live as they, think as they, be as they."

Baley said, "The Spacers? Impossible."

"You are quite right," said R. Daneel. "Despite his views, Dr. Sarton himself could not have brought himself to enter any of the Cities, and he knew it. He would have been unable to bear the hugeness and the crowds. Even if he had been forced inside at the point of a blaster, the externals would have weighed him down so that he could never have penetrated the inner truths for which he sought."

"What about the way they're always worrying about disease?" demanded Baley. "Don't forget that. I don't think there's one of them that would risk entering a City on that account alone."

"There is that, too. Disease in the Earthly sense is unknown on the Outer Worlds and the fear of the unknown is always morbid. Dr. Sarton appreciated all of this, but, nevertheless, he insisted on the necessity of growing to know the Earthman and his way of life intimately."

"He seems to have worked himself into a corner."

"Not quite. The objections to entering the City hold for human Spacers. Robot Spacers are another thing entirely."

Baley thought: I keep forgetting, damn it. Aloud, he said, "Oh?"

"Yes," said R. Daneel. "We are more flexible, naturally. At least in this respect. We can be designed for adaptation to an Earthly life. By being built into a particularly close similarity to the human externals, we could be accepted by Earthmen and allowed a closer view of their life."

"And you yourself——" began Baley in sudden enlightenment.

"Am just such a robot. For a year, Dr. Sarton had been working upon the design and construction of such robots. I was the first of his robots and so far the only one. Unfortunately, my education is not yet complete. I have been hurried into my role prematurely as a result of the murder."

"Then not all Spacer robots are like you? I mean, some look more like robots and less like humans. Right?"

"Why, naturally. The outward appearance is dependent on a robot's function. My own function requires a very manlike appearance, and I have it. Others are different, although all are humanoid. Certainly they are more humanoid than the distressingly primitive models I saw at the shoe counter. Are all your robots like that?"

"More or less," said Baley. "You don't approve?"

"Of course not. It is difficult to accept a gross parody of the human form as an intellectual equal. Can your factories do no better?"

"I'm sure they can, Daneel. I think we just prefer to know when we're dealing with a robot and when we're not." He stared directly into the robot's eyes as he said that. They were bright and moist, as a human's would be, but it seemed to Baley that their gaze was steady and did not flicker slightly from point to point as a man's would.

R. Daneel said, "I am hopeful that in time I will grow to understand that point of view."

For a moment, Baley thought there was sarcasm in the sentence, then dismissed the possibility.

"In any case," said R. Daneel, "Dr. Sarton saw clearly the fact that it was a case for C/Fe."

"See fee? What's that?"

"Just the chemical symbols for the elements carbon and iron, Elijah. Carbon is the basis of human life and iron of robot life. It becomes easy to speak of C/Fe when you wish to express a culture that combines the best of the two on an equal but parallel basis."

"See fee. Do you write it with a hyphen? Or how?"

"No, Elijah. A diagonal line between the two is the accepted way. It symbolizes neither one nor the other, but a mixture of the two, without priority."

Against his will, Baley found himself interested. Formal education on Earth included virtually no information on Outer World history or sociology after the Great Rebellion that made them independent of the mother planet. The popular book-film romances, to be sure, had their stock Outer World characters: the visiting tycoon, choleric and eccentric; the beautiful heiress, invariably smitten by the Earthman's charms and drowning disdain in love; the arrogant Spacer rival, wicked and forever beaten. These were worthless pictures, since they denied even the most elementary and well-known truths: that Spacers never entered Cities and Spacer women virtually never visited Earth.

For the first time in his life, Baley was stirred by an odd curiosity. What was Spacer life really like?

He brought his mind back to the issue at hand with something of an effort. He said, "I think I get what you're driving at. Your Dr. Sarton was attacking the problem of Earth's conversion to C/Fe from a new and promising angle. Our conservative groups or Medievalists, as they call themselves, were perturbed. They were afraid he might succeed. So they killed him. That's the motivation that makes it an organized plot and not an isolated outrage. Right?"

"I would put it about like that, Elijah. Yes."

Baley whistled thoughtfully under his breath. His long fingers tapped lightly against the table. Then he shook his head. "It won't wash. It won't wash at all."

"Pardon me. I do not understand you."

"I'm trying to get the picture. An Earthman walks into Spacetown, walks up to Dr. Sarton, blasts him, and walks out. I just don't see it. Surely the entrance to Spacetown is guarded."

R. Daneel nodded. "I think it is safe to say that no Earthman can possibly have passed through the entrance illegally."

"Then where does that leave you?"

"It would leave us in a confusing position, Elijah, if the entrance were the only way of reaching Spacetown from New York City."

Baley watched his partner thoughtfully. "I don't get you. It's the only connection between the two."

"Directly between the two, yes." R. Daneel waited a moment, then said, "You do not follow me. Is that not so?"

"That *is* so. I don't get you at all."

"Well, if it will not offend you, I will try to explain myself. May I have a piece of paper and a writer? Thank you. Look here, partner Elijah. I will draw a big circle and label it 'New York City.' Now, tangent to it, I will draw a small circle and label it 'Spacetown.' Here, where they touch, I draw an arrowhead and label it 'Barrier.' Now do you see no other connection?"

Baley said, "Of course not. There is no other connection."

"In a way," said the robot, "I am glad to hear you say this. It is in accordance with what I have been taught about Terrestrial ways of thinking. The barrier is the only *direct* connection. But both the City and Spacetown are open to the countryside in all directions. It is possible for a Terrestrial to leave the City at any of numerous exits and strike out cross country to Spacetown, where no barrier will stop him."

The tip of Baley's tongue touched his upper lip and for a moment stayed there. Then he said, "Cross country?"

"Yes."

"Cross *country!* Alone?"

"Why not?"

"Walking?"

"Undoubtedly walking. Walking would offer the least chance of detection. The murder took place early in the working day and the trip was undoubtedly negotiated in the hours before dawn."

"Impossible! There isn't a man in the City who would do it. Leave the City? Alone?"

"Ordinarily, it would seem unlikely. Yes. We Spacers know that. It is why we guard only the entrance. Even in the Great Riot, your people attacked only at the barrier that then protected the entrance. Not one left the City."

"Well, then?"

"But now we are dealing with an unusual situation. It is not the blind attack of a mob following the line of least resistance, but the organized attempt of a small group to strike, deliberately, at the unguarded point. It explains why, as you say, a Terrestrial could enter Spacetown, walk up to his victim, kill him, and walk away. The man attacked through a complete blind spot on our part."

Baley shook his head. "It's too unlikely. Have your people done anything to check that theory?"

"Yes, we have. Your Commissioner of Police was present almost at the time of the murder——"

"I know. He told me so."

"That, Elijah, is another example of the timeliness of the murder. Your Commissioner has co-operated with Dr. Sarton in the past and he was the Earthman with whom Dr. Sarton planned to make initial arrangements concerning the infiltration of your city by R's such as myself. The appointment for that morning was to concern that. The murder, of course, stopped those plans, at least temporarily, and the fact that it happened when your own Commissioner of Police was actually within Spacetown made the entire situation more difficult and embarrassing for Earth, and for our own people, too.

"But that is not what I started to say. Your Commissioner was present. We said to him, 'The man must have come cross country.' Like you, he said, 'Impossible,' or perhaps, 'Unthinkable.' He was quite disturbed, of course, and perhaps that may have made it difficult for him to see the essential point. Nevertheless, we forced him to begin checking that possibility almost at once."

Baley thought of the Commissioner's broken glasses and, even in the middle of somber thoughts, a corner of his mouth twitched. Poor Julius! Yes, he *would* be disturbed. Of course, there would be no way for Enderby to have explained the situation to the lofty Spacers, who looked upon physical disability as a peculiarly disgusting attribute of the non-genetically selected Earthmen. At least, he couldn't without losing face, and face was valuable to Police Commissioner Julius Enderby. Well, Earthmen had to stick together in some respects. The robot would never find out about Enderby's nearsightedness from Baley.

R. Daneel continued, "One by one, the various exit points from the City were investigated. Do you know how many there are, Elijah?"

Baley shook his head, then hazarded, "Twenty?"

"Five hundred and two."

"What?"

"Originally, there were many more. Five hundred and two are all that remain functional. Your City represents a slow growth, Elijah. It was once open to the sky and people crossed from City to country freely."

"Of course. I know that."

"Well, when it was first enclosed, there were many exits left. Five hundred and two still remain. The rest are built over or blocked up. We are not counting, of course, the entrance points for air freight."

"Well, what of the exit points?"

"It was hopeless. They are unguarded. We could find no official who was in charge or who considered them under his jurisdiction. It seemed as though no one even knew they existed. A man could have walked out of any of them at any time and returned at will. He would never have been detected."

"Anything else? The weapon was gone, I suppose."

"Oh, yes."

"Any clues of any sort?"

"None. We have investigated the grounds surrounding Spacetown thoroughly. The robots on the truck farms were quite useless as possible witnesses. They are little more than automatic farm machinery, scarcely humanoid. And there were no humans."

"Uh-huh. What next?"

"Having failed, so far, at one end, Spacetown, we will work at the other, New York City. It will be our duty to track down all possible subversive groups, to sift all dissident organizations——"

"How much time do you intend to spend?" interrupted Baley.

"As little as possible, as much as necessary."

"Well," said Baley, thoughtfully, "I wish you had another partner in this mess."

"I do not," said R. Daneel. "The Commissioner spoke very highly of your loyalty and ability."

"It was nice of him," said Baley sardonically. He thought: Poor Julius. I'm on his conscience and he tries hard.

"We didn't rely entirely on him," said R. Daneel. "We checked your records. You have expressed yourself openly against the use of robots in your department."

"Oh? Do you object?"

"Not at all. Your opinions are, obviously, your own. But it made it necessary for us to check your psychological profile very closely. We know that, although you dislike R's intensely, you *will* work with one if you conceive it to be your duty. You have an extraordinarily high loyalty aptitude and a respect for legitimate authority. It is what we need. Commissioner Enderby judged you well."

"You have no personal resentment toward my anti-robot sentiments?"

R. Daneel said, "If they do not prevent you from working with me and helping me do what is required of me, how can they matter?"

Baley felt stopped. He said, belligerently, "Well, then, if I pass the test, how about you? What makes you a detective?"

"I do not understand you."

"You were designed as an information-gathering machine. A man-imitation to record the facts of human life for the Spacers."

"That is a good beginning for an investigator, is it not? To be an information-gathering machine?"

"A beginning, maybe. But it's not all there is, by a long shot."

"To be sure, there has been a final adjustment of my circuits."

"I'd be curious to hear the details of that, Daneel."

"That is easy enough. A particularly strong drive has been inserted into my motivation banks; a desire for justice."

"*Justice!*" cried Baley. The irony faded from his face and was replaced by a look of the most earnest distrust.

But R. Daneel turned swiftly in his chair and stared at the door. "Someone is out there."

Someone was. The door opened and Jessie, pale and thin-lipped, walked in.

Baley was startled. "Why, Jessie! Is anything wrong?"

She stood there, eyes not meeting his. "I'm sorry. I had to . . ." Her voice trailed off.

"Where's Bentley?"

"He's to stay the night in the Youth Hall."

Baley said, "Why? I didn't tell you to do that."

"You said your partner would stay the night. I felt he would need Bentley's room."

R. Daneel said, "There was no necessity, Jessie."

Jessie lifted her eyes to R. Daneel's face, staring at it earnestly.

Baley looked at his fingertips, sick at what might follow, somehow unable to interpose. The momentary silence pressed thickly on his eardrums and then, far away, as though through folds of plastex, he heard his wife say, "I think you are a robot, Daneel."

And R. Daneel replied, in a voice as calm as ever, "I am."

6

Whispers in a Bedroom

ON THE uppermost levels of some of the wealthiest subsections of the City are the natural Solariums, where a partition of quartz with a movable metal shield excludes the air but lets in the sunlight. There the wives and daughters of the City's highest administrators and executives may tan themselves. There a unique thing happens every evening.

Night falls.

In the rest of the City (including the UV-Solariums, where the millions, in strict sequence of allotted time, may occasionally expose themselves to the artificial wavelengths of arc lights) there are only the arbitrary cycles of hours.

The business of the City might easily continue in three eight-hour or four six-hour shifts, by "day" and "night" alike. Light and work could easily proceed endlessly. There are always civic reformers who periodically suggest such a thing in the interests of economy and efficiency.

The notion is never accepted.

Much of the earlier habits of Earthly society have been given up in the interests of that same economy and efficiency: space, privacy, even much of free will. They are the products of civilization, however, and not more than ten thousand years old.

The adjustment of sleep to night, however, is as old as man: a million years. The habit is not easy to give up. Although the evening is unseen, apartment lights dim as the hours of darkness pass and the City's pulse sinks. Though no one can tell noon from midnight by any cosmic phenomenon along the enclosed avenues of the City, mankind follows the mute partitionings of the hour hand.

The expressways empty, the noise of life sinks, the moving mob among the colossal alleys melts away; New York City lies in Earth's unnoticed shadow, and its population sleeps.

Elijah Baley did not sleep. He lay in bed and there was no light in his apartment, but that was as far as it went.

Jessie lay next to him, motionless in the darkness. He had not felt nor heard her move.

On the other side of the wall sat, stood, lay (Baley wondered which) R. Daneel Olivaw.

Baley whispered, "Jessie!" Then again, "Jessie!"

The dark figure beside him stirred slightly under the sheet. "What do you want?"

"Jessie, don't make it worse for me."

"You might have told me."

"How could I? I was planning to, when I could think of a way. Jehoshaphat, Jessie——"

"Sh!"

Baley's voice returned to its whisper. "How did you find out? Won't you tell me?"

Jessie turned toward him. He could sense her eyes looking through the darkness at him.

"Lije." Her voice was scarcely more than a stirring of air. "Can he hear us? That thing?"

"Not if we whisper."

"How do you know? Maybe he has special ears to pick up tiny sounds. Spacer robots can do all sorts of things."

Baley knew that. The prorobot propaganda was forever stressing the miraculous feats of the Spacer robots, their endurance, their extra senses, their service to humanity in a hundred novel ways. Personally, he thought that approach defeated itself. Earthmen hated the robots all the more for their superiority.

He whispered, "Not Daneel. They made him human-type on purpose. They wanted him to be accepted as a human being, so he must have only human senses."

"How do you know?"

"If he had extra senses, there would be too much danger of his giving himself away as non-human by accident. He would do too much, know too much."

"Well, maybe."

Silence fell again.

A minute passed and Baley tried a second time. "Jessie, if you'll just let things be until—until . . . Look, dear, it's unfair of you to be angry."

"Angry? Oh, Lije, you fool. I'm not angry. I'm scared; I'm scared clean to death."

She made a gulping sound and clutched at the neck of his pajamas. For a while, they clung together, and Baley's growing sense of injury evaporated into a troubled concern.

"Why, Jessie? There's nothing to be worried about. He's harmless. I swear he is."

"Can't you get rid of him, Lije?"

"You know I can't. It's Department business. How can I?"

"What kind of business, Lije? Tell me."

"Now, Jessie, I'm surprised at you." He groped for her cheek in the darkness and patted it. It was wet. Using his pajama sleeve, he carefully wiped her eyes.

"Now, look," he said tenderly, "you're being a baby."

"Tell them at the Department to have someone else do it, whatever it is. Please, Lije."

Baley's voice hardened a bit. "Jessie, you've been a policeman's wife long enough to know an assignment is an assignment."

"Well, why did it have to be you?"

"Julius Enderby——"

She stiffened in his arms. "I might have known. Why can't you tell Julius Enderby to have someone else do the dirty work just once. You stand for too much, Lije, and this is just——"

"All right, all right," he said, soothingly.

She subsided, quivering.

Baley thought: She'll never understand.

Julius Enderby had been a fighting word with them since their engagement. Enderby had been two classes ahead of Baley at the City School of Administrative Studies. They had been friends. When Baley had taken his battery of aptitude tests and neuroanalysis and found himself in line for the police force, he found Enderby there ahead of him. Enderby had already moved into the plain-clothes division.

Baley followed Enderby, but at a continually greater distance. It was no one's fault, precisely. Baley was capable enough, efficient enough, but he lacked something that Enderby had. Enderby fit the administrative machine perfectly. He was one of those persons who was born for a hierarchy, who was just naturally comfortable in a bureaucracy.

The Commissioner wasn't a great brain, and Baley knew it. He had his childish peculiarities, his intermittent rash of ostentatious Medievalism, for instance. But he was smooth with others; he offended no one; he took orders gracefully; he gave them with the proper mixture of gentleness and firmness. He even got along with the Spacers. He was perhaps overobsequious to them (Baley himself could never have dealt with them for half a day without getting into a state of bristle; he was sure of that, even though he had never really spoken to a Spacer), but they trusted him, and that made him extremely useful to the City.

So, in a Civil Service where smooth and sociable performance was more useful than an individualistic competence, Enderby went up the scale quickly, and was at the Commissioner level when Baley himself was nothing more than a C-5. Baley did not resent the contrast, though he was human enough to regret it. Enderby did not forget their earlier friendship and, in his queer way, tried to make up for his success by doing what he could for Baley.

The assignment of partnership with R. Daneel was an example of it. It was tough and unpleasant, but there was no question that it carried within it the germs of tremendous advance. The Commissioner might have given the chance to someone else. His own talk, that morning, of needing a favor masked but did not hide that fact.

Jessie never saw things that way. On similar occasions in the past, she had said, "It's your silly loyalty index. I'm so tired of hearing everyone praise you for being so full of a sense of duty. Think of yourself once in a while. I notice the ones on top don't bring up the topic of their *own* loyalty index."

Baley lay in bed in a state of stiff wakefulness, letting Jessie calm down. He had to *think*. He had to be certain of his suspicions.

Little things chased one another and fitted together in his mind. Slowly, they were building into a pattern.

He felt the mattress give as Jessie stirred.

"Lije?" Her lips were at his ear.

"What?"

"Why don't you resign?"

"Don't be crazy."

"Why not?" She was suddenly almost eager. "You can get rid of that horrible robot that way. Just walk in and tell Enderby you're through."

Baley said coldly, "I can't resign in the middle of an important case. I can't throw the whole thing down the disposal tube just any time I feel like it. A trick like that means declassification for cause."

"Even so. You can work your way up again. You can do it, Lije. There are a dozen places where you'd fit into Service."

"Civil Service doesn't take men who are declassified for cause. Manual labor is the only thing I can do; the only thing you could do. Bentley would lose all inherited status. For God's sake, Jessie, you don't know what it's like."

"I've read about it. I'm not afraid of it," she mumbled.

"You're crazy. You're plain crazy." Baley could feel himself trembling. There was a familiar, flashing picture of his father in his mind's eye. His father, moldering away toward death.

Jessie sighed heavily.

Baley's mind turned savagely away from her. In desperation, it returned to the pattern it was constructing.

He said, tightly, "Jessie, you've got to tell me. How did you find out Daneel was a robot? What made you decide that?"

She began, "Well . . ." and just ran down. It was the third time she had begun to explain and failed.

He crushed her hand in his, willing her to speak. "Please, Jessie. What's frightening you?"

She said, "I just guessed he was a robot, Lije."

He said, "There wasn't anything to make you guess that, Jessie. You didn't think he was a robot before you left, now did you?"

"No-o, but I got to thinking . . ."

"Come on, Jessie. What was it?"

"Well . . . Look, Lije, the girls were talking in the Personal. You know how they are. Just talking about everything."

Women! thought Baley.

"Anyway," said Jessie. "The rumor is all over town. It must be."

"All over town?" Baley felt a quick and savage touch of triumph, or nearly that. Another piece in place!

"It was the way they sounded. They said there was talk about a Spacer robot loose in the City. He was supposed to look just like a man and to be working with the police. They even asked *me* about it. They laughed and said, 'Does your Lije know anything about it, Jessie?' and I laughed, and said, 'Don't be silly!'

"Then we went to the etherics and I got to thinking about your new partner. Do you remember those pictures you brought home, the ones Julius Enderby took in Spacetown, to show me what Spacers looked like? Well, I got to thinking that's what your partner looked like. It just came to me that that's what he looked like and I said to myself, oh, my God, someone must've recognized him in the shoe department and he's with Lije and I just said I had a headache and I ran——"

Baley said, "Now, Jessie, stop, stop. Get hold of yourself. Now why are you afraid? You're not afraid of Daneel himself. You faced up to him when you came home. You faced up to him fine. So——"

He stopped speaking. He sat up in bed, eyes uselessly wide in the darkness.

′ He felt his wife move against his side. His hand leaped, found her lips and pressed against them. She heaved against his grip, her hands grasping his wrist and wrenching, but he leaned down against her the more heavily.

Then, suddenly, he released her. She whimpered.

He said, huskily, "Sorry, Jessie. I was listening."

He was getting out of bed, pulling warm Plastofilm over the soles of his feet.

"Lije, where are you going? Don't leave me."

"It's all right. I'm just going to the door."

The Plastofilm made a soft, shuffling noise as he circled the bed. He cracked the door to the living room and waited a long moment. Nothing happened. It was so quiet, he could hear the thin whistle of Jessie's breath from their bed. He could hear the dull rhythm of blood in his ears.

Baley's hand crept through the opening of the door, snaking out to the spot he needed no light to find. His fingers closed upon the knob that controlled the ceiling illumination. He exerted the smallest pressure he could and the ceiling gleamed dimly, so dimly that the lower half of the living room remained in semidusk.

He saw enough, however. The main door was closed and the living room lay lifeless and quiet.

He turned the knob back into the off position and moved back to bed.

It was all he needed. The pieces fit. The pattern was complete. Jessie pleaded with him. "Lije, what's wrong?"

"Nothing's wrong, Jessie. Everything's all right. He's not here."

"The robot? Do you mean he's gone? For good?"

"No, no. He'll be back. And before he does, answer my question."

"What question?"

"What are you afraid of?"

Jessie said nothing.

Baley grew more insistent. "You said you were scared to death."

"Of him."

"No, we went through that. You weren't afraid of him and, besides, you know quite well a robot cannot hurt a human being."

Her words came slowly. "I thought if everyone knew he was a robot there might be a riot. We'd be killed."

"Why kill us?"

"You know what riots are like."

"They don't even know where the robot is, do they?"

"They might find out."

"And that's what you're afraid of, a riot?"

"Well——"

"Sh!" He pressed Jessie down to the pillow.

Then he put his lips to her ear. "He's come back. Now listen and don't say a word. Everything's fine. He'll be gone in the morning and he won't be back. There'll be no riot, nothing."

He was almost contented as he said that, almost completely contented. He felt he could sleep.

He thought again: No riot, nothing. And no declassification.

And just before he actually fell asleep, he thought: Not even a murder investigation. Not even that. The whole thing's solved. . . .

He slept.

7

Excursion Into Spacetown

POLICE COMMISSIONER Julius Enderby polished his glasses with exquisite care and placed them upon the bridge of his nose.

Baley thought: It's a good trick. Keeps you busy while you're thinking what to say, and it doesn't cost money the way lighting up a pipe does.

And because the thought had entered his mind, he drew out his pipe and dipped into his pinched store of rough-cut. One of the few luxury crops still grown on Earth was tobacco, and its end was visibly approaching. Prices had gone up, never down, in Baley's lifetime; quotas down, never up.

Enderby, having adjusted his glasses, felt for the switch at one end of his desk and flicked his door into one-way transparency for a moment. "Where is he now, by the way?"

"He told me he wanted to be shown through the Department, and I let Jack Tobin do the honors." Baley lit his pipe and tightened its baffle carefully. The Commissioner, like most non-indulgers, was petty about tobacco smoke.

"I hope you didn't tell him Daneel was a robot."

"Of course I didn't."

The Commissioner did not relax. One hand remained aimlessly busy with the automatic calendar on his desk.

"How is it?" he asked, without looking at Baley.

"Middling rough."

"I'm sorry, Lije."

Baley said, firmly, "You might have warned me that he looked completely human."

The Commissioner looked surprised. "I didn't?" Then, with sudden petulance, "Damn it, you should have known. I wouldn't have asked you to have him stay at your house if he looked like R. Sammy. Now would I?"

"I know, Commissioner, but I'd never seen a robot like that and you had. I didn't even know such things were possible. I just wish you'd mentioned it, that's all."

"Look, Lije, I'm sorry. I should have told you. You're right. It's just that this job, this whole deal, has me so on edge that half the time I'm just snapping at people for no reason. He, I mean this Daneel thing, is a new-type robot. It's still in the experimental stage."

"So he explained himself."

"Oh. Well, that's it, then."

Baley tensed a little. This was it, now. He said, casually, teeth clenched on pipestem. "R. Daneel has arranged a trip to Spacetown for me."

"To Spacetown!" Enderby looked up with instant indignation.

"Yes. It's the logical next move, Commissioner. I'd like to see the scene of the crime, ask a few questions."

Enderby shook his head decidedly. "I don't think that's a good idea, Lije. We've gone over the ground. I doubt there's anything new to be learned. And they're strange people. Kid gloves! They've got to be handled with kid gloves. You don't have the experience."

He put a plump hand to his forehead and added, with unexpected fervor, "I hate them."

Baley inserted hostility into his voice. "Damn it, the robot came here and I should go there. It's bad enough sharing a front seat with a robot; I hate to take a back seat. Of course, if you don't think I'm capable of running this investigation, Commissioner——"

"It isn't that, Lije. It's not you, it's the Spacers. You don't know what they're like."

Baley deepened his frown. "Well, then, Commissioner, suppose you come along." His right hand rested on his knee, and two of his fingers crossed automatically as he said that.

The Commissioner's eyes widened. "No, Lije. I won't go there. Don't ask me to." He seemed visibly to catch hold of his runaway words. More quietly, he said, with an unconvincing smile, "Lots of work here, you know. I'm days behind."

Baley regarded him thoughtfully. "I tell you what, then. Why not get into it by trimension later on. Just for a while, you understand. In case I need help."

"Well, yes. I suppose I can do that." He sounded unenthusiastic.

"Good." Baley looked at the wall clock, nodded, and got up. "I'll be in touch with you."

Baley looked back as he left the office, keeping the door open for part of an additional second. He saw the Commissioner's head begin bending down toward the crook of one elbow as it rested on the desk. The plain-clothes man could almost swear he heard a sob.

Jehoshaphat! he thought, in outright shock.

He paused in the common room and sat on the corner of a nearby desk, ignoring its occupant, who looked up, murmured a casual greeting, and returned to his work.

Baley unclipped the baffle from the bowl of the pipe and blew into it. He inverted the pipe itself over the desk's small ash vacuum and let the powdery white tobacco ash vanish. He looked regretfully at the empty pipe, readjusted the baffle, and put it away. Another pipeful gone forever!

He reconsidered what had just taken place. In one way, Enderby had not surprised him. He had expected resistance to any attempt on his own part to enter Spacetown. He had heard the Commissioner talk often enough about the difficulties of dealing with Spacers, about the dangers of allowing any but experienced negotiators to have anything to do with them, even over trifles.

He had not expected, however, to have the Commissioner give in so easily. He had supposed, at the very least, that Enderby would have insisted on accompanying him. The pressure of other work was meaningless in the face of the importance of this problem.

And that was not what Baley wanted. He wanted exactly what he had gotten. He wanted the Commissioner to be present by trimensional personification so that he could witness the proceedings from a point of safety.

Safety was the key word. Baley would need a witness that could not be put out of the way immediately. He needed that much as the minimum guarantee of his own safety.

The Commissioner had agreed to that at once. Baley remembered the parting sob, or ghost of one, and thought: Jehoshaphat, the man's into this past his depth.

A cheerful, slurring voice sounded just at Baley's shoulder and Baley started.

"What the devil do you want?" he demanded savagely.

The smile on R. Sammy's face remained foolishly fixed. "Jack says to tell you Daneel is ready, Lije."

"All right. Now get out of here."

He frowned at the robot's departing back. There was nothing so irritating as having that clumsy metal contraption forever making free with your front name. He'd complained about that when R. Sammy first arrived and the Commissioner had shrugged his shoulders and said, "You can't have it both ways, Lije. The public insists that City robots be built with a strong friendship circuit. All right, then. He is drawn to you. He calls you by the friendliest name he knows."

Friendship circuit! No robot built, of any type, could possibly hurt a human being. That was the First Law of Robotics:

"A robot may not injure a human being, or, through inaction, allow a human being to come to harm."

No positronic brain was ever built without that injunction driven so deeply into its basic circuits that no conceivable derangement could displace it. There was no need for specialized friendship circuits.

Yet the Commissioner was right. The Earthman's distrust for robots was something quite irrational and friendship circuits had to be incorporated, just as all robots had to be made smiling. On Earth, at any rate.

R. Daneel, now, never smiled.

Sighing, Baley rose to his feet. He thought: Spacetown, next stop— or, maybe, last stop!

The police forces of the City, as well as certain high officials, could still make use of individual squad cars along the corridors of the City and even along the ancient underground motorways that were barred to foot traffic. There were perennial demands on the part of the Liberals that these motorways be converted to children's playgrounds, to new shopping areas, or to expressway or local-way extensions.

The strong pleas of "Civic safety!" remained unvanquished, how-ever. In cases of fires too large to be handled by local devices, in cases of massive breakdowns in power lines or ventilators, most of all in cases of serious riot, there had to be some means whereby the forces of the City could be mobilized at the stricken point in a hurry. No substitute for the motorways existed or could exist.

Baley had traveled along a motorway several times before in his life, but its indecent emptiness always depressed him. It seemed a million miles from the warm, living pulsation of the City. It stretched out like a blind and hollow worm before his eyes as he sat at the controls of the squad car. It opened continuously into new stretches as he moved around this gentle curve or that. Behind him, he knew without looking, another blind and hollow worm continually contracted and closed. The motorway was well lit, but lighting was meaningless in the silence and emptiness.

R. Daneel did nothing to break that silence or fill that emptiness. He looked straight ahead, as unimpressed by the empty motorway as by the bulging expressway.

In one sounding moment, to the tune of a wild whine of the squad car's siren, they popped out of the motorway and curved gradually into the vehicular lane of a City corridor.

The vehicular lanes were still conscientiously marked down each major corridor in reverence for one vestigial portion of the past. There were no vehicles any longer, except for squad cars, fire engines, and maintenance trucks, and pedestrians used the lanes in complete self-assurance. They scattered in indignant hurry before the advance of Baley's squealing car.

Baley, himself, drew a freer breath as noise surged in about him, but it was an interval only. In less than two hundred yards they turned into the subdued corridors that led to Spacetown Entrance.

They were expected. The guards obviously knew R. Daneel by sight and, although themselves human, nodded to him without the least self-consciousness.

One approached Baley and saluted with perfect, if frigid, military courtesy. He was tall and grave, though not the perfect specimen of Spacer physique that R. Daneel was.

He said, "Your identification card, if you please, sir."

It was inspected quickly but thoroughly. Baley noticed that the guard wore flesh-colored gloves and had an all but unnoticeable filter in each nostril.

The guard saluted again and returned the card. He said, "There is a small Men's Personal here which we would be pleased to have you use if you wish to shower."

It was in Baley's mind to deny the necessity, but R. Daneel plucked gently at his sleeve, as the guard stepped back to his place.

R. Daneel said, "It is customary, partner Elijah, for City dwellers to shower before entering Spacetown. I tell you this since I know you have no desire, through lack of information on this matter, to render yourself or ourselves uncomfortable. It is also advisable for you to attend to any matters of personal hygiene you may think advisable. There will be no facilities within Spacetown for that purpose."

"No facilities!" said Baley, strenuously. "But that's impossible."

"I mean, of course," said R. Daneel, "none for use by City dwellers."

Baley's face filled with a clearly hostile astonishment.

R. Daneel said, "I regret the situation, but it is a matter of custom."

Wordlessly, Baley entered the Personal. He felt, rather than saw, R. Daneel entering behind him.

He thought: Checking on me? Making sure I wash the City dust off myself?

For a furious moment, he reveled in the thought of the shock he was preparing for Spacetown. It seemed to him suddenly minor that he might, in effect, be pointing a blaster at his own chest.

The Personal was small, but it was well appointed and antiseptic in its cleanliness. There was a trace of sharpness in the air. Baley sniffed at it, momentarily puzzled.

Then he thought: Ozone! They've got ultraviolet radiation flooding the place.

A little sign blinked on and off several times, then remained steadily lit. It said, "Visitor will please remove all clothing, including shoes, and place it in the receptacle below."

Baley acquiesced. He unhitched his blaster and blaster strap and recircled it about his naked waist. It felt heavy and uncomfortable.

The receptacle closed and his clothing was gone. The lighted sign blanked out. A new sign flashed ahead.

It said: "Visitor will please tend to personal needs, then make use of the shower indicated by arrow."

Baley felt like a machine tool being shaped by long-distance force edges on an assembly line.

His first act upon entering the small shower cubicle was to draw up the moisture-proof flap on his blaster holster and clip it down firmly all about. He knew by long-standing test that he could still draw and use it in less than five seconds.

There was no knob or hook on which to hang his blaster. There was not even a visible shower head. He placed it in a corner away from the cubicle's entrance door.

Another sign flashed: "Visitor will please hold arms directly out from his body and stand in the central circle with feet in the indicated positions."

As he placed his feet in the small depressions allowed for them, the sign blanked out. As it did so, a stinging, foaming spray hit him from ceiling, floor, and four walls. He felt the water welling up even beneath the soles of his feet. For a full minute it lasted, his skin reddening under the combined force of the heat and pressure and his lungs gasping for air in the warm dampness. There followed another minute of cool, low-pressure spray, and then finally a minute of warm air that left him dry and refreshed.

He picked up his blaster and blaster strap and found that they, too, were dry and warm. He strapped them on and stepped out of the cubicle in time to see R. Daneel emerge from a neighboring shower. Of course! R. Daneel was not a City dweller, but he had accumulated City dust.

Quite automatically, Baley looked away. Then, with the thought that, after all, R. Daneel's customs were not City customs, he forced his unwilling eyes back for one moment. His lips quirked in a tiny smile. R. Daneel's resemblance to humanity was not restricted to his face and hands but had been carried out with painstaking accuracy over the entire body.

Baley stepped forward in the direction he had been traveling continuously since entering the Personal. He found his clothes waiting for him, neatly folded. They had a warm, clean odor to them.

A sign said, "Visitor will please resume his clothing and place his hand in the indicated depression."

Baley did so. He felt a definite tingling in the ball of his middle finger as he laid it down upon the clean, milky surface. He lifted his hand hastily and found a little drop of blood oozing out. As he watched, it stopped flowing.

He shook it off and pinched the finger. No more blood was flowing even then.

Obviously, they were analyzing his blood. He felt a definite pang of anxiety. His own yearly routine examination by Department doctors, he felt sure, was not carried on with the thoroughness or, perhaps, with the knowledge of these cold robot-makers from outer space. He was not sure he wanted too probing an inquiry into the state of his health.

The time of waiting seemed long to Baley, but when the light flashed again, it said simply, "Visitor will proceed."

Baley drew a long breath of relief. He walked onward and stepped through an archway. Two metal rods closed in before him and, written in luminous air, were the words: "Visitor is warned to proceed no further."

"What the devil——" called out Baley, forgetting in his anger the fact that he was still in the Personal.

R. Daneel's voice was in his ear. "The sniffers have detected a power source, I imagine. Are you carrying your blaster, Elijah?"

Baley whirled, his face a deep crimson. He tried twice, then managed to croak out, "A police officer has his blaster on him or in easy reach at all times, on duty and off."

It was the first time he had spoken in a Personal, proper, since he was ten years old. That had been in his uncle Boris's presence and had merely been an automatic complaint when he stubbed his toe. Uncle Boris had beaten him well when he reached home and had lectured him strongly on the necessities of public decency.

R. Daneel said, "No visitor may be armed. It is our custom, Elijah. Even your Commissioner leaves his blaster behind on all visits."

Under almost any other circumstances, Baley would have turned on his heel and walked away, away from Spacetown and away from that robot. Now, however, he was almost mad with desire to go through with his exact plan and have his revenge to the brim in that way.

This, he thought, was the unobtrusive medical examination that had replaced the more detailed one of the early days. He could well understand, he could understand to overflowing, the indignation and anger that had led to the Barrier Riots of his youth.

In black anger, Baley unhitched his blaster belt. R. Daneel took it from him and placed it within a recess in the wall. A thin metal plate slithered across it.

"If you will put your thumb in the depression," said R. Daneel, "only your thumb will open it later on."

Baley felt undressed, far more so, in fact, than he had felt in the shower. He stepped across the point at which the rods had lately barred him, and, finally, out of the Personal.

He was back in a corridor again, but there was an element of strangeness about it. Up ahead, the light had an unfamiliar quality to it. He felt a whiff of air against his face and, automatically, he thought a squad car had passed.

R. Daneel must have read his uneasiness in his face. He said, "You are essentially in open air now, Elijah. It is unconditioned."

Baley felt faintly sick. How could the Spacers be so rigidly careful of a human body, merely because it came from the City, and then breathe the dirty air of the open fields? He tightened his nostrils, as though by pulling them together he could the more effectively screen the ingoing air.

R. Daneel said, "I believe you will find that open air is not deleterious to human health."

"All right," said Baley, faintly.

The air currents hit annoyingly against his face. They were gentle enough, but they were erratic. That bothered him.

Worse came. The corridor opened into blueness and as they approached its end, strong white light washed down. Baley had seen sunlight. He had been in a natural Solarium once in the line of duty. But there, protecting glass had enclosed the place and the sun's own image had been refracted into a generalized glow. Here, all was open.

Automatically, he looked up at the sun, then turned away. His dazzled eyes blinked and watered.

A Spacer was approaching. A moment of misgiving struck Baley.

R. Daneel, however, stepped forward to greet the approaching man with a handshake. The Spacer turned to Baley and said, "Won't you come with me, sir? I am Dr. Han Fastolfe."

Things were better inside one of the domes. Baley found himself goggling at the size of the rooms and the way in which space was so carelessly distributed, but was thankful for the feel of the conditioned air.

Fastolfe said, sitting down and crossing his long legs, "I'm assuming that you prefer conditioning to unobstructed wind."

He seemed friendly enough. There were fine wrinkles on his forehead and a certain flabbiness to the skin below his eyes and just under his chin. His hair was thinning, but showed no signs of gray. His large ears stood away from his head, giving him a humorous and homely appearance that comforted Baley.

Early that morning, Baley had looked once again at those pictures of Spacetown that Enderby had taken. R. Daneel had just arranged the Spacetown appointment and Baley was absorbing the notion that he was to meet Spacers in the flesh. Somehow that was considerably different from speaking to them across miles of carrier wave, as he had done on several occasions before.

The Spacers in those pictures had been, generally speaking, like those that were occasionally featured in the book-films: tall, redheaded, grave, coldly handsome. Like R. Daneel Olivaw, for instance.

R. Daneel named the Spacers for Baley and when Baley suddenly pointed and said, in surprise, "That isn't you, is it?" R. Daneel answered, "No, Elijah, that is my designer, Dr. Sarton."

He said it unemotionally.

"You were made in your maker's image?" asked Baley, sardonically, but there was no answer to that and, in truth, Baley scarcely expected one. The Bible, as he knew, circulated only to the most limited extent on the Outer Worlds.

And now Baley looked at Han Fastolfe, a man who deviated very noticeably from the Spacer norm in looks, and the Earthman felt a pronounced gratitude for that fact.

"Won't you accept food?" asked Fastolfe.

He indicated the table that separated himself and R. Daneel from the Earthman. It bore nothing but a bowl of varicolored spheroids. Baley felt vaguely startled. He had taken them for table decorations.

R. Daneel explained. "These are the fruits of natural plant life grown on Aurora. I suggest you try this kind. It is called an apple and is reputed to be pleasant."

Fastolfe smiled. "R. Daneel does not know this by personal experience, of course, but he is quite right."

Baley brought an apple to his mouth. Its surface was red and green. It was cool to the touch and had a faint but pleasant odor. With an effort, he bit into it and the unexpected tartness of the pulpy contents hurt his teeth.

He chewed it gingerly. City dwellers ate natural food, of course, whenever rations allowed it. He himself had eaten natural meat and bread often. But such food had always been processed in some way. It had been cooked or ground, blended or compounded. Fruit, now, properly speaking, should come in the form of sauce or preserve. What he was holding now must have come straight from the dirt of a planet's soil.

He thought: I hope they've washed it at least.

Again he wondered at the spottiness of Spacer notions concerning cleanliness.

Fastolfe said, "Let me introduce myself a bit more specifically. I am in charge of the investigation of the murder of Dr. Sarton at the Spacetown end as Commissioner Enderby is at the City end. If I can help you in any way, I stand ready to do so. We are as eager for a quiet solution of the affair and prevention of future incidents of the sort as any of you City men can be."

"Thank you, Dr. Fastolfe," said Baley. "Your attitude is appreciated."

So much, he thought, for the amenities. He bit into the center of the apple and hard, dark little ovoids popped into his mouth. He spat automatically. They flew out and fell to the ground. One would have struck Fastolfe's leg had not the Spacer moved it hastily.

Baley reddened, started to bend.

Fastolfe said, pleasantly, "It is quite all right, Mr. Baley. Just leave them, please."

Baley straightened again. He put the apple down gingerly. He had the uncomfortable feeling that once he was gone, the lost little objects would be found and picked up by suction; the bowl of fruit would be burnt or discarded far from Spacetown; the very room they were sitting in would be sprayed with viricide.

He covered his embarrassment with brusqueness. He said, "I would like to ask permission to have Commissioner Enderby join our conference by trimensional personification."

Fastolfe's eyebrows raised. "Certainly, if you wish it. Daneel, would you make the connection?"

Baley sat in stiff discomfort until the shiny surface of the large parallelepiped in one corner of the room dissolved away to show Commissioner Julius Enderby and part of his desk. At that moment, the discomfort eased and Baley felt nothing short of love for that familiar figure, and a longing to be safely back in that office with him, or anywhere in the City, for that matter. Even in the least prepossessing portion of the Jersey yeast-vat districts.

Now that he had his witness, Baley saw no reason for delay. He said, "I believe I have penetrated the mystery surrounding the death of Dr. Sarton."

Out of the corner of his eye, he saw Enderby springing to his feet and grabbing wildly (and successfully) at his flying spectacles. By standing, the Commissioner thrust his head out of the limits of the trimensic receiver and was forced to sit down again, red-faced and speechless.

In a much quieter way, Dr. Fastolfe, head inclined to one side, was as startled. Only R. Daneel was unmoved.

"Do you mean," said Fastolfe, "that you know the murderer?"

"No," said Baley, "I mean there was no murder."

"What!" screamed Enderby.

"One moment, Commissioner Enderby," said Fastolfe, raising a hand. His eyes held Baley's and he said, "Do you mean that Dr. Sarton is alive?"

"Yes, sir, and I believe I know where he is."

"Where?"

"Right there," said Baley, and pointed firmly at R. Daneel Olivaw.

8

Debate Over a Robot

AT THE MOMENT, Baley was most conscious of the thud of his own pulse. He seemed to be living in a moment of suspended time. R. Daneel's expression was, as always, empty of emotion. Han Fastolfe wore a look of well-bred astonishment on his face and nothing more.

It was Commissioner Julius Enderby's reaction that most concerned Baley, however. The trimensic receiver out of which his face stared did not allow of perfect reproduction. There was always that tiny flicker and that not-quite-ideal resolution. Through that imperfection and through the further masking of the Commissioner's spectacles, Enderby's eyes were unreadable.

Baley thought: Don't go to pieces on me, Julius. I need you.

He didn't really think that Fastolfe would act in haste or under emotional impulse. He had read somewhere once that Spacers had no religion, but substituted, instead, a cold and phlegmatic intellectualism raised to the heights of a philosophy. He believed that and counted on it. They would make a point of acting slowly and then only on the basis of reason.

If he were alone among them and had said what he had said, he was certain that he would never have returned to the City. Cold reason would have dictated that. The Spacers' plans were worth more to them, many times over, than the life of a City dweller. There would be some excuse made to Julius Enderby. Maybe they would present his corpse to the Commissioner, shake their heads, and speak of an Earthman conspiracy having struck again. The Commissioner would believe them. It was the way he was built. If he hated Spacers, it was a hatred based on fear. He wouldn't dare disbelieve them.

That was why he had to be an actual witness of events, a witness, moreover, safely out of reach of the Spacers' calculated safety measures.

The Commissioner said, chokingly, "Lije, you're all wrong. I saw Dr. Sarton's corpse."

"You saw the charred remnants of something you were told was Dr. Sarton's corpse," retorted Baley, boldly. He thought grimly of the Commissioner's broken glasses. That had been an unexpected favor for the Spacers.

"No, no, Lije. I knew Dr. Sarton well and his head was undamaged. It was he." The Commissioner put his hand to his glasses uneasily, as though he, too, remembered, and added, "I looked at him closely, very closely."

"How about this one, Commissioner?" asked Baley, pointing to R. Daneel again. "Doesn't he resemble Dr. Sarton?"

"Yes, the way a statue would."

"An expressionless attitude can be assumed, Commissioner. Suppose that were a robot you had seen blasted to death. You say you looked closely. Did you look closely enough to see whether the charred surface at the edge of the blast was really decomposed organic tissue or a deliberately introduced layer of carbonization over fused metal."

The Commissioner looked revolted. He said, "You're being ridiculous."

Baley turned to the Spacer. "Are you willing to have the body exhumed for examination, Dr. Fastolfe?"

Dr. Fastolfe smiled. "Ordinarily, I would have no objection, Mr. Baley, but I'm afraid we do not bury our dead. Cremation is a universal custom among us."

"Very convenient," said Baley.

"Tell me, Mr. Baley," said Dr. Fastolfe, "just how did you arrive at this very extraordinary conclusion of yours?"

Baley thought: He isn't giving up. He'll brazen it out, if he can.

He said, "It wasn't difficult. There's more to imitating a robot than just putting on a frozen expression and adopting a stilted style of conversation. The trouble with you men of the Outer Worlds is that you're too used to robots. You've gotten to accept them almost as human beings. You've grown blind to the differences. On Earth, it's different. We're very conscious of what a robot is.

"Now in the first place, R. Daneel is too good a human to be a robot. My first impression of him was that he was a Spacer. It was quite an effort for me to adjust myself to his statement that he was a robot. And of course, the reason for that was that he *was* a Spacer and *wasn't* a robot."

R. Daneel interrupted, without any sign of self-consciousness at being himself so intimately the topic of debate. He said, "As I told you, partner Elijah, I was designed to take a temporary place in a human society. The resemblance to humanity is purposeful."

"Even," asked Baley, "down to the painstaking duplication of those portions of the body which, in the ordinary course of events, would always be covered by clothes? Even to the duplication of organs which, in a robot, would have no conceivable function?"

Enderby said suddenly, "How did you find that out?"

Baley reddened. "I couldn't help noticing in the—in the Personal."

Enderby looked shocked.

Fastolfe said, "Surely you understand that a resemblance must be complete if it is to be useful. For our purposes, half measures are as bad as nothing at all."

Baley asked abruptly, "May I smoke?"

Three pipefuls in one day was a ridiculous extravagance, but he was riding a rolling torrent of recklessness and needed the release of tobacco. After all, he was talking back to Spacers. He was going to force their lies down their own throats.

Fastolfe said, "I'm sorry, but I'd prefer that you didn't."

It was a "preference" that had the force of a command. Baley felt that. He thrust back the pipe, the bowl of which he had already taken into his hand in anticipation of automatic permission.

Of course not, he thought bitterly. Enderby didn't warn me, because he doesn't smoke himself, but it's obvious. It follows. They don't smoke on their hygienic Outer Worlds, or drink, or have any human vices. No wonder they accept robots in their damned—what did R. Daneel call it?—C/Fe society? No wonder R. Daneel can play the robot as well as he does. They're all robots out there to begin with.

He said, "The too complete resemblance is just one point out of a number. There was a near riot in my section as I was taking *him* home." (He had to point. He could not bring himself to say either

R. Daneel or Dr. Sarton.) "It was he that stopped the trouble and he did it by pointing a blaster at the potential rioters."

"Good Lord," said Enderby, energetically, "the report stated that it was you——"

"I know, Commissioner," said Baley. "The report was based on information that I gave. I didn't want to have it on the record that a robot had threatened to blast men and women."

"No, no. Of course not." Enderby was quite obviously horrified. He leaned forward to look at something that was out of the range of the trimensic receiver.

Baley could guess what it was. The Commissioner was checking the power gauge to see if the transmitter were being tapped.

"Is that a point in your argument?" asked Fastolfe.

"It certainly is. The First Law of Robotics states that a robot cannot harm a human being."

"But R. Daneel did no harm."

"True. He even stated afterward that he wouldn't have fired under any circumstances. Still, no robot I ever heard of could have violated the spirit of the First Law to the extent of threatening to blast a man, even if he really had no intention to do so."

"I see. Are you a robotics expert, Mr. Baley?"

"No, sir. But I've had a course in general robotics and in positronic analysis. I'm not completely ignorant."

"That's nice," said Fastolfe, agreeably, "but you see, I *am* a robotics expert, and I assure you that the essence of the robot mind lies in a completely literal interpretation of the universe. It recognizes no spirit in the First Law, only the letter. The simple models you have on Earth may have their First Law so overlaid with additional safeguards that, to be sure, they may well be incapable of threatening a human. An advanced model such as R. Daneel is another matter. If I gather the situation correctly, Daneel's threat was necessary to prevent a riot. It was intended then to prevent harm to human beings. He was obeying the First Law, not defying it."

Baley squirmed inwardly, but maintained a tight external calm. It would go hard, but he would match this Spacer at his own game.

He said, "You may counter each point separately, but they add up just the same. Last evening in our discussion of the so-called murder, this alleged robot claimed that he had been converted into a detective by the installation of a new drive into his positronic circuits. A drive, if you please, for justice."

"I'll vouch for that," said Fastolfe. "It was done to him three days ago under my own supervision."

"A drive for *justice?* Justice, Dr. Fastolfe, is an abstraction. Only a human being can use the term."

"If you define 'justice' in such a way that it is an abstraction, if you say that it is the rendering of each man his due, that it is adhering to the right, or anything of the sort, I grant you your argument, Mr. Baley. A human understanding of abstractions cannot be built into a positronic brain in the present state of our knowledge."

"You admit that, then—as an expert in robotics?"

"Certainly. The question is, what did R. Daneel mean by using the term 'justice'?"

"From the context of our conversation, he meant what you and I and any human being would mean, but what no robot could mean."

"Why don't you ask him, Mr. Baley, to define the term?"

Baley felt a certain loss of confidence. He turned to R. Daneel. "Well?"

"Yes, Elijah?"

"What is your definition of justice?"

"Justice, Elijah, is that which exists when all the laws are enforced."

Fastolfe nodded. "A good definition, Mr. Baley, for a robot. The desire to see all laws enforced has been built into R. Daneel, now. Justice is a very concrete term to him since it is based on law enforcement, which is in turn based upon the existence of specific and definite laws. There is nothing abstract about it. A human being can recognize the fact that, on the basis of an abstract moral code, some laws may be bad ones and their enforcement unjust. What do you say, R. Daneel?"

"An unjust law," said R. Daneel evenly, "is a contradiction in terms."

"To a robot it is, Mr. Baley. So you see, you mustn't confuse your justice and R. Daneel's."

Baley turned to R. Daneel sharply and said, "You left my apartment last night."

R. Daneel replied, "I did. If my leaving disturbed your sleep, I am sorry."

"Where did you go?"

"To the Men's Personal."

For a moment, Baley was staggered. It was the answer he had already decided was the truth, but he had not expected it to be the answer R. Daneel would give. He felt a little more of his certainty oozing away, yet he held firmly on his track. The Commissioner was watching, his lensed eyes flicking from one to the other as they spoke. Baley *couldn't* back down now, no matter what sophistries they used against him. He had to hold to his point.

He said, "On reaching my section, *he* insisted on entering Personal with me. His excuse was a poor one. During the night, he left to visit Personal again as he has just admitted. If he were a man, I'd say he had every reason and right to do so. Obviously. As a robot, however, the trip was meaningless. The conclusion can only be that he is a man."

Fastolfe nodded. He seemed not in the least put out. He said, "This is most interesting. Suppose we ask Daneel why he made his trip to Personal last night."

Commissioner Enderby leaned forward. "Please, Dr. Fastolfe," he muttered, "it is not proper to——"

"You need not be concerned, Commissioner," said Fastolfe, his thin lips curving back in something that looked like a smile but wasn't, "I am certain that Daneel's answer will not offend your sensibilities or those of Mr. Baley. Won't you tell us, Daneel?"

R. Daneel said, "Elijah's wife, Jessie, left the apartment last night on friendly terms with me. It was quite obvious that she had no reason for thinking me to be other than human. She returned to the apartment knowing I was a robot. The obvious conclusion is that the information to that effect exists outside the apartment. It followed that my conversation with Elijah last night had been overheard. In no other way could the secret of my true nature have become common knowledge.

"Elijah told me that the apartments were well insulated. We spoke together in low voices. Ordinary eavesdropping would not do. Still, it was known that Elijah is a policeman. If a conspiracy exists within the City sufficiently well organized to have planned the murder of Dr. Sarton, they may well have been aware that Elijah had been placed in charge of the murder investigation. It would fall within the realm of possibility then, even of probability, that his apartment had been spybeamed.

"I searched the apartment as well as I could after Elijah and Jessie had gone to bed, but could find no transmitter. This complicated matters. A focused duo-beam could do the trick even in the absence of a transmitter, but that requires rather elaborate equipment.

"Analysis of the situation led to the following conclusion. The one place where a City dweller can do almost anything without being disturbed or questioned is in the Personals. He could even set up a duo-beam. The custom of absolute privacy in the Personals is very strong and other men would not even look at him. The Section Personal is quite close to Elijah's apartment, so that the distance factor is not important. A suitcase model could be used. I went to the Personal to investigate."

"And what did you find?" asked Baley quickly.

"Nothing, Elijah. No sign of a duo-beam."

Dr. Fastolfe said, "Well, Mr. Baley, does this sound reasonable to you?"

But Baley's uncertainty was gone, now. He said, "Reasonable as far as it goes, perhaps, but it stops short of perfection by a hell of a way. What *he* doesn't know is that my wife told me where she got the information and *when*. She learned he was a robot shortly after she left the house. Even then, the rumor had been circulating for hours. So the fact that he was a robot could not have leaked out through spying on our last evening's conversation."

"Nevertheless," said Dr. Fastolfe, "his action last night of going to the Personal stands explained, I think."

"But something is brought up that is *not* explained," retorted Baley, heatedly. "When, where, and how was the leak? How did the news get about that there was a Spacer robot in the City? As far as I know, only two of us knew about the deal, Commissioner Enderby and myself, and we told no one.—Commissioner, did anyone else in the Department know?"

"No," said Enderby, anxiously. "Not even the Mayor. Only we, and Dr. Fastolfe."

"And *he*," added Baley, pointing.

"I?" asked R. Daneel.

"Why not?"

"I was with you at all times, Elijah."

"You were *not*," cried Baley, fiercely. "I was in Personal for half an hour or more before we went to my apartment. During that time, we two were completely out of contact with one another. It was then that you got in touch with your group in the City."

"What group?" asked Fastolfe.

And "What group?" echoed Commissioner Enderby almost simultaneously.

Baley rose from his chair and turned to the trimensic receiver. "Commissioner, I want you to listen closely to this. Tell me if it doesn't all fall into a pattern. A murder is reported and by a curious coincidence it happens just as you are entering Spacetown to keep an appointment with the murdered man. You are shown the corpse of something supposed to be human, but the corpse has since been disposed of and is not available for close examination.

"The Spacers insist an Earthman did the killing, even though the only way they can make such an accusation stick is to suppose that a City man had left the City and cut cross country to Spacetown alone and at night. You know damn well how unlikely that is.

"Next they send a supposed robot into the City; in fact, they *insist* on sending him. The first thing the robot does is to threaten a crowd of human beings with a blaster. The second is to set in motion the rumor that there is a Spacer robot in the City. In fact, the rumor is so specific that Jessie told me it was known that he was working with the police. That means that before long it will be known that it was the robot who handled the blaster. Maybe even now the rumor is spreading across the yeast-vat country and down the Long Island hydroponic plants that there's a killer robot on the loose."

"This is impossible. Impossible!" groaned Enderby.

"No, it isn't. It's exactly what's happening, Commissioner. Don't you see it? There's a conspiracy in the City, all right, but it's run from Spacetown. The Spacers *want* to be able to report a murder. They *want* riots. They *want* an assault on Spacetown. The worse things get, the better the incident—and Spacer ships come down and occupy the Cities of Earth."

Fastolfe said, mildly, "We had an excuse in the Barrier Riots of twenty-five years ago."

"You weren't ready then. You are now." Baley's heart was pounding madly.

"This is quite a complicated plot you're attributing to us, Mr. Baley. If we wanted to occupy Earth, we could do so in much simpler fashion."

"Maybe not, Dr. Fastolfe. Your so-called robot told me that public opinion concerning Earth is by no means unified on your Outer Worlds. I think he was telling the truth at that time, anyway. Maybe an outright occupation wouldn't sit well with the people at home. Maybe an incident is an absolute necessity. A good shocking incident."

"Like a murder, eh? Is that it? You'll admit it would have to be a pretended murder. You won't suggest, I hope, that we'd really kill one of ourselves for the sake of an incident."

"You built a robot to look like Dr. Sarton, blasted the robot, and showed the remains to Commissioner Enderby."

"And then," said Dr. Fastolfe, "having used R. Daneel to impersonate Dr. Sarton in the false murder, we have to use Dr. Sarton to impersonate R. Daneel in the false investigation of the false murder."

"Exactly. I am telling you this in the presence of a witness who is not here in the flesh and whom you cannot blast out of existence and who is important enough to be believed by the City government and by Washington itself. We will be prepared for you and we know what your intentions are. If necessary, our government will report directly to your people, expose the situation for exactly what it is. I doubt if this sort of interstellar rape will be tolerated."

Fastolfe shook his head. "Please, Mr. Baley, you are being unreasonable. Really, you have the most astonishing notions. Suppose now, just quietly suppose, that R. Daneel is really R. Daneel. Suppose he is actually a robot. Wouldn't it follow that the corpse Commissioner Enderby saw was really Dr. Sarton? It would be scarcely reasonable to believe that the corpse were still another robot. Commissioner Enderby witnessed R. Daneel under construction and can vouch for the fact that only one existed."

"If it comes to that," said Baley, stubbornly, "the Commissioner is not a robotics expert. You might have had a dozen such robots."

"Stick to the point, Mr. Baley. What if R. Daneel is really R. Daneel? Would not the entire structure of your reasoning fall to the ground? Would you have any further basis for your belief in this completely melodramatic and implausible interstellar plot you have constructed?"

"*If* he is a robot! I say he is human."

"Yet you haven't really investigated the problem, Mr. Baley," said Fastolfe. "To differentiate a robot, even a very humanoid robot, from a human being, it isn't necessary to make elaborately shaky deductions from little things he says and does. For instance, have you tried sticking a pin into R. Daneel?"

"What?" Baley's mouth fell open.

"It's a simple experiment. There are others perhaps not quite so simple. His skin and hair look real, but have you tried looking at them under adequate magnification. Then again, he seems to breathe, particularly when he is using air to talk, but have you noticed that his breathing is irregular, that minutes may go by during which he has no breath at all. You might even have trapped some of his expired air and measured the carbon dioxide content. You might have tried to draw a sample of blood. You might have tried to detect a pulse in his wrist, or a heartbeat under his shirt. Do you see what I mean, Mr. Baley?"

"That's just talk," said Baley, uneasily. "I'm not going to be bluffed. I might have tried any of those things, but do you suppose this alleged robot would have let me bring a hypodermic to him, or a stethoscope or a microscope?"

"Of course. I see your point," said Fastolfe. He looked at R. Daneel and gestured slightly.

R. Daneel touched the cuff of his right shirt sleeve and the diamagnetic seam fell apart the entire length of his arm. A smooth, sinewy, and apparently entirely human limb lay exposed. Its short, bronze hairs, both in quantity and distribution, were exactly what one would expect of a human being.

Baley said, "So?"

R. Daneel pinched the ball of his right middle finger with the thumb and forefinger of his left hand. Exactly what the details of the manipulation that followed were, Baley could not see.

But, just as the fabric of the sleeve had fallen in two when the diamagnetic field of its seam had been interrupted, so now the arm itself fell in two.

There, under a thin layer of fleshlike material, was the dull blue gray of stainless steel rods, cords, and joints.

"Would you care to examine Daneel's workings more closely, Mr. Baley?" asked Dr. Fastolfe politely.

Baley could scarcely hear the remark for the buzzing in his ears and for the sudden jarring of the Commissioner's high-pitched and hysterical laughter.

9

Elucidation by a Spacer

THE MINUTES PASSED and the buzzing grew louder and drowned out the laughter. The dome and all it contained wavered and Baley's time sense wavered, too.

At least, he found himself sitting in an unchanged position but with a definite feeling of lost time. The Commissioner was gone; the trimensic receiver was milky and opaque; and R. Daneel sat at his side, pinching up the skin of Baley's bared upper arm. Baley could see, just beneath the skin, the small thin darkness of a hypo-sliver. It vanished as he watched, soaking and spreading away into the intercellular fluid, from that into the blood stream and the neighboring cells, from that into all the cells of his body.

His grip on reality heightened.

"Do you feel better, partner Elijah?" asked R. Daneel.

Baley did. He pulled at his arm and the robot let him take it away. He rolled down his sleeve and looked about. Dr. Fastolfe sat where he had been, a small smile softening the homeliness of his face.

Baley said, "Did I black out?"

Dr. Fastolfe said, "In a way, yes. You received a sizable shock, I'm afraid."

It came back to Baley quite clearly. He seized R. Daneel's nearer arm quickly, forcing up the sleeve as far as it would go, exposing the wrist. The robot's flesh felt soft to his fingers, but underneath was the hardness of something more than bone.

R. Daneel let his arm rest easily in the plain-clothes man's grip. Baley stared at it, pinching the skin along the median line. Was there a faint seam?

It was logical, of course, that there should be. A robot, covered with synthetic skin, and deliberately made to look human, could not be repaired in the ordinary fashion. A chest plate could not be un-riveted for the purpose. A skull could not be hinged up and out-ward. Instead, the various parts of the mechanical body would have to be put together along a line of micromagnetic fields. An arm, a head, an entire body, must fall in two at the proper touch, then come together again at a contrary touch.

Baley looked up. "Where's the Commissioner?" he mumbled, hot with mortification.

"Pressing business," said Dr. Fastolfe. "I encouraged him to leave, I'm afraid. I assured him we would take care of you."

"You've taken care of me quite nicely already, thank you," said Baley, grimly. "I think our business is done."

He lifted himself erect on tired joints. He felt an old man, very suddenly. Too old to start over again. He needed no deep insight to foresee that future.

The Commissioner would be half frightened and half furious. He would face Baley whitely, taking his glasses off to wipe them every fifteen seconds. His soft voice (Julius Enderby almost never shouted) would explain carefully that the Spacers had been mor-tally offended.

"You *can't* talk to Spacers that way, Lije. They won't take it." (Baley could hear Enderby's voice very plainly down to the finest shade of intonation.) "I warned you. No saying how much damage you've done. I can see your point, mind you. I see what you were trying to do. If they were Earthmen, it would be different. I'd say yes, chance it. Run the risk. Smoke them out. But *Spacers!* You might have told me, Lije. You might have consulted me. I know them. I know them inside and out."

And what would Baley be able to say? That Enderby was exactly the man he couldn't tell. That the project was one of tremendous risk and Enderby a man of tremendous caution. That it had been Enderby himself who had pointed up the supreme dangers of either outright failure or of the wrong kind of success. That the one way of defeating declassification was to show that guilt lay in Spacetown itself. . . .

Enderby would say, "There'll have to be a report on this, Lije. There'll be all sorts of repercussions. I know the Spacers. They'll demand your removal from the case, and it'll have to be that way. You understand that, Lije, don't you? I'll try to make it easy on you. You can count on that. I'll protect you as far as I can, Lije."

Baley knew that would be exactly true. The Commissioner would protect him, but only as far as he could, not to the point, for instance, of infuriating further an angry Mayor.

He could hear the Mayor, too. "Damn it, Enderby, what *is* all this? Why wasn't I consulted? Who's running the City? Why was an unauthorized robot allowed inside the City? And just what the devil did this Baley . . ."

If it came to a choice between Baley's future in the Department and the Commissioner's own, what possible result could Baley expect? He could find no reasonable way of blaming Enderby.

The least he could expect was demotion, and that was bad enough. The mere act of living in a modern City insured the bare possibility of existence, even for those entirely declassified. How bare that possibility was he knew only too well.

It was the addition of status that brought the little things: a more comfortable seat here, a better cut of meat there, a shorter wait in line at the other place. To the philosophical mind, these items might seem scarcely worth any great trouble to acquire.

Yet no one, however philosophical, could give up those privileges, *once acquired*, without a pang. That was the point.

What a trifling addition to the convenience of the apartment an activated washbasin was when for thirty years previously the trip to Personal had been an automatic and unregarded one. How useless it was even as a device to prove "status" when it was considered the height of ill form to parade "status." Yet were the washbasin to be deactivated, how humiliating and unbearable would each added trip to Personal be! How yearningly attractive the memory of the bedroom shave! How filled with a sense of lost luxury!

It was fashionable for modern political writers to look back with a smug disapproval at the "fiscalism" of Medieval times, when economy was based on money. The competitive struggle for existence, they said, was brutal. No truly complex society could be maintained because of the strains introduced by the eternal "fight-for-the-buck." (Scholars had varying interpretations of the word "buck," but there was no dispute over the meaning as a whole.)

By contrast, modern "civism" was praised highly as efficient and enlightened.

Maybe so. There were historical novels both in the romantic and the sensational tradition, and the Medievalists thought "fiscalism" had bred such things as individualism and initiative.

Baley wouldn't commit himself, but now he wondered sickly if ever a man fought harder for that buck, whatever it was, or felt its loss more deeply, than a City dweller fought to keep from losing his Sunday night option on a chicken drumstick—a real-flesh drumstick from a once-living bird.

Baley thought: Not me so much. There's Jessie and Ben.

Dr. Fastolfe's voice broke in upon his thoughts. "Mr. Baley, do you hear me?"

Baley blinked. "Yes?" How long had he been standing there like a frozen fool?

"Won't you sit down, sir? Having taken care of the matter on your mind, you may now be interested in some films we have taken of the scene of the crime and of the events immediately following."

"No, thank you. I have business in the City."

"Surely the case of Dr. Sarton comes first."

"Not with me. I imagine I'm off the case already." Suddenly, he boiled over. "Damn it, if you could prove R. Daneel was a robot, why didn't you do it at once? Why did you make such a farce of it all?"

"My dear Mr. Baley, I was very interested in your deductions. As for being off the case, I doubt it. Before the Commissioner left, I made a special point of asking that you be retained. I believe he will co-operate."

Baley sat down, not entirely voluntarily. He said, sharply, "Why?"

Dr. Fastolfe crossed his legs and sighed. "Mr. Baley, in general I have met two kinds of City dwellers, rioters and politicians. Your Commissioner is useful to us, but he is a politician. He tells us what we want to hear. He *handles* us, if you know what I mean. Now you came here and boldly accused us of tremendous crimes and tried to prove your case. I enjoyed the process. I found it a hopeful development."

"How hopeful?" asked Baley sardonically.

"Hopeful enough. You are someone I can deal with frankly. Last night, Mr. Baley, R. Daneel reported to me by shielded subether.

Some things about you interested me very much. For instance, there was the point concerning the nature of the book-films in your apartment."

"What about them?"

"A good many dealt with historical and archaeological subjects. It makes it appear that you are interested in human society and that you know a little about its evolution."

"Even policemen can spend their free time on book-films, if they so choose."

"Quite. I'm glad of your choice in viewing matter. It will help me in what I am trying to do. In the first place, I want to explain, or try to, the exclusivism of the men of the Outer Worlds. We live here in Spacetown; we don't enter the City; we mingle with you City dwellers only in a very rigidly limited fashion. We breathe the open air, but when we do, we wear filters. I sit here now with filters in my nostrils, gloves on my hands, and a fixed determination to come no closer to you than I can help. Why do you suppose that is?"

Baley said, "There's no point in guessing." Let *him* talk now.

"If you guessed as some of your people do, you would say that it was because we despised the men of Earth and refused to lose caste by allowing their shadow to fall upon us. That is not so. The true answer is really quite obvious. The medical examination you went through, as well as the cleansing procedures, were not matters of ritual. They were dictated by necessity."

"Disease?"

"Yes, disease. My dear Mr. Baley, the Earthmen who colonized the Outer Worlds found themselves on planets entirely free of Terrestrial bacteria and viruses. They brought in their own, of course, but they also brought with them the latest medical and microbiological techniques. They had a small community of micro-organisms to deal with and no intermediate hosts. There were no mosquitoes to spread malaria, no snails to spread schistosomiasis. Disease agents were wiped out and symbiotic bacteria allowed to grow. Gradually, the Outer Worlds became disease-free. Naturally, as time went on, entrance requirements for immigrant Earthmen were made more and more rigorous, since less and less could the Outer Worlds endure the possible introduction of disease."

"You've never been sick, Dr. Fastolfe?"

"Not with a parasitic disease, Mr. Baley. We are all liable to degenerative diseases such as atherosclerosis, of course, but I have never had what you would call a cold. If I were to contract one, I might die of it. I've built up no resistance to it whatsoever. That's what's wrong with us here in Spacetown. Those of us who come here run a definite risk. Earth is riddled with diseases to which we have no defense, no *natural* defense. You yourself are carrying the germs of almost every known disease. You are not aware of it, since you keep them all under control at almost all times through the antibodies your body has developed over the years. I, myself, lack the antibodies. Do you wonder that I come no closer to you? Believe me, Mr. Baley, I act aloof only in self-defense."

Baley said, "If this is so, why isn't the fact made known on Earth? I mean, that it is not just queasiness on your part, but a defense against an actual physical danger."

The Spacer shook his head. "We are few, Mr. Baley, and are disliked as foreigners anyway. We maintain our own safety on the basis of a rather shaky prestige as a superior class of being. We cannot afford to lose face by admitting that we are *afraid* to approach an Earthman. Not at least until there is a better understanding between Earthmen and Spacers."

"There won't be, on present terms. It's your supposed superiority that we—they hate you for."

"It is a dilemma. Don't think we aren't aware of it."

"Does the Commissioner know of this?"

"We have never explained it to him flatly, as I have just done to you. He may guess it, however. He is quite an intelligent man."

"If he guessed it, he might have told me," Baley said reflectively.

Dr. Fastolfe lifted his eyebrows. "If he had, then you wouldn't have considered the possibility of R. Daneel being a human Spacer. Is that it?"

Baley shrugged slightly, tossing the matter to one side.

But Dr. Fastolfe went on, "That's quite true, you know. Putting the psychological difficulties to one side, the terrible effect of the noise and crowds upon us, the fact remains that for one of us to enter the City is the equivalent of a death sentence. It is why Dr. Sarton initiated his project of humanoid robots. They were substitute men, designed to enter the City instead of us——"

"Yes. R. Daneel explained this to me."

"Do you disapprove?"

"Look," said Baley, "since we're talking to one another so freely, let me ask a question in simple words. Why have you Spacers come to Earth anyway? Why don't you leave us alone?"

Dr. Fastolfe said, with obvious surprise, "Are you *satisfied* with life on Earth?"

"We get along."

"Yes, but for how long will that continue? Your population goes up continuously; the available calories meet the needs only as a result of greater and greater effort. Earth is in a blind alley, man."

"We get along," repeated Baley stubbornly.

"Barely. A City like New York must spend every ounce of effort getting water in and waste out. The nuclear power plants are kept going by uranium supplies that are constantly more difficult to obtain even from the other planets of the system, and the supply needed goes up steadily. The life of the City depends every moment on the arrival of wood pulp for the yeast vats and minerals for the hydroponic plants. Air must be circulated unceasingly. The balance is a very delicate one in a hundred directions, and growing more delicate each year. What would happen to New York if the tremendous flow of input and outgo were to be interrupted for even a single hour?"

"It never has been."

"Which is no security for the future. In primitive times, individual population centers were virtually self-supporting, living on the produce of neighboring farms. Nothing but immediate disaster, a flood or a pestilence or crop failure, could harm them. As the centers grew and technology improved, localized disasters could be overcome by drawing on help from distant centers, but at the cost of making ever larger areas interdependent. In Medieval times, the open cities, even the largest, could subsist on food stores and on emergency supplies of all sorts for a week at least. When New York first became a City, it could have lived on itself for a day. Now it cannot do so for an hour. A disaster that would have been uncomfortable ten thousand years ago, merely serious a thousand years ago, and acute a hundred years ago would now be surely fatal."

Baley moved restlessly in his chair. "I've heard all this before. The Medievalists want an end to Cities. They want us to get back to the soil and to natural agriculture. Well, they're mad; we can't. There are too many of us and you can't go backward in history, only forward. Of course, if emigration to the Outer Worlds were not re-stricted——"

"You know why it must be restricted."

"Then what is there to do? You're tapping a dead power line."

"What about emigration to new worlds? There are a hundred billion stars in the Galaxy. It is estimated that there are a hundred million planets that are inhabitable or can be made inhabitable."

"That's ridiculous."

"Why?" asked Dr. Fastolfe, with vehemence. "Why is the suggestion ridiculous? Earthmen have colonized planets in the past. Over thirty of the fifty Outer Worlds, including my native Aurora, were directly colonized by Earthmen. Is colonization no longer possible?"

"Well . . ."

"No answer? Let me suggest that if it *is* no longer possible, it is because of the development of City culture on Earth. Before the Cities, human life on Earth wasn't so specialized that they couldn't break loose and start all over on a raw world. They did it thirty times. But now, Earthmen are all so coddled, so enwombed in their imprisoning caves of steel, that they are caught forever. You, Mr. Baley, won't even believe that a City dweller is capable of crossing country to get to Spacetown. Crossing space to get to a new world must represent impossibility squared to you. Civism is ruining Earth, sir."

Baley said angrily, "And if it does? How does it concern you people? It's our problem. We'll solve it. If not, it's our own particular road to hell."

"Better your own road to hell than another's road to heaven, eh? I know how you must feel. It is not pleasant to listen to the preaching of a stranger. Yet I wish your people could preach to us, for we, too, have a problem, one that is quite analogous to yours."

Baley smiled crookedly. "Overpopulation?"

"Analogous, not identical. Ours is underpopulation. How old would you say I was?"

The Earthman considered for a moment and then deliberately overestimated. "Sixty, I'd say."

"A hundred and sixty, you should say."

"What!"

"A hundred and sixty-three next birthday, to be exact. There's no trick to that. I'm using the Standard Earth year as the unit. If I'm fortunate, if I take care of myself, most of all, if I catch no disease on Earth, I may double that age. Men on Aurora have been known to live over three hundred and fifty years. And life expectancy is still increasing."

Baley looked to R. Daneel (who throughout the conversation had been listening in stolid silence), as though he were seeking confirmation.

He said, "How is that possible?"

"In an underpopulated society, it is practical to concentrate study on gerontology, to do research on the aging process. In a world such as yours, a lengthened life expectancy would be disastrous. You couldn't afford the resulting rise in population. On Aurora, there is room for tricentenarians. Then, of course, a long life becomes doubly and triply precious.

"If you were to die now, you would lose perhaps forty years of your life, probably less. If I were to die, I would lose a hundred fifty years, probably more. In a culture such as ours, then, individual life is of prime importance. Our birth rate is low and population increase is rigidly controlled. We maintain a definite robot/man ratio designed to maintain the individual in the greatest comfort. Logically, developing children are carefully screened for physical and mental defects before being allowed to mature."

Baley interrupted. "You mean you kill them if they don't——"

"If they don't measure up. Quite painlessly, I assure you. The notion shocks you, just as the Earthman's uncontrolled breeding shocks us."

"We're controlled, Dr. Fastolfe. Each family is allowed so many children."

Dr. Fastolfe smiled tolerantly. "So many of any kind of children; not so many *healthy* children. And even so, there are many illegitimates and your population increases."

"Who's to judge which children should live?"

"That's rather complicated and not to be answered in a sentence. Some day we may talk it out in detail."

"Well, where's your problem? You sound satisfied with your society."

"It is stable. That's the trouble. It is too stable."

Baley said, "Nothing pleases you. Our civilization is at the ragged edge of chaos, according to you, and your own is too stable."

"It is possible to be too stable. No Outer World has colonized a new planet in two and a half centuries. There is no prospect for colonization in the future. Our lives in the Outer Worlds are too long to risk and too comfortable to upset."

"I don't know about that, Dr. Fastolfe. You've come to Earth. You risk disease."

"Yes, I do. There are some of us, Mr. Baley, who feel that the future of the human race is even worth the possible loss of an extended lifetime. Too few of us, I am sorry to say."

"All right. We're coming to the point. How is Spacetown helping matters?"

"In trying to introduce robots here on Earth, we're doing our best to upset the balance of your City economy."

"That's your way of helping?" Baley's lips quivered. "You mean you're creating a growing group of displaced and declassified men on purpose?"

"Not out of cruelty or callousness, believe me. A group of displaced men, as you call them, are what we need to serve as a nucleus for colonization. Your ancient America was discovered by ships fitted out with men from the prisons. Don't you see that the City's womb has failed the displaced man. He has nothing to lose and worlds to gain by leaving Earth."

"But it isn't working."

"No, it isn't," said Dr. Fastolfe, sadly. "There is something wrong. The resentment of the Earthman for the robot blocks things. Yet those very robots can accompany humans, smooth the difficulties of initial adjustment to a raw world, make colonization practical."

"Then what? More Outer Worlds?"

"No. The Outer Worlds were established before Civism had spread over Earth, before the Cities. The new colonies will be built by humans who have the City background plus the beginnings of a C/Fe culture. It will be a synthesis, a crossbreeding. As it stands now, Earth's own structure must go ricketing down in the near future, the Outer Worlds will slowly degenerate and decay in a somewhat further future, but the new colonies will be a new and healthy strain, combining the best of both cultures. By their reaction upon the older worlds, including Earth, we ourselves may gain new life."

"I don't know. It's all misty, Dr. Fastolfe."

"It's a dream, yes. Think about it." Abruptly the Spacer rose to his feet. "I have spent more time with you than I intended. In fact, more time than our health ordinances allow. You will excuse me?"

Baley and R. Daneel left the dome. Sunlight, at a different angle, somewhat yellower, washed down upon them once again. In Baley, there was a vague wonder whether sunlight might not seem different on another world. Less harsh and brazen perhaps. More acceptable.

Another world? The ugly Spacer with the prominent ears had filled his mind with queer imaginings. Did the doctors of Aurora once look at the child Fastolfe and wonder if he ought to be allowed to mature? Wasn't he too ugly? Or did their criteria include physical appearance at all? When did ugliness become a deformity and what deformities . . .

But when the sunlight vanished and they entered the first door that led to the Personal, the mood became harder to maintain.

Baley shook his head with exasperation. It was all ridiculous. Forcing Earthmen to emigrate, to set up a new society! It was nonsense! What were these Spacers *really* after?

He thought about it and came to no conclusion.

Slowly, their squad car rolled down the vehicular lane. Reality was surging all about Baley. His blaster was a warm and comfortable weight against his hip. The noise and vibrant life of the City was just as warm, just as comfortable.

For a moment, as the City closed in, his nose tingled to a slight and fugitive pungence.

He thought wonderingly: The City smells.

He thought of the twenty million human beings crammed into the steel walls of the great cave and for the first time in his life he smelled them with nostrils that had been washed clean by outdoor air.

He thought: Would it be different on another world? Less people and more air—cleaner?

But the afternoon roar of the City was all around them, the smell faded and was gone, and he felt a little ashamed of himself.

He let the drive rod in slowly and tapped a larger share of the beamed power. The squad car accelerated sharply as it slanted down into the empty motorway.

"Daneel," he said.

"Yes, Elijah."

"Why was Dr. Fastolfe telling me all he did?"

"It seems probable to me, Elijah, that he wished to impress you with the importance of the investigation. We are not here just to solve a murder, but to save Spacetown and with it, the future of the human race."

Baley said dryly, "I think he'd have been better off if he'd let me see the scene of the crime and interview the men who first found the body."

"I doubt if you could have added anything, Elijah. We have been quite thorough."

"Have you? You've got nothing. Not a clue. Not a suspect."

"No, you are right. The answer must be in the City. To be accurate, though, we did have one suspect."

"What? You said nothing of this before."

"I did not feel it to be necessary, Elijah. Surely it is obvious to you that one suspect automatically existed."

"Who? In the devil's name, who?"

"The one Earthman who was on the scene. Commissioner Julius Enderby."

10

Afternoon of a Plain-clothes Man

THE SQUAD CAR veered to one side, halted against the impersonal concrete wall of the motorway. With the humming of its motor stopped, the silence was dead and thick.

Baley looked at the robot next to him and said in an incongruously quiet voice, "What?"

Time stretched while Baley waited for an answer. A small and lonesome vibration rose and reached a minor peak, then faded. It was the sound of another squad car, boring its way past them on some unknown errand, perhaps a mile away. Or else it was a fire car hurrying along toward its own appointment with combustion.

A detached portion of Baley's mind wondered if any one man any longer knew all the motorways that twisted about in New York City's bowels. At no time in the day or night could the entire motorway system be completely empty, and yet there must be individual passages that no man had entered in years. With sudden, devastating clarity, he remembered a short story he had viewed as a youngster.

It concerned the motorways of London and began, quietly enough, with a murder. The murderer fled toward a prearranged hideout in the corner of a motorway in whose dust his own shoeprints had been the only disturbance for a century. In that abandoned hole, he could wait in complete safety till the search died.

But he took a wrong turning and in the silence and loneness of those twisting corridors he swore a mad and blaspheming oath that, in spite of the Trinity and all the saints, he would yet reach his haven.

From that time on, no turning was right. He wandered through an unending maze from the Brighton Sector on the Channel to Norwich and from Coventry to Canterbury. He burrowed endlessly beneath the great City of London from end to end of its sprawl across the southeastern corner of Medieval England. His clothes were rags and his shoes ribbons, his strength wore down but never left him. He was tired, tired, but unable to stop. He could only go on and on with only wrong turnings ahead of him.

Sometimes he heard the sound of passing cars, but they were always in the next corridor, and however fast he rushed (for he would gladly have given himself up by then) the corridors he reached were always empty. Sometimes he saw an exit far ahead that would lead to the City's life and breath, but it always glimmered further away as he approached until he would turn—and it would be gone.

Occasionally, Londoners on official business through the underground would see a misty figure limping silently toward them, a semitransparent arm lifted in pleading, a mouth open and moving, but soundless. As it approached, it would waver and vanish.

It was a story that had lost the attributes of ordinary fiction and had entered the realm of folklore. The "Wandering Londoner" had become a familiar phrase to all the world.

In the depths of New York City, Baley remembered the story and stirred uneasily.

R. Daneel spoke and there was a small echo to his voice. He said, "We may be overheard."

"Down here? Not a chance. Now what about the Commissioner?"

"He was on the scene, Elijah. He is a City dweller. He was inevitably a suspect."

"Was! Is he still a suspect?"

"No. His innocence was quickly established. For one thing, there was no blaster in his possession. There could not very well be one. He had entered Spacetown in the usual fashion; that was quite certain; and, as you know, blasters are removed as a matter of course."

"Was the murder weapon found at all, by the way?"

"No, Elijah. Every blaster in Spacetown was checked and none had been fired for weeks. A check of the radiation chambers was quite conclusive."

"Then whoever had committed the murder had either hidden the weapon so well——"

"It could not have been hidden anywhere in Spacetown. We were quite thorough."

Baley said impatiently, "I'm trying to consider all possibilities. It was either hidden or it was carried away by the murderer when he left."

"Exactly."

"And if you admit only the second possibility, then the Commissioner is cleared."

"Yes. As a precaution, of course, he was cerebroanalyzed."

"What?"

"By cerebroanalysis, I mean the interpretation of the electromagnetic fields of the living brain cells."

"Oh," said Baley, unenlightened. "And what does that tell you?"

"It gives us information concerning the temperamental and emotional makeup of an individual. In the case of Commissioner Enderby, it told us that he was incapable of killing Dr. Sarton. Quite incapable."

"No," agreed Baley. "He isn't the type. I could have told you that."

"It is better to have objective information. Naturally, all our people in Spacetown allowed themselves to be cerebroanalyzed as well."

"All incapable, I suppose."

"No question. It is why we know that the murderer must be a City dweller."

"Well, then, all we have to do is pass the whole City under your cute little process."

"It would not be very practical, Elijah. There might be millions temperamentally capable of the deed."

"Millions," grunted Baley, thinking of the crowds of that long ago day who had screamed at the dirty Spacers, and of the threatening and slobbering crowds outside the shoe store the night before.

He thought: Poor Julius. A suspect!

He could hear the Commissioner's voice describing the period after the discovery of the body: "It was brutal, brutal." No wonder he broke his glasses in shock and dismay. No wonder he did not want to return to Spacetown. "I hate them," he had ground out between his teeth.

Poor Julius. The man who could handle Spacers. The man whose greatest value to the City lay in his ability to get along with them. How much did that contribute to his rapid promotions?

No wonder the Commissioner had wanted Baley to take over. Good old loyal, close-mouthed Baley. College chum! He would keep quiet if he found out about that little incident. Baley wondered how cerebroanalysis was carried out. He imagined huge electrodes, busy pantographs skidding inklines across graphed paper, self-adjusting gears clicking into place now and then.

Poor Julius. If his state of mind were as appalled as it almost had a right to be, he might already be seeing himself at the end of his career with a forced letter of resignation in the hands of the Mayor.

The squad car slanted up into the sublevels of City Hall.

It was 14:30 when Baley arrived back at his desk. The Commissioner was out. R. Sammy, grinning, did not know where the Commissioner was.

Baley spent some time thinking. The fact that he was hungry didn't register.

At 15:20 R. Sammy came to his desk and said, "The Commissioner is in now, Lije."

Baley said, "Thanks."

For once he listened to R. Sammy without being annoyed. R. Sammy, after all, was a kind of relation to R. Daneel, and R. Daneel obviously wasn't a person—or thing, rather—to get annoyed with. Baley wondered how it would be on a new planet with men and robots starting even in a City culture. He considered the situation quite dispassionately.

The Commissioner was going through some documents as Baley entered, stopping occasionally to make notations.

He said, "That was a fairly giant-size blooper you pulled out in Spacetown."

It flooded back strongly. The verbal duel with Fastolfe . . .

His long face took on a lugubrious expression of chagrin. "I'll admit I did, Commissioner. I'm sorry."

Enderby looked up. His expression was keen through his glasses. He seemed more himself than at any time these thirty hours. He said, "No real matter. Fastolfe didn't seem to mind, so we'll forget it. Unpredictable, these Spacers. You don't deserve your luck, Lije. Next time you talk it over with me before you make like a one-man subether hero."

Baley nodded. The whole thing rolled off his shoulders. He had tried a grandstand stunt and it hadn't worked. Okay. He was a little surprised that he could be so casual about it, but there it was.

He said, "Look, Commissioner. I want to have a two-man apartment assigned to Daneel and myself. I'm not taking him home tonight."

"What's all this?"

"The news is out that he's a robot. Remember? Maybe nothing will happen, but if there is a riot, I don't want my family in the middle of it."

"Nonsense, Lije. I've had the thing checked. There's no such rumor in the City."

"Jessie got the story somewhere, Commissioner."

"Well, there's no organized rumor. Nothing dangerous. I've been checking this ever since I got off the trimensic at Fastolfe's dome. It was why I left. I had to track it down, naturally, and fast. Anyway, here are the reports. See for yourself. There's Doris Gillid's report. She went through a dozen Women's Personals in different parts of the City. You know Doris. She's a competent girl. Well, nothing showed. Nothing showed anywhere."

"Then how did Jessie get the rumor, Commissioner?"

"It can be explained. R. Daneel made a show of himself in the shoe store. Did he really pull a blaster, Lije, or were you stretching it a little?"

"He really pulled one. Pointed it, too."

Commissioner Enderby shook his head. "All right. Someone recognized him. As a robot, I mean."

"Hold on," said Baley, indignantly. "You can't tell him for a robot."

"Why not?"

"Could you? I couldn't."

"What does that prove? We're no experts. Suppose there was a technician out of the Westchester robot factories in the crowd. A professional. A man who has spent his life building and designing robots. He notices something queer about R. Daneel. Maybe in the way he talks or holds himself. He speculates about it. Maybe he tells his wife. She tells a few friends. Then it dies. It's too improbable. People don't believe it. Only it got to Jessie before it died."

"Maybe," said Baley, doubtfully. "But how about an assignment to a bachelor room for two, anyway?"

The Commissioner shrugged, lifted the intercom. After a while, he said, "Section Q-27 is all they can do. It's not a very good neighborhood."

"It'll do," said Baley.

"Where's R. Daneel now, by the way?"

"He's at our record files. He's trying to collect information on Medievalist agitators."

"Good Lord, there are millions."

"I know, but it keeps him happy."

Baley was nearly at the door, when he turned, half on impulse, and said, "Commissioner, did Dr. Sarton ever talk to you about Spacetown's program? I mean, about introducing the C/Fe culture?"

"The what?"

"Introducing robots."

"Occasionally." The Commissioner's tone was not one of any particular interest.

"Did he ever explain what Spacetown's point was?"

"Oh, improve health, raise the standard of living. The usual talk; it didn't impress me. Oh, I agreed with him. I nodded my head and all that. What could I do? It's just a matter of humoring them and hoping they'll keep within reason in their notions. Maybe some day . . ."

Baley waited but he didn't say what maybe-some-day might bring.

Baley said, "Did he ever mention anything about emigration?"

"Emigration! Never. Letting an Earthman into an Outer World is like finding a diamond asteroid in the rings of Saturn."

"I mean emigration to new worlds."

But the Commissioner answered that one with a simple stare of incredulousness.

Baley chewed that for a moment, then said with sudden bluntness, "What's cerebroanalysis, Commissioner? Ever hear of it?"

The Commissioner's round face didn't pucker; his eyes didn't blink. He said evenly, "No, what's it supposed to be?"

"Nothing. Just picked it up."

He left the office and at his desk continued thinking. Certainly, the Commissioner wasn't *that* good an actor. Well, then . . .

At 16:05 Baley called Jessie and told her he wouldn't be home that night nor probably any night for a while. It took a while after that to disengage her.

"Lije, is there trouble? Are you in danger?"

A policeman is always in a certain amount of danger, he explained lightly. It didn't satisfy her. "Where will you be staying?"

He didn't tell her. "If you're going to be lonely tonight," he said, "stay at your mother's." He broke connections abruptly, which was probably just as well.

At 16:20 he made a call to Washington. It took a certain length of time to reach the man he wanted and an almost equally long time to convince him he ought to make an air trip to New York the next day. By 16:40, he had succeeded.

At 16:55 the Commissioner left, passing him with an uncertain smile. The day shift left en masse. The sparser population that filled the offices in the evening and through the night made its way in and greeted him in varied tones of surprise.

R. Daneel came to his desk with a sheaf of papers.

"And those are?" asked Baley.

"A list of men and women who might belong to a Medievalist organization."

"How many does the list include?"

"Over a million," said R. Daneel. "These are just part of them."

"Do you expect to check them all, Daneel?"

"Obviously that would be impractical, Elijah."

"You see, Daneel, almost all Earthmen are Medievalists in one way or another. The Commissioner, Jessie, myself. Look at the Commissioner's——" (He almost said, "spectacles," then remembered that Earthmen must stick together and that the Commissioner's face must be protected in the figurative as well as the literal sense.) He concluded, lamely, "eye ornaments."

"Yes," said R. Daneel, "I had noticed them, but thought it indelicate, perhaps, to refer to them. I have not seen such ornaments on other City dwellers."

"It is a very old-fashioned sort of thing."

"Does it serve a purpose of any sort?"

Baley said, abruptly, "How did you get your list?"

"It was a machine that did it for me. Apparently, one sets it for a particular type of offense and it does the rest. I let it scan all disorderly conduct cases involving robots over the past twenty-five years.

Another machine scanned all City newspapers over an equal period for the names of those involved in unfavorable statements concerning robots or men of the Outer Worlds. It is amazing what can be done in three hours. The machine even eliminated the names of non-survivors from the lists."

"You are amazed? Surely you've got computers on the Outer Worlds?"

"Of many sorts, certainly. Very advanced ones. Still, none are as massive and complex as the ones here. You must remember, of course, that even the largest Outer World scarcely has the population of one of your Cities and extreme complexity is not necessary."

Baley said, "Have you ever been on Aurora?"

"No," said R. Daneel, "I was assembled here on Earth."

"Then how do you know about Outer World computers?"

"But surely that is obvious, partner Elijah. My data store is drawn from that of the late Dr. Sarton. You may take it for granted that it is rich in factual material concerning the Outer Worlds."

"I see. Can you eat, Daneel?"

"I am nuclear-powered. I had thought you were aware of that."

"I'm perfectly aware of it. I didn't ask if you needed to eat. I asked if you *could* eat. If you could put food in your mouth, chew it, and swallow it. I should think that would be an important item in seeming to be a man."

"I see your point. Yes, I can perform the mechanical operations of chewing and swallowing. My capacity is, of course, quite limited, and I would have to remove the ingested material from what you might call my stomach sooner or later."

"All right. You can regurgitate, or whatever you do, in the quiet of our room tonight. The point is that I'm hungry. I've missed lunch, damn it, and I want you with me when I eat. And you can't sit there and *not* eat without attracting attention. So if you can eat, that's what I want to hear. Let's go!"

Section kitchens were the same all over the City. What's more, Baley had been in Washington, Toronto, Los Angeles, London, and Budapest in the way of business, and they had been the same there, too. Perhaps it had been different in Medieval times when languages had varied and dietaries as well. Nowadays, yeast products were just the same from Shanghai to Tashkent and from Winnipeg to Buenos

Aires; and English might not be the "English" of Shakespeare or Churchill, but it was the final potpourri that was current over all the continents and, with some modification, on the Outer Worlds as well.

But language and dietary aside, there were the deeper similarities. There was always that particular odor, undefinable but completely characteristic of "kitchen." There was the waiting triple line moving slowly in, converging at the door and splitting up again, right, left, center. There was the rumble of humanity, speaking and moving, and the sharper clatter of plastic on plastic. There was the gleam of simulated wood, highly polished, highlights on glass, long tables, the touch of steam in the air.

Baley inched slowly forward as the line moved (with all possible staggering of meal hours, a wait of at least ten minutes was almost unavoidable) and said to R. Daneel in sudden curiosity, "Can you smile?"

R. Daneel, who had been gazing at the interior of the kitchen with cool absorption, said, "I beg your pardon, Elijah."

"I'm just wondering, Daneel. Can you smile?" He spoke in a casual whisper.

R. Daneel smiled. The gesture was sudden and surprising. His lips curled back and the skin about either end folded. Only the mouth smiled, however. The rest of the robot's face was untouched.

Baley shook his head. "Don't bother, R. Daneel. It doesn't do a thing for you."

They were at the entrance. Person after person thrust his metal food tag through the appropriate slot and had it scanned. Click—click—click—

Someone once calculated that a smoothly running kitchen could allow the entrance of two hundred persons a minute, the tags of each one being fully scanned to prevent kitchen-jumping, meal-jumping, and ration-stretching. They had also calculated how long a waiting line was necessary for maximum efficiency and how much time was lost when any one person required special treatment.

It was therefore always a calamity to interrupt that smooth click—click by stepping to the manual window, as Baley and R. Daneel did, in order to thrust a special-permit pass at the official in charge.

Jessie, filled with the knowledge of an assistant dietitian, had explained it once to Baley.

"It upsets things completely," she had said. "It throws off consumption figures and inventory estimates. It means special checks. You have to match slips with all the different Section kitchens to make sure the balance isn't too unbalanced, if you know what I mean. There's a separate balance sheet to be made out each week. Then if anything goes wrong and you're overdrawn, it's always your fault. It's never the fault of the City Government for passing out special tickets to everybody and his kid sister. Oh, no. And when we have to say that free choice is suspended for the meal, don't the people in line make a fuss. It's always the fault of the people behind the counter. . . ."

Baley had the story in the fullest detail and so he quite understood the dry and poisonous look he received from the woman behind the window. She made a few hurried notes. Home Section, occupation, reason for meal displacement ("official business," a very irritating reason indeed, but quite irrefutable). Then she folded the slip with firm motions of her fingers and pushed it into a slot. A computer seized it, devoured the contents, and digested the information.

She turned to R. Daneel.

Baley let her have the worst. He said, "My friend is out-of-City."

The woman looked finally and completely outraged. She said, "Home City, please."

Baley intercepted the ball for Daneel once again. "All records are to be credited to the Police Department. No details necessary. Official business."

The woman brought down a pad of slips with a jerk of her arm and filled in the necessary matter in dark-light code with practiced pressings of the first two fingers of her right hand.

She said, "How long will you be eating here?"

"Till further notice," said Baley.

"Press fingers here," she said, inverting the information blank.

Baley had a short qualm as R. Daneel's even fingers with their glistening nails pressed downward. Surely, they wouldn't have forgotten to supply him with fingerprints.

The woman took the blank away and fed it into the all-consuming machine at her elbow. It belched nothing back and Baley breathed more easily.

She gave them little metal tags that were in the bright red that meant "temporary."

She said, "No free choices. We're short this week. Take table DF."
They made their way toward DF.

R. Daneel said, "I am under the impression that most of your people eat in kitchens such as these regularly."

"Yes. Of course, it's rather gruesome eating in a strange kitchen. There's no one about whom you know. In your own kitchen, it's quite different. You have your own seat which you occupy all the time. You're with your family, your friends. Especially when you're young, mealtimes are the bright spot of the day." Baley smiled in brief reminiscence.

Table DF was apparently among those reserved for transients. Those already seated watched their plates uneasily and did not talk with one another. They looked with sneaking envy at the laughing crowds at the other tables.

There is no one so uncomfortable, thought Baley, as the man eating out-of-Section. Be it ever so humble, the old saying went, there's no place like home-kitchen. Even the food tastes better, no matter how many chemists are ready to swear it to be no different from the food in Johannesburg.

He sat down on a stool and R. Daneel sat down next to him.

"No free choice," said Baley, with a wave of his fingers, "so just close the switch there and wait."

It took two minutes. A disc slid back in the table top and a dish lifted.

"Mashed potatoes, zymoveal sauce, and stewed apricots. Oh, well," said Baley.

A fork and two slices of whole yeast bread appeared in a recess just in front of the low railing that went down the long center of the table.

R. Daneel said in a low voice, "You may help yourself to my serving, if you wish."

For a moment, Baley was scandalized. Then he remembered and mumbled, "That's bad manners. Go on. Eat."

Baley ate industriously but without the relaxation that allows complete enjoyment. Carefully, he flicked an occasional glance at R. Daneel. The robot ate with precise motions of his jaws. Too precise. It didn't look quite natural.

Strange! Now that Baley knew for a fact that R. Daneel was in truth a robot, all sorts of little items showed up clearly. For instance, there was no movement of an Adam's apple when R. Daneel swallowed.

Yet he didn't mind so much. Was he getting used to the creature? Suppose people started afresh on a new world (how that ran through his mind ever since Dr. Fastolfe had put it there); suppose Bentley, for instance, were to leave Earth; could he get so he didn't mind working and living alongside robots? Why not? The Spacers themselves did it.

R. Daneel said, "Elijah, is it bad manners to watch another man while he is eating?"

"If you mean stare directly at him, of course. That's only common sense, isn't it? A man has a right to his privacy. Ordinary conversation is entirely in order, but you don't peer at a man while he's swallowing."

"I see. Why is it then that I count eight people watching us closely, very closely?"

Baley put down his fork. He looked about as though he were searching for the salt-pinch dispenser. "I see nothing out of the ordinary."

But he said it without conviction. The mob of diners was only a vast conglomeration of chaos to him. And when R. Daneel turned his impersonal brown eyes upon him, Baley suspected uncomfortably that those were not eyes he saw, but scanners capable of noting, with photographic accuracy and in split seconds of time, the entire panorama.

"I am quite certain," said R. Daneel, calmly.

"Well, then, what of it? It's crude behavior, but what does it prove?"

"I cannot say, Elijah, but is it coincidence that six of the watchers were in the crowd outside the shoe store last night?"

11

Escape Along The Strips

BALEY'S GRIP tightened convulsively on his fork.

"Are you sure?" he asked automatically, and as he said it, he realized the uselessness of the question. You don't ask a computer if it is sure of the answer it disgorges; not even a computer with arms and legs.

R. Daneel said, "Quite!"

"Are they close to us?"

"Not very. They are scattered."

"All right, then." Baley returned to his meal, his fork moving mechanically. Behind the frown on his long face, his mind worked furiously.

Suppose the incident last night had been organized by a group of anti-robot fanatics, that it had not been the spontaneous trouble it had seemed. Such a group of agitators could easily include men who had studied robots with the intensity born of deep opposition. One of them might have recognized R. Daneel for what he was. (The Commissioner had suggested that, in a way. Damn it, there were surprising depths to that man.)

It worked itself out logically. Granting they had been unable to act in an organized manner on the spur of last evening's moment, they would still have been able to plan for the future. If they could recognize a robot such as R. Daneel, they could certainly realize that Baley himself was a police officer. A police officer in the unusual company of a humanoid robot would very likely be a responsible man in the organization. (With the wisdom of hindsight, Baley followed the line of reasoning with no trouble at all.)

It followed then that observers at City Hall (or perhaps agents within City Hall) would be bound to spot Baley, R. Daneel, or both before too long a time had passed. That they had done so within twenty-four hours was not surprising. They might have done so in less time if so much of Baley's day had not been spent in Spacetown and along the motorway.

R. Daneel had finished his meal. He sat quietly waiting, his perfect hands resting lightly on the end of the table.

"Had we not better do something?" he asked.

"We're safe here in the kitchen," said Baley. "Now leave this to me. Please."

Baley looked about him cautiously and it was as though he saw a kitchen for the first time.

People! Thousands of them. What was the capacity of an average kitchen? He had once seen the figure. Two thousand two hundred, he thought. This one was larger than average.

Suppose the cry, "Robot," were sent out into the air. Suppose it were tossed among the thousands like a . . .

He was at a loss for a comparison, but it didn't matter. It wouldn't happen.

A spontaneous riot could flare anywhere, in the kitchens as easily as in the corridors or in the elevators. More easily, perhaps. There was a lack of inhibition at mealtimes, a sense of horseplay that could degenerate into something more serious at a trifle.

But a planned riot would be different. Here in the kitchen, the planners would themselves be trapped in a large and mob-filled room. Once the dishes went flying and the tables cracking there would be no easy way to escape. Hundreds would certainly die and they themselves might easily be among them.

No, a safe riot would have to be planned in the avenues of the City, in some relatively narrow passageway. Panic and hysteria would travel slowly along the constriction and there would be time for the quick, prepared fadeaway along the side passage or the unobtrusive step onto an escalating localway that would move them to a higher level and disappearance.

Baley felt trapped. There were probably others waiting outside. Baley and R. Daneel were to be followed to a proper point and the fuse would be set off.

R. Daneel said, "Why not arrest them?"

"That would only start the trouble sooner. You know their faces, don't you? You won't forget?"

"I am not capable of forgetting."

"Then we'll nab them another time. For now, we'll break their net. Follow me. Do exactly as I do."

He rose, turned his dish carefully upside down, centering it on the movable disc from below which it had risen. He put his fork back in its recess. R. Daneel, watching, matched his action. The dishes and utensils dropped out of sight.

R. Daneel said, "They are getting up, too."

"All right. It's my feeling they won't get too close. Not here."

The two moved into line now, drifting toward an exit where the click—click—click of the tags sounded ritualistically, each click recording the expenditure of a ration unit.

Baley looked back through the steamy haze and the noise and, with incongruous sharpness, thought of a visit to the City Zoo with Ben six or seven years ago. No, eight, because Ben had just passed his eighth birthday then. (Jehoshaphat! Where did the time go?)

It had been Ben's first visit and he had been excited. After all, he had never actually seen a cat or a dog before. Then, on top of that, there was the bird cage! Even Baley himself, who had seen it a dozen times before, was not immune to its fascination.

There is something about the first sight of living objects hurtling through air that is incomparably startling. It was feeding time in the sparrow cage and an attendant was dumping cracked oats into a long trough (human beings had grown used to yeast substitutes, but animals, more conservative in their way, insisted on real grain).

The sparrows flocked down in what seemed like hundreds. Wing to wing, with an ear-splitting twitter, they lined the trough. . . .

That was it; that was the picture that came to Baley's mind as he looked back at the kitchen he was leaving. Sparrows at the trough. The thought repelled him.

He thought: Jehoshaphat, there must be a better way.

But what better way? What was wrong with this way? It had never bothered him before.

He said abruptly to R. Daneel, "Ready, Daneel?"

"I am ready, Elijah."

They left the kitchen and escape was now clearly and flatly up to Baley.

There is a game that youngsters know called "running the strips." Its rules vary in trivial fashion from City to City, but its essentials are eternal. A boy from San Francisco can join the game in Cairo with no trouble.

Its object is to get from point A to point B via the City's rapid transit system in such a way that the "leader" manages to lose as many of his followers as possible. A leader who arrives at the destination alone is skillful indeed, as is a follower who refuses to be shaken.

The game is usually conducted during the evening rush hour when the increased density of the commuters makes it at once more hazardous and more complicated. The leader sets off, running up and down the accelerating strips. He does his best to do the unexpected, remaining standing on a given strip as long as possible, then leaping off suddenly in either direction. He will run quickly through several strips, then remain waiting once more.

Pity the follower who incautiously careens forward one strip too far. Before he has caught his mistake, unless he is extraordinarily nimble, he has driven past the leader or fallen behind. The clever leader will compound the error by moving quickly in the appropriate direction.

A move designed to increase the complexity of the task tenfold involves boarding the localways or the expressways themselves, and hurtling off the other side. It is bad form to avoid them completely and also bad form to linger on them.

The attraction of the game is not easy for an adult to understand, particularly for an adult who has never himself been a teen-age strip-runner. The players are roughly treated by legitimate travelers into whose path they find themselves inevitably flying. They are persecuted bitterly by the police and punished by their parents. They are denounced in the schools and on the subetherics. No year passes without its four or five teen-agers killed at the game, its dozens hurt, its cases of innocent bystanders meeting tragedy of varying degree.

Yet nothing can be done to wipe out the strip-running gangs. The greater the danger, the more the strip-runners have that most valuable of all prizes, honor in the eyes of their fellows. A successful one may well swagger; a well-known leader is cock-of-the-walk.

Elijah Baley, for instance, remembered with satisfaction even now that he had been a strip-runner once. He had led a gang of twenty from the Concourse Sector to the borders of Queens, crossing three expressways. In two tireless and relentless hours, he had shaken off some of the most agile followers of the Bronx, and arrived at the destination point alone. They talked about that run for months.

Baley was in his forties now, of course. He hadn't run the strips for over twenty years, but he remembered some of the tricks. What he had lost in agility, he made up in another respect. He was a policeman. No one but another policeman as experienced as himself could possibly know the City as well, know where almost every metal-bordered alley began and ended.

He walked away from the kitchen briskly, but not too rapidly. Each moment he expected the cry of "Robot, robot" to ring out behind him. That initial set of moments was the riskiest. He counted the steps until he felt the first accelerating strip moving under him.

He stopped for a moment, while R. Daneel moved smoothly up beside him.

"Are they still behind us, Daneel?" asked Baley in a whisper.

"Yes. They're moving closer."

"That won't last," said Baley confidently. He looked at the strips stretching to either side, with their human cargo whipping to his left more and more rapidly as their distance from him increased. He had felt the strips beneath his feet many times a day almost all the days of his life, but he had not bent his knees in anticipation of running them in seven thousand days and more. He felt the old familiar thrill and his breath grew more rapid.

He quite forgot the one time he had caught Ben at the game. He had lectured him interminably and threatened to have him put under police surveillance.

Lightly, quickly, at double the "safe" rate, he went up the strips. He leaned forward sharply against the acceleration. The localway was humming past. For a moment, it looked as though he would mount, but suddenly he was fading backward, backward, dodging through the crowd to left and right as it thickened on the slower strips.

He stopped, and let himself be carried along at a mere fifteen miles an hour.

"How many are with us, Daneel?"

"Only one, Elijah." The robot was at his side, unruffled, unbreathing.

"He must have been a good one in his day, too, but he won't last either."

Full of self-confidence, he felt a half-remembered sensation of his younger days. It consisted partly of the feeling of immersion in a mystic rite to which others did not belong, partly of the purely physical sensation of wind against hair and face, partly of a tenuous sense of danger.

"They call this the side shuffle," he said to R. Daneel in a low voice.

His long stride ate distance, but he moved along a single strip, dodging the legitimate crowd with a minimum of effort. He kept it up, moving always closer to the strip's edge, until the steady movement of his head through the crowd must have been hypnotic in its constant velocity—as it was intended to be.

And then, without a break in his step, he shifted two inches sideways and was on the adjoining strip. He felt an aching in his thigh muscles as he kept his balance.

He whipped through a cluster of commuters and was on the forty-five-mile strip.

"How is it now, Daneel?" he asked.

"He is still with us," was the calm answer.

Baley's lips tightened. There was nothing for it but to use the moving platforms themselves, and that really required co-ordination; more, perhaps, than he still retained.

He looked about quickly. Exactly where were they now? B-22d Street flashed by. He made rapid calculations and was off. Up the remaining strips, smoothly and steadily, a swing onto the localway platform.

The impersonal faces of men and women, calloused with the ennui of way-riding, were jolted into something like indignation as Baley and R. Daneel clambered aboard and squeezed through the railings.

"Hey, now," called a woman shrilly, clutching at her hat.

"Sorry," said Baley, breathlessly.

He forced his way through the standees and with a wriggle was off on the other side. At the last moment, a jostled passenger thumped his back in anger. He went staggering.

Desperately he tried to regain his footing. He lurched across a strip boundary and the sudden change in velocity forced him to his knees and then over on his side.

He had the sudden, panicky vision of men colliding with him and bowling over, of a spreading confusion on the strips, one of the dreaded "man-jams" that would not fail to put dozens in the hospital with broken limbs.

But R. Daneel's arm was under his back. He felt himself lifted with more than a man's strength.

"Thanks," gasped Baley, and there was no time for more.

Off he went and down the decelerating strips in a complicated pattern so designed that his feet met the V-joint strips of an expressway at the exact point of crossover. Without the loss of rhythm, he was accelerating again, then up and over an expressway.

"Is he with us, Daneel?"

"Not one in sight, Elijah."

"Good. But what a strip-runner you would have been, Daneel!— Oops, now, now!"

Off onto another localway in a whirl and down the strips with a clatter to a doorway, large and official in appearance. A guard rose to his feet.

Baley flashed his identification. "Official business."

They were inside.

"Power plant," said Baley, curtly. "This breaks our tracks completely."

He had been in power plants before, including this one. Familiarity did not lessen his feeling of uncomfortable awe. The feeling was heightened by the haunting thought that once his father had been high in the hierarchy of a plant such as this. That is, before . . .

There was the surrounding hum of the tremendous generators hidden in the central well of the plant, the faint sharpness of ozone in the air, the grim and silent threat of the red lines that marked the limits beyond which no one could pass without protective clothing.

Somewhere in the plant (Baley had no idea exactly where) a pound of fissionable material was consumed each day. Every so often, the radioactive fission products, the so-called "hot ash," were forced by air pressure through leaden pipes to distant caverns ten miles out in the ocean and a half mile below the ocean floor. Baley sometimes wondered what would happen when the caverns were filled.

He said to R. Daneel with sudden gruffness, "Stay away from the red lines." Then, he bethought himself and added sheepishly, "But I suppose it doesn't matter to you."

"Is it a question of radioactivity?" asked Daneel.

"Yes."

"Then it does matter to me. Gamma radiation destroys the delicate balance of a positronic brain. It would affect me much sooner than it would affect you."

"You mean it would *kill* you?"

"I would require a new positronic brain. Since no two can be alike, I would be a new individual. The Daneel you now speak to would be, in a manner of speaking, dead."

Baley looked at the other doubtfully. "I never knew that.—Up these ramps."

"The point isn't stressed. Spacetown wishes to convince Earthmen of the usefulness of such as myself, not of our weaknesses."

"Then why tell me?"

R. Daneel turned his eyes full on his human companion. "You are my partner, Elijah. It is well that you know my weaknesses and shortcomings."

Baley cleared his throat and had nothing more to say on the subject.

"Out in this direction," he said a moment later, "and we're a quarter of a mile from our apartment."

It was a grim, lower-class apartment. One small room and two beds. Two fold-in chairs and a closet. A built-in subetheric screen that allowed no manual adjustment, and would be working only at stated hours, but *would* be working then. No washbasin, not even an unactivated one, and no facilities for cooking or even boiling water. A small trash-disposal pipe was in one corner of the room, an ugly, unadorned, unpleasantly functional object.

Baley shrugged. "This is it. I guess we can stand it."

R. Daneel walked to the trash-disposal pipe. His shirt unseamed at a touch, revealing a smooth and, to all appearances, well-muscled chest.

"What are you doing?" asked Baley.

"Getting rid of the food I ingested. If I were to leave it, it would putrefy and I would become an object of distaste."

R. Daneel placed two fingers carefully under one nipple and pushed in a definite pattern of pressure. His chest opened longitudinally. R. Daneel reached in and from a welter of gleaming metal withdrew a thin, translucent sac, partly distended. He opened it while Baley watched with a kind of horror.

R. Daneel hesitated. He said, "The food is perfectly clean. I do not salivate or chew. It was drawn in through the gullet by suction, you know. It is edible."

"That's all right," said Baley, gently. "I'm not hungry. You just get rid of it."

R. Daneel's food sac was of fluorocarbon plastic, Baley decided. At least the food did not cling to it. It came out smoothly and was placed little by little into the pipe. A waste of good food at that, he thought.

He sat down on one bed and removed his shirt. He said, "I suggest an early start tomorrow."

"For a specific reason?"

"The location of this apartment isn't known to our friends yet. Or at least I hope not. If we leave early, we are that much safer. Once in City Hall, we will have to decide whether our partnership is any longer practical."

"You think it is perhaps not?"

Baley shrugged and said dourly, "We can't go through this sort of thing every day."

"But it seems to me——"

R. Daneel was interrupted by the sharp scarlet sliver of the door signal.

Baley rose silently to his feet and unlimbered his blaster. The door signal flashed once more.

He moved silently to the door, put his thumb on the blaster contact while he threw the switch that activated the one-way transparency patch. It wasn't a good view-patch; it was small and had a distorting effect, but it was quite good enough to show Baley's youngster, Ben, outside the door.

Baley acted quickly. He flung the door open, snatched brutally at Ben's wrist as the boy raised his hand to signal a third time, and pulled him in.

The look of fright and bewilderment faded only slowly from Ben's eyes as he leaned breathlessly against the wall toward which he had been hurled. He rubbed his wrist.

"Dad!" he said in grieved tones. "You didn't have to grab me like that."

Baley was staring through the view-patch of the once-again-closed door. As nearly as he could tell, the corridor was empty.

"Did you see anyone out there, Ben?"

"No. Gee, Dad, I just came to see if you were all right."

"Why shouldn't I be all right?"

"I don't know. It was Mom. She was crying and all like that. She said I had to find you. If I didn't go, she said she would go herself, and then she didn't know what would happen. She *made* me go, Dad."

Baley said, "How did you find me? Did your mother know where I was?"

"No, she didn't. I called up your office."

"And they told you?"

Ben looked startled at his father's vehemence. He said, in a low voice, "Sure. Weren't they supposed to?"

Baley and Daneel looked at one another.

Baley rose heavily to his feet. He said, "Where's your mother now, Ben? At the apartment?"

"No, we went to Grandma's for dinner and stayed there. I'm supposed to go back there now. I mean, as long as you're all right, Dad."

"You'll stay here. Daneel, did you notice the exact location of the floor communo?"

The robot said, "Yes. Do you intend leaving the room to use it?"

"I've got to. I've got to get in touch with Jessie."

"Might I suggest that it would be more logical to let Bentley do that. It is a form of risk and he is less valuable."

Baley stared. "Why, you——"

He thought: Jehoshaphat, what am I getting angry about?

He went on more calmly, "You don't understand, Daneel. Among us, it is not customary for a man to send his young son into possible danger, even if it is logical to do so."

"Danger!" squeaked Ben in a sort of horrified pleasure. "What's going on, Dad? Huh, Dad?"

"Nothing, Ben. Now, this isn't any of your business. Understand?

Get ready for bed. I want you in bed when I get back. You hear me?"

"Aw, gosh. You could tell a fellow. I won't say anything."

"In bed!"

"Gosh!"

Baley hitched his jacket back as he stood at the floor communo, so that his blaster butt was ready for snatching. He spoke his personal number into the mouthpiece and waited while a computer fifteen miles away checked it to make sure the call was permissible. It was a very short wait that was involved, since a plain-clothes man had no limit on the number of his business calls. He spoke the code number of his mother-in-law's apartment.

The small screen at the base of the instrument lit up, and her face looked out at him.

He said, in a low voice, "Mother, put on Jessie."

Jessie must have been waiting for him. She was on at once. Baley looked at her face and then darkened the screen deliberately.

"All right, Jessie. Ben's here. Now, what's the matter?" His eyes roved from side to side continuously, watching.

"Are you all right? You aren't in trouble?"

"I'm obviously all right, Jessie. Now stop it."

"Oh, Lije, I've been so worried."

"What about?" he asked tightly.

"You know. Your friend."

"What about him?"

"I told you last night. There'll be trouble."

"Now, that's nonsense. I'm keeping Ben with me for tonight and you go to bed. Good-by, dear."

He broke connections and waited for two breaths before starting back. His face was gray with apprehension and fear.

Ben was standing in the middle of the room when Baley returned. One of his contact lenses was neatly pocketed in a little suction cup. The other was still in his eye.

Ben said, "Gosh, Dad, isn't there any water in the place? Mr. Olivaw says I can't go to the Personal."

"He's right. You can't. Put that thing back in your eye, Ben. It won't hurt you to sleep with them for one night."

"All right." Ben put it back, put away his suction cup and climbed into bed. "Boy, what a mattress!"

Baley said to R. Daneel, "I suppose you won't mind sitting up."

"Of course not. I was interested, by the way, in the queer glass Bentley wears close to his eyes. Do all Earthmen wear them?"

"No. Just some," said Baley, absently. "I don't, for instance."

"For what reason is it worn?"

Baley was too absorbed with his own thoughts to answer. His own uneasy thoughts.

The lights were out.

Baley remained wakeful. He was dimly aware of Ben's breathing as it turned deep and regular and became a bit rough. When he turned his head, he grew somehow conscious of R. Daneel, sitting in a chair with grave immobility, face turned toward the door.

Then he fell asleep, and when he slept, he dreamed.

He dreamed Jessie was falling into the fission chamber of a nuclear power plant, falling and falling. She held out her arms to him, shrieking, but he could only stand frozenly just outside a scarlet line and watch her distorted figure turn as it fell, growing smaller until it was only a dot.

He could only watch her, in the dream, knowing that it was he, himself, who had pushed her.

12

Words From an Expert

ELIJAH BALEY looked up as Commissioner Julius Enderby entered the office. He nodded wearily.

The Commissioner looked at the clock and grunted, "Don't tell me you've been here all night!"

Baley said, "I won't."

The Commissioner said in a low voice, "Any trouble last night?"

Baley shook his head.

The Commissioner said, "I've been thinking that I could be minimizing the possibility of riots. If there's anything to——"

Baley said tightly, "For God's sake, Commissioner, if anything happened, I'd tell you. There was no trouble of any sort."

"All right." The Commissioner moved away, passing beyond the door that marked off the unusual privacy that became his exalted position.

Baley looked after him and thought: *He* must have slept last night.

Baley bent to the routine report he was trying to write as a cover-up for the real activities of the last two days, but the words he had tapped out by finger touch blurred and danced. Slowly, he became aware of an object standing by his desk.

He lifted his head. "What do you want?"

It was R. Sammy. Baley thought: Julius's private flunky. It pays to be a Commissioner.

R. Sammy said through his fatuous grin, "The Commissioner wants to see you, Lije. He says right away."

Baley waved his hand. "He just saw me. Tell him I'll be in later."

R. Sammy said, "He says right away."

"All right. All right. Go away."

The robot backed away, saying, "The Commissioner wants to see you right away, Lije. He says right away."

"Jehoshaphat," said Baley between his teeth. "I'm going. I'm going." He got up from his desk, headed for the office, and R. Sammy was silent.

Baley said as he entered, "Damn it, Commissioner, *don't* send that thing after me, will you?"

But the Commissioner only said, "Sit down, Lije. Sit down."

Baley sat down and stared. Perhaps he had done old Julius an injustice. Perhaps the man hadn't slept after all. He looked fairly beat.

The Commissioner was tapping the paper before him. "There's a record of a call you made to a Dr. Gerrigel at Washington by insulated beam."

"That's right, Commissioner."

"There's no record of the conversation, naturally, since it was insulated. What's it all about?"

"I'm after background information."

"He's a roboticist, isn't he?"

"That's right."

The Commissioner put out a lower lip and suddenly looked like a child about to pout. "But what's the point? What kind of information are you after?"

"I'm not sure, Commissioner. I just have a feeling that in a case like this, information on robots might help." Baley clamped his mouth shut after that. He wasn't going to be specific, and that was that.

"I wouldn't, Lije. I wouldn't. I don't think it's wise."

"What's your objection, Commissioner?"

"The fewer the people who know about all this, the better."

"I'll tell him as little as I can. Naturally."

"I still don't think it's wise."

Baley was feeling just sufficiently wretched to lose patience.

He said, "Are you ordering me not to see him?"

"No. No. You do as you see fit. You're heading this investigation. Only . . ."

"Only what?"

The Commissioner shook his head. "Nothing.—Where is *he?* You know who I mean."

Baley did. He said, "Daneel's still at the files."

The Commissioner paused a long moment, then said, "We're not making much progress, you know."

"We're not making any so far. Still, things may change."

"All right, then," said the Commissioner, but he didn't look as though he really thought it were all right.

R. Daneel was at Baley's desk, when the latter returned.

"Well, and what have *you* got?" Baley asked gruffly.

"I have completed my first, rather hasty, search through the files, partner Elijah, and I have located two of the people who tried to track us last night and who, moreover, were at the shoe store during the former incident."

"Let's see."

R. Daneel placed the small, stamp-size cards before Baley. They were mottled with the small dots that served as code. The robot also produced a portable decoder and placed one of the cards into an appropriate slot. The dots possessed electrical conduction properties different from that of the card as a whole. The electric field passing through the card was therefore distorted in a highly specific manner and in response to that specification the three-by-six screen above the decoder was filled with words. Words which, uncoded, would have filled several sheets of standard size report paper. Words, moreover, which could not possibly be interpreted by anyone not in possession of an official police decoder.

Baley read through the material stolidly. The first person was Francis Clousarr, age thirty-three at time of arrest two years before; cause of arrest, inciting to riot; employee at New York Yeast; home address, so-and-so; parentage, so-and-so; hair, eyes, distinguishing marks, educational history, employment history, psychoanalytic profile, physical profile, data here, data there, and finally reference to tri-photo in the rogues' gallery.

"You checked the photograph?" asked Baley.

"Yes, Elijah."

The second person was Gerhard Paul. Baley glanced at the material on that card and said, "This is all no good."

R. Daneel said, "I am sure that cannot be so. If there is an organization of Earthmen who are capable of the crime we are investigating, these are members. Is that not an obvious likelihood? Should they then not be questioned?"

"We'd get nothing out of them."

"They were there, both at the shoe store and in the kitchen. They cannot deny it."

"Just being there's no crime. Besides which, they *can* deny it. They can just say they weren't there. It's as simple as that. How can we prove they're lying?"

"I saw them."

"That's no proof," said Baley, savagely. "No court, if it ever came to that, would believe that you could remember two faces in a blur of a million."

"It is obvious that *I* can."

"Sure. Tell them what you are. As soon as you do that, you're no witness. Your kind have no status in any court of law on Earth."

R. Daneel said, "I take it, then, that you have changed your mind."

"What do you mean?"

"Yesterday, in the kitchen, you said there was no need to arrest them. You said that as long as I remembered their faces, we could arrest them at any time."

"Well, I didn't think it through," said Baley. "I was crazy. It can't be done."

"Not even for psychological reasons? They would not know we had no legal proof of their complicity in conspiracy."

Baley said, tensely, "Look, I am expecting Dr. Gerrigel of Washington in half an hour. Do you mind waiting till he's been here and gone? Do you mind?"

"I will wait," said R. Daneel.

Anthony Gerrigel was a precise and very polite man of middle height, who looked far from being one of the most erudite roboticists on Earth. He was nearly twenty minutes late, it turned out, and quite apologetic about it. Baley, white with an anger born of apprehension, shrugged off the apologies gracelessly. He checked his reservation on Conference Room D, repeated his instructions that they were not to be disturbed on any account for an hour, and led Dr. Gerrigel and R. Daneel down the corridor, up a ramp, and through a door that led to one of the spy-beam-insulated chambers.

Baley checked the walls carefully before sitting down, listening to the soft burr of the pulsometer in his hand, waiting for any fading of the steady sound which would indicate a break, even a small one, in the insulation. He turned it on the ceiling, floor, and, with particular care, on the door. There was no break.

Dr. Gerrigel smiled a little. He looked like a man who never smiled more than a little. He was dressed with a neatness that could only be described as fussy. His iron-gray hair was smoothed carefully back and his face looked pink and freshly washed. He sat with a posture of prim stiffness as though repeated maternal advice in his younger years concerning the desirability of good posture had rigidified his spine forever.

He said to Baley, "You make this all seem very formidable."

"It's quite important, Doctor. I need information about robots that only you can give me, perhaps. Anything we say here, of course, is top secret and the City will expect you to forget it all when you leave." Baley looked at his watch.

The little smile on the roboticist's face winked away. He said, "Let me explain why I am late." The matter obviously weighed upon him. "I decided not to go by air. I get airsick."

"That's too bad," said Baley. He put away the pulsometer, after checking its standard settings to make last-minute certain that there was nothing wrong with *it*, and sat down.

"Or at least not exactly airsick, but nervous. A mild agoraphobia. It's nothing particularly abnormal, but there it is. So I took the expressways."

Baley felt a sudden sharp interest. "Agoraphobia?"

"I make it sound worse than it is," the roboticist said at once. "It's just the feeling you get in a plane. Have you ever been in one, Mr. Baley?"

"Several times."

"Then you must know what I mean. It's that feeling of being surrounded by nothing; of being separated from—from empty air by a mere inch of metal. It's very uncomfortable."

"So you took the expressway?"

"Yes."

"All the way from Washington to New York?"

"Oh, I've done it before. Since they built the Baltimore-Philadelphia tunnel, it's quite simple."

So it was. Baley had never made the trip himself, but he was perfectly aware that it was possible. Washington, Baltimore, Philadelphia, and New York had grown, in the last two centuries, to the point where all nearly touched. The Four-City Area was almost the official name for the entire stretch of coast, and there were a considerable number of people who favored administrational consolidation and the formation of a single super-City. Baley disagreed with that, himself. New York City by itself was almost too large to be handled by a centralized government. A larger City, with over fifty million population, would break down under its own weight.

"The trouble was," Dr. Gerrigel was saying, "that I missed a connection in Chester Sector, Philadelphia, and lost time. That, and a little difficulty in getting a transient room assignment, ended by making me late."

"Don't worry about that, Doctor. What you say, though, is interesting. In view of your dislike for planes, what would you say to going outside City limits on foot, Dr. Gerrigel?"

"For what reason?" He looked startled and more than a little apprehensive.

"It's just a rhetorical question. I'm not suggesting that you really should. I want to know how the notion strikes you, that's all."

"It strikes me very unpleasantly."

"Suppose you had to leave the City at night and walk cross country for half a mile or more."

"I—I don't think I could be persuaded to."

"No matter how important the necessity?"

"If it were to save my life or the lives of my family, I might try. . . ." He looked embarrassed. "May I ask the point of these questions, Mr. Baley?"

"I'll tell you. A serious crime has been committed, a particularly disturbing murder. I'm not at liberty to give you the details. There is a theory, however, that the murderer, in order to commit the crime, did just what we were discussing; he crossed open country at night and alone. I was just wondering what kind of man could do that."

Dr. Gerrigel shuddered. "No one I know. Certainly not I. Of

course, among millions I suppose you could find a few hardy individuals."

"But you wouldn't say it was a very likely thing for a human being to do?"

"No. Certainly not likely."

"In fact, if there's any other explanation for the crime, any other *conceivable* explanation, it should be considered."

Dr. Gerrigel looked more uncomfortable than ever as he sat bolt upright with his well-kept hands precisely folded in his lap. "Do you have an alternate explanation in mind?"

"Yes. It occurs to me that a robot, for instance, would have no difficulty at all in crossing open country."

Dr. Gerrigel stood up. "Oh, my dear sir!"

"What's wrong?"

"You mean a robot may have committed the crime?"

"Why not?"

"Murder? Of a human being?"

"Yes. Please sit down, Doctor."

The roboticist did as he was told. He said, "Mr. Baley, there are two acts involved: walking cross country, and murder. A human being could commit the latter easily, but would find difficulty in doing the former. A robot could do the former easily, but the latter act would be completely impossible. If you're going to replace an unlikely theory by an impossible one——"

"Impossible is a hell of a strong word, Doctor."

"You've heard of the First Law of Robotics, Mr. Baley?"

"Sure. I can even quote it: A robot may not injure a human being, or, through inaction, allow a human being to come to harm." Baley suddenly pointed a finger at the roboticist and went on, "Why can't a robot be built without the First Law? What's so sacred about it?"

Dr. Gerrigel looked startled, then tittered, "Oh, Mr. Baley."

"Well, what's the answer?"

"Surely, Mr. Baley, if you even know a little about robotics, you must know the gigantic task involved, both mathematically and electronically, in building a positronic brain."

"I have an idea," said Baley. He remembered well his visit to a robot factory once in the way of business. He had seen their library of book-films, long ones, each of which contained the mathematical analysis of a single type of positronic brain. It took more than an hour for the average such film to be viewed at standard scanning speed, condensed though its symbolisms were. And no two brains were alike, even when prepared according to the most rigid specifications. That, Baley understood, was a consequence of Heisenberg's Uncertainty Principle. This meant that each film had to be supplemented by appendices involving possible variations.

Oh, it was a job, all right. Baley wouldn't deny that.

Dr. Gerrigel said, "Well, then, you must understand that a design for a new type of positronic brain, even one where only minor innovations are involved, is not the matter of a night's work. It usually involves the entire research staff of a moderately sized factory and takes anywhere up to a year of time. Even this large expenditure of work would not be nearly enough if it were not that the basic theory of such circuits has already been standardized and may be used as a foundation for further elaboration. The standard basic theory involves the Three Laws of Robotics: the First Law, which you've quoted; the Second Law, which states, 'A robot must obey the orders given it by human beings except where such orders would conflict with the First Law,' and the Third Law, which states, 'A robot must protect its own existence as long as such protection does not conflict with the First or Second Law.' Do you understand?"

R. Daneel, who, to all appearances, had been following the conversation with close attention, broke in. "If you will excuse me, Elijah, I would like to see if I follow Dr. Gerrigel. What you imply, sir, is that any attempt to build a robot, the working of whose positronic brain is not oriented about the Three Laws, would require first the setting up of a new basic theory and that this, in turn, would take many years."

The roboticist looked very gratified. "That is exactly what I mean, Mr. . . ."

Baley waited a moment, then carefully introduced R. Daneel: "This is Daneel Olivaw, Dr. Gerrigel."

"Good day, Mr. Olivaw." Dr. Gerrigel extended his hand and shook Daneel's. He went on, "It is my estimation that it would take fifty years to develop the basic theory of a non-Asenion positronic brain—that is, one in which the basic assumptions of the Three Laws are disallowed—and bring it to the point where robots similar to modern models could be constructed."

"And this has never been done?" asked Baley. "I mean, Doctor, that we've been building robots for several thousand years. In all that time, hasn't anybody or any group had fifty years to spare?"

"Certainly," said the roboticist, "but it is not the sort of work that anyone would care to do."

"I find that hard to believe. Human curiosity will undertake anything."

"It hasn't undertaken the non-Asenion robot. The human race, Mr. Baley, has a strong Frankenstein complex."

"A what?"

"That's a popular name derived from a Medieval novel describing a robot that turned on its creator. I never read the novel myself. But that's beside the point. What I wish to say is that robots without the First Law are simply not built."

"And no theory for it even exists?"

"Not to my knowledge, and my knowledge," he smiled self-consciously, "is rather extensive."

"And a robot with a First Law built in could not kill a man?"

"Never. Unless such killing were completely accidental or unless it were necessary to save the lives of two or more men. In either case, the positronic potential built up would ruin the brain past recovery."

"All right," said Baley. "All this represents the situation on Earth. Right?"

"Yes. Certainly."

"What about the Outer Worlds?"

Some of Dr. Gerrigel's self-assurance seemed to ooze away. "Oh dear, Mr. Baley, I couldn't say of my own knowledge, but I'm sure that if non-Asenion positronic brains were ever designed or if the mathematical theory were worked out, we'd hear of it."

"Would we? Well, let me follow up another thought in my mind, Dr. Gerrigel. I hope you don't mind."

"No. Not at all." He looked helplessly first at Baley, then at R. Daneel. "After all, if it is as important as you say, I'm glad to do all I can."

"Thank you, Doctor. My question is, why humanoid robots? I mean that I've been taking them for granted all my life, but now it occurs to me that I don't know the reason for their existence. Why should a robot have a head and four limbs? Why should he look more or less like a man?"

"You mean, why shouldn't he be built functionally, like any other machine?"

"Right," said Baley. "Why not?"

Dr. Gerrigel smiled a little. "Really, Mr. Baley, you are born too late. The early literature of robotics is riddled with a discussion of that very matter and the polemics involved were something frightful. If you would like a very good reference to the disputations among the functionalists and anti-functionalists, I can recommend Hanford's 'History of Robotics.' Mathematics is kept to a minimum. I think you'd find it very interesting."

"I'll look it up," said Baley, patiently. "Meanwhile, could you give me an idea?"

"The decision was made on the basis of economics. Look here, Mr. Baley, if you were supervising a farm, would you care to buy a tractor with a positronic brain, a reaper, a harrow, a milker, an automobile, and so on, each with a positronic brain; or would you rather have ordinary unbrained machinery with a single positronic robot to run them all. I warn you that the second alternative represents only a fiftieth or a hundredth the expense."

"But why the human form?"

"Because the human form is the most successful generalized form in all nature. We are not a specialized animal, Mr. Baley, except for our nervous systems and a few odd items. If you want a design capable of doing a great many widely various things, all fairly well, you could do no better than to imitate the human form. Besides that, our entire technology is based on the human form. An automobile, for instance, has its controls so made as to be grasped and manipulated most easily by human hands and feet of a certain size and shape, attached to the body by limbs of a certain length and joints of a certain type. Even such simple objects as chairs and tables or knives and forks are designed to meet the requirements of human measurements and manner of working. It is easier to have robots imitate the human shape than to redesign radically the very philosophy of our tools."

"I see. That makes sense. Now isn't it true, Doctor, that the roboticists of the Outer World manufacture robots that are much more humanoid than our own?"

"I believe that is true."

"Could they manufacture a robot so humanoid that it would pass for human under ordinary conditions?"

Dr. Gerrigel lifted his eyebrows and considered that. "I think they could, Mr. Baley. It would be terribly expensive. I doubt that the return could be profitable."

"Do you suppose," went on Baley, relentlessly, "that they could make a robot that would fool *you* into thinking it was human?"

The roboticist tittered. "Oh, my dear Mr. Baley. I doubt that. Really. There's more to a robot than just his appear——"

Dr. Gerrigel froze in the middle of the word. Slowly, he turned to R. Daneel, and his pink face went very pale.

"Oh, dear me," he whispered. "Oh, dear me."

He reached out one hand and touched R. Daneel's cheek gingerly. R. Daneel did not move away but gazed at the roboticist calmly.

"Dear me," said Dr. Gerrigel, with what was almost a sob in his voice, "you *are* a robot."

"It took you a long time to realize that," said Baley, dryly.

"I wasn't expecting it. I never saw one like this. Outer World manufacture?"

"Yes," said Baley.

"It's obvious now. The way he holds himself. The manner of his speaking. It is not a perfect imitation, Mr. Baley."

"It's pretty good though, isn't it?"

"Oh, it's marvelous. I doubt that anyone could recognize the imposture at sight. I am very grateful to you for having me brought face to face with him. May I examine him?" The roboticist was on his feet, eager.

Baley put out a hand. "Please, Doctor. In a moment. First, the matter of the murder, you know."

"Is that real, then?" Dr. Gerrigel was bitterly disappointed and showed it. "I thought perhaps that was just a device to keep my mind engaged and to see how long I could be fooled by——"

"It is not a device, Dr. Gerrigel. Tell me, now, in constructing a robot as humanoid as this one, with the deliberate purpose of having it pass as human, is it not necessary to make its brain possess properties as close to that of the human brain as possible?"

"Certainly."

"Very well. Could not such a humanoid brain lack the First Law? Perhaps it is left out accidentally. You say the theory is unknown. The very fact that it is unknown means that the constructors might set up a brain without the First Law. They would not know what to avoid."

Dr. Gerrigel was shaking his head vigorously. "No. No. Impossible."

"Are you sure? We can test the Second Law, of course.—Daneel, let me have your blaster."

Baley's eyes never left the robot. His own hand, well to one side, gripped his own blaster tightly.

R. Daneel said calmly, "Here it is, Elijah," and held it out, butt first.

Baley said, "A plain-clothes man must never abandon his blaster, but a robot has no choice but to obey a human."

"Except, Mr. Baley," said Dr. Gerrigel, "when obedience involves breaking the First Law."

"Do you know, Doctor, that Daneel drew his blaster on an unarmed group of men and women and threatened to shoot?"

"But I did not shoot," said R. Daneel.

"Granted, but the threat was unusual in itself, wasn't it, Doctor?"

Dr. Gerrigel bit his lip. "I'd need to know the exact circumstances to judge. It sounds unusual."

"Consider this, then. R. Daneel was on the scene at the time of the murder, and if you omit the possibility of an Earthman having moved across open country, carrying a weapon with him, Daneel and Daneel alone of all the persons on the scene could have hidden the weapon."

"Hidden the weapon?" asked Dr. Gerrigel.

"Let me explain. The blaster that did the killing was not found. The scene of the murder was searched minutely and it was not found. Yet it could not have vanished like smoke. There is only one place it could have been, only one place they would not have thought to look."

"Where, Elijah?" asked R. Daneel.

Baley brought his blaster into view, held its barrel firmly in the robot's direction.

"In your food sac," he said. "In your food sac, Daneel!"

13

Shift to the Machine

"THAT IS not so," said R. Daneel, quietly.

"Yes? We'll let the Doctor decide. Dr. Gerrigel?"

"Mr. Baley?" The roboticist, whose glance had been alternating wildly between the plain-clothes man and the robot as they spoke, let it come to rest upon the human being.

"I've asked you here for an authoritative analysis of this robot. I can arrange to have you use the laboratories of the City Bureau of Standards. If you need any piece of equipment they don't have, I'll get it for you. What I want is a quick and definite answer and hang the expense and trouble."

Baley rose. His words had emerged calmly enough, but he felt a rising hysteria behind them. At the moment, he felt that if he could only seize Dr. Gerrigel by the throat and choke the necessary statements out of him, he would forgo all science.

He said, "Well, Dr. Gerrigel?"

Dr. Gerrigel tittered nervously and said, "My dear Mr. Baley, I won't need a laboratory."

"Why not?" asked Baley apprehensively. He stood there, muscles tense, feeling himself twitch.

"It's not difficult to test the First Law. I've never had to, you understand, but it's simple enough."

Baley pulled air in through his mouth and let it out slowly. He said, "Would you explain what you mean? Are you saying that you can test him here?"

"Yes, of course. Look, Mr. Baley, I'll give you an analogy. If I were a Doctor of Medicine and had to test a patient's blood sugar,

I'd need a chemical laboratory. If I needed to measure his basal metabolic rate, or test his cortical function, or check his genes to pinpoint a congenital malfunction, I'd need elaborate equipment. On the other hand, I could check whether he were blind by merely passing my hand before his eyes and I could test whether he were dead by merely feeling for his pulse.

"What I'm getting at is that the more important and fundamental the property being tested, the simpler the needed equipment. It's the same in a robot. The First Law is fundamental. It affects everything. If it were absent, the robot could not react properly in two dozen obvious ways."

As he spoke, he took out a flat, black object which expanded into a small book-viewer. He inserted a well-worn spool into the receptacle. He then took out a stop watch and a series of white, plastic slivers that fitted together to form something that looked like a slide rule with three independent movable scales. The notations upon it struck no chord of familiarity to Baley.

Dr. Gerrigel tapped his book-viewer and smiled a little, as though the prospect of a bit of field work cheered him.

He said, "It's my *Handbook of Robotics*. I never go anywhere without it. It's part of my clothes." He giggled self-consciously.

He put the eyepiece of the viewer to his eyes and his finger dealt delicately with the controls. The viewer whirred and stopped, whirred and stopped.

"Built-in index," the roboticist said, proudly, his voice a little muffled because of the way in which the viewer covered his mouth. "I constructed it myself. It saves a great deal of time. But then, that's not the point now, is it? Let's see. Umm, won't you move your chair near me, Daneel."

R. Daneel did so. During the roboticist's preparations, he had watched closely and unemotionally.

Baley shifted his blaster.

What followed confused and disappointed him. Dr. Gerrigel proceeded to ask questions and perform actions that seemed without meaning, punctuated by references to his triple slide rule and occasionally to the viewer.

At one time, he asked, "If I have two cousins, five years apart in age, and the younger is a girl, what sex is the older?"

Daneel answered (inevitably, Baley thought), "It is impossible to say on the information given."

To which Dr. Gerrigel's only response, aside from a glance at his stop watch, was to extend his right hand as far as he could sideways and to say, "Would you touch the tip of my middle finger with the tip of the third finger of your left hand?"

Daneel did that promptly and easily.

In fifteen minutes, not more, Dr. Gerrigel was finished. He used his slide rule for a last silent calculation, then disassembled it with a series of snaps. He put away his stop watch, withdrew the *Handbook* from the viewer, and collapsed the latter.

"Is that all?" said Baley, frowning.

"That's all."

"But it's ridiculous. You've asked nothing that pertains to the First Law."

"Oh, my dear Mr. Baley, when a doctor hits your knee with a little rubber mallet and it jerks, don't you accept the fact that it gives information concerning the presence or absence of some degenerative nerve disease? When he looks closely at your eyes and considers the reaction of your iris to light, are you surprised that he can tell you something concerning your possible addiction to the use of certain alkaloids?"

Baley said, "Well, then? What's your decision?"

"Daneel is fully equipped with the First Law!" The roboticist jerked his head in a sharp affirmative.

"You can't be right," said Baley huskily.

Baley would not have thought that Dr. Gerrigel could stiffen into a rigidity that was greater than his usual position. He did so, however, visibly. The man's eyes grew narrow and hard.

"Are you teaching me my job?"

"I don't mean you're incompetent," said Baley. He put out a large, pleading hand. "But couldn't you be mistaken? You've said yourself nobody knows anything about the theory of non-Asenion robots. A blind man could read by using Braille or a sound-scriber. Suppose you didn't know that Braille or sound-scribing existed. Couldn't you, in all honesty, say that a man had eyes because he knew the contents of a certain book-film, and be mistaken?"

"Yes," the roboticist grew genial again, "I see your point. But still a blind man could not read by use of his eyes and it is that which I was testing, if I may continue the analogy. Take my word for it, regardless of what a non-Asenion robot could or could not do, it is certain that R. Daneel is equipped with First Law."

"Couldn't he have falsified his answers?" Baley was floundering, and knew it.

"Of course not. That is the difference between a robot and a man. A human brain, or any mammalian brain, cannot be completely analyzed by any mathematical discipline now known. No response can therefore be counted upon as a certainty. The robot brain is completely analyzable, or it could not be constructed. We know exactly what the responses to given stimuli must be. No robot can truly falsify answers. The thing you call falsification just doesn't exist in the robot's mental horizon."

"Then let's get down to cases. R. Daneel did point a blaster at a crowd of human beings. I saw that. I was there. Granted that he didn't shoot, wouldn't the First Law still have forced him into a kind of neurosis? It didn't, you know. He was perfectly normal afterward."

The roboticist put a hesitant hand to his chin. "That *is* anomalous."

"Not at all," said R. Daneel, suddenly. "Partner Elijah, would you look at the blaster that you took from me?"

Baley looked down upon the blaster he held cradled in his left hand.

"Break open the charge chamber," urged R. Daneel. "Inspect it."

Baley weighed his chances, then slowly put his own blaster on the table beside him. With a quick movement, he opened the robot's blaster.

"It's empty," he said, blankly.

"There is no charge in it," agreed R. Daneel. "If you will look closer, you will see that there has never been a charge in it. The blaster has no ignition bud and cannot be used."

Baley said, "You held an uncharged blaster on the crowd?"

"I had to have a blaster or fail in my role as plain-clothes man," said R. Daneel. "Yet to carry a charged and usable blaster might have made it possible for me to hurt a human being by accident, a thing which is, of course, unthinkable. I would have explained this at the time, but you were angry and would not listen."

Baley stared bleakly at the useless blaster in his hand and said in a low voice, "I think that's all, Dr. Gerrigel. Thank you for helping out."

Baley sent out for lunch, but when it came (yeast-nut cake and a rather extravagant slice of fried chicken on cracker) he could only stare at it.

Round and round went the currents of his mind. The lines on his long face were etched in deep gloom.

He was living in an unreal world, a cruel, topsy-turvy world.

How had it happened? The immediate past stretched behind him like a misty improbable dream dating back to the moment he had stepped into Julius Enderby's office and found himself suddenly immersed in a nightmare of murder and robotics.

Jehoshaphat! It had begun only fifty hours before.

Persistently, he had sought the solution in Spacetown. Twice he had accused R. Daneel, once as a human being in disguise, and once as an admitted and actual robot, each time as a murderer. Twice the accusation had been bent back and broken.

He was being driven back. Against his will he was forced to turn his thoughts into the City, and since last night he dared not. Certain questions battered at his conscious mind, but he would not listen; he felt he could not. If he heard them, he couldn't help but answer them and, oh God, he didn't want to face the answers.

"Lije! Lije!" A hand shook Baley's shoulder roughly.

Baley stirred and said, "What's up, Phil?"

Philip Norris, Plain-clothes man C-5, sat down, put his hands on his knees, and leaned forward, peering at Baley's face. "What happened to you? Been living on knockout drops lately? You were sitting there with your eyes open and, near as I could make out, you were dead."

He rubbed his thinning, pale blond hair, and his close-set eyes appraised Baley's cooling lunch greedily. "Chicken!" he said. "It's getting so you can't get it without a doctor's prescription."

"Take some," said Baley, listlessly.

Decorum won out and Norris said, "Oh, well, I'm going out to eat in a minute. You keep it.—Say, what's doing with the Commish?"

"What?"

Norris attempted a casual attitude, but his hands were restless. He said, "Go on. You know what I mean. You've been living with him ever since he got back. What's up? A promotion in the works?"

Baley frowned and felt reality return somewhat at the touch of office politics. Norris had approximately his own seniority and he was bound to watch most assiduously for any sign of official preference in Baley's direction.

Baley said, "No promotion. Believe me. It's nothing. Nothing. And if it's the Commissioner you're wanting, I wish I could give him to you. Jehoshaphat! Take him!"

Norris said, "Don't get me wrong. I don't care if you get promoted. I just mean that if you've got any pull with the Commish, how about using it for the kid?"

"What kid?"

There was no need of any answer to that. Vincent Barrett, the youngster who had been moved out of his job to make room for R. Sammy, was shuffling up from an unnoticed corner of the room. A skull cap turned restlessly in his hands and the skin over his high cheekbones moved as he tried to smile.

"Hello, Mr. Baley."

"Oh, hello, Vince. How're you doing?"

"Not so good, Mr. Baley."

He was looking about hungrily. Baley thought: He looks lost, half dead—declassified.

Then, savagely, his lips almost moving with the force of his emotion, he thought: But what does he want from me?

He said, "I'm sorry, kid." What else was there to say?

"I keep thinking—maybe something has turned up."

Norris moved in close and spoke into Baley's ear. "Someone's got to stop this sort of thing. They're going to move out Chen-low now."

"What?"

"Haven't you heard?"

"No, I haven't. Damn it, he's a C-3. He's got ten years behind him."

"I grant that. But a machine with legs can do his work. Who's next?"

Young Vince Barrett was oblivious to the whispers. He said out of the depths of his own thinking, "Mr. Baley?"

"Yes, Vince?"

"You know what they say? They say Lyrane Millane, the sub-etherics dancer, is really a robot."

"That's silly."

"Is it? They say they can make robots look just like humans; with a special plastic skin, sort of."

Baley thought guiltily of R. Daneel and found no words. He shook his head.

The boy said, "Do you suppose anyone will mind if I just walk around. It makes me feel better to see the old place."

"Go ahead, kid."

The youngster wandered off. Baley and Norris watched him go. Norris said, "It looks as though the Medievalists are right."

"You mean back to the soil? Is that it, Phil?"

"*No.* I mean about the robots. Back to the soil. Huh! Old Earth has an unlimited future. We don't need robots, that's all."

Baley muttered, "Eight billion people and the uranium running out! What's unlimited about it?"

"What if the uranium does run out. We'll import it. Or we'll discover other nuclear processes. There's no way you can stop mankind, Lije. You've got to be optimistic about it and have faith in the old human brain. Our greatest resource is ingenuity and we'll never run out of that, Lije."

He was fairly started now. He went on, "For one thing, we can use sunpower and that's good for billions of years. We can build space stations inside Mercury's orbit to act as energy accumulators. We'll transmit energy to Earth by direct beam."

This project was not new to Baley. The speculative fringe of science had been playing with the notion for a hundred and fifty years at least. What was holding it up was the impossibility so far of projecting a beam tight enough to reach fifty million miles without dispersal to uselessness. Baley said as much.

Norris said, "When it's necessary, it'll be done. Why worry?"

Baley had the picture of an Earth of unlimited energy. Population could continue to increase. The yeast farms could expand, hydroponic culture intensify. Energy was the only thing indispensable. The raw minerals could be brought in from the uninhabited rocks of the System. If ever water became a bottleneck, more could be brought in from the moons of Jupiter. Hell, the oceans could be frozen and dragged out into Space where they could circle Earth as moonlets of ice. There they would be, always available for use, while the ocean bottoms would represent more land for exploitation, more room to live. Even carbon and oxygen could be maintained and increased on Earth through utilization of the methane atmosphere of Titan and the frozen oxygen of Umbriel.

Earth's population could reach a trillion or two. Why not? There was a time when the current population of eight billion would have been viewed as impossible. There was a time when a population of a single billion would have been unthinkable. There had always been prophets of Malthusian doom in every generation since Medieval times and they had always been proven wrong.

But what would Fastolfe say? A world of a trillion? Surely! But they would be dependent on imported air and water and upon an energy supply from complicated storehouses fifty million miles away. How incredibly unstable that would be. Earth would be, and remain, a feather's weight away from complete catastrophe at the slightest failure of any part of the System-wide mechanism.

Baley said, "I think it would be easier to ship off some of the surplus population, myself." It was more an answer to the picture he had himself conjured up than to anything Norris had said.

"Who'd have us?" said Norris with a bitter lightness.

"Any uninhabited planet."

Norris rose, patted Baley on the shoulder. "Lije, you eat your chicken, and recover. You *must* be living on knockout pills." He left, chuckling.

Baley watched him leave with a humorless twist to his mouth. Norris would spread the news and it would be weeks before the humor boys of the office (every office has them) would lay off. But at least it got him off the subject of young Vince, of robots, of declassification.

He sighed as he put a fork into the now cold and somewhat stringy chicken.

Baley finished the last of the yeast-nut and it was only then that R. Daneel left his own desk (assigned him that morning) and approached.

Baley eyed him uncomfortably. "Well?"

R. Daneel said, "The Commissioner is not in his office and it is not known when he'll be back. I've told R. Sammy we will use it and that he is to allow no one but the Commissioner to enter."

"What are we going to use it for?"

"Greater privacy. Surely you agree that we must plan our next move. After all, you do not intend to abandon the investigation, do you?"

That was precisely what Baley most longed to do, but obviously, he could not say so. He rose and led the way to Enderby's office.

Once in the office, Baley said, "All right, Daneel. What is it?"

The robot said, "Partner Elijah, since last night, you are not yourself. There is a definite alteration in your mental aura."

A horrible thought sprang full-grown into Baley's mind. He cried, "Are you telepathic?"

It was not a possibility he would have considered at a less disturbed moment.

"No. Of course not," said R. Daneel.

Baley's panic ebbed. He said, "Then what the devil do you mean by talking about my mental aura?"

"It is merely an expression I use to describe a sensation that you do not share with me."

"What sensation?"

"It is difficult to explain, Elijah. You will recall that I was originally designed to study human psychology for our people back in Spacetown."

"Yes, I know. You were adjusted to detective work by the simple installation of a justice-desire circuit." Baley did not try to keep the sarcasm out of his voice.

"Exactly, Elijah. But my original design remains essentially unaltered. I was constructed for the purpose of cerebroanalysis."

"For analyzing brain waves?"

"Why, yes. It can be done by field-measurements without the necessity of direct electrode contact, if the proper receiver exists. My mind is such a receiver. Is that principle not applied on Earth?"

Baley didn't know. He ignored the question and said, cautiously, "If you measure the brain waves, what do you get out of it?"

"Not thoughts, Elijah. I get a glimpse of emotion and most of all, I can analyze temperament, the underlying drives and attitudes of a man. For instance, it was I who was able to ascertain that Commissioner Enderby was incapable of killing a man under the circumstances prevailing at the time of the murder."

"And they eliminated him as a suspect on your say-so."

"Yes. It was safe enough to do so. I am a very delicate machine in that respect."

Again a thought struck Baley. "Wait! Commissioner Enderby didn't know he was being cerebroanalyzed, did he?"

"There was no necessity of hurting his feelings."

"I mean you just stood there and looked at him. No machinery. No electrodes. No needles and graphs."

"Certainly not. I am a self-contained unit."

Baley bit his lower lip in anger and chagrin. It had been the one remaining inconsistency, the one loophole through which a forlorn stab might yet be made in an attempt to pin the crime on Spacetown.

R. Daneel had stated that the Commissioner had been cerebroanalyzed and one hour later the Commissioner himself had, with apparent candor, denied any knowledge of the term. Certainly no man could have undergone the shattering experience of electroencephalographic measurements by electrode and graph under the suspicion of murder without an unmistakable impression of what cerebroanalysis must be.

But now that discrepancy had evaporated. The Commissioner had been cerebroanalyzed and had never known it. R. Daneel told the truth; so had the Commissioner.

"Well," said Baley, sharply, "what does cerebroanalysis tell you about me?"

"You are disturbed."

"That's a great discovery, isn't it? Of course, I'm disturbed."

"Specifically, though, your disturbance is due to a clash between motivations within you. On the one hand your devotion to the principles of your profession urges you to look deeply into this conspiracy of Earthmen who lay siege to us last night. Another motivation, equally strong, forces you in the opposite direction. This much is clearly written in the electric field of your cerebral cells."

"My cerebral cells, *nuts*," said Baley, feverishly. "Look, I'll tell you why there's no point in investigating your so-called conspiracy. It has nothing to do with the murder. I thought it might have. I'll admit that. Yesterday in the kitchen, I thought we were in danger. But what happened? They followed us out, were quickly lost on the strips, and that was that. That was not the action of well-organized and desperate men.

"My own son found out where we were staying easily enough. He called the Department. He didn't even have to identify himself. Our precious conspirators could have done the same if they had really wanted to hurt us."

"Didn't they?"

"Obviously not. If they had wanted riots, they could have started one at the shoe counter, and yet they backed out tamely enough before one man and a blaster. One *robot*, and a blaster which they must have known you would be unable to fire once they recognized what you were. They're Medievalists. They're harmless crackpots. You wouldn't know that, but I should have. And I would have, if it weren't for the fact that this whole business has me thinking in—in foolish melodramatic terms.

"I tell you I know the type of people that become Medievalists. They're soft, dreamy people who find life too hard for them here and get lost in an ideal world of the past that never really existed. If you could cerebroanalyze a movement as you do an individual, you would find they are no more capable of murder than Julius Enderby himself."

R. Daneel said slowly, "I cannot accept your statements at face value."

"What do you mean?"

"Your conversion to this view is too sudden. There are certain discrepancies, too. You arranged the appointment with Dr. Gerrigel hours before the evening meal. You did not know of my food sac then and could not have suspected me as the murderer. Why *did* you call him, then?"

"I suspected you even then."

"And last night you spoke as you slept."

Baley's eyes widened. "What did I say?"

"Merely the one word 'Jessie' several times repeated. I believe you were referring to your wife."

Baley let his tight muscles loosen. He said, shakily, "I had a nightmare. Do you know what that is?"

"I do not know by personal experience, of course. The dictionary definition has it that it is a bad dream."

"And do you know what a dream is?"

"Again, the dictionary definition only. It is an illusion of reality experienced during the temporary suspension of conscious thought which you call sleep."

"All right. I'll buy that. An illusion. Sometimes the illusions can seem damned real. Well, I dreamed my wife was in danger. It's the sort of dream people often have. I called her name. That happens under such circumstances, too. You can take my word for it."

"I am only too glad to do so. But it brings up a thought. How did Jessie find out I was a robot?"

Baley's forehead went moist again. "We're not going into that again, are we? The rumor——"

"I am sorry to interrupt, partner Elijah, but there is no rumor. If there were, the City would be alive with unrest today. I have checked reports coming into the Department and this is not so. There simply is no rumor. Therefore, how did your wife find out?"

"Jehoshaphat! What are you trying to say? Do you think my wife is one of the members of—of . . ."

"Yes, Elijah."

Baley gripped his hands together tightly. "Well, she isn't, and we won't discuss that point any further."

"This is not like you, Elijah. In the course of duty, you accused me of murder twice."

"And is this your way of getting even?"

"I am not sure I understand what you mean by the phrase. Certainly, I approve your readiness to suspect me. You had your reasons. They were wrong, but they might easily have been right. Equally strong evidence points to your wife."

"As a murderess? Why, damn you, Jessie wouldn't hurt her worst enemy. She couldn't set foot outside the City. She couldn't . . . Why, if you were flesh and blood I'd——"

"I merely say that she is a member of the conspiracy. I say that she should be questioned."

"Not on your life. Not on whatever it is you call your life. Now, listen to me. The Medievalists aren't after our blood. It's not the way they do things. But they are trying to get you out of the City. That much is obvious. And they're trying to do it by a kind of psychological attack. They're trying to make life unpleasant for you and for me, since I'm with you. They could easily have found out Jessie was my wife, and it was an obvious move for them to let the news leak to her. She's like any other human being. She doesn't *like* robots. She wouldn't want me to associate with one, especially if she thought it involved danger, and surely they would imply that. I tell you it worked. She begged all night to have me abandon the case or to get you out of the City somehow."

"Presumably," said R. Daneel, "you have a very strong urge to protect your wife against questioning. It seems obvious to me that you are constructing this line of argument without really believing it."

"What the hell do you think you are?" ground out Baley. "You're not a detective. You're a cerebroanalysis machine like the electro-encephalographs we have in this building. You've got arms, legs, a head, and can talk, but you're not one inch more than that machine. Putting a lousy circuit into you doesn't make you a detective, so what do you know? You keep your mouth shut, and let me do the figuring out."

The robot said quietly, "I think it would be better if you lowered your voice, Elijah. Granted that I am not a detective in the sense that you are, I would still like to bring one small item to your attention."

"I'm not interested in listening."

"Please do. If I am wrong, you will tell me so, and it will do no harm. It is only this. Last night you left our room to call Jessie by corridor phone. I suggested that your son go in your place. You told me it was not the custom among Earthmen for a father to send his son into danger. Is it then the custom for a mother to do so?"

"No, of cour——" began Baley, and stopped.

"You see my point," said R. Daneel. "Ordinarily, if Jessie feared for your safety and wished to warn you, she would risk her own life, *not* send her son. The fact that she did send Bentley could only mean that she felt that he would be safe while she herself would not. If the conspiracy consisted of people unknown to Jessie, that would not be the case, or at least she would have no reason to think it to be the case. On the other hand, if she were a member of the conspiracy, she would know, she would *know*, Elijah, that she would be watched for and recognized, whereas Bentley might get through unnoticed."

"Wait now," said Baley, sick at heart, "that's feather-fine reasoning, but——"

There was no need to wait. The signal on the Commissioner's desk was flickering madly. R. Daneel waited for Baley to answer, but the latter could only stare at it helplessly. The robot closed contact.

"What is it?"

R. Sammy's slurring voice said, "There is a lady here who wishes to see Lije. I told her he was busy, but she will not go away. She says her name is Jessie."

"Let her in," said R. Daneel calmly, and his brown eyes rose unemotionally to meet the panicky glare of Baley's.

14

Power of a Name

BALEY REMAINED standing in a tetany of shock, as Jessie ran to him, seizing his shoulders, huddling close.

His pale lips formed the word, "Bentley?"

She looked at him and shook her head, her brown hair flying with the force of her motion. "He's all right."

"Well, then . . ."

Jessie said through a sudden torrent of sobs, in a low voice that could scarcely be made out, "I can't go on, Lije. I can't. I can't sleep or eat. I've got to tell you."

"Don't say anything," Baley said in anguish. "For God's sake, Jessie, not now."

"I must. I've done a terrible thing. Such a terrible thing. Oh, Lije . . ." She lapsed into incoherence.

Baley said, hopelessly, "We're not alone, Jessie."

She looked up and stared at R. Daneel with no signs of recognition. The tears in which her eyes were swimming might easily be refracting the robot into a featureless blur.

R. Daneel said in a low murmur, "Good afternoon, Jessie."

She gasped. "Is it the—the robot?"

She dashed the back of her hand across her eyes and stepped out of Baley's encircling right arm. She breathed deeply and, for a moment, a tremulous smile wavered on her lips. "It *is* you, isn't it?"

"Yes, Jessie."

"You don't mind being called a robot?"

"No, Jessie. It is what I am."

"And I don't mind being called a fool and an idiot and a—a subversive agent, because it's what *I* am."

"Jessie!" groaned Baley.

"It's no use, Lije," she said. "He might as well know if he's your partner. I can't live with it any more. I've had such a time since yesterday. I don't care if I go to jail. I don't care if they send me down to the lowest levels and make me live on raw yeast and water. I don't care if . . . You won't let them, will you, Lije? Don't let them do anything to me. I'm fuh—frightened."

Baley patted her shoulder and let her cry.

He said to R. Daneel, "She isn't well. We can't keep her here. What time is it?"

R. Daneel said without any visible signs of consulting a timepiece, "Fourteen-forty-five."

"The Commissioner could be back any minute. Look, commandeer a squad car and we can talk about this in the motorway."

Jessie's head jerked upright. "The motorway? Oh, no, Lije."

He said, in as soothing a tone as he could manage, "Now, Jessie, don't be superstitious. You can't go on the expressway the way you are. Be a good girl and calm down or we won't even be able to go through the common room. I'll get you some water."

She wiped her face with a damp handkerchief and said drearily, "Oh, look at my makeup."

"Don't worry about your makeup," said Baley. "Daneel, what about the squad car?"

"It's waiting for us now, partner Elijah."

"Come on, Jessie."

"Wait. Wait just a minute, Lije. I've got to do something to my face."

"It doesn't matter now."

But she twisted away. "Please. I can't go through the common room like this. I won't take a second."

The man and the robot waited, the man with little jerky clenchings of his fists, the robot impassively.

Jessie rummaged through her purse for the necessary equipment. (If there were one thing, Baley had once said solemnly, that had resisted mechanical improvement since Medieval times, it was a woman's purse. Even the substitution of magnetic clotures for metal clasps had not proven successful.) Jessie pulled out a small mirror and the silver-chased cosmetokit that Baley had bought her on the occasion of three birthdays before.

The cosmetokit had several orifices and she used each in turn. All but the last spray were invisible. She used them with that fineness of touch and delicacy of control that seems to be the birthright of women even at times of the greatest stress.

The base went on first in a smooth even layer that removed all shininess and roughness from the skin and left it with the faintly golden glow which long experience had taught Jessie was just the shade most suited to the natural coloring of her hair and eyes. Then the touch of tan along the forehead and chin, a gentle brush of rouge on either cheek, tracing back to the angle of the jaw; and a delicate drift of blue on the upper eyelids and along the earlobes. Finally there was the application of the smooth carmine to the lips. That involved the one visible spray, a faintly pink mist that glistened liquidly in air, but dried and deepened richly on contact with the lips.

"There," said Jessie, with several swift pats at her hair and a look of deep dissatisfaction. "I suppose that will do."

The process had taken more than the promised second, but less than fifteen seconds. Nevertheless, it had seemed interminable to Baley.

"Come," he said.

She barely had time to return the cosmetokit to the purse before he had pushed her through the door.

The eerie silence of the motorway lay thick on either side.

Baley said, "All right, Jessie."

The impassivity that had covered Jessie's face since they first left the Commissioner's office showed signs of cracking. She looked at her husband and at Daneel with a helpless silence.

Baley said, "Get it over with, Jessie. Please. Have you committed a crime? An actual crime?"

"A crime?" She shook her head uncertainly.

"Now hold on to yourself. No hysterics. Just say yes or no, Jessie. Have you—" he hesitated a trifle, "killed anyone?"

The look on Jessie's face was promptly transmuted to indignation. "Why, Lije Baley!"

"Yes or no, Jessie."

"No, of course not."

The hard knot in Baley's stomach softened perceptibly. "Have you stolen anything? Falsified ration data? Assaulted anyone? Destroyed property? Speak up, Jessie."

"I haven't done anything—anything specific. I didn't mean anything like that." She looked over her shoulder. "Lije, do we have to stay down here?"

"Right here until this is over. Now, start at the beginning. What did you come to tell us?" Over Jessie's bowed head, Baley's eyes met R. Daneel's.

Jessie spoke in a soft voice that gained in strength and articulateness as she went on.

"It's these people, these Medievalists; *you* know, Lije. They're always around, always talking. Even in the old days when I was an assistant dietitian, it was like that. Remember Elizabeth Thornbowe? She was a Medievalist. She was always talking about how all our troubles came from the City and how things were better before the Cities started.

"I used to ask her how she was so sure that was so, especially after you and I met, Lije (remember the talks we used to have), and then she would quote from those small book-reels that are always floating around. You know, like *Shame of the Cities* that the fellow wrote. I don't remember his name."

Baley said, absently, "Ogrinsky."

"Yes, only most of them were lots worse. Then, when I married you, she was really sarcastic. She said, 'I suppose you're going to be a real City woman now that you've married a policeman.' After that, she didn't talk to me much and then I quit the job and that was that. Lots of things she used to say were just to shock me, I think, or to make herself look mysterious and glamorous. She was an old maid, you know; never got married till the day she died. Lots of those Medievalists don't fit in, one way or another. Remember, you once said, Lije, that people sometimes mistake their own shortcomings for those of society and want to fix the Cities because they don't know how to fix themselves."

Baley remembered, and his words now sounded flip and superficial in his own ears. He said, gently, "Keep to the point, Jessie."

She went on, "Anyway, Lizzy was always talking about how there'd come a day and people had to get together. She said it was all the fault of the Spacers because they wanted to keep Earth weak and decadent. That was one of her favorite words, 'decadent.' She'd look at the menus I'd prepare for the next week and sniff and say, 'Decadent, decadent.' Jane Myers used to imitate her in the cook room and we'd die laughing. She said, Elizabeth did, that someday we were going to break up the Cities and go back to the soil and have an accounting with the Spacers who were trying to tie us forever to the Cities by forcing robots on us. Only she never called them robots. She used to say 'soulless monster-machines,' if you'll excuse the expression, Daneel."

The robot said, "I am not aware of the significance of the adjective you used, Jessie, but in any case, the expression is excused. Please go on."

Baley stirred restlessly. It was that way with Jessie. No emergency, no crisis could make her tell a story in any way but her own circuitous one.

She said, "Elizabeth always tried to talk as though there were lots of people in it with her. She would say, 'At the last meeting,' and then stop and look at me sort of half proud and half scared as though she wanted me to ask about it so she could look important, and yet scared I might get her in trouble. Of course, I never asked her. I wouldn't give her the satisfaction.

"Anyway, after I married you, Lije, it was all over, until . . ."

She stopped.

"Go on, Jessie," said Baley.

"You remember, Lije, that argument we had? About Jezebel, I mean?"

"What about it?" It took a second or two for Baley to remember that it was Jessie's own name, and not a reference to another woman.

He turned to R. Daneel in an automatically defensive explanation. "Jessie's full name is Jezebel. She is not fond of it and doesn't use it."

R. Daneel nodded gravely and Baley thought: Jehoshaphat, why waste worry on *him?*

"It bothered me a lot, Lije," Jessie said. "It really did. I guess it was silly, but I kept thinking and thinking about what you said. I mean about your saying that Jezebel was only a conservative who fought for the ways of her ancestors against the strange ways the newcomers had brought. After all, *I* was Jezebel and I always . . ."

She groped for a word and Baley supplied it. "Identified yourself?"

"Yes." But she shook her head almost immediately and looked away. "Not really, of course. Not literally. The way I thought she was, you know. I wasn't like that."

"I know that, Jessie. Don't be foolish."

"But still I thought of her a lot and, somehow, I got to thinking, it's just the same now as it was then. I mean, we Earth people had our old ways and here were the Spacers coming in with a lot of new ways and trying to encourage the new ways we had stumbled into ourselves and maybe the Medievalists were right. Maybe we *should* go back to our old, good ways. So I went back and found Elizabeth."

"Yes. Go on."

"She said she didn't know what I was talking about and besides I was a cop's wife. I said that had nothing to do with it and finally she said, well, she'd speak to somebody, and then about a month later she came to me and said it was all right and I joined and I've been at meetings ever since."

Baley looked at her sadly. "And you never told me?"

Jessie's voice trembled. "I'm sorry, Lije."

"Well, that won't help. Being sorry, I mean. I want to know about the meetings. In the first place, where were they held?"

A sense of detachment was creeping over him, a numbing of emotions. What he had tried not to believe was so, was openly so, was unmistakably so. In a sense, it was a relief to have the uncertainty over.

She said, "Down here."

"Down here? You mean on this spot? What *do* you mean?"

"Here in the motorway. That's why I didn't want to come down here. It was a wonderful place to meet, though. We'd get together——"

"How many?"

"I'm not sure. About sixty or seventy. It was just a sort of local branch. There'd be folding chairs and some refreshments and someone would make a speech, mostly about how wonderful life was in the old days and how someday we'd do away with the monsters, the robots, that is, and the Spacers, too. The speeches were sort of dull really, because they were all the same. We just endured them. Mostly, it was the fun of getting together and feeling important.

We would pledge ourselves to oaths and there'd be secret ways we could greet each other on the outside."

"Weren't you ever interrupted? No squad cars or fire engines passed?"

"No. Never."

R. Daneel interrupted, "Is that unusual, Elijah?"

"Maybe not," Baley answered thoughtfully. "There are some side-passages that are practically never used. It's quite a trick, knowing which they are, though. Is that all you did at the meetings, Jessie? Make speeches and play at conspiracy?"

"It's about all. And sing songs, sometimes. And of course, re-freshments. Not much. Sandwiches, usually, and juice."

"In that case," he said, almost brutally, "what's bothering you now?"

Jessie winced. "You're angry."

"Please," said Baley, with iron patience, "answer my question. If it were all as harmless as that, why have you been in such a panic for the last day and a half?"

"I thought they would hurt you, Lije. For heaven's sake, why do you act as though you don't understand? I've explained it to you."

"No, you haven't. Not yet. You've told me about a harmless little secret kaffee-klatsch you belonged to. Did they ever hold open dem-onstrations? Did they ever destroy robots? Start riots? Kill people?"

"*Never!* Lije, I wouldn't do any of those things. I wouldn't stay a member if they tried it."

"Well, then, why do you say you've done a terrible thing? Why do you expect to be sent to jail?"

"Well . . . Well, they used to talk about someday when they'd put pressure on the government. We were supposed to get organized and then afterward there would be huge strikes and work stoppages. We could force the government to ban all robots and make the Spac-ers go back where they came from. I thought it was just talk and then, this thing started; about you and Daneel, I mean. Then they said, 'Now we'll see action,' and 'We're going to make an example of them and put a stop to the robot invasion right now.' Right there in Personal they said it, not knowing it was you they were talking about. But I knew. Right away."

Her voice broke.

Baley softened. "Come on, Jessie. It was all nothing. It was just talk. You can see for yourself that nothing has happened."

"I was so—so suh—scared. And I thought: *I'm* part of it. If there were going to be killing and destruction, *you* might be killed and Bentley and somehow it would be all muh—my fault for taking part in it, and I ought to be sent to jail."

Baley let her sob herself out. He put his arm about her shoulder and stared tight-lipped at R. Daneel, who gazed calmly back.

He said, "Now, I want you to think, Jessie. Who was the head of your group?"

She was quieter now, patting the corners of her eyes with a handkerchief. "A man called Joseph Klemin was the leader, but he wasn't really anybody. He wasn't more than five feet four inches tall and I think he was terribly henpecked at home. I don't think there's any harm in him. You aren't going to arrest him, are you, Lije? On my say-so?" She looked guiltily troubled.

"I'm not arresting anyone just yet. How did Klemin get *his* instructions?"

"I don't know."

"Did any strangers come to meeting? You know what I mean: big shots from Central Headquarters?"

"Sometimes people would come to make speeches. That wasn't very often, maybe twice a year or so."

"Can you name them?"

"No. They were always just introduced as 'one of us' or 'a friend from Jackson Heights' or wherever."

"I see. Daneel!"

"Yes, Elijah," said R. Daneel.

"Describe the men you think you've tabbed. We'll see if Jessie can recognize them."

R. Daneel went through the list with clinical exactness. Jessie listened with an expression of dismay as the categories of physical measurements lengthened and shook her head with increasing firmness.

"It's no use. It's no use," she cried. "How can I remember? I can't remember how any of them looked. I can't——"

She stopped, and seemed to consider. Then she said, "Did you say one of them was a yeast farmer?"

"Francis Clousarr," said R. Daneel, "is an employee at New York Yeast."

"Well, you know, once a man was making a speech and I happened to be sitting in the first row and I kept getting a whiff, just a whiff, really, of raw yeast smell. You know what I mean. The only reason that I remember is that I had an upset stomach that day and the smell kept making me sick. I had to stand up and move to the back and of course I couldn't explain what was wrong. It was so embarrassing. Maybe that's the man you're speaking of. After all, when you work with yeast all the time, the odor gets to stick to your clothes." She wrinkled her nose.

"You don't remember what he looked like?" said Baley.

"No," she replied, with decision.

"All right, then. Look, Jessie, I'm going to take you to your mother's. Bentley will stay with you, and none of you will leave the Section. Ben can stay away from school and I'll arrange to have meals sent in and the corridors around the apartment watched by the police."

"What about you?" quavered Jessie.

"I'll be in no danger."

"But how long?"

"I don't know. Maybe just a day or two." The words sounded hollow even to himself.

They were back in the motorway, Baley and R. Daneel, alone now. Baley's expression was dark with thought.

"It would seem to me," he said, "that we are faced with an organization built up on two levels. First, a ground level with no specific program, designed only to supply mass support for an eventual coup. Secondly, a much smaller elite dedicated to a well-planned program of action. It is this elite we must find. The comic-opera groups that Jessie spoke of can be ignored."

"All this," said R. Daneel, "follows, perhaps, if we can take Jessie's story at face value."

"I think," Baley said stiffly, "that Jessie's story can be accepted as completely true."

"So it would seem," said R. Daneel. "There is nothing about her cerebro-impulses that would indicate a pathological addiction to lying."

Baley turned an offended look upon the robot. "I should say not. And there will be no necessity to mention her name in our reports. Do you understand that?"

"If you wish it so, partner Elijah," said R. Daneel calmly, "but our report will then be neither complete nor accurate."

Baley said, "Well, maybe so, but no real harm will be done. She has come to us with whatever information she had and to mention her name will only put her in the police records. I do not want that to happen."

"In that case, certainly not, provided we are certain that nothing more remains to be found out."

"Nothing remains as far as she's concerned. My guarantee."

"Could you then explain why the word, Jezebel, the mere sound of a name, should lead her to abandon previous convictions and assume a new set? The motivation seems obscure."

They were traveling slowly through the curving, empty tunnel.

Baley said, "It is hard to explain. Jezebel is a rare name. It belonged once to a woman of very bad reputation. My wife treasured that fact. It gave her a vicarious feeling of wickedness and compensated for a life that was uniformly proper."

"Why should a law-abiding woman wish to feel wicked?"

Baley almost smiled. "Women are women, Daneel. Anyway, I did a very foolish thing. In a moment of irritation, I insisted that the historic Jezebel was not particularly wicked and was, if anything, a good wife. I've regretted that ever since.

"It turned out," he went on, "that I had made Jessie bitterly unhappy. I had spoiled something for her that couldn't be replaced. I suppose what followed was her way of revenge. I imagine she wished to punish me by engaging in activity of which she knew I wouldn't approve. I don't say the wish was a conscious one."

"Can a wish be anything but conscious? Is that not a contradiction in terms?"

Baley stared at R. Daneel and despaired at attempting to explain the unconscious mind. He said, instead, "Besides that, the Bible has a great influence on human thought and emotion."

"What is the Bible?"

For a moment Baley was surprised, and then was surprised at himself for having felt surprised. The Spacers, he knew, lived under a thoroughly mechanistic personal philosophy, and R. Daneel could know only what the Spacers knew; no more.

He said, curtly, "It is the sacred book of about half of Earth's population."

"I do not grasp the meaning here of the adjective."

"I mean that it is highly regarded. Various portions of it, when properly interpreted, contain a code of behavior which many men consider best suited to the ultimate happiness of mankind."

R. Daneel seemed to consider that. "Is this code incorporated into your laws?"

"I'm afraid not. The code doesn't lend itself to legal enforcement. It must be obeyed spontaneously by each individual out of a longing to do so. It is in a sense higher than any law can be."

"Higher than law? Is that not a contradiction in terms?"

Baley smiled wryly. "Shall I quote a portion of the Bible for you? Would you be curious to hear it?"

"Please do."

Baley let the car slow to a halt and for a few moments sat with his eyes closed, remembering. He would have liked to use the sonorous Middle English of the Medieval Bible, but to R. Daneel, Middle English would be gibberish.

He began, speaking almost casually in the words of the Modern Revision, as though he were telling a story of contemporary life, instead of dredging a tale out of Man's dimmest past:

" 'Jesus went to the mount of Olives, and at dawn returned to the temple. All the people came to him, and he sat down and preached to them. And the scribes and Pharisees brought to him a woman caught in adultery, and when they had placed her before him, they said to him, "Master, this woman was caught in adultery, in the very act. Now Moses, in the law, commanded us to stone such offenders. What do you say?"

" 'They said this, hoping to trap him, that they might have grounds for accusations against him. But Jesus stooped down, and with his finger wrote on the ground, as though he had not heard them. But when they continued asking him, he stood up and said to them, "He that is without sin among you, let him first cast a stone at her."

" 'And again he stooped down and wrote on the ground. And those that heard this, being convicted by their own conscience, went away one by one, beginning with the oldest, down to the last: and

Jesus was left alone, with the woman standing before him. When Jesus stood up and saw no one but the woman, he said to her, "Woman, where are your accusers? Has no one condemned you?"

" 'She said, "No one, Lord."

" 'And Jesus said to her, "Nor do I condemn you. Go, and sin no more." ' "

R. Daneel listened attentively. He said, "What is adultery?"

"That doesn't matter. It was a crime and at the time, the accepted punishment was stoning; that is, stones were thrown at the guilty one until she was killed."

"And the woman was guilty?"

"She was."

"Then why was she not stoned?"

"None of the accusers felt he could after Jesus's statement. The story is meant to show that there is something even higher than the justice which you have been filled with. There is a human impulse known as mercy; a human act known as forgiveness."

"I am not acquainted with those words, partner Elijah."

"I know," muttered Baley. "I know."

He started the squad car with a jerk and let it tear forward savagely. He was pressed back against the cushions of the seat.

"Where are we going?" asked R. Daneel.

"To Yeast-town," said Baley, "to get the truth out of Francis Clousarr, conspirator."

"You have a method for doing this, Elijah?"

"Not I, exactly. But you have, Daneel. A simple one."

They sped onward.

15

Arrest of a Conspirator

BALEY COULD sense the vague aroma of Yeast-town growing stronger, more pervasive. He did not find it as unpleasant as some did; Jessie, for instance. He even liked it, rather. It had pleasant connotations.

Every time he smelled raw yeast, the alchemy of sense perception threw him more than three decades into the past. He was a ten-year-old again, visiting his Uncle Boris, who was a yeast farmer. Uncle Boris always had a little supply of yeast delectables: small cookies, chocolaty things filled with sweet liquid, hard confections in the shape of cats and dogs. Young as he was, he knew that Uncle Boris shouldn't really have had them to give away and he always ate them very quietly, sitting in a corner with his back to the center of the room. He would eat them quickly for fear of being caught.

They tasted all the better for that.

Poor Uncle Boris! He had an accident and died. They never told him exactly how, and he had cried bitterly because he thought Uncle Boris had been arrested for smuggling yeast out of the plant. He expected to be arrested and executed himself. Years later, he poked carefully through police files and found the truth. Uncle Boris had fallen beneath the treads of a transport. It was a disillusioning ending to a romantic myth.

Yet the myth would always arise in his mind, at least momentarily, at the whiff of raw yeast.

Yeast-town was not the official name of any part of New York City. It could be found in no gazetteer and on no official map. What was called Yeast-town in popular speech was, to the Post Office, merely the boroughs of Newark, New Brunswick, and Trenton. It was a broad strip across what was once Medieval New Jersey, dotted with residential areas, particularly in Newark Center and Trenton Center, but given over mostly to the many-layered farms in which a thousand varieties of yeast grew and multiplied.

One fifth of the City's population worked in the yeast farms; another fifth worked in the subsidiary industries. Beginning with the mountains of wood and coarse cellulose that were dragged into the City from the tangled forests of the Alleghenies, through the vats of acid that hydrolyzed it to glucose, the carloads of niter and phosphate rock that were the most important additives, down to the jars of organics supplied by the chemical laboratories—it all came to only one thing, yeast and more yeast.

Without yeast, six of Earth's eight billions would starve in a year.

Baley felt cold at the thought. Three days before the possibility existed as deeply as it did now, but three days before it would never have occurred to him.

They whizzed out of the motorway through an exit on the Newark outskirts. The thinly populated avenues, flanked on either side by the featureless blocks that were the farms, offered little to act as a brake on their speed.

"What time is it, Daneel?" asked Baley.

"Sixteen-oh-five," replied R. Daneel.

"Then he'll be at work, if he's on day shift."

Baley parked the squad car in a delivery recess and froze the controls.

"This is New York Yeast then, Elijah?" asked the robot.

"Part of it," said Baley.

They entered into a corridor flanked by a double row of offices. A receptionist at a bend in the corridor was instantly smiles. "Whom do you wish to see?"

Baley opened his wallet. "Police. Is there a Francis Clousarr working for New York Yeast?"

The girl looked perturbed. "I can check."

She connected her switchboard through a line plainly marked "Personnel," and her lips moved slightly, though no sound could be heard.

Baley was no stranger to the throat phones that translated the small movements of the larynx into words. He said, "Speak up, please. Let me hear you."

Her words became audible, but consisted only of, ". . . he says he's a policeman, sir."

A dark, well-dressed man came out a door. He had a thin mustache and his hairline was beginning to retreat. He smiled whitely, and said, "I'm Prescott of Personnel. What's the trouble, Officer?"

Baley stared at him coldly and Prescott's smile grew strained.

Prescott said, "I just don't want to upset the workers. They're touchy about the police."

Baley said, "Tough, isn't it? Is Clousarr in the building now?"

"Yes, Officer."

"Let's have a rod, then. And if he's gone when we get there, I'll be speaking to you again."

The other's smile was quite dead. He muttered, "I'll get you a rod, Officer."

The guide rod was set for Department CG, Section 2. What that meant in factory terminology, Baley didn't know. He didn't have to. The rod was an inconspicuous thing which could be palmed in the hand. Its tip warmed gently when lined up in the direction for which it was set, cooled quickly when turned away. The warmth increased as the final goal was approached.

To an amateur, the guide rod was almost useless, with its quick little differences of heat content, but few City dwellers were amateurs at this particular game. One of the most popular and perennial of the games of childhood was hide-and-seek through the school-level corridors with the use of toy guide rods. ("Hot or Not, Let Hot-Spot Spot. Hot-Spot Guide Rods Are Keen.")

Baley had found his way through hundreds of massive piles by guide rod, and he could follow the shortest course with one of them in his hand as though it had been mapped out for him.

When he stepped into a large and brilliantly lit room after ten minutes, the guide rod's tip was almost hot.

Baley said to the worker nearest the door, "Francis Clousarr here?"

The worker jerked his head. Baley walked in the indicated direction. The odor of yeast was sharply penetrating, despite the laboring air pumps whose humming made a steady background noise.

A man had risen at the other end of the room, and was taking off an apron. He was of moderate height, his face deeply lined despite his comparative youth, and his hair just beginning to grizzle. He had large, knobby hands which he wiped slowly on a celltex towel.

"I'm Francis Clousarr," he said.

Baley looked briefly at R. Daneel. The robot nodded.

"Okay," said Baley. "Anywhere here we can talk?"

"Maybe," said Clousarr slowly, "but it's just about the end of my shift. How about tomorrow?"

"Lots of hours between now and tomorrow. Let's make it now." Baley opened his wallet and palmed it at the yeast farmer.

But Clousarr's hands did not waver in their somber wiping motions. He said, coolly, "I don't know the system in the Police Department, but around here you get tight eating hours with no leeway. I eat at 17:00 to 17:45, or I don't eat."

"It's all right," said Baley. "I'll arrange to have your supper brought to you."

"Well, well," said Clousarr, joylessly. "Just like an aristocrat, or a C-class copper. What's next? Private bath?"

"You just answer questions, Clousarr," said Baley, "and save your big jokes for your girl friend. Where can we talk?"

"If you want to talk, how about the balance room? Suit yourself about that. Me, I've got nothing to say."

Baley thumbed Clousarr into the balance room. It was square and antiseptically white, air-conditioned independently of the larger room (and more efficiently), and with its walls lined with delicate electronic balances, glassed off and manipulable by field forces only. Baley had used cheaper models in his college days. One make, which he recognized, could weigh a mere billion atoms.

Clousarr said, "I don't expect anyone will be in here for a while."

Baley grunted, then turned to Daneel and said, "Would you step out and have a meal sent up here? And if you don't mind, wait outside for it."

He watched R. Daneel leave, then said to Clousarr, "You're a chemist?"

"I'm a zymologist, if you don't mind."

"What's the difference?"

Clousarr looked lofty. "A chemist is a soup-pusher, a stink-operator. A zymologist is a man who helps keep a few billion people alive. I'm a yeast-culture specialist."

"All right," said Baley.

But Clousarr went on, "This laboratory keeps New York Yeast going. There isn't one day, not one damned hour, that we haven't got cultures of every strain of yeast in the company growing in our kettles. We check and adjust the food factor requirements. We make sure it's breeding true. We twist the genetics, start the new strains and weed them out, sort out their properties and mold them again.

"When New Yorkers started getting strawberries out of season a couple of years back, those weren't strawberries, fella. Those were a special high-sugar yeast culture with true-bred color and just a dash of flavor additive. It was developed right here in this room.

"Twenty years ago *Saccharomyces olei Benedictae* was just a scrub strain with a lousy taste of tallow and good for nothing. It still tastes of tallow, but its fat content has been pushed up from 15 per cent to 87 per cent. If you used the expressway today, just remember that it's greased strictly with *S. O. Benedictae, Strain AG-7*. Developed right here in this room.

"So don't call me a chemist. I'm a zymologist."

Despite himself, Baley retreated before the fierce pride of the other.

He said abruptly, "Where were you last night between the hours of eighteen and twenty?"

Clousarr shrugged. "Walking. I like to take a little walk after dinner."

"You visited friends? Or a subetheric?"

"No. Just walked."

Baley's lips tightened. A visit to the subetherics would have involved a notch in Clousarr's ration plack. A meeting with a friend would have involved naming a man or woman, and a cross check.

"No one saw you, then?"

"Maybe someone did. I don't know. Not that I know of, though."

"What about the night before last?"

"Same thing."

"You have no alibi then for either night?"

"If I had done anything criminal, Officer, I'd have one. What do I need an alibi for?"

Baley didn't answer. He consulted his little book. "You were up before the magistrate once. Inciting to riot."

"All right. One of the R things pushed past me and I tripped him up. Is that inciting to riot?"

"The court thought so. You were convicted and fined."

"That ends it, doesn't it? Or do you want to fine me again?"

"Night before last, there was a near riot at a shoe department in the Bronx. You were seen there."

"By whom?"

Baley said, "It was at mealtime for you here. Did you eat the evening meal night before last?"

Clousarr hesitated, then shook his head. "Upset stomach. Yeast gets you that way sometimes. Even an old-timer."

"Last night, there was a near riot in Williamsburg and you were seen *there*."

"By whom?"

"Do you deny you were present on both occasions?"

"You're not giving me anything to deny. Exactly where did these things happen and who says he saw me?"

Baley stared at the zymologist levelly. "I think you know exactly what I'm talking about. I think you're an important man in an unregistered Medievalist organization."

"I can't stop you from thinking, Officer, but thinking isn't evidence. Maybe you know that." Clousarr was grinning.

"Maybe," said Baley, his long face stony, "I can get a little truth out of you right now."

Baley stepped to the door of the balance room and opened it. He said to R. Daneel, who was waiting stolidly outside, "Has Clousarr's evening meal arrived?"

"It is coming now, Elijah."

"Bring it in, will you, Daneel?"

R. Daneel entered a moment later with a metal compartmented tray.

"Put it down in front of Mr. Clousarr, Daneel," said Baley. He sat down on one of the stools lining the balance wall, legs crossed, one shoe swinging rhythmically. He watched Clousarr edge stiffly away as R. Daneel placed the tray on a stool near the zymologist.

"Mr. Clousarr," said Baley. "I want to introduce you to my partner, Daneel Olivaw."

Daneel put out his hand and said, "How do you do, Francis."

Clousarr said nothing. He made no move to grasp Daneel's extended hand. Daneel maintained his position and Clousarr began to redden.

Baley said softly, "You are being rude, Mr. Clousarr. Are you too proud to shake hands with a policeman?"

Clousarr muttered, "If you don't mind, I'm hungry." He unfolded a pocket fork out of a clasp knife he took from his pocket and sat down, eyes bent on his meal.

Baley said, "Daneel, I think our friend is offended by your cold attitude. You are not angry with him, are you?"

"Not at all, Elijah," said R. Daneel.

"Then show that there are no hard feelings. Put your arm about his shoulder."

"I will be glad to," said R. Daneel, and stepped forward.

Clousarr put down his fork. "What is this? What's going on?"

R. Daneel, unruffled, put out his arm.

Clousarr swung backhanded, wildly, knocking R. Daneel's arm to one side. "Damn it, don't touch me."

He jumped up and away, the tray of food tipping and hitting the floor in a messy clatter.

Baley, hard-eyed, nodded curtly to R. Daneel, who thereupon continued a stolid advance toward the retreating zymologist. Baley stepped in front of the door.

Clousarr yelled, "Keep that thing off me."

"That's no way to speak," said Baley with equanimity. "The man's my partner."

"You mean he's a damned robot," shrieked Clousarr.

"Get away from him, Daneel," said Baley promptly.

R. Daneel stepped back and stood quietly against the door just behind Baley. Clousarr, panting harshly, fists clenched, faced Baley.

Baley said, "All right, smart boy. What makes you think Daneel's a robot?"

"Anyone can tell!"

"We'll leave that to a judge. Meanwhile, I think we want you at headquarters, Clousarr. We'd like to have you explain exactly how you knew Daneel was a robot. And lots more, mister, lots more. Daneel, step outside and get through to the Commissioner. He'll be at his home by now. Tell him to come down to the office. Tell him I have a fellow who can't wait to be questioned."

R. Daneel stepped out.

Baley said, "What makes your wheels go round, Clousarr?"

"I want a lawyer."

"You'll get one. Meanwhile, suppose you tell me what makes you Medievalists tick?"

Clousarr looked away in a determined silence.

Baley said, "Jehoshaphat, man, we know all about you *and* your organization. I'm not bluffing. Just tell me for my own curiosity: What do you Medievalists *want?*"

"Back to the soil," said Clousarr in a stifled voice. "That's simple, isn't it?"

"It's simple to say," said Baley. "But it isn't simple to do. How's the soil going to feed eight billions?"

"Did I say back to the soil overnight? Or in a year? Or in a hundred years? Step by step, mister policeman. It doesn't matter how long it takes, but let's get started out of these caves we live in. Let's get out into the fresh air."

"Have *you* ever been out into the fresh air?"

Clousarr squirmed. "All right, so I'm ruined, too. But the children aren't ruined yet. There are babies being born continuously. Get them out, for God's sake. Let them have space and open air and sun. If we've got to, we'll cut our population little by little, too."

"Backward, in other words, to an impossible past." Baley did not really know why he was arguing, except for the strange fever that was burning in his own veins. "Back to the seed, to the egg, to the womb. Why not move forward? Don't cut Earth's population. Use it for export. Go back to the soil, but go back to the soil of other planets. Colonize!"

Clousarr laughed harshly. "And make more Outer Worlds? More Spacers?"

"We won't. The Outer Worlds were settled by Earthmen who came from a planet that did not have Cities, by Earthmen who were individualists and materialists. Those qualities were carried to an unhealthy extreme. We can now colonize out of a society that has built co-operation, if anything, too far. Now environment and tradition can interact to form a new middle way, distinct from either old Earth or the Outer Worlds. Something newer and better."

He was parroting Dr. Fastolfe, he knew, but it was coming out as though he himself had been thinking of it for years.

Clousarr said, "Nuts! Colonize desert worlds with a world of our own at our fingertips? What fools would try?"

"Many. And they wouldn't be fools. There'd be robots to help."

"No," said Clousarr, fiercely. "Never! No robots!"

"Why not, for the love of Heaven? I don't like them, either, but I'm not going to knife myself for the sake of a prejudice. What are we afraid of in robots? If you want my guess, it's a sense of inferiority. We, all of us, feel inferior to the Spacers and hate it. We've got to feel superior somehow, somewhere, to make up for it, and it kills us that we can't at least feel superior to robots. They seem to be better than us—only they're *not*. That's the damned irony of it."

Baley felt his blood heating as he spoke. "Look at this Daneel I've been with for over two days. He's taller than I am, stronger, handsomer. He looks like a Spacer, in fact. He's got a better memory and knows more facts. He doesn't have to sleep or eat. He's not troubled by sickness or panic or love or guilt.

"But he's a machine. I can do anything I want to him, the way I can to that microbalance right there. If I slam the microbalance, it won't hit me back. Neither will Daneel. I can order him to take a blaster to himself and he'll do it.

"We can't ever build a robot that will be even as good as a human being in anything that counts, let alone better. We can't create a robot with a sense of beauty or a sense of ethics or a sense of religion. There's no way we can raise a positronic brain one inch above the level of perfect materialism.

"We can't, damn it, we can't. Not as long as we don't understand what makes our own brains tick. Not as long as things exist that science can't measure. What *is* beauty, or goodness, or art, or love, or God? We're forever teetering on the brink of the unknowable, and trying to understand what can't be understood. It's what makes us men.

"A robot's brain must be finite or it can't be built. It must be calculated to the final decimal place so that it has an end. Jehoshaphat, what are you afraid of? A robot can look like Daneel, he can look like a god, and be no more human than a lump of wood is. Can't you see that?"

Clousarr had tried to interrupt several times and failed against Baley's furious torrent. Now, when Baley paused in sheer emotional exhaustion, he said weakly, "Copper turned philosopher. What do you know?"

R. Daneel re-entered.

Baley looked at him and frowned, partly with the anger that had not yet left him, partly with new annoyance.

He said, "What kept you?"

R. Daneel said, "I had trouble in reaching Commissioner Enderby, Elijah. It turned out he was still at his office."

Baley looked at his watch. *"Now?* What for?"

"There is a certain confusion at the moment. A corpse has been discovered in the Department."

"What! For God's sake, who?"

"The errand boy, R. Sammy."

Baley gagged. He stared at the robot and said in an outraged voice, "I thought you said a corpse."

R. Daneel amended smoothly, "A robot with a completely deactivated brain, if you prefer."

Clousarr laughed suddenly and Baley turned on him, saying huskily, "Nothing out of you! Understand?" Deliberately, he unlimbered his blaster. Clousarr was very silent.

Baley said, "Well, what of it? R. Sammy blew a fuse. So what?"

"Commissioner Enderby was evasive, Elijah, but while he did not say so outright, my impression is that the Commissioner believes R. Sammy to have been deliberately deactivated."

Then, as Baley absorbed that silently, R. Daneel added gravely, "Or, if you prefer the phrase—murdered."

16

Questions Concerning a Motive

Baley replaced his blaster, but kept his hand unobtrusively upon its butt.

He said, "Walk ahead of us, Clousarr, to Seventeenth Street Exit B."

Clousarr said, "I haven't eaten."

"Tough," said Baley, impatiently. "There's your meal on the floor where you dumped it."

"I have a right to eat."

"You'll eat in detention, or you'll miss a meal. You won't starve. Get going."

All three were silent as they threaded the maze of New York Yeast, Clousarr moving stonily in advance, Baley right behind him, and R. Daneel in the rear.

It was after Baley and R. Daneel had checked out at the receptionist's desk, after Clousarr had drawn a leave of absence and requested that a man be sent in to clean up the balance room, after they were out in the open just to one side of the parked squad car, that Clousarr said, "Just a minute."

He hung back, turned toward R. Daneel, and, before Baley could make a move to stop him, stepped forward and swung his open hand full against the robot's cheek.

"What the devil," cried Baley, snatching violently at Clousarr.

Clousarr did not resist the plain-clothes man's grasp. "It's all right. I'll go. I just wanted to see for myself." He was grinning.

R. Daneel, having faded with the slap, but not having escaped it entirely, gazed quietly at Clousarr. There was no reddening of his cheek, no mark of any blow.

He said, "That was a dangerous action, Francis. Had I not moved backward, you might easily have damaged your hand. As it is, I regret that I must have caused you pain."

Clousarr laughed.

Baley said, "Get in, Clousarr. You, too, Daneel. Right in the back seat with him. And make sure he doesn't move. I don't care if it means breaking his arm. That's an order."

"What about the First Law?" mocked Clousarr.

"I think Daneel is strong enough and fast enough to stop you without hurting you, but it might do you good to have an arm or two broken at that."

Baley got behind the wheel and the squad car gathered speed. The empty wind ruffled his hair and Clousarr's, but R. Daneel's remained smoothly in place.

R. Daneel said quietly to Clousarr, "Do you fear robots for the sake of your job, Mr. Clousarr?"

Baley could not turn to see Clousarr's expression, but he was certain it would be a hard and rigid mirror of detestation, that he would be sitting stiffly apart, as far as he might, from R. Daneel.

Clousarr's voice said, "And my kids' jobs. And everyone's kids."

"Surely adjustments are possible," said the robot. "If your children, for instance, were to accept training for emigration——"

Clousarr broke in. "You, too? The policeman talked about emigration. He's got good robot training. Maybe he *is* a robot."

Baley growled, "That's enough, you!"

R. Daneel said, evenly, "A training school for emigrants would involve security, guaranteed classification, an assured career. If you are concerned over your children, that is something to consider."

"I wouldn't take anything from a robot, or a Spacer, or any of your trained hyenas in the Government."

That was all. The silence of the motorway engulfed them and there was only the soft whirr of the squad-car motor and the hiss of its wheels on the pavement.

Back at the Department, Baley signed a detention certificate for Clousarr and left him in appropriate hands. Following that, he and R. Daneel took the motospiral up the levels to Headquarters.

R. Daneel showed no surprise that they had not taken the elevators, nor did Baley expect him to. He was becoming used to the robot's queer mixture of ability and submissiveness and tended to leave him out of his calculations. The elevator was the logical method of leaping the vertical gap between Detention and Headquarters. The long moving stairway that was the motospiral was useful only for short climbs or drops of two or three levels at most. People of all sorts and varieties of administrative occupation stepped on and then off in less than a minute. Only Baley and R. Daneel remained on continuously, moving upward in a slow and stolid measure.

Baley felt that he needed the time. It was only minutes at best, but up in Headquarters he would be thrown violently into another phase of the problem and he wanted a rest. He wanted time to think and orient himself. Slowly as it moved, the motospiral went too quickly to satisfy him.

R. Daneel said, "It seems then we will not be questioning Clousarr just yet."

"He'll keep," said Baley, irritably. "Let's find out what the R. Sammy thing is all about." He added in a mutter, far more to himself than to R. Daneel, "It can't be independent; there must be a connection."

R. Daneel said, "It is a pity. Clousarr's cerebric qualities——"

"What about them?"

"They have changed in a strange way. What was it that took place between the two of you in the balance room while I was not present?"

Baley said, absently, "The only thing I did was to preach at him. I passed along the gospel according to St. Fastolfe."

"I do not understand you, Elijah."

Baley sighed and said, "Look, I tried to explain that Earth might as well make use of robots and get its population surplus onto other planets. I tried to knock some of the Medievalist hogwash out of his head. God knows why. I've never thought of myself as the missionary type. Anyway, that's all that happened."

"I see. Well, that makes some sense. Perhaps that can be fitted in. Tell me, Elijah, what did you tell him about robots?"

"You really want to know? I told him robots were simply machines. That was the gospel according to St. Gerrigel. There are any number of gospels, I think."

"Did you by any chance tell him that one could strike a robot without fear of a return blow, much as one could strike any other mechanical object?"

"Except a punching bag, I suppose. Yes. But what made you guess that?" Baley looked curiously at the robot.

"It fits the cerebric changes," said R. Daneel, "and it explains his blow to my face just after we left the factory. He must have been thinking of what you said, so he simultaneously tested your statement, worked off his aggressive feelings, and had the pleasure of seeing me placed in what seemed to him a position of inferiority. In order to be so motivated and allowing for the delta variations in his quintic . . ."

He paused a long moment and said, "Yes, it is quite interesting, and now I believe I can form a self-consistent whole of the data."

Headquarters level was approaching. Baley said, "What time is it?"

He thought, pettishly: Nuts, I could look at my watch and take less time that way.

But he knew why he asked him, nevertheless. The motive was not so different from Clousarr's in punching R. Daneel. To give the robot a trivial order that he must fulfill emphasized his roboticity and, contrariwise, Baley's humanity.

Baley thought: We're all brothers. Under the skin, over it, everywhere. Jehoshaphat!

R. Daneel said, "Twenty-ten."

They stepped off the motospiral and for a few seconds Baley had the usual queer sensation that went with the necessary adjustment to non-motion after long minutes of steady movement.

He said, "And I haven't eaten. Damn this job, anyway."

Baley saw and heard Commissioner Enderby through the open door of his office. The common room was empty, as though it had been wiped clean, and Enderby's voice rang through it with unusual hollowness. His round face looked bare and weak without its glasses, which he held in his hand, while he mopped his smooth forehead with a flimsy paper napkin.

His eyes caught Baley just as the latter reached the door and his voice rose into a petulant tenor.

"Good God, Baley, where the devil were you?"

Baley shrugged off the remark and said, "What's doing? Where's the night shift?" and then caught sight of the second person in the office with the Commissioner.

He said, blankly, "Dr. Gerrigel!"

The gray-haired roboticist returned the involuntary greeting by nodding briefly. "I'm glad to see you again, Mr. Baley."

The Commissioner readjusted his glasses and stared at Baley through them. "The entire staff is being questioned downstairs. Signing statements. I was going mad trying to find you. It looked queer, your being away."

"*My* being away!" cried Baley, strenuously.

"Anybody's being away. Someone in the Department did it and there's going to be hell to pay for that. What an unholy mess! What an unholy, *rotten* mess!"

He raised his hands as though in expostulation to heaven and as he did so, his eyes fell on R. Daneel.

Baley thought sardonically: First time you've looked Daneel in the face. Take a good look, Julius!

The Commissioner said in a subdued voice, "*He'll* have to sign a statement. Even *I've* had to do it. I!"

Baley said, "Look, Commissioner, what makes you so sure that R. Sammy didn't blow a gasket all by himself? What makes it deliberate destruction?"

The Commissioner sat down heavily. "Ask him," he said, and pointed to Dr. Gerrigel.

Dr. Gerrigel cleared his throat. "I scarcely know how to go about this, Mr. Baley. I take it from your expression that you are surprised to see me."

"Moderately," admitted Baley.

"Well, I was in no real hurry to return to Washington and my visits to New York are few enough to make me wish to linger. And what's more important, I had a growing feeling that it would be criminal for me to leave the City without having made at least one more effort to be allowed to analyze your fascinating robot, whom, by the way," (he looked very eager) "I see you have with you."

Baley stirred restlessly. "That's quite impossible."

The roboticist looked disappointed. "Now, yes. Perhaps later?"

Baley's long face remained woodenly unresponsive.

Dr. Gerrigel went on. "I called you, but you weren't in and no one knew where you could be located. I asked for the Commissioner and he asked me to come to headquarters and wait for you."

The Commissioner interposed quickly. "I thought it might be important. I knew you wanted to see the man."

Baley nodded. "Thanks."

Dr. Gerrigel said, "Unfortunately my guide rod was somewhat off, or perhaps in my overanxiety I misjudged its temperature. In either case I took a wrong turning and found myself in a small room——"

The Commissioner interrupted again. "One of the photographic supply rooms, Lije."

"Yes," said Dr. Gerrigel. "And in it was the prone figure of what was obviously a robot. It was quite clear to me after a brief examination that he was irreversibly deactivated. Dead, you might say. Nor was it very difficult to determine the cause of the deactivation."

"What was it?" asked Baley.

"In the robot's partly clenched right fist," said Dr. Gerrigel, "was a shiny ovoid about two inches long and half an inch wide with a mica window at one end. The fist was in contact with his skull as though the robot's last act had been to touch his head. The thing he was holding was an alpha-sprayer. You know what they are, I suppose?"

Baley nodded. He needed neither dictionary nor handbook to be told what an alpha-sprayer was. He had handled several in his lab courses in physics: a lead-alloy casing with a narrow pit dug into it longitudinally, at the bottom of which was a fragment of a plutonium salt. The pit was capped with a sliver of mica, which was transparent to alpha particles. In that one direction, hard radiation sprayed out.

An alpha-sprayer had many uses, but killing robots was not one of them, not a legal one, at least.

Baley said, "He held it to his head mica first, I take it."

Dr. Gerrigel said, "Yes, and his positronic brain paths were immediately randomized. Instant death, so to speak."

Baley turned to the pale Commissioner. "No mistake? It really *was* an alpha-sprayer?"

The Commissioner nodded, his plump lips thrust out. "Absolutely. The counters could spot it ten feet away. Photographic film in the storeroom was fogged. Cut and dried."

He seemed to brood about it for a moment or two, then said

abruptly, "Dr. Gerrigel, I'm afraid you'll have to stay in the City a day or two until we can get your evidence down on wire-film. I'll have you escorted to a room. You don't mind being under guard, I hope?"

Dr. Gerrigel said nervously, "Do you think it's necessary?"

"It's safer."

Dr. Gerrigel, seeming quite abstracted, shook hands all around, even with R. Daneel, and left.

The Commissioner heaved a sigh. "It's one of us, Lije. That's what bothers me. No outsider would come into the Department just to knock off a robot. Plenty of them outside where it's safer. And it had to be somebody who could pick up an alpha-sprayer. They're hard to get hold of."

R. Daneel spoke, his cool, even voice cutting through the agitated words of the Commissioner. He said, "But what is the motive for this murder?"

The Commissioner glanced at R. Daneel with obvious distaste, then looked away. "We're human, too. I suppose policemen can't get to like robots any more than anyone else can. He's gone now and maybe it's a relief to somebody. He used to annoy you considerably, Lije, remember?"

"That is scarcely murder motive," said R. Daneel.

"No," agreed Baley, with decision.

"It isn't murder," said the Commissioner. "It's property damage. Let's keep our legal terms straight. It's just that it was done inside the Department. Anywhere else it would be nothing. Nothing. Now it could be a first-class scandal. Lije!"

"Yes?"

"When did you last see R. Sammy?"

Baley said, "R. Daneel spoke to R. Sammy after lunch. I should judge it was about 13:30. He arranged to have us use your office, Commissioner."

"My office? What for?"

"I wanted to talk over the case with R. Daneel in moderate privacy. You weren't in, so your office was an obvious place."

"I see." The Commissioner looked dubious, but let the matter ride. "You didn't see him yourself?"

"No, but I heard his voice perhaps an hour afterward."

"Are you sure it was he?"

"Perfectly."

"That would be about 14:30?"

"Or a little sooner."

The Commissioner bit his pudgy lower lip thoughtfully. "Well, that settles one thing."

"It does?"

"Yes. The boy, Vincent Barrett, was here today. Did you know that?"

"Yes. But, Commissioner, he wouldn't do anything like this."

The Commissioner lifted his eyes to Baley's face. "Why not? R. Sammy took his job away. I can understand how he feels. There would be a tremendous sense of injustice. He would want a certain revenge. Wouldn't you? But the fact is that he left the building at 14:00 and you heard R. Sammy alive at 14:30. Of course, he might have given the alpha-sprayer to R. Sammy before he left with instructions not to use it for an hour, but then where could he have gotten an alpha-sprayer? It doesn't bear thinking of. Let's get back to R. Sammy. When you spoke to him at 14:30, what did he say?"

Baley hesitated a perceptible moment, then said carefully, "I don't remember. We left shortly afterward."

"Where did you go?"

"Yeast-town, eventually. I want to talk about that, by the way."

"Later. Later." The Commissioner rubbed his chin. "Jessie was in today, I noticed. I mean, we were checking on all visitors today and I just happened to see her name."

"She was here," said Baley, coldly.

"What for?"

"Personal family matters."

"She'll have to be questioned as a pure formality."

"I understand police routine, Commissioner. Incidentally, what about the alpha-sprayer itself? Has it been traced?"

"Oh, yes. It came from one of the power plants."

"How do they account for having lost it?"

"They don't. They have no idea. But look, Lije, except for routine statements, this has nothing to do with you. You stick to your case. It's just that . . . Well, you stick to the Spacetown investigation."

Baley said, "May I give my routine statements later, Commissioner? The fact is, I haven't eaten yet."

Commissioner Enderby's glassed eyes turned full on Baley. "By all means get something to eat. But stay inside the Department, will you? Your partner's right, though, Lije"—he seemed to avoid addressing R. Daneel or using his name—"it's the motive we need. The motive."

Baley felt suddenly frozen.

Something outside himself, something completely alien, took up the events of this day and the day before and the day before and juggled them. Once again pieces began to dovetail; a pattern began to form.

He said, "Which power plant did the alpha-sprayer come from, Commissioner?"

"The Williamsburg plant. Why?"

"Nothing. Nothing."

The last word Baley heard the Commissioner mutter as he strode out of the office, with R. Daneel immediately behind him, was, "Motive. Motive."

Baley ate a sparse meal in the small and infrequently used Department lunchroom. He devoured the stuffed tomato on lettuce without being entirely aware of its nature and for a second or so after he had gulped down the last mouthful his fork still slithered aimlessly over the slick cardboard of his plate, searching automatically for something that was no longer there.

He became aware of that and put down his fork with a muffled, "Jehoshaphat!"

"He said, "Daneel!"

R. Daneel had been sitting at another table, as though he wished to leave the obviously preoccupied Baley in peace, or as though he required privacy himself. Baley was past caring which.

Daneel stood up, moved to Baley's table, and sat down again. "Yes, partner Elijah?"

Baley did not look at him. "Daneel, I'll need your co-operation."

"In what way?"

"They will question Jessie and myself. That is certain. Let me answer the questions in my own way. Do you understand?"

"I understand what you say, of course. Nevertheless, if I am asked a direct question, how is it possible for me to say anything but what is so?"

"*If* you are asked a direct question, that's another matter. I ask only that you don't volunteer information. You can do that, can't you?"

"I believe so, Elijah, provided it does not appear that I am hurting a human being by remaining silent."

Baley said, grimly, "You will hurt *me* if you don't. I assure you of that."

"I do not quite understand your point of view, partner Elijah. Surely the matter of R. Sammy cannot concern you."

"No? It all centers about motive, doesn't it? You've questioned the motive. The Commissioner questioned it. I do, for that matter. Why should anyone want to kill R. Sammy? Mind you, it's not just a question of who would want to smash up robots in general. Any Earthman, practically, would want to do that. The question is, who would want to single out R. Sammy. Vincent Barrett might, but the Commissioner said he couldn't get hold of an alpha-sprayer, and he's right. We have to look somewhere else, and it so happens that one other person has a motive. It glares out. It yells. It stinks to top level."

"Who is the person, Elijah?"

And Baley said, softly, "I am, Daneel."

R. Daneel's expressionless face did not change under the impact of the statement. He merely shook his head.

Baley said, "You don't agree. My wife came to the office today. They know that already. The Commissioner is even curious. If I weren't a personal friend, he wouldn't have stopped his questioning so soon. Now they'll find out why. That's certain. She was part of a conspiracy; a foolish and harmless one, but a conspiracy just the same. And a policeman can't afford to have his wife mixed up with anything like that. It would be to my obvious interest to see that the matter was hushed up.

"Well, who knew about it? You and I, of course, and Jessie—*and R. Sammy.* He saw her in a state of panic. When he told her that we had left orders not to be disturbed, she must have lost control. You saw the way she was when she first came in."

R. Daneel said, "It is unlikely that she said anything incriminating to him."

"That may be so. But I'm reconstructing the case the way they will. They'll say she did. There's my motive. I killed him to keep him quiet."

"They will not think so."

"They *will* think so. The murder was arranged deliberately in order to throw suspicion on me. Why use an alpha-sprayer? It's a rather risky way. It's hard to get and it can be traced. I think that those were the very reasons it *was* used. The murderer even ordered R. Sammy to go into the photographic supply room and kill himself there. It seems obvious to me that the reason for that was to have the method of murder unmistakable. Even if everyone was so infantile as not to recognize the alpha-sprayer immediately, someone would be bound to notice fogged photographic film in fairly short order."

"How does that all relate to you, Elijah?"

Baley grinned tightly, his long face completely devoid of humor. "Very neatly. The alpha-sprayer was taken from the Williamsburg power plant. You and I passed through the Williamsburg power plant yesterday. We were seen, and the fact will come out. That gives me opportunity to get the weapon as well as motive for the crime. And it may turn out that we were the last ones to see or hear R. Sammy alive, except for the real murderer, of course."

"I was with you in the power plant and I can testify that you did not have the opportunity to steal an alpha-sprayer."

"Thanks," said Baley sadly, "but you're a robot and your testimony will be invalid."

"The Commissioner is your friend. He will listen."

"The Commissioner has a job to keep, and he already is a bit uneasy about me. There's only one chance of saving myself from this very nasty situation."

"Yes?"

"I ask myself, *why* am I being framed? Obviously to get rid of me. But why? Again obviously, because I am dangerous to someone. I am doing my best to be dangerous to whoever killed Dr. Sarton in Spacetown. That might mean the Medievalists, of course, or at least, the inner group among them. It would be this inner group that would know I had passed through the power plant; at least one of them might have followed me along the strips that far, even though you thought we had lost them.

"So the chances are that if I find the murderer of Dr. Sarton, I find the man or men who are trying to get me out of the way. If I think it through, if I crack the case, if I can only crack it, I'll be safe. And Jessie. I couldn't stand to have her . . . But I don't have much time." His fist clenched and unclenched spasmodically. "I don't have much time."

Baley looked at R. Daneel's chiseled face with a sudden burning hope. Whatever the creature was, he was strong and faithful, animated by no selfishness. What more could you ask of any friend? Baley needed a friend and he was in no mood to cavil at the fact that a gear replaced a blood vessel in this particular one.

But R. Daneel was shaking his head.

The robot said, "I am sorry, Elijah"—there was no trace of sorrow on his face, of course—"but I anticipated none of this. Perhaps my action was to your harm. I am sorry if the general good requires that."

"What general good?" stammered Baley.

"I have been in communication with Dr. Fastolfe."

"Jehoshaphat! When?"

"While you were eating."

Baley's lips tightened.

"Well?" he managed to say. "What happened?"

"You will have to clear yourself of suspicion of the murder of R. Sammy through some means other than the investigation of the murder of my designer, Dr. Sarton. Our people at Spacetown, as a result of my information, have decided to bring that investigation to an end, as of today, and to begin plans for leaving Spacetown and Earth."

17

Conclusion of a Project

BALEY LOOKED at his watch with something approaching detachment. It was 21:45. In two and a quarter hours it would be midnight. He had been awake since before six and had been under tension now for two and a half days. A vague sense of unreality pervaded everything.

He kept his voice painfully steady as he reached for his pipe and for the little bag that held his precious crumbs of tobacco. He said, "What's it all about, Daneel?"

R. Daneel said, "Do you not understand? Is it not obvious?"

Baley said, patiently, "I do not understand. It is not obvious."

"We are here," said the robot, "and by we, I mean our people at Spacetown, to break the shell surrounding Earth and force its people into new expansion and colonization."

"I know that. Please don't labor the point."

"I must, since it is the essential one. If we were anxious to exact punishment for the murder of Dr. Sarton, it was not that in doing so we expected to bring Dr. Sarton back to life, you understand; it was only that failure to do so would strengthen the position of our home planet politicians who are against the very idea of Spacetown."

"But now," said Baley, with sudden violence, "you say you're getting ready to go home of your own accord. Why? In heaven's name, why? The answer to the Sarton case is close. It *must* be close or they wouldn't be trying so hard to blast me out of the investigation. I have a feeling I have all the facts I need to work out the answer. It must be in here somewhere." He knuckled his temple wildly. "A sentence might bring it out. A word."

He clenched his eyes fiercely shut, as though the quivering opaque jelly of the last sixty hours were indeed on the point of clarifying and becoming transparent. But it did not. It did not.

Baley drew a shuddering breath and felt ashamed. He was making a weak spectacle of himself before a cold and unimpressed machine that could only stare at him silently.

He said harshly, "Well, never mind that. Why are the Spacers breaking off?"

The robot said, "Our project is concluded. We are satisfied that Earth will colonize."

"You've switched to optimism then?" The plain-clothes man drew in his first calming puff of tobacco smoke and felt his grip upon his own emotions grow firmer.

"I have. For a long time now, we of Spacetown have tried to change Earth by changing its economy. We have tried to introduce our own C/Fe culture. Your planetary and various City governments co-operated with us because it was expedient to do so. Still, in twenty-five years, we have failed. The harder we tried, the stronger the opposing party of the Medievalists grew."

"I know all this," said Baley. He thought: No use. He's got to tell this in his own way, like a field recording. He yelled silently at R. Daneel: *Machine!*

R. Daneel went on, "It was Dr. Sarton who first theorized that we must reverse our tactics. We must first find a segment of Earth's population that desired what we desired or could be persuaded to do so. By encouraging and helping them, we could make the movement a native one rather than a foreign one. The difficulty was in finding the native element best suited for our purposes. You, yourself, Elijah, were an interesting experiment."

"I? I? What do you mean?" demanded Baley.

"We were glad your Commissioner recommended you. From your psychic profile we judged you to be a useful specimen. Cerebroanalysis, a process I conducted upon you as soon as I met you, confirmed our judgment. You are a practical man, Elijah. You do not moon romantically over Earth's past, despite your healthy interest in it. Nor do you stubbornly embrace the City culture of Earth's present day. We felt that people such as yourself were the ones that could lead Earthmen to the stars once more. It was one reason Dr. Fastolfe was anxious to see you yesterday morning.

"To be sure, your practical nature was embarrassingly intense. You refused to understand that the fanatical service of an ideal, even a mistaken ideal, could make a man do things quite beyond his ordinary capacity, as, for instance, crossing open country at night to destroy someone he considered an archenemy of his cause. We were not overly surprised, therefore, that you were stubborn enough and daring enough to attempt to prove the murder a fraud. In a way, it proved you were the man we wanted for our experiment."

"For God's sake, what experiment?" Baley brought his fist down on the table.

"The experiment of persuading you that colonization was the answer to Earth's problems."

"Well, I was persuaded. I'll grant you that."

"Yes, under the influence of the appropriate drug."

Baley's teeth loosened their grip on his pipestem. He caught the pipe as it fell. Once again, he was seeing that scene in the Spacetown dome. Himself swimming back to awareness after the shock of learning that R. Daneel was a robot after all; R. Daneel's smooth fingers pinching up the flesh of his arm; a hypo-sliver standing out darkly under his skin and then fading away.

He said, chokingly, "What was in the hypo-sliver?"

"Nothing that need alarm you, Elijah. It was a mild drug intended only to make your mind more receptive."

"And so I believed whatever was told me. Is that it?"

"Not quite. You would not believe anything that was foreign to the basic pattern of your thought. In fact, the results of the experiment were disappointing. Dr. Fastolfe had hoped you would become fanatical and single-minded on the subject. Instead you became rather distantly approving, no more. Your practical nature stood in the way of anything further. It made us realize that our only hope was the romantics after all, and the romantics, unfortunately, were all Medievalists, actual or potential."

Baley felt incongruously proud of himself, glad of his stubbornness, and happy that he had disappointed them. Let them experiment with someone else.

He grinned savagely. "And so now you've given up and are going home?"

"Why, that is not it. I said a few moments ago that we were satisfied Earth would colonize. It was you that gave us the answer."

"*I* gave it to you? How?"

"You spoke to Francis Clousarr of the advantages of colonization. You spoke rather fervently, I judge. At least our experiment on you had *that* result. And Clousarr's cerebroanalytic properties changed. Very subtly, to be sure, but they changed."

"You mean I convinced him that I was right? I don't believe that."

"No, conviction does not come that easily. But the cerebroanalytic changes demonstrated conclusively that the Medievalist mind is *open* to that sort of conviction. I experimented further myself. When leaving Yeast-town, guessing what might have happened between you two from his cerebric changes, I made the proposition of a school for emigrants as a way of insuring his children's future. He rejected that, but again his aura changed, and it seemed to me quite obvious that it was the proper method of attack."

R. Daneel paused, then spoke on.

"The thing called Medievalism shows a craving for pioneering. To be sure, the direction in which that craving turns itself is toward Earth itself, which is near and which has the precedent of a great past. But the vision of worlds beyond is a similar something and the romantic can turn to it easily, just as Clousarr felt the attraction as a result of one lecture from you.

"So you see, we of Spacetown had already succeeded without knowing it. We ourselves, rather than anything we tried to introduce, were the unsettling factor. We crystallized the romantic impulses on Earth into Medievalism and induced an organization in them. After all, it is the Medievalist who wishes to break the cake of custom, not the City officials who have most to gain from preserving the *status quo*. If we leave Spacetown now, if we do not irritate the Medievalist by our continued presence until he has committed himself to Earth, and only Earth, past redemption, if we leave behind a few obscure individuals or robots such as myself who, together with sympathetic Earthmen such as yourself, can establish the training schools for emigrants that I spoke of, the Medievalist will eventually turn away from Earth. He will need robots and will either get them from us or build his own. He will develop a C/Fe culture to suit himself."

It was a long speech for R. Daneel. He must have realized that himself, for, after another pause, he said, "I tell you all this to explain why it is necessary to do something that may hurt you."

Baley thought bitterly: A robot must not hurt a human being, unless he can think of a way to prove it is for the human being's ultimate good after all.

Baley said, "Just a minute. Let me introduce a practical note. You'll go back to your worlds and say that an Earthman killed a Spacer and is unpunished. The Outer Worlds will demand an indemnity from Earth, and I warn you, Earth is no longer in a mood to endure such treatment. There will be trouble."

"I am sure that will not happen, Elijah. The elements on our planets that would be most interested in pressing for an indemnity would be also most interested in forcing an end to Spacetown. We can easily offer the latter as an inducement to abandon the former. It is what we plan to do, anyway. Earth will be left in peace."

And Baley broke out, his voice hoarse with sudden despair, "And where does that leave me? The Commissioner will drop the Sarton investigation at once if Spacetown is willing, but the R. Sammy thing will have to continue, since it points to corruption inside the Department. He'll be in any minute with a ream of evidence against me. I know that. It's been arranged. I'll be declassified, Daneel. There's Jessie to consider. She'll be smeared as a criminal. There's Bentley——"

R. Daneel said, "You must not think, Elijah, that I do not understand the position in which you find yourself. In the service of humanity's good, the minor wrongs must be tolerated. Dr. Sarton has a surviving wife, two children, parents, a sister, many friends. All must grieve at his death and be saddened at the thought that his murderer has not been found and punished."

"Then why not stay and find him?"

"It is no longer necessary."

Baley said, bitterly, "Why not admit that the entire investigation was an excuse to study us under field conditions? You never gave a damn who killed Dr. Sarton."

"We would have liked to know," said R. Daneel, coolly, "but we were never under any delusions as to which was more important, an individual or humanity. To continue the investigation now would involve interfering with a situation which we now find satisfactory. We could not foretell what damage we might do."

"You mean the murderer might turn out to be a prominent Medievalist and right now the Spacers don't want to do anything to antagonize their new friends."

"It is not as I would say it, but there is truth in your words."

"Where's your justice circuit, Daneel? Is this justice?"

"There are degrees of justice, Elijah. When the lesser is incompatible with the greater, the lesser must give way."

It was as though Baley's mind were circling the impregnable logic of R. Daneel's positronic brain, searching for a loophole, a weakness.

He said, "Have you no personal curiosity, Daneel? You've called yourself a detective. Do you know what that implies? Do you understand that an investigation is more than a job of work? It is a challenge. Your mind is pitted against that of the criminal. It is a clash of intellect. Can you abandon the battle and admit defeat?"

"If no worthy end is served by a continuation, certainly."

"Would you feel no loss? No wonder? Would there be no little speck of dissatisfaction? Frustrated curiosity?"

Baley's hopes, not strong in the first place, weakened as he spoke. The word "curiosity," second time repeated, brought back his own remarks to Francis Clousarr four hours before. He had known well enough then the qualities that marked off a man from a machine. Curiosity *had* to be one of them. A six-week-old kitten was curious, but how could there be a curious machine, be it ever so humanoid?

R. Daneel echoed those thoughts by saying, "What do you mean by curiosity?"

Baley put the best face on it. "Curiosity is the name we give to a desire to extend one's knowledge."

"Such a desire exists within me, when the extension of knowledge is necessary for the performance of an assigned task."

"Yes," said Baley, sarcastically, "as when you ask questions about Bentley's contact lenses in order to learn more of Earth's peculiar customs."

"Precisely," said R. Daneel, with no sign of any awareness of sarcasm. "Aimless extension of knowledge, however, which is what I think you really mean by the term curiosity, is merely inefficiency. I am designed to avoid inefficiency."

It was in that way that the "sentence" he had been waiting for came to Elijah Baley, and the opaque jelly shuddered and settled and changed into luminous transparency.

While R. Daneel spoke, Baley's mouth opened and stayed so.

It could not all have burst full-grown into his mind. Things did not work so. Somewhere, deep inside his unconscious, he had built a case, built it carefully and in detail, but had been brought up short by a single inconsistency. One inconsistency that could be neither jumped over, burrowed under, nor shunted aside. While that inconsistency existed, the case remained buried below his thoughts, beyond the reach of his conscious probing.

But the sentence had come; the inconsistency had vanished; the case was his.

The glare of mental light appeared to have stimulated Baley mightily. At least he suddenly knew what R. Daneel's weakness must be, the weakness of any thinking machine. He thought feverishly, hopefully: The thing *must* be literal-minded.

He said, "Then Project Spacetown is concluded as of today and with it the Sarton investigation. Is that it?"

"That is the decision of our people at Spacetown," agreed R. Daneel, calmly.

"But today is not yet over." Baley looked at his watch. It was 22:30. "There is an hour and a half until midnight."

R. Daneel said nothing. He seemed to consider.

Baley spoke rapidly. "Until midnight, the project continues then. You are my partner and the investigation continues." He was becoming almost telegraphic in his haste. "Let us go on as before. Let me work. It will do your people no harm. It will do them great good. My word upon it. If, in your judgment, I am doing harm, stop me. It is only an hour and a half I ask."

R. Daneel said, "What you say is correct. Today is not over. I had not thought of that, partner Elijah."

Baley was "partner Elijah" again.

He grinned, and said, "Didn't Dr. Fastolfe mention a film of the scene of the murder when I was in Spacetown?"

"He did," said R. Daneel.

Baley said, "Can you get a copy of the film?"

"Yes, partner Elijah."

"I mean now! Instantly!"

"In ten minutes, if I can use the Department transmitter."

The process took less time than that. Baley stared at the small aluminum block he held in his trembling hands. Within it the subtle forces transmitted from Spacetown had strongly fixed a certain atomic pattern.

And at that moment, Commissioner Julius Enderby stood in the doorway. He saw Baley and a certain anxiety passed from his round face, leaving behind it a look of growing thunder.

He said, uncertainly, "Look here, Lije, you're taking a devil of a time, eating."

"I was bone-tired, Commissioner. Sorry if I've delayed you."

"I wouldn't mind, but . . . You'd better come to my office."

Baley's eyes flicked toward R. Daneel, but met no answering look. Together they moved out of the lunchroom.

Julius Enderby tramped the floor before his desk, up and down, up and down. Baley watched him, himself far from composed. Occasionally, he glanced at his watch.

22:45.

The Commissioner moved his glasses up onto his forehead and rubbed his eyes with thumb and forefinger. He left red splotches in the flesh around them, then restored the glasses to their place, blinking at Baley from behind them.

"Lije," he said suddenly, "when were you last in the Williamsburg power plant?"

Baley said, "Yesterday, after I left the office. I should judge at about eighteen or shortly thereafter."

The Commissioner shook his head. "Why didn't you say so?"

"I was going to. I haven't given an official statement yet."

"What were you doing there?"

"Just passing through on my way to our temporary sleeping quarters."

The Commissioner stopped short, standing before Baley, and said, "That's no good, Lije. No one just passes through a power plant to get somewhere else."

Baley shrugged. There was no point in going through the story of the pursuing Medievalists, of the dash along the strips. Not now.

He said, "If you're trying to hint that I had an opportunity to get the alpha-sprayer that knocked out R. Sammy, I'll remind you that

Daneel was with me and will testify that I went right through the plant without stopping and that I had no alpha-sprayer on me when I left."

Slowly, the Commissioner sat down. He did not look in R. Daneel's direction or offer to speak to him. He put his pudgy white hands on the desk before him and regarded them with a look of acute misery on his face.

He said, "Lije, I don't know what to say or what to think. And it's no use having your—your partner as alibi. He can't give evidence."

"I still deny that I took an alpha-sprayer."

The Commissioner's fingers intertwined and writhed. He said, "Lije, why did Jessie come to see you here this afternoon?"

"You asked me that before, Commissioner. Same answer. Family matters."

"I've got information from Francis Clousarr, Lije."

"What kind of information?"

"He claims that a Jezebel Baley is a member of a Medievalist society dedicated to the overthrow of the government by force."

"Are you sure he has the right person? There are many Baleys."

"There aren't many Jezebel Baleys."

"He used her name, did he?"

"He said Jezebel. I heard him, Lije. I'm not giving you a second-hand report."

"All right. Jessie was a member of a harmless lunatic-fringe organization. She never did anything but attend meetings and feel devilish about it."

"It won't look that way to a board of review, Lije."

"You mean I'm going to be suspended and held on suspicion of destroying government property in the form of R. Sammy?"

"I hope not, Lije, but it looks awfully bad. Everyone knows you didn't like R. Sammy. Your wife was seen talking to him this afternoon. She was in tears and some of her words were heard. They were harmless in themselves, but two and two can be added up, Lije. You might feel it was dangerous to leave him in a position to talk. *And* you had an opportunity to obtain the weapon."

Baley interrupted. "If I were wiping out all evidence against Jessie, would I bring in Francis Clousarr? He seems to know a lot more about her than R. Sammy could have. Another thing. I passed through the power plant eighteen hours before R. Sammy spoke to Jessie. Did I know that long in advance that I would have to destroy him and pick up an alpha-sprayer out of clairvoyance?"

The Commissioner said, "Those are good points. I'll do my best. I'm sorry about this, Lije."

"Yes? Do you really believe I didn't do it, Commissioner?"

Enderby said slowly, "I don't know what to think, Lije. I'll be frank with you."

"Then I'll tell you what to think. Commissioner, this is all a careful and elaborate frame."

The Commissioner stiffened. "Now, wait, Lije. Don't strike out blindly. You won't get any sympathy with that line of defense. It's been used by too many bad eggs."

"I'm not after sympathy. I'm just telling the truth. I'm being taken out of circulation to prevent me from learning the facts about the Sarton murder. Unfortunately for my framing pal, it's too late for that."

"*What!*"

Baley looked at his watch. It was 23:00.

He said, "I know who is framing me, and I know how Dr. Sarton was killed and by whom, and I have one hour to tell you about it, catch the man, and end the investigation."

18

End of an Investigation

COMMISSIONER ENDERBY's eyes narrowed and he glared at Baley. "What are you going to do? You tried something like this in Fastolfe's dome yesterday morning. Not again. Please."

Baley nodded. "I know. I was wrong the first time."

He thought, fiercely: Also the second time. But not now, not *this* time, not . . .

The thought faded out, spluttering like a micropile under a positronic damper.

He said, "Judge for yourself, Commissioner. Grant that the evidence against me has been planted. Go that far with me and see where it takes you. Ask yourself who could have planted that evidence. Obviously only someone who'd known I was in the Williamsburg plant yesterday evening."

"All right. Who would that be?"

Baley said, "I was followed out of the kitchen by a Medievalist group. I lost them, or I thought I did, but obviously at least one of them saw me pass through the plant. My only purpose in doing so, you understand, was to help me lose them."

The Commissioner considered. "Clousarr? Was he with them?"

Baley nodded.

Enderby said, "All right, we'll question him. If he's got anything in him, we'll have it out of him. What more can I do, Lije?"

"Wait, now. Don't quit on me. Do you see my point?"

"Well, let's see if I do?" The Commissioner clasped his hands. "Clousarr saw you go into the Williamsburg power plant, or else someone in his group did and passed the information along to him,

He decided to utilize that fact to get you into trouble and off the investigation. Is that what you're saying?"

"It's close to it."

"Good." The Commissioner seemed to warm to the task. "He knew your wife was a member of his organization, naturally, and so he knew you wouldn't face a really close probe into your private life. He thought you would resign rather than fight circumstantial evidence. By the way, Lije, what about a resignation? I mean, if things looked really bad. We could keep things quiet——"

"Not in a million years, Commissioner."

Enderby shrugged. "Well, where was I? Oh, yes, so he got an alpha-sprayer, presumably through a confederate in the plant, and had another confederate arrange the destruction of R. Sammy." His fingers drummed lightly on the desk. "No good, Lije."

"Why not?"

"Too farfetched. Too many confederates. And he has a cast-iron alibi for the night and morning of the Spacetown murder, by the way. We checked that almost right away, though I was the only one who knew the reason for checking that particular time."

Baley said, "I never said it was Clousarr, Commissioner. *You* did. It could be anyone in the Medievalist organization. Clousarr is just the owner of a face that Daneel happened to recognize. I don't even think he's particularly important in the organization. Though there is one queer thing about him."

"What?" asked Enderby, suspiciously.

"He did know Jessie was a member. Does he know every member in the organization, do you suppose?"

"I don't know. He knew about Jessie, anyway. Maybe she was important because she was the wife of a policeman. Maybe he remembered her for that reason."

"You say he came right out and said that Jezebel Baley was a member. Just like that? Jezebel Baley?"

Enderby nodded. "I keep telling you I heard him."

"That's the funny thing, Commissioner. Jessie hasn't used her full first name since before Bentley was born. Not once. I know that for certain. She joined the Medievalists after she dropped her full name. I know that for sure, too. How would Clousarr come to know her as Jezebel, then?"

The Commissioner flushed and said, hastily, "Oh well, if it comes to that, he probably said Jessie. I just filled it in automatically and gave her full name. In fact, I'm sure of that. He said Jessie."

"Until now you were quite sure he said Jezebel. I asked several times."

The Commissioner's voice rose. "You're not saying I'm a liar, are you?"

"I'm just wondering if Clousarr, perhaps, said nothing at all. I'm wondering if you made that up. You've known Jessie for twenty years, and *you* knew her name was Jezebel."

"You're off your head, man."

"Am I? Where were you after lunch today? You were out of your office for two hours at least."

"Are you questioning *me*?"

"I'll answer for you, too. You were in the Williamsburg power plant."

The Commissioner rose from his seat. His forehead glistened and there were dry, white flecks at the corners of his lips. "What the hell are you trying to say?"

"Weren't you?"

"Baley, you're suspended. Hand me your credentials."

"Not yet. Hear me out."

"I don't intend to. You're guilty. You're guilty as the devil, and what gets me is your cheap attempt to make me, *me*, look as though I were conspiring against you." He lost his voice momentarily in a squeak of indignation. He managed to gasp out, "In fact, you're under arrest."

"No," said Baley, tightly, "not yet. Commissioner, I've got a blaster on you. It's pointed straight and it's cocked. Don't fool with me, please, because I'm desperate and I *will* have my say. Afterward, you can do what you please."

With widening eyes, Julius Enderby stared at the wicked muzzle in Baley's hands.

He stammered, "Twenty years for this, Baley, in the deepest prison level in the City."

R. Daneel moved suddenly. His hand clamped down on Baley's wrist. He said, quietly, "I cannot permit this, partner Elijah. You must do no harm to the Commissioner."

For the first time since R. Daneel had entered the City, the Commissioner spoke directly to him. "Hold him, you. First Law!"

Baley said quickly, "I have no intention of hurting him, Daneel, if you will keep him from arresting me. You said you would help me clear this up. I have forty-five minutes."

R. Daneel, without releasing Baley's wrist, said, "Commissioner, I believe Elijah should be allowed to speak. I am in communication with Dr. Fastolfe at this moment——"

"How? How?" demanded the Commissioner, wildly.

"I possess a self-contained subetheric unit," said R. Daneel. The Commissioner stared.

"I am in communication with Dr. Fastolfe," the robot went on inexorably, "and it would make a bad impression, Commissioner, if you were to refuse to listen to Elijah. Damaging inferences might be drawn."

The Commissioner fell back in his chair, quite speechless.

Baley said, "I say you were in the Williamsburg power plant today, Commissioner, and you got the alpha-sprayer and gave it to R. Sammy. You deliberately chose the Williamsburg power plant in order to incriminate me. You even seized Dr. Gerrigel's reappearance to invite him down to the Department and give him a deliberately maladjusted guide rod to lead him to the photographic supply room and allow him to find R. Sammy's remains. You counted on him to make a correct diagnosis."

Baley put away his blaster. "If you want to have me arrested now, go ahead, but Spacetown won't take that for an answer."

"Motive," spluttered Enderby breathlessly. His glasses were fogged and he removed them, looking once again curiously vague and helpless in their absence. "What motive could I have for this?"

"You got me into trouble, didn't you? It will put a spoke in the Sarton investigation, won't it? And all that aside, R. Sammy knew too much."

"About *what*, in Heaven's name?"

"About the way in which a Spacer was murdered five and a half days ago. You see, Commissioner, *you* murdered Dr. Sarton of Spacetown."

It was R. Daneel who spoke. Enderby could only clutch feverishly at his hair and shake his head.

The robot said, "Partner Elijah, I am afraid that this theory is quite untenable. As you know, it is impossible for Commissioner Enderby to have murdered Dr. Sarton."

"Listen, then. Listen to me. Enderby begged *me* to take the case, not any of the men who overranked me. He did that for several reasons. In the first place, we were college friends and he thought he could count on its never occurring to me that an old buddy and respected superior could be a criminal. He counted on my well-known loyalty, you see. Secondly, he knew Jessie was a member of an underground organization and expected to be able to maneuver me out of the investigation or blackmail me into silence if I got too close to the truth. And he wasn't really worried about that. At the very beginning he did his best to arouse my distrust of you, Daneel, and make certain that the two of us worked at cross-purposes. He knew about my father's declassification. He could guess how I would react. You see, it is an advantage for the murderer to be in charge of the murder investigation."

The Commissioner found his voice. He said, weakly, "How could I know about Jessie?" He turned to the robot. "You! If you're transmitting this to Spacetown, tell them it's a lie! It's all a lie!"

Baley broke in, raising his voice for a moment and then lowering it into a queer sort of tense calm. "Certainly you would know about Jessie. You're a Medievalist, and part of the organization. Your old-fashioned spectacles! Your windows! It's obvious your temperament is turned that way. But there's better evidence than that.

"How did Jessie find out Daneel was a robot? It puzzled me at the time. Of course we know now that she found out through her Medievalist organization, but that just shoves the problem one step backward. How did *they* know? You, Commissioner, dismissed it with a theory that Daneel was recognized as a robot during the incident at the shoe counter. I didn't quite believe that. I couldn't. I took him for human when I first saw him, and there's nothing wrong with my eyes.

"Yesterday, I asked Dr. Gerrigel to come in from Washington. Later I decided I needed him for several reasons, but, at the time I first called him, my only purpose was to see if he would recognize Daneel for what he was with no prompting on my part.

"Commissioner, he didn't! I introduced him to Daneel, he shook hands with him, we all talked together, and it was only after the subject got around to humanoid robots that he suddenly caught on. Now, that was Dr. Gerrigel, Earth's greatest expert on robots. Do you mean to say a few Medievalist rioters could do better than he under conditions of confusion and tension, and be so certain about it that they would throw their entire organization into activity based on the feeling that Daneel was a robot?

"It's obvious now that the Medievalists must have known Daneel to be a robot to begin with. The incident at the shoe counter was deliberately designed to show Daneel and, through him, Spacetown, the extent of antirobot feeling in the City. It was meant to confuse the issue, to turn suspicion away from individuals and toward the population as a whole.

"Now, if they knew the truth about Daneel to begin with, who told them? I didn't. I once thought it was Daneel himself, but that's out. The only other Earthman who knew about it was you, Commissioner."

Enderby said, with surprising energy, "There could be spies in the Department, too. The Medievalists could have us riddled with them. Your wife was one, and if you don't find it impossible that I should be one, why not others in the Department?"

The corners of Baley's lips pulled back a savage trifle. "Let's not bring up mysterious spies until we see where the straightforward solution leads us. I say you're the obvious informer and the real one.

"It's interesting now that I look back on it, Commissioner, to see how your spirits rose and fell accordingly as I seemed to be far from a solution or possibly close to it. You were nervous to begin with. When I wanted to visit Spacetown yesterday morning and wouldn't tell you the reason, you were practically in a state of collapse. Did you think I had you pinned, Commissioner? That it was a trap to get you into their hands? You hated them, you told me. You were virtually in tears. For a time, I thought that to be caused by the memory of humiliation in Spacetown when you yourself were a suspect, but then Daneel told me that your sensibilities had been carefully regarded. You had never known you were a suspect. Your panic was due to fear, not humiliation.

"Then when I came out with my completely wrong solution, while you listened over trimensional circuit, and you saw how far, how immensely far, from the truth I was, you were confident again. You even argued with me, defended the Spacers. After that, you were quite master of yourself for a while, quite confident. It surprised me at the time that you so easily forgave my false accusations against the Spacers when earlier you had so lectured me on their sensitivity. You enjoyed my mistake.

"Then I put in my call for Dr. Gerrigel and you wanted to know why and I wouldn't tell you. That plunged you into the abyss again because you feared——"

R. Daneel suddenly raised his hand. "Partner Elijah!"

Baley looked at his watch. 23:42! He said, "What is it?"

R. Daneel said, "He might have been disturbed at thinking you would find out his Medievalist connections, if we grant their existence. There is nothing, though, to connect him with the murder. He cannot have had anything to do with that."

Baley said, "You're quite wrong, Daneel. He didn't know what I wanted Dr. Gerrigel for, but it was quite safe to assume that it was in connection with information about robots. This frightened the Commissioner, because a robot had an intimate connection with his greater crime. Isn't that so, Commissioner?"

Enderby shook his head. "When this is over——" he began, but choked into inarticulacy.

"How was the murder committed?" demanded Baley with a suppressed fury. "C/Fe, damn it! C/Fe! I use your own term, Daneel. You're so full of the benefits of a C/Fe culture, yet you don't see where an Earthman might have used it for at least a temporary advantage. Let me sketch it in for you.

"There is no difficulty in the notion of a robot crossing open country. Even at night. Even alone. The Commissioner put a blaster into R. Sammy's hand, told him where to go and when. He himself entered Spacetown through the Personal and was relieved of his own blaster. He received the other from R. Sammy's hands, killed Dr. Sarton, returned the blaster to R. Sammy, who took it back across the fields to New York City. And today he destroyed R. Sammy, whose knowledge had become dangerous.

"That explains everything. The presence of the Commissioner, the absence of a weapon. And it makes it unnecessary to suppose any human New Yorker had crawled a mile under the open sky at night."

But at the end of Baley's recitation, R. Daneel said, "I am sorry, partner Elijah, though happy for the Commissioner, that your story explains nothing. I have told you that the cerebroanalytic properties of the Commissioner are such that it is impossible for him to have committed deliberate murder. I don't know what English word would be applied to the psychological fact: cowardice, conscience, or compassion. I know the dictionary meanings of all these, but I cannot judge. At any rate, the Commissioner did not murder."

"Thank you," muttered Enderby. His voice gained strength and confidence. "I don't know what your motives are, Baley, or why you should try to ruin me this way, but I'll get to the bottom——"

"Wait," said Baley. "I'm not through. I've got this."

He slammed the aluminum cube on Enderby's desk, and tried to feel the confidence he hoped he was radiating. For half an hour now, he had been hiding from himself one little fact: that he did *not* know what the picture showed. He was gambling, but it was all that was left to do.

Enderby shrank away from the small object. "What is it?"

"It isn't a bomb," said Baley, sardonically. "Just an ordinary micro-projector."

"Well? What will that prove?"

"Suppose we see." His fingernail probed at one of the slits in the cube, and a corner of the Commissioner's office blanked out, then lit up in an alien scene in three dimensions.

It reached from floor to ceiling and extended out past the walls of the room. It was awash with a gray light of a sort the City's utilities never provided.

Baley thought, with a pang of mingled distaste and perverse attraction: It must be the dawn they talk about.

The pictured scene was of Dr. Sarton's dome. Dr. Sarton's dead body, a horrible, broken remnant, filled its center.

Enderby's eyes bulged as he stared.

Baley said, "I know the Commissioner isn't a killer. I don't need you to tell me that, Daneel. If I could have gotten around that one fact earlier, I would have had the solution earlier. Actually, I didn't see a way out of it until an hour ago when I carelessly said to you that you had once been curious about Bentley's contact lenses.— That was it, Commissioner. It occurred to me then that your near-sightedness and your glasses were the key. They don't have near-sightedness on the Outer Worlds, I suppose, or they might have reached the true solution of the murder almost at once. Commissioner, when did you break your glasses?"

The Commissioner said, "What do you mean?"

Baley said, "When I first saw you about this case, you told me you had broken your glasses in Spacetown. I assumed that you broke them in your agitation on hearing the news of the murder, but *you* never said so, and I had no reason for making that assumption. Actually, if you were entering Spacetown with crime on your mind, you were already sufficiently agitated to drop and break your glasses *before* the murder. Isn't that so, and didn't that, in fact, happen?"

R. Daneel said, "I do not see the point, partner Elijah."

Baley thought: I'm partner Elijah for ten minutes more. Fast! Talk fast! And think fast!

He was manipulating Sarton's dome image as he spoke. Clumsily, he expanded it, his fingernails unsure in the tension that was overwhelming him. Slowly, in jerks, the corpse widened, broadened, heightened, came closer. Baley could almost smell the stench of its scorched flesh. Its head, shoulders, and one upper arm lolled crazily, connected to hips and legs by a blackened remnant of spine from which charred rib stumps jutted.

Baley cast a side glance at the Commissioner. Enderby had closed his eyes. He looked sick. Baley felt sick, too, but he *had* to look. Slowly he circled the trimensional image by means of the transmitter controls, rotating it, bringing the ground about the corpse to view in successive quadrants. His fingernail slipped and the imaged floor tilted suddenly and expanded till floor and corpse alike were a hazy mass, beyond the resolving power of the transmitter. He brought the expansion down, let the corpse slide away.

He was still talking. He had to. He couldn't stop till he found what he was looking for. And if he didn't, all his talk might be useless. Worse than useless. His heart was throbbing, and so was his head.

He said, "The Commissioner can't commit deliberate murder. True! *Deliberate.* But any man can kill by accident. The Commissioner didn't enter Spacetown to kill Dr. Sarton. He came in to kill you, Daneel, *you!* Is there anything in his cerebroanalysis that says he is incapable of wrecking a machine? *That's* not murder, merely sabotage.

"He is a Medievalist, an earnest one. He worked with Dr. Sarton and knew the purpose for which you were designed, Daneel. He feared that purpose might be achieved, that Earthmen would eventually be weaned away from Earth. So he decided to destroy you,

Daneel. You were the only one of your type manufactured as yet and he had good reason to think that by demonstrating the extent and determination of Medievalism on Earth, he would discourage the Spacers. He knew how strong popular opinion was on the Outer Worlds to end the Spacetown project altogether. Dr. Sarton must have discussed that with him. This, he thought, would be the last nudge in the proper direction.

"I don't say even the thought of killing you, Daneel, was a pleasant one. He would have had R. Sammy do it, I imagine, if you didn't look so human that a primitive robot such as Sammy could not have told the difference, or understood it. First Law would stop him. Or the Commissioner would have had another human do it if he, himself, were not the only one who had ready access to Spacetown at all times.

"Let me reconstruct what the Commissioner's plan might have been. I'm guessing, I admit, but I think I'm close. He made the appointment with Dr. Sarton, but deliberately came early, at dawn, in fact. Dr. Sarton would be sleeping, I imagine, but you, Daneel, would be awake. I assume, by the way, you were living with Dr. Sarton, Daneel."

The robot nodded. "You are quite right, partner Elijah."

Baley said, "Then let me go on. You would come to the dome door, Daneel, receive a blaster charge in the chest or head, and be done with. The Commissioner would leave quickly, through the deserted streets of Spacetown's dawn, and back to where R. Sammy waited. He would give him back the blaster, then slowly walk again to Dr. Sarton's dome. If necessary, he would 'discover' the body himself, though he would prefer to have someone else do that. If questioned concerning his early arrival, he could say, I suppose, that he had come to tell Dr. Sarton of rumors of a Medievalist attack on Spacetown, urge him to take secret precautions to avoid open trouble between Spacers and Earthmen. The dead robot would lend point to his words.

"If they asked about the long interval between your entering Spacetown, Commissioner, and your arrival at Dr. Sarton's dome, you could say—let's see—that you saw someone lurking through the streets and heading for open country. You pursued for a while. That would also encourage them along a false path. As for R. Sammy, no one would notice him. A robot among the truck farms outside the City is just another robot.

"How close am I, Commissioner?"

Enderby writhed, "I didn't——"

"No," said Baley, "you didn't kill Daneel. He's here, and in all the time he's been in the City, you haven't been able to look him in the face or address him by name. Look at him now, Commissioner."

Enderby couldn't. He covered his face with shaking hands.

Baley's shaking hands almost dropped his transmitter. He had found it.

The image was now centered upon the main door to Dr. Sarton's dome. The door was open; it had been slid into its wall receptacle along its shining metal runner grooves. Down within them. There! There!

The sparkle was unmistakable.

"I'll tell you what happened," said Baley. "You were at the dome when you dropped your glasses. You must have been nervous and I've seen you when you're nervous. You take them off; you wipe them. You did that then. But your hands were shaking and you dropped them; maybe you stepped on them. Anyway, they were broken, and just then, the door opened and a figure that looked like Daneel faced you.

"You blasted him, scrabbled up the remains of your glasses, and ran. *They* found the body, not you, and when they came to find you, you discovered that it was not Daneel, but the early-rising Dr. Sarton, that you had killed. Dr. Sarton had designed Daneel in his own image, to his great misfortune, and without your glasses in that moment of tension, you could not tell them apart.

"And if you want the tangible proof, it's there!" The image of Sarton's dome quivered and Baley put the transmitter carefully upon the desk, his hand tightly upon it.

Commissioner Enderby's face was distorted with terror and Baley's with tension. R. Daneel seemed indifferent.

Baley's finger was pointing. "That glitter in the grooves of the door. What was it, Daneel?"

"Two small slivers of glass," said the robot, coolly. "It meant nothing to us."

"It will now. They're portions of concave lenses. Measure their optical properties and compare them with those of the glasses Enderby is wearing now. *Don't smash them, Commissioner!*"

He lunged at the Commissioner and wrenched the spectacles from the other's hand. He held them out to R. Daneel, panting, "That's proof enough, I think, that he was at the dome earlier than he was thought to be."

R. Daneel said, "I am quite convinced. I can see now that I was thrown completely off the scent by the Commissioner's cerebroanalysis. I congratulate you, partner Elijah."

Baley's watch said 24:00. A new day was beginning.

Slowly, the Commissioner's head went down on his arms. His words were muffled wails. "It was a mistake. A mistake. I never meant to kill him." Without warning, he slipped from the chair and lay crumpled on the floor.

R. Daneel sprang to him, saying, "You have hurt him, Elijah. That is too bad."

"He isn't dead, is he?"

"No. But unconscious."

"He'll come to. It was too much for him, I suppose. I had to do it, Daneel, I had to. I had no evidence that would stand up in court, only inferences. I had to badger him and badger him and let it out little by little, hoping he would break down. He did, Daneel. You heard him confess, didn't you?"

"Yes."

"Now, then, I promised this would be to the benefit of Spacetown's project, so—— Wait, he's coming to."

The Commissioner groaned. His eyes fluttered and opened. He stared speechlessly at the two.

Baley said, "Commissioner, do you hear me?"

The Commissioner nodded listlessly.

"All right, then. Now, the Spacers have more on their minds than your prosecution. If you co-operate with them——"

"What? What?" There was a dawning flicker of hope in the Commissioner's eyes.

"You must be a big wheel in New York's Medievalist organization, maybe even in the planetary setup. Maneuver them in the direction of the colonization of space. You can see the propaganda line, can't you? We can go back to the soil all right—but on other planets."

"I don't understand," mumbled the Commissioner.

"It's what the Spacers are after. And God help me, it's what I'm after now, too, since a small conversation I had with Dr. Fastolfe. It's what they want more than anything. They risk death continually by coming to Earth and staying here for that purpose. If Dr. Sarton's murder will make it possible for you to swing Medievalism into line for the resumption of Galactic colonization, they'll probably consider it a worth-while sacrifice. Do you understand now?"

R. Daneel said, "Elijah is quite correct. Help us, Commissioner, and we will forget the past. I am speaking for Dr. Fastolfe and our people generally in this. Of course, if you should agree to help and later betray us, we would always have the fact of your guilt to hold over your head. I hope you understand that, too. It pains me to have to mention that."

"I won't be prosecuted?" asked the Commissioner.

"Not if you help us."

Tears filled his eyes. "I'll do it. It was an accident. Explain that. An accident. I did what I thought right."

Baley said, "If you help us, you *will* be doing right. The colonization of space is the only possible salvation of Earth. You'll realize that if you think about it without prejudice. If you find you cannot, have a short talk with Dr. Fastolfe. And now, you can begin helping by quashing the R. Sammy business. Call it an accident or something. End it!"

Baley got to his feet. "And remember, I'm not the only one who knows the truth, Commissioner. Getting rid of me will ruin you. All Spacetown knows. You see that, don't you?"

R. Daneel said, "It is unnecessary to say more, Elijah. He is sincere and he will help. So much is obvious from his cerebroanalysis."

"All right. Then I'll go home. I want to see Jessie and Bentley and take up a natural existence again. And I want to sleep.— Daneel, will you stay on Earth after the Spacers go?"

R. Daneel said, "I have not been informed. Why do you ask?"

Baley bit his lip, then said, "I didn't think I would ever say anything like this to anyone like you, Daneel, but I trust you. I even— admire you. I'm too old ever to leave Earth myself, but when schools for emigrants are finally established, there's Bentley. If someday, perhaps, Bentley and you, together . . ."

"Perhaps." R. Daneel's face was emotionless.

The robot turned to Julius Enderby, who was watching them with a flaccid face into which a certain vitality was only now beginning to return.

The robot said, "I have been trying, friend Julius, to understand some remarks Elijah made to me earlier. Perhaps I am beginning to, for it suddenly seems to me that the destruction of what should not be, that is, the destruction of what you people call evil, is less just and desirable than the conversion of this evil into what you call good."

He hesitated, then, almost as though he were surprised at his own words, he said, "Go, and sin no more!"

Baley, suddenly smiling, took R. Daneel's elbow, and they walked out the door, arm in arm.

The Naked Sun

To Noreen and Nick Falasca, for inviting me,
To Tony Boucher, for introducing me, and
To One Hundred Unusual Hours.

Contents

1

A Question Is Asked

STUBBORNLY Elijah Baley fought panic.

For two weeks it had been building up. Longer than that, even. It had been building up ever since they had called him to Washington and there calmly told him he was being reassigned.

The call to Washington had been disturbing enough in itself. It came without details, a mere summons; and that made it worse. It included travel slips directing round trip by plane and that made it still worse.

Partly it was the sense of urgency introduced by any order for plane travel. Partly it was the thought of the plane; simply that. Still, that was just the beginning of uneasiness and, as yet, easy to suppress.

After all, Lije Baley had been in a plane four times before. Once he had even crossed the continent. So, while plane travel is never pleasant, it would, at least, not be a complete step into the unknown.

And then, the trip from New York to Washington would take only an hour. The take-off would be from New York Runway Number 2, which, like all official Runways, was decently enclosed, with a lock opening to the unprotected atmosphere only after air speed had been achieved. The arrival would be at Washington Runway Number 5, which was similarly protected.

Furthermore, as Baley well knew, there would be no windows on the plane. There would be good lighting, decent food, all necessary conveniences. The radio-controlled flight would be smooth; there would scarcely be any sensation of motion once the plane was airborne.

He explained all this to himself, and to Jessie, his wife, who had never been air-borne and who approached such matters with terror.

She said, "But I don't *like* you to take a plane, Lije. It isn't natural. Why can't you take the Expressways?"

"Because that would take ten hours"—Baley's long face was set in dour lines—"and because I'm a member of the City Police Force and have to follow the orders of my superiors. At least, I do if I want to keep my C-6 rating."

There was no arguing with that.

Baley took the plane and kept his eyes firmly on the news-strip that unreeled smoothly and continuously from the eye-level dispenser. The City was proud of that service: news, features, humorous articles, educational bits, occasional fiction. Someday the strips would be converted to film, it was said, since enclosing the eyes with a viewer would be an even more efficient way of distracting the passenger from his surroundings.

Baley kept his eyes on the unreeling strip, not only for the sake of distraction, but also because etiquette required it. There were five other passengers on the plane (he could not help noticing that much) and each one of them had his private right to whatever degree of fear and anxiety his nature and upbringing made him feel.

Baley would certainly resent the intrusion of anyone else on his own uneasiness. He wanted no strange eyes on the whiteness of his knuckles where his hands gripped the armrest, or the dampish stain they would leave when he took them away.

He told himself: I'm enclosed. This plane is just a little City.

But he didn't fool himself. There was an inch of steel at his left; he could feel it with his elbow. Past that, nothing——

Well, air! But that was nothing, really.

A thousand miles of it in one direction. A thousand in another. One mile of it, maybe two, straight down.

He almost wished he could see straight down, glimpse the top of the buried Cities he was passing over; New York, Philadelphia, Baltimore, Washington. He imagined the rolling, low-slung cluster-complexes of domes he had never seen but knew to be there. And under them, for a mile underground and dozens of miles in every direction, would be the Cities.

The endless, hiving corridors of the Cities, he thought, alive with people; apartments, community kitchens, factories, Expressways; all comfortable and warm with the evidence of man.

And he himself was isolated in the cold and featureless air in a small bullet of metal, moving through emptiness.

His hands trembled, and he forced his eyes to focus on the strip of paper and read a bit.

It was a short story dealing with Galactic exploration and it was quite obvious that the hero was an Earthman.

Baley muttered in exasperation, then held his breath momentarily in dismay at his boorishness in making a sound.

It was completely ridiculous, though. It was pandering to child-ishness, this pretense that Earthmen could invade space. Galactic exploration! The Galaxy was closed to Earthmen. It was pre-empted by the Spacers, whose ancestors had been Earthmen centuries before. Those ancestors had reached the Outer Worlds first, found themselves comfortable, and their descendants had lowered the bars to immigration. They had penned in Earth and their Earthman cousins. And Earth's City civilization completed the task, imprisoning Earthmen within the Cities by a wall of fear of open spaces that barred them from the robot-run farming and mining areas of their own planet; from even that.

Baley thought bitterly: Jehoshaphat! If we don't like it, let's do something about it. Let's not just waste time with fairy tales.

But there was nothing to do about it, and he knew it.

Then the plane landed. He and his fellow-passengers emerged and scattered away from one another, never looking.

Baley glanced at his watch and decided there was time for fresh-ening before taking the Expressway to the Justice Department. He was glad there was. The sound and clamor of life, the huge vaulted chamber of the airport with City corridors leading off on numerous levels, everything else he saw and heard, gave him the feeling of being safely and warmly enclosed in the bowels and womb of the City. It washed away anxiety and only a shower was necessary to complete the job.

He needed a transient's permit to make use of one of the com-munity bathrooms, but presentation of his travel orders eliminated any difficulties. There was only the routine stamping, with private-stall privileges (the date carefully marked to prevent abuse) and a slim strip of directions for getting to the assigned spot.

Baley was thankful for the feel of the strips beneath his feet. It was with something amounting to luxury that he felt himself accelerate as he moved from strip to moving strip inward toward the speeding Expressway. He swung himself aboard lightly, taking the seat to which his rating entitled him.

It wasn't a rush hour; seats were available. The bathroom, when he reached it, was not unduly crowded either. The stall assigned to him was in decent order with a launderette that worked well.

With his water ration consumed to good purpose and his clothing freshened he felt ready to tackle the Justice Department. Ironically enough, he even felt cheerful.

Undersecretary Albert Minnim was a small, compact man, ruddy of skin, and graying, with the angles of his body smoothed down and softened. He exuded an air of cleanliness and smelled faintly of tonic. It all spoke of the good things of life that came with the liberal rations obtained by those high in Administration.

Baley felt sallow and rawboned in comparison. He was conscious of his own large hands, deep-set eyes, a general sense of cragginess.

Minnim said cordially, "Sit down, Baley. Do you smoke?"

"Only a pipe, sir," said Baley.

He drew it out as he spoke, and Minnim thrust back a cigar he had half drawn.

Baley was instantly regretful. A cigar was better than nothing and he would have appreciated the gift. Even with the increased tobacco ration that went along with his recent promotion from C-5 to C-6 he wasn't exactly swimming in pipe fixings.

"Please light up, if you care to," said Minnim, and waited with a kind of paternal patience while Baley measured out a careful quantity of tobacco and affixed the pipe baffle.

Baley said, his eyes on his pipe, "I have not been told the reason for my being called to Washington, sir."

"I know that," said Minnim. He smiled. "I can fix that right now. You are being reassigned temporarily."

"Outside New York City?"

"Quite a distance."

Baley raised his eyebrows and looked thoughtful. "How temporarily, sir?"

"I'm not sure."

Baley was aware of the advantages and disadvantages of reassignment. As a transient in a City of which he was not a resident, he would probably live on a scale better than his official rating entitled him to. On the other hand, it would be very unlikely that Jessie and their son, Bentley, would be allowed to travel with him. They would be taken care of, to be sure, there in New York, but Baley was a domesticated creature and he did not enjoy the thought of separation.

Then, too, a reassignment meant a specific job of work, which was good, and a responsibility greater than that ordinarily expected of the individual detective, which could be uncomfortable. Baley had, not too many months earlier, survived the responsibility of the investigation of the murder of a Spacer just outside New York. He was not overjoyed at the prospect of another such detail, or anything approaching it.

He said, "Would you tell me where I'm going? The nature of the reassignment? What it's all about?"

He was trying to weigh the Undersecretary's "Quite a distance" and make little bets with himself as to his new base of operations. The "Quite a distance" had sounded emphatic and Baley thought: Calcutta? Sydney?

Then he noticed that Minnim was taking out a cigar after all and was lighting it carefully.

Baley thought: Jehoshaphat! He's having trouble telling me. He doesn't want to say.

Minnim withdrew his cigar from between his lips. He watched the smoke and said, "The Department of Justice is assigning you to temporary duty on Solaria."

For a moment Baley's mind groped for an illusive identification: Solaria, Asia; Solaria, Australia . . . ?

Then he rose from his seat and said tightly, "You mean, one of the Outer Worlds?"

Minnim didn't meet Baley's eyes. "That is right!"

Baley said, "But that's impossible. They wouldn't allow an Earthman on an Outer World."

"Circumstances do alter cases, Plainclothesman Baley. There has been a murder on Solaria."

Baley's lips quirked into a sort of reflex smile. "That's a little out of our jurisdiction, isn't it?"

"They've requested help."

"From us? From Earth?" Baley was torn between confusion and disbelief. For an Outer World to take any attitude other than contempt toward the despised mother planet or, at best, a patronizing social benevolence was unthinkable. To come for help?

"From Earth?" he repeated.

"Unusual," admitted Minnim, "but there it is. They want a Terrestrial detective assigned to the case. It's been handled through diplomatic channels on the highest levels."

Baley sat down again. "Why me? I'm not a young man. I'm forty-three. I've got a wife and child. I couldn't leave Earth."

"That's not our choice, Plainclothesman. You were specifically asked for."

"I?"

"Plainclothesman Elijah Baley, C-6, of the New York City Police Force. They knew what they wanted. Surely you see why."

Baley said stubbornly, "I'm not qualified."

"They think you are. The way you handled the Spacer murder has apparently reached them."

"They must have got it all mixed up. It must have seemed better than it was."

Minnim shrugged. "In any case, they've asked for you and we have agreed to send you. You are reassigned. The papers have all been taken care of and you must go. During your absence, your wife and child will be taken care of at a C-7 level since that will be your temporary rating during your discharge of this assignment." He paused significantly. "Satisfactory completion of the assignment may make the rating permanent."

It was happening too quickly for Baley. None of this could be so. He *couldn't* leave Earth. Didn't they see that?

He heard himself ask in a level voice that sounded unnatural in his own ears. "What kind of a murder? What are the circumstances? Why can't they handle it themselves?"

Minnim rearranged small objects on his desk with carefully kept fingers. He shook his head. "I don't know anything about the murder. I don't know the circumstances."

"Then who does, sir? You don't expect me to go there cold, do you?" And again a despairing inner voice: But I *can't* leave Earth.

"Nobody knows anything about it. Nobody on Earth. The Solarians didn't tell us. That will be your job; to find out what is so important about the murder that they must have an Earthman to solve it. Or, rather, that will be *part* of your job."

Baley was desperate enough to say, "What if I refuse?" He knew the answer, of course. He knew exactly what declassification would mean to himself and, more than that, to his family.

Minnim said nothing about declassification. He said softly, "You can't refuse, Plainclothesman. You have a job to do."

"For Solaria? The hell with them."

"For *us*, Baley. For us." Minnim paused. Then he went on, "You know the position of Earth with respect to the Spacers. I don't have to go into that."

Baley knew the situation and so did every man on Earth. The fifty Outer Worlds, with a far smaller population, in combination, than that of Earth alone, nevertheless maintained a military potential perhaps a hundred times greater. With their underpopulated worlds resting on a positronic robot economy, their energy production per human was thousands of times that of Earth. And it was the amount of energy a single human could produce that dictated military potential, standard of living, happiness, and all besides.

Minnim said, "One of the factors that conspires to keep us in that position is ignorance. Just that. Ignorance. The Spacers know all about us. They send missions enough to Earth, heaven knows. We know nothing about them except what they tell us. No man on Earth has ever as much as set foot on an Outer World. *You* will, though."

Baley began, "I can't . . ."

But Minnim repeated, "You *will*. Your position will be unique. You will be on Solaria on their invitation, doing a job to which they will assign you. When you return, you will have information useful to Earth."

Baley watched the Undersecretary through somber eyes. "You mean I'm to spy for Earth."

"No question of spying. You need do nothing they don't ask you to do. Just keep your eyes and mind open. Observe! There will be specialists on Earth when you return to analyze and interpret your observations."

Baley said, "I take it there's a crisis, sir."

"Why do you say that?"

"Sending an Earthman to an Outer World is risky. The Spacers hate us. With the best will in the world and even though I'm there on invitation, I could cause an interstellar incident. The Terrestrial Government could easily avoid sending me if they chose. They could say I was ill. The Spacers are pathologically afraid of disease. They wouldn't want me for any reason if they thought I were ill."

"Do you suggest," said Minnim, "we try that trick?"

"No. If the government had no other motive for sending me, they would think of that or something better without my help. So it follows that it is the question of spying that is the real essential. And if that is so, there must be more to it than just a see-what-you-can-see to justify the risk."

Baley half expected an explosion and would have half welcomed one as a relief of pressure, but Minnim only smiled frostily and said, "You can see past the non-essentials, it seems. But then, I expected no less."

The Undersecretary leaned across his desk toward Baley. "Here is certain information which you will discuss with no one, not even with other government officials. Our sociologists have been coming to certain conclusions concerning the present Galactic situation. Fifty Outer Worlds, underpopulated, roboticized, powerful, with people that are healthy and long-lived. We ourselves, crowded, technologically underdeveloped, short-lived, under their domination. It is unstable."

"Everything is in the long run."

"This is unstable in the short run. A hundred years is the most we're allowed. The situation will last our time, to be sure, but we have children. Eventually we will become too great a danger to the Outer Worlds to be allowed to survive. There are eight billions on Earth who hate the Spacers."

Baley said, "The Spacers exclude us from the Galaxy, handle our trade to their own profit, dictate to our government, and treat us with contempt. What do they expect? Gratitude?"

"True, and yet the pattern is fixed. Revolt, suppression, revolt, suppression—and within a century Earth will be virtually wiped out as a populated world. So the sociologists say."

Baley stirred uneasily. One didn't question sociologists and their computers. "But what do you expect me to accomplish if all this is so?"

"Bring us information. The big flaw in sociological forecast is our lack of data concerning the Spacers. We've had to make assumptions on the basis of the few Spacers they sent out here. We've had to rely on what they choose to tell us of themselves, so it follows we know their strengths and only their strengths. Damn it, they have their robots and their low numbers and their long lives. But do they have weaknesses? Is there some factor or factors which, if we but knew, would alter the sociologic inevitability of destruction; something that could guide our actions and better the chance of Earth's survival."

"Hadn't you better send a sociologist, sir?"

Minnim shook his head. "If we could send whom we pleased, we would have sent someone out ten years ago, when these conclusions were first being arrived at. This is our first excuse to send someone and they ask for a detective and that suits us. A detective is a sociologist, too; a rule-of-thumb, practicing sociologist, or he wouldn't be a good detective. Your record proves you a good one."

"Thank you, sir," said Baley mechanically. "And if I get into trouble?"

Minnim shrugged. "That's the risk of a policeman's job." He dismissed the point with a wave of his hand and added, "In any case, you must go. Your time of departure is set. The ship that will take you is waiting."

Baley stiffened. "Waiting? When do I leave?"

"In two days."

"I've got to get back to New York then. My wife——"

"*We* will see your wife. She can't know the nature of your job, you know. She will be told not to expect to hear from you."

"But this is inhuman. I must see her. I may never see her again."

Minnim said, "What I say now may sound even more inhuman, but isn't it true that there is never a day you set about your duties on which you cannot tell yourself she may never see you again? Plainclothesman Baley, we must all do our duty."

Baley's pipe had been out for fifteen minutes. He had never noticed it.

No one had more to tell him. No one knew anything about the murder. Official after official simply hurried him on to the moment when he stood at the base of a spaceship, all unbelieving still.

It was like a gigantic cannon aimed at the heavens, and Baley shivered spasmodically in the raw, open air. The night closed in (for which Baley was thankful) like dark black walls melting into a black ceiling overhead. It was cloudy, and though he had been to Planetaria, a bright star, stabbing through a rift in the cloud, startled him when it caught his eyes.

A little spark, far, far away. He stared curiously, almost unafraid of it. It looked quite close, quite insignificant, and yet around things like that circled planets of which the inhabitants were lords of the Galaxy. The sun was a thing like that, he thought, except much closer, shining now on the other side of the Earth.

He thought of the Earth suddenly as a ball of stone with a film of moisture and gas, exposed to emptiness on every side, with its Cities barely dug into the outer rim, clinging precariously between rock and air. His skin crawled!

The ship was a Spacer vessel, of course. Interstellar trade was entirely in Spacer hands. He was alone now, just outside the rim of the City. He had been bathed and scraped and sterilized until he was considered safe, by Spacer standards, to board the ship. Even so, they sent only a robot out to meet him, bearing as he did a hundred varieties of disease germs from the sweltering City to which he himself was resistant but to which the eugenically hothoused Spacers were not.

The robot bulked dimly in the night, its eyes a dull red glow. "Plainclothesman Elijah Baley?"

"That's right," said Baley crisply, the hair on the nape of his neck stirring a bit. He was enough of an Earthman to get angry goose flesh at the sight of a robot doing a man's job. There had been R. Daneel Olivaw, who had partnered with him in the Spacer murder affair, but that had been different. Daneel had been——

"You will follow me, please," said the robot, and a white light flooded a path toward the ship.

Baley followed. Up the ladder and into the ship he went, along corridors, and into a room.

The robot said, "This will be your room, Plainclothesman Baley. It is requested that you remain in it for the duration of the trip."

Baley thought: Sure, seal me off. Keep me safe. Insulated.

The corridors along which he had traveled had been empty. Robots were probably disinfecting them now. The robot facing him would probably step through a germicidal bath when it left.

The robot said, "There is a water supply and plumbing. Food will be supplied. You will have viewing matter. The ports are controlled from this panel. They are closed now but if you wish to view space——"

Baley said with some agitation, "That's all right, boy. Leave the ports closed."

He used the "boy" address that Earthmen always used for robots, but the robot showed no adverse response. It couldn't, of course. Its responses were limited and controlled by the Laws of Robotics.

The robot bent its large metal body in the travesty of a respectful bow and left.

Baley was alone in his room and could take stock. It was better than the plane, at least. He could see the plane from end to end. He could see its limits. The spaceship was large. It had corridors, levels, rooms. It was a small City in itself. Baley could almost breathe freely.

Then lights flashed and a robot's metallic voice sounded over the communo and gave him specific instructions for guarding himself against take-off acceleration.

There was the push backward against webbing and a yielding hydraulic system, a distant rumble of force-jets heated to fury by the proton micro-pile. There was the hiss of tearing atmosphere, growing thinner and high-pitched and fading into nothingness after an hour.

They were in space.

It was as though all sensation had numbed, as though nothing were real. He told himself that each second found him thousands of miles farther from the Cities, from Jessie, but it didn't register.

On the second day (the third?—there was no way of telling time except by the intervals of eating and sleeping) there was a queer momentary sensation of being turned inside out. It lasted an instant and Baley knew it was a Jump, that oddly incomprehensible, almost mystical, momentary transition through hyperspace that transferred a ship and all it contained from one point in space to another, light-years away. Another lapse of time and another Jump, still another lapse, still another Jump.

Baley told himself now that he was light-years away, tens of light-years, hundreds, thousands.

He didn't know how many. No one on Earth as much as knew

Solaria's location in space. He would bet on that. They were ignorant, every one of them.

He felt terribly alone.

There was the feel of deceleration and the robot entered. Its somber, ruddy eyes took in the details of Baley's harness. Efficiently it
tightened a wing nut; quickly it surveyed the details of the hydraulic
system.

It said, "We will be landing in three hours. You will remain, if
you please, in this room. A man will come to escort you out and to
take you to your place of residence."

"Wait," said Baley tensely. Strapped in as he was, he felt helpless. "When we land, what time of day will it be?"

The robot said at once, "By Galactic Standard Time, it will be——"

"Local time, boy. Local time! Jehoshaphat!"

The robot continued smoothly, "The day on Solaria is twenty-
eight point thirty-five Standard hours in length. The Solarian hour
is divided into ten decads, each of which is divided into a hundred
centads. We are scheduled to arrive at an airport at which the day
will be at the twentieth centad of the fifth decad."

Baley hated that robot. He hated it for its obtuseness in not understanding; for the way it was making him ask the question directly and exposing his own weakness.

He had to. He said flatly, "Will it be daytime?"

And after all that the robot answered, "Yes, sir," and left.

It would be day! He would have to step out onto the unprotected
surface of a planet in daytime.

He was not quite sure how it would be. He had seen glimpses of
planetary surfaces from certain points within the City; he had even
been out upon it for moments. Always, though, he had been surrounded by walls or within reach of one. There was always safety
at hand.

Where would there be safety now? Not even the false walls of
darkness.

And because he would not display weakness before the Spacers—
he'd be damned if he would—he stiffened his body against the webbing that held him safe against the forces of deceleration, closed his
eyes, and stubbornly fought panic.

2

A Friend Is Encountered

BALEY WAS losing his fight. Reason alone was not enough.

Baley told himself over and over: Men live in the open all their lives. The Spacers do so now. Our ancestors on Earth did it in the past. There is no real harm in wall-lessness. It is only my mind that tells me differently, and it is wrong.

But all that did not help. Something above and beyond reason cried out for walls and would have none of space.

As time passed, he thought he would not succeed. He would be cowering at the end, trembling and pitiful. The Spacer they would send for him (with filters in his nose to keep out germs, and gloves on his hands to prevent contact) would not even honestly despise him. The Spacer would feel only disgust.

Baley held on grimly.

When the ship stopped and the deceleration harness automatically uncoupled, while the hydraulic system retracted into the wall, Baley remained in his seat. He was afraid, and determined not to show it.

He looked away at the first quiet sound of the door of his room opening. There was the eye-corner flash of a tall, bronze-haired figure entering; a Spacer, one of those proud descendants of Earth who had disowned their heritage.

The Spacer spoke. "Partner Elijah!"

Baley's head turned toward the speaker with a jerk. His eyes rounded and he rose almost without volition.

He stared at the face; at the broad, high cheekbones, the absolute calm of the facial lines, the symmetry of the body, most of all at that level look out of nerveless blue eyes.

"D-daneel."

The Spacer said, "It is pleasant that you remember me, Partner Elijah."

"Remember you!" Baley felt relief wash over him. This being was a bit of Earth, a friend, a comfort, a savior. He had an almost unbearable desire to rush to the Spacer and embrace him, to hug him wildly, and laugh and pound his back and do all the foolish things old friends did when meeting once again after a separation.

But he didn't. He couldn't. He could only step forward, and hold out his hand and say, "I'm not likely to forget you, Daneel."

"That is pleasant," said Daneel, nodding gravely. "As you are well aware, it is quite impossible for me, while in working order, to forget you. It is well that I see you again."

Daneel took Baley's hand and pressed it with firm coolness, his fingers closing to a comfortable but not painful pressure and then releasing it.

Baley hoped earnestly that the creature's unreadable eyes could not penetrate Baley's mind and see that wild moment, just past and not yet entirely subsided, when all of Baley had concentrated into a feeling of an intense friendship that was almost love.

After all, one could not love as a friend this Daneel Olivaw, who was not a man at all, but only a robot.

The robot that looked so like a man said, "I have asked that a robot-driven ground-transport vessel be connected to this ship by airtube——"

Baley frowned. "An air-tube?"

"Yes. It is a common technique, frequently used in space, in order that personnel and matériel be transferred from one vessel to another without the necessity of special equipment against vacuum. It would seem then that you are not acquainted with the technique."

"No," said Baley, "but I get the picture."

"It is, of course, rather complicated to arrange such a device between spaceship and ground vehicle, but I have requested that it be done. Fortunately, the mission on which you and I are engaged is one of high priority. Difficulties are smoothed out quickly."

"Are you assigned to the murder case too?"

"Have you not been informed of that? I regret not having told you at once." There was, of course, no sign of regret on the robot's perfect face. "It was Dr. Han Fastolfe, whom you met on Earth during our previous partnership and whom I hope you remember, who first suggested you as an appropriate investigator in this case. He made it a condition that I be assigned to work with you once more."

Baley managed a smile. Dr. Fastolfe was a native of Aurora and Aurora was the strongest of the Outer Worlds. Apparently the advice of an Auroran bore weight.

Baley said, "A team that works shouldn't be broken up, eh?" (The first exhilaration of Daneel's appearance was fading and the compression about Baley's chest was returning.)

"I do not know if that precise thought was in his mind, Partner Elijah. From the nature of his orders to me, I should think that he was interested in having assigned to work with you one who would have experience with your world and would know of your consequent peculiarities."

"Peculiarities!" Baley frowned and felt offended. It was not a term he liked in connection with himself.

"So that I could arrange the air-tube, for example. I am well aware of your aversion to open spaces as a result of your upbringing in the Cities of Earth."

Perhaps it was the effect of being called "peculiar," the feeling that he had to counterattack or lose caste to a machine, that drove Baley to change the subject sharply. Perhaps it was just that lifelong training prevented him from leaving any logical contradiction undisturbed.

He said, "There was a robot in charge of my welfare on board this ship; a robot" (a touch of malice intruded itself here) "that looks like a robot. Do you know it?"

"I spoke to it before coming on board."

"What's its designation? How do I make contact with it?"

"It is RX-2475. It is customary on Solaria to use only serial numbers for robots." Daneel's calm eyes swept the control panel near the door. "This contact will signal it."

Baley looked at the control panel himself and, since the contact to which Daneel pointed was labeled RX, its identification seemed quite unmysterious.

Baley put his finger over it and in less than a minute, the robot, the one that looked like a robot, entered.

Baley said, "You are RX-2475."

"Yes, sir."

"You told me earlier that someone would arrive to escort me off the ship. Did you mean him?" Baley pointed at Daneel.

The eyes of the two robots met. RX-2475 said, "His papers identify him as the one who was to meet you."

"Were you told in advance anything about him other than his papers? Was he described to you?"

"No, sir. I was given his name, however."

"Who gave you the information?"

"The captain of the ship, sir."

"Who is a Solarian?"

"Yes, sir."

Baley licked his lips. The next question would be decisive.

He said, "What were you told would be the name of the one you were expecting?"

RX-2475 said, "Daneel Olivaw, sir."

"Good boy! You may leave now."

There was the robotic bow and then the sharp about-face. RX-2475 left.

Baley turned to his partner and said thoughtfully, "You are not telling me all the truth, Daneel."

"In what way, Partner Elijah?" asked Daneel.

"While I was talking to you earlier, I recalled an odd point. RX-2475, when it told me I would have an escort said a *man* would come for me. I remember that quite well."

Daneel listened quietly and said nothing.

Baley went on. "I thought the robot might have made a mistake. I thought also that perhaps a man had indeed been assigned to meet me and had later been replaced by you, RX-2475 not being informed of the change. But you heard me check that. Your papers were described to it and it was given your name. But it was not quite given your name at that, was it, Daneel?"

"Indeed, it was not given my entire name," agreed Daneel.

"Your name is not Daneel Olivaw, but R. Daneel Olivaw, isn't it? Or, in full, Robot Daneel Olivaw."

"You are quite correct, Partner Elijah."

"From which it all follows that RX-2475 was never informed that you are a robot. It was allowed to think of you as a man. With your manlike appearance, such a masquerade is possible."

"I have no quarrel with your reasoning."

"Then let's proceed." Baley was feeling the germs of a kind of savage delight. He was on the trace of something. It couldn't be anything much, but this was the kind of tracking he could do well. It was something he could do well enough to be called half across space to do. He said, "Now why should anyone want to deceive a miserable robot? It doesn't matter to it whether you are man or robot. It follows orders in either case. A reasonable conclusion then is that the Solarian captain who informed the robot and the Solarian officials who informed the Captain did not themselves know you were a robot. As I say, that is one reasonable conclusion, but perhaps not the only one. Is this one true?"

"I believe it is."

"All right, then. Good guess. Now why? Dr. Han Fastolfe, in recommending you as my partner allows the Solarians to think you are a human. Isn't that a dangerous thing? The Solarians, if they find out, may be quite angry. Why was it done?"

The humanoid robot said, "It was explained to me thus, Partner Elijah. Your association with a human of the Outer Worlds would raise your status in the eyes of the Solarians. Your association with a robot would lower it. Since I was familiar with your ways and could work with you easily, it was thought reasonable to allow the Solarians to accept me as a man without actually deceiving them by a positive statement to that effect."

Baley did not believe it. It seemed like the kind of careful consideration for an Earthman's feelings that did not come naturally to a Spacer, not even to as enlightened a one as Fastolfe.

He considered an alternative and said, "Are the Solarians well known among the Outer Worlds for the production of robots?"

"I am glad," said Daneel, "that you have been briefed concerning the inner economy of Solaria."

"Not a word," said Baley. "I can guess the spelling of the word Solaria and there my knowledge stops."

"Then I do not see, Partner Elijah, what it was that impelled you to ask that question, but it is a most pertinent one. You have hit the mark. My mind-store of information includes the fact that, of the fifty Outer Worlds, Solaria is by far the best known for the variety and excellence of robot models it turns out. It exports specialized models to all the other Outer Worlds."

Baley nodded in grim satisfaction. Naturally Daneel did not follow an intuitive mental leap that used human weakness as a starting point. Nor did Baley feel impelled to explain the reasoning. If Solaria turned out to be a world expert in robotics, Dr. Han Fastolfe and his associates might have purely personal and very human motives for demonstrating their own prize robot. It would have nothing at all to do with an Earthman's safety or feelings.

They would be asserting their own superiority by allowing the expert Solarians to be fooled into accepting a robot of Auroran handiwork as a fellow-man.

Baley felt much better. Strange that all the thought, all the intellectual powers he could muster, could not succeed in lifting him out of panic; and yet a sop to his own vainglory succeeded at once.

The recognition of the vainglory of the Spacers helped too.

He thought: Jehoshaphat, we're all human; even the Spacers.

Aloud he said, almost flippantly, "How long do we have to wait for the ground-car? I'm ready."

The air-tube gave signs of not being well adapted to its present use. Man and humanoid stepped out of the spaceship erect, moving along flexible mesh that bent and swayed under their weight. (In space, Baley imagined hazily, men transferring weightlessly from ship to ship might easily skim along the length of the tube, impelled by an initial Jump.)

Toward the other end the tube narrowed clumsily, its meshing bunching as though some giant hand had constricted it. Daneel, carrying the flashlight, got down on all fours and so did Baley. They traveled the last twenty feet in that fashion, moving at last into what was obviously a ground-car.

Daneel closed the door through which they had entered, sliding it shut carefully. There was a heavy, clicking noise that might have been the detachment of the air-tube.

Baley looked about curiously. There was nothing too exotic about the ground-car. There were two seats in tandem, each of which could hold three. There were doors at each end of each seat. The glossy sections that might ordinarily have been windows were black and opaque, as a result, undoubtedly, of appropriate polarization. Baley was acquainted with that.

The interior of the car was lit by two round spots of yellow illumination in the ceiling and, in short, the only thing Baley felt to be strange was the transmitter set into the partition immediately before the front seat and, of course, the added fact that there were no visible controls.

Baley said, "I suppose the driver is on the other side of this partition."

Daneel said, "Exactly so, Partner Elijah. And we can give our orders in this fashion." He leaned forward slightly and flicked a toggle switch that set a spot of red light to flickering. He said quietly, "You may start now. We are ready."

There was a muted whir that faded almost at once, a very slight, very transitory pressing against the back of the seat, and then nothing.

Baley said in surprise, "Are we moving?"

Daneel said, "We are. The car does not move on wheels but glides along a diamagnetic force-field. Except for acceleration and deceleration, you will feel nothing."

"What about curves?"

"The car will bank automatically to compensate. Its level is maintained when traveling up- or downhill."

"The controls must be complicated," said Baley dryly.

"Quite automatic. The driver of the vehicle is a robot."

"Umm." Baley had about all he wanted on the ground-car. He said, "How long will this take?"

"About an hour. Air travel would have been speedier, but I was concerned to keep you enclosed and the aircraft models available on Solaria do not lend themselves to complete enclosure as does a ground-car such as that in which we are now riding."

Baley felt annoyed at the other's "concern." He felt like a baby in the charge of its nurse. He felt almost as annoyed, oddly enough, at Daneel's sentences. It seemed to him that such needlessly formal sentence structure might easily betray the robotic nature of the creature.

For a moment Baley stared curiously at R. Daneel Olivaw. The robot, looking straight ahead, was motionless and unself-conscious under the other's gaze.

Daneel's skin texture was perfect, the individual hairs on head and body had been lovingly and intricately manufactured and placed. The muscle movement under the skin was most realistic. No pains, however extravagant, had been spared. Yet Baley knew, from personal knowledge, that limbs and chest could be split open along invisible seams so that repairs might be made. He knew there was metal and silicone under that realistic skin. He knew a positronic brain, most advanced but only positronic, nestled in the hollow of the skull. He knew that Daneel's "thoughts" were only short-lived positronic currents flowing along paths rigidly designed and foreordained by the manufacturer.

But what were the signs that would give that away to the expert eye that had no foreknowledge? The trifling unnaturalness of Daneel's manner of speech? The unemotional gravity that rested so steadily upon him? The very perfection of his humanity?

But he was wasting time. Baley said, "Let's get on with it, Daneel. I suppose that before arriving here, you were briefed on matters Solarian?"

"I was, Partner Elijah."

"Good. That's more than they did for me. How large is the world?"

"Its diameter is 9500 miles. It is the outermost of three planets and the only inhabited one. In climate and atmosphere it resembles Earth; its percentage of fertile land is higher; its useful mineral content lower, but of course less exploited. The world is self-supporting and can, with the aid of its robot exports, maintain a high standard of living."

Baley said, "What's the population?"

"Twenty thousand people, Partner Elijah."

Baley accepted that for a moment, then he said mildly, "You mean twenty million, don't you?" His scant knowledge of the Outer Worlds was enough to tell him that, although the worlds were underpopulated by Earthly standards, the individual populations *were* in the millions.

"Twenty thousand people, Partner Elijah," said the robot again.

"You mean the planet has just been settled?"

"Not at all. It has been independent for nearly two centuries, and it was settled for a century or more before that. The population is deliberately maintained at twenty thousand, that being considered optimum by the Solarians themselves."

"How much of the planet do they occupy?"

"All the fertile portions."

"Which is, in square miles?"

"Thirty million square miles, including marginal areas."

"For twenty thousand people?"

"There are also some two hundred million working positronic robots, Partner Elijah."

"Jehoshaphat! That's—that's ten thousand robots per human."

"It is by far the highest such ratio among the Outer Worlds, Partner Elijah. The next highest, on Aurora, is only fifty to one."

"What can they use so many robots for? What do they want with all that food?"

"Food is a relatively minor item. The mines are more important, and power production more important still."

Baley thought of all those robots and felt a trifle dizzy. Two hundred million robots! So many among so few humans. The robots must litter the landscape. An observer from without might think Solaria a world of robots altogether and fail to notice the thin human leaven.

He felt a sudden need to see. He remembered the conversation with Minnim and the sociologic prediction of Earth's danger. It seemed far off, a bit unreal, but he remembered. His personal dangers and difficulties since leaving Earth dimmed the memory of Minnim's voice stating enormities with cool and precise enunciation, but never blotted it out altogether.

Baley had lived too long with duty to allow even the overwhelming fact of open space to stop him in its performance. Data collected from a Spacer's words, or from those of a Spacer robot for that matter, was the sort of thing that was already available to Earth's sociologists. What was needed was direct observation and it was his job, however unpleasant, to collect it.

He inspected the upper portion of the ground-car. "Is this thing a convertible, Daneel?"

"I beg your pardon, Partner Elijah, but I do not follow your meaning."

"Can the car's top be pushed back? Can it be made open to the—the sky?" (He had almost said "dome" out of habit.)

"Yes, it can."

"Then have that done, Daneel. I would like to take a look."

The robot responded gravely, "I am sorry, but I cannot allow that."

Baley felt astonished. He said, "Look, R. Daneel" (he stressed the R.). "Let's rephrase that. I order you to lower the top."

The creature was a robot, manlike or not. It *had* to follow orders.

But Daneel did not move. He said, "I must explain that it is my first concern to spare you harm. It has been clear to me on the basis both of my instructions and of my own personal experience that you would suffer harm at finding yourself in large, empty spaces. I cannot, therefore, allow you to expose yourself to that."

Baley could feel his face darkening with an influx of blood and at the same time could feel the complete uselessness of anger. The creature *was* a robot, and Baley knew the First Law of Robotics well.

It went: *A robot may not injure a human being, or, through inaction, allow a human being to come to harm.*

Everything else in a robot's positronic brain—that of any robot on any world in the Galaxy—had to bow to that prime consideration. Of course a robot had to follow orders, but with one major, all-important qualification. Following orders was only the Second Law of Robotics.

It went: *A robot must obey the orders given it by human beings except where such orders would conflict with the First Law.*

Baley forced himself to speak quietly and reasonably. "I think I can endure it for a short time, Daneel."

"That is not my feeling, Partner Elijah."

"Let me be the judge, Daneel."

"If that is an order, Partner Elijah, I cannot follow it."

Baley let himself lounge back against the softly upholstered seat. The robot would, of course, be quite beyond the reach of force. Daneel's strength, if exerted fully, would be a hundred times that of flesh and blood. He would be perfectly capable of restraining Baley without ever hurting him.

Baley was armed. He could point a blaster at Daneel, but, except for perhaps a momentary sensation of mastery, that action would only succeed in greater frustration. A threat of destruction was useless against a robot. Self-preservation was only the Third Law.

It went: *A robot must protect its own existence, as long as such protection does not conflict with the First or Second Laws.*

It would not trouble Daneel to be destroyed if the alternative were breaking the First Law. And Baley did not wish to destroy Daneel. Definitely not.

Yet he did want to see out the car. It was becoming an obsession with him. He couldn't allow this nurse-infant relationship to build up.

For a moment he thought of pointing the blaster at his own temple. Open the car top or I'll kill myself. Oppose one application of the First Law by a greater and more immediate one.

Baley knew he couldn't do it. Too undignified. He disliked the picture conjured up by the thought.

He said wearily, "Would you ask the driver how close in miles we are to destination?"

"Certainly, Partner Elijah."

Daneel bent forward and pushed the toggle switch. But as he did so, Baley leaned forward too, crying out, "Driver! Lower the top of the car!"

And it was the human hand that moved quickly to the toggle switch and closed it again. The human hand held its place firmly thereafter.

Panting a bit, Baley stared at Daneel.

For a second Daneel was motionless, as though his positronic paths were momentarily out of stability in their effort to adjust to the new situation. But that passed quickly and then the robot's hand was moving.

Baley had anticipated that. Daneel would remove the human hand from the switch (gently, not hurting it), reactivate the transmitter, and countermand the order.

Baley said, "You won't get my hand away without hurting me. I warn you. You will probably have to break my finger."

That was not so. Baley knew that. But Daneel's movements stopped. Harm against harm. The positronic brain had to weigh probabilities and translate them into opposing potentials. It meant just a bit more hesitation.

Baley said, "It's too late."

His race was won. The top was sliding back and pouring into the car, now open, was the harsh white light of Solaria's sun.

Baley wanted to shut his eyes in initial terror, but fought the sensation. He faced the enormous wash of blue and green, incredible quantities of it. He could feel the undisciplined rush of air against his face, but could make out no details of anything. A moving something flashed past. It might have been a robot or an animal or an unliving something caught in a puff of air. He couldn't tell. The car went past it too quickly.

Blue, green, air, noise, motion—and over it all, beating down, furiously, relentlessly, frighteningly, was the white light that came from a ball in the sky.

For one fleeting split moment he bent his head back and stared directly at Solaria's sun. He stared at it, unprotected by the diffusing glass of the Cities' uppermost-Level sun-porches. He stared at the naked sun.

And at the very moment he felt Daneel's hands clamping down upon his shoulders. His mind crowded with thought during that unreal, whirling moment. He had to see! He had to see all he could. And Daneel must be there with him to keep him from seeing.

But surely a robot would not dare use violence on a man. That thought was dominant. Daneel could not prevent him forcibly, and yet Baley felt the robot's hands forcing him down.

Baley lifted his arms to force those fleshless hands away and lost all sensation.

3

A Victim Is Named

BALEY WAS back in the safety of enclosure. Daneel's face wavered before his eyes, and it was splotched with dark spots that turned to red when he blinked.

Baley said, "What happened?"

"I regret," said Daneel, "that you have suffered harm despite my presence. The direct rays of the sun are damaging to the human eye, but I believe that the damage from the short exposure you suffered will not be permanent. When you looked up, I was forced to pull you down and you lost consciousness."

Baley grimaced. That left the question open as to whether he had fainted out of overexcitement (or fright?) or had been knocked unconscious. He felt his jaw and head and found no pain. He forbore asking the question direct. In a way he didn't want to know.

He said, "It wasn't so bad."

"From your reactions, Partner Elijah, I should judge you had found it unpleasant."

"Not at all," said Baley stubbornly. The splotches before his eyes were fading and they weren't tearing so. "I'm only sorry I saw so little. We were moving too fast. Did we pass a robot?"

"We passed a number of them. We are traveling across the Kinbald estate, which is given over to fruit orchards."

"I'll have to try again," said Baley.

"You must not, in my presence," said Daneel. "Meanwhile, I have done as you requested."

"As I requested?"

"You will remember, Partner Elijah, that before you ordered the driver to lower the top of the car, you had ordered me to ask the driver how close in miles we were to destination. We are ten miles away now and shall be there in some six minutes."

Baley felt the impulse to ask Daneel if he were angry at having been outwitted if only to see that perfect face become imperfect, but he repressed it. Of course Daneel would simply answer no, without rancor or annoyance. He would sit there as calm and as grave as ever, unperturbed and imperturbable.

Baley said quietly, "Just the same, Daneel, I'll have to get used to it, you know."

The robot regarded his human partner. "To what is it that you refer?"

"Jehoshaphat! To the—the outdoors. It's all this planet is made of."

"There will be no necessity for facing the outdoors," said Daneel. Then, as though that disposed of the subject, he said, "We are slowing down, Partner Elijah. I believe we have arrived. It will be necessary to wait now for the connection of another air-tube leading to the dwelling that will serve as our base of operations."

"An air-tube is unnecessary, Daneel. If I am to be working outdoors, there is no point in delaying the indoctrination."

"There will be no reason for you to work outdoors, Partner Elijah."

The robot started to say more, but Baley waved him quiet with a peremptory motion of the hand.

At the moment he was not in the mood for Daneel's careful consolations, for soothings, for assurances that all would be well and that he would be taken care of.

What he really wanted was an inner knowledge that he could take care of himself and fulfill his assignment. The sight and feel of the open had been hard to take. It might be that when the time came he would lack the hardihood to dare face it again, at the cost of his self-respect and, conceivably, of Earth's safety. All over a small matter of emptiness.

His face grew grim even at the glancing touch of that thought. He would face air, sun, and empty space yet!

Elijah Baley felt like an inhabitant of one of the smaller Cities, say Helsinki, visiting New York and counting the Levels in awe. He had thought of a "dwelling" as something like an apartment unit, but this was nothing like it at all. He passed from room to room endlessly. Panoramic windows were shrouded closely, allowing no hint of disturbing day to enter. Lights came to life noiselessly from hidden sources as they stepped into a room and died again as quietly when they left.

"So many rooms," said Baley with wonder. "So many. It's like a very tiny City, Daneel."

"It would seem so, Partner Elijah," said Daneel with equanimity.

It seemed strange to the Earthman. Why was it necessary to crowd so many Spacers together with him in close quarters? He said, "How many will be living here with me?"

Daneel said, "There will be myself, of course, and a number of robots."

Baley thought: He ought to have said, a number of *other* robots.

Again he found it obvious that Daneel had the intention of playing the man thoroughly even for no other audience than Baley, who knew the truth so well.

And then that thought popped into nothing under the force of a second, more urgent one. He cried, "*Robots? How many humans?*"

"None, Partner Elijah."

They had just stepped into a room, crowded from floor to ceiling with book films. Three fixed viewers with large twenty-four-inch viewing panels set vertically were in three corners of the room. The fourth contained an animation screen.

Baley looked about in annoyance. He said, "Did they kick everyone out just to leave me rattling around alone in this mausoleum?"

"It is meant only for you. A dwelling such as this for one person is customary on Solaria."

"Everyone lives like this?"

"Everyone."

"What do they need all the rooms for?"

"It is customary to devote a single room to a single purpose. This is the library. There is also a music room, a gymnasium, a kitchen, a bakery, a dining room, a machine shop, various robot-repair and testing rooms, two bedrooms——"

"Stop! How do you know all this?"

"It is part of the information pattern," said Daneel smoothly, "made available to me before I left Aurora."

"Jehoshaphat! Who takes care of all of this?" He swung his arm in a wide arc.

"There are a number of household robots. They have been assigned to you and will see to it that you are comfortable."

"But I don't need all this," said Baley. He had the urge to sit down and refuse to budge. He wanted to see no more rooms.

"We can remain in one room if you so desire, Partner Elijah. That was visualized as a possibility from the start. Nevertheless, Solarian customs being what they are, it was considered wiser to allow this house to be built——"

"*Built!*" Baley stared. "You mean this was built for me? All this? Specially?"

"A thoroughly roboticized economy——"

"Yes, I see what you're going to say. What will they do with the house when all this is over?"

"I believe they will tear it down."

Baley's lips clamped together. Of course! Tear it down! Build a tremendous structure for the special use of one Earthman and then tear down everything he touched. Sterilize the soil the house stood on! Fumigate the air he breathed! The Spacers might seem strong, but they, too, had their foolish fears.

Daneel seemed to read his thoughts, or to interpret his expression at any rate. He said, "It may appear to you, Partner Elijah, that it is to escape contagion that they will destroy the house. If such are your thoughts, I suggest that you refrain from making yourself uncomfortable over the matter. The fear of disease on the part of Spacers is by no means so extreme. It is just that the effort involved in building the house is, to them, very little. Nor does the waste involved in tearing it down once more seem great to them.

"And by law, Partner Elijah, this place cannot be allowed to remain standing. It is on the estate of Hannis Gruer and there can only be one legal dwelling place on any estate, that of the owner. This house was built by special dispensation, for a specific purpose. It is meant to house us for a specific length of time, till our mission is completed."

"And who is Hannis Gruer?" asked Baley.

"The head of Solarian security. We are to see him on arrival."

"Are we? Jehoshaphat, Daneel, when do I begin to learn anything at all about anything? I'm working in a vacuum and I don't like it. I might as well go back to Earth. I might as well——"

He felt himself working up into resentment and cut himself short.

Daneel never wavered. He merely waited his chance to speak. He said, "I regret the fact that you are annoyed. My general knowledge of Solaria does seem to be greater than yours. My knowledge of the murder case itself is as limited as is your own. It is Agent Gruer who will tell us what we must know. The Solarian Government has arranged this."

"Well, then, let's get to this Gruer. How long a trip will it be?" Baley winced at the thought of more travel and the familiar constriction in his chest was making itself felt again.

Daneel said, "No travel is necessary, Partner Elijah. Agent Gruer will be waiting for us in the conversation room."

"A room for conversation, too?" Baley murmured wryly. Then, in a louder voice, "Waiting for us now?"

"I believe so."

"Then let's get to him, Daneel!"

Hannis Gruer was bald, and that without qualification. There was not even a fringe of hair at the sides of his skull. It was completely naked.

Baley swallowed and tried, out of politeness, to keep his eyes off that skull, but couldn't. On Earth there was the continuous acceptance of Spacers at the Spacers' own evaluation. The Spacers were the unquestioned lords of the Galaxy; they were tall, bronze of skin and hair, handsome, large, cool, aristocratic.

In short, they were all R. Daneel Olivaw was, but with the fact of humanity in addition.

And the Spacers who were sent to Earth often did look like that; perhaps were deliberately chosen for that reason.

But here was a Spacer who might have been an Earthman for all his appearance. He was bald. And his nose was misshapen, too. Not much, to be sure, but on a Spacer even a slight asymmetry was noteworthy.

Baley said, "Good afternoon, sir. I am sorry if we kept you waiting."

No harm in politeness. He would have to work with these people.

He had the momentary urge to step across the expanse of room (how ridiculously large) and offer his hand in greeting. It was an urge easy to fight off. A Spacer certainly would not welcome such a greeting: a hand covered with Earthly germs?

Gruer sat gravely, as far away from Baley as he could get, his hands resting within long sleeves, and probably there were filters in his nostrils, although Baley couldn't see them.

It even seemed to him that Gruer cast a disapproving look at Daneel as though to say: You're a queer Spacer, standing that close to an Earthman.

That would mean Gruer simply did not know the truth. Then Baley noticed suddenly that Daneel was standing at some distance, at that; farther than he usually did.

Of course! Too close, and Gruer might find the proximity unbelievable. Daneel was intent on being accepted as human.

Gruer spoke in a pleasant, friendly voice, but his eyes tended to remain furtively on Daneel; looking away, then drifting back. He said, "I haven't been waiting long. Welcome to Solaria, gentlemen. Are you comfortable?"

"Yes, sir. Quite," said Baley. He wondered if etiquette would require that Daneel as the "Spacer" should speak for the two, but rejected that possibility resentfully. Jehoshaphat! It was he, himself, who had been requested for the investigation and Daneel had been added afterward. Under the circumstances Baley felt he would not play the secondary to a genuine Spacer; it was out of the question when a robot was involved, even such a robot as Daneel.

But Daneel made no attempt to take precedence over Baley, nor did Gruer seem surprised or displeased at that. Instead, he turned his attention at once to Baley to the exclusion of Daneel.

Gruer said, "You have been told nothing, Plainclothesman Baley, about the crime for which your services have been solicited. I imagine you are quite curious about that." He shook his arms so that the sleeves fell backward and clasped his hands loosely in his lap. "Won't you gentlemen sit down?"

They did so and Baley said, "We *are* curious." He noted that Gruer's hands were not protected by gloves.

Gruer went on. "That was on purpose, Plainclothesman. We wanted you to arrive here prepared to tackle the problem with a fresh mind. We wanted no preconceived notions. You will have available to you shortly a full report of the details of the crime and of the investigations we have been able to conduct. I am afraid, Plainclothesman, that you will find our investigations ridiculously incomplete from the standpoint of your own experience. We have no police force on Solaria."

"None at all?" asked Baley.

Gruer smiled and shrugged. "No crime, you see. Our population is tiny and widely scattered. There is no occasion for crime; therefore no occasion for police."

"I see. But for all that, you *do* have crime now."

"True, but the first crime of violence in two centuries of history."

"Unfortunate, then, that you must begin with murder."

"Unfortunate, yes. More unfortunately still, the victim was a man we could scarcely afford to lose. A most inappropriate victim. And the circumstances of the murder were particularly brutal."

Baley said, "I suppose the murderer is completely unknown." (Why else would the crime be worth the importation of an Earthly detective?)

Gruer looked particularly uneasy. He glanced sideways at Daneel, who sat motionless, an absorptive, quiet mechanism. Baley knew that Daneel would, at any time in the future, be able to reproduce any conversation he heard, of whatever length. He was a recording machine that walked and talked like a man.

Did Gruer know that? His look at Daneel had certainly something of the furtive about it.

Gruer said, "No, I cannot say the murderer is completely unknown. In fact, there is only one person that can possibly have done the deed."

"Are you sure you don't mean only one person who is *likely* to have done the deed?" Baley distrusted overstatement and had no liking for the armchair deducer who discovered certainty rather than probability in the workings of logic.

But Gruer shook his bald head. "No. Only one possible person. Anyone else is impossible. Completely impossible."

"Completely?"

"I assure you."

"Then you have no problem."

"On the contrary. We do have a problem. That one person couldn't have done it either."

Baley said calmly, "Then no one did it."

"Yet the deed was done. Rikaine Delmarre is dead."

That's something, thought Baley. Jehoshaphat, I've got *something*. I've got the victim's name.

He brought out his notebook and solemnly made note of it, partly out of a wry desire to indicate that he had scraped up, at last, a nubbin of fact, and partly to avoid making it too obvious that he sat by the side of a recording machine who needed no notes.

He said, "How is the victim's name spelled?"

Gruer spelled it.

"His profession, sir?"

"Fetologist."

Baley spelled that as it sounded and let it go. He said, "Now who would be able to give me a personal account of the circumstances surrounding the murder? As firsthand as possible."

Gruer's smile was grim and his eyes shifted to Daneel again, and then away. "His wife, Plainclothesman."

"His wife . . . ?"

"Yes. Her name is Gladia." Gruer pronounced it in three syllables, accenting the second.

"Any children?" Baley's eyes were fixed on his notebook. When no answer came, he looked up. "Any children?"

But Gruer's mouth had pursed up as though he had tasted something sour. He looked sick. Finally he said, "I would scarcely know."

Baley said, "What?"

Gruer added hastily, "In any case, I think you had better postpone actual operations till tomorrow. I know you've had a hard trip, Mr. Baley, and that you are tired and probably hungry."

Baley, about to deny it, realized suddenly that the thought of food had an uncommon attraction for him at the moment. He said, "Will you join us at our meal?" He didn't think Gruer would, being a Spacer. (Yet he had been brought to the point of saying "Mr. Baley" rather than "Plainclothesman Baley," which was something.)

As expected, Gruer said, "A business engagement makes that impossible. I will have to leave. I am sorry."

Baley rose. The polite thing would be to accompany Gruer to the door. In the first place, however, he wasn't at all anxious to approach the door and the unprotected open. And in the second he wasn't sure where the door was.

He remained standing in uncertainty.

Gruer smiled and nodded. He said, "I will see you again. Your robots will know the combination if you wish to talk to me."

And he was gone.

Baley exclaimed sharply.

Gruer and the chair he was sitting on were simply not there. The wall behind Gruer, the floor under his feet changed with explosive suddenness.

Daneel said calmly, "He was not there in the flesh at any time. It was a trimensional image. It seemed to me you would know. You have such things on Earth."

"Not like this," muttered Baley.

A trimensional image on Earth was encased in a cubic force-field that glittered against the background. The image itself had a tiny flicker. On Earth there was no mistaking image for reality. Here . . .

No wonder Gruer had worn no gloves. He needed no nose filters, for that matter.

Daneel said, "Would you care to eat now, Partner Elijah?"

Dinner was an unexpected ordeal. Robots appeared. One set the table. One brought in the food.

"How many are there in the house, Daneel?" Baley asked.

"About fifty, Partner Elijah."

"Will they stay here while we eat?" (One had backed into a corner, his glossy, glowing-eyed face turned toward Baley.)

"It is the usual practice," said Daneel, "for one to do so in case its service is called upon. If you do not wish that, you have only to order it to leave."

Baley shrugged. "Let it stay!"

Under normal conditions Baley might have found the food delicious. Now he ate mechanically. He noted abstractedly that Daneel ate also, with a kind of unimpassioned efficiency. Later on, of course, he would empty the fluorocarbon sac within him into which the "eaten" food was now being stored. Meanwhile Daneel maintained his masquerade.

"Is it night outside?" asked Baley.

"It is," replied Daneel.

Baley stared somberly at the bed. It was too large. The whole bedroom was too large. There were no blankets to burrow under, only sheets. They would make a poor enclosure.

Everything was difficult! He had already gone through the unnerving experience of showering in a stall that actually adjoined the bedroom. It was the height of luxury in a way, yet, on the other hand, it seemed an unsanitary arrangement.

He said abruptly, "How is the light put out?" The headboard of the bed gleamed with a soft light. Perhaps that was to facilitate book viewing before sleeping, but Baley was in no mood for that.

"It will be taken care of once you're in bed, if you compose yourself for sleep."

"The robots watch, do they?"

"It is their job."

"Jehoshaphat! What do these Solarians do for *themselves?*" Baley muttered. "I wonder now why a robot didn't scrub my back in the shower."

With no trace of humor Daneel said, "One would have, had you required it. As for the Solarians, they do what they choose. No robot performs his duty if ordered not to, except, of course, where the performance is necessary to the well-being of the human."

"Well, good night, Daneel."

"I will be in another bedroom, Partner Elijah. If, at any time during the night, you need anything——"

"I know. The robots will come."

"There is a contact patch on the side table. You have only to touch it. I will come too."

Sleep eluded Baley. He kept picturing the house he was in, balanced precariously at the outer skin of the world, with emptiness waiting just outside like a monster.

On Earth his apartment—his snug, comfortable, crowded apartment—sat nestled beneath many others. There were dozens of Levels and thousands of people between himself and the rim of Earth.

Even on Earth, he tried to tell himself, there were people on the topmost Level. They would be immediately adjacent to the outside. Sure! But that's what made those apartments low-rent.

Then he thought of Jessie, a thousand light-years away.

He wanted terribly to get out of bed right now, dress, and walk to her. His thoughts grew mistier. If there were only a tunnel, a nice, safe tunnel burrowing its way through safe, solid rock and metal from Solaria to Earth, he would walk and walk and walk. . . .

He would walk back to Earth, back to Jessie, back to comfort and security. . . .

Security.

Baley's eyes opened. His arms grew rigid and he rose up on his elbow, scarcely aware that he was doing so.

Security! This man, Hannis Gruer, was head of Solarian security. So Daneel had said. What did "security" mean? If it meant the same as it meant on Earth, and surely it must, this man Gruer was responsible for the protection of Solaria against invasion from without and subversion from within.

Why was he interested in a murder case? Was it because there were no police on Solaria and the Department of Security would come the closest to knowing what to do about a murder?

Gruer had seemed at ease with Baley, yet there had been those furtive glances, again and again, in the direction of Daneel.

Did Gruer suspect the motives of Daneel? Baley, himself, had been ordered to keep his eyes open and Daneel might very likely have received similar instructions.

It would be natural for Gruer to suspect that espionage was possible. His job made it necessary for him to suspect that in any case where it was conceivable. And he would not fear Baley overmuch, an Earthman, representative of the least formidable world in the Galaxy.

But Daneel was a native of Aurora, the oldest and largest and strongest of the Outer Worlds. That would be different.

Gruer, as Baley now remembered, had not addressed one word to Daneel.

For that matter, why should Daneel pretend so thoroughly to be a man? The earlier explanation that Baley had posed for himself, that it was a vainglorious game on the part of Daneel's Auroran designers, seemed trivial. It seemed obvious now that the masquerade was something more serious.

A man could be expected to receive diplomatic immunity; a certain courtesy and gentleness of treatment. A robot could not. But then why did not Aurora send a real man in the first place. Why gamble so desperately on a fake? The answer suggested itself instantly to Baley. A real man of Aurora, a real Spacer, would not care to associate too closely or for too long a time with an Earthman.

But if all this were true, why should Solaria find a single murder so important that it must allow an Earthman and an Auroran to come to their planet?

Baley felt trapped.

He was trapped on Solaria by the necessities of his assignment. He was trapped by Earth's danger, trapped in an environment he could scarcely endure, trapped by a responsibility he could not shirk. And, to add to all this, he was trapped somehow in the midst of a Spacer conflict the nature of which he did not understand.

4

A Woman Is Viewed

HE SLEPT at last. He did not remember when he actually made the transition to sleep. There was just a period when his thoughts grew more erratic and then the headboard of his bed was shining and the ceiling was alight with a cool, daytime glow. He looked at his watch.

Hours had passed. The robots who ran the house had decided it was time for him to wake up and had acted accordingly.

He wondered if Daneel were awake and at once realized the illogic of the thought. Daneel could not sleep. Baley wondered if he had counterfeited sleep as part of the role he was playing. Had he undressed and put on nightclothes?

As though on cue Daneel entered. "Good morning, Partner Elijah."

The robot was completely dressed and his face was in perfect repose. He said, "Did you sleep well?"

"Yes," said Baley dryly, "did you?"

He got out of bed and tramped into the bathroom for a shave and for the remainder of the morning ritual. He shouted, "If a robot comes in to shave me, send him out again. They get on my nerves. Even if I don't see them, they get on my nerves."

He stared at his own face as he shaved, marveling a bit that it looked so like the mirrored face he saw on Earth. If only the image were another Earthman with whom he could consult instead of only the light-mimicry of himself. If he could go over what he had already learned, small as it was . . .

"Too small! Get more," he muttered to the mirror.

He came out, mopping his face, and pulled trousers over fresh shorts. (Robots supplied everything, damn them.)

He said, "Would you answer a few questions, Daneel?"

"As you know, Partner Elijah, I answer all questions to the best of my knowledge."

Or to the letter of your instructions, thought Baley. He said, "Why are there only twenty thousand people on Solaria?"

"That is a mere fact," said Daneel. "A datum. A figure that is the result of a counting process."

"Yes, but you're evading the matter. The planet can support millions; why, then, only twenty thousand? You said the Solarians consider twenty thousand optimum. Why?"

"It is their way of life."

"You mean they practice birth control?"

"Yes."

"And leave the planet empty?" Baley wasn't sure why he was pounding away at this one point, but the planet's population was one of the few hard facts he had learned about it and there was little else he could ask about.

Daneel said, "The planet is not empty. It is parceled out into estates, each of which is supervised by a Solarian."

"You mean each lives on his estate. Twenty thousand estates, each with a Solarian."

"Fewer estates than those, Partner Elijah. Wives share the estate."

"No Cities?" Baley felt cold.

"None at all, Partner Elijah. They live completely apart and never see one another except under the most extraordinary circumstances."

"Hermits?"

"In a way, yes. In a way, no."

"What does that mean?"

"Agent Gruer visited you yesterday by trimensional image. Solarians visit one another freely that way and in no other way."

Baley stared at Daneel. He said, "Does that include us? Are we expected to live that way?"

"It is the custom of the world."

"Then how do I investigate this case? If I want to see someone——"

"From this house, Partner Elijah, you can obtain a trimensional view of anyone on the planet. There will be no problem. In fact, it will save you the annoyance of leaving this house. It was why I said when we arrived that there would be no occasion for you to feel it necessary to grow accustomed to facing the outdoors. And that is well. Any other arrangement would be most distasteful to you."

"I'll judge what's distasteful to me," said Baley. "First thing today, Daneel, I get in touch with the Gladia woman, the wife of the murdered man. If the trimensional business is unsatisfactory, I will go out to her place, personally. It's a matter for my decision."

"We shall see what is best and most feasible, Partner Elijah," said Daneel noncommittally. "I shall arrange for breakfast." He turned to leave.

Baley stared at the broad robotic back and was almost amused. Daneel Olivaw acted the master. If his instructions had been to keep Baley from learning any more than was absolutely necessary, a trump card had been left in Baley's hand.

The other was only R. Daneel Olivaw, after all. All that was necessary was to tell Gruer, or any Solarian, that Daneel was a robot and not a man.

And yet, on the other hand, Daneel's pseudo humanity could be of great use, too. A trump card need not be played at once. Sometimes it was more useful in the hand.

Wait and see, he thought, and followed Daneel out to breakfast.

Baley said, "Now how does one go about establishing trimensional contact?"

"It is done for us, Partner Elijah," said Daneel, and his finger sought out one of the contact patches that summoned robots.

A robot entered at once.

Where do they come from, Baley wondered. As one wandered aimlessly about the uninhabited maze that constituted the mansion, not one robot was ever visible. Did they scramble out of the way as humans approached? Did they send messages to one another and clear the path?

Yet whenever a call went out, one appeared without delay.

Baley stared at the robotic newcomer. It was sleek, but not glossy. Its surface had a muted, grayish finish, with a checkerboard pattern on the right shoulder as the only bit of color. Squares in white and yellow (silver and gold, really, from the metallic luster) were placed in what seemed an aimless pattern.

Daneel said, "Take us to the conversation room."

The robot bowed and turned, but said nothing.

Baley said, "Wait, boy. What's your name?"

The robot faced Baley. It spoke in clear tones and without hesitation. "I have no name, master. My serial number"—and a metal finger lifted and rested on the shoulder patch—"is ACX-2745."

Daneel and Baley followed into a large room, which Baley recognized as having held Gruer and his chair the day before.

Another robot was waiting for them with the eternal, patient nonboredom of the machine. The first bowed and left.

Baley compared shoulder patches of the two as the first bowed and started out. The pattern of silver and gold was different. The checkerboard was made up of a six-by-six square. The number of possible arrangements would be 2^{36} then, or seventy billion. More than enough.

Baley said, "Apparently, there is one robot for everything. One to show us here. One to run the viewer."

Daneel said, "There is much robotic specialization in Solaria, Partner Elijah."

"With so many of them, I can understand why." Baley looked at the second robot. Except for the shoulder patch, and, presumably, for the invisible positronic patterns within its spongy platinum-iridium brain it was the duplicate of the first. He said, "And your serial number?"

"ACC-1129, master."

"I'll just call you boy. Now I want to speak to a Mrs. Gladia Delmarre, wife of the late Rikaine Delmarre—— Daneel, is there an address, some way of pin-pointing her location?"

Daneel said gently, "I do not believe any further information is necessary. If I may question the robot——"

"Let me do that," Baley said. "All right, boy, do you know how the lady is to be reached?"

"Yes, master. I have knowledge of the connection pattern of all masters." This was said without pride. It was a mere fact, as though it were saying: I am made of metal, master.

Daneel interposed, "That is not surprising, Partner Elijah. There are less than ten thousand connections that need be fed into the memory circuits, and that is a small number."

Baley nodded. "Is there more than one Gladia Delmarre, by any chance? There might be that chance of confusion."

"Master?" After the question the robot remained blankly silent.

"I believe," said Daneel, "that this robot does not understand your question. It is my belief that duplicate names do not occur on Solaria. Names are registered at birth and no name may be adopted unless it is unoccupied at the time."

"All right," said Baley, "we learn something every minute. Now see here, boy, you tell me how to work whatever it is I am supposed to work; give me the connection pattern, or whatever you call it, and then step out."

There was a perceptible pause before the robot answered. It said, "Do you wish to make contact yourself, sir?"

"That's right."

Daneel touched Baley's sleeve gently. "One moment, Partner Elijah."

"Now what is it?"

"It is my belief that the robot could make the necessary contact with greater ease. It is his specialization."

Baley said grimly, "I'm sure he can do it better than I can. Doing it myself, I may make a mess of it." He stared levelly at the impassive Daneel. "Just the same, I prefer to make contact myself. Do I give the orders or don't I?"

Daneel said, "You give the orders, Partner Elijah, and your orders, where First Law permits, will be obeyed. However, with your permission, I would like to give you what pertinent information I have concerning the Solarian robots. Far more than on any other world, the robots on Solaria are specialized. Although Solarian robots are physically capable of many things, they are heavily equipped mentally for one particular type of job. To perform functions outside their specialty requires the high potentials produced by direct application of one of the Three Laws. Again, for them *not* to perform the duty for which they *are* equipped also requires the direct application of the Three Laws."

"Well, then, a direct order from me brings the Second Law into play, doesn't it?"

"True. Yet the potential set up by it is 'unpleasant' to the robot. Ordinarily, the matter would not come up, since almost never does a Solarian interfere with the day-to-day workings of a robot. For one thing, he would not care to do a robot's work; for another, he would feel no need to."

"Are you trying to tell me, Daneel, that it hurts the robot to have me do its work?"

"As you know, Partner Elijah, pain in the human sense is not applicable to robotic reactions."

Baley shrugged. "Then?"

"Nevertheless," went on Daneel, "the experience which the robot undergoes is as upsetting to it as pain is to a human, as nearly as I can judge."

"And yet," said Baley, "I'm not a Solarian. I'm an Earthman. I don't like robots doing what I want to do."

"Consider, too," said Daneel, "that to cause distress to a robot might be considered on the part of our hosts to be an act of impoliteness since in a society such as this there must be a number of more or less rigid beliefs concerning how it is proper to treat a robot and how it is not. To offend our hosts would scarcely make our task easier."

"All right," said Baley. "Let the robot do its job."

He settled back. The incident had not been without its uses. It was an educational example of how remorseless a robotic society could be. Once brought into existence, robots were not so easily removed, and a human who wished to dispense with them even temporarily found he could not.

His eyes half closed, he watched the robot approach the wall. Let the sociologists on Earth consider what had just occurred and draw their conclusions. He was beginning to have certain notions of his own.

Half a wall slid aside and the control panel that was revealed would have done justice to a City Section power station.

Baley longed for his pipe. He had been briefed that smoking on non-smoking Solaria would be a terrible breach of decorum, so he had not even been allowed to take his fixings. He sighed. There were moments when the feel of pipestem between teeth and a warm bowl in his hand would have been infinitely comforting.

The robot was working quickly, adjusting variable resistances a trifle here and there and intensifying field-forces in proper pattern by quick finger pressures.

Daneel said, "It is necessary first to signal the individual one desires to view. A robot will, of course, receive the message. If the individual being signaled is available and wishes to receive the view, full contact is established."

"Are all those controls necessary?" asked Baley. "The robot's hardly touching most of the panel."

"My information on the matter is not complete, Partner Elijah. There is, however, the necessity of arranging, upon occasion, for multiple viewings and for mobile viewings. The latter, particularly, call for complicated and continuing adjustment."

The robot said, "Masters, contact is made and approved. When you are ready, it will be completed."

"Ready," growled Baley, and as though the word were a signal, the far half of the room was alive with light.

Daneel said at once, "I neglected to have the robot specify that all visible openings to the outside be draped. I regret that and we must arrange——"

"Never mind," said Baley, wincing. "I'll manage. Don't interfere."

It was a bathroom he was staring at, or he judged it to be so from its fixtures. One end of it was, he guessed, a kind of beautician's establishment and his imagination pictured a robot (or robots?) working with unerring swiftness on the details of a woman's coiffure and on the externals that made up the picture she presented to the world.

Some gadgets and fittings he simply gave up on. There was no way of judging their purpose in the absence of experience. The walls were inlaid with an intricate pattern that all but fooled the eye into believing some natural object was being represented before fading away into an abstraction. The result was soothing and almost hypnotic in the way it monopolized attention.

What might have been the shower stall, a large one, was shielded off by nothing that seemed material, but rather by a trick of lighting that set up a wall of flickering opacity. No human was in sight.

Baley's glance fell to the floor. Where did his room end and the other begin? It was easy to tell. There was a line where the quality of the light changed and that must be it.

He stepped toward the line and after a moment's hesitation pushed his hand beyond it.

He felt nothing, any more than he would have had he shoved the hand into one of Earth's crude trimensionals. There, at least, he would have seen his own hand still; faintly, perhaps, and overlaid by the image, but he would have seen it. Here it was lost completely. To his vision, his arm ended sharply at the wrist.

What if he stepped across the line altogether? Probably his own vision would become inoperative. He would be in a world of complete blackness. The thought of such efficient enclosure was almost pleasant.

A voice interrupted him. He looked up and stepped backward with an almost clumsy haste.

Gladia Delmarre was speaking. At least Baley assumed it was she. The upper portion of the flickering light across the shower stall had faded and a head was clearly visible.

It smiled at Baley. "I said hello, and I'm sorry to keep you waiting. I'll be dry soon."

Hers was a triangular face, rather broad at the cheekbones (which grew prominent when she smiled) and narrowing with a gentle curve past full lips to a small chin. Her head was not high above the ground. Baley judged her to be about five feet two in height. (This was not typical. At least not to Baley's way of thinking. Spacer women were supposed to lean toward the tall and stately.) Nor was her hair the Spacer bronze. It was light brown, tinging toward yellow, and worn moderately long. At the moment it was fluffed out in what Baley imagined must be a stream of warm air. The whole picture was quite pleasing.

Baley said in confusion, "If you want us to break contact and wait till you're through——"

"Oh no. I'm almost done, and we can talk meanwhile. Hannis Gruer told me you would be viewing. You're from Earth, I understand." Her eyes rested full on him, seemed to drink him in.

Baley nodded and sat down. "My companion is from Aurora."

She smiled and kept her glance fixed on Baley as though *he* remained the curiosity nevertheless, and of course, Baley thought, so he was.

She lifted her arms above her head, running her fingers through the hair and spreading it out as though to hasten drying. Her arms were slim and graceful. Very attractive, Baley thought.

Then he thought uneasily: Jessie wouldn't like this.

Daneel's voice broke in. "Would it be possible, Mrs. Delmarre, to have the window we see polarized or draped. My partner is disturbed by the sight of daylight. On Earth, as you may have heard——"

The young woman (Baley judged her to be twenty-five but had the doleful thought that the apparent ages of Spacers could be most deceptive) put her hands to her cheeks and said, "Oh my, yes. I know all about that. How ridiculously silly of me. Forgive me, please, but it won't take a moment. I'll have a robot in here——"

She stepped out of the drying cabinet, her hand extended toward the contact-patch, still talking. "I'm always thinking I ought to have more than one contact-patch in this room. A house is just no good if it doesn't have a patch within reach no matter where you stand— say not more than five feet away. It just—— Why, what's the matter?"

She stared in shock at Baley, who, having jumped out of his chair and upset it behind him, had reddened to his hairline and hastily turned away.

Daneel said calmly, "It would be better, Mrs. Delmarre, if, after you have made contact with the robot, you would return to the stall or, failing that, proceed to put on some articles of clothing."

Gladia looked down at her nudity in surprise and said, "Well, of course."

5

A Crime Is Discussed

"It was only viewing, you see," said Gladia contritely. She was wrapped in something that left her arms and shoulders free. One leg showed to mid-thigh, but Baley, entirely recovered and feeling an utter fool, ignored it stoically.

He said, "It was the surprise, Mrs. Delmarre——"

"Oh, please. You can call me Gladia, unless—unless that's against your customs."

"Gladia, then. It's all right. I just want to assure you there was nothing repulsive about it, you understand. Just the surprise." Bad enough for him to have acted the fool, he thought, without having the poor girl think he found her unpleasant. As a matter of fact, it had been rather—rather . . .

Well, he didn't have the phrase, but he knew quite certainly that there was no way he would ever be able to talk of this to Jessie.

"I know I offended you," Gladia said, "but I didn't mean to. I just wasn't thinking. Of course I realize one must be careful about the customs of other planets, but the customs are so queer sometimes; at least, not queer," she hastened to add, "I don't mean queer. I mean strange, you know, and it's so easy to forget. As I forgot about keeping the windows darkened."

"Quite all right," muttered Baley. She was in another room now with all the windows draped and the light had the subtly different and more comfortable texture of artificiality.

"But about the other thing," she went on earnestly, "it's just *viewing,* you see. After all, you didn't mind talking to me when I was in the drier and I wasn't wearing anything then, either."

"Well," said Baley, wishing she would run down as far as that subject was concerned, "hearing you is one thing, and seeing you is another."

"But that's exactly it. Seeing isn't involved." She reddened a trifle and looked down. "I hope you don't think I'd ever do anything like that, I mean, just step out of the drier, if anyone were *seeing* me. It was just *viewing*."

"Same thing, isn't it?" said Baley.

"Not at all the same thing. You're viewing me right now. You can't touch me, can you, or smell me, or anything like that. You could if you were seeing me. Right now, I'm two hundred miles away from you at *least*. So how can it be the same thing?"

Baley grew interested. "But I see you with my eyes."

"No, you don't see me. You see my image. You're viewing me."

"And that makes a difference?"

"All the difference there is."

"I see." In a way he did. The distinction was not one he could make easily, but it had a kind of logic to it.

She said, bending her head a little to one side, "Do you *really* see?"

"Yes."

"Does that mean you wouldn't mind if I took off my wrapper?" She was smiling.

He thought: She's teasing and I ought to take her up on it.

But aloud he said, "No, it would take my mind off my job. We'll discuss it another time."

"Do you mind my being in the wrapper, rather than something more formal? Seriously."

"I don't mind."

"May I call you by your first name?"

"If you have the occasion."

"What is your first name?"

"Elijah."

"All right." She snuggled into a chair that looked hard and almost ceramic in texture, but it slowly gave as she sat until it embraced her gently.

Baley said, "To business, now."

She said, "To business."

Baley found it all extraordinarily difficult. There was no way even to make a beginning. On Earth he would ask name, rating, City and Sector of dwelling, a million different routine questions. He might even know the answers to begin with, yet it would be a device to ease into the serious phase. It would serve to introduce him to the person, make his judgment of the tactics to pursue something other than a mere guess.

But here? How could he be certain of anything? The very verb "to see" meant different things to himself and to the woman. How many other words would be different? How often would they be at cross-purposes without his being aware of it?

He said, "How long were you married, Gladia?"

"Ten years, Elijah."

"How old are you?"

"Thirty-three."

Baley felt obscurely pleased. She might easily have been a hundred thirty-three.

He said, "Were you happily married?"

Gladia looked uneasy. "How do you mean that?"

"Well——" For a moment Baley was at a loss. How do you define a happy marriage. For that matter, what would a Solarian consider a happy marriage? He said, "Well, you saw one another often?"

"What? I should hope not. We're not animals, you know."

Baley winced. "You did live in the same mansion? I thought——"

"Of course, we did. We were married. But I had my quarters and he had his. He had a very important career which took much of his time and I have my own work. We viewed each other whenever necessary."

"He *saw* you, didn't he?"

"It's not a thing one talks about but he *did* see me."

"Do you have any children?"

Gladia jumped to her feet in obvious agitation. "That's too much. Of all the indecent——"

"Now wait. *Wait!*" Baley brought his fist down on the arm of his chair. "Don't be difficult. This is a murder investigation. Do you understand? Murder. And it was your husband who was murdered. Do you want to see the murderer found and punished or don't you?"

"Then *ask* about the murder, not about—about——"

"I have to ask all sorts of things. For one thing I want to know whether you're sorry your husband is dead." He added with calculated brutality, "You don't seem to be."

She stared at him haughtily. "I'm sorry when anyone dies, especially when he's young and useful."

"Doesn't the fact that he was your husband make it just a little more than that?"

"He was assigned to me and, well, we *did* see each other when scheduled and—and"—she hurried the next words—"and, if you must know, we don't have children because none have been assigned us yet. I don't see what all that has to do with being sorry over someone being dead."

Maybe it had nothing to do with it, Baley thought. It depended on the social facts of life and with those he was not acquainted.

He changed the subject. "I'm told you have personal knowledge of the circumstances of the murder."

For a moment she seemed to grow taut. "I—discovered the body. Is that the way I should say it?"

"Then you didn't witness the actual murder?"

"Oh no," she said faintly.

"Well, suppose you tell me what happened. Take your time and use your own words." He sat back and composed himself to listen.

She began, "It was on three-two of the fifth——"

"When was that in Standard Time?" asked Baley quickly.

"I'm not sure. I really don't know. You can check, I suppose."

Her voice seemed shaky and her eyes had grown large. They were a little too gray to be called blue, he noted.

She said, "He came to my quarters. It was our assigned day for seeing and I knew he'd come."

"He always came on the assigned day?"

"Oh yes. He was a very conscientious man, a good Solarian. He never skipped an assigned day and always came at the same time. Of course, he didn't stay long. We have not been assigned ch——"

She couldn't finish the word, but Baley nodded.

"Anyway," she said, "he always came at the same time, you know, so that everything would be comfortable. We spoke a few minutes; seeing *is* an ordeal, but he always spoke quite normally to me. It was his way. Then he left to attend to some project he was involved with; I'm not sure what. He had a special laboratory in my quarters to which he could retire on seeing days. He had a much bigger one in his quarters, of course."

Baley wondered what he did in those laboratories. Fetology, perhaps, whatever that was.

He said, "Did he seem unnatural in any way? Worried?"

"No. No. He was never worried." She came to the edge of a small laugh and buried it at the last moment. "He always had perfect control, like your friend there." For a brief moment her small hand reached out and indicated Daneel, who did not stir.

"I see. Well, go on."

Gladia didn't. Instead she whispered, "Do you mind if I have myself a drink?"

"Please do."

Gladia's hand slipped along the arm of her chair momentarily. In less than a minute, a robot moved in silently and a warm drink (Baley could see the steam) was in her hand. She sipped slowly, then set the drink down.

She said, "That's better. May I ask a personal question?"

Baley said, "You may always ask."

"Well, I've read a lot about Earth. I've always been interested, you know. It's such a *queer* world." She gasped and added immediately, "I didn't mean that."

Baley frowned a little. "Any world is queer to people who don't live on it."

"I mean it's different. You know. Anyway, I want to ask a rude question. At least, I hope it doesn't seem rude to an Earthman. I wouldn't ask it of a Solarian, of course. Not for anything."

"Ask what, Gladia?"

"About you and your friend—Mr. Olivaw, is it?"

"Yes."

"You two aren't viewing, are you?"

"How do you mean?"

"I mean each other. You're seeing. You're there, both of you."

Baley said, "We're physically together. Yes."

"You could touch him, if you wanted to."

"That's right."

She looked from one to the other and said, "Oh."

It might have meant anything. Disgust? Revulsion?

Baley toyed with the idea of standing up, walking to Daneel and placing his hand flat on Daneel's face. It might be interesting to watch her reaction.

He said, "You were about to go on with the events of that day when your husband came to see you." He was morally certain that her digression, however interesting it might have been intrinsically to her, was primarily motivated by a desire to avoid just that.

She returned to her drink for a moment. Then: "There isn't much to tell. I saw he would be engaged, and I knew he would be, anyway, because he was always at some sort of constructive work, so I went back to my own work. Then, perhaps fifteen minutes later, I heard a shout."

There was a pause and Baley prodded her. "What kind of a shout?"

She said, "Rikaine's. My husband's. Just a shout. No words. A kind of fright. No! Surprise, shock. Something like that. I'd never heard him shout before."

She lifted her hands to her ears as though to shut out even the memory of the sound and her wrapper slipped slowly down to her waist. She took no notice and Baley stared firmly at his notebook.

He said, "What did you do?"

"I ran. I ran. I didn't know where he was——"

"I thought you said he had gone to the laboratory he maintained in your quarters."

"He did, E-Elijah, but *I* didn't know where that was. Not for sure, anyway. I never went there. It was his. I had a general idea of its direction. I knew it was somewhere in the west, but I was so upset, I didn't even think to summon any robot. One of them would have guided me easily, but of course none came without being summoned. When I did get there—I found it somehow—he was dead."

She stopped suddenly and, to Baley's acute discomfort, she bent her head and wept. She made no attempt to obscure her face. Her eyes simply closed and tears slowly trickled down her cheeks. It was quite soundless. Her shoulders barely trembled.

Then her eyes opened and looked at him through swimming tears. "I never saw a dead man before. He was all bloody and his head was—just—all—— I managed to get a robot and he called others and I suppose they took care of me and of Rikaine. I don't remember. I don't——"

Baley said, "What do you mean, they took care of Rikaine?"

"They took him away and cleaned up." There was a small wedge of indignation in her voice, the lady of the house careful of its condition. "Things were a mess."

"And what happened to the body?"

She shook her head. "I don't know. Burned, I suppose. Like any dead body."

"You didn't call the police?"

She looked at him blankly and Baley thought: No police!

He said, "You told somebody, I suppose. People found out about the matter."

She said, "The robots called a doctor. And I had to call Rikaine's place of work. The robots there had to know he wouldn't be back."

"The doctor was for you, I suppose."

She nodded. For the first time, she seemed to notice her wrapper draped about her hips. She pulled it up into position, murmuring forlornly, "I'm sorry. I'm sorry."

Baley felt uncomfortable, watching her as she sat there helpless, shivering, her face contorted with the absolute terror that had come over her with the memory.

She had never seen a dead body before. She had never seen blood and a crushed skull. And if the husband-wife relationship on Solaria was something thin and shallow, it was still a dead human being with whom she had been confronted.

Baley scarcely knew what to say or do next. He had the impulse to apologize, and yet, as a policeman, he was doing only his duty.

But there were no police on this world. Would she understand that this was his duty?

Slowly, and as gently as he could, he said, "Gladia, did you hear anything at all? Anything besides your husband's shout."

She looked up, her face as pretty as ever, despite its obvious distress—perhaps because of it. She said, "Nothing."

"No running footsteps? No other voice?"

She shook her head. "I didn't hear anything."

"When you found your husband, he was completely alone? You two were the only ones present?"

"Yes."

"No signs of anyone else having been there?"

"None that I could see. I don't see how anyone could have been there, anyway."

"Why do you say that?"

For a moment she looked shocked. Then she said dispiritedly, "You're from Earth. I keep forgetting. Well, it's just that nobody could have been there. My husband never saw anybody except me; not since he was a boy. He certainly wasn't the sort to see anybody. Not Rikaine. He was very strict; very custom-abiding."

"It might not have been his choice. What if someone had just come to see him without an invitation, without your husband knowing anything about it? He couldn't have helped seeing the intruder regardless of how custom-abiding he was."

She said, "Maybe, but he would have called robots at once and had the man taken away. He would have! Besides no one would try to see my husband without being invited to. I couldn't conceive of such a thing. And Rikaine certainly would never invite anyone to see him. It's ridiculous to think so."

Baley said softly, "Your husband was killed by being struck on the head, wasn't he? You'll admit that."

"I suppose so. He was—all——"

"I'm not asking for the details at the moment. Was there any sign of some mechanical contrivance in the room that would have enabled someone to crush his skull by remote control."

"Of course not. At least, I didn't see any."

"If anything like that had been there, I imagine you would have seen it. It follows then that a hand held something capable of crushing a man's skull and that hand swung it. Some person had to be within four feet of your husband to do that. So someone did see him."

"No one would," she said earnestly. "A Solarian just wouldn't see anyone."

"A Solarian who would commit murder wouldn't stick at a bit of seeing, would he?"

(To himself that statement sounded dubious. On Earth he had known the case of a perfectly conscienceless murderer who had been caught only because he could not bring himself to violate the custom of absolute silence in the community bathroom.)

Gladia shook her head. "You don't understand about seeing. Earthmen just see anybody they want to all the time, so you don't understand it. . . ."

Curiosity seemed to be struggling within her. Her eyes lightened a bit. "Seeing does seem perfectly normal to you, doesn't it?"

"I've always taken it for granted," said Baley.

"It doesn't trouble you?"

"Why should it?"

"Well, the films don't say, and I've always wanted to know——Is it all right if I ask a question?"

"Go ahead," said Baley stolidly.

"Do you have a wife assigned to you?"

"I'm married. I don't know about the assignment part."

"And I know you see your wife any time you want to and she sees you and neither of you thinks anything of it."

Baley nodded.

"Well, when you see her, suppose you just want to——" She lifted her hands elbow-high, pausing as though searching for the proper phrase. She tried again, "Can you just—any time . . ." She let it dangle.

Baley didn't try to help.

She said, "Well, never mind. I don't know why I should bother you with that sort of thing now anyway. Are you through with me?" She looked as though she might cry again.

Baley said, "One more try, Gladia. Forget that no one would see your husband. Suppose someone *did*. Who might it have been?"

"It's just useless to guess. It couldn't be anyone."

"It has to be someone. Agent Gruer says there is reason to suspect some one person. So you see there must be someone."

A small, joyless smile flickered over the girl's face. "I know who he thinks did it."

"All right. Who?"

She put a small hand on her breast. "I."

6

A Theory Is Refuted

"I should have said, Partner Elijah," said Daneel, speaking suddenly, "that that is an obvious conclusion."

Baley cast a surprised look at his robot partner. "Why obvious?" he asked.

"The lady herself," said Daneel, "states that she was the only person who did or who would see her husband. The social situation on Solaria is such that even she cannot plausibly present anything else as the truth. Certainly Agent Gruer would find it reasonable, even obligatory, to believe that a Solarian husband would be seen only by his wife. Since only one person could be in seeing range, only one person could strike the blow and only one person could be the murderer. Or murderess, rather. Agent Gruer, you will remember, said that only one person could have done it. Anyone else he considered impossible. Well?"

"He also said," said Baley, "that that one person couldn't have done it, either."

"By which he probably meant that there was no weapon found at the scene of the crime. Presumably Mrs. Delmarre could explain that anomaly."

He gestured with cool robotic politeness toward where Gladia sat, still in viewing focus, her eyes cast down, her small mouth compressed.

Jehoshaphat, thought Baley, we're forgetting the lady.

Perhaps it was annoyance that had caused him to forget. It was Daneel who annoyed him, he thought, with his unemotional approach to problems. Or perhaps it was himself, with his emotional approach. He did not stop to analyze the matter.

He said, "That will be all for now, Gladia. However one goes about it, break contact. Good-by."

She said softly, "Sometimes one says, 'Done viewing,' but I like 'Good-by' better. You seem disturbed, Elijah. I'm sorry, because I'm used to having people think I did it, so you don't need to feel disturbed."

Daneel said, "*Did* you do it, Gladia?"

"No," she said angrily.

"Good-by, then."

With the anger not yet washed out of her face she was gone. For a moment, though, Baley could still feel the impact of those quite extraordinary gray eyes.

She might say she was used to having people think her a murderess, but that was very obviously a lie. Her anger spoke more truly than her words. Baley wondered of how many other lies she was capable.

And now Baley found himself alone with Daneel. He said, "All right, Daneel, I'm not altogether a fool."

"I have never thought you were, Partner Elijah."

"Then tell me what made you say there was no murder weapon found at the site of the crime? There was nothing in the evidence so far, nothing in anything I've heard that would lead us to that conclusion."

"You are correct. I have additional information not yet available to you."

"I was sure of that. What kind?"

"Agent Gruer said he would send a copy of the report of their own investigation. I have that copy. It arrived this morning."

"Why haven't you shown it to me?"

"I felt that it would perhaps be more fruitful for you to conduct your investigation, at least in the initial stages, according to your own ideas, without being prejudiced by the conclusions of other people who, self-admittedly, have reached no satisfactory conclusion. It was because I, myself, felt my logical processes might be influenced by those conclusions that I contributed nothing to the discussion."

Logical processes! Unbidden, there leaped into Baley's mind the fragment of a conversation he had once had with a roboticist. A robot, the man had said, is logical but not reasonable.

He said, "You entered the discussion at the end."

"So I did, Partner Elijah, but only because by that time I had independent evidence bearing out Agent Gruer's suspicions."

"What kind of independent evidence?"

"That which could be deduced from Mrs. Delmarre's own behavior."

"Let's be specific, Daneel."

"Consider that if the lady were guilty and were attempting to prove herself innocent, it would be useful to her to have the detective in the case believe her innocent."

"Well?"

"If she could warp his judgment by playing upon a weakness of his, she might do so, might she not?"

"Strictly hypothetical."

"Not at all," was the calm reply. "You will have noticed, I think, that she concentrated her attention entirely on you."

"I was doing the talking," said Baley.

"Her attention was on you from the start; even before she could guess that you would be doing the talking. In fact, one might have thought she would, logically, have expected that I, as an Auroran, would take the lead in the investigation. Yet she concentrated on you."

"And what do you deduce from this?"

"That it was upon you, Partner Elijah, that she pinned her hopes. You were the Earthman."

"What of that?"

"She had studied Earth. She implied that more than once. She knew what I was talking about when I asked her to blank out the outer daylight at the very start of the interview. She did not act surprised or uncomprehending, as she would most certainly have done had she not had actual knowledge of conditions on Earth."

"Well?"

"Since she has studied Earth, it is quite reasonable to suppose that she discovered one weakness Earthmen possess. She must know of the nudity tabu, and of how such a display must impress an Earthman."

"She—she explained about viewing——"

"So she did. Yet did it seem entirely convincing to you? Twice she allowed herself to be seen in what you would consider a state of improper clothing——"

"Your conclusion," said Baley, "is that she was trying to seduce me. Is that it?"

"Seduce you away from your professional impersonality. So it would seem to me. And though I cannot share human reactions to stimuli, I would judge, from what has been imprinted on my instruction circuits, that the lady meets any reasonable standard of physical attractiveness. From your behavior, moreover, it seems to me that you were aware of that and that you approved her appearance. I would even judge that Mrs. Delmarre acted rightly in thinking her mode of behavior would predispose you in her favor."

"Look," said Baley uncomfortably, "regardless of what effect she might have had on me, I am still an officer of the law in full possession of my sense of professional ethics. Get that straight. Now let's see the report."

Baley read through the report in silence. He finished, turned back, and read it through a second time.

"This brings in a new item," he said. "The robot."

Daneel Olivaw nodded.

Baley said thoughtfully, "She didn't mention it."

Daneel said, "You asked the wrong question. You asked if he was alone when she found the body. You asked if anyone else had been present at the death scene. A robot isn't 'anybody else.'"

Baley nodded. If he himself were a suspect and were asked who else had been at the scene of a crime, he would scarcely have replied: "No one but this table."

He said, "I suppose I should have asked if any robots were present?" (Damn it, what questions does one ask anyway on a strange world?) He said, "How legal is robotic evidence, Daneel?"

"What do you mean?"

"Can a robot bear witness on Solaria? Can it give evidence?"

"Why should you doubt it?"

"A robot isn't human, Daneel. On Earth, it cannot be a legal witness."

"And yet a footprint can, Partner Elijah, although that is much less a human than a robot is. The position of your planet in this respect is illogical. On Solaria, robotic evidence, when competent, is admissible."

Baley did not argue the point. He rested his chin on the knuckles of one hand and went over this matter of the robot in his mind.

In the extremity of terror Gladia Delmarre, standing over her husband's body, had summoned robots. By the time they came she was unconscious.

The robots reported having found her there together with the dead body. And something else was present as well; a robot. That robot had not been summoned; it was already there. It was not one of the regular staff. No other robot had seen it before or knew its function or assignment.

Nor could anything be discovered from the robot in question. It was not in working order. When found, its motions were disorganized and so, apparently, was the functioning of its positronic brain. It could give none of the proper responses, either verbal or mechanical, and after exhaustive investigation by a robotics expert it was declared a total loss.

Its only activity that had any trace of organization was its constant repetition of "You're going to kill me—you're going to kill me—you're going to kill me . . ."

No weapon that could possibly have been used to crush the dead man's skull was located.

Baley said suddenly, "I'm going to eat, Daneel, and then we see Agent Gruer again—or view him, anyway."

Hannis Gruer was still eating when contact was established. He ate slowly, choosing each mouthful carefully from a variety of dishes, peering at each anxiously as though searching for some hidden combination he would find most satisfactory.

Baley thought: He may be a couple of centuries old. Eating may be getting dull for him.

Gruer said, "I greet you, gentlemen. You received our report, I believe." His bald head glistened, as he leaned across the table to reach a titbit.

"Yes. We have spent an interesting session with Mrs. Delmarre also," said Baley.

"Good, good," said Gruer. "And to what conclusion, if any, did you come?"

Baley said, "That she is innocent, sir."

Gruer looked up sharply. "Really?"

Baley nodded.

Gruer said, "And yet she was the only one who could see him, the only one who could possibly be within reach. . . ."

Baley said, "That's been made clear to me, and no matter how firm social customs are on Solaria, the point is not conclusive. May I explain?"

Gruer had returned to his dinner. "Of course."

"Murder rests on three legs," said Baley, "each equally important. They are motive, means, and opportunity. For a good case against any suspect, each of the three must be satisfied. Now I grant you that Mrs. Delmarre had the opportunity. As for the motive, I've heard of none."

Gruer shrugged. "We know of none." For a moment his eyes drifted to the silent Daneel.

"All right. The suspect has no known motive, but perhaps she's a pathological killer. We can let the matter ride for a while, and continue. She is in his laboratory with him and there's some reason why she wants to kill him. She waves some club or other heavy object threateningly. It takes him a while to realize that his wife really intends to hurt him. He shouts in dismay, 'You're going to kill me,' and so she does. He turns to run as the blow descends and it crushes the back of his head. Did a doctor examine the body, by the way?"

"Yes and no. The robots called a doctor to attend Mrs. Delmarre and, as a matter of course, he looked at the dead body, too."

"That wasn't mentioned in the report."

"It was scarcely pertinent. The man was dead. In fact, by the time the doctor could view the body, it had been stripped, washed, and prepared for cremation in the usual manner."

"In other words, the robots had destroyed evidence," said Baley, annoyed. Then: "Did you say he *viewed* the body? He didn't *see* it?"

"Great Space," said Gruer, "what a morbid notion. He viewed it, of course, from all necessary angles and at close focus, I'm sure. Doctors can't avoid seeing patients under some conditions, but I can't conceive of any reason why they should have to see corpses. Medicine is a dirty job, but even doctors draw the line somewhere."

"Well, the point is this. Did the doctor report anything about the nature of the wound that killed Dr. Delmarre?"

"I see what you're driving at. You think that perhaps the wound was too severe to have been caused by a woman."

"A woman is weaker than a man, sir. And Mrs. Delmarre is a small woman."

"But quite athletic, Plainclothesman. Given a weapon of the proper type, gravity and leverage would do most of the work. Even not allowing for that, a woman in frenzy can do surprising things."

Baley shrugged. "You speak of a weapon. Where is it?"

Gruer shifted position. He held out his hand toward an empty glass and a robot entered the viewing field and filled it with a colorless fluid that might have been water.

Gruer held the filled glass momentarily, then put it down as though he had changed his mind about drinking. He said, "As is stated in the report, we have not been able to locate it."

"I know the report says that. I want to make absolutely certain of a few things. The weapon was searched for?"

"Thoroughly."

"By yourself?"

"By robots, but under my own viewing supervision at all times. We could locate nothing that might have been the weapon."

"That weakens the case against Mrs. Delmarre, doesn't it?"

"It does," said Gruer calmly. "It is one of several things about the case we don't understand. It is one reason why we have not acted against Mrs. Delmarre. It is one reason why I told you that the guilty party could not have committed the crime, either. Perhaps I should say that she apparently could not have committed the crime."

"Apparently?"

"She must have disposed of the weapon someway. So far, we have lacked the ingenuity to find it."

Baley said dourly, "Have you considered all possibilities?"

"I think so."

"I wonder. Let's see. A weapon has been used to crush a man's skull and it is not found at the scene of the crime. The only alternative is that it has been carried away. It could not have been carried away by Rikaine Delmarre. He was dead. Could it have been carried away by Gladia Delmarre?"

"It must have been," said Gruer.

"How? When the robots arrived, she was on the floor unconscious. Or she may have been feigning unconsciousness, but anyway she was there. How long a time between the murder and the arrival of the first robot?"

"That depends upon the exact time of the murder, which we don't know," said Gruer uneasily.

"I read the report, sir. One robot reported hearing a disturbance and a cry it identified as Dr. Delmarre's. It was apparently the closest to the scene. The summoning signal flashed five minutes afterward. It would take the robot less than a minute to appear on the scene." (Baley remembered his own experiences with the rapid-fire appearance of robots when summoned.) "In five minutes, even ten, how far could Mrs. Delmarre have carried a weapon and returned in time to assume unconsciousness?"

"She might have destroyed it in a disposer unit."

"The disposer unit was investigated, according to the report, and the residual gamma-ray activity was quite low. Nothing sizable had been destroyed in it for twenty-four hours."

"I know that," said Gruer. "I simply present it as an example of what might have been done."

"True," said Baley, "but there may be a very simple explanation. I suppose the robots belonging to the Delmarre household have been checked and all were accounted for."

"Oh yes."

"And all in reasonable working order?"

"Yes."

"Could any of those have carried away the weapon, perhaps without being aware of what it was?"

"Not one of them had removed anything from the scene of the crime. Or touched anything, for that matter."

"That's not so. They certainly removed the body and prepared it for cremation."

"Well, yes, of course, but that scarcely counts. You would expect them to do that."

"Jehoshaphat!" muttered Baley. He had to struggle to keep calm. He said, "Now suppose someone else had been on the scene."

"Impossible," said Gruer. "How could someone invade Dr. Delmarre's personal presence?"

"Suppose!" cried Baley. "Now there was never any thought in the robots' minds that an intruder might have been present. I don't suppose any of them made an immediate search of the grounds about the house. It wasn't mentioned in the report."

"There was no search till we looked for the weapon, but that was a considerable time afterward."

"Nor any search for signs of a ground-car or an air vehicle on the grounds?"

"No."

"Then if someone had nerved himself to invade Dr. Delmarre's personal presence, as you put it, he could have killed him and then walked away leisurely. No one would have stopped him or even seen him. Afterward, he could rely on everyone being sure no one could have been there."

"And no one could," said Gruer positively.

Baley said, "One more thing. Just one more. There was a robot involved. A robot was at the scene."

Daneel interposed for the first time. "The robot was not at the scene. Had it been there, the crime would not have been committed."

Baley turned his head sharply. And Gruer, who had lifted his glass a second time as though about to drink, put it down again to stare at Daneel.

"Is that not so?" asked Daneel.

"Quite so," said Gruer. "A robot would have stopped one person from harming another. First Law."

"All right," said Baley. "Granted. But it must have been close. It was on the scene when the other robots arrived. Say it was in the next room. The murderer is advancing on Delmarre and Delmarre cries out, 'You're going to kill me.' The robots of the household did not hear those words; at most they heard a cry, so, unsummoned, they did not come. But this particular robot heard the words and First Law made it come unsummoned. It was too late. Probably, it actually saw the murder committed."

"It must have seen the last stages of the murder," agreed Gruer. "That is what disordered it. Witnessing harm to a human without having prevented it is a violation of the First Law and, depending upon circumstances, more or less damage to the positronic brain is induced. In this case, it was a great deal of damage."

Gruer stared at his fingertips as he turned the glass of liquid to and fro, to and fro.

Baley said, "Then the robot was a witness. Was it questioned?"

"What use? He was disordered. It could only say 'You're going to kill me.' I agree with your reconstruction that far. They were probably Delmarre's last words burned into the robot's consciousness when everything else was destroyed."

"But I'm told Solaria specializes in robots. Was there no way in which the robot could be repaired? No way in which its circuits could be patched?"

"None," said Gruer sharply.

"And where is the robot, now?"

"Scrapped," said Gruer.

Baley raised his eyebrows. "This is a rather peculiar case. No motive, no means, no witnesses, no evidence. Where there was some evidence to begin with, it was destroyed. You have only one suspect and everyone seems convinced of her guilt; at least, everyone is certain no one else can be guilty. That's your opinion, too, obviously. The question then is: Why was I sent for?"

Gruer frowned. "You seem upset, Mr. Baley." He turned abruptly to Daneel. "Mr. Olivaw."

"Yes, Agent Gruer."

"Won't you please go through the dwelling and make sure all windows are closed and blanked out? Plainclothesman Baley may be feeling the effects of open space."

The statement astonished Baley. It was his impulse to deny Gruer's assumption and order Daneel to keep his place when, on the brink, he caught something of panic in Gruer's voice, something of glittering appeal in his eyes.

He sat back and let Daneel leave the room.

It was as though a mask had dropped from Gruer's face, leaving it naked and afraid. Gruer said, "That was easier than I had thought. I'd planned so many ways of getting you alone. I never thought the Auroran would leave at a simple request, and yet I could think of nothing else to do."

Baley said, "Well, I'm alone now."

Gruer said, "I couldn't speak freely in his presence. He's an Auroran and he is here because he was forced on us as the price of having you." The Solarian leaned forward. "There's something more to this than murder. I am not concerned only with the matter of who did it. There are parties on Solaria, secret organizations. . . ."

Baley stared. "Surely, I can't help you there."

"Of course you can. Now understand this: Dr. Delmarre was a Traditionalist. He believed in the old ways, the good ways. But there are new forces among us, forces for change, and Delmarre has been silenced."

"By Mrs. Delmarre?"

"Hers must have been the hand. That doesn't matter. There is an organization behind her and that is the important matter."

"Are you sure? Do you have evidence?"

"Vague evidence, only. I can't help that. Rikaine Delmarre was on the track of something. He assured me *his* evidence was good, and I believe him. I knew him well enough to know him as neither fool nor child. Unfortunately, he told me very little. Naturally, he wanted to complete his investigation before laying the matter completely open to the authorities. He must have gotten close to completion, too, or they wouldn't have dared the risk of having him openly slaughtered by violence. One thing Delmarre told me, though. The whole human race is in danger."

Baley felt himself shaken. For a moment it was as though he were listening to Minnim again, but on an even larger scale. Was *everyone* going to turn to him with cosmic dangers?

"Why do you think I can help?" he asked.

"Because you're an Earthman," said Gruer. "Do you understand? We on Solaria have no experience with these things. In a way, we don't understand people. There are too few of us here."

He looked uneasy. "I don't like to say this, Mr. Baley. My colleagues laugh at me and some grow angry, but it is a definite feeling I have. It seems to me that you Earthmen *must* understand people far better than we do, just by living among such crowds of them. And a detective more than anyone. Isn't that so?"

Baley half nodded and held his tongue.

Gruer said, "In a way, this murder was fortunate. I have not dared speak to the others about Delmarre's investigation, since I wasn't sure who might be involved in the conspiracy, and Delmarre himself was not ready to give any details till his investigation was complete. And even if Delmarre had completed his work, how would we deal with the matter afterward? How does one deal with hostile human beings? I don't know. From the beginning, I felt we needed an Earthman. When I heard of your work in connection with the murder in Spacetown on Earth, I knew we needed you. I got in touch with Aurora, with whose men you had worked most closely, and through them approached the Earth government. Yet my own colleagues could not be persuaded into agreeing to this. Then came the murder and that was enough of a shock to give me the agreement I needed. At the moment, they would have agreed to anything."

Gruer hesitated, then added, "It's not easy to ask an Earthman to help, but I must do so. Remember, whatever it is, the human race is in danger. Earth, too."

Earth was doubly in danger, then. There was no mistaking the desperate sincerity in Gruer's voice.

But then, if the murder were so fortunate a pretext for allowing Gruer to do what he so desperately wanted to do all the time, was it entirely fortune? It opened new avenues of thought that were not reflected in Baley's face, eyes, or voice.

Baley said, "I have been sent here, sir, to help. I will do so to the best of my ability."

Gruer finally lifted his long-delayed drink and looked over the rim of the glass at Baley. "Good," he said. "Not a word to the Auroran, please. Whatever this is about, Aurora may be involved. Certainly they took an unusually intense interest in the case. For instance, they insisted on including Mr. Olivaw as your partner. Aurora is powerful; we had to agree. They say they include Mr. Olivaw only because he worked with you before, but it may well be that they wish a reliable man of their own on the scene, eh?"

He sipped slowly, his eyes on Baley.

Baley passed the knuckles of one hand against his long cheek, rubbing it thoughtfully. "Now if that——"

He didn't finish, but leaped from his chair and almost hurled himself toward the other, before remembering it was only an image he was facing.

For Gruer, staring wildly at his drink, clutched his throat, whispering hoarsely, "Burning . . . burning . . ."

The glass fell from his hand, its contents spilling. And Gruer dropped with it, his face distorted with pain.

7

A Doctor Is Prodded

DANEEL STOOD in the doorway. "What happened, Partner Eli——"

But no explanation was needed. Daneel's voice changed to a loud ringing shout. "Robots of Hannis Gruer! Your master is hurt! Robots!"

At once a metal figure strode into the dining room and after it, in a minute or two, a dozen more entered. Three carried Gruer gently away. The others busily engaged in straightening the disarray and picking up the tableware strewn on the floor.

Daneel called out suddenly, "You there, robots, never mind the crockery. Organize a search. Search the house for any human being. Alert any robots on the grounds outside. Have them go over every acre of the estate. If you find a master, hold him. Do not hurt him" (unnecessary advice) "but do not let him leave, either. If you find no master present, let me know. I will remain at this viewer combination."

Then, as robots scattered, Elijah muttered to Daneel, "That's a beginning. It was poison, of course."

"Yes. That much is obvious, Partner Elijah." Daneel sat down queerly, as though there were a weakness in his knees. Baley had never seen him give way so, not for an instant, to any action that resembled anything so human as a weakness in the knees.

Daneel said, "It is not well with my mechanism to see a human being come to harm."

"There was nothing you could do."

"That I understand and yet it is as though there were certain cloggings in my thought paths. In human terms what I feel might be the equivalent to shock."

"If that's so, get over it." Baley felt neither patience nor sympathy for a queasy robot. "We've got to consider the little matter of responsibility. There is no poison without a poisoner."

"It might have been food-poisoning."

"Accidental food-poisoning? On a world this neatly run? Never. Besides, the poison was in a liquid and the symptoms were sudden and complete. It was a poisoned dose and a large one. Look, Daneel, I'll go into the next room to think this out a bit. You get Mrs. Delmarre. Make sure she's at home and check the distance between her estate and Gruer's."

"Is it that you think she——"

Baley held up a hand. "Just find out, will you?"

He strode out of the room, seeking solitude. Surely there could not be two independent attempts at murder so close together in time on a world like Solaria. And if a connection existed, the easiest assumption to make was that Gruer's story of a conspiracy was true.

Baley felt a familiar excitement growing within him. He had come to this world with Earth's predicament in his mind, and his own. The murder itself had been a faraway thing, but now the chase was really on. The muscles in his jaw knotted.

After all, the murderer or murderers (or murderess) had struck in his presence and he was stung by that. Was he held in so little account? It was professional pride that was hurt and Baley knew it and welcomed the fact. At least it gave him a firm reason to see this thing through as a murder case, simply, even without reference to Earth's dangers.

Daneel had located him now and was striding toward him. "I have done as you asked me to, Partner Elijah. I have viewed Mrs. Delmarre. She is at her home, which is somewhat over a thousand miles from the estate of Agent Gruer."

Baley said, "I'll see her myself later. View her, I mean." He stared thoughtfully at Daneel. "Do you think she has any connection with this crime?"

"Apparently not a direct connection, Partner Elijah."

"Does that imply there might be an indirect connection?"

"She might have persuaded someone else to do it."

"Someone else?" Baley asked quickly. "Who?"

"That, Partner Elijah, I cannot say."

"If someone were acting for her, that someone would have to be at the scene of the crime."

"Yes," said Daneel, "someone must have been there to place the poison in the liquid."

"Isn't it possible that the poisoned liquid might have been prepared earlier in the day? Perhaps much earlier?"

Daneel said quietly, "I had thought of that, Partner Elijah, which is why I used the word 'apparently' when I stated that Mrs. Delmarre had no direct connection with the crime. It is within the realm of possibility for her to have been on the scene earlier in the day. It would be well to check her movements."

"We will do that. We will check whether she was physically present at any time."

Baley's lips twitched. He had guessed that in some ways robotic logic must fall short and he was convinced of it now. As the roboticist had said: Logical but not reasonable.

He said, "Let's get back into the viewing room and get Gruer's estate back in view."

The room sparkled with freshness and order. There was no sign at all that less than an hour before a man had collapsed in agony.

Three robots stood, backs against the wall, in the usual robotic attitude of respectful submission.

Baley said, "What news concerning your master?"

The middle robot said, "The doctor is attending him, master."

"Viewing or seeing?"

"Viewing, master."

"What does the doctor say? Will your master live?"

"It is not yet certain, master."

Baley said, "Has the house been searched?"

"Thoroughly, master."

"Was there any sign of another master beside your own?"

"No, master."

"Were there any signs of such presence in the near past?"

"Not at all, master."

"Are the grounds being searched?"

"Yes, master."

"Any results so far?"

"No, master."

Baley nodded and said, "I wish to speak to the robot that served at the table this night."

"It is being held for inspection, master. Its reactions are erratic."

"Can it speak?"

"Yes, master."

"Then get it here without delay."

There *was* delay and Baley began again. "I said——"

Daneel interrupted smoothly. "There is interradio communication among these Solarian types. The robot you desire is being summoned. If it is slow in coming, it is part of the disturbance that has overtaken it as the result of what has occurred."

Baley nodded. He might have guessed at interradio. In a world so thoroughly given over to robots some sort of intimate communication among them would be necessary if the system were not to break down. It explained how a dozen robots could follow when one robot had been summoned, but only when needed and not otherwise.

A robot entered. It limped, one leg dragging. Baley wondered why and then shrugged. Even among the primitive robots on Earth reactions to injury of the positronic paths were never obvious to the layman. A disrupted circuit might strike a leg's functioning, as here, and the fact would be most significant to a roboticist and completely meaningless to anyone else.

Baley said cautiously, "Do you remember a colorless liquid on your master's table, some of which you poured into a goblet for him?"

The robot said, "Yeth, mathter."

A defect in oral articulation, too!

Baley said, "What was the nature of the liquid?"

"It wath water, mathter."

"Just water? Nothing else?"

"Jutht water, mathter."

"Where did you get it?"

"From the rethervoir tap, mathter."

"Had it been standing in the kitchen before you brought it in?"

"The mathter preferred it not too cold, mathter. It wath a thtanding order that it be poured an hour before mealth."

How convenient, thought Baley, for anyone who knew that fact.

He said, "Have one of the robots connect me with the doctor viewing your master as soon as he is available. And while that is being done, I want another one to explain how the reservoir tap works. I want to know about the water supply here."

The doctor was available with little delay. He was the oldest Spacer Baley had ever seen, which meant, Baley thought, that he might be over three hundred years old. The veins stood out on his hands and his close-cropped hair was pure white. He had a habit of tapping his ridged front teeth with a fingernail, making a little clicking noise that Baley found annoying. His name was Altim Thool.

The doctor said, "Fortunately, he threw up a good deal of the dose. Still, he may not survive. It is a tragic event." He sighed heavily.

"What was the poison, Doctor?" asked Baley.

"I'm afraid I don't know." (Click-click-click.)

Baley said, "What? Then how are you treating him?"

"Direct stimulation of the neuromuscular system to prevent paralysis, but except for that I am letting nature take its course." His face, with its faintly yellow skin, like well-worn leather of superior quality, wore a pleading expression. "We have very little experience with this sort of thing. I don't recall another case in over two centuries of practice."

Baley stared at the other with contempt. "You know there are such things as poisons, don't you?"

"Oh yes." (Click-click.) "Common knowledge."

"You have book-film references where you can gain some knowledge."

"It would take days. There are numerous mineral poisons. We make use of insecticides in our society, and it is not impossible to obtain bacterial toxins. Even with descriptions in the films it would take a long time to gather the equipment and develop the techniques to test for them."

"If no one on Solaria knows," said Baley grimly, "I'd suggest you get in touch with one of the other worlds and find out. Meanwhile, you had better test the reservoir tap in Gruer's mansion for poison. Get there in person, if you have to, and do it."

Baley was prodding a venerable Spacer roughly, ordering him about like a robot and was quite unconscious of the incongruity of it. Nor did the Spacer make any protest.

Dr. Thool said doubtfully, "How could the reservoir tap be poisoned? I'm sure it couldn't be."

"Probably not," agreed Baley, "but test it anyway to make sure."

The reservoir tap was a dim possibility indeed. The robot's explanation had shown it to be a typical piece of Solarian self-care. Water might enter it from whatever source and be tailored to suit. Microorganisms were removed and non-living organic matter eliminated. The proper amount of aeration was introduced, as were various ions in just those trace amounts best suited to the body's needs. It was very unlikely that any poison could survive one or another of the control devices.

Still, if the safety of the reservoir were directly established, then the time element would be clear. There would be the matter of the hour before the meal, when the pitcher of water (exposed to *air*, thought Baley sourly) was allowed to warm slowly, thanks to Gruer's idiosyncrasy.

But Dr. Thool, frowning, was saying, "But how would I test the reservoir tap?"

"Jehoshaphat! Take an animal with you. Inject some of the water you take out of the tap into its veins, or have it drink some. Use your head, man. And do the same for what's left in the pitcher, and if that's poisoned, as it must be, run some of the tests the reference films describe. Find some simple ones. Do *something*."

"Wait, wait. What pitcher?"

"The pitcher in which the water was standing. The pitcher from which the robot poured the poisoned drink."

"Well, dear me—I presume it has been cleaned up. The household retinue would surely not leave it standing about."

Baley groaned. Of course not. It was *impossible* to retain evidence with eager robots forever destroying it in the name of household duty. He should have *ordered* it preserved, but of course, this society was not his own and he never reacted properly to it.

Jehoshaphat!

Word eventually came through that the Gruer estate was clear; no sign of any unauthorized human present anywhere.

Daneel said, "That rather intensifies the puzzle, Partner Elijah, since it seems to leave no one in the role of poisoner."

Baley, absorbed in thought, scarcely heard. He said, "What? . . . Not at all. Not at all. It clarifies the matter." He did not explain, knowing quite well that Daneel would be incapable of understanding or believing what Baley was certain was the truth.

Nor did Daneel ask for an explanation. Such an invasion of a human's thoughts would have been most unrobotic.

Baley prowled back and forth restlessly, dreading the approach of the sleep period, when his fears of the open would rise and his longing for Earth increase. He felt an almost feverish desire to keep things happening.

He said to Daneel, "I might as well see Mrs. Delmarre again. Have the robot make contact."

They walked to the viewing room and Baley watched a robot work with deft metal fingers. He watched through a haze of obscuring thought that vanished in startled astonishment when a table, elaborately spread for dinner, suddenly filled half the room.

Gladia's voice said, "Hello." A moment later she stepped into view and sat down. "Don't look surprised, Elijah. It's just dinnertime. And I'm very carefully dressed. See?"

She was. The dominant color of her dress was a light blue and it shimmered down the length of her limbs to wrists and ankles. A yellow ruff clung about her neck and shoulders, a little lighter than her hair, which was now held in disciplined waves.

Baley said, "I did not mean to interrupt your meal."

"I haven't begun yet. Why don't you join me?"

He eyed her suspiciously. "Join you?"

She laughed. "You Earthmen are so funny. I don't mean join me in personal presence. How could you do that? I mean, go to your own dining room and then you and the other one can dine with me."

"But if I leave——"

"Your viewing technician can maintain contact."

Daneel nodded gravely at that, and with some uncertainty Baley turned and walked toward the door. Gladia, together with her table, its setting, and its ornaments moved with him.

Gladia smiled encouragingly. "See? Your viewing technician is keeping us in contact."

Baley and Daneel traveled up a moving ramp that Baley did not recall having traversed before. Apparently there were numerous possible routes between any two rooms in this impossible mansion and he knew only few of them. Daneel, of course, knew them all.

And, moving through walls, sometimes a bit below floor level, sometimes a bit above, there was always Gladia and her dinner table.

Baley stopped and muttered, "This takes getting used to."

Gladia said at once, "Does it make you dizzy?"

"A little."

"Then I tell you what. Why don't you have your technicians freeze me right here. Then when you're in your dining room and all set, he can join us up."

Daneel said, "I will order that done, Partner Elijah."

Their own dinner table was set when they arrived, the plates steaming with a dark brown soup in which diced meat was bobbing, and in the center a large roast fowl was ready for the carving. Daneel spoke briefly to the serving robot and, with smooth efficiency, the two places that had been set were drawn to the same end of the table.

As though that were a signal, the opposite wall seemed to move outward, the table seemed to lengthen and Gladia was seated at the opposite end. Room joined to room and table to table so neatly that but for the varying pattern in wall and floor covering and the differing designs in tableware it would have been easy to believe they were all dining together in actual fact.

"There," said Gladia with satisfaction. "Isn't this comfortable?"

"Quite," said Baley. He tasted his soup gingerly, found it delicious, and helped himself more generously. "You know about Agent Gruer?"

Trouble shadowed her face at once and she put her spoon down. "Isn't it terrible? Poor Hannis."

"You use his first name. Do you know him?"

"I know almost all the important people on Solaria. Most Solarians do know one another. Naturally."

Naturally, indeed, thought Baley. How many of them were there, after all?

Baley said, "Then perhaps you know Dr. Altim Thool. He's taking care of Gruer."

Gladia laughed gently. Her serving robot sliced meat for her and added small, browned potatoes and slivers of carrots. "Of course I know him. He treated me."

"Treated you when?"

"Right after the—the trouble. About my husband, I mean."

Baley said in astonishment, "Is he the only doctor on the planet?"

"Oh no." For a moment her lips moved as though she were count-ing to herself. "There are at least ten. And there's one youngster I know of who's studying medicine. But Dr. Thool is one of the best. He has the most experience. Poor Dr. Thool."

"Why poor?"

"Well, you know what I mean. It's such a nasty job, being a doc-tor. Sometimes you just have to see people when you're a doctor and even touch them. But Dr. Thool seems so resigned to it and he'll always do some seeing when he feels he must. He's always treated me since I was a child and was always so friendly and kind and I honestly feel I almost wouldn't mind if he did have to see me. For instance, he saw me this last time."

"After your husband's death, you mean?"

"Yes. You can imagine how he felt when he saw my husband's dead body and me lying there."

"I was told he viewed the body," said Baley.

"The body, yes. But after he made sure I was alive and in no real danger, he ordered the robots to put a pillow under my head and give me an injection of something or other, and then get out. He came over by jet. Really! By jet. It took less than half an hour and he took care of me and made sure all was well. I was so woozy when I came to that I was sure I was only viewing him, you know, and it wasn't till he touched me that I knew we were seeing, and I screamed. Poor Dr. Thool. He was awfully embarrassed, but I knew he meant well."

Baley nodded. "I suppose there's not much use for doctors on Solaria?"

"I should hope *not.*"

"I know there are no germ diseases to speak of. What about meta-bolic disorders? Atherosclerosis? Diabetes? Things like that?"

"It happens and it's pretty awful when it does. Doctors can make life more livable for such people in a physical way, but that's the least of it."

"Oh?"

"Of course. It means the gene analysis was imperfect. You don't suppose we allow defects like diabetes to develop on purpose. Any-one who develops such things has to undergo very detailed re-analysis. The mate assignment has to be retracted, which is terribly embarrassing for the mate. And it means no—no"—her voice sank to a whisper—"children."

Baley said in a normal voice, "No children?"

Gladia flushed. "It's a terrible thing to say. Such a word! Ch-children!"

"It comes easy after a while," said Baley dryly.

"Yes, but if I get into the habit, I'll say it in front of another Solarian someday and I'll just sink into the ground. . . . Anyway, if the two of them have had children (see, I've said it again) already, the children have to be found and examined—that was one of Rikaine's jobs, by the way—and well, it's just a mess."

So much for Thool, thought Baley. The doctor's incompetence was a natural consequence of the society, and held nothing sinister. Nothing *necessarily* sinister. Cross him off, he thought, but lightly.

He watched Gladia as she ate. She was neat and precisely delicate in her movements and her appetite seemed normal. (His own fowl was delightful. In one respect, anyway—food—he could easily be spoiled by these Outer Worlds.)

He said, "What is your opinion of the poisoning, Gladia?"

She looked up. "I'm trying not to think of it. There are so many horrors lately. Maybe it wasn't poisoning."

"It was."

"But there wasn't anyone around?"

"How do you know?"

"There couldn't have been. He has no wife, these days, since he's all through with his quota of ch—you know what. So there was no one to put the poison in anything, so how could he be poisoned?"

"But he was poisoned. That's a fact and must be accepted."

Her eyes clouded over. "Do you suppose," she said, "he did it himself?"

"I doubt it. Why should he? And so publicly?"

"Then it couldn't be done, Elijah. It just couldn't."

Baley said, "On the contrary, Gladia. It could be done very easily. And I'm sure I know exactly how."

8

A Spacer Is Defied

GLADIA SEEMED to be holding her breath for a moment. It came out through puckered lips in what was almost a whistle. She said, "I'm sure *I* don't see how. Do you know *who* did it?"

Baley nodded. "The same one who killed your husband."

"Are you sure?"

"Aren't you? Your husband's murder was the first in the history of Solaria. A month later there is another murder. Could that be a coincidence? Two separate murderers striking within a month of each other on a crime-free world? Consider, too, that the second victim was investigating the first crime and therefore represented a violent danger to the original murderer."

"Well!" Gladia applied herself to her dessert and said between mouthfuls, "If you put it that way, I'm innocent."

"How so, Gladia?"

"Why, Elijah. I've never been near the Gruer estate, never in my whole life. So I certainly couldn't have poisoned Agent Gruer. And if I haven't—why, neither did I kill my husband."

Then, as Baley maintained a stern silence, her spirit seemed to fade and the corners of her small mouth drooped. "Don't you think so, Elijah?"

"I can't be sure," said Baley. "I've told you I know the method used to poison Gruer. It's an ingenious one and anyone on Solaria could have used it, whether they were on the Gruer estate or not; whether they were ever on the Gruer estate or not."

Gladia clenched her hands into fists. "Are you saying I did it?"

"I'm not saying that."

"You're implying it." Her lips were thin with fury and her high cheekbones were splotchy. "Is that all your interest in viewing me? To ask me sly questions? To trap me?"

"Now wait——"

"You seemed so sympathetic. So understanding. You—you Earthman!"

Her contralto had become a tortured rasp with the last word.

Daneel's perfect face leaned toward Gladia and he said, "If you will pardon me, Mrs. Delmarre, you are holding a knife rather tightly and may cut yourself. Please be careful."

Gladia stared wildly at the short, blunt, and undoubtedly quite harmless knife she held in her hand. With a spasmodic movement she raised it high.

Baley said, "You couldn't reach me, Gladia."

She gasped. "Who'd want to reach you? Ugh!" She shuddered in exaggerated disgust and called out, "Break contact at once!"

The last must have been to a robot out of the line of sight, and Gladia and her end of the room were gone and the original wall sprang back.

Daneel said, "Am I correct in believing you now consider this woman guilty?"

"No," said Baley flatly. "Whoever did this needed a great deal more of certain characteristics than this poor girl has."

"She has a temper."

"What of that? Most people do. Remember, too, that she has been under a considerable strain for a considerable time. If I had been under a similar strain and someone had turned on me as she imagined I had turned on her, I might have done a great deal more than wave a foolish little knife."

Daneel said, "I have not been able to deduce the technique of poisoning at a distance, as you say you have."

Baley found it pleasant to be able to say, "I know you haven't. You lack the capacity to decipher this particular puzzle."

He said it with finality and Daneel accepted the statement as calmly and as gravely as ever.

Baley said, "I have two jobs for you, Daneel."

"And what are they, Partner Elijah?"

"First, get in touch with this Dr. Thool and find out Mrs. Delmarre's condition at the time of the murder of her husband. How long she required treatment and so on."

"Do you want to determine something in particular?"

"No. I'm just trying to accumulate data. It isn't easy on this world. Secondly, find out who will be taking Gruer's place as head of security and arrange a viewing session for me first thing in the morning. As for me," he said without pleasure in his mind, and with none in his voice, "I'm going to bed and eventually, I hope, I'll sleep." Then, almost petulantly, "Do you suppose I could get a decent book-film in this place?"

Daneel said, "I would suggest that you summon the robot in charge of the library."

Baley felt only irritation at having to deal with the robot. He would much rather have browsed at will.

"No," he said, "not a classic; just an ordinary piece of fiction dealing with everyday life on contemporary Solaria. About half a dozen of them."

The robot submitted (it would have to) but even as it manipulated the proper controls that plucked the requisite book-films out of their niches and transferred them first to an exit slot and then to Baley's hand, it rattled on in respectful tones about all the other categories in the library.

The master might like an adventure romance of the days of exploration, it suggested, or an excellent view of chemistry, perhaps, with animated atom models, or a fantasy, or a Galactography. The list was endless.

Baley waited grimly for his half dozen, said, "These will do," reached with his own hands (his *own* hands) for a scanner and walked away.

When the robot followed and said, "Will you require help with the adjustment, master?" Baley turned and snapped, "No. Stay where you are."

The robot bowed and stayed.

Lying in bed, with the headboard aglow, Baley almost regretted his decision. The scanner was like no model he had ever used and he began with no idea at all as to the method for threading the film. But he worked at it obstinately, and, eventually, by taking it apart and working it out bit by bit, he managed something.

At least he could view the film and, if the focus left a bit to be desired, it was small payment for a moment's independence from the robots.

In the next hour and a half he had skipped and switched through four of the six films and was disappointed.

He had had a theory. There was no better way, he had thought, to get an insight into Solarian ways of life and thought than to read their novels. He needed that insight if he were to conduct the investigation sensibly.

But now he had to abandon his theories. He had viewed novels and had succeeded only in learning of people with ridiculous problems who behaved foolishly and reacted mysteriously. Why should a woman abandon her job on discovering her child had entered the same profession and refuse to explain her reasons until unbearable and ridiculous complications had resulted? Why should a doctor and an artist be humiliated at being assigned to one another and what was so noble about the doctor's insistence on entering robotic research?

He threaded the fifth novel into the scanner and adjusted it to his eyes. He was bone-weary.

So weary, in fact, that he never afterward recalled anything of the fifth novel (which he believed to be a suspense story) except for the opening in which a new estate owner entered his mansion and looked through the past account films presented him by a respectful robot.

Presumably he fell asleep then with the scanner on his head and all lights blazing. Presumably a robot, entering respectfully, had gently removed the scanner and put out the lights.

In any case, he slept and dreamed of Jessie. All was as it had been. He had never left Earth. They were ready to travel to the community kitchen and then to see a subetheric show with friends. They would travel over the Expressways and see people and neither of them had a care in the world. He was happy.

And Jessie was beautiful. She had lost weight somehow. Why should she be so slim? And so beautiful?

And one other thing was wrong. Somehow the sun shone down on them. He looked up and there was only the vaulted base of the upper Levels visible, yet the sun shone down, blazing brightly on everything, and no one was afraid.

Baley woke up, disturbed. He let the robots serve breakfast and did not speak to Daneel. He said nothing, asked nothing, downed excellent coffee without tasting it.

Why had he dreamed of the visible-invisible sun? He could understand dreaming of Earth and of Jessie, but what had the sun to do with it? And why should the thought of it bother him, anyway?

"Partner Elijah," said Daneel gently.

"What?"

"Corwin Attlebish will be in viewing contact with you in half an hour. I have arranged that."

"Who the hell is Corwin Whatchamacullum?" asked Baley sharply, and refilled his coffee cup.

"He was Agent Gruer's chief aide, Partner Elijah, and is now Acting Head of Security."

"Then get him now."

"The appointment, as I explained, is for half an hour from now."

"I don't care when it's for. Get him now. That's an order."

"I will make the attempt, Partner Elijah. He may not, however, agree to receive the call."

"Let's take the chance, and get on with it, Daneel."

The Acting Head of Security accepted the call and, for the first time on Solaria, Baley saw a Spacer who looked like the usual Earthly conception of one. Attlebish was tall, lean, and bronze. His eyes were a light brown, his chin large and hard.

He looked faintly like Daneel. But whereas Daneel was idealized, almost godlike, Corwin Attlebish had lines of humanity in his face.

Attlebish was shaving. The small abrasive pencil gave out its spray of fine particles that swept over cheek and chin, biting off the hair neatly and then disintegrating into impalpable dust.

Baley recognized the instrument through hearsay but had never seen one used before.

"You the Earthman?" asked Attlebish slurringly through barely cracked lips, as the abrasive dust passed under his nose.

Baley said, "I'm Elijah Baley, Plainclothesman C-7. I'm from Earth."

"You're early." Attlebish snapped his shaver shut and tossed it somewhere outside Baley's range of vision. "What's on your mind, Earthman?"

Baley would not have enjoyed the other's tone of voice at the best of times. He burned now. He said, "How is Agent Gruer?"

Attlebish said, "He's still alive. He may stay alive."

Baley nodded. "Your poisoners here on Solaria don't know dosages. Lack of experience. They gave Gruer too much and he threw it up. Half the dose would have killed him."

"Poisoners? There is no evidence for poison."

Baley stared. "Jehoshaphat! What else do you think it is?"

"A number of things. Much can go wrong with a person." He rubbed his face, looking for roughness with his fingertips. "You would scarcely know the metabolic problems that arise past the age of two fifty."

"If that's the case, have you obtained competent medical advice?"

"Dr. Thool's report——"

That did it. The anger that had been boiling inside Baley since waking burst through. He cried at the top of his voice, "I don't care about Dr. Thool. I said competent medical advice. Your doctors don't know anything, any more than your detectives would, if you had any. You had to get a detective from Earth. Get a doctor as well."

The Solarian looked at him coolly. "Are you telling me what to do?"

"Yes, and without charge. Be my guest. Gruer *was* poisoned. I witnessed the process. He drank, retched, and yelled that his throat was burning. What do you call it when you consider that he was investigating——" Baley came to a sudden halt.

"Investigating what?" Attlebish was unmoved.

Baley was uncomfortably aware of Daneel at his usual position some ten feet away. Gruer had not wanted Daneel, as an Auroran, to know of the investigation. He said lamely, "There were political implications."

Attlebish crossed his arms and looked distant, bored, and faintly hostile. "We have no politics on Solaria in the sense we hear of it on other worlds. Hannis Gruer has been a good citizen, but he is imaginative. It was he who, having heard some story about you, urged that we import you. He even agreed to accept an Auroran companion for you as a condition. I did not think it necessary. There is no mystery. Rikaine Delmarre was killed by his wife and we shall find out how and why. Even if we do not, she will be genetically analyzed and the proper measures taken. As for Gruer, your fantasy concerning poisoning is of no importance."

Baley said incredulously, "You seem to imply that I'm not needed here."

"I believe not. If you wish to return to Earth, you may do so. I may even say we urge you to."

Baley was amazed at his own reaction. He cried, "No, sir. I don't budge."

"We hired you, Plainclothesman. We can discharge you. You will return to your home planet."

"*No!* You listen to me. I'd advise you to. You're a big-time Spacer and I'm an Earthman, but with all respect, with deepest and most humble apologies, you're scared."

"Withdraw that statement!" Attlebish drew himself to his six-foot-plus, and stared down at the Earthman haughtily.

"You're scared as hell. You think you'll be next if you pursue this thing. You're giving in so they'll let you alone; so they'll leave you your miserable life." Baley had no notion who the "they" might be or if there were any "they" at all. He was striking out blindly at an arrogant Spacer and enjoying the thud his phrases made as they hit against the other's self-control.

"You will leave," said Attlebish, pointing his finger in cold anger, "within the hour. There'll be no diplomatic considerations about this, I assure you."

"Save your threats, Spacer. Earth is nothing to you, I admit, but I'm not the only one here. May I introduce my partner, Daneel Olivaw. He's from Aurora. He doesn't talk much. He's not here to talk. I handle that department. But he listens awfully well. He doesn't miss a word.

"Let me put it straight, Attlebish"—Baley used the unadorned name with relish—"whatever monkeyshines are going on here on Solaria, Aurora and forty-odd other Outer Worlds are interested. If you kick us off, the next deputation to visit Solaria will consist of warships. I'm from Earth and I know how the system works. Hurt feelings mean warships by return trip."

Attlebish transferred his regard to Daneel and seemed to be considering. His voice was gentler. "There is nothing going on here that need concern anyone outside the planet."

"Gruer thought otherwise and my partner heard him." This was no time to cavil at a lie.

Daneel turned to look at Baley, at the Earthman's last statement, but Baley paid no attention. He drove on: "I intend to pursue this investigation. Ordinarily, there's nothing I wouldn't do to get back to Earth. Even just dreaming about it gets me so restless I can't sit. If I owned this robot-infested palace I'm living in now, I'd give it with the robots thrown in and you and all your lousy world to boot for a ticket home.

"But I won't be ordered off by you. Not while there's a case to which I've been assigned that's still open. Try getting rid of me against my will and you'll be looking down the throats of space-based artillery.

"What's more, from now on, this murder investigation is going to be run *my* way. I'm in charge. I see the people I want to see. I *see* them. I don't view them. I'm used to seeing and that's the way it's going to be. I'll want the official approval of your office for all of that."

"This is impossible, unbearable——"

"Daneel, you tell him."

The humanoid's voice said dispassionately, "As my partner has informed you, Agent Attlebish, we have been sent here to conduct a murder investigation. It is essential that we do so. We, of course, do not wish to disturb any of your customs and perhaps actual seeing will be unnecessary, although it would be helpful if you were to give approval for such seeing as becomes necessary as Plainclothesman Baley has requested. As to leaving the planet against our will, we feel that would be inadvisable, although we regret any feeling on your part or on the part of any Solarian that our remaining would be unpleasant."

Baley listened to the stilted sentence structure with a dour stretching of his lips that was not a smile. To one who knew Daneel as a robot, it was all an attempt to do a job without giving offense to any human, not to Baley and not to Attlebish. To one who thought Daneel was an Auroran, a native of the oldest and most powerful militarily of the Outer Worlds, it sounded like a series of subtly courteous threats.

Attlebish put the tips of his fingers to his forehead. "I'll think about it."

"Not too long," said Baley, "because I have some visiting to do within the hour, and not by viewer. Done viewing!"

He signaled the robot to break contact, then he stared with surprise and pleasure at the place where Attlebish had been. None of this had been planned. It had all been impulse born of his dream and of Attlebish's unnecessary arrogance. But now that it had happened, he was glad. It was what he had wanted, really—to take control.

He thought: Anyway, that was telling the dirty Spacer!

He wished the entire population of Earth could have been here to watch. The man *looked* such a Spacer, and that made it all the better, of course. All the better.

Only, why this feeling of vehemence in the matter of seeing? Baley scarcely understood that. He knew what he planned to do, and seeing (not viewing) was part of it. All right. Yet there had been the tight lift to his spirit when he spoke of seeing, as though he were ready to break down the walls of this mansion even though it served no purpose.

Why?

There was something impelling him beside the case, something that had nothing to do even with the question of Earth's safety. But what?

Oddly, he remembered his dream again; the sun shining down through all the opaque layers of the gigantic underground Cities of Earth.

Daneel said with thoughtfulness (as far as his voice could carry a recognizable emotion), "I wonder, Partner Elijah, if this is entirely safe."

"Bluffing this character? It worked. And it wasn't really a bluff. I think it *is* important to Aurora to find out what's going on on Solaria, and that Aurora knows it. Thank you, by the way, for not catching me out in a misstatement."

"It was the natural decision. To have borne you out did Agent Attlebish a certain rather subtle harm. To have given you the lie would have done you a greater and more direct harm."

"Potentials countered and the higher one won out, eh, Daneel?"

"So it was, Partner Elijah. I understand that this process, in a less definable way, goes on within the human mind. I repeat, however, that this new proposal of yours is not safe."

"Which new proposal is this?"

"I do not approve your notion of seeing people. By that I mean seeing as opposed to viewing."

"I understand you. I'm not asking for your approval."

"I have my instructions, Partner Elijah. What it was that Agent Hannis Gruer told you during my absence last night I cannot know. That he did say something is obvious from the change in your attitude toward this problem. However, in the light of my instructions, I can guess. He must have warned you of the possibility of danger to other planets arising from the situation on Solaria."

Slowly Baley reached for his pipe. He did that occasionally and always there was the feeling of irritation when he found nothing and remembered he could not smoke. He said, "There are only twenty thousand Solarians. What danger can they represent?"

"My masters on Aurora have for some time been uneasy about Solaria. I have not been told all the information at their disposal——"

"And what little you have been told you have been told not to repeat to me. Is that it?" demanded Baley.

Daneel said, "There is a great deal to find out before this matter can be discussed freely."

"Well, what are the Solarians doing? New weapons? Paid subversion? A campaign of individual assassination? What can twenty thousand people do against hundreds of millions of Spacers?"

Daneel remained silent.

Baley said, "I intend to find out, you know."

"But not the way you have now proposed, Partner Elijah. I have been instructed most carefully to guard your safety."

"You would have to anyway. First Law!"

"Over and above that, as well. In conflict between your safety and that of another I must guard yours."

"Of course. I understand that. If anything happens to me, there is no further way in which you can remain on Solaria without complications that Aurora is not yet ready to face. As long as I'm alive, I'm here at Solaria's original request and so we can throw our weight around, if necessary, and make them keep us. If I'm dead, the whole situation is changed. Your orders are, then, to keep Baley alive. Am I right, Daneel?"

Daneel said, "I cannot presume to interpret the reasoning behind my orders."

Baley said, "All right, don't worry. The open space won't kill me, if I do find it necessary to see anyone. I'll survive. I may even get used to it."

"It is not the matter of open space alone, Partner Elijah," said Daneel. "It is this matter of seeing Solarians. I do not approve of it."

"You mean the Spacers won't like it. Too bad if they don't. Let them wear nose filters and gloves. Let them spray the air. And if it offends their nice morals to see me in the flesh, let them wince and blush. But I intend to see them. I consider it necessary to do so and I *will* do so."

"But I cannot allow you to."

"*You* can't allow *me?*"

"Surely you see why, Partner Elijah."

"I do not."

"Consider, then, that Agent Gruer, the key Solarian figure in the investigation of this murder, has been poisoned. Does it not follow that if I permit you to proceed in your plan for exposing yourself indiscriminately in actual person, the next victim will necessarily be you yourself. How then can I possibly permit you to leave the safety of this mansion?"

"How will you stop me, Daneel?"

"By force, if necessary, Partner Elijah," said Daneel calmly. "Even if I must hurt you. If I do not do so, you will surely die."

9

A Robot Is Stymied

BALEY SAID, "So the higher potential wins out again, Daneel. You will hurt me to keep me alive."

"I do not believe hurting you will be necessary, Partner Elijah. You know that I am superior to you in strength and you will not attempt a useless resistance. If it should become necessary, however, I will be compelled to hurt you."

"I could blast you down where you stand," said Baley. "Right now! There is nothing in *my* potentials to prevent me."

"I had thought you might take this attitude at some time in our present relationship, Partner Elijah. Most particularly, the thought occurred to me during our trip to this mansion, when you grew momentarily violent in the ground-car .The destruction of myself is unimportant in comparison with your safety, but such destruction would cause you distress eventually and disturb the plans of my masters. It was one of my first cares, therefore, during your first sleeping period, to deprive your blaster of its charge."

Baley's lips tightened. He was left without a charged blaster! His hand dropped instantly to his holster. He drew his weapon and stared at the charge reading. It hugged zero.

For a moment he balanced the lump of useless metal as though to hurl it directly into Daneel's face. What good? The robot would dodge efficiently.

Baley put the blaster back. It could be recharged in good time.

Slowly, thoughtfully, he said, "I'm not fooled by you, Daneel."

"In what way, Partner Elijah."

"You are too much the master. I am too completely stopped by you. Are you a robot?"

"You have doubted me before," said Daneel.

"On Earth last year, I doubted whether R. Daneel Olivaw was truly a robot. It turned out he was. I believe he still is. My question, however is this: Are you R. Daneel Olivaw?"

"I am."

"Yes? Daneel was designed to imitate a Spacer closely. Why could not a Spacer be made up to imitate Daneel closely?"

"For what reason?"

"To carry on an investigation here with greater initiative and capacity than ever a robot could. And yet by assuming Daneel's role, you could keep me safely under control by giving me a false consciousness of mastery. After all, you are working through me and I must be kept pliable."

"All this is not so, Partner Elijah."

"Then why do all the Solarians we meet assume you to be human? They are robotic experts. Are they so easily fooled? It occurs to me that I cannot be one right against many wrong. It is far more likely that I am one wrong against many right."

"Not at all, Partner Elijah."

"Prove it," said Baley, moving slowly toward an end table and lifting a scrap-disposal unit. "You can do that easily enough, if you *are* a robot. Show the metal beneath your skin."

Daneel said, "I assure you——"

"Show the metal," said Baley crisply. "That is an order! Or don't you feel compelled to obey orders?"

Daneel unbuttoned his shirt. The smooth, bronze skin of his chest was sparsely covered with light hair. Daneel's fingers exerted a firm pressure just under the right nipple, and flesh and skin split bloodlessly the length of the chest, with the gleam of metal showing beneath.

And as that happened, Baley's fingers, resting on the end table, moved half an inch to the right and stabbed at a contact patch. Almost at once a robot entered.

"Don't move, Daneel," cried Baley. "That's an order! Freeze!"

Daneel stood motionless, as though life, or the robotic imitation thereof, had departed from him.

Baley shouted to the robot, "Can you get two more of the staff in here without yourself leaving? If so, do it."

The robot said, "Yes, master."

Two more robots entered, answering a radioed call. The three lined up abreast.

"Boys!" said Baley. "Do you see this creature whom you thought a master?"

Six ruddy eyes had turned solemnly on Daneel. They said in unison, "We see him, master."

Baley said, "Do you also see that this so-called master is actually a robot like yourself since it is metal within. It is only designed to look like a man."

"Yes, master."

"You are not required to obey any order it gives you. Do you understand that?"

"Yes, master."

"I, on the other hand," said Baley, "am a true man."

For a moment the robots hesitated. Baley wondered if, having had it shown to them that a thing might seem a man yet be a robot, they would accept *anything* in human appearance as a man, anything at all.

But then one robot said, "You are a man, master," and Baley drew breath again.

He said, "Very well, Daneel. You may relax."

Daneel moved into a more natural position and said calmly, "Your expressed doubt as to my identity, then, was merely a feint designed to exhibit my nature to these others, I take it."

"So it was," said Baley, and looked away. He thought: The thing is a machine, not a man. You can't double-cross a machine.

And yet he couldn't entirely repress a feeling of shame. Even as Daneel stood there, chest open, there seemed something so human about him, something capable of being betrayed.

Baley said, "Close your chest, Daneel, and listen to me. Physically, you are no match for three robots. You see that, don't you?"

"That is clear, Partner Elijah."

"Good! . . . Now you boys," and he turned to the other robots again. "You are to tell no one, human or master, that this creature is a robot. Never at any time, without further instructions from myself and myself alone."

"I thank you," interposed Daneel softly.

"However," Baley went on, "this manlike robot is not to be allowed to interfere with my actions in any way. If it attempts any such interference, you will restrain it by force, taking care not to damage it unless absolutely necessary. Do not allow it to establish contact with humans other than myself, or with robots other than yourselves, either by seeing or by viewing. And do not leave it at any time. Keep it in this room and remain here yourselves. Your other duties are suspended until further notice. Is all this clear?"

"Yes, master," they chorused.

Baley turned to Daneel again. "There is nothing you can do now, so don't try to stop me."

Daneel's arms hung loosely at his side. He said, "I may not, through inaction, allow you to come to harm, Partner Elijah. Yet under the circumstances, nothing but inaction is possible. The logic is unassailable. I shall do nothing. I trust you will remain safe and in good health."

There it was, thought Baley. Logic was logic and robots had nothing else. Logic told Daneel he was completely stymied. Reason might have told him that all factors are rarely predictable, that the opposition might make a mistake.

None of that. A robot is logical only, not reasonable.

Again Baley felt a twinge of shame and could not forbear an attempt at consolation. He said, "Look, Daneel, even if I were walking into danger, *which I'm not*" (he added that hurriedly, with a quick glance at the other robots) "it would only be my job. It is what I'm paid to do. It is as much my job to prevent harm to mankind as a whole as yours is to prevent harm to man as an individual. Do you see?"

"I do not, Partner Elijah."

"Then that is because you're not made to see. Take my word for it that if you were a man, you would see."

Daneel bowed his head in acquiescence and remained standing, motionless, while Baley walked slowly toward the door of the room. The three robots parted to make room for him and kept their photoelectric eyes fixed firmly on Daneel.

Baley was walking to a kind of freedom and his heart beat rapidly in anticipation of the fact, then skipped a beat. Another robot was approaching the door from the other side.

Had something gone wrong?

"What is it, boy?" he snapped.

"A message has been forwarded to you, master, from the office of Acting Head of Security Attlebish."

Baley took the personal capsule handed to him and it opened at once. A finely inscribed strip of paper unrolled. (He wasn't startled. Solaria would have his fingerprints on file and the capsule would be adjusted to open at the touch of his particular convolutions.)

He read the message and his long face mirrored satisfaction. It was his official permission to arrange "seeing" interviews, subject to the wishes of the interviewees, who were nevertheless urged to give "Agents Baley and Olivaw" every possible co-operation.

Attlebish had capitulated, even to the extent of putting the Earthman's name first. It was an excellent omen with which to begin, finally, an investigation conducted as it should be conducted.

Baley was in an air-borne vessel again, as he had been on that trip from New York to Washington. This time, however, there was a difference. The vessel was not closed in. The windows were left transparent.

It was a clear, bright day and from where Baley sat the windows were so many patches of blue. Unrelieved, featureless. He tried not to huddle. He buried his head in his knees only when he could absolutely no longer help it.

The ordeal was of his own choosing. His state of triumph, his unusual sense of freedom at having beaten down first Attlebish and then Daneel, his feeling of having asserted the dignity of Earth against the Spacers, almost demanded it.

He had begun by stepping across open ground to the waiting plane with a kind of lightheaded dizziness that was almost enjoyable, and he had ordered the windows left unblanked in a kind of manic self-confidence.

I have to get used to it, he thought, and stared at the blue until his heart beat rapidly and the lump in his throat swelled beyond endurance.

He had to close his eyes and bury his head under the protective cover of his arms at shortening intervals. Slowly his confidence trickled away and even the touch of the holster of his freshly recharged blaster could not reverse the flow.

He tried to keep his mind on his plan of attack. First, learn the ways of the planet. Sketch in the background against which everything must be placed or fail to make sense.

See a sociologist!

He had asked a robot for the name of the Solarian most eminent as a sociologist. And there was that comfort about robots; they asked no questions.

The robot gave the name and vital statistics, and paused to remark that the sociologist would most probably be at lunch and would, therefore, possibly ask to delay contact.

"Lunch!" said Baley sharply. "Don't be ridiculous. It's not noon by two hours."

The robot said, "I am using local time, master."

Baley stared, then understood. On Earth, with its buried Cities, day and night, waking and sleeping, were man-made periods, adjusted to suit the needs of the community and the planet. On a planet such as this one, exposed nakedly to the sun, day and night were not a matter of choice at all, but were imposed on man willy-nilly.

Baley tried to picture a world as a sphere being lit and unlit as it turned. He found it hard to do and felt scornful of the so-superior Spacers who let such an essential thing as time be dictated to them by the vagaries of planetary movements.

He said, "Contact him anyway."

Robots were there to meet the plane when it landed and Baley, stepping out into the open again, found himself trembling badly.

He muttered to the nearest of the robots, "Let me hold your arm, boy."

The sociologist waited for him down the length of a hall, smiling tightly. "Good afternoon, Mr. Baley."

Baley nodded breathlessly. "Good evening, sir. Would you blank out the windows?"

The sociologist said, "They are blanked out already. I know something of the ways of Earth. Will you follow me?"

Baley managed it without robotic help, following at a considerable distance, across and through a maze of hallways. When he finally sat down in a large and elaborate room, he was glad of the opportunity to rest.

The walls of the room were set with curved, shallow alcoves. Statuary in pink and gold occupied each niche; abstract figures that pleased the eye without yielding instant meaning. A large, boxlike affair with white and dangling cylindrical objects and numerous pedals suggested a musical instrument.

Baley looked at the sociologist standing before him. The Spacer looked precisely as he had when Baley had viewed him earlier that day. He was tall and thin and his hair was pure white. His face was strikingly wedge-shaped, his nose prominent, his eyes deep-set and alive.

His name was Anselmo Quemot.

They stared at one another until Baley felt he could trust his voice to be reasonably normal. And then his first remark had nothing to do with the investigation. In fact it was nothing he had planned.

He said, "May I have a drink?"

"A drink?" The sociologist's voice was a trifle too high-pitched to be entirely pleasant. He said, "You wish water?"

"I'd prefer something alcoholic."

The sociologist's look grew sharply uneasy, as though the obligations of hospitality were something with which he was unacquainted.

And that, thought Baley, was literally so. In a world where viewing was the thing, there would be no sharing of food and drink.

A robot brought him a small cup of smooth enamel. The drink was a light pink in color. Baley sniffed at it cautiously and tasted it even more cautiously. The small sip of liquid evaporated warmly in his mouth and sent a pleasant message along the length of his esophagus. His next sip was more substantial.

Quemot said, "If you wish more——"

"No, thank you, not now. It is good of you, sir, to agree to see me."

Quemot tried a smile and failed rather markedly, "It has been a long time since I've done anything like this. Yes."

He almost squirmed as he spoke.

Baley said, "I imagine you find this rather hard."

"Quite." Quemot turned away sharply and retreated to a chair at the opposite end of the room. He angled the chair so that it faced more away from Baley than toward him and sat down. He clasped his gloved hands and his nostrils seemed to quiver.

Baley finished his drink and felt warmth in his limbs and even the return of something of his confidence.

He said, "Exactly how *does* it feel to have me here, Dr. Quemot?"

The sociologist muttered, "That is an uncommonly personal question."

"I know it is. But I think I explained when I viewed you earlier that I was engaged in a murder investigation and that I would have to ask a great many questions, some of which were bound to be personal."

"I'll help if I can," said Quemot. "I hope the questions will be decent ones." He kept looking away as he spoke. His eyes, when they struck Baley's face, did not linger, but slipped away.

Baley said, "I don't ask about your feelings out of curiosity only. This is essential to the investigation."

"I don't see how."

"I've got to know as much as I can about this world. I must understand how Solarians feel about ordinary matters. Do you see that?"

Quemot did not look at Baley at all now. He said slowly, "Ten years ago, my wife died. Seeing her was never very easy, but, of course, it is something one learns to bear in time and she was not the intrusive sort. I have been assigned no new wife since I am past the age of—of"—he looked at Baley as though requesting him to supply the phrase, and when Baley did not do so, he continued in a lower voice—"siring. Without even a wife, I have grown quite unused to this phenomenon of seeing."

"But how does it feel?" insisted Baley. "Are you in panic?" He thought of himself on the plane.

"No. Not in panic." Quemot angled his head to catch a glimpse of Baley and almost instantly withdrew. "But I will be frank, Mr. Baley. I imagine I can smell you."

Baley automatically leaned back in his chair, painfully self-conscious. "Smell me?"

"Quite imaginary, of course," said Quemot. "I cannot say whether you do have an odor or how strong it is, but even if you had a strong one, my nose filters would keep it from me. Yet, imagination . . ." He shrugged.

"I understand."

"It's worse. You'll forgive me, Mr. Baley, but in the actual presence of a human, I feel strongly as though something slimy were about to touch me. I keep shrinking away. It is most unpleasant."

Baley rubbed his ear thoughtfully and fought to keep down annoyance. After all, it was the other's neurotic reaction to a simple state of affairs.

He said, "If all this is so, I'm surprised you agreed to see me so readily. Surely you anticipated this unpleasantness."

"I did. But you know, I was curious. You're an Earthman."

Baley thought sardonically that that should have been another argument against seeing, but he said only, "What does that matter?"

A kind of jerky enthusiasm entered Quemot's voice. "It's not something I can explain easily. Not even to myself, really. But I've worked on sociology for ten years now. Really worked. I've developed propositions that are quite new and startling, and yet basically true. It is one of these propositions that makes me most extraordinarily interested in Earth and Earthmen. You see, if you were to consider Solaria's society and way of life carefully, it will become obvious to you that the said society and way of life is modeled directly and closely on that of Earth itself."

10

A Culture Is Traced

BALEY COULD not prevent himself from crying out, "What!"

Quemot looked over his shoulder as the moments of silence passed and said finally, "Not Earth's present culture. No."

Baley said, "Oh."

"But in the past, yes. Earth's ancient history. As an Earthman, you know it, of course."

"I've viewed books," said Baley cautiously.

"Ah. Then you understand."

Baley, who did not, said, "Let me explain exactly what I want, Dr. Quemot. I want you to tell me what you can about why Solaria is so different from the other Outer Worlds, why there are so many robots, why you behave as you do. I'm sorry if I seem to be changing the subject."

Baley most definitely wanted to change the subject. Any discussion of a likeness or unlikeness between Solaria's culture and Earth's would prove too absorbing by half. He might spend the day there and come away none the wiser as far as useful information was concerned.

Quemot smiled. "You want to compare Solaria and the other Outer Worlds and not Solaria and Earth."

"I know Earth, sir."

"As you wish." The Solarian coughed slightly. "Do you mind if I turn my chair completely away from you? It would be more—more comfortable."

"As you wish, Dr. Quemot," said Baley stiffly.

"Good." A robot turned the chair at Quemot's low-voiced order, and as the sociologist sat there, hidden from Baley's eyes by the substantial chair back, his voice took on added life and even deepened and strengthened in tone.

Quemot said, "Solaria was first settled about three hundred years ago. The original settlers were Nexonians. Are you acquainted with Nexon?"

"I'm afraid not."

"It is close to Solaria, only about two parsecs away. In fact, Solaria and Nexon represent the closest pair of inhabited worlds in the Galaxy. Solaria, even when uninhabited by man, was life-bearing and eminently suited for human occupation. It represented an obvious attraction to the well-to-do of Nexon, who found it difficult to maintain a proper standard of living as their own planet filled up."

Baley interrupted. "Filled up? I thought Spacers practiced population control."

"Solaria does, but the Outer Worlds in general control it rather laxly. Nexon was completing its second million of population at the time I speak of. There was sufficient crowding to make it necessary to regulate the number of robots that might be owned by a particular family. So those Nexonians who could established summer homes on Solaria, which was fertile, temperate, and without dangerous fauna.

"The settlers on Solaria could still reach Nexon without too much trouble and while on Solaria they could live as they pleased. They could use as many robots as they could afford or felt a need for. Estates could be as large as desired since, with an empty planet, room was no problem, and with unlimited robots, exploitation was no problem.

"Robots grew to be so many that they were outfitted with radio contact and that was the beginning of our famous robot industries. We began to develop new varieties, new attachments, new capabilities. Culture dictates invention; a phrase I believe I have invented." Quemot chuckled.

A robot, responding to some stimulus Baley could not see beyond the barrier of the chair, brought Quemot a drink similar to that Baley had had earlier. None was brought to Baley, and he decided not to ask for one.

Quemot went on, "The advantages of life on Solaria were obvious to all who watched. Solaria became fashionable. More Nexonians established homes, and Solaria became what I like to call a 'villa planet.' And of the settlers, more and more took to remaining on the planet all year round and carrying on their business on Nexon through proxies. Robot factories were established on Solaria. Farms and mines began to be exploited to the point where exports were possible.

"In short, Mr. Baley, it became obvious that Solaria, in the space of a century or less, would be as crowded as Nexon had been. It seemed ridiculous and wasteful to find such a new world and then lose it through lack of foresight.

"To spare you a great deal of complicated politics, I need say only that Solaria managed to establish its independence and make it stick without war. Our usefulness to other Outer Worlds as a source of specialty robots gained us friends and helped us, of course.

"Once independent, our first care was to make sure that population did not grow beyond reasonable limits. We regulate immigration and births and take care of all needs by increasing and diversifying the robots we use."

Baley said, "Why is it the Solarians object to seeing one another?" He felt annoyed at the manner in which Quemot chose to expound sociology.

Quemot peeped around the corner of his chair and retreated almost at once. "It follows inevitably. We have huge estates. An estate ten thousand square miles in area is not uncommon, although the largest ones contain considerable unproductive areas. My own estate is nine hundred fifty square miles in area but every bit of it is good land.

"In any case, it is the size of an estate, more than anything else, that determines a man's position in society. And one property of a large estate is this: You can wander about in it almost aimlessly with little or no danger of entering a neighbor's territory and thus encountering your neighbor. You see?"

Baley shrugged. "I suppose I do."

"In short, a Solarian takes pride in not meeting his neighbor. At the same time, his estate is so well run by robots and so self-sufficient that there is no reason for him to have to meet his neighbor. The desire not to do so led to the development of ever more perfect viewing equipment, and as the viewing equipment grew better there was less and less need ever to see one's neighbor. It was a reinforcing cycle, a kind of feed-back. Do you see?"

Baley said, "Look here, Dr. Quemot. You don't have to make all this so simple for me. I'm not a sociologist but I've had the usual elementary courses in college. It's only an Earth college, of course," Baley added with a reluctant modesty designed to ward off the same comment, in more insulting terms, from the other, "but I can follow mathematics."

"Mathematics?" said Quemot, his voice squeaking the last syllable.

"Well, not the stuff they use in robotics, which I *wouldn't* follow, but sociological relationships I can handle. For instance, I'm familiar with the Teramin Relationship."

"The what, sir?"

"Maybe you have a different name for it. The differential of inconveniences suffered with privileges granted: dee eye sub jay taken to the nth——"

"What are you talking about?" It was the sharp and peremptory tone of a Spacer that Baley heard and he was silenced in bewilderment.

Surely the relationship between inconveniences suffered and privileges granted was part of the very essentials of learning how to handle people without an explosion. A private stall in the community bathroom for one person, given for cause, would keep x persons waiting patiently for the same lightning to strike them, the value of x varying in known ways with known variations in environment and human temperament, as quantitatively described in the Teramin Relationship.

But then again, in a world where all was privilege and nothing inconvenience, the Teramin Relationship might reduce to triviality. Perhaps he had chosen the wrong example.

He tried again. "Look, sir, it's one thing to get a qualitative fill-in on the growth of this prejudice against seeing, but it isn't helpful for my purposes. I want to know the exact analysis of the prejudice so I can counteract it effectively. I want to persuade people to see me, as you are doing now."

"Mr. Baley," said Quemot, "you can't treat human emotions as though they were built about a positronic brain."

"I'm not saying you can. Robotics is a deductive science and sociology an inductive one. But mathematics can be made to apply in either case."

There was silence for a moment. Then Quemot spoke in a voice that trembled. "You have admitted you are not a sociologist."

"I know. But I was told you *were* one. The best on the planet."

"I am the only one. You might almost say I have invented the science."

"Oh?" Baley hesitated over the next question. It sounded impertinent even to himself. "Have you viewed books on the subject?"

"I've looked at some Auroran books."

"Have you looked at books from Earth?"

"Earth?" Quemot laughed uneasily. "It wouldn't have occurred to me to read any of Earth's scientific productions. No offense intended."

"Well, I'm sorry. I had thought I would be able to get specific data that would make it possible for me to interview others face to face without having to——"

Quemot made a queer, grating, inarticulate sound and the large chair in which he sat scraped backward, then went over with a crash.

A muffled "My apologies" was caught by Baley.

Baley had a momentary glimpse of Quemot running with an ungainly stride, then he was out the room and gone.

Baley's eyebrows lifted. What the devil had he said this time? Jehoshaphat! What wrong button had he pushed?

Tentatively he rose from his seat, and stopped halfway as a robot entered.

"Master," said the robot, "I have been directed to inform you that the master will view you in a few moments."

"*View* me, boy?"

"Yes, master. In the meanwhile, you may desire further refreshment."

Another beaker of the pink liquid was at Baley's elbow and this time a dish of some confectionary, warm and fragrant, was added.

Baley took his seat again, sampled the liquor cautiously and put it down. The confectionary was hard to the touch and warm, but the crust broke easily in the mouth and the inner portion was at once considerably warmer and softer. He could not identify the components of the taste and wondered if it might not be a product of the native spices or condiments of Solaria.

Then he thought of the restricted, yeast-derived dietary of Earth and wondered if there might be a market for yeast strains designed to imitate the tastes of Outer World products.

But his thoughts broke off sharply as sociologist Quemot appeared out of nowhere and faced him. *Faced* him this time! He sat in a smaller chair in a room in which the walls and floor clashed sharply with those surrounding Baley. And he was smiling now, so that fine wrinkles in his face deepened and, paradoxically, gave him a more youthful appearance by accentuating the life in his eyes.

He said, "A thousand pardons, Mr. Baley. I thought I was enduring personal presence so well, but that was a delusion. I was quite on edge and your phrase pushed me over it, in a manner of speaking."

"What phrase was that, sir?"

"You said something about interviewing people face to——" He shook his head, his tongue dabbing quickly at his lips. "I would rather not say it. I think you know what I mean. The phrase conjured up the most striking picture of the two of us breathing—breathing one another's breath." The Solarian shuddered. "Don't you find that repulsive?"

"I don't know that I've ever thought of it so."

"It seems so filthy a habit. And as you said it and the picture arose in my mind, I realized that after all we *were* in the same room and even though I was not facing you, puffs of air that had been in your lungs must be reaching me and entering mine. With my sensitive frame of mind——"

Baley said, "Molecules all over Solaria's atmosphere have been in thousands of lungs. Jehoshaphat! They've been in the lungs of animals and the gills of fish."

"That *is* true," said Quemot with a rueful rub of his cheek, "and I'd just as soon not think of that, either. However there was a sense of immediacy to the situation with yourself actually there and with both of us inhaling and exhaling. It's amazing the relief I feel in viewing."

"I'm still in the same house, Dr. Quemot."

"That's precisely what is so amazing about the relief. You are in the same house and yet just the use of the trimensionals makes all the difference. At least I know what seeing a stranger feels like now. I won't try it again."

"That sounds as though you were experimenting with seeing."

"In a way," said the Spacer, "I suppose I was. It was a minor motivation. And the results were interesting, even if they were disturbing as well. It was a good test and I may record it."

"Record what?" asked Baley, puzzled.

"My feelings!" Quemot returned puzzled stare for puzzled stare.

Baley sighed. Cross-purposes. Always cross-purposes. "I only asked because somehow I assumed you would have instruments of some sort to measure emotional responses. An electroencephalograph, perhaps." He looked about fruitlessly, "Though I suppose you could have a pocket version of the same that works without direct electrical connection. We don't have anything like that on Earth."

"I trust," said the Solarian stiffly, "that I am able to estimate the nature of my own feelings without an instrument. They were pronounced enough."

"Yes, of course, but for quantitative analysis . . ." began Baley.

Quemot said querulously, "I don't know what you're driving at. Besides I'm trying to tell you something else, my own theory, in fact, something I have viewed in no books, something I am quite proud of——"

Baley said, "Exactly what is that, sir?"

"Why, the manner in which Solaria's culture is based on one existing in Earth's past."

Baley sighed. If he didn't allow the other to get it off his chest, there might be very little co-operation thereafter. He said, "And that is?"

"Sparta!" said Quemot, lifting his head so that for a moment his white hair glistened in the light and seemed almost a halo. "I'm sure you've heard of Sparta!"

Baley felt relieved. He had been mightily interested in Earth's ancient past in his younger days (it was an attractive study to many Earthmen—an Earth supreme because it was an Earth alone; Earthmen the masters because there were no Spacers), but Earth's past was a large one. Quemot might well have referred to some phase with which Baley was unacquainted and that would have been embarrassing.

As it was, he could say cautiously, "Yes. I've viewed films on the subject."

"Good. Good. Now Sparta in its heydey consisted of a relatively small number of Spartiates, the only full citizens, plus a somewhat larger number of second-class individuals, the Perioeci, and a really large number of outright slaves, the Helots. The Helots outnumbered the Spartiates a matter of twenty to one, and the Helots were men with human feelings and human failings.

"In order to make certain that a Helot rebellion could never be successful despite their overwhelming numbers, the Spartans became military specialists. Each lived the life of a military machine, and the society achieved its purpose. There was never a successful Helot revolt.

"Now we human beings on Solaria are equivalent, in a way, to the Spartiates. We have our Helots, but our Helots aren't men but machines. They cannot revolt and need not be feared even though they outnumber us a thousand times as badly as the Spartans' human Helots outnumbered them. So we have the advantage of Spartiate exclusiveness without any need to sacrifice ourselves to rigid mastery. We can, instead, model ourselves on the artistic and cultural way of life of the Athenians, who were contemporaries of the Spartans and who——"

Baley said, "I've viewed films on the Athenians, too."

Quemot grew warmer as he spoke. "Civilizations have always been pyramidal in structure. As one climbs toward the apex of the social edifice, there is increased leisure and increasing opportunity to pursue happiness. As one climbs, one finds also fewer and fewer people to enjoy this more and more. Invariably, there is a preponderance of the dispossessed. And remember this, no matter how well off the bottom layers of the pyramid might be on an absolute scale, they are always dispossessed in comparison with the apex. For instance, even the most poorly off humans on Aurora are better off than Earth's aristocrats, but they are dispossessed with respect to Aurora's aristocrats, and it is with the masters of their own world that they compare themselves.

"So there is always social friction in ordinary human societies. The action of social revolution and the reaction of guarding against such revolution or combating it once it has begun are the causes of a great deal of the human misery with which history is permeated.

"Now here on Solaria, for the first time, the apex of the pyramid stands alone. In the place of the dispossessed are the robots. We have the first new society, the first really new one, the first great social invention since the farmers of Sumeria and Egypt invented cities."

He sat back now, smiling.

Baley nodded. "Have you published this?"

"I may," said Quemot with an affectation of carelessness, "someday. I haven't yet. This is my third contribution."

"Were the other two as broad as this?"

"They weren't in sociology. I have been a sculptor in my time. The work you see about you"—he indicated the statuary—"is my own. And I have been a composer, too. But I am getting older and Rikaine Delmarre always argued strongly in favor of the applied arts rather than the fine arts and I decided to go into sociology."

Baley said, "That sounds as though Delmarre was a good friend of yours."

"We knew one another. At my time in life, one knows all adult Solarians. But there is no reason not to agree that Rikaine Delmarre and I were well acquainted."

"What sort of a man was Delmarre?" (Strangely enough, the name of the man brought up the picture of Gladia in Baley's mind and he was plagued with a sudden, sharp recall of her as he had last seen her, furious, her face distorted with anger at him.)

Quemot looked a bit thoughtful. "He was a worthy man; devoted to Solaria and to its way of life."

"An idealist, in other words."

"Yes. Definitely. You could see that in the fact that he volunteered for his job as—as fetal engineer. It was an applied art, you see, and I told you his feelings about that."

"Was volunteering unusual?"

"Wouldn't *you* say—— But I forget you're an Earthman. Yes, it is unusual. It's one of those jobs that must be done, yet finds no voluntary takers. Ordinarily, someone must be assigned to it for a period of so many years and it isn't pleasant to be the one chosen. Delmarre volunteered, and for life. He felt the position was too important to be left to reluctant draftees, and he persuaded me into that opinion, too. Yet I certainly would never have volunteered. I couldn't possibly make the personal sacrifice. And it was more of a sacrifice for him, since he was almost a fanatic in personal hygiene."

"I'm still not certain I understand the nature of his job."

Quemot's old cheeks flushed gently. "Hadn't you better discuss that with his assistant?"

Baley said, "I would certainly have done so by now, sir, if anyone had seen fit to tell me before this moment that he had an assistant."

"I'm sorry about that," said Quemot, "but the existence of the assistant is another measure of his social responsibility. No previous occupant of the post provided for one. Delmarre, however, felt it necessary to find a suitable youngster and conduct the necessary training himself so as to leave a professional heir behind when the time came for him to retire or, well, to die." The old Solarian sighed heavily. "Yet I outlived him and he was so much younger. I used to play chess with him. Many times."

"How did you manage that?"

Quemot's eyebrows lifted. "The usual way."

"You saw one another?"

Quemot looked horrified. "What an idea! Even if I could stomach it, Delmarre would never allow it for an instant. Being fetal engineer didn't blunt his sensibilities. He was a finicky man."

"Then how——"

"With two boards as any two people would play chess." The Solarian shrugged in a sudden gesture of tolerance. "Well, you're an Earthman. My moves registered on his board, and his on mine. It's a simple matter."

Baley said, "Do you know Mrs. Delmarre?"

"We've viewed one another. She's a field colorist, you know, and I've viewed some of her showings. Fine work in a way but more interesting as curiosities than as creations. Still, they're amusing and show a perceptive mind."

"Is she capable of killing her husband, would you say?"

"I haven't given it thought. Women are surprising creatures. But then, there's scarcely room for argument, is there? Only Mrs. Delmarre could have been close enough to Rikaine to kill him. Rikaine would never, under any circumstances, have allowed anyone else seeing privileges for any reason. Extremely finicky. Perhaps finicky is the wrong word. It was just that he lacked any trace of abnormality; anything of the perverse. He was a good Solarian."

"Would you call your granting me seeing privileges perverse?" asked Baley.

Quemot said, "Yes, I think I would. I should say there was a bit of scatophilia involved."

"Could Delmarre have been killed for political reasons?"

"What?"

"I've heard him called a Traditionalist."

"Oh, we all are."

"You mean there is no group of Solarians who are *not* Traditionalists?"

"I dare say there are some," said Quemot slowly, "who think it is dangerous to be too Traditionalist. They are overconscious of our small population, of the way the other worlds outnumber us. They think we are defenseless against possible aggression from the other Outer Worlds. They're quite foolish to think so and there aren't many of them. I don't think they're a force."

"Why do you say they are foolish? Is there anything about Solaria that would affect the balance of power in spite of the great disadvantage of numbers? Some new type of weapon?"

"A weapon, certainly. But not a new one. The people I speak of are more blind than foolish not to realize that such a weapon is in operation continuously and cannot be resisted."

Baley's eyes narrowed. "Are you serious?"

"Certainly."

"Do you know the nature of the weapon?"

"All of us must. *You* do, if you stop to think of it. I see it a trifle easier than most, perhaps, since I am a sociologist. To be sure, it isn't used as a weapon ordinarily is used. It doesn't kill or hurt, but it is irresistible even so. All the more irresistible because no one notices it."

Baley said with annoyance, "And just what is this non-lethal weapon?"

Quemot said, "The positronic robot."

11

A Farm Is Inspected

FOR A MOMENT Baley went cold. The positronic robot was the symbol of Spacer superiority over Earthmen. That was weapon enough.

He kept his voice steady. "It's an economic weapon. Solaria is important to the other Outer Worlds as a source of advanced models and so it will not be harmed by them."

"That's an obvious point," said Quemot indifferently. "That helped us establish our independence. What I have in mind is something else, something more subtle and more cosmic." Quemot's eyes were fixed on his fingers' ends and his mind was obviously fixed on abstractions.

Baley said, "Is this another of your sociological theories?"

Quemot's poorly suppressed look of pride all but forced a short smile out of the Earthman.

The sociologist said, "It is indeed mine. Original, as far as I know, and yet obvious if population data on the Outer Worlds is carefully studied. To begin with, ever since the positronic robot was invented, it has been used more and more intensively everywhere."

"Not on Earth," said Baley.

"Now, now, Plainclothesman. I don't know much of your Earth, but I know enough to know that robots are entering your economy. You people live in large Cities and leave most of your planetary surface unoccupied. Who runs your farms and mines, then?"

"Robots," admitted Baley. "But if it comes to that, Doctor, Earthmen invented the positronic robot in the first place."

"They did? Are you sure?"

"You can check. It's true."

"Interesting. Yet robots made the least headway there." The sociologist said thoughtfully, "Perhaps that is because of Earth's large population. It would take that much longer. Yes . . . Still, you have robots even in your Cities."

"Yes," said Baley.

"More now than, say, fifty years ago."

Baley nodded impatiently. "Yes."

"Then it fits. The difference is only one of time. Robots tend to displace human labor. The robot economy moves in only one direction. More robots and fewer humans. I've studied population data *very* carefully and I've plotted it and made a few extrapolations." He paused in sudden surprise. "Why, that's rather an application of mathematics to sociology, isn't it?"

"It is," said Baley.

"There may be something to it, at that. I will have to give the matter thought. In any case, these are the conclusions I have come to, and I am convinced there is no doubt as to their correctness. The robot-human ratio in any economy that has accepted robot labor tends continuously to increase despite any laws that are passed to prevent it. The increase is slowed, but never stopped. At first the human population increases, but the robot population increases much more quickly. Then, after a certain critical point is reached . . ."

Quemot stopped again, then said, "Now let's see. I wonder if the critical point could be determined exactly; if you could really put a figure to it. There's your mathematics again."

Baley stirred restlessly. "What happens after the critical point is reached, Dr. Quemot?"

"Eh? Oh, the human population begins actually to decline. A planet approaches a true social stability. Aurora will have to. Even your Earth will have to. Earth may take a few more centuries, but it is inevitable."

"What do you mean by social stability?"

"The situation here. In Solaria. A world in which the humans are the leisure class only. So there is no reason to fear the other Outer Worlds. We need only wait a century perhaps and they shall all be Solarias. I suppose that will be the end of human history, in a way; at least, its fulfillment. Finally, finally, all men will have all they can need and want. You know, there is a phrase I once picked up; I don't know where it comes from; something about the pursuit of happiness."

Baley said thoughtfully, "All men are 'endowed by their Creator with certain unalienable rights . . . among these are life, liberty, and the pursuit of happiness.'"

"You've hit it. Where's that from?"

"Some old document," said Baley.

"Do you see how that is changed here on Solaria and eventually in all the Galaxy? The pursuit will be over. The rights mankind will be heir to will be life, liberty, and happiness. Just that. Happiness."

Baley said dryly, "Maybe so, but a man has been killed on your Solaria and another may yet die."

He felt regret almost the moment he spoke, for the expression on Quemot's face was as though he had been struck with an open palm. The old man's head bowed. He said without looking up, "I have answered your questions as well as I could. Is there anything else you wish?"

"I have enough. Thank you, sir. I am sorry to have intruded on your grief at your friend's death."

Quemot looked up slowly. "It will be hard to find another chess partner. He kept our appointments most punctually and he played an extraordinarily even game. He was a good Solarian."

"I understand," said Baley softly. "May I have your permission to use your viewer to make contact with the next person I must see?"

"Of course," said Quemot. "My robots are yours. And now I will leave you. Done viewing."

A robot was at Baley's side within thirty seconds of Quemot's disappearance and Baley wondered once again how these creatures were managed. He had seen Quemot's fingers move toward a contact as he had left and that was all.

Perhaps the signal was quite a generalized one, saying only, "Do your duty!" Perhaps robots listened to all that went on and were always aware of what a human might desire at any given moment, and if the particular robot was not designed for a particular job in either mind or body, the radio web that united all robots went into action and the correct robot was spurred into action.

For a moment Baley had the vision of Solaria as a robotic net with holes that were small and continually growing smaller, with every human being caught neatly in place. He thought of Quemot's picture of worlds turning into Solarias; of nets forming and tightening even on Earth, until——

His thoughts were disrupted as the robot who had entered spoke with the quiet and even respect of the machine.

"I am ready to help you, master."

Baley said, "Do you know how to reach the place where Rikaine Delmarre once worked?"

"Yes, master."

Baley shrugged. He would never teach himself to avoid asking useless questions. The robots knew. Period. It occurred to him that, to handle robots with true efficiency, one must needs be expert, a sort of roboticist. How well did the average Solarian do, he wondered? Probably only so-so.

He said, "Get Delmarre's place and contact his assistant. If the assistant is not there, locate him wherever he is."

"Yes, master."

As the robot turned to go, Baley called after it, "Wait! What time is it at the Delmarre workplace?"

"About 0630, master."

"In the morning?"

"Yes, master."

Again Baley felt annoyance at a world that made itself victim of the coming and going of a sun. It was what came of living on bare planetary surface.

He thought fugitively of Earth, then tore his mind away. While he kept firmly to the matter in hand, he managed well. Slipping into homesickness would ruin him.

He said, "Call the assistant, anyway, boy, and tell him it's government business—and have one of the other boys bring something to eat. A sandwich and a glass of milk will do."

He chewed thoughtfully at the sandwich, which contained a kind of smoked meat, and with half his mind thought that Daneel Olivaw would certainly consider every article of food suspect after what had happened to Gruer. And Daneel might be right, too.

He finished the sandwich without ill effects, however (immediate ill effects, at any rate), and sipped at the milk. He had not learned from Quemot what he had come to learn, but he had learned something. As he sorted it out in his mind, it seemed he had learned a good deal.

Little about the murder, to be sure, but more about the larger matter.

The robot returned. "The assistant will accept contact, master."

"Good. Was there any trouble about it?"

"The assistant was asleep, master."

"Awake now, though?"

"Yes, master."

The assistant was facing him suddenly, sitting up in bed and wearing an expression of sullen resentment.

Baley reared back as though a force-barrier had been raised before him without warning. Once again a piece of vital information had been withheld from him. Once again he had not asked the right questions.

No one had thought to tell him that Rikaine Delmarre's assistant was a woman.

Her hair was a trifle darker than ordinary Spacer bronze and there was a quantity of it, at the moment in disorder. Her face was oval, her nose a trifle bulbous, and her chin large. She scratched slowly at her side just above the waist and Baley hoped the sheet would remain in position. He remembered Gladia's free attitude toward what was permitted while viewing.

Baley felt a sardonic amusement at his own disillusion at that moment. Earthmen assumed, somehow, that all Spacer women were beautiful, and certainly Gladia had reinforced that assumption. This one, though, was plain even by Earthly standards.

It therefore surprised Baley that he found her contralto attractive when she said, "See here, do you know what time it is?"

"I do," said Baley, "but since I will be seeing you, I felt I should warn you."

"*Seeing* me? Skies above——" Her eyes grew wide and she put a hand to her chin. (She wore a ring on one finger, the first item of personal adornment Baley had yet seen on Solaria.) "Wait, you're not my new assistant, are you?"

"No. Nothing like that. I'm here to investigate the death of Rikaine Delmarre."

"Oh? Well, investigate, then."

"What is your name?"

"Klorissa Cantoro."

"And how long have you been working with Dr. Delmarre?"

"Three years."

"I assume you're now at the place of business." (Baley felt uncomfortable at that noncommittal phrase, but he did not know what to call a place where a fetal engineer worked.)

"If you mean, am I at the farm?" said Klorissa discontentedly, "I certainly am. I haven't left it since the old man was done in, and I won't leave it, looks like, till an assistant is assigned me. Can *you* arrange that, by the way?"

"I'm sorry, ma'am. I have no influence with anyone here."

"Thought I'd ask."

Klorissa pulled off the sheet and climbed out of bed without any self-consciousness. She was wearing a one-piece sleeping suit and her hand went to the notch of the seam, where it ended at the neck.

Baley said hurriedly, "Just one moment. If you'll agree to see me, that will end my business with you for now and you may dress in privacy."

"In privacy?" She put out her lower lip and stared at Baley curiously. "You're finicky, aren't you? Like the boss."

"Will you see me? I would like to look over the farm."

"I don't get this business about seeing, but if you want to view the farm I'll tour you. If you'll give me a chance to wash and take care of a few things and wake up a little, I'll enjoy the break in routine."

"I don't want to view anything. I want to *see*."

The woman cocked her head to one side and her keen look had something of professional interest in it. "Are you a pervert or something? When was the last time you underwent a gene analysis?"

"Jehoshaphat!" muttered Baley. "Look, I'm Elijah Baley. I'm from Earth."

"From Earth?" She cried vehemently. "Skies above! Whatever are you doing here? Or is this some kind of complicated joke?"

"I'm not joking. I was called in to investigate Delmarre's death. I'm a plainclothesman, a detective."

"You mean that kind of investigation. But I thought everyone knew his wife did it."

"No, ma'am, there's some question about it in my mind. May I have your permission to see the farm and you. As an Earthman, you understand, I'm not accustomed to viewing. It makes me uncomfortable. I have permission from the Head of Security to see people who might help me. I will show you the document, if you wish."

"Let's see it."

Baley held the official strip up before her imaged eyes.

She shook her head. "Seeing! It's filthy. Still, skies above, what's a little more filth in this filthy job? Look here, though, don't you come close to me. You stay a good distance away. We can shout or send messages by robot, if we have to. You understand?"

"I understand."

Her sleeping suit split open at the seam just as contact broke off and the last word he heard from her was a muttered: "Earthman!"

"That's close enough," said Klorissa.

Baley, who was some twenty-five feet from the woman, said, "It's all right this distance, but I'd like to get indoors quickly."

It had not been so bad this time, somehow. He had scarcely minded the plane trip, but there was no point in overdoing it. He kept himself from yanking at his collar to allow himself to breathe more freely.

Klorissa said sharply, "What's wrong with you? You look kind of beat."

Baley said, "I'm not used to the outdoors."

"That's right! Earthman! You've got to be cooped up or something. Skies above!" Her tongue passed over her lips as though it tasted something unappetizing. "Well, come in, then, but let me move out of the way first. All right. Get in."

Her hair was in two thick braids that wound about her head in a complicated geometrical pattern. Baley wondered how long it took to arrange like that and then remembered that, in all probability, the unerring mechanical fingers of a robot did the job.

The hair set off her oval face and gave it a kind of symmetry that made it pleasant if not pretty. She did not wear any facial make-up, nor, for that matter, were her clothes meant to do more than cover her serviceably. For the most part they were a subdued dark blue except for her gloves, which covered her to mid-arm and were a badly clashing lilac in color. Apparently they were not part of her ordinary costume. Baley noted the thickening of one finger of the gloves owing to the presence of the ring underneath.

They remained at opposite ends of the room, facing one another.

Baley said, "You don't like this, do you, ma'am?"

Klorissa shrugged. "Why should I like it? I'm not an animal. But I can stand it. You get pretty hardened, when you deal with—with"—she paused, and then her chin went up as though she had made up her mind to say what she had to say without mincing—"with children." She pronounced the word with careful precision.

"You sound as though you don't like the job you have."

"It's an important job. It must be done. Still, I don't like it."

"Did Rikaine Delmarre like it?"

"I suppose he didn't, but he never showed it. He was a good Solarian."

"And he was finicky."

Klorissa looked surprised.

Baley said, "You yourself said so. When we were viewing and I said you might dress in private, you said I was finicky like the boss."

"Oh. Well, he *was* finicky. Even viewing he never took any liberties. Always proper."

"Was that unusual?"

"It shouldn't be. Ideally, you're supposed to be proper, but no one ever is. Not when viewing. There's no personal presence involved so why take any pains? You know? I don't take pains when viewing, except with the boss. You had to be formal with him."

"Did you admire Dr. Delmarre?"

"He was a good Solarian."

Baley said, "You've called this place a farm and you've mentioned children. Do you bring up children here?"

"From the age of a month. Every fetus on Solaria comes here."

"Fetus?"

"Yes." She frowned. "We get them a month after conception. Does this embarrass you?"

"No," Baley said shortly. "Can you show me around?"

"I can. But keep your distance."

Baley's long face took on a stony grimness as he looked down the length of the long room from above. There was glass between the room and themselves. On the other side, he was sure, was perfectly controlled heat, perfectly controlled humidity, perfectly controlled asepsis. Those tanks, row on row, each contained its little creature floating in a watery fluid of precise composition, infused with a nutrient mixture of ideal proportions. Life and growth went on.

Little things, some smaller than half his fist, curled on themselves, with bulging skulls and tiny budding limbs and vanishing tails.

Klorissa, from her position twenty feet away, said, "How do you like it, Plainclothesman?"

Baley said, "How many do you have?"

"As of this morning, one hundred and fifty-two. We receive fifteen to twenty each month and we graduate as many to independence."

"Is this the only such institution on the planet?"

"That's right. It's enough to keep the population steady, counting on a life expectancy of three hundred years and a population of twenty thousand. This building is quite new. Dr. Delmarre supervised its construction and made many changes in our procedures. Our fetal death rate now is virtually zero."

Robots threaded their way among the tanks. At each tank they stopped and checked controls in a tireless, meticulous way, looking in at the tiny embryos within.

"Who operates on the mother?" asked Baley. "I mean, to get the little things."

"Doctors," answered Klorissa.

"Dr. Delmarre?"

"Of course not. *Medical* doctors. You don't think Dr. Delmarre would ever stoop to—— Well, never mind."

"Why can't robots be used?"

"Robots in surgery? First Law makes that very difficult, Plainclothesman. A robot might perform an appendectomy to save a human life, if he knew how, but I doubt that he'd be usable after that without major repairs. Cutting human flesh would be quite a traumatic experience for a positronic brain. Human doctors can manage to get hardened to it. Even to the personal presence required."

Baley said, "I notice that robots tend the fetuses, though. Do you and Dr. Delmarre ever interfere?"

"We have to, sometimes, when things go wrong. If a fetus has developmental trouble, for instance. Robots can't be trusted to judge the situation accurately when human life is involved."

Baley nodded. "Too much risk of a misjudgment and a life lost, I suppose."

"Not at all. Too much risk of overvaluing a life and saving one improperly." The woman looked stern. "As fetal engineers, Baley, we see to it that healthy children are born; *healthy* ones. Even the best gene analysis of parents can't assure that all gene permutations and combinations will be favorable, to say nothing of the possibility of mutations. That's our big concern, the unexpected mutation. We've got the rate of those down to less than one in a thousand, but that means that, on the average, once a decade, we have trouble."

She motioned him along the balcony and he followed her.

She said, "I'll show you the infants' nurseries and the youngsters' dormitories. They're much more a problem than the fetuses are. With them, we can rely on robot labor only to a limited extent."

"Why is that?"

"You would know, Baley, if you ever tried to teach a robot the importance of discipline. First Law makes them almost impervious to that fact. And don't think youngsters don't learn that about as soon as they can talk. I've seen a three-year-old holding a dozen robots motionless by yelling, 'You'll hurt me. I'm hurt.' It takes an extremely advanced robot to understand that a child might be deliberately lying."

"Could Delmarre handle the children?"

"Usually."

"How did he do that? Did he get out among them and shake sense into them?"

"Dr. Delmarre? Touch them? Skies above! Of course not! But he could *talk* to them. And he could give a robot specific orders. I've seen him viewing a child for fifteen minutes, and keeping a robot in spanking position all that time, getting it to spank—spank—spank. A few like that and the child would risk fooling with the boss no more. And the boss was skillful enough about it so that usually the robot didn't need more than a routine readjustment afterward."

"How about you? Do you get out among the children?"

"I'm afraid I have to sometimes. I'm not like the boss. Maybe someday I'll be able to handle the long-distance stuff, but right now if I tried, I'd just ruin robots. There's an art to handling robots really well, you know. When I think of it, though. Getting out among the children. Little animals!"

She looked back at him suddenly. "I suppose you wouldn't mind seeing them."

"It wouldn't bother me."

She shrugged and stared at him with amusement. "Earthman!"

She walked on again. "What's all this about, anyway? You'll have to end up with Gladia Delmarre as murderess. You'll *have* to."

"I'm not quite sure of that," said Baley.

"How could you be anything else but sure? Who else could it possibly be?"

"There are possibilities, ma'am."

"Who, for instance?"

"Well, you, for instance!"

And Klorissa's reaction to that quite surprised Baley.

12

A Target Is Missed

SHE LAUGHED.

The laughter grew and fed on itself till she was gasping for breath and her plump face had reddened almost to purple. She leaned against the wall and gasped for breath.

"No, don't come—closer," she begged. "I'm all right."

Baley said gravely, "Is the possibility that humorous?"

She tried to answer and laughed again. Then, in a whisper, she said, "Oh, you *are* an Earthman? How could it ever be me?"

"You knew him well," said Baley. "You knew his habits. You could have planned it."

"And you think I would *see* him? That I would get close enough to bash him over the head with something? You just don't know anything at all about it, Baley."

Baley felt himself redden. "Why couldn't you get close enough to him, ma'am. You've had practice—uh—mingling."

"With the *children*."

"One thing leads to another. You seem to be able to stand my presence."

"At twenty feet," she said contemptuously.

"I've just visited a man who nearly collapsed because he had to endure my presence for a while."

Klorissa sobered and said, "A difference in degree."

"I suggest that a difference in degree is all that is necessary. The habit of seeing children makes it possible to endure seeing Delmarre just long enough."

"I would like to point out, Mr. Baley," said Klorissa, no longer appearing the least amused, "that it doesn't matter a speck what I can endure. Dr. Delmarre was the finicky one. He was almost as bad as Leebig himself. Almost. Even if I could endure seeing him, he would never endure seeing me. Mrs. Delmarre is the only one he could possibly have allowed within seeing distance."

Baley said, "Who's this Leebig you mentioned?"

Klorissa shrugged. "One of these odd-genius types, if you know what I mean. He's done work with the boss on robots."

Baley checked that off mentally and returned to the matter at hand. He said, "It could also be said you had a motive."

"What motive?"

"His death put you in charge of this establishment, gave you position."

"You call that a motive? Skies above, who could *want* this position? Who on Solaria? This is a motive for keeping him alive. It's a motive for hovering over him and protecting him. You'll have to do better than that, Earthman."

Baley scratched his neck uncertainly with one finger. He saw the justice of that.

Klorissa said, "Did you notice my ring, Mr. Baley?"

For a moment it seemed she was about to strip the glove from her right hand, but she refrained.

"I noticed it," said Baley.

"You don't know its significance, I suppose?"

"I don't." (He would never have done with ignorance, he thought bitterly.)

"Do you mind a small lecture, then?"

"If it will help me make sense of this damned world," blurted out Baley, "by all means."

"Skies above!" Klorissa smiled. "I suppose we seem to you as Earth would seem to us. Imagine. Say, here's an empty chamber. Come in here and we'll sit down—no, the room's not big enough. Tell you what, though. You take a seat in there and I'll stand out here."

She stepped farther down the corridor, giving him space to enter the room, then returned, taking up her stand against the opposite wall at a point from which she could see him.

Baley took his seat with only the slightest quiver of chivalry countering it. He thought rebelliously: Why not? Let the Spacer woman stand.

Klorissa folded her muscular arms across her chest and said, "Gene analysis is the key to our society. We don't analyze for genes directly, of course. Each gene, however, governs one enzyme, and we can analyze for enzymes. Know the enzymes, know the body chemistry. Know the body chemistry, know the human being. You see all that?"

"I understand the theory," said Baley. "I don't know how it's applied."

"That part's done here. Blood samples are taken while the infant is still in the late fetal stage. That gives us our rough first approximation. Ideally, we should catch all mutations at that point and judge whether birth can be risked. In actual fact, we still don't quite know enough to eliminate all possibility of mistake. Someday, maybe. Anyway, we continue testing after birth; biopsies as well as body fluids. In any case, long before adulthood, we know exactly what our little boys and girls are made of."

(Sugar and spice . . . A nonsense phrase went unbidden through Baley's mind.)

"We wear coded rings to indicate our gene constitution," said Klorissa. "It's an old custom, a bit of the primitive left behind from the days when Solarians had not yet been weeded eugenically. Nowadays, we're all healthy."

Baley said, "But you still wear yours. Why?"

"Because I'm exceptional," she said with an unembarrassed, unblunted pride. "Dr. Delmarre spent a long time searching for an assistant. He *needed* someone exceptional. Brains, ingenuity, industry, stability. Most of all, stability. Someone who could learn to mingle with children and not break down."

"He couldn't, could he? Was that a measure of his instability?"

Klorissa said, "In a way, it was, but at least it was a desirable type of instability under most circumstances. You wash your hands, don't you?"

Baley's eyes dropped to his hands. They were as clean as need be. "Yes," he said.

"All right. I suppose it's a measure of instability to feel such revulsion at dirty hands as to be unable to clean an oily mechanism by hand even in an emergency. Still, in the *ordinary* course of living, the revulsion keeps you clean, which is good."

"I see. Go ahead."

"There's nothing more. My genic health is the third-highest ever recorded on Solaria, so I wear my ring. It's a record I enjoy carrying with me."

"I congratulate you."

"You needn't sneer. It may not be my doing. It may be the blind permutation of parental genes, but it's a proud thing to own, anyway. And no one would believe me capable of so seriously psychotic an act as murder. Not with my gene make-up. So don't waste accusations on me."

Baley shrugged and said nothing. The woman seemed to confuse gene make-up and evidence and presumably the rest of Solaria would do the same.

Klorissa said, "Do you want to see the youngsters now?"

"Thank you. Yes."

The corridors seemed to go on forever. The building was obviously a tremendous one. Nothing like the huge banks of apartments in the Cities of Earth, of course, but for a single building clinging to the outside skin of a planet it must be a mountainous structure.

There were hundreds of cribs, with pink babies squalling, or sleeping, or feeding. Then there were playrooms for the crawlers.

"They're not too bad even at this age," said Klorissa grudgingly, "though they take up a tremendous sum of robots. It's practically a robot per baby till walking age."

"Why is that?"

"They sicken if they don't get individual attention."

Baley nodded. "Yes, I suppose the requirement for affection is something that can't be done away with."

Klorissa frowned and said brusquely, "Babies require attention."

Baley said, "I'm surprised you can counter an instinct so thorfor affection."

She whirled toward him, the distance between them not sufficing to hide her displeasure. "See here, Baley, if you're trying to shock me by using unpleasant terms, you won't succeed. Skies above, don't be childish."

"Shock you?"

"I can use the word too. Affection! Do you want a short word, a good four-letter word. I can say that, too. Love! Love! Now if it's out of your system, behave yourself."

Baley did not trouble to dispute the matter of obscenity. He said, "Can robots really give the necessary attention, then?"

"Obviously, or this farm would not be the success it is. They fool with the child. They nuzzle it and snuggle it. The child doesn't care that it's only a robot. But then, things grow more difficult between three and ten."

"Oh?"

"During that interval, the children insist on playing with one another. Quite indiscriminately."

"I take it you let them."

"We have to, but we never forget our obligation to teach them the requirements of adulthood. Each has a separate room that can be closed off. Even from the first, they must sleep alone. We insist on that. And then we have an isolation time every day and that increases with the years. By the time a child reaches ten, he is able to restrict himself to viewing for a week at a time. Of course, the viewing arrangements are elaborate. They can view outdoors, under mobile conditions, and can keep it up all day."

Baley said, "I'm surprised you can counter an instinct so thoroughly. You do counter it; I see that. Still, it surprises me."

"What instinct?" demanded Klorissa.

"The instinct of gregariousness. There is one. You say yourself that as children they insist on playing with each other."

Klorissa shrugged. "Do you call that instinct? But then, what if it is? Skies above, a child has an instinctive fear of falling, but adults can be trained to work in high places even where there is constant danger of falling. Haven't you ever seen gymnastic exhibitions on high wires? There are some worlds where people live in tall buildings. And children have instinctive fear of loud noises, too, but are you afraid of them?"

"Not within reason," said Baley.

"I'm willing to bet that Earth people couldn't sleep if things were really quiet. Skies above, there isn't an instinct around that can't give way to a good, persistent education. Not in human beings, where instincts are weak anyway. In fact, if you go about it right, education gets easier with each generation. It's a matter of evolution."

Baley said, "How is that?"

"Don't you see? Each individual repeats his own evolutionary history as he develops. Those fetuses back there have gills and a tail for a time. Can't skip those steps. The youngster has to go through the social-animal stage in the same way. But just as a fetus can get through in one month a stage that evolution took a hundred million years to get through, so our children can hurry through the social-animal stage. Dr. Delmarre was of the opinion that with the generations, we'd get through that stage faster and faster."

"Is that so?"

"In three thousand years, he estimated, at the present rate of progress, we'd have children who'd take to viewing at once. The boss had other notions, too. He was interested in improving robots to the point of making them capable of disciplining children without becoming mentally unstable. Why not? Discipline today for a better life tomorrow is a true expression of First Law if robots could only be made to see it."

"Have such robots been developed yet?"

Klorissa shook her head. "I'm afraid not. Dr. Delmarre and Leebig had been working hard on some experimental models."

"Did Dr. Delmarre have some of the models sent out to his estate? Was he a good enough roboticist to conduct tests himself?"

"Oh yes. He tested robots frequently."

"Do you know that he had a robot with him when he was murdered?"

"I've been told so."

"Do you know what kind of a model it was?"

"You'll have to ask Leebig. As I told you, he's the roboticist who worked with Dr. Delmarre."

"You know nothing about it?"

"Not a thing."

"If you think of anything, let me know."

"I will. And don't think new robot models are all that Dr. Delmarre was interested in. Dr. Delmarre used to say the time would come when unfertilized ova would be stored in banks at liquid-air temperatures and utilized for artificial insemination. In that way, eugenic principles could be truly applied and we could get rid of the last vestige of any need for seeing. I'm not sure that I quite go along with him so far, but he was a man of advanced notions; a very good Solarian."

She added quickly, "Do you want to go outside? The five-through-eight group are encouraged to take part in outdoor play and you could see them in action."

Baley said cautiously, "I'll try that. I may have to come back inside on rather short notice."

"Oh yes, I forgot. Maybe you'd rather not go out at all?"

"No." Baley forced a smile. "I'm trying to grow accustomed to the outdoors."

The wind was hard to bear. It made breathing difficult. It wasn't cold, in a direct physical sense, but the feel of it, the feel of his clothes moving against his body, gave Baley a kind of chill.

His teeth chattered when he tried to talk and he had to force his words out in little bits. It hurt his eyes to look so far at a horizon so hazy green and blue and there was only limited relief when he looked at the pathway immediately before his toes. Above all, he avoided looking up at the empty blue, empty, that is, but for the piled-up white of occasional clouds and the glare of the naked sun.

And yet he could fight off the urge to run, to return to enclosure.

He passed a tree, following Klorissa by some ten paces, and he reached out a cautious hand to touch it. It was rough and hard to the touch. Frondy leaves moved and rustled overhead, but he did not raise his eyes to look at them. A living tree!

Klorissa called out. "How do you feel?"

"All right."

"You can see a group of youngsters from here," she said. "They're involved in some kind of game. The robots organize the games and see to it that the little animals don't kick each other's eyes out. With personal presence you can do just that, you know."

Baley raised his eyes slowly, running his glance along the cement of the pathway out to the grass and down the slope, farther and farther out—very carefully—ready to snap back to his toes if he grew frightened—feeling with his eyes . . .

There were the small figures of boys and girls racing madly about, uncaring that they raced at the very outer rim of a world with nothing but air and space above them. The glitter of an occasional robot moved nimbly among them. The noise of the children was a far-off incoherent squeaking in the air.

"They love it," said Klorissa. "Pushing and pulling and squabbling and falling down and getting up and just generally contacting. Skies above! How do children ever manage to grow up?"

"What are those older children doing?" asked Baley. He pointed at a group of isolated youngsters standing to one side.

"They're viewing. They're not in a state of personal presence. By viewing, they can walk together, talk together, race together, play together. Anything except physical contact."

"Where do children go when they leave here?"

"To estates of their own. The number of deaths is, on the average, equal to the number of graduations."

"To their parents' estates?"

"Skies above, no! It would be an amazing coincidence, wouldn't it, to have a parent die just as a child is of age. No, the children take any one that falls vacant. I don't know that any of them would be particularly happy, anyway, living in a mansion that once belonged to their parents, supposing, of course, they knew who their parents were."

"Don't they?"

She raised her eyebrows. "Why should they?"

"Don't parents visit their children here?"

"What a mind you have. Why should they want to?"

Baley said, "Do you mind if I clear up a point for myself? Is it bad manners to ask a person if they have had children?"

"It's an intimate question, wouldn't you say?"

"In a way."

"I'm hardened. Children are my business. Other people aren't."

Baley said, "Have you any children?"

Klorissa's Adam's apple made a soft but clearly visible motion in her throat as she swallowed. "I deserve that, I suppose. And you deserve an answer. I haven't."

"Are you married?"

"Yes, and I have an estate of my own and I would be there but for the emergency here. I'm just not confident of being able to control all the robots if I'm not here in person."

She turned away unhappily, and then pointed. "Now there's one of them gone tumbling and of course he's crying."

A robot was running with great space-devouring strides.

Klorissa said, "He'll be picked up and cuddled and if there's any real damage, I'll be called in." She added nervously, "I hope I don't have to be."

Baley took a deep breath. He noted three trees forming a small triangle fifty feet to the left. He walked in that direction, the grass soft and loathsome under his shoes, disgusting in its softness (like walking through corrupting flesh, and he nearly retched at the thought).

He was among them, his back against one trunk. It was almost like being surrounded by imperfect walls. The sun was only a wavering series of glitters through the leaves, so disconnected as almost to be robbed of horror.

Klorissa faced him from the path, then slowly shortened the distance by half.

"Mind if I stay here awhile?" asked Baley.

"Go ahead," said Klorissa.

Baley said, "Once the youngsters graduate out of the farm, how do you get them to court one another?"

"Court?"

"Get to know one another," said Baley, vaguely wondering how the thought could be expressed safely, "so they can marry."

"That's not their problem," said Klorissa. "They're matched by gene analysis, usually when they are quite young. That's the sensible way, isn't it?"

"Are they always willing?"

"To be married? They never are! It's a very traumatic process. At first they have to grow accustomed to one another, and a little bit of seeing each day, once the initial queasiness is gone, can do wonders."

"What if they just don't like their partner?"

"What? If the gene analysis indicates a partnership what difference does it——"

"I understand," said Baley hastily. He thought of Earth and sighed.

Klorissa said, "Is there anything else you would like to know?"

Baley wondered if there were anything to be gained from a longer stay. He would not be sorry to be done with Klorissa and fetal engineering so that he might pass on to the next stage.

He had opened his mouth to say as much, when Klorissa called out at some object far off, "You, child, you there! What are you doing?" Then, over her shoulder: "Earthman! Baley! Watch out! Watch *out!*"

Baley scarcely heard her. He responded to the note of urgency in her voice. The nervous effort that held his emotions taut snapped wide and he flamed into panic. All the terror of the open air and the endless vault of heaven broke in upon him.

Baley gibbered. He heard himself mouth meaningless sounds and felt himself fall to his knees and slowly roll over to his side as though he were watching the process from a distance.

Also from a distance he heard the sighing hum piercing the air above him and ending with a sharp thwack.

Baley closed his eyes and his fingers clutched a thin tree root that skimmed the surface of the ground and his nails burrowed into dirt.

He opened his eyes (it must only have been moments after). Klorissa was scolding sharply at a youngster who remained at a distance. A robot, silent, stood closer to Klorissa. Baley had only time to notice the youngster held a stringed object in his hand before his eyes sheered away.

Breathing heavily, Baley struggled to his feet. He stared at the shaft of glistening metal that remained in the trunk of the tree against which he had been standing. He pulled at it and it came out readily. It had not penetrated far. He looked at the point but did not touch it. It was blunted, but it would have sufficed to tear his skin had he not dropped when he did.

It took him two tries to get his legs moving. He took a step toward Klorissa and called, "You. Youngster."

Klorissa turned, her face flushed. She said, "It was an accident. Are you hurt?"

"No! What is this thing?"

"It's an arrow. It is fired by a bow, which makes a taut string do the work."

"Like this," called the youngster impudently, and he shot another arrow into the air, then burst out laughing. He had light hair and a lithe body.

Klorissa said, "You will be disciplined. Now leave!"

"Wait, wait," cried Baley. He rubbed his knee where a rock had caught and bruised him as he had fallen. "I have some questions. What is your name?"

"Bik," he said carelessly.

"Did you shoot that arrow at me, Bik?"

"That's right," said the boy.

"Do you realize you would have hit me if I hadn't been warned in time to duck?"

Bik shrugged. "I was aiming to hit."

Klorissa spoke hurriedly. "You must let me explain. Archery is an encouraged sport. It is competitive without requiring contact. We have contests among the boys using viewing only. Now I'm afraid some of the boys will aim at robots. It amuses them and it doesn't hurt the robots. I'm the only adult human on the estate and when the boy saw you, he must have assumed you were a robot."

Baley listened. His mind was clearing, and the natural dourness of his long face intensified. He said, "Bik, did you think I was a robot?"

"No," said the youngster. "You're an Earthman."

"All right. Go now."

Bik turned and raced off whistling. Baley turned to the robot. "You! How did the youngster know I was an Earthman, or weren't you with him when he shot?"

"I was with him, master. I told him you were an Earthman."

"Did you tell him what an Earthman was?"

"Yes, master."

"What is an Earthman?"

"An inferior sort of human that ought not to be allowed on Solaria because he breeds disease, master."

"And who told you that, boy?"

The robot maintained silence.

Baley said, "Do you know who told you?"

"I do not, master. It is in my memory store."

"So you told the boy I was a disease-breeding inferior and he immediately shot at me. Why didn't you stop him?"

"I would have, master. I would not have allowed harm to come to a human, even an Earthman. He moved too quickly and I was not fast enough."

"Perhaps you thought I was just an Earthman, not completely a human, and hesitated a bit."

"No, master."

It was said with quiet calm, but Baley's lips quirked grimly. The robot might deny it in all faith, but Baley felt that was exactly the factor involved.

Baley said, "What were you doing with the boy?"

"I was carrying his arrows, master."

"May I see them?"

He held out his hand. The robot approached and delivered a dozen of them. Baley put the original arrow, the one that had hit the tree, carefully at his feet, and looked the others over one by one. He handed them back and lifted the original arrow again.

He said, "Why did you give this particular arrow to the boy?"

"No reason, master. He had asked for an arrow some time earlier and this was the one my hand touched first. He looked about for a target, then noticed you and asked who the strange human was. I explained——"

"I know what you explained. This arrow you handed him is the only one with gray vanes at the rear. The others have black vanes."

The robot simply stared.

Baley said, "Did you guide the youngster here?"

"We walked randomly, master."

The Earthman looked through the gap between two trees through which the arrow had hurled itself toward its mark. He said, "Would it happen, by any chance, that this youngster, Bik, was the best archer you have here?"

The robot bent his head. "He is the best, master."

Klorissa gaped. "How did you ever come to guess that?"

"It follows," said Baley dryly. "Now please observe this gray-vaned arrow and the others. The gray-vaned arrow is the only one that seems oily at the point. I'll risk melodrama, ma'am, by saying that your warning saved my life. This arrow that missed me is poisoned."

13

A Roboticist Is Confronted

Klorissa said, "Impossible! Skies above, absolutely impossible!"

"Above or below or any way you wish it. Is there an animal on the farm that's expendable? Get it and scratch it with the arrow and see what happens."

"But why should anyone want to——"

Baley said harshly, "I know why. The question is, who?"

"No one."

Baley felt the dizziness returning and he grew savage. He threw the arrow at her and she eyed the spot where it fell.

"Pick it up," Baley cried, "and if you don't want to test it, destroy it. Leave it there and you'll have an accident if the children get at it."

She picked it up hurriedly, holding it between forefinger and thumb.

Baley ran for the nearest entrance to the building and Klorissa was still holding the arrow, gingerly, when she followed him back indoors.

Baley felt a certain measure of equanimity return with the comfort of enclosure. He said, "Who poisoned the arrow?"

"I can't imagine."

"I suppose it isn't likely the boy did it himself. Would you have any way of telling who his parents were?"

"We could check the records," said Klorissa gloomily.

"Then you do keep records of relationships?"

"We have to for gene analysis."

"Would the youngster know who his parents were?"

"Never," said Klorissa energetically.

"Would he have any way of finding out?"

"He would have to break into the records room. Impossible."

"Suppose an adult visited the estate and wanted to know who his child was——"

Klorissa flushed. "Very unlikely."

"But suppose. Would he be told if he were to ask?"

"I don't know. It isn't exactly illegal for him to know. It certainly isn't customary."

"Would *you* tell him?"

"I'd try not to. I know Dr. Delmarre wouldn't have. He believed knowledge of relationship was for gene analysis only. Before him things may have been looser. . . . Why do you ask all this, anyway?"

"I don't see how the youngster could have a motive on his own account. I thought that through his parents he might have."

"This is all horrible." In her disturbed state of mind Klorissa approached more closely than at any previous time. She even stretched out an arm in his direction. "How can it all be happening? The boss killed; you nearly killed. We have no motives for violence on Solaria. We all have all we can want, so there is no personal ambition. We have no knowledge of relationship, so there is no family ambition. We are all in good genic health."

Her face cleared all at once. "Wait. This arrow can't be poisoned. I shouldn't let you convince me it is."

"Why have you suddenly decided that?"

"The robot with Bik. He would never have allowed poison. It's inconceivable that he could have done anything that might bring harm to a human being. The First Law of Robotics makes sure of that."

Baley said, "Does it? What is the First Law, I wonder?"

Klorissa stared blankly. "What do you mean?"

"Nothing. You have the arrow tested and you will find it poisoned." Baley himself was scarcely interested in the matter. He knew it for poison beyond any internal questionings. He said, "Do you still believe Mrs. Delmarre to have been guilty of her husband's death?"

"She was the only one present."

"I see. And you are the only other human adult present on this estate at a time when I have just been shot at with a poisoned arrow."

She cried energetically, "I had nothing to do with it."

"Perhaps not. And perhaps Mrs. Delmarre is innocent as well. May I use your viewing apparatus?"

"Yes, of course."

Baley knew exactly whom he intended to view and it was *not* Gladia. It came as a surprise to himself then to hear his voice say, "Get Gladia Delmarre."

The robot obeyed without comment, and Baley watched the manipulations with astonishment, wondering why he had given the order.

Was it that the girl had just been the subject of discussion, or was it that he had been a little disturbed over the manner of the end of their last viewing, or was it simply the sight of the husky, almost overpoweringly practical figure of Klorissa that finally enforced the necessity of a glimpse of Gladia as a kind of counterirritant?

He thought defensively: Jehoshaphat! Sometimes a man has to play things by ear.

She was there before him all at once, sitting in a large, upright chair that made her appear smaller and more defenseless than ever. Her hair was drawn back and bound into a loose coil. She wore pendant earrings bearing gems that looked like diamonds. Her dress was a simple affair that clung tightly at the waist.

She said in a low voice, "I'm glad you viewed, Elijah. I've been trying to reach you."

"Good morning, Gladia." (Afternoon? Evening? He didn't know Gladia's time and he couldn't tell from the manner in which she was dressed what time it might be.) "Why have you been trying to reach me?"

"To tell you I was sorry I had lost my temper last time we viewed. Mr. Olivaw didn't know where you were to be reached."

Baley had a momentary vision of Daneel still bound fast by the overseeing robots and almost smiled. He said, "That's all right. In a few hours, I'll be seeing you."

"Of course, if—— *Seeing* me?"

"Personal presence," said Baley gravely.

Her eyes grew wide and her fingers dug into the smooth plastic of the chair arms. "Is there any reason for that?"

"It is necessary."

"I don't think——"

"Would you allow it?"

She looked away. "Is it absolutely necessary?"

"It is. First, though, there is someone else I must see. Your husband was interested in robots. You told me that, and I have heard it from other sources, but he wasn't a roboticist, was he?"

"That wasn't his training, Elijah." She still avoided his eyes.

"But he worked with a roboticist, didn't he?"

"Jothan Leebig," she said at once. "He's a good friend of mine."

"He is?" said Baley energetically.

Gladia looked startled. "Shouldn't I have said that?"

"Why not, if it's the truth?"

"I'm always afraid that I'll say things that will make me seem as though—— You don't know what it's like when everyone is sure you've done something."

"Take it easy. How is it that Leebig is a friend of yours?"

"Oh, I don't know. He's in the next estate, for one thing. Viewing energy is just about nil, so we can just view all the time in free motion with hardly any trouble. We go on walks together all the time; or we did, anyway."

"I didn't know you could go on walks together with anyone."

Gladia flushed. "I said *viewing*. Oh well, I keep forgetting you're an Earthman. Viewing in free motion means we focus on ourselves and we can go anywhere we want to without losing contact. I walk on my estate and he walks on his and we're together." She held her chin high. "It can be pleasant."

Then, suddenly, she giggled. "Poor Jothan."

"Why do you say that?"

"I was thinking of you thinking we walked together without viewing. He'd die if he thought anyone could think that."

"Why?"

"He's terrible that way. He told me that when he was five years old he stopped seeing people. Insisted on viewing only. Some children are like that. Rikaine"—she paused in confusion, then went on —"Rikaine, my husband, once told me, when I talked about Jothan, that more and more children would be like that too. He said it was a kind of social evolution that favored survival of pro-viewing. Do you think that's so?"

"I'm no authority," said Baley.

"Jothan won't even get married. Rikaine was angry with him, told him he was anti-social and that he had genes that were necessary in the common pool, but Jothan just refused to consider it."

"Has he a right to refuse?"

"No-o," said Gladia hesitantly, "but he's a very brilliant roboticist, you know, and roboticists are valuable on Solaria. I suppose they stretched a point. Except I think Rikaine was going to stop working with Jothan. He told me once Jothan was a bad Solarian."

"Did he tell Jothan that?"

"I don't know. He was working with Jothan to the end."

"But he thought Jothan was a bad Solarian for refusing to marry?"

"Rikaine once said that marriage was the hardest thing in life, but that it had to be endured."

"What did you think?"

"About what, Elijah?"

"About marriage. Did you think it was the hardest thing in life?"

Her expression grew slowly blank as though she were painstakingly washing emotion out of it. She said, "I never thought about it."

Baley said, "You said you go on walks with Jothan Leebig all the time, then corrected yourself and put that in the past. You don't go on walks with him any more, then?"

Gladia shook her head. Expression was back in her face. Sadness. "No. We don't seem to. I viewed him once or twice. He always seemed busy and I didn't like to—— You know."

"Was this since the death of your husband?"

"No, even some time before. Several months before."

"Do you suppose Dr. Delmarre ordered him not to pay further attention to you?"

Gladia looked startled. "Why should he? Jothan isn't a robot and neither am I. How can we take orders and why should Rikaine give them?"

Baley did not bother to try to explain. He could have done so only in Earth terms and that would make things no clearer to her. And if it did manage to clarify, the result could only be disgusting to her.

Baley said, "Only a question. I'll view you again, Gladia, when I'm done with Leebig. What time do you have, by the way?" He was sorry at once for asking the question. Robots would answer in Terrestrial equivalents, but Gladia might answer in Solarian units and Baley was weary of displaying ignorance.

But Gladia answered in purely qualitative terms. "Midafternoon," she said.

"Then that's it for Leebig's estate also?"

"Oh yes."

"Good. I'll view you again as soon as I can and we'll make arrangements for seeing."

Again she grew hesitant. "Is it absolutely necessary?"

"It is."

She said in a low voice, "Very well."

There was some delay in contacting Leebig and Baley utilized it in consuming another sandwich, one that was brought to him in its original packaging. But he had grown more cautious. He inspected the seal carefully before breaking it, then looked over the contents painstakingly.

He accepted a plastic container of milk, not quite unfrozen, bit an opening with his own teeth, and drank from it directly. He thought gloomily that there were such things as odorless, tasteless, slow-acting poisons that could be introduced delicately by means of hypodermic needles or high-pressure needle jets, then put the thought aside as being childish.

So far murders and attempted murders had been committed in the most direct possible fashion. There was nothing delicate or subtle about a blow on the head, enough poison in a glass to kill a dozen men, or a poisoned arrow shot openly at the victim.

And then he thought, scarcely less gloomily, that as long as he hopped between time zones in this fashion, he was scarcely likely to have regular meals. Or, if this continued, regular sleep.

The robot approached him. "Dr. Leebig directs you to call sometime tomorrow. He is engaged in important work."

Baley bounced to his feet and roared, "You tell that guy——"

He stopped. There was no use in yelling at a robot. That is, you could yell if you wished, but it would achieve results no sooner than a whisper.

He said in a conversational tone, "You tell Dr. Leebig, or his robot if that is as far as you've reached, that I am investigating the murder of a professional associate of his and a good Solarian. You tell him that I cannot wait on his work. You tell him that if I am not viewing him in five minutes, I will be in a plane and at his estate *seeing* him in less than an hour. You use that word, seeing, so there's no mistake."

He returned to his sandwich.

The five minutes were not quite gone, when Leebig, or at least a Solarian whom Baley presumed to be Leebig, was glaring at him.

Baley glared back. Leebig was a lean man, who held himself rigidly erect. His dark, prominent eyes had a look of intense abstraction about them, compounded now with anger. One of his eyelids drooped slightly.

He said, "Are you the Earthman?"

"Elijah Baley," said Baley, "Plainclothesman C-7, in charge of the investigation into the murder of Dr. Rikaine Delmarre. What is your name?"

"I'm Dr. Jothan Leebig. Why do you presume to annoy me at my work?"

"It's easy," said Baley quietly. "It's my business."

"Then take your business elsewhere."

"I have a few questions to ask first, Doctor. I believe you were a close associate of Dr. Delmarre. Right?"

One of Leebig's hands clenched suddenly into a fist and he strode hastily toward a mantelpiece on which tiny clockwork contraptions went through complicated periodic motions that caught hypnotically at the eye.

The viewer kept focused on Leebig so that his figure did not depart from central projection as he walked. Rather the room behind him seemed to move backward in little rises and dips as he strode.

Leebig said, "If you are the foreigner whom Gruer threatened to bring in——"

"I am."

"Then you are here against my advice. Done viewing."

"Not yet. Don't break contact." Baley raised his voice sharply and a finger as well. He pointed it directly at the roboticist, who shrank visibly away from it, full lips spreading into an expression of disgust.

Baley said, "I wasn't bluffing about seeing you, you know."

"No Earthman vulgarity, please."

"A straightforward statement is what it is intended to be. I will see you, if I can't make you listen any other way. I will grab you by the collar and make you listen."

Leebig stared back. "You are a filthy animal."

"Have it your way, but I will do as I say."

"If you try to invade my estate, I will—I will——"

Baley lifted his eyebrows. "Kill me? Do you often make such threats?"

"I made no threat."

"Then talk now. In the time you have wasted, a good deal might have been accomplished. You were a close associate of Dr. Delmarre. Right?"

The roboticist's head lowered. His shoulders moved slightly to a slow, regular breathing. When he looked up, he was in command of himself. He even managed a brief, sapless smile.

"I was."

"Delmarre was interested in new types of robots, I understand."

"He was."

"What kind?"

"Are you a roboticist?"

"No. Explain it for the layman."

"I doubt that I can."

"Try! For instance, I think he wanted robots capable of disciplining children. What would that involve?"

Leebig raised his eyebrows briefly and said, "To put it very simply, skipping all the subtle details, it means a strengthening of the C-integral governing the Sikorovich tandem route response at the W-65 level."

"Double-talk," said Baley.

"The truth."

"It's double-talk to me. How else can you put it?"

"It means a certain weakening of the First Law."

"Why so? A child is disciplined for its own future good. Isn't that the theory?"

"Ah, the future good!" Leebig's eyes glowed with passion and he seemed to grow less conscious of his listener and correspondingly more talkative. "A simple concept, you think. How many human beings are willing to accept a trifling inconvenience for the sake of a large future good? How long does it take to train a child that what tastes good now means a stomach-ache later, and what tastes bad now will correct the stomach-ache later? Yet you want a robot to be able to understand?

"Pain inflicted by a robot on a child sets up a powerful disruptive potential in the positronic brain. To counteract that by an anti-potential triggered through a realization of future good requires enough paths and bypaths to increase the mass of the positronic brain by 50 per cent, unless other circuits are sacrificed."

Baley said, "Then you haven't succeeded in building such a robot."

"No, nor am I likely to succeed. Nor anyone."

"Was Dr. Delmarre testing an experimental model of such a robot at the time of his death?"

"Not of *such* a robot. We were interested in other more practical things also."

Baley said quietly, "Dr. Leebig, I am going to have to learn a bit more about robotics and I am going to ask you to teach me."

Leebig shook his head violently, and his drooping eyelid dipped further in a ghastly travesty of a wink. "It should be obvious that a course in robotics takes more than a moment. I lack the time."

"Nevertheless, you must teach me. The smell of robots is the one thing that pervades everything on Solaria. If it is time we require, then more than ever I must see you. I am an Earthman and I cannot work or think comfortably while viewing."

It would not have seemed possible to Baley for Leebig to stiffen his stiff carriage further, but he did. He said, "Your phobias as an Earthman don't concern me. Seeing is impossible."

"I think you will change your mind when I tell you what I chiefly want to consult you about."

"It will make no difference. Nothing can."

"No? Then listen to this. It is my belief that throughout the history of the positronic robot, the First Law of Robotics has been deliberately misquoted."

Leebig moved spasmodically. "Misquoted? Fool! Madman! Why?"

"To hide the fact," said Baley with complete composure, "that robots can commit murder."

14

A Motive Is Revealed

LEEBIG'S MOUTH widened slowly. Baley took it for a snarl at first and then, with considerable surprise, decided that it was the most unsuccessful attempt at a smile that he had ever seen.

Leebig said, "Don't say that. Don't ever say that."

"Why not?"

"Because anything, however small, that encourages distrust of robots is harmful. Distrusting robots is a human *disease!*"

It was as though he were lecturing a small child. It was as though he were saying something gently that he wanted to yell. It was as though he were trying to persuade when what he really wanted was to enforce on penalty of death.

Leebig said, "Do you know the history of robotics?"

"A little."

"On Earth, you should. Yes. Do you know robots started with a Frankenstein complex against them? They were suspect. Men distrusted and feared robots. Robotics was almost an undercover science as a result. The Three Laws were first built into robots in an effort to overcome distrust and even so Earth would never allow a robotic society to develop. One of the reasons the first pioneers left Earth to colonize the rest of the Galaxy was so that they might establish societies in which robots would be allowed to free men of poverty and toil. Even *then*, there remained a latent suspicion not far below, ready to pop up at any excuse."

"Have you yourself had to counter distrust of robots?" asked Baley.

"Many times," said Leebig grimly.

"Is that why you and other roboticists are willing to distort the facts just a little in order to avoid suspicion as much as possible?"

"There is no distortion!"

"For instance, aren't the Three Laws misquoted?"

"*No!*"

"I can demonstrate that they are, and unless you convince me otherwise, I will demonstrate it to the whole Galaxy, if I can."

"You're mad. Whatever argument you may think you have is fallacious, I assure you."

"Shall we discuss it?"

"If it does not take too long."

"Face to face? Seeing?"

Leebig's thin face twisted. "*No!*"

"Good-by, Dr. Leebig. Others will listen to me."

"Wait. Great Galaxy, man, wait!"

"Seeing?"

The roboticist's hands wandered upward, hovered about his chin. Slowly a thumb crept into his mouth and remained there. He stared, blankly, at Baley.

Baley thought: Is he regressing to the pre-five-year-old stage so that it will be legitimate for him to see me?

"Seeing?" he said.

But Leebig shook his head slowly. "I can't. I can't," he moaned, the words all but stifled by the blocking thumb. "Do whatever you want."

Baley stared at the other and watched him turn away and face the wall. He watched the Solarian's straight back bend and the Solarian's face hide in shaking hands.

Baley said, "Very well, then, I'll agree to view."

Leebig said, back still turned, "Excuse me a moment. I'll be back."

Baley tended to his own needs during the interval and stared at his fresh-washed face in the bathroom mirror. Was he getting the feel of Solaria and Solarians? He wasn't sure.

He sighed and pushed a contact and a robot appeared. He didn't turn to look at it. He said, "Is there another viewer at the farm, besides the one I'm using?"

"There are three other outlets, master."

"Then tell Klorissa Cantoro—tell your mistress that I will be using this one till further notice and that I am not to be disturbed."

"Yes, master."

Baley returned to his position where the viewer remained focused on the empty patch of room in which Leebig had stood. It was still empty and he settled himself to wait.

It wasn't long. Leebig entered and the room once more jiggled as the man walked. Evidently focus shifted from room center to man center without delay. Baley remembered the complexity of viewing controls and began to feel a kind of appreciation of what was involved.

Leebig was quite master of himself now, apparently. His hair was slicked back and his costume had been changed. His clothes fitted loosely and were of a material that glistened and caught highlights. He sat down in a slim chair that folded out of the wall.

He said soberly, "Now what is this notion of yours concerning First Law?"

"Will we be overheard?"

"No. I've taken care."

Baley nodded. He said, "Let me quote the First Law."

"I scarcely need that."

"I know, but let me quote it, anyway: A robot may not harm a human being or, through inaction, allow a human being to come to harm."

"Well?"

"Now when I first landed on Solaria, I was driven to the estate assigned for my use in a ground-car. The ground-car was a specially enclosed job designed to protect me from exposure to open space. As an Earthman——"

"I know about that," said Leebig impatiently. "What has this to do with the matter?"

"The robots who drove the car did *not* know about it. I asked that the car be opened and was at once obeyed. Second Law. They had to follow orders. I was uncomfortable, of course, and nearly collapsed before the car was enclosed again. Didn't the robots harm me?"

"At your order," snapped Leebig.

"I'll quote the Second Law: A robot must obey the orders given it by human beings except where such orders would conflict with the First Law. So you see, my order should have been ignored."

"This is nonsense. The robot lacked knowledge——"

Baley leaned forward in his chair. "Ah! We have it. Now let's recite the First Law as it should be stated: A robot may do nothing that, *to its knowledge,* will harm a human being; nor, through inaction, *knowingly* allow a human being to come to harm."

"This is all understood."

"I think not by ordinary men. Otherwise, ordinary men would realize robots could commit murder."

Leebig was white. "Mad! Lunacy!"

Baley stared at his finger ends. "A robot may perform an innocent task, I suppose; one that has no damaging effect on a human being?"

"If ordered to do so," said Leebig.

"Yes, of course. If ordered to do so. And a second robot may perform an innocent task, also, I suppose; one that also can have no damaging effect on a human being? If ordered to do so?"

"Yes."

"And what if the two innocent tasks, each completely innocent, completely, amount to murder when added together?"

"What?" Leebig's face puckered into a scowl.

"I want your expert opinion on the matter," said Baley. "I'll set you a hypothetical case. Suppose a man says to a robot, 'Place a small quantity of this liquid into a glass of milk that you will find in such and such a place. The liquid is harmless. I wish only to know its effect on milk. Once I know the effect, the mixture will be poured out. After you have performed this action, forget you have done so.'"

Leebig, still scowling, said nothing.

Baley said, "If I had told the robot to add a mysterious liquid to milk and then offer it to a man, First Law would force it to ask, 'What is the nature of the liquid? Will it harm a man?' And if it were assured the liquid was harmless, First Law might still make the robot hesitate and refuse to offer the milk. Instead, however, it is told the milk will be poured out. First Law is not involved. Won't the robot do as it is told?"

Leebig glared.

Baley said, "Now a second robot has poured out the milk in the first place and is unaware that the milk has been tampered with. In all innocence, it offers the milk to a man and the man dies."

Leebig cried out, "*No!*"

"Why not? Both actions are innocent in themselves. Only together are they murder. Do you deny that that sort of thing can happen?"

"The murderer would be the man who gave the order," cried Leebig.

"If you want to be philosophical, yes. The robots would have been the immediate murderers, though, the instruments of murder."

"No man would give such orders."

"A man would. A man has. It was exactly in this way that the murder attempt on Dr. Gruer must have been carried through. You've heard about that, I suppose."

"On Solaria," muttered Leebig, "one hears about everything."

"Then you know Gruer was poisoned at his dinner table before the eyes of myself and my partner, Mr. Olivaw of Aurora. Can you suggest any other way in which the poison might have reached him? There was no other human on the estate. As a Solarian, you must appreciate that point."

"I'm not a detective. I have no theories."

"I've presented you with one. I want to know if it is a possible one. I want to know if two robots might not perform two separate actions, each one innocent in itself, the two together resulting in murder. You're the expert, Dr. Leebig. *Is it possible?*"

And Leebig, haunted and harried, said, "Yes," in a voice so low that Baley scarcely heard him.

Baley said, "Very well, then. So much for the First Law."

Leebig stared at Baley and his drooping eyelid winked once or twice in a slow tic. His hands, which had been clasped, drew apart, though the fingers maintained their clawed shape as though each hand still entwined a phantom hand of air. Palms turned downward and rested on knees and only then did the fingers relax.

Baley watched it all in abstraction.

Leebig said, "Theoretically, yes. Theoretically! But don't dismiss the First Law that easily, Earthman. Robots would have to be ordered very cleverly in order to circumvent the First Law."

"Granted," said Baley. "I am only an Earthman. I know next to nothing about robots and my phrasing of the orders was only by way of example. A Solarian would be much more subtle and do much better. I'm sure of that."

Leebig might not have been listening. He said loudly, "If a robot can be manipulated into doing harm to a man, it means only that we must extend the powers of the positronic brain. One *might* say we ought to make the human better. That is impossible, so we will make the robot more foolproof.

"We advance continuously. Our robots are more varied, more specialized, more capable, and more unharming than those of a century ago. A century hence, we will have still greater advances. Why have a robot manipulate controls when a positronic brain can be built into the controls itself? That's specialization, but we can generalize, also. Why not a robot with replaceable and interchangeable limbs. Eh? Why not? If we——"

Baley interrupted. "Are you the only roboticist on Solaria?"

"Don't be a fool."

"I only wondered. Dr. Delmarre was the only—uh—fetal engineer, except for an assistant."

"Solaria has over twenty roboticists."

"Are you the best?"

"I am," Leebig said without self-consciousness.

"Delmarre worked with you."

"He did."

Baley said, "I understand that he was planning to break the partnership toward the end."

"No sign of it. What gave you the idea?"

"I understand he disapproved of your bachelorhood."

"He may have. He was a thorough Solarian. However, it did not affect our business relationships."

"To change the subject. In addition to developing new model robots, do you also manufacture and repair existing types?"

Leebig said, "Manufacture and repair are largely robot-conducted. There is a large factory and maintenance shop on my estate."

"Do robots require much in the way of repair, by the way?"

"Very little."

"Does that mean that robot repair is an undeveloped science?"

"Not at all." Leebig said that stiffly.

"What about the robot that was at the scene of Dr. Delmarre's murder?"

Leebig looked away, and his eyebrows drew together as though a painful thought were being barred entrance to his mind. "It was a complete loss."

"Really complete? Could it answer any questions at all?"

"None at all. It was absolutely useless. Its positronic brain was completely short-circuited. Not one pathway was left intact. Consider! It had witnessed a murder it had been unable to halt——"

"Why was it unable to halt the murder, by the way?"

"Who can tell? Dr. Delmarre was experimenting with that robot. I do not know in what mental condition he had left it. He might have ordered it, for instance, to suspend all operations while he checked one particular circuit element. If someone whom neither Dr. Delmarre nor the robot suspected of harm were suddenly to launch a homicidal attack, there might be a perceptible interval before the robot could use First Law potential to overcome Dr. Delmarre's freezing order. The length of the interval would depend on the nature of the attack and the nature of Dr. Delmarre's freezing order. I could invent a dozen other ways of explaining why the robot was unable to prevent the murder. Being unable to do so was a First Law violation, however, and that was sufficient to blast every positronic pathway in the robot's mind."

"But if the robot was physically unable to prevent the murder, was it responsible? Does the First Law ask impossibilities?"

Leebig shrugged. "The First Law, despite your attempts to make little of it, protects humanity with every atom of possible force. It allows no excuses. If the First Law is broken, the robot is ruined."

"That is a universal rule, sir?"

"As universal as robots."

Baley said, "Then I've learned something."

"Then learn something else. Your theory of murder by a series of robotic actions, each innocent in itself, will not help you in the case of Dr. Delmarre's death."

"Why not?"

"The death was not by poisoning, but by bludgeoning. Something had to hold the bludgeon, and that had to be a human arm. No robot could swing a club and smash a skull."

"Suppose," said Baley, "a robot were to push an innocent button which dropped a booby-trap weight on Delmarre's head."

Leebig smiled sourly. "Earthman, I've viewed the scene of the crime. I've heard all the news. The murder was a big thing here on Solaria, you know. So I know there was no sign of any machinery at the scene of the crime, or of any fallen weight."

Baley said, "Or of any blunt instrument, either."

Leebig said scornfully, "You're a detective. Find it."

"Granting that a robot was not responsible for Dr. Delmarre's death, who was, then?"

"Everyone knows who was," shouted Leebig. "His wife! Gladia!"

Baley thought: At least there's a unanimity of opinion.

Aloud he said, "And who was the mastermind behind the robots who poisoned Gruer?"

"I suppose . . ." Leebig trailed off.

"You don't think there are two murderers, do you? If Gladia was responsible for one crime, she must be responsible for the second attempt, also."

"Yes. You must be right." His voice gained assurance. "No doubt of it."

"No doubt?"

"Nobody else could get close enough to Dr. Delmarre to kill him. He allowed personal presence no more than I did, except that he made an exception in favor of his wife, and I make no exceptions. The wiser I." The roboticist laughed harshly.

"I believe you knew her," said Baley abruptly.

"Whom?"

"Her. We are discussing only one 'her.' Gladia!"

"Who told you I knew her any more than I know anyone else?" demanded Leebig. He put his hand to his throat. His fingers moved slightly and opened the neck-seam of his garment for an inch downward, leaving more freedom to breathe.

"Gladia herself did. You two went for walks."

"So? We were neighbors. It is a common thing to do. She seemed a pleasant person."

"You approved of her, then?"

Leebig shrugged. "Talking to her was relaxing."

"What did you talk about?"

"Robotics." There was a flavor of surprise about the word as though there were wonder that the question could be asked.

"And she talked robotics too?"

"She knew nothing about robotics. Ignorant! But she listened. She has some sort of field-force rigmarole she plays with; field coloring, she calls it. I have no patience with that, but I listened."

"All this without personal presence?"

Leebig looked revolted and did not answer.

Baley tried again, "Were you attracted to her?"

"What?"

"Did you find her attractive? Physically?"

Even Leebig's bad eyelid lifted and his lips quivered. "Filthy animal," he muttered.

"Let me put it this way, then. When did you cease finding Gladia pleasant? You used that word yourself, if you remember."

"What do you mean?"

"You said you found her pleasant. Now you believe she murdered her husband. That isn't the mark of a pleasant person."

"I was mistaken about her."

"But you decided you were mistaken before she killed her husband, if she did so. You stopped walking with her some time before the murder. Why?"

Leebig said, "Is that important?"

"Everything is important till proven otherwise."

"Look, if you want information from me as a roboticist, ask it. I won't answer personal questions."

Baley said, "You were closely associated with both the murdered man and the chief suspect. Don't you see that personal questions are unavoidable? Why did you stop walking with Gladia?"

Leebig snapped, "There came a time when I ran out of things to say; when I was too busy; when I found no reason to continue the walks."

"When you no longer found her pleasant, in other words."

"All right. Put it so."

"Why was she no longer pleasant?"

Leebig shouted, "I have no reason."

Baley ignored the other's excitement. "You are still someone who has known Gladia well. What could her motive be?"

"Her motive?"

"No one has suggested any motive for the murder. Surely Gladia wouldn't commit murder without a motive."

"Great Galaxy!" Leebig leaned his head back as though to laugh, but didn't. "No one told you? Well, perhaps no one knew. I knew, though. She told me. She told me frequently."

"Told you what, Dr. Leebig?"

"Why, that she quarreled with her husband. Quarreled bitterly and frequently. She hated him, Earthman. Didn't anyone tell you that? Didn't *she* tell you?"

15

A Portrait Is Colored

Baley took it between the eyes and tried not to show it.

Presumably, living as they did, Solarians considered one another's private lives to be sacrosanct. Questions concerning marriage and children were in bad taste. He supposed then that chronic quarreling could exist between husband and wife and be a matter into which curiosity was equally forbidden.

But even when murder had been committed? Would no one commit the social crime of asking the suspect if she quarreled with her husband? Or of mentioning the matter if they happened to know of it?

Well, Leebig had.

Baley said, "What did the quarrels concern?"

"You had better ask her, I think."

He better had, thought Baley. He rose stiffly, "Thank you, Dr. Leebig, for your co-operation. I may need your help again later. I hope you will keep yourself available."

"Done viewing," said Leebig, and he and the segment of his room vanished abruptly.

For the first time Baley found himself not minding a plane flight through open space. Not minding it at all. It was almost as though he were in his own element.

He wasn't even thinking of Earth or of Jessie. He had been away from Earth only a matter of weeks, yet it might as well have been years. He had been on Solaria only the better part of three days and yet it seemed forever.

How fast could a man adapt to nightmare?

Or was it Gladia? He would be seeing her soon, not viewing her. Was that what gave him confidence and this odd feeling of mixed apprehension and anticipation?

Would she endure it? he wondered. Or would she slip away after a few moments of seeing, begging off as Quemot had done?

She stood at the other end of a long room when he entered. She might almost have been an impressionistic representation of herself, she was reduced so to essentials.

Her lips were faintly red, her eyebrows lightly penciled, her earlobes faintly blue, and, except for that, her face was untouched. She looked pale, a little frightened, and very young.

Her brown-blond hair was drawn back, and her gray-blue eyes were somehow shy. Her dress was a blue so dark as to be almost black, with a thin white edging curling down each side. She wore long sleeves, white gloves, and flat-heeled shoes. Not an inch of skin showed anywhere but in her face. Even her neck was covered by a kind of unobtrusive ruching.

Baley stopped where he was. "Is this close enough, Gladia?"

She was breathing with shallow quickness. She said, "I had forgotten what to expect really. It's just like viewing, isn't it? I mean, if you don't think of it as seeing."

Baley said, "It's all quite normal to me."

"Yes, on Earth." She closed her eyes. "Sometimes I try to imagine it. Just crowds of people everywhere. You walk down a road and there are others walking with you and still others walking in the other direction. Dozens——"

"Hundreds," said Baley. "Did you ever view scenes on Earth in a book-film? Or view a novel with an Earth setting?"

"We don't have many of those, but I've viewed novels set on the other Outer Worlds where seeing goes on all the time. It's different in a novel. It just seems like a multiview."

"Do people ever kiss in novels?"

She flushed painfully. "I don't read that kind."

"Never?"

"Well—there are always a few dirty films around, you know, and sometimes, just out of curiosity—— It's sickening, really."

"Is it?"

She said with sudden animation, "But Earth is so different. So many people. When you walk, Elijah, I suppose you even t-touch people. I mean, by accident."

Baley half smiled. "You even knock them down by accident." He thought of the crowds on the Expressways, tugging and shoving, bounding up and down the strips, and for a moment, inevitably, he felt the pang of homesickness.

Gladia said, "You don't have to stay way out there."

"Would it be all right if I came closer?"

"I think so. I'll tell you when I'd rather you wouldn't any more."

Stepwise Baley drew closer, while Gladia watched him, wide-eyed.

She said suddenly, "Would you like to see some of my field colorings?"

Baley was six feet away. He stopped and looked at her. She seemed small and fragile. He tried to visualize her, something in her hand (what?), swinging furiously at the skull of her husband. He tried to picture her, mad with rage, homicidal with hate and anger.

He had to admit it could be done. Even a hundred and five pounds of woman could crush a skull if she had the proper weapon and were wild enough. And Baley had known murderesses (on Earth, of course) who, in repose, were bunny rabbits.

He said, "What are field colorings, Gladia?"

"An art form," she said.

Baley remembered Leebig's reference to Gladia's art. He nodded. "I'd like to see some."

"Follow me, then."

Baley maintained a careful six-foot distance between them. At that, it was less than a third the distance Klorissa had demanded.

They entered a room that burst with light. It glowed in every corner and every color.

Gladia looked pleased, proprietary. She looked up at Baley, eyes anticipating.

Baley's response must have been what she expected, though he said nothing. He turned slowly, trying to make out what he saw, for it was light only, no material object at all.

The gobbets of light sat on embracing pedestals. They were living geometry, lines and curves of color, entwined into a coalescing whole yet maintaining distinct identities. No two specimens were even remotely alike.

Baley groped for appropriate words and said, "Is it supposed to mean anything?"

Gladia laughed in her pleasant contralto. "It means whatever you like it to mean. They're just light-forms that might make you feel angry or happy or curious or whatever *I* felt when I constructed one. I could make one for you, a kind of portrait. It might not be very good, though, because I would just be improvising quickly."

"Would you? I would be very interested."

"All right," she said, and half-ran to a light-figure in one corner, passing within inches of him as she did so. She did not seem to notice.

She touched something on the pedestal of the light-figure and the glory above died without a flicker.

Baley gasped and said, "Don't do that."

"It's all right. I was tired of it, anyway. I'll just fade the others temporarily so they don't distract me." She opened a panel along one featureless wall and moved a rheostat. The colors faded to something scarcely visible.

Baley said, "Don't you have a robot to do this? Closing contacts?"

"Shush, now," she said impatiently. "I don't keep robots in here. This is *me*." She looked at him, frowning. "I don't know you well enough. That's the trouble."

She wasn't looking at the pedestal, but her fingers rested lightly on its smooth upper surface. All ten fingers were curved, tense, waiting.

One finger moved, describing a half curve over smoothness. A bar of deep yellow light grew and slanted obliquely across the air above. The finger inched backward a fraction and the light grew slightly less deep in shade.

She looked at it momentarily. "I suppose that's it. A kind of strength without weight."

"Jehoshaphat," said Baley.

"Are you offended?" Her fingers lifted and the yellow slant of light remained solitary and stationary.

"No, not at all. But what is it? How do you do it?"

"That's hard to explain," said Gladia, looking at the pedestal thoughtfully, "considering I don't really understand it myself. It's a kind of optical illusion, I've been told. We set up force-fields at different energy levels. They're extrusions of hyperspace, really, and don't have the properties of ordinary space at all. Depending on the energy level, the human eye sees light of different shades. The shapes and colors are controlled by the warmth of my fingers against appropriate spots on the pedestal. There are all sorts of controls inside each pedestal."

"You mean if I were to put my finger there——" Baley advanced and Gladia made way for him. He put a hesitant forefinger down upon the pedestal and felt a soft throbbing.

"Go ahead. Move your finger, Elijah," said Gladia.

Baley did so and a dirty-gray jag of light lifted upward, skewing the yellow light. Baley withdrew his finger sharply and Gladia laughed and then was instantly contrite.

"I shouldn't laugh," she said. "It's really very hard to do, even for people who've tried a long time." Her own hand moved lightly and too quickly for Baley to follow and the monstrosity he had set up disappeared, leaving the yellow light in isolation again.

"How did you learn to do this?" asked Baley.

"I just kept on trying. It's a new art form, you know, and only one or two really know how——"

"And you're the best," said Baley somberly. "On Solaria everyone is either the only or the best or both."

"You needn't laugh. I've had some of my pedestals on display. I've given shows." Her chin lifted. There was no mistaking her pride.

She continued, "Let me go on with your portrait." Her fingers moved again.

There were few curves in the light-form that grew under her ministrations. It was all sharp angles. And the dominant color was blue.

"That's Earth, somehow," said Gladia, biting her lower lip. "I always think of Earth as blue. All those people and seeing, seeing, seeing. Viewing is more rose. How does it seem to you?"

"Jehoshaphat, I can't picture things as colors."

"Can't you?" she asked abstractedly. "Now you say 'Jehoshaphat' sometimes and that's just a little blob of violet. A little sharp blob because it usually comes out ping, like that." And the little blob was there, glowing just off-center.

"And then," she said, "I can finish it like this." And a flat, luster-less hollow cube of slate gray sprang up to enclose everything. The light within shone through it, but dimmer; imprisoned, somehow.

Baley felt a sadness at it, as though it were something enclosing him, keeping him from something he wanted. He said, "What's that last?"

Gladia said, "Why, the walls about you. That's what's most in you, the way you can't go outside, the way you have to be inside. You *are* inside there. Don't you see?"

Baley saw and somehow he disapproved. He said, "Those walls aren't permanent. I've been out today."

"You have? Did you mind?"

He could not resist a counterdig. "The way you mind seeing me. You don't like it but you can stand it."

She looked at him thoughtfully. "Do you want to come out now? With me? For a walk?"

It was Baley's impulse to say: Jehoshaphat, no.

She said, "I've never walked with anyone, seeing. It's still daytime, and it's pleasant weather."

Baley looked at his abstractionist portrait and said, "If I go, will you take away the gray?"

She smiled and said, "I'll see how you behave."

The structure of light remained as they left the room. It stayed behind, holding Baley's imprisoned soul fast in the gray of the Cities.

Baley shivered slightly. Air moved against him and there was a chill to it.

Gladia said, "Are you cold?"

"It wasn't like this before," muttered Baley.

"It's late in the day now, but it isn't really cold. Would you like a coat? One of the robots could bring one in a minute."

"No. It's all right." They stepped forward along a narrow paved path. He said, "Is this where you used to walk with Dr. Leebig?"

"Oh no. We walked way out among the fields, where you only see an occasional robot working and you can hear the animal sounds. You and I will stay near the house though, just in case."

"In case what?"

"Well, in case you want to go in."

"Or in case you get weary of seeing?"

"It doesn't bother me," she said recklessly.

There was the vague rustle of leaves above and an all-pervading yellowness and greenness. There were sharp, thin cries in the air about, plus a strident humming, and shadows, too.

He was especially aware of the shadows. One of them stuck out before him, in shape like a man, that moved as he did in horrible mimicry. Baley had heard of shadows, of course, and he knew what they were, but in the pervasive indirect lighting of the Cities he had never been specifically aware of one.

Behind him, he knew, was the Solarian sun. He took care not to look at it, but he knew it was there.

Space was large, space was lonely, yet he found it drawing him. His mind pictured himself striding the surface of a world with thousands of miles and light-years of room all about him.

Why should he find attraction in this thought of loneliness? He didn't want loneliness. He wanted Earth and the warmth and companionship of the man-crammed Cities.

The picture failed him. He tried to conjure up New York in his mind, all the noise and fullness of it, and found he could remain conscious only of the quiet, air-moving chill of the surface of Solaria.

Without quite willing it Baley moved closer to Gladia until he was two feet away, then grew aware of her startled face.

"I beg your pardon," he said at once, and drew off.

She gasped, "It's all right. Won't you walk this way? We have some flower beds you might like."

The direction she indicated lay away from the sun. Baley followed silently.

Gladia said, "Later in the year, it will be wonderful. In the warm weather I can run down to the lake and swim, or just run across the fields, run as fast as I can until I'm just glad to fall down and lie still."

She looked down at herself. "But this is no costume for it. With all this on, I've *got* to walk. Sedately, you know."

"How would you prefer to dress?" asked Baley.

"Halter and shorts at the *most,*" she cried, lifting her arms as though feeling the freedom of that in her imagination. "Sometimes less. Sometimes just sandals so you can feel the air with every inch—— Oh, I'm sorry. I've offended you."

Baley said, "No. It's all right. Was that your costume when you went walking with Dr. Leebig?"

"It varied. It depended on the weather. Sometimes I wore very little, but it was viewing, you know. You *do* understand, I hope."

"I understand. What about Dr. Leebig, though? Did he dress lightly too?"

"Jothan dress lightly?" Gladia smiled flashingly. "Oh no. He's very solemn, always." She twisted her face into a thin look of gravity and half winked, catching the very essence of Leebig and forcing a short grunt of appreciation out of Baley.

"This is the way he talks," she said. " 'My dear Gladia, in considering the effect of a first-order potential on positron flow——' "

"Is that what he talked to you about? Robotics?"

"Mostly. Oh, he takes it so seriously, you know. He was always trying to teach me about it. He never gave up."

"Did you learn anything?"

"Not one thing. Nothing. It's just all a complete mix-up to me. He'd get angry with me sometimes, but when he'd scold, I'd dive into the water, if we were anywhere near the lake, and splash him."

"*Splash* him? I thought you were viewing."

She laughed. "You're *such* an Earthman. I'd splash where he was standing in his own room or on his own estate. The water couldn't touch him, but he would duck just the same. Look at that."

Baley looked. They had circled a wooded patch and now came upon a clearing, centered about an ornamental pond. Small bricked walks penetrated the clearing and broke it up. Flowers grew in profusion and order. Baley knew them for flowers from book-films he had viewed.

In a way the flowers were like the light-patterns that Gladia constructed and Baley imagined that she constructed them in the spirit of flowers. He touched one cautiously, then looked about. Reds and yellows predominated.

In turning to look about Baley caught a glimpse of the sun.

He said uneasily, "The sun is low in the sky."

"It's late afternoon," called Gladia back to him. She had run toward the pond and was sitting on a stone bench at its edge. "Come here," she shouted, waving. "You can stand if you don't like to sit on stone."

Baley advanced slowly. "Does it get this low every day?" and at once he was sorry he asked. If the planet rotated, the sun must be low in the sky both mornings and afternoons. Only at midday could it be high.

Telling himself this couldn't change a lifetime of pictured thought. He knew there was such a thing as night and had even experienced it, with a planet's whole thickness interposing safely between a man and the sun. He knew there were clouds and a protective grayness hiding the worst of outdoors. And still, when he thought of planetary surfaces, it was always a picture of a blaze of light with a sun high in the sky.

He looked over his shoulder, just quickly enough to get a flash of sun, and wondered how far the house was if he should decide to return.

Gladia was pointing to the other end of the stone bench.

Baley said, "That's pretty close to you, isn't it?"

She spread out her little hands, palms up. "I'm getting used to it. Really."

He sat down, facing toward her to avoid the sun.

She leaned over backward toward the water and pulled a small cup-shaped flower, yellow without and white-streaked within, not at all flamboyant. She said, "This is a native plant. Most of the flowers here are from Earth originally."

Water dripped from its severed stem as she extended it gingerly toward Baley.

Baley reached for it as gingerly. "You killed it," he said.

"It's only a flower. There are thousands more." Suddenly, before his fingers more than touched the yellow cup, she snatched it away, her eyes kindling. "Or are you trying to imply I could kill a human being because I pulled a flower?"

Baley said in soft conciliation, "I wasn't implying anything. May I see it?"

Baley didn't really want to touch it. It had grown in wet soil and there was still the effluvium of mud about it. How could these people, who were so careful in contact with Earthmen and even with one another, be so careless in their contact with ordinary dirt?

But he held the stalk between thumb and forefinger and looked at it. The cup was formed of several thin pieces of papery tissue, curving up from a common center. Within it was a white convex swelling, damp with liquid and fringed with dark hairs that trembled lightly in the wind.

She said, "Can you smell it?"

At once Baley was aware of the odor that emanated from it. He leaned toward it and said, "It smells like a woman's perfume."

Gladia clapped her hands in delight. "How like an Earthman. What you really mean is that a woman's perfume smells like *that*."

Baley nodded ruefully. He was growing weary of the outdoors. The shadows were growing longer and the land was becoming somber. Yet he was determined not to give in. He wanted those gray walls of light that dimmed his portrait removed. It was quixotic, but there it was.

Gladia took the flower from Baley, who let it go without reluctance. Slowly she pulled its petals apart. She said, "I suppose every woman smells different."

"It depends on the perfume," said Baley indifferently.

"Imagine being close enough to tell. I don't wear perfume because no one is close enough. Except now. But I suppose you smell perfume often, all the time. On Earth, your wife is always with you, isn't she?" She was concentrating very hard on the flower, frowning as she plucked it carefully to pieces.

"She's not always with me," said Baley. "Not every minute."

"But most of the time. And whenever you want to——"

Baley said suddenly, "Why did Dr. Leebig try so hard to teach you robotics, do you suppose?"

The dismembered flower consisted now of a stalk and the inner swelling. Gladia twirled it between her fingers, then tossed it away, so that it floated for a moment on the surface of the pond. "I think he wanted me to be his assistant," she said.

"Did he tell you so, Gladia?"

"Toward the end, Elijah. I think he grew impatient. Anyway, he asked me if I didn't think it would be exciting to work in robotics. Naturally, I told him I could think of nothing duller. He was quite angry."

"And he never walked with you again after that."

She said, "You know, I think that may have been it. I suppose his feelings were hurt. Really, though, what could I do?"

"It was before that, though, that you told him about your quarrels with Dr. Delmarre."

Her hands became fists and held so in a tight spasm. Her body held stiffly to its position, head bent and a little to one side. Her voice was unnaturally high. "What quarrels?"

"Your quarrels with your husband. I understand you hated him."

Her face was distorted and blotched as she glared at him. "Who told you that? Jothan?"

"Dr. Leebig mentioned it. I think it's true."

She was shaken. "You're still trying to prove I killed him. I keep thinking you're my friend and you're only—only a detective."

She raised her fists and Baley waited.

He said, "You know you can't touch me."

Her hands dropped and she began crying without a sound. She turned her head away.

Baley bent his own head and closed his eyes, shutting out the disturbing long shadows. He said, "Dr. Delmarre was not a very affectionate man, was he?"

She said in a strangled way, "He was a very busy man."

Baley said, "You *are* affectionate, on the other hand. You find a man interesting. Do you understand?"

"I c-can't help it. I know it's disgusting, but I can't help it. It's even disgusting t-to talk about it."

"You did talk about it to Dr. Leebig, though?"

"I *had* to do something and Jothan was handy and he didn't seem to mind and it made me feel better."

"Was this the reason you quarreled with your husband? Was it that he was cold and unaffectionate and you resented it?"

"Sometimes I hated him." She shrugged her shoulders helplessly. "He was just a good Solarian and we weren't scheduled for ch—for ch——" She broke down.

Baley waited. His own stomach was cold and open air pressed down heavily upon him. When Gladia's sobs grew quieter, he asked, as gently as he could, "Did you kill him, Gladia?"

"N-no." Then, suddenly, as though all resistance had corroded within her: "I haven't told you everything."

"Well, then, please do so now."

"We were quarreling that time, the time he died. The old quarrel. I screamed at him but he never shouted back. He hardly ever even said anything and that just made it worse. I was so angry, so angry. I don't remember after that."

"Jehoshaphat!" Baley swayed slightly and his eyes sought the neutral stone of the bench. "What do you mean you don't remember?"

"I mean he was dead and I was screaming and the robots came——"

"Did you kill him?"

"I don't remember it, Elijah, and I would remember it if I did, wouldn't I? Only I don't remember anything else, either, and I've been so frightened, so frightened. Help me, please, Elijah."

"Don't worry, Gladia. I'll help you." Baley's reeling mind fastened on the murder weapon. What happened to it? It must have been removed. If so, only the murderer could have done it. Since Gladia was found immediately after the murder on the scene, she could not have done it. The murderer would have to be someone else. No matter how it looked to everyone on Solaria, it had to be someone else.

Baley thought sickly: I've got to get back to the house.

He said, "Gladia——"

Somehow he was staring at the sun. It was nearly at the horizon. He had to turn his head to look at it and his eyes locked with a morbid fascination. He had never seen it so. Fat, red, and dim somehow, so that one could look at it without blinding, and see the bleeding clouds above it in thin lines, with one crossing it in a bar of black.

Baley mumbled, "The sun is so red."

He heard Gladia's choked voice say drearily, "It's always red at sunset, red and dying."

Baley had a vision. The sun was moving down to the horizon because the planet's surface was moving away from it, a thousand miles an hour, spinning under that naked sun, spinning with nothing to guard the microbes called men that scurried over its spinning surface, spinning madly forever, spinning—spinning . . .

It was his head that was spinning and the stone bench that was slanting beneath him and the sky heaving, blue, dark blue, and the sun was gone, with the tops of trees and the ground rushing up and Gladia screaming thinly and another sound . . .

16

A Solution Is Offered

BALEY WAS aware first of enclosure, the absence of the open, and then of a face bending over him.

He stared for a moment without recognition. Then: *"Daneel!"*

The robot's face showed no sign of relief or of any other recognizable emotion at being addressed. He said, "It is well that you have recovered consciousness, Partner Elijah. I do not believe you have suffered physical injury."

"I'm all right," said Baley testily, struggling to his elbows. "Jehoshaphat, am I in bed? What for?"

"You have been exposed to the open a number of times today. The effects upon you have been cumulative and you need rest."

"I need a few answers first." Baley looked about and tried to deny to himself that his head was spinning just a little. He did not recognize the room. The curtains were drawn. Lights were comfortably artificial. He was feeling much better. "For instance, where am I?"

"In a room of Mrs. Delmarre's mansion."

"Next, let's get something straight. What are *you* doing here? How did you get away from the robots I set over you?"

Daneel said, "It had seemed to me that you would be displeased at this development and yet in the interests of your safety and of my orders, I felt that I had no choice but——"

"What did you *do*? Jehoshaphat!"

"It seems Mrs. Delmarre attempted to view you some hours ago."

"Yes." Baley remembered Gladia saying as much earlier in the day. "I know that."

"Your order to the robots that held me prisoner was, in your words: 'Do not allow him' (meaning myself) 'to establish contact with other humans or other robots, either by seeing or by viewing.' However, Partner Elijah, you said nothing about forbidding other humans or robots to contact me. You see the distinction?"

Baley groaned.

Daneel said, "No need for distress, Partner Elijah. The flaw in your orders was instrumental in saving your life, since it brought me to the scene. You see, when Mrs. Delmarre viewed me, being allowed to do so by my robot guardians, she asked after you and I answered, quite truthfully, that I did not know of your whereabouts, but that I could attempt to find out. She seemed anxious that I do so. I said I thought it possible you might have left the house temporarily and that I would check that matter and would she, in the meanwhile, order the robots in the room with me, to search the mansion for your presence."

"Wasn't she surprised that you didn't deliver the orders to the robots yourself?"

"I gave her the impression, I believe, that as an Auroran I was not as accustomed to robots as she was; that she might deliver the orders with greater authority and effect a more speedy consummation. Solarians, it is quite clear, are vain of their skill with robots and contemptuous of the ability of natives of other planets to handle them. Is that not your opinion as well, Partner Elijah?"

"And she ordered them away, then?"

"With difficulty. They protested previous orders but, of course, could not state the nature thereof since you had ordered them to tell no one of my own true identity. She overrode them, although the final orders had to be shrilled out in fury."

"And then you left."

"I did, Partner Elijah."

A pity, thought Baley, that Gladia did not consider that episode important enough to relay to him when he viewed her. He said, "It took you long enough to find me, Daneel."

"The robots on Solaria have a network of information through subetheric contact. A skilled Solarian could obtain information readily, but, mediated as it is through millions of individual machines, one such as myself, without experience in the matter, must take time to unearth a single datum. It was better than an hour before the information as to your whereabouts reached me. I lost further time by visiting Dr. Delmarre's place of business after you had departed."

"What were you doing there?"

"Pursuing researches of my own. I regret that this had to be done in your absence, but the exigencies of the investigation left me no choice."

Baley said, "Did you view Klorissa Cantoro, or see her?"

"I viewed her, but from another part of her building, not from our own estate. There were records at the farm I had to see. Ordinarily viewing would have been sufficient, but it might have been inconvenient to remain on our own estate since three robots knew my real nature and might easily have imprisoned me once more."

Baley felt almost well. He swung his legs out of bed and found himself in a kind of nightgown. He stared at it with distaste. "Get me my clothes."

Daneel did so.

As Baley dressed, he said, "Where's Mrs. Delmarre?"

"Under house arrest, Partner Elijah."

"What? By whose order?"

"By my order. She is confined to her bedroom under robotic guard and her right to give orders other than to meet personal needs has been neutralized."

"By yourself?"

"The robots on this estate are not aware of my identity."

Baley finished dressing. "I know the case against Gladia," he said. "She had the opportunity; more of it, in fact, than we thought at first. She did not rush to the scene at the sound of her husband's cry, as she first said. She was there all along."

"Does she claim to have witnessed the murder and seen the murderer?"

"No. She remembers nothing of the crucial moments. That happens sometimes. It turns out, also, that she has a motive."

"What was it, Partner Elijah?"

"One that I had suspected as a possibility from the first. I said to myself, if this were Earth, and Dr. Delmarre were as he was described to be and Gladia Delmarre as she seemed to be, I would say that she was in love with him, or had been, and that he was in love only with himself. The difficulty was to tell whether Solarians felt love or reacted to love in any Earthly sense. My judgment as to their emotions and reactions wasn't to be trusted. It was why I had to see a few. *Not* view them, but see them."

"I do not follow you, Partner Elijah."

"I don't know if I can explain it to you. These people have their gene possibilities carefully plotted before birth and the actual gene distribution tested after birth."

"I know that."

"But genes aren't everything. Environment counts too, and environment can bend into actual psychosis where genes indicate only a potentiality for a particular psychosis. Did you notice Gladia's interest in Earth?"

"I remarked upon it, Partner Elijah, and considered it an assumed interest designed to influence your opinions."

"Suppose it were a real interest, even a fascination. Suppose there were something about Earth's crowds that excited her. Suppose she were attracted against her will by something she had been taught to consider filthy. There was possible abnormality. I had to test it by seeing Solarians and noticing how they reacted to it, and seeing her and noticing how *she* reacted to it. It was why I had to get away from you, Daneel, at any cost. It was why I had to abandon viewing as a method for carrying on the investigation."

"You did not explain this, Partner Elijah."

"Would the explanation have helped against what you conceived your duty under First Law to be?"

Daneel was silent.

Baley said, "The experiment worked. I saw or tried to see several people. An old sociologist tried to see me and had to give up midway. A roboticist refused to see me at all even under terrific force. The bare possibility sent him into an almost infantile frenzy. He sucked his finger and wept. Dr. Delmarre's assistant was used to personal presence in the way of her profession and so she tolerated me, but at twenty feet only. Gladia, on the other hand——"

"Yes, Partner Elijah?"

"Gladia consented to see me without more than a slight hesitation. She tolerated my presence easily and actually showed signs of decreasing strain as time went on. It all fits into a pattern of psychosis. She didn't mind seeing me; she was interested in Earth; she might have felt an abnormal interest in her husband. All of it could be explained by a strong and, for this world, psychotic interest in the personal presence of members of the opposite sex. Dr. Delmarre, himself, was not the type to encourage such a feeling or co-operate with it. It must have been very frustrating for her."

Daneel nodded. "Frustrating enough for murder in a moment of passion."

"In spite of everything, I don't think so, Daneel."

"Are you perhaps being influenced by extraneous motives of your own, Partner Elijah? Mrs. Delmarre is an attractive woman and you are an Earthman in whom a preference for the personal presence of an attractive woman is not psychotic."

"I have better reasons," said Baley uneasily. (Daneel's cool glance was too penetrating and soul-dissecting by half. Jehoshaphat! The thing was only a machine.) He said, "If she were the murderess of her husband, she would also have to be the attempted murderess of Gruer." He had almost the impulse to explain the way murder could be manipulated through robots, but held back. He was not sure how Daneel would react to a theory that made unwitting murderers of robots.

Daneel said, "And the attempted murderess of yourself as well."

Baley frowned. He had had no intention of telling Daneel of the poisoned arrow that had missed; no intention of strengthening the other's already too strong protective complex vis-à-vis himself.

He said angrily, "What did Klorissa tell you?" He ought to have warned her to keep quiet, but then, how was he to know that Daneel would be about, asking questions?

Daneel said calmly, "Mrs. Cantoro had nothing to do with the matter. I witnessed the murder attempt myself."

Baley was thoroughly confused. "You were nowhere about."

Daneel said, "I caught you myself and brought you here an hour ago."

"What are you talking about?"

"Do you not remember, Partner Elijah? It was almost a perfect murder. Did not Mrs. Delmarre suggest that you go into the open? I was not a witness to that, but I feel certain she did."

"She did suggest it. Yes."

"She may even have enticed you to leave the house."

Baley thought of the "portrait" of himself, of the enclosing gray walls. Could it have been clever psychology? Could a Solarian have that much intuitive understanding of the psychology of an Earthman?

"No," he said.

Daneel said, "Was it she who suggested you go down to the ornamental pond and sit on the bench?"

"Well, yes."

"Does it occur to you that she might have been watching you, noticing your gathering dizziness?"

"She asked once or twice if I wanted to go back."

"She might not have meant it seriously. She might have been watching you turn sicker on that bench. She might even have pushed you, or perhaps a push wasn't necessary. At the moment I reached you and caught you in my arms, you were in the process of falling backward off the stone bench and into three feet of water, in which you would surely have drowned."

For the first time Baley recalled those last fugitive sensations. "Jehoshaphat!"

"Moreover," said Daneel with calm relentlessness, "Mrs. Delmarre sat beside you, watching you fall, without a move to stop you. Nor would she have attempted to pull you out of the water. She would have let you drown. She might have called a robot, but the robot would surely have arrived too late. And afterward, she would explain merely that, of course, it was impossible for her to touch you even to save your life."

True enough, thought Baley. No one would question her inability to touch a human being. The surprise, if any, would come at her ability to be as close to one as she was.

Daneel said, "You see, then, Partner Elijah, that her guilt can scarcely be in question. You stated that she would have to be the attempted murderess of Agent Gruer as though this were an argument against her guilt. You see now that she must have been. Her only motive to murder you was the same as her motive for trying to murder Gruer; the necessity of getting rid of an embarrassingly persistent investigator of the first murder."

Baley said, "The whole sequence might have been an innocent one. She might never have realized how the outdoors would affect me."

"She studied Earth. She knew the peculiarities of Earthmen."

"I assured her I had been outdoors today and that I was growing used to it."

"She may have known better."

Baley pounded fist against palm. "You're making her too clever. It doesn't fit and I don't believe it. In any case, no murder accusation can stick unless and until the absence of the murder weapon can be accounted for."

Daneel looked steadily at the Earthman, "I can do that, too, Partner Elijah."

Baley looked at his robot partner with a stunned expression. "How?"

"Your reasoning, you will remember, Partner Elijah, was this. Were Mrs. Delmarre the murderess, then the weapon, whatever it was, must have remained at the scene of the murder. The robots, appearing almost at once, saw no sign of such a weapon, hence it must have been removed from the scene, hence the murderer must have removed it, hence the murderer could not be Mrs. Delmarre. Is all that correct?"

"Correct."

"Yet," continued the robot, "there is one place where the robots did not look for the weapon."

"Where?"

"Under Mrs. Delmarre. She was lying in a faint, brought on by the excitement and passion of the moment, whether murderess or not, and the weapon, whatever it was, lay under her and out of sight."

Baley said, "Then the weapon would have been discovered as soon as she was moved."

"Exactly," said Daneel, "but she was not moved by the robots. She herself told us yesterday at dinner that Dr. Thool ordered the robots to put a pillow under her head and leave her. She was first moved by Dr. Altim Thool, himself, when he arrived to examine her."

"So?"

"It follows, therefore, Partner Elijah, that a new possibility arises. Mrs. Delmarre was the murderess, the weapon was at the scene of the crime, but Dr. Thool carried it off and disposed of it to protect Mrs. Delmarre."

Baley felt contemptuous. He had almost been seduced into expecting something reasonable. He said, "Completely motiveless. Why should Dr. Thool do such a thing?"

"For a very good reason. You remember Mrs. Delmarre's remarks concerning him: 'He always treated me since I was a child and was always so friendly and kind.' I wondered if he might have some motive for being particularly concerned about her. It was for that reason that I visited the baby farm and inspected the records. What I had merely guessed at as a possibility turned out to be the truth."

"What?"

"Dr. Altim Thool was the father of Gladia Delmarre, and what is more, he knew of the relationship."

Baley had no thought of disbelieving the robot. He felt only a deep chagrin that it had been Robot Daneel Olivaw and not himself that had carried through the necessary piece of logical analysis. Even so, it was not complete.

He said, "Have you spoken to Dr. Thool?"

"Yes. I have placed him under house arrest, also."

"What does he say?"

"He admits that he is the father of Mrs. Delmarre. I confronted him with the records of the fact and the records of his inquiries into her health when she was a youngster. As a doctor, he was allowed more leeway in this respect than another Solarian might have been allowed."

"Why should he have inquired into her health?"

"I have considered that, too, Partner Elijah. He was an old man when he was given special permission to have an additional child and, what is more, he succeeded in producing one. He considers this a tribute to his genes and to his physical fitness. He is prouder of the result, perhaps, than is quite customary on this world. Moreover, his position as physician, a profession little regarded on Solaria because it involves personal presences, made it the more important to him to nurture this sense of pride. For that reason, he maintained unobtrusive contact with his offspring."

"Does Gladia know anything of it?"

"As far as Dr. Thool is aware, Partner Elijah, she does not."

Baley said, "Does Thool admit removing the weapon?"

"No. That he does not."

"Then you've got nothing, Daneel."

"Nothing?"

"Unless you can find the weapon and prove he took it, or at the very least induce him to confess, you have no evidence. A chain of deduction is pretty, but it isn't evidence."

"The man would scarcely confess without considerable questioning of a type I myself could not carry through. His daughter is dear to him."

"Not at all," said Baley. "His feeling for his daughter is not at all what you and I are accustomed to. Solaria is different!"

He strode the length of the room and back, letting himself cool. He said, "Daneel, you have worked out a perfect exercise in logic, but none of it is reasonable, just the same." (Logical but not reasonable. Wasn't that the definition of a robot?)

He went on, "Dr. Thool is an old man and past his best years, regardless of whether he was capable of siring a daughter thirty years or so ago. Even Spacers get senile. Picture him then examining his daughter in a faint and his son-in-law dead by violence. Can you imagine the unusual nature of the situation for him? Can you suppose he could have remained master of himself? So much the master of himself, in fact, as to carry out a series of amazing actions?

"Look! First, he would have had to notice a weapon under his daughter, one that must have been so well covered by her body that the robots never noticed it. Secondly, from whatever small scrap of object he noted, he must have deduced the presence of the weapon and seen at once that if he could but sneak off with that weapon, unseen, a murder accusation against his daughter would be hard to substantiate. That's pretty subtle thinking for an old man in a panic. Then, thirdly, he would have had to carry the plan through, also tough for an old man in a panic. And now, lastly, he would have to dare to compound the felony further by sticking to his lie. It all may be the result of logical thinking, but none of it is reasonable."

Daneel said, "Do you have an alternate solution to the crime, Partner Elijah?"

Baley had sat down during the course of his last speech and now he tried to rise again, but a combination of weariness and the depth of the chair defeated him. He held out his hand petulantly. "Give me a hand, will you, Daneel?"

Daneel stared at his own hand. "I beg your pardon, Partner Elijah?"

Baley silently swore at the other's literal mind and said, "Help me out of the chair."

Daneel's strong arm lifted him out of the chair effortlessly.

Baley said, "Thanks. No, I haven't an alternate solution. At least, I have, but the whole thing hinges on the location of the weapon."

He walked impatiently to the heavy curtains that lined most of one wall and lifted a corner without quite realizing what he was doing. He stared at the black patch of glass until he became aware of the fact that he was looking out into the early night, and then dropped the curtain just as Daneel, approaching quietly, took it out of his fingers.

In the split fraction of a moment in which Baley watched the robot's hand take the curtain away from him with the loving caution of a mother protecting her child from the fire, a revolution took place within him.

He snatched the curtain back, yanking it out of Daneel's grasp. Throwing his full weight against it, he tore it away from the window, leaving shreds behind.

"Partner Elijah!" said Daneel softly. "Surely you know now what the open will do to you."

"I know," said Baley, "what it will do *for* me."

He stared out the window. There was nothing to see, only blackness, but that blackness was open air. It was unbroken, unobstructed space, even if unlit, and he was facing it.

And for the first time he faced it freely. It was no longer bravado, or perverse curiosity, or the pathway to a solution of a murder. He faced it because he knew he wanted to and because he needed to. That made all the difference.

Walls were crutches! Darkness and crowds were crutches! He must have thought them so, unconsciously, and hated them even when he most thought he loved and needed them. Why else had he so resented Gladia's gray enclosure of his portrait?

He felt himself filling with a sense of victory, and, as though victory were contagious, a new thought came, bursting like an inner shout.

Baley turned dizzily to Daneel. "I know," he whispered. "Jehoshaphat! I know!"

"Know what, Partner Elijah?"

"I know what happened to the weapon; I know who is responsible. All at once, everything falls into place."

17

A Meeting Is Held

DANEEL WOULD allow no immediate action.

"Tomorrow!" he had said with respectful firmness. "That is my suggestion, Partner Elijah. It is late and you are in need of rest."

Baley had to admit the truth of it, and besides there was the need of preparation; a considerable quantity of it. He had the solution of the murder, he felt sure of that, but it rested on deduction, as much as had Daneel's theory, and it was worth as little as evidence. Solarians would have to help him.

And if he were to face them, one Earthman against half a dozen Spacers, he would have to be in full control. That meant rest and preparation.

Yet he would not sleep. He was certain he would not sleep. Not all the softness of the special bed set up for him by smoothly functioning robots nor all the soft perfume and softer music in the special room of Gladia's mansion would help. He was sure of it.

Daneel sat unobtrusively in one darkened corner.

Baley said, "Are you still afraid of Gladia?"

The robot said, "I do not think it wise to allow you to sleep alone and unprotected."

"Well, have your way. Are you clear as to what I want you to do, Daneel?"

"I am, Partner Elijah."

"You have no reservations under the First Law, I hope."

"I have some with respect to the conference you wish arranged. Will you be armed and careful of your own safety?"

"I assure you, I will."

Daneel delivered himself of a sigh that was somehow so human that for a moment Baley found himself trying to penetrate the darkness that he might study the machine-perfect face of the other.

Daneel said, "I have not always found human behavior logical."

"We need Three Laws of our own," said Baley, "but I'm glad we don't have them."

He stared at the ceiling. A great deal depended on Daneel and yet he could tell him very little of the whole truth. Robots were too involved. The planet, Aurora, had its reasons for sending a robot as representative of their interests, but it was a mistake. Robots had their limitations.

Still, if all went right, this could all be over in twelve hours. He could be heading back to Earth in twenty-four, bearing hope. A strange kind of hope. A kind he could scarcely believe himself, yet it was Earth's way out. It must be Earth's way out.

Earth! New York! Jessie and Ben! The comfort and familiarity and dearness of home!

He dwelled on it, half asleep, and the thought of Earth failed to conjure the comfort he expected. There was an estrangement between himself and the Cities.

And at some unknown point in time it all faded and he slept.

Baley, having slept and then wakened, showered and dressed. Physically he was quite prepared. Yet he was unsure. It was not that his reasoning seemed any less cogent to himself in the pallor of morning. It was rather the necessity of facing Solarians.

Could he be sure of their reactions after all? Or would he still be working blind?

Gladia was the first to appear. It was simple for her, of course. She was on an intramural circuit, since she was in the mansion itself. She was pale and expressionless, in a white gown that draped her into a cold statue.

She stared helplessly at Baley. Baley smiled back gently and she seemed to take comfort from that.

One by one, they appeared now. Attlebish, the Acting Head of Security, appeared next after Gladia, lean and haughty, his large chin set in disapproval. Then Leebig, the roboticist, impatient and angry, his weak eyelid fluttering periodically. Quemot, the sociologist, a little tired, but smiling at Baley out of deep-set eyes in a condescending way, as though to say: We have seen one another, we have been intimate.

Klorissa Cantoro, when she appeared, seemed uneasy in the presence of the others. She glanced at Gladia for a moment with an audible sniff, then stared at the floor. Dr. Thool, the physician, appeared last. He looked haggard, almost sick.

They were all there, all but Gruer, who was slowly recovering and for whom attendance was physically impossible. (Well, thought Baley, we'll do without him.) All were dressed formally; all sat in rooms that were well curtained into enclosure.

Daneel had arranged matters well. Baley hoped fervently that what remained for Daneel to do would work as well.

Baley looked from one Spacer to the other. His heart thudded. Each figure viewed him out of a different room and the clash of lighting, furniture, and wall decoration was dizzying.

Baley said, "I want to discuss the matter of the killing of Dr. Rikaine Delmarre under the heading of motive, opportunity, and means, in that order——"

Attlebish interrupted. "Will this be a long speech?"

Baley said sharply, "It may be. I have been called here to investigate a murder and such a job is my specialty and my profession. I know best how to go about it." (Take nothing from them now, he thought, or this whole thing won't work. Dominate! Dominate!)

He went on, making his words as sharp and incisive as he could. "Motive first. In a way, motive is the most unsatisfactory of the three items. Opportunity and means are objective. They can be investigated factually. Motive is subjective. It may be something that can be observed by others; revenge for a known humiliation, for instance. But it may also be completely unobservable; an irrational, homicidal hate on the part of a well-disciplined person who never lets it show.

"Now almost all of you have told me at one time or another that you believed Gladia Delmarre to have committed the crime. Certainly, no one has suggested an alternate suspect. Has Gladia a motive? Dr. Leebig suggested one. He said that Gladia quarreled frequently with her husband and Gladia later admitted this to me. The rage that can arise out of a quarrel can, conceivably, move a person to murder. Very well.

"The question remains, though, whether she is the only one with a motive. I wonder. Dr. Leebig, himself——"

The roboticist almost jumped. His hand extended rigidly in the direction of Baley. "Watch what you say, Earthman."

"I am only theorizing," said Baley coldly. "You, Dr. Leebig, were working with Dr. Delmarre on new robot models. You are the best man in Solaria as far as robotics is concerned. You say so and I believe it."

Leebig smiled with open condescension.

Baley went on. "But I have heard that Dr. Delmarre was about to break off relations with you for matters concerning yourself of which he disapproved."

"False! False!"

"Perhaps. But what if it were true? Wouldn't you have a motive to get rid of him before he humiliated you publicly by breaking with you? I have a feeling you could not easily bear such humiliation."

Baley went on rapidly to give Leebig no chance to retort. "And you, Mrs. Cantoro. Dr. Delmarre's death leaves you in charge of fetal engineering, a responsible position."

"Skies above, we talked about that before," cried Klorissa in anguish.

"I know we did, but it's a point that must be considered, anyway. As for Dr. Quemot, he played chess with Dr. Delmarre regularly. Perhaps he grew annoyed at losing too many games."

The sociologist interposed quietly. "Losing a chess game is insufficient motive surely, Plainclothesman."

"It depends on how seriously you take your chess. Motives can seem all the world to the murderer and completely insignificant to everyone else. Well, it doesn't matter. My point is that motive alone is insufficient. Anyone can have a motive, particularly for the murder of a man such as Dr. Delmarre."

"What do you mean by that remark," demanded Quemot in indignation.

"Why, only that Dr. Delmarre was a 'good Solarian.' You all described him as such. He rigidly fulfilled all the requirements of Solarian custom. He was an ideal man, almost an abstraction. Who could feel love, or even liking, for such a man? A man without weaknesses serves only to make everyone else conscious of his own imperfections. A primitive poet named Tennyson once wrote: 'He is all fault who has no fault at all.'"

"No one would kill a man for being too good," said Klorissa, frowning.

"You little know," said Baley, and went on without amplification. "Dr. Delmarre was aware of a conspiracy on Solaria, or thought he was; a conspiracy that was preparing an assault on the rest of the Galaxy for purposes of conquest. He was interested in preventing that. For that reason, those concerned in the conspiracy might find it necessary to do away with him. Anyone here could be a member of the conspiracy, including, to be sure, Mrs. Delmarre, but including even the Acting Head of Security, Corwin Attlebish."

"I?" said Attlebish, unmoved.

"You certainly attempted to end the investigation as soon as Gruer's mishap put you in charge."

Baley took a few slow sips at his drink (straight from its original container, untouched by human hands others than his own, or robotic hands, either) and gathered his strength. So far, this was a waiting game, and he was thankful the Solarians were sitting still for it. They hadn't the Earthman's experience of dealing with people at close quarters. They weren't in-fighters.

He said, "Opportunity next. It is the general opinion that only Mrs. Delmarre had opportunity since only she could approach her husband in actual personal presence.

"Are we sure of that? Suppose someone other than Mrs. Delmarre had made up his or her mind to kill Dr. Delmarre? Would not such a desperate resolution make the discomfort of personal presence secondary? If any of you were set on murder, wouldn't you bear personal presence just long enough to do the job? Couldn't you sneak into the Delmarre mansion——"

Attlebish interposed frigidly. "You are ignorant of the matter, Earthman. Whether we would or would not doesn't matter. The fact is that Dr. Delmarre himself would not allow seeing, I assure you. If anyone came into his personal presence, regardless of how valued and long-standing a friendship there was between them, Dr. Delmarre would order him away and, if necessary, call robots to help with the ejection."

"True," said Baley, "*if* Dr. Delmarre were aware that personal presence was involved."

"What do you mean by that?" demanded Dr. Thool in surprise, his voice quavering.

"When you treated Mrs. Delmarre at the scene of the murder," replied Baley, looking full at his questioner, "she assumed you were viewing her, until you actually touched her. So she told me and so I believe. I am, myself, accustomed only to seeing. When I arrived at Solaria and met Security Head Gruer, I assumed I was seeing him. When at the end of our interview, Gruer disappeared, I was taken completely by surprise.

"Now assume the reverse. Suppose that for all a man's adult life, he had been viewing only; never seeing anyone, except on rare occasions his wife. Now suppose someone other than his wife walked up to him in personal presence. Would he not automatically assume that it was a matter of viewing, particularly if a robot had been instructed to advise Delmarre that viewing contact was being set up?"

"Not for a minute," said Quemot. "The sameness of background would give it away."

"Maybe, but how many of you are aware of background now? There would be a minute or so, at least, before Dr. Delmarre would grow aware that something was wrong and in that time, his friend, whoever he was, could walk up to him, raise a club, and bring it down."

"Impossible," said Quemot stubbornly.

"I think not," said Baley. "I think opportunity must be canceled out as absolute proof that Mrs. Delmarre is the murderess. She had opportunity, but so might others."

Baley waited again. He felt perspiration on his forehead, but wiping it away would have made him look weak. He must maintain absolute charge of the proceedings. The person at whom he was aiming must be placed in self-convinced inferiority. It was hard for an Earthman to do that to a Spacer.

Baley looked from face to face and decided that matters were at least progressing satisfactorily. Even Attlebish looked quite humanly concerned.

"And so we come," he said, "to means, and that is the most puzzling factor of all. The weapon with which the murder was committed was never found."

"We know that," said Attlebish. "If it were not for that point, we would have considered the case against Mrs. Delmarre conclusive. We would never have required an investigation."

"Perhaps," said Baley. "Let's analyze the matter of means, then.

There are two possibilities. Either Mrs. Delmarre committed the murder, or someone else did. If Mrs. Delmarre committed the murder, the weapon would have had to remain at the scene of the crime, unless it were removed later. It has been suggested by my partner, Mr. Olivaw of Aurora, who is not present at the moment, that Dr. Thool had the opportunity to remove the weapon. I ask Dr. Thool now, in the presence of all of us, if he did this, if he removed a weapon while examining the unconscious Mrs. Delmarre?"

Dr. Thool was shaking. "No, no. I swear it. I'll abide any questioning. I swear I removed nothing."

Baley said, "Is there anyone who wishes to suggest at this point that Dr. Thool is lying?"

There was a silence, during which Leebig looked at an object outside of Baley's field of vision and muttered something about the time.

Baley said, "The second possibility is that someone else committed the crime and carried the weapon off with him. But if that were so, one must ask why. Carrying the weapon away is an advertisement of the fact that Mrs. Delmarre was not the murderess. If an outsider were the murderer, he would have to be a complete imbecile not to leave the weapon with the corpse to convict Mrs. Delmarre. Either way, then, *the weapon must be there!* Yet it was not seen."

Attlebish said, "Do you take us for fools or for blind men?"

"I take you for Solarians," said Baley calmly, "and therefore incapable of recognizing the particular weapon that was left at the scene of the crime as a weapon."

"I don't understand a word," muttered Klorissa in distress.

Even Gladia, who had scarcely moved a muscle during the course of the meeting, was staring at Baley in surprise.

Baley said, "Dead husband and unconscious wife were not the only individuals on the scene. There was also a disorganized robot."

"Well?" said Leebig angrily.

"Isn't it obvious, then, that, in having eliminated the impossible, what remains, however improbable, is the truth. The robot at the scene of the crime was the murder weapon, a murder weapon none of you could recognize by force of your training."

They all talked at once; all but Gladia, who simply stared.

Baley raised his arms. "Hold it. Quiet! Let me explain!" And once again he told the story of the attempt on Gruer's life and the method by which it could have been accomplished. This time he added the attempt on his own life at the baby farm.

Leebig said impatiently, "I suppose that was managed by having one robot poison an arrow without knowing it was using poison, and having a second robot hand the poisoned arrow to the boy after telling him that you were an Earthman, without its knowing that the arrow was poisoned."

"Something like that. Both robots would be completely instructed."

"Very farfetched," said Leebig.

Quemot was pale and looked as though he might be sick at any moment. "No Solarian could possibly use robots to harm a human."

"Maybe so," said Baley with a shrug, "but the point is that robots can be so manipulated. Ask Dr. Leebig. He is the roboticist."

Leebig said, "It does not apply to the murder of Dr. Delmarre. I told you that yesterday. How can anyone arrange to have a robot smash a man's skull?"

"Shall I explain how?"

"Do so if you can."

Baley said, "It was a new-model robot that Dr. Delmarre was testing. The significance of that wasn't plain to me until last evening, when I had occasion to say to a robot, in asking for his help in rising out of a chair, 'Give me a hand!' The robot looked at his own hand in confusion as though he thought he was expected to detach it and give it to me. I had to repeat my order less idiomatically. But it reminded me of something Dr. Leebig had told me earlier that day. There was experimentation among robots with replaceable limbs.

"Suppose this robot that Dr. Delmarre had been testing was one such, capable of using any of a number of interchangeable limbs of various shapes for different kinds of specialized tasks. Suppose the murderer knew this and suddenly said to the robot, 'Give me your arm.' The robot would detach its arm and give it to him. The detached arm would make a splendid weapon. With Dr. Delmarre dead, it could be snapped back into place."

Stunned horror gave way to a babble of objection as Baley talked. His last sentence had to be shouted, and, even so, was all but drowned out.

Attlebish, face flushed, raised himself from his chair and stepped forward. "Even if what you say is so, then Mrs. Delmarre is the murderess. She was there, she quarreled with him, she would be watching her husband working with the robot, and would know of the replaceable-limb situation—which I don't believe, by the way. No matter what you do, Earthman, everything points to her."

Gladia began to weep softly.

Baley did not look at her. He said, "On the contrary, it is easy to show that, whoever committed the murder, Mrs. Delmarre did not."

Jothan Leebig suddenly folded his arms and allowed an expression of contempt to settle on his face.

Baley caught that and said, "You'll help me do so, Dr. Leebig. As a roboticist, you know that maneuvering robots into actions such as indirect murder takes enormous skill. I had occasion yesterday to try to put an individual under house arrest. I gave three robots detailed instructions intended to keep this individual safe. It was a simple thing, but I am a clumsy man with robots. There were loopholes in my instructions and my prisoner escaped."

"Who was the prisoner?" demanded Attlebish.

"Beside the point," said Baley impatiently. "What *is* the point is the fact that amateurs can't handle robots well. And some Solarians may be pretty amateurish as Solarians go. For instance, what does Gladia Delmarre know about robotics? . . . Well, Dr. Leebig?"

"What?" The roboticist stared.

"You tried to teach Mrs. Delmarre robotics. What kind of a pupil was she? Did she learn anything?"

Leebig looked about uneasily. "She didn't . . ." and stalled.

"She was completely hopeless, wasn't she? Or would you prefer not to answer?"

Leebig said stiffly, "She might have pretended ignorance."

"Are you prepared to say, as a roboticist, that you think Mrs. Delmarre is sufficiently skilled to drive robots to indirect murder?"

"How can I answer that?"

"Let me put it another way. Whoever tried to have me killed at the baby farm must have had to locate me by using interrobot communications. After all, I told no human where I was going and only the robots who conveyed me from point to point knew of my whereabouts. My partner, Daneel Olivaw, managed to trace me later in the day, but only with considerable difficulty. The murderer, on the other hand, must have done it easily, since, in addition to locating me, he had to arrange for arrow poisoning and arrow shooting, all before I left the farm and moved on. Would Mrs. Delmarre have the skill to do that?"

Corwin Attlebish leaned forward. "Who do you suggest would have the necessary skill, Earthman?"

Baley said, "Dr. Jothan Leebig is self-admittedly the best robot man on the planet."

"Is that an accusation?" cried Leebig.

"Yes!" shouted Baley.

The fury in Leebig's eyes faded slowly. It was replaced not by calm, exactly, but by a kind of clamped-down tension. He said, "I studied the Delmarre robot after the murder. It had no detachable limbs. At least, they were detachable only in the usual sense of requiring special tools and expert handling. So the robot wasn't the weapon used in killing Delmarre and you have no argument."

Baley said, "Who else can vouch for the truth of your statement?"

"My word is not to be questioned."

"It is here. I'm accusing you, and your unsupported word concerning the robot is valueless. If someone else will bear you out, that would be different. Incidentally, you disposed of that robot quickly. Why?"

"There was no reason to keep it. It was completely disorganized. It was useless."

"Why?"

Leebig shook his finger at Baley and said violently, "You asked me that once before, Earthman, and I told you why. It had witnessed a murder which it had been powerless to stop."

"And you told me that that always brought about complete collapse; that that was a universal rule. Yet when Gruer was poisoned, the robot that had presented him with the poisoned drink was harmed only to the extent of a limp and a lisp. It had actually itself been the agent of what looked like murder at the moment, and not merely a witness, and yet it retained enough sanity to be questioned.

"This robot, the robot in the Delmarre case, must therefore have been still more intimately concerned with murder than the Gruer robot. This Delmarre robot must have had its own arm used as the murder weapon."

"All nonsense," gasped out Leebig. "You know nothing about robotics."

Baley said, "That's as may be. But I will suggest that Security Head Attlebish impound the records of your robot factory and maintenance shop. Perhaps we can find out whether you have built robots with detachable limbs and, if so, whether any were sent to Dr. Delmarre, and, if so, when."

"No one will tamper with my records," cried Leebig.

"Why? If you have nothing to hide, why?"

"But why on Solaria should I want to kill Delmarre? Tell me that. What's my motive?"

"I can think of two," said Baley. "You were friendly with Mrs. Delmarre. Overly friendly. Solarians are human, after a fashion. You never consorted with women, but that didn't keep you immune from, shall we say, animal urges. You saw Mrs. Delmarre—I beg your pardon, you viewed her—when she was dressed rather informally and——"

"No," cried Leebig in agony.

And Gladia whispered energetically, "No."

"Perhaps you didn't recognize the nature of your feelings yourself," said Baley, "or if you had a dim notion of it, you despised yourself for your weakness, and hated Mrs. Delmarre for inspiring it. And yet you might have hated Delmarre, too, for having her. You did ask Mrs. Delmarre to be your assistant. You compromised with your libido that far. She refused and your hatred was the keener for that. By killing Dr. Delmarre in such a way as to throw suspicion on Mrs. Delmarre, you could be avenged on both at once."

"Who would believe that cheap, melodramatic filth?" demanded Leebig in a hoarse whisper. "Another Earthman, another animal, maybe. No Solarian."

"I don't depend on that motive," said Baley. "I think it was there, unconsciously, but you had a plainer motive, too. Dr. Rikaine Delmarre was in the way of your plans, and had to be removed."

"What plans?" demanded Leebig.

"Your plans aiming at the conquest of the Galaxy, Dr. Leebig," said Baley.

18

A Question Is Answered

"The Earthman is mad," cried Leebig, turning to the others. "Isn't that obvious?"

Some stared at Leebig wordlessly, some at Baley.

Baley gave them no chance to come to decisions. He said, "You know better, Dr. Leebig. Dr. Delmarre was going to break off with you. Mrs. Delmarre thought it was because you wouldn't marry. I don't think so. Dr. Delmarre himself was planning a future in which ectogenesis would be possible and marriage unnecessary. But Dr. Delmarre was working with you; he would know, and guess, more about your work than anyone else. He would know if you were attempting dangerous experiments and he would try to stop you. He hinted about such matters to Agent Gruer, but gave no details, because he was not yet certain of the details. Obviously, you discovered his suspicions and killed him."

"Mad!" said Leebig again. "I will have nothing more to do with this."

But Attlebish interrupted. "Hear him out, Leebig!"

Baley bit his lip to keep from a premature display of satisfaction at the obvious lack of sympathy in the Security Head's voice. He said, "In the same discussion with me in which you mentioned robots with detachable limbs, Dr. Leebig, you mentioned spaceships with built-in positronic brains. You were definitely talking too much then. Was it that you thought I was only an Earthman and incapable of understanding the implications of robotics? Or was it that you had just been threatened with personal presence, had the threat lifted, and were a little delirious with relief? In any case, Dr.

Quemot had already told me that the secret weapon of Solaria against the Outer Worlds was the positronic robot."

Quemot, thus unexpectedly referred to, started violently, and cried, "I meant——"

"You meant it sociologically, I know. But it gives rise to thoughts. Consider a spaceship with a built-in positronic brain as compared to a manned spaceship. A manned spaceship could not use robots in active warfare. A robot could not destroy humans on enemy spaceships or on enemy worlds. It could not grasp the distinction between friendly humans and enemy humans.

"Of course, a robot could be told that the opposing spaceship had no humans aboard. It could be told that it was an uninhabited planet that was being bombarded. That would be difficult to manage. A robot could see that its own ship carried humans; it would know its own world held humans. It would assume that the same was true of enemy ships and worlds. It would take a real expert in robotics, such as you, Dr. Leebig, to handle them properly in that case, and there are very few such experts.

"But a spaceship that was equipped with its own positronic brain would cheerfully attack any ship it was directed to attack, it seems to me. It would naturally assume all other ships were unmanned. A positronic-brained ship could easily be made incapable of receiving messages from enemy ships that might undeceive it. With its weapons and defenses under the immediate control of a positronic brain, it would be more maneuverable than any manned ship. With no room necessary for crewmen, for supplies, for water or air purifiers, it could carry more armor, more weapons and be more invulnerable than any ordinary ship. One ship with a positronic brain could defeat fleets of ordinary ships. Am I wrong?"

The last question was shot at Dr. Leebig, who had risen from his seat and was standing, rigid, almost cataleptic with—what? Anger? Horror?

There was no answer. No answer could have been heard. Something tore loose and the others were yelling madly. Klorissa had the face of a Fury and even Gladia was on her feet, her small fist beating the air threateningly.

And all had turned on Leebig.

Baley relaxed and closed his eyes. He tried for just a few moments to unknot his muscles, unfreeze his tendons.

It had worked. He had pressed the right button at last. Quemot had made an analogy between the Solarian robots and the Spartan Helots. He said the robots could not revolt so that the Solarians could relax.

But what if some human threatened to teach the robots how to harm humans; to make them, in other words, capable of revolting?

Would that not be the ultimate crime? On a world such as Solaria would not every last inhabitant turn fiercely against anyone even suspected of making a robot capable of harming a human; on Solaria, where robots outnumbered humans by twenty thousand to one?

Attlebish cried, "You are under arrest. You are absolutely forbidden to touch your books or records until the government has a chance to inspect them——" He went on, almost incoherent, scarcely heard in the pandemonium.

A robot approached Baley. "A message, master, from the master Olivaw."

Baley took the message gravely, turned, and cried, "One moment."

His voice had an almost magical effect. All turned to look at him solemnly and in no face (outside Leebig's frozen glare) was there any sign of anything but the most painful attention to the Earthman.

Baley said, "It is foolish to expect Dr. Leebig to leave his records untouched while waiting for some official to reach them. So even before this interview began, my partner, Daneel Olivaw, left for Dr. Leebig's estate. I have just heard from him. He is on the grounds now and will be with Dr. Leebig in a moment in order that he may be put under restraint."

"*Restraint!*" howled Leebig in an almost animal terror. His eyes widened into staring holes in his head. "Someone coming here? Personal presence? No! No!" The second "No" was a shriek.

"You will not be harmed," said Baley coldly, "if you co-operate."

"But I won't see him. I can't see him." The roboticist fell to his knees without seeming aware of the motion. He put his hands together in a desperate clasped gesture of appeal. "What do you want? Do you want a confession? Delmarre's robot had detachable limbs. Yes. Yes. Yes. I arranged Gruer's poisoning. I arranged the arrow meant for you. I even planned the spaceships as you said. I haven't succeeded, but, yes, I planned it. Only keep the man away. Don't let him come. Keep him away!"

He was babbling.

Baley nodded. Another right button. The threat of personal presence would do more to induce confession than any physical torture.

But then, at some noise or movement outside the field of sound or vision of any of the others, Leebig's head twisted and his mouth opened. He lifted a pair of hands, holding something off.

"Away," he begged. "Go away. Don't come. Please don't come. Please——"

He scrambled away on hands and knees, then his hand went suddenly to a pocket in his jacket. It came out with something and moved rapidly to his mouth. Swaying twice, he fell prone.

Baley wanted to cry: You fool, it isn't a human that's approaching; only one of the robots you love.

Daneel Olivaw darted into the field of vision and for a moment stared down at the crumpled figure.

Baley held his breath. If Daneel should realize it was his own pseudo humanity that had killed Leebig, the effect on his First Law-enslaved brain might be drastic.

But Daneel only knelt and his delicate fingers touched Leebig here and there. Then he lifted Leebig's head as though it were infinitely precious to him, cradling it, caressing it.

His beautifully chiseled face stared out at the others and he whispered, "A human is dead!"

Baley was expecting her; she had asked for a last interview; but his eyes widened when she appeared.

He said, "I'm seeing you."

"Yes," said Gladia, "how can you tell?"

"You're wearing gloves."

"Oh." She looked at her hands in confusion. Then, softly, "Do you mind?"

"No, of course not. But why have you decided to see, rather than view?"

"Well"—she smiled weakly—"I've got to get used to it, don't I, Elijah? I mean, if I'm going to Aurora."

"Then it's all arranged?"

"Mr. Olivaw seems to have influence. It's all arranged. I'll never come back."

"Good. You'll be happier, Gladia. I know you will."

"I'm a little afraid."

"I know. It will mean seeing all the time and you won't have all the comforts you had on Solaria. But you'll get used to it and, what's more, you'll forget all the terror you've been through."

"I don't want to forget everything," said Gladia softly.

"You will." Baley looked at the slim girl who stood before him and said, not without a momentary pang, "And you will be married someday, too. Really married, I mean."

"Somehow," she said mournfully, "that doesn't seem so attractive to me—right now."

"You'll change your mind."

And they stood there, looking at each other for a wordless moment.

Gladia said, "I've never thanked you."

Baley said, "It was only my job."

"You'll be going back to Earth now, won't you?"

"Yes."

"I'll never see you again."

"Probably not. But don't feel badly about that. In forty years at most, I'll be dead and you won't look a bit different from the way you do now."

Her face twisted. "Don't say that."

"It's true."

She said rapidly, as though forced to change the subject, "It's all true about Jothan Leebig, you know."

"I know. Other roboticists went over his records and found experiments toward unmanned intelligent spaceships. They also found other robots with replaceable limbs."

Gladia shuddered, "Why did he do such a horrible thing, do you suppose?"

"He was afraid of people. He killed himself to avoid personal presence and he was ready to kill other worlds to make sure that Solaria and its personal-presence taboo would never be touched."

"How could he feel so," she murmured, "when personal presence can be so very——"

Again a silent moment while they faced each other at ten paces.

Then Gladia cried suddenly, "Oh, Elijah, you'll think it abandoned of me."

"Think what abandoned?"

"May I touch you? I'll never see you again, Elijah."

"If you want to."

Step by step, she came closer, her eyes glowing, yet looking apprehensive, too. She stopped three feet away, then slowly, as though in a trance, she began to remove the glove on her right hand.

Baley started a restraining gesture. "Don't be foolish, Gladia."

"I'm not afraid," said Gladia.

Her hand was bare. It trembled as she extended it.

And so did Baley's as he took her hand in his. They remained so for one moment, her hand a shy thing, frightened as it rested in his. He opened his hand and hers escaped, darted suddenly and without warning toward his face until her fingertips rested feather-light upon his cheek for the barest moment.

She said, "Thank you, Elijah. Good-by."

He said, "Good-by, Gladia," and watched her leave.

Even the thought that a ship was waiting to take him back to Earth did not wipe out the sense of loss he felt at that moment.

Undersecretary Albert Minnim's look was intended to be one of prim welcome. "I am glad to see you back on Earth. Your report, of course, arrived before you did and is being studied. You did a good job. The matter will look well in your record."

"Thank you," said Baley. There was no room for further elation in him. Being back on Earth; being safe in the Caves; being in hearing of Jessie's voice (he had spoken to her already) had left him strangely empty.

"However," said Minnim, "your report concerned only the murder investigation. There was another matter we were interested in. May I have a report on that, verbally?"

Baley hesitated and his hand moved automatically toward the inner pocket where the warm comfort of his pipe could once more be found.

Minnim said at once, "You may smoke, Baley."

Baley made of the lighting process a rather drawn-out ritual. He said, "I am not a sociologist."

"Aren't you?" Minnim smiled briefly. "It seems to me we discussed that once. A successful detective must be a good rule-of-thumb sociologist even if he never heard of Hackett's Equation. I think, from your discomfort at the moment, that you have notions concerning the Outer Worlds but aren't sure how it will sound to me?"

"If you put it that way, sir . . . When you ordered me to Solaria, you asked a question; you asked what the weaknesses of the Outer Worlds were. Their strengths were their robots, their low population, their long lives, but what were their weaknesses?"

"Well?"

"I believe I know the weaknesses of the Solarians, sir."

"You can answer my question? Good. Go ahead."

"Their weaknesses, sir, are their robots, their low population, their long lives."

Minnim stared at Baley without any change of expression. His hands worked in jerky finger-drawn designs along the papers on his desk.

He said, "Why do you say that?"

Baley had spent hours organizing his thoughts on the way back from Solaria; had confronted officialdom, in imagination, with balanced, well-reasoned arguments. Now he felt at a loss.

He said, "I'm not sure I can put them clearly."

"No matter. Let me hear. This is first approximation only."

Baley said, "The Solarians have given up something mankind has had for a million years; something worth more than atomic power, cities, agriculture, tools, fire, everything; because it's something that made everything else possible."

"I don't want to guess, Baley. What is it?"

"The tribe, sir. Co-operation between individuals. Solaria has given it up entirely. It is a world of isolated individuals and the planet's only sociologist is delighted that this is so. That sociologist, by the way, never heard of sociomathematics, because he is inventing his own science. There is no one to teach him, no one to help him, no one to think of something he himself might miss. The only science that really flourishes on Solaria is robotics and there are only a handful of men involved in that, and when it came to an analysis of the interaction of robots and men, they had to call in an Earthman to help."

"Solarian art, sir, is abstract. We have abstract art on Earth as *one* form of art; but on Solaria it is the *only* form. The human touch is gone. The looked-for future is one of ectogenesis and complete isolation from birth."

Minnim said, "It all sounds horrible. But is it harmful?"

"I think so. Without the interplay of human against human, the chief interest in life is gone; most of the intellectual values are gone; most of the reason for living is gone. Viewing is no substitute for seeing. The Solarians, themselves, are conscious that viewing is a long-distance sense.

"And if isolation isn't enough to induce stagnation, there is the matter of their long lives. On Earth, we have a continuous influx of young people who are willing to change because they haven't had time to grow hard-set in their ways. I suppose there's some optimum. A life long enough for real accomplishment and short enough to make way for youth at a rate that's not too slow. On Solaria, the rate *is* too slow."

Minnim still drew patterns with his finger. "Interesting! Interesting!" He looked up, and it was as though a mask had fallen away. There was glee in his eyes. "Plainclothesman, you're a man of penetration."

"Thank you," said Baley stiffly.

"Do you know why I encouraged you to describe your views to me?" He was almost like a little boy, hugging his pleasure. He went on without waiting for an answer. "Your report has already undergone preliminary analysis by our sociologists and I was wondering if you had any idea yourself as to the excellent news for Earth you had brought with you. I see you have."

"But wait," said Baley. "There's more to this."

"There is, indeed," agreed Minnim jubilantly. "Solaria cannot possibly correct its stagnation. It has passed a critical point and their dependence on robots has gone too far. Individual robots can't discipline an individual child, even though discipline may do the child eventual good. The robot can't see past the immediate pain. And robots collectively cannot discipline a planet by allowing its institutions to collapse when the institutions have grown harmful. They can't see past the immediate chaos. So the only end for the Outer Worlds is perpetual stagnation and Earth will be freed of their domination. This new data changes everything. Physical revolt will not even be necessary. Freedom will come of itself."

"Wait," said Baley again, more loudly. "It's only Solaria we're discussing, not any other Outer World."

"It's the same thing. Your Solarian sociologist—Kimot——"

"Quemot, sir."

"Quemot, then. He said, did he not, that the other Outer Worlds were moving in the direction of Solaria?"

"He did, but he knew nothing about the other Outer Worlds first-hand, and he was no sociologist. Not really. I thought I made that clear."

"Our own men will check."

"They'll lack data too. We know nothing about the really big Outer Worlds. Aurora, for instance; Daneel's world. To me, it doesn't seem reasonable to expect them to be anything like Solaria. In fact, there's only one world in the Galaxy which resembles Solaria——"

Minnim was dismissing the subject with a small, happy wave of his neat hand. "Our men will check. I'm sure they will agree with Quemot."

Baley's stare grew somber. If Earth's sociologists were anxious enough for happy news, they would find themselves agreeing with Quemot, at that. Anything could be found in figures if the search were long enough and hard enough and if the proper pieces of information were ignored or overlooked.

He hesitated. Was it best now to speak while he had the ear of a man high in the government or——

He hesitated a trifle too long. Minnim was speaking again, shuffling a few papers and growing more matter-of-fact. "A few minor matters, Plainclothesman, concerning the Delmarre case itself and then you will be free to go. Did you intend to have Leebig commit suicide?"

"I intended to force a confession, sir. I had not anticipated suicide at the approach, ironically, of someone who was only a robot and who would not really be violating the taboo against personal presence. But, frankly, I don't regret his death. He was a dangerous man. It will be a long time before there will be another man who will combine his sickness and his brilliance."

"I agree with that," said Minnim dryly, "and consider his death fortunate, but didn't you consider your danger if the Solarians had stopped to realize that Leebig couldn't possibly have murdered Delmarre?"

Baley took his pipe out of his mouth and said nothing.

"Come, Plainclothesman," said Minnim. "You know he didn't.

The murder required personal presence and Leebig would die rather than allow that. He *did* die rather than allow it."

Baley said, "You're right, sir. I counted on the Solarians being too horrified at his misuse of robots to stop to think of that."

"Then who did kill Delmarre?"

Baley said slowly, "If you mean who struck the actual blow, it was the person everyone knew had done so. Gladia Delmarre, the man's wife."

"And you let her go?"

Baley said, "Morally, the responsibility wasn't hers. Leebig knew Gladia quarreled bitterly with her husband, and often. He must have known how furious she could grow in moments of anger. Leebig wanted the death of the husband under circumstances that would incriminate the wife. So he supplied Delmarre with a robot and, I imagine, instructed it with all the skill he possessed to hand Gladia one of its detachable limbs at the moment of her full fury. With a weapon in her hand at the crucial moment, she acted in a temporary black-out before either Delmarre or the robot could stop her. Gladia was as much Leebig's unwitting instrument as the robot itself."

Minnim said, "The robot's arm must have been smeared with blood and matted hair."

"It probably was," said Baley, "but it was Leebig who took the murder robot in charge. He could easily have instructed any other robots who might have noticed the fact to forget it. Dr. Thool might have noticed it, but he inspected only the dead man and the unconscious woman. Leebig's mistake was to think that guilt would rest so obviously on Gladia that the matter of the absence of an obvious weapon at the scene wouldn't save her. Nor could he anticipate that an Earthman would be called in to help with the investigation."

"So with Leebig dead, you arranged to have Gladia leave Solaria. Was that to save her in case any Solarians began thinking about the case?"

Baley shrugged. "She had suffered enough. She had been victimized by everyone; by her husband, by Leebig, by the world of Solaria."

Minnim said, "Weren't you bending the law to suit a personal whim?"

Baley's craggy face grew hard. "It was not a whim. I was not bound by Solarian law. Earth's interests were paramount, and for the sake of those interests, I had to see that Leebig, the dangerous one, was dealt with. As for Mrs. Delmarre." He faced Minnim now, and felt himself taking a crucial step. He *had* to say this. "As for Mrs. Delmarre, I made her the basis of an experiment."

"What experiment?"

"I wanted to know if she would consent to face a world where personal presence was permitted and expected. I was curious to know if she had the courage to face disruption of habits so deeply settled in her. I was afraid she might refuse to go; that she might insist on remaining on Solaria, which was purgatory to her, rather than bring herself to abandon her distorted Solarian way of life. But she chose change and I was glad she did, because to me it seemed symbolic. It seemed to open the gates of salvation for *us.*"

"For *us?*" said Minnim with energy. "What the devil do you mean?"

"Not for you and me, particularly, sir," said Baley gravely, "but for all mankind. You're wrong about the other Outer Worlds. They have few robots; they permit personal presence; and they have been investigating Solaria. R. Daneel Olivaw was there with me, you know, and he'll bring back a report. There is a danger they may become Solarias someday, but they will probably recognize that danger and work to keep themselves in a reasonable balance and in that way remain the leaders of mankind."

"That is your opinion," said Minnim testily.

"And there's more to it. There *is* one world like Solaria and that's Earth."

"Plainclothesman Baley!"

"It's so, sir. We're Solaria inside out. They retreated into isolation from one another. We retreated into isolation from the Galaxy. They are at the dead end of their inviolable estates. We are at the dead end of underground Cities. They're leaders without followers, only robots who can't talk back. We're followers without leaders, only enclosing Cities to keep us safe." Baley's fists clenched.

Minnim disapproved. "Plainclothesman, you have been through an ordeal. You need a rest and you will have one. A month's vacation, full pay, and a promotion at the end of it."

"Thank you, but that's not all I want. I want you to listen. There's only one direction out of our dead end and that's outward, toward Space. There are a million worlds out there and the Spacers own only fifty. They are few and long-lived. We are many and short-lived. We are better suited than they for exploration and colonization. We have population pressure to push us and a rapid turnover of generation to keep us supplied with the young and reckless. It was our ancestors who colonized the Outer Worlds in the first place."

"Yes, I see—but I'm afraid our time is up."

Baley could feel the other's anxiety to be rid of him and he remained stolidly in place. He said, "When the original colonization established worlds superior to our own in technology, we escaped by building wombs beneath the ground for ourselves. The Spacers made us feel inferior and we hid from them. That's no answer. To avoid the destructive rhythm of rebellion and suppression, we must *compete* with them, follow them, if we must, lead them, if we can. To do that, we must face the open; we must teach ourselves to face the open. If it is too late to teach ourselves, then we must teach our children. It's vital!"

"You need a rest, Plainclothesman."

Baley said violently, "Listen to me, sir. If the Spacers are strong and we remain as we are, then Earth will be destroyed within a century. That has been computed, as you yourself told me. If the Spacers are really weak and are growing weaker, then we may escape, but who says the Spacers are weak? The Solarians, yes, but that's all we know."

"But——"

"I'm not through. One thing we *can* change, whether the Spacers are weak or strong. We can change the way we are. Let us face the open and we'll never need rebellion. We can spread out into our own crowd of worlds and become Spacers ourselves. If we stay here on Earth, cooped up, then useless and fatal rebellion can't be stopped. It will be all the worse if the people build any false hopes because of supposed Spacer weakness. Go ahead, ask the sociologists. Put my argument to them. And if they're still in doubt, find a way to send me to Aurora. Let me bring back a report on the *real* Spacers, and you'll see what Earth must do."

Minnim nodded. "Yes, yes. Good day, now, Plainclothesman Baley."

Baley left with a feeling of exaltation. He had not expected an open victory over Minnim. Victories over ingrained patterns of thought are not won in a day or a year. But he had seen the look of pensive uncertainty that had crossed Minnim's face and had blotted out, at least for a while, the earlier uncritical joy.

He felt he could see into the future. Minnim would ask the sociologists and one or two of them would be uncertain. They would wonder. They would consult Baley.

Give it one year, thought Baley, one year, and I'll be on my way to Aurora. One generation, and we'll be out in space once more.

Baley stepped onto the northbound Expressway. Soon he would see Jessie. Would *she* understand? And his son, Bentley, now seventeen. When Ben had a seventeen-year-old of his own, would he be standing on some empty world, building a spacious life?

It was a frightening thought. Baley still feared the open. But he no longer feared the fear! It was not something to run from, that fear, but something to fight.

Baley felt as though a touch of madness had come over him. From the very first the open had had its weird attraction over him; from the time in the ground-car when he had tricked Daneel in order to have the top lowered so that he might stand up in the open air.

He had failed to understand then. Daneel thought he was being perverse. Baley himself thought he was facing the open out of professional necessity, to solve a crime. Only on that last evening on Solaria, with the curtain tearing away from the window, did he realize his need to face the open for the open's own sake; for its attraction and its promise of freedom.

There must be millions on Earth who would feel that same urge, if the open were only brought to their attention, if they could be made to take the first step.

He looked about.

The Expressway was speeding on. All about him was artificial light and huge banks of apartments gliding backward and flashing signs and store windows and factories and lights and noise and crowds and more noise and people and people and people . . .

It was all he had loved, all he had hated and feared to leave, all he had thought he longed for on Solaria.

And it was all strange to him.

He couldn't make himself fit back in.

He had gone out to solve a murder and something had happened to him.

He had told Minnim the Cities were wombs, and so they were. And what was the first thing a man must do before he can be a man? He must be born. He must leave the womb. And once left, it could not be re-entered.

Baley had left the City and could not re-enter. The City was no longer his; the Caves of Steel were alien. This *had* to be. And it would be so for others and Earth would be born again and reach outward.

His heart beat madly and the noise of life about him sank to an unheard murmur.

He remembered his dream on Solaria and he understood it at last. He lifted his head and he could see through all the steel and concrete and humanity above him. He could see the beacon set in space to lure men outward. He could see it shining down. The naked sun!

THE
COMPLETE
ROBOT

BY ISAAC ASIMOV

DOUBLEDAY & COMPANY, INC.
GARDEN CITY, NEW YORK

Acknowledgments:

"A Boy's Best Friend, Copyright © 1975 by the Boy Scouts of America. First appeared in *Boys' Life*, March 1975. Not included in any other collection.

"Sally," copyright 1953 by Ziff-Davis Publishing Company, renewed Copyright © 1981 by Isaac Asimov. First appeared in *Fantastic*, May–June 1953. Included in NIGHTFALL AND OTHER STORIES.

"Someday," Copyright © 1956 by Royal Publications, Inc. First appeared in *Infinity Science Fiction*, August 1956. Included in EARTH IS ROOM ENOUGH.

"Point of View," Copyright © 1975 by the Boy Scouts of America. First appeared in *Boys' Life*, July 1975. Not included in any other collection.

"Think!" Copyright © 1977 by Davis Publications, Inc. First Appeared in *Isaac Asimov's Science Fiction Magazine*, Spring 1977. Not included in any other collection.

"True Love," Copyright © 1977 by *The American Way*. First appeared in *The American Way*, February 1977. Not included in any other collection.

"Robot AL–76 Goes Astray," copyright 1941 by Ziff-Davis Publishing Company, renewed Copyright © 1968 by Isaac Asimov. First appeared in *Amazing Stories*, February 1942. Included in THE REST OF THE ROBOTS.

"Victory Unintentional," copyright 1942 by Fictioneers, Inc., renewed Copyright © 1969 by Isaac Asimov. First appeared in *Super Science Stories*, August 1942. Included in THE REST OF THE ROBOTS.

"Stranger in Paradise," Copyright © 1974 by UPD Publishing Corporation. First appeared in *Worlds of If Science Fiction*, May–June 1974. Included in The BICENTENNIAL MAN AND OTHER STORIES.

"Light Verse," Copyright © 1973 by The Saturday Evening Post Company. First appeared in *The Saturday Evening Post*, September–October 1973. Included in BUY JUPITER AND OTHER STORIES.

"Segregationist," Copyright © 1967 by Abbott Universal Ltd. First appeared in *Abbottempo 4*. Included in NIGHTFALL AND OTHER STORIES.

"Robbie," copyright 1940 by Fictioneers, Inc., renewed Copyright © 1967 by Isaac Asimov. First appeared under title "Strange Playfellow" in *Super Science Stories*, September 1940. Included in I, ROBOT.

"Let's Get Together," Copyright © 1956 by Royal Publications, Inc. First appeared in *Infinity Science Fiction*, February 1957. Included in THE REST OF THE ROBOTS.

"Mirror Image," Copyright © 1972 by Condé Nast Publications, Inc. First appeared in *Analog: Science Fiction—Science Fact*, May 1972. Included in THE BEST OF ISAAC ASIMOV.

"The Tercentenary Incident," Copyright © 1976 by Isaac Asimov. First appeared in *Ellery Queen's Mystery Magazine*, August 1976. Included in THE BICENTENNIAL MAN AND OTHER STORIES.

Dedicated to:

Marjorie Goldstein

David Bearinger

Hugh O'Neill

    for whom books are in progress

CONTENTS

INTRODUCTION

By the time I was in my late teens and already a hardened science fiction reader, I had read many robot stories and found that they fell into two classes.

In the first class there was Robot-as-Menace. I don't have to explain that overmuch. Such stories were a mixture of "clank-clank" and "aarghh" and "There are some things man was not meant to know." After a while, they palled dreadfully and I couldn't stand them.

In the second class (a much smaller one) there was Robot-as-Pathos. In such stories the robots were lovable and were usually put upon by cruel human beings. These charmed me. In late 1938 two such stories hit the stands that particularly impressed me. One was a short story by Eando Binder entitled "I, Robot," about a saintly robot named Adam Link; another was a story by Lester del Rey, entitled "Helen O'Loy," that touched me with its portrayal of a robot that was everything a loyal wife should be.

When, therefore, on June 10, 1939 (yes, I do keep meticulous records), I sat down to write my first robot story, there was no question that I fully intended to write a Robot-as-Pathos story. I wrote "Robbie," about a robot nurse and a little girl and love and a prejudiced mother and a weak father and a broken heart and a tearful reunion. (It originally appeared under the title—one I hated—of "Strange Playfellow.")

But something odd happened as I wrote this first story. I managed to get the dim vision of a robot as neither Menace nor Pathos. I began to think of robots as industrial products built by matter-of-fact engineers. They were built with safety features so they weren't Menaces and they were fashioned for certain jobs so that no Pathos was necessarily involved.

As I continued to write robot stories, this notion of carefully engineered industrial robots permeated my stories more and more until the whole character of robot stories in serious printed science fiction changed—not only that of my own stories, but of just about everybody's.

That made me feel good and for many years, decades even, I went about freely admitting that I was "the father of the modern robot story."

As time went by, I made other discoveries that delighted me. I found, for instance, that when I used the word "robotics" to describe the study of robots, I was *not* using a word that already existed but had invented a word that had never been used before. (That was in my story "Runaround," published in 1942.)

The word has now come into general use. There are journals and books with the word in the title and it is generally known in the field that I invented the term. Don't think I'm not proud of *that*. There are not many people who have coined a useful scientific term, and although I did it unknowingly, I have no intention of letting anyone in the world forget it.

What's more, in "Runaround" I listed my "Three Laws of Robotics" in explicit detail for the first time, and these, too, became famous. At least, they are quoted in and out of season, in all sorts of places that have nothing primarily to do with science fiction, even in general quotation references. And people who work in the field of artificial intelligence sometimes take occasion to tell me that they think the Three Laws will serve as a good guide.

We can go even beyond that—

When I wrote my robot stories I had no thought that robots would come into existence in my lifetime. In fact, I was certain they would not, and would have wagered vast sums that they would not. (At least, I would have wagered 15 cents, which is my betting limit on sure things.)

Yet here I am, forty-three years after I wrote my first robot story, and we *do* have robots. Indeed, we do. What's more, they are what I envisaged them to be in a way—industrial robots, created by engineers to do specific jobs and with safety features built in. They are to be found in numerous factories, particularly in Japan, where there are automobile factories that are entirely roboticized. The assembly line in such places is "manned" by robots at every stage.

To be sure, these robots are not as intelligent as my robots are—they are not positronic; they are not even humanoid. However, they are evolving rapidly and becoming steadily more capable and versatile. Who knows where they'll be in another forty years?

One thing we can be sure of. Robots are changing the world and driving it in directions we cannot clearly foresee.

Where are these robots-in-reality coming from? The most important single source is a firm called Unimation, Inc., of Danbury, Connecticut. It is the leading manufacturer of industrial robots and is responsible for perhaps one third of all robots that have been installed. The president of the firm is Joseph F. Engelberger, who founded it in the late 1950s because he was so interested in robots that he decided to make their production his life work.

But how in the world did he become so interested in robots so early in the game? According to his own words, he grew interested in robots in the 1940s when he was a physics-major undergraduate at Columbia University, reading the robot stories of his fellow Columbian Isaac Asimov.

My goodness!

You know, I didn't write my robot stories with much in the way of ambition back in those old, old days. All I wanted was to sell them to the magazines in order to earn a few hundred dollars to help pay my college tuition—and to see my name in print besides.

If I had been writing in any other field of literature, that's all I would have attained. But because I was writing science fiction, and *only* because I was writing science fiction, I—without knowing it—was starting a chain of events that is changing the face of the world.

Joseph F. Engelberger, by the way, published a book in 1980 called *Robotics in Practice: Management and Application of Industrial Robots* (American Management Associations), and he was kind enough to invite me to write the foreword.

All this set the nice people at Doubleday to thinking—

My various robot short stories have appeared in no less than seven different collections of mine. Why should they be so separated?

Since they appear to be far more important than anyone dreamed they would be (least of all, I) at the time they were written, why not pull them together in a single book?

It wasn't hard to get me to agree, so here are thirty-one short stories, totaling some 200,000 words, written over a time period stretching from 1939 to 1977.

Some Non-human Robots

I am not having the robot stories appear in the order in which they were written. Rather, I am grouping them by the nature of the contents. In this first division, for instance, I deal with robots that have a non-human shape—a dog, an automobile, a box. Why not? The industrial robots that have come into existence in reality are non-human in appearance.

The very first story, "A Boy's Best Friend," is not in any of my earlier collections. It was written on September 10, 1974, and you may find in it a distant echo of "Robbie," written thirty-five years earlier, which appears later in this volume. Don't think I'm not aware of that.

You will note, by the way, that in these three stories, the concept of Robot-as-Pathos is clearly marked. You may also notice, however, that in "Sally" there seems to be no hint of the Three Laws and that there is more than a hint of Robot-as-Menace. Well, if I want to do that once in a while, I can, I suppose. Who's there to stop me?

A Boy's Best Friend

Mr. Anderson said, "Where's Jimmy, dear?"

"Out on the crater," said Mrs. Anderson. "He'll be all right. Robutt is with him.—Did he arrive?"

"Yes. He's at the rocket station, going through the tests. Actually, I can hardly wait to see him myself. I haven't really seen one since I left Earth 15 years ago. You can't count films."

"Jimmy has never seen one," said Mrs. Anderson.

"Because he's Moonborn and can't visit Earth. That's why I'm bringing one here. I think it's the first one ever on the Moon."

"It cost enough," said Mrs. Anderson, with a small sigh.

"Maintaining Robutt isn't cheap, either," said Mr. Anderson.

Jimmy was out on the crater, as his mother had said. By Earth standards, he was spindly, but rather tall for a 10-year-old. His arms and legs were long and agile. He looked thicker and stubbier with his spacesuit on, but he could handle the lunar gravity as no Earth-born human being could. His father couldn't begin to keep up with him when Jimmy stretched his legs and went into the kangaroo hop.

The outer side of the crater sloped southward and the Earth, which was low in the southern sky (where it always was, as seen from Lunar City) was nearly full, so that the entire crater-slope was brightly lit.

The slope was a gentle one and even the weight of the spacesuit couldn't keep Jimmy from racing up it in a floating hop that made the gravity seem nonexistent.

"Come on, Robutt," he shouted.

Robutt, who could hear him by radio, squeaked and bounded after.

Jimmy, expert though he was, couldn't outrace Robutt, who didn't need a spacesuit, and had four legs and tendons of steel. Robutt sailed over Jimmy's head, somersaulting and landing almost under his feet.

"Don't show off, Robutt," said Jimmy, "and stay in sight."

Robutt squeaked again, the special squeak that meant "Yes."

"I don't trust you, you faker," shouted Jimmy, and up he went in one last bound that carried him over the curved upper edge of the crater wall and down onto the inner slope.

The Earth sank below the top of the crater wall and at once it was pitch-dark around him. A warm, friendly darkness that wiped out the difference between ground and sky except for the glitter of stars.

Actually, Jimmy wasn't supposed to exercise along the dark side of the crater wall. The grownups said it was dangerous, but that was because they were never there. The ground was smooth and crunchy and Jimmy knew the exact location of every one of the few rocks.

Besides, how could it be dangerous racing through the dark when Robutt was right there with him, bouncing around and squeaking and glowing? Even without the glow, Robutt could tell where he was, and where Jimmy was, by radar. Jimmy couldn't go wrong while Robutt was around, tripping him when he was too near a rock, or jumping on him to show how much he loved him, or circling around and squeaking low and scared when Jimmy hid behind a rock, when all the time Robutt knew well enough where he was. Once Jimmy had lain still and pretended he was hurt and Robutt had sounded the radio alarm and people from Lunar City got there in a hurry. Jimmy's father had let him hear about that little trick, and Jimmy never tried it again.

Just as he was remembering that, he heard his father's voice on his private wavelength. "Jimmy, come back. I have something to tell you."

Jimmy was out of his spacesuit now and washed up. You always had to wash up after coming in from outside. Even Robutt had to be sprayed, but he loved it. He stood there on all fours, his little foot-long body quivering and glowing just a tiny bit, and his small head, with no mouth, with two large glassed-in eyes, and with a bump where the brain was. He squeaked until Mr. Anderson said, "Quiet, Robutt."

Mr. Anderson was smiling. "We have something for you, Jimmy. It's at the rocket station now, but we'll have it tomorrow after all the tests are over. I thought I'd tell you now."

"From Earth, Dad?"

"A *dog* from Earth, son. A real dog. A Scotch terrier puppy. The first dog on the Moon. You won't need Robutt any more. We can't keep them both, you know, and some other boy or girl will have Robutt." He seemed to be waiting for Jimmy to say something, then he said, "You know what a dog is, Jimmy. It's the real thing. Robutt's only a mechanical imitation, a robot-mutt. That's how he got his name."

Jimmy frowned. "Robutt isn't an imitation, Dad. He's my dog."

"Not a real one, Jimmy. Robutt's just steel and wiring and a simple positronic brain. It's not alive."

"He does everything I want him to do, Dad. He understands me. Sure, he's alive."

"No, son. Robutt is just a machine. It's just programmed to act the way it does. A dog *is* alive. You won't want Robutt after you have the dog."

"The dog will need a spacesuit, won't he?"

"Yes, of course. But it will be worth the money and he'll get used to it. And he won't need one in the City. You'll see the difference once he gets here."

Jimmy looked at Robutt, who was squeaking again, a very low, slow squeak, that seemed frightened. Jimmy held out his arms and Robutt was in them in one bound. Jimmy said, "What will the difference be between Robutt and the dog?"

"It's hard to explain," said Mr. Anderson, "but it will be easy to see. The dog will *really* love you. Robutt is just adjusted to act as though it loves you."

"But, Dad, we don't know what's inside the dog, or what his feelings are. Maybe it's just acting, too."

Mr. Anderson frowned. "Jimmy, you'll *know* the difference when you experience the love of a living thing."

Jimmy held Robutt tightly. He was frowning, too, and the desperate look on his face meant that he wouldn't change his mind. He said, "But what's the difference how *they* act? How about how *I* feel? I love Robutt and *that's* what counts."

And the little robot-mutt, which had never been held so tightly in all its existence, squeaked high and rapid squeaks—happy squeaks.

Sally

Sally was coming down the lake road, so I waved to her and called her by name. I always liked to see Sally. I liked all of them, you understand, but Sally's the prettiest one of the lot. There just isn't any question about it.

She moved a little faster when I waved to her. Nothing undignified. She was never that. She moved just enough faster to show that she was glad to see me, too.

I turned to the man standing beside me. "That's Sally," I said.

He smiled at me and nodded.

Mrs. Hester had brought him in. She said, "This is Mr. Gellhorn, Jake. You remember he sent you the letter asking for an appointment."

That was just talk, really. I have a million things to do around the Farm, and one thing I just can't waste my time on is mail. That's why I have Mrs. Hester around. She lives pretty close by, she's good at attending to foolishness without running to me about it, and most of all, she likes Sally and the rest. Some people don't.

"Glad to see you, Mr. Gellhorn," I said.

"Raymond J. Gellhorn," he said, and gave me his hand, which I shook and gave back.

He was a largish fellow, half a head taller than I and wider, too. He was about half my age, thirtyish. He had black hair, plastered down slick, with a part in the middle, and a thin mustache, very neatly trimmed. His jawbones got big under his ears and made him look as if he had a slight case of mumps. On video he'd be a natural to play the villain, so I assumed he was a nice fellow. It goes to show that video can't be wrong all the time.

"I'm Jacob Folkers," I said. "What can I do for you?"

He grinned. It was a big, wide, white-toothed grin. "You can tell me a little about your Farm here, if you don't mind."

I heard Sally coming up behind me and I put out my hand. She slid right into it and the feel of the hard, glossy enamel of her fender was warm in my palm.

"A nice automatobile," said Gellhorn.

That's one way of putting it. Sally was a 2045 convertible with a Hennis-Carleton positronic motor and an Armat chassis. She had the cleanest, finest lines I've ever seen on any model, bar none. For five years, she'd been my favorite, and I'd put everything into her I could dream up. In all that time, there'd never been a human being behind her wheel.

Not once.

"Sally," I said, patting her gently, "meet Mr. Gellhorn."

Sally's cylinder-purr keyed up a little. I listened carefully for any knocking. Lately, I'd been hearing motor-knock in almost all the cars and changing the gasoline hadn't done a bit of good. Sally was as smooth as her paint job this time, however.

"Do you have names for all your cars?" asked Gellhorn.

He sounded amused, and Mrs. Hester doesn't like people to sound as though they were making fun of the Farm. She said, sharply, "Certainly. The cars have real personalities, don't they, Jake? The sedans are all males and the convertibles are females."

Gellhorn was smiling again. "And do you keep them in separate garages, ma'am?"

Mrs. Hester glared at him.

Gellhorn said to me, "And now I wonder if I can talk to you alone, Mr. Folkers?"

"That depends," I said. "Are you a reporter?"

"No, sir. I'm a sales agent. Any talk we have is not for publication. I assure you I am interested in strict privacy."

"Let's walk down the road a bit. There's a bench we can use."

We started down. Mrs. Hester walked away. Sally nudged along after us.

I said, "You don't mind if Sally comes along, do you?"

"Not at all. She can't repeat what we say, can she?" He laughed at his own joke, reached over and rubbed Sally's grille.

Sally raced her motor and Gellhorn's hand drew away quickly.

"She's not used to strangers," I explained.

We sat down on the bench under the big oak tree where we could look across the small lake to the private speedway. It was the warm part of the day and the cars were out in force, at least thirty of them. Even at this distance I could see that Jeremiah was pulling his usual stunt of sneaking up behind some staid older model, then putting on a jerk of speed and yowling past with deliberately squealing brakes. Two weeks before he had crowded old Angus off the asphalt altogether, and I had turned off his motor for two days.

It didn't help though, I'm afraid, and it looks as though there's nothing to be done about it. Jeremiah is a sports model to begin with and that kind is awfully hot-headed.

"Well, Mr. Gellhorn," I said. "Could you tell me why you want the information?"

But he was just looking around. He said, "This *is* an amazing place, Mr. Folkers."

"I wish you'd call me Jake. Everyone does."

"All right, Jake. How many cars do you have here?"

"Fifty-one. We get one or two new ones every year. One year we got five. We haven't lost one yet. They're all in perfect running order. We even have a '15 model Mat-O-Mot in working order. One of the original automatics. It was the first car here."

Good old Matthew. He stayed in the garage most of the day now, but then he was the granddaddy of all positronic-motored cars. Those were the days when blind war veterans, paraplegics and heads of state were the only ones who drove automatics. But Samson Harridge was my boss and he was rich enough to be able to get one. I was his chauffeur at the time.

The thought makes me feel old. I can remember when there wasn't an automobile in the world with brains enough to find its own way home. I chauffeured dead lumps of machines that needed a man's hand at their controls every minute. Every year machines like that used to kill tens of thousands of people.

The automatics fixed that. A positronic brain can react much faster than a human one, of course, and it paid people to keep hands off the controls. You got in, punched your destination and let it go its own way.

We take it for granted now, but I remember when the first laws came out forcing the old machines off the highways and limiting travel to automatics. Lord, what a fuss. They called it everything from communism to fascism, but it emptied the highways and stopped the killing, and still more people get around more easily the new way.

Of course, the automatics were ten to a hundred times as expensive as the hand-driven ones, and there weren't many that could afford a private vehicle. The industry specialized in turning out omnibus-automatics. You could always call a company and have one stop at your door in a matter of minutes and take you where you wanted to go. Usually, you had to drive with others who were going your way, but what's wrong with that?

Samson Harridge had a private car though, and I went to him the minute it arrived. The car wasn't Matthew to me then. I didn't know it was going to be the dean of the Farm some day. I only knew it was taking my job away and I hated it.

I said, "You won't be needing me any more, Mr. Harridge?"

He said, "What are you dithering about, Jake? You don't think I'll trust myself to a contraption like that, do you? You stay right at the controls."

I said, "But it works by itself, Mr. Harridge. It scans the road, reacts properly to obstacles, humans, and other cars, and remembers routes to travel."

"So they say. So they say. Just the same, you're sitting right behind the wheel in case anything goes wrong."

Funny how you can get to like a car. In no time I was calling it Matthew and was spending all my time keeping it polished and humming. A positronic brain stays in condition best when it's got control of its chassis at all times, which means it's worth keeping the gas tank filled so that the motor can turn over slowly day and night. After a while, it got so I could tell by the sound of the motor how Matthew felt.

In his own way, Harridge grew fond of Matthew, too. He had no one else to like. He'd divorced or outlived three wives and outlived five children and three grandchildren. So when he died, maybe it wasn't surprising that he had his estate converted into a Farm for Retired Automobiles, with me in charge and Matthew the first member of a distinguished line.

It's turned out to be my life. I never got married. You can't get married and still tend to automatics the way you should.

The newspapers thought it was funny, but after a while they

stopped joking about it. Some things you can't joke about. Maybe you've never been able to afford an automatic and maybe you never will, either, but take it from me, you get to love them. They're hard-working and affectionate. It takes a man with no heart to mistreat one or to see one mistreated.

It got so that after a man had an automatic for a while, he would make provisions for having it left to the Farm, if he didn't have an heir he could rely on to give it good care.

I explained that to Gellhorn.

He said, "Fifty-one cars! That represents a lot of money."

"Fifty thousand minimum per automatic, original investment," I said. "They're worth a lot more now. I've done things for them."

"It must take a lot of money to keep up the Farm."

"You're right there. The Farm's a non-profit organization, which gives us a break on taxes and, of course, new automatics that come in usually have trust funds attached. Still, costs are always going up. I have to keep the place landscaped; I keep laying down new asphalt and keeping the old in repair; there's gasoline, oil, repairs, and new gadgets. It adds up."

"And you've spent a long time at it."

"I sure have, Mr. Gellhorn. Thirty-three years."

"You don't seem to be getting much out of it yourself."

"I don't? You surprise me, Mr. Gellhorn. I've got Sally and fifty others. Look at her."

I was grinning. I couldn't help it. Sally was so clean, it almost hurt. Some insect must have died on her windshield or one speck of dust too many had landed, so she was going to work. A little tube protruded and spurted Tergosol over the glass. It spread quickly over the silicone surface film and squeegees snapped into place instantly, passing over the windshield and forcing the water into the little channel that led it, dripping, down to the ground. Not a speck of water got onto her glistening apple-green hood. Squeegee and detergent tube snapped back into place and disappeared.

Gellhorn said, "I never saw an automatic do that."

"I guess not," I said. "I fixed that up specially on our cars. They're clean. They're always scrubbing their glass. They like it. I've even got Sally fixed up with wax jets. She polishes herself every night till you can see your face in any part of her and shave by it. If I can scrape up the money, I'd be putting it on the rest of the girls. Convertibles are very vain."

"I can tell you how to scrape up the money, if that interests you."

"That always does. How?"

"Isn't it obvious, Jake? Any of your cars is worth fifty thousand minimum, you said. I'll bet most of them top six figures."

"So?"

"Ever think of selling a few?"

I shook my head. "You don't realize it, I guess, Mr. Gellhorn, but I can't sell any of these. They belong to the Farm, not to me."

"The money would go to the Farm."

"The incorporation papers of the Farm provide that the cars receive perpetual care. They can't be sold."

"What about the motors, then?"

"I don't understand you."

Gellhorn shifted position and his voice got confidential. "Look here, Jake, let me explain the situation. There's a big market for private automatics if they could only be made cheaply enough. Right?"

"That's no secret."

"And ninety-five per cent of the cost is the motor. Right? Now, I know where we can get a supply of bodies. I also know where we can sell automatics at a good price—twenty or thirty thousand for the cheaper models, maybe fifty or sixty for the better ones. All I need are the motors. You see the solution?"

"I don't, Mr. Gellhorn." I did, but I wanted him to spell it out.

"It's right here. You've got fifty-one of them. You're an expert automatobile mechanic, Jake. You must be. You could unhook a motor and place it in another car so that no one would know the difference."

"It wouldn't be exactly ethical."

"You wouldn't be harming the cars. You'd be doing them a favor. Use your older cars. Use that old Mat-O-Mot."

"Well, now, wait a while, Mr. Gellhorn. The motors and bodies aren't two separate items. They're a single unit. Those motors are used to their own bodies. They wouldn't be happy in another car."

"All right, that's a point. That's a very good point, Jake. It would be like taking your mind and putting it in someone else's skull. Right? You don't think you would like that?"

"I don't think I would. No."

"But what if I took your mind and put it into the body of a young athlete. What about that, Jake? You're not a youngster anymore. If you had the chance, wouldn't you enjoy being twenty again? That's what I'm offering some of your positronic motors. They'll be put into new '57 bodies. The latest construction."

I laughed. "That doesn't make much sense, Mr. Gellhorn. Some of our cars may be old, but they're well-cared for. Nobody drives them. They're allowed their own way. They're *retired*, Mr. Gellhorn. I wouldn't want a twenty-year-old body if it meant I had to dig ditches for the rest of my new life and never have enough to eat. . . . What do you think, Sally?"

Sally's two doors opened and then shut with a cushioned slam.

"What's that?" said Gellhorn.

"That's the way Sally laughs."

Gellhorn forced a smile. I guess he thought I was making a bad joke. He said, "Talk sense, Jake. Cars are *made* to be driven. They're probably not happy if you don't drive them."

I said, "Sally hasn't been driven in five years. She looks happy to me."

"I wonder."

He got up and walked toward Sally slowly. "Hi, Sally, how'd you like a drive?"

Sally's motor revved up. She backed away.

"Don't push her, Mr. Gellhorn," I said. "She's liable to be a little skittish."

Two sedans were about a hundred yards up the road. They had stopped. Maybe, in their own way, they were watching. I didn't bother about them. I had my eyes on Sally, and I kept them there.

Gellhorn said, "Steady now, Sally." He lunged out and seized the door handle. It didn't budge, of course.

He said, "It opened a minute ago."

I said, "Automatic lock. She's got a sense of privacy, Sally has."

He let go, then said, slowly and deliberately, "A car with a sense of privacy shouldn't go around with its top down."

He stepped back three or four paces, then quickly, so quickly I couldn't take a step to stop him, he ran forward and vaulted into the car. He caught Sally completely by surprise, because as he came down, he shut off the ignition before she could lock it in place.

For the first time in five years, Sally's motor was dead.

I think I yelled, but Gellhorn had the switch on "Manual" and locked that in place, too. He kicked the motor into action. Sally was alive again but she had no freedom of action.

He started up the road. The sedans were still there. They turned and drifted away, not very quickly. I suppose it was all a puzzle to them.

One was Giuseppe, from the Milan factories, and the other was Stephen. They were always together. They were both new at the Farm, but they'd been here long enough to know that our cars just didn't have drivers.

Gellhorn went straight on, and when the sedans finally got it through their heads that Sally wasn't going to slow down, that she *couldn't* slow down, it was too late for anything but desperate measures.

They broke for it, one to each side, and Sally raced between them like a streak. Steve crashed through the lakeside fence and rolled to a halt on the grass and mud not six inches from the water's edge. Giuseppe bumped along the land side of the road to a shaken halt.

I had Steve back on the highway and was trying to find out what harm, if any, the fence had done him, when Gellhorn came back.

Gellhorn opened Sally's door and stepped out. Leaning back, he shut off the ignition a second time.

"There," he said. "I think I did her a lot of good."

I held my temper. "Why did you dash through the sedans? There was no reason for that."

"I kept expecting them to turn out."

"They did. One went through a fence."

"I'm sorry, Jake," he said. "I thought they'd move more quickly. You know how it is. I've been in lots of buses, but I've only been in a private automatic two or three times in my life, and this is the first time I ever drove one. That just shows you, Jake. It got me, driving one, and I'm pretty hard-boiled. I tell you, we don't have to go more than twenty per cent below list price to reach a good market, and it would be ninety per cent profit."

"Which we would split?"

"Fifty-fifty. And I take all the risks, remember."

"All right. I listened to you. Now you listen to me." I raised my voice because I was just too mad to be polite anymore. "When you turn off Sally's motor, you hurt her. How would you like to be kicked unconscious? That's what you do to Sally, when you turn her off."

"You're exaggerating, Jake. The automatobuses get turned off every night."

"Sure, that's why I want none of my boys or girls in your fancy '57 bodies, where I won't know what treatment they'll get. Buscs nccd major repairs in their positronic circuits every couple of years. Old Matthew hasn't had his circuits touched in twenty years. What can you offer him compared with that?"

"Well, you're excited now. Suppose you think over my proposition when you've cooled down and get in touch with me."

"I've thought it over all I want to. If I ever see you again, I'll call the police."

His mouth got hard and ugly. He said, "Just a minute, old-timer."

I said, "Just a minute, you. This is private property and I'm ordering you off."

He shrugged. "Well, then, goodbye."

I said, "Mrs. Hester will see you off the property. Make that goodbye permanent."

But it wasn't permanent. I saw him again two days later. Two and a half days, rather, because it was about noon when I saw him first and a little after midnight when I saw him again.

I sat up in bed when he turned the light on, blinking blindly till I made out what was happening. Once I could see, it didn't take much explaining. In fact, it took none at all. He had a gun in his right fist, the nasty little needle barrel just visible between two fingers. I knew that all he had to do was to increase the pressure of his hand and I would be torn apart.

He said, "Put on your clothes, Jake."

I didn't move. I just watched him.

He said, "Look, Jake, I know the situation. I visited you two days ago, remember. You have no guards on this place, no electrified fences, no warning signals. Nothing."

I said, "I don't need any. Meanwhile there's nothing to stop you from leaving, Mr. Gellhorn. I would if I were you. This place can be very dangerous."

He laughed a little. "It is, for anyone on the wrong side of a fist gun."

"I see it," I said. "I know you've got one."

"Then get a move on. My men are waiting."

"No, sir, Mr. Gellhorn. Not unless you tell me what you want, and probably not then."

"I made you a proposition day before yesterday."

"The answer's still no."

"There's more to the proposition now. I've come here with some men and an automatobus. You have your chance to come with me and disconnect twenty-five of the positronic motors. I don't care which twenty-five you choose. We'll load them on the bus and take them away. Once they're disposed of, I'll see to it that you get your fair share of the money."

"I have your word on that, I suppose."

He didn't act as if he thought I was being sarcastic. He said, "You have."

I said, "No."

"If you insist on saying no, we'll go about it in our own way. I'll disconnect the motors myself, only I'll disconnect all fifty-one. Every one of them."

"It isn't easy to disconnect positronic motors, Mr. Gellhorn. Are you a robotics expert? Even if you are, you know, these motors have been modified by me."

"I know that, Jake. And to be truthful, I'm not an expert. I may ruin quite a few motors trying to get them out. That's why I'll have to work over all fifty-one if you don't cooperate. You see, I may only end up with twenty-five when I'm through. The first few I'll tackle will probably suffer the most. Till I get the hang of it, you see. And if I go it myself, I think I'll put Sally first in line."

I said, "I can't believe you're serious, Mr. Gellhorn."

He said, "I'm serious, Jake." He let it all dribble in. "If you want to help, you can keep Sally. Otherwise, she's liable to be hurt very badly. Sorry."

I said, "I'll come with you, but I'll give you one more warning. You'll be in trouble, Mr. Gellhorn."

He thought that was very funny. He was laughing very quietly as we went down the stairs together.

There was an automatobus waiting outside the driveway to the garage apartments. The shadows of three men waited beside it, and their flash beams went on as we approached.

Gellhorn said in a low voice, "I've got the old fellow. Come on. Move the truck up the drive and let's get started."

One of the others leaned in and punched the proper instructions on the control panel. We moved up the driveway with the bus following submissively.

"It won't go inside the garage," I said. "The door won't take it. We don't have buses here. Only private cars."

"All right," said Gellhorn. "Pull it over onto the grass and keep it out of sight."

I could hear the thrumming of the cars when we were still ten yards from the garage.

Usually they quieted down if I entered the garage. This time they didn't. I think they knew that strangers were about, and once the faces of Gellhorn and the others were visible they got noisier. Each motor was a warm rumble, and each motor was knocking irregularly until the place rattled.

The lights went up automatically as we stepped inside. Gellhorn didn't seem bothered by the car noise, but the three men with him looked surprised and uncomfortable. They had the look of the hired thug about them, a look that was not compounded of physical features so much as of a certain wariness of eye and hang-dogness of face. I knew the type and I wasn't worried.

One of them said, "Damn it, they're burning gas."

"My cars always do," I replied stiffly.

"Not tonight," said Gellhorn. "Turn them off."

"It's not that easy, Mr. Gellhorn," I said.

"Get started!" he said.

I stood there. He had his fist gun pointed at me steadily. I said, "I told you, Mr. Gellhorn, that my cars have been well-treated while they've been at the Farm. They're used to being treated that way, and they resent anything else."

"You have one minute," he said. "Lecture me some other time."

"I'm trying to explain something. I'm trying to explain that my cars can understand what I say to them. A positronic motor will learn to do that with time and patience. My cars have learned. Sally understood your proposition two days ago. You'll remember she laughed when I asked her opinion. She also knows what you did to her and so do the two sedans you scattered. And the rest know what to do about trespassers in general."

"Look, you crazy old fool—"

"All I have to say is—" I raised my voice. "Get them!"

One of the men turned pasty and yelled, but his voice was drowned completely in the sound of fifty-one horns turned loose at once. They held their notes, and within the four walls of the garage the echoes rose to a wild, metallic call. Two cars rolled forward, not hurriedly, but with no possible mistake as to their target. Two cars fell in line behind the first two. All the cars were stirring in their separate stalls.

The thugs stared, then backed.

I shouted, "Don't get up against a wall."

Apparently, they had that instinctive thought themselves. They rushed madly for the door of the garage.

At the door one of Gellhorn's men turned, brought up a fist gun of his own. The needle pellet tore a thin, blue flash toward the first car. The car was Giuseppe.

A thin line of paint peeled up Giuseppe's hood, and the right half of his windshield crazed and splintered but did not break through.

The men were out the door, running, and two by two the cars crunched out after them into the night, their horns calling the charge.

I kept my hand on Gellhorn's elbow, but I don't think he could have moved in any case. His lips were trembling.

I said, "That's why I don't need electrified fences or guards. My property protects itself."

Gellhorn's eyes swiveled back and forth in fascination as, pair by pair, they whizzed by. He said, "They're killers!"

"Don't be silly. They won't kill your men."

"They're killers!"

"They'll just give your men a lesson. My cars have been specially trained for cross-country pursuit for just such an occasion; I think what your men will get will be worse than an outright quick kill. Have you ever been chased by an automatobile?"

Gellhorn didn't answer.

I went on. I didn't want him to miss a thing. "They'll be shadows going no faster than your men, chasing them here, blocking them there, blaring at them, dashing at them, missing with a screech of brake and a thunder of motor. They'll keep it up till your men drop, out of breath and half-dead, waiting for the wheels to crunch over their breaking bones. The cars won't do that. They'll turn away. You can bet, though, that your men will never return here in their lives. Not for all the money you or ten like you could give them. Listen—"

I tightened my hold on his elbow. He strained to hear.

I said, "Don't you hear car doors slamming?"

It was faint and distant, but unmistakable.

I said, "They're laughing. They're enjoying themselves."

His face crumpled with rage. He lifted his hand. He was still holding his fist gun.

I said, "I wouldn't. One automatocar is still with us."

I don't think he had noticed Sally till then. She had moved up so quietly. Though her right front fender nearly touched me, I couldn't hear her motor. She might have been holding her breath.

Gellhorn yelled.

I said, "She won't touch you, as long as I'm with you. But if you kill me. . . . You know, Sally doesn't like you."

Gellhorn turned the gun in Sally's direction.

"Her motor is shielded," I said, "and before you could ever squeeze the gun a second time she would be on top of you."

"All right, then," he yelled, and suddenly my arm was bent behind my back and twisted so I could hardly stand. He held me between Sally and himself, and his pressure didn't let up. "Back out with me and don't try to break loose, old-timer, or I'll tear your arm out of its socket."

I had to move. Sally nudged along with us, worried, uncertain what to do. I tried to say something to her and couldn't. I could only clench my teeth and moan.

Gellhorn's automatobus was still standing outside the garage. I was forced in. Gellhorn jumped in after me, locking the doors.

He said, "All right, now. We'll talk sense."

I was rubbing my arm, trying to get life back into it, and even as I did I was automatically and without any conscious effort studying the control board of the bus.

I said, "This is a rebuilt job."

"So?" he said caustically. "It's a sample of my work. I picked up a discarded chassis, found a brain I could use and spliced me a private bus. What of it?"

I tore at the repair panel, forcing it aside.

He said, "What the hell. Get away from that." The side of his palm came down numbingly on my left shoulder.

I struggled with him. "I don't want to do this bus any harm. What kind of a person do you think I am? I just want to take a look at some of the motor connections."

It didn't take much of a look. I was boiling when I turned to him. I said, "You're a hound and a bastard. You had no right installing this motor yourself. Why didn't you get a robotics man?"

He said, "Do I look crazy?"

"Even if it was a stolen motor, you had no right to treat it so. I wouldn't treat a man the way you treated that motor. Solder, tape, and pinch clamps! It's brutal!"

"It works, doesn't it?"

"Sure it works, but it must be hell for the bus. You could live with migraine headaches and acute arthritis, but it wouldn't be much of a life. This car is *suffering*."

"Shut up!" For a moment he glanced out the window at Sally, who had rolled up as close to the bus as she could. He made sure the doors and windows were locked.

He said, "We're getting out of here now, before the other cars come back. We'll stay away."

"How will that help you?"

"Your cars will run out of gas someday, won't they? You haven't got them fixed up so they can tank up on their own, have you? We'll come back and finish the job."

"They'll be looking for me," I said. "Mrs. Hester will call the police."

He was past reasoning with. He just punched the bus in gear. It lurched forward. Sally followed.

He giggled. "What can she do if you're here with me?"

Sally seemed to realize that, too. She picked up speed, passed us and was gone. Gellhorn opened the window next to him and spat through the opening.

The bus lumbered on over the dark road, its motor rattling unevenly. Gellhorn dimmed the periphery light until the phosphorescent green stripe down the middle of the highway, sparkling in the moonlight, was all that kept us out of the trees. There was virtually no traffic. Two cars passed ours, going the other way, and there was none at all on our side of the highway, either before or behind.

I heard the door-slamming first. Quick and sharp in the silence, first on the right and then on the left. Gellhorn's hands quivered as he punched savagely for increased speed. A beam of light shot out from among a scrub of trees, blinding us. Another beam plunged at us from behind the guard rails on the other side. At a crossover, four hundred yards ahead, there was a sque-e-e-e as a car darted across our path.

"Sally went for the rest," I said. "I think you're surrounded."

"So what? What can they do?"

He hunched over the controls, peering through the windshield.

"And don't *you* try anything, old-timer," he muttered.

I couldn't. I was bone-weary; my left arm was on fire. The motor sounds gathered and grew closer. I could hear the motors missing in odd patterns; suddenly it seemed to me that my cars were speaking to one another.

A medley of horns came from behind. I turned and Gellhorn looked quickly into the rear-view mirror. A dozen cars were following in both lanes.

Gellhorn yelled and laughed madly.

I cried, "Stop! Stop the car!"

Because not a quarter of a mile ahead, plainly visible in the light beams of two sedans on the roadside was Sally, her trim body plunked square across the road. Two cars shot into the opposite lane to our left, keeping perfect time with us and preventing Gellhorn from turning out.

But he had no intention of turning out. He put his finger on the full-speed-ahead button and kept it there.

He said, "There'll be no bluffing here. This bus outweighs her five to one, old-timer, and we'll just push her off the road like a dead kitten."

I knew he could. The bus was on manual and his finger was on the button. I knew he would.

I lowered the window, and stuck my head out. "Sally," I screamed. "Get out of the way. *Sally!*"

It was drowned out in the agonized squeal of maltreated brake-bands. I felt myself thrown forward and heard Gellhorn's breath puff out of his body.

I said, "What happened?" It was a foolish question. We had stopped. That was what had happened. Sally and the bus were five feet apart. With five times her weight tearing down on her, she had not budged. The guts of her.

Gellhorn yanked at the Manual toggle switch. "It's got to," he kept muttering. "It's got to."

I said, "Not the way you hooked up the motor, expert. Any of the circuits could cross over."

He looked at me with a tearing anger and growled deep in his throat. His hair was matted over his forehead. He lifted his fist.

"That's all the advice out of you there'll ever be, old-timer."

And I knew the needle gun was about to fire.

I pressed back against the bus door, watching the fist come up, and when the door opened I went over backward and out, hitting the ground with a thud. I heard the door slam closed again.

I got to my knees and looked up in time to see Gellhorn struggle uselessly with the closing window, then aim his fist-gun quickly through the glass. He never fired. The bus got under way with a tremendous roar, and Gellhorn lurched backward.

Sally wasn't in the way any longer, and I watched the bus's rear lights flicker away down the highway.

I was exhausted. I sat down right there, right on the highway, and put my head down in my crossed arms, trying to catch my breath.

I heard a car stop gently at my side. When I looked up, it was Sally. Slowly—lovingly, you might say—her front door opened.

No one had driven Sally for five years—except Gellhorn, of course —and I know how valuable such freedom was to a car. I appreciated the gesture, but I said, "Thanks, Sally, but I'll take one of the newer cars."

I got up and turned away, but skillfully and neatly as a pirouette, she wheeled before me again. I couldn't hurt her feelings. I got in. Her front seat had the fine, fresh scent of an automatobile that kept itself spotlessly clean. I lay down across it, thankfully, and with even, silent, and rapid efficiency, my boys and girls brought me home.

Mrs. Hester brought me the copy of the radio transcript the next evening with great excitement.

"It's Mr. Gellhorn," she said. "The man who came to see you."

"What about him?"

I dreaded her answer.

"They found him dead," she said. "Imagine that. Just lying dead in a ditch."

"It might be a stranger altogether," I mumbled.

"Raymond J. Gellhorn," she said, sharply. "There can't be two, can there? The description fits, too. Lord, what a way to die! They found tire marks on his arms and body. Imagine! I'm glad it turned out to be a bus; otherwise they might have come poking around here."

"Did it happen near here?" I asked, anxiously.

"No . . . Near Cooksville. But, goodness, read about it yourself if you—What happened to Giuseppe?"

I welcomed the diversion. Giuseppe was waiting patiently for me to complete the repaint job. His windshield had been replaced.

After she left, I snatched up the transcript. There was no doubt about it. The doctor reported he had been running and was in a state of totally spent exhaustion. I wondered for how many miles the bus had played with him before the final lunge. The transcript had no notion of anything like that, of course.

They had located the bus and identified it by the tire tracks. The police had it and were trying to trace its ownership.

There was an editorial in the transcript about it. It had been the first traffic fatality in the state for that year and the paper warned strenuously against manual driving after night.

There was no mention of Gellhorn's three thugs and for that, at least, I was grateful. None of our cars had been seduced by the pleasure of the chase into killing.

That was all. I let the paper drop. Gellhorn had been a criminal. His treatment of the bus had been brutal. There was no question in my mind he deserved death. But still I felt a bit queasy over the manner of it.

A month has passed now and I can't get it out of my mind.

My cars talk to one another. I have no doubt about it anymore. It's as though they've gained confidence; as though they're not bothering to keep it secret anymore. Their engines rattle and knock continuously.

And they don't talk among themselves only. They talk to the cars and buses that come into the Farm on business. How long have they been doing that?

They must be understood, too. Gellhorn's bus understood them, for all it hadn't been on the grounds more than an hour. I can close my eyes and bring back that dash along the highway, with our cars flanking the bus on either side, clacking their motors at it till it understood, stopped, let me out, and ran off with Gellhorn.

Did my cars tell him to kill Gellhorn? Or was that his idea?

Can cars have such ideas? The motor designers say no. But they mean under ordinary conditions. Have they foreseen *everything*?

Cars get ill-used, you know.

Some of them enter the Farm and observe. They get told things.

They find out that cars exist whose motors are never stopped, whom no one ever drives, whose every need is supplied.

Then maybe they go out and tell others. Maybe the word is spreading quickly. Maybe they're going to think that the Farm way should be the way all over the world. They don't understand. You couldn't expect them to understand about legacies and the whims of rich men.

There are millions of automatobiles on Earth, tens of millions. If the thought gets rooted in them that they're slaves; that they should do something about it . . . If they begin to think the way Gellhorn's bus did. . . .

Maybe it won't be till after my time. And then they'll have to keep a few of us to take care of them, won't they? They wouldn't kill us all.

And maybe they would. Maybe they wouldn't understand about how someone would have to care for them. Maybe they won't wait.

Every morning I wake up and think, Maybe today. . . .

I don't get as much pleasure out of my cars as I used to. Lately, I notice that I'm even beginning to avoid Sally.

Someday

Niccolo Mazetti lay stomach down on the rug, chin buried in the palm of one small hand, and listened to the Bard disconsolately. There was even the suspicion of tears in his dark eyes, a luxury an eleven-year-old could allow himself only when alone.

The Bard said, "Once upon a time in the middle of a deep wood, there lived a poor woodcutter and his two motherless daughters, who were each as beautiful as the day is long. The older daughter had long hair as black as a feather from a raven's wing, but the younger daughter had hair as bright and golden as the sunlight of an autumn afternoon.

"Many times while the girls were waiting for their father to come home from his day's work in the wood, the older girl would sit before a mirror and sing—"

What she sang, Niccolo did not hear, for a call sounded from outside the room: "Hey, Nickie."

And Niccolo, his face clearing on the moment, rushed to the window and shouted, "Hey, Paul."

Paul Loeb waved an excited hand. He was thinner than Niccolo and not as tall, for all he was six months older. His face was full of repressed tension which showed itself most clearly in the rapid blinking of his eyelids. "Hey, Nickie, let me in. I've got an idea and a *half*. Wait till you hear it." He looked rapidly about him as though to check on the possibility of eavesdroppers, but the front yard was quite patently empty. He repeated, in a whisper, "Wait till you hear it."

"All right. I'll open the door."

The Bard continued smoothly, oblivious to the sudden loss of attention on the part of Niccolo. As Paul entered, the Bard was saying, ". . . Thereupon, the lion said, 'If you will find me the lost egg of the bird which flies over the Ebony Mountain once every ten years, I will—"

Paul said, "Is that a Bard you're listening to? I didn't know you had one."

Niccolo reddened and the look of unhappiness returned to his face. "Just an old thing I had when I was a kid. It ain't much good." He kicked at the Bard with his foot and caught the somewhat scarred and discolored plastic covering a glancing blow.

The Bard hiccupped as its speaking attachment was jarred out of contact a moment, then it went on: "—for a year and a day until the iron shoes were worn out. The princess stopped at the side of the road. . . ."

Paul said, "Boy, that *is* an old model," and looked at it critically.

Despite Niccolo's own bitterness against the Bard, he winced at the other's condescending tone. For the moment, he was sorry he had allowed Paul in, at least before he had restored the Bard to its usual resting place in the basement. It was only in the desperation of a dull day and a fruitless discussion with his father that he had resurrected it. And it turned out to be just as stupid as he had expected.

Nickie was a little afraid of Paul anyway, since Paul had special courses at school and everyone said he was going to grow up to be a Computing Engineer.

Not that Niccolo himself was doing badly at school. He got adequate marks in logic, binary manipulations, computing and elementary circuits; all the usual grammar-school subjects. But that was it! They were just the usual subjects and he would grow up to be a control-board guard like everyone else.

Paul, however, knew mysterious things about what he called electronics and theoretical mathematics and programing. Especially programing. Niccolo didn't even try to understand when Paul bubbled over about it.

Paul listened to the Bard for a few minutes and said, "You been using it much?"

"No!" said Niccolo, offended. "I've had it in the basement since before you moved into the neighborhood. I just got it out today—"

He lacked an excuse that seemed adequate to himself, so he concluded, "I just got it out."

Paul said, "Is that what it tells you about: woodcutters and princesses and talking animals?"

Niccolo said, "It's terrible. My dad says we can't afford a new one. I said to him this morning—" The memory of the memory of the morning's fruitless pleadings brought Niccolo dangerously near tears, which he repressed in a panic. Somehow, he felt that Paul's thin cheeks never felt the stain of tears and that Paul would have only contempt for anyone else less strong than himself. Niccolo went on, "So I thought I'd try this old thing again, but it's no good."

Paul turned off the Bard, pressed the contact that led to a nearly instantaneous reorientation and recombination of the vocabulary, characters, plot lines and climaxes stored within it. Then he reactivated it.

The Bard began smoothly, "Once upon a time there was a little boy named Willikins whose mother had died and who lived with a stepfather and a stepbrother. Although the stepfather was very well-to-do, he begrudged poor Willikins the very bed he slept in so that Willikins was forced to get such rest as he could on a pile of straw in the stable next to the horses—"

"Horses!" cried Paul.

"They're a kind of animal," said Niccolo. "I think."

"I know that! I just mean imagine stories about *horses*."

"It tells about horses all the time," said Niccolo. "There are things called cows, too. You milk them but the Bard doesn't say how."

"Well, gee, why don't you fix it up?"

"I'd like to know how."

The Bard was saying, "Often Willikins would think that if only he were rich and powerful, he would show his stepfather and stepbrother what it meant to be cruel to a little boy, so one day he decided to go out into the world and seek his fortune."

Paul, who wasn't listening to the Bard, said, "It's *easy*. The Bard has memory cylinders all fixed up for plot lines and climaxes and things. We don't have to worry about that. It's just vocabulary we've got to fix so it'll know about computers and automation and electronics and real things about today. Then it can tell interesting stories, you know, instead of about princesses and things."

Niccolo said despondently, "I wish we could do that."

Paul said, "Listen, my dad says if I get into special computing school next year, he'll get me a *real* Bard, a late model. A big one with an attachment for space stories and mysteries. And a visual attachment, too!"

"You mean *see* the stories?"

"Sure. Mr. Daugherty at school says they've got things like that, now, but not for just everybody. Only if I get into computing school, Dad can get a few breaks."

Niccolo's eyes bulged with envy. "Gee. *Seeing* a story."

"You can come over and watch anytime, Nickie."

"Oh, boy. Thanks."

"That's all right. But remember, I'm the guy who says what kind of story we hear."

"Sure. Sure." Niccolo would have agreed readily to much more onerous conditions.

Paul's attention returned to the Bard.

It was saying, "'If that is the case,' said the king, stroking his beard and frowning till clouds filled the sky and lightning flashed, 'you will see to it that my entire land is freed of flies by this time day after tomorrow or—'"

"All we've got to do," said Paul, "is open it up—" He shut the Bard off again and was prying at its front panel as he spoke.

"Hey," said Niccolo, in sudden alarm. "Don't break it."

"I won't break it," said Paul impatiently. "I know all about these things." Then, with sudden caution, "Your father and mother home?"

"No."

"All right, then." He had the front panel off and peered in. "Boy, this *is* a one-cylinder thing."

He worked away at the Bard's innards. Niccolo, who watched with painful suspense, could not make out what he was doing.

Paul pulled out a thin, flexible metal strip, powdered with dots. "That's the Bard's memory cylinder. I'll bet its capacity for stories is under a trillion."

"What are you going to do, Paul?" quavered Niccolo.

"I'll give it vocabulary."

"How?"

"Easy. I've got a book here. Mr. Daugherty gave it to me at school."

Paul pulled the book out of his pocket and pried at it till he had its plastic jacket off. He unreeled the tape a bit, ran it through the vocalizer, which he turned down to a whisper, then placed it within the Bard's vitals. He made further attachments.

"What'll that do?"

"The book will talk and the Bard will put it all on its memory tape."

"What good will that do?"

"Boy, you're a dope! This book is all about computers and automation and the Bard will get all that information. Then he can stop talking about kings making lightning when they frown."

Niccolo said, "And the good guy always wins anyway. There's no excitement."

"Oh, well," said Paul, watching to see if his setup was working properly, "that's the way they make Bards. They got to have the good guy win and make the bad guys lose and things like that. I heard my father talking about it once. He says that without censorship there'd be no telling what the younger generation would come to. He says it's bad enough as it is. . . . There, it's working fine."

Paul brushed his hands against one another and turned away from the Bard. He said, "But listen, I didn't tell you my idea yet. It's the best thing you ever heard, I bet. I came right to you, because I figured you'd come in with me."

"Sure, Paul, sure."

"Okay. You know Mr. Daugherty at school? You know what a funny kind of guy he is. Well, he likes me, kind of."

"I know."

"I was over his house after school today."

"You *were?*"

"Sure. He says I'm going to be entering computer school and he wants to encourage me and things like that. He says the world needs more people who can design advanced computer circuits and do proper programing."

"Oh?"

Paul might have caught some of the emptiness behind that monosyllable. He said impatiently, "Programing! I told you a hundred times. That's when you set up problems for the giant computers like Multivac to work on. Mr. Daugherty says it gets harder all the time to find people who can really run computers. He says anyone can keep an eye on the controls and check off answers and put through routine problems. He says the trick is to expand research and figure out ways to ask the right questions, and that's hard.

"Anyway, Nickie, he took me to his place and showed me his collection of old computers. It's kind of a hobby of his to collect old computers. He had tiny computers you had to push with your hand, with little knobs all over it. And he had a hunk of wood he called a slide rule with a little piece of it that went in and out. And some wires with balls on them. He even had a hunk of paper with a kind of thing he called a multiplication table."

Niccolo, who found himself only moderately interested, said, "A paper table?"

"It wasn't really a table like you eat on. It was different. It was to help people compute. Mr. Daugherty tried to explain but he didn't have much time and it was kind of complicated, anyway."

"Why didn't people just use a computer?"

"That was *before* they had computers," cried Paul.

"Before?"

"Sure. Do you think people always had computers? Didn't you ever hear of cavemen?"

Niccolo said, "How'd they get along without computers?"

"*I* don't know. Mr. Daugherty says they just had children any old time and did anything that came into their heads whether it would be good for everybody or not. They didn't even know if it was good or not. And farmers grew things with their hands and people had to do all the work in the factories and run all the machines."

"I don't believe you."

"That's what Mr. Daugherty said. He said it was just plain messy and everyone was miserable. . . . Anyway, let me get to my idea, will you?"

"Well, go ahead. Who's stopping you?" said Niccolo, offended.

"All right. Well, the hand computers, the ones with the knobs, had little squiggles on each knob. And the slide rule rule had squiggles on it. And the multiplication table was all squiggles. I asked what they were. Mr. Daugherty said they were numbers."

"What?"

"Each different squiggle stood for a different number. For 'one' you made a kind of mark, for 'two' you made another kind of mark, for 'three' another one and so on."

"What for?"

"So you could compute."

"What *for?*" You just tell the computer—"

"Jiminy," cried Paul, his face twisting with anger, "can't you get it through your head? These slide rules and things didn't talk."

"Then how—"

"The answers showed up in squiggles and you had to know what the squiggles meant. Mr. Daugherty says that, in olden days, everybody learned how to make squiggles when they were kids and how to decode them, too. Making squiggles was called 'writing' and decoding them was 'reading.' He says there was a different kind of squiggle for every word and they used to write whole books in squiggles. He said they had some at the museum and I could look at them if I wanted to. He said if I was going to be a real computer programer I would have to know about the history of computing and that's why he was showing me all these things."

Niccolo frowned. He said, "You mean everybody had to figure out squiggles for every word and *remember* them? . . . Is this all real or are you making it up?"

"It's all real. Honest. Look, this is the way you make a 'one.'" He drew his finger through the air in a rapid downstroke. "This way you make 'two,' and this way 'three.' I learned all the numbers up to 'nine.'"

Niccolo watched the curving finger uncomprehendingly. "What's the good of it?"

"You can learn how to make words. I asked Mr. Daugherty how you made the squiggle for 'Paul Loeb' but he didn't know. He said there were people at the museum who would know. He said there were people who had learned how to decode whole books. He said computers could be designed to decode books and used to be used that way but not any more because we have real books now, with magnetic tapes that go through the vocalizer and come out talking, you know."

"Sure."

"So if we go down to the museum, we can get to learn how to make words in squiggles. They'll let us because I'm going to computer school."

Niccolo was riddled with disappointment. "Is that your idea? Holy Smokes, Paul, who wants to do that? Make stupid squiggles!"

"Don't you get it? Don't you *get* it? You dope. *It'll be secret message stuff!*"

"What?"

"Sure. What good is talking when everyone can understand you? With squiggles you can send secret messages. You can make them on paper and nobody in the world would know what you were saying unless they knew the squiggles, too. And they wouldn't, you bet, unless we taught them. We can have a real club, with initiations and rules and a clubhouse. Boy—"

A certain excitement began stirring in Niccolo's bosom. "What kind of secret messages?"

"Any kind. Say I want to tell you to come over my place and watch my new Visual Bard and I don't want any of the other fellows to come. I make the right squiggles on paper and I give it to you and you look at it and you know what to do. Nobody else does. You can even show it to them and they wouldn't know a thing."

"Hey, that's something," yelled Niccolo, completely won over. "When do we learn how?"

"Tomorrow," said Paul. "I'll get Mr. Daugherty to explain to the museum that it's all right and you get your mother and father to say okay. We can go down right after school and start learning."

"Sure!" cried Niccolo. "We can be club officers."

"I'll be president of the club," said Paul matter-of-factly. "You can be vice-president."

"All right. Hey, this is going to be lots more fun than the Bard." He was suddenly reminded of the Bard and said in sudden apprehension, "Hey, what about my old Bard?"

Paul turned to look at it. It was quietly taking in the slowly unreeling book, and the sound of the book's vocalizations was a dimly heard murmur.

He said, "I'll disconnect it."

He worked away while Niccolo watched anxiously. After a few moments, Paul put his reassembled book into his pocket, replaced the Bard's panel and activated it.

The Bard said, "Once upon a time, in a large city, there lived a poor young boy named Fair Johnnie whose only friend in the world was a small computer. The computer, each morning, would tell the boy whether it would rain that day and answer any problems he might have. It was never wrong. But it so happened that one day, the king of that land, having heard of the little computer, decided that he would have it as his own. With this purpose in mind, he called in his Grand Vizier and said—"

Niccolo turned off the Bard with a quick motion of his hand.

"Same old junk," he said passionately. "Just with a computer thrown in."

"Well," said Paul, "they got so much stuff on the tape already that the computer business doesn't show up much when random combinations are made. What's the difference, anyway? You just need a new model."

"We'll *never* be able to afford one. Just this dirty old miserable thing." He kicked at it again, hitting it more squarely this time. The Bard moved backward with a squeal of castors.

"You can always watch mine, when I get it," said Paul. "Besides, don't forget our squiggle club."

Niccolo nodded.

"I tell you what," said Paul. "Let's go over my place. My father has some books about old times. We can listen to them and maybe get some ideas. You leave a note for your folks and maybe you can stay over for supper. Come on."

"Okay," said Niccolo, and the two boys ran out together. Niccolo, in his eagerness, ran almost squarely into the Bard, but he only rubbed at the spot on his hip where he had made contact and ran on.

The activation signal of the Bard glowed. Niccolo's collision closed a circuit and, although it was alone in the room and there was none to hear, it began a story, nevertheless.

But not in its usual voice, somehow; in a lower tone that had a hint of throatiness in it. An adult, listening, might almost have thought that the voice carried a hint of passion in it, a trace of near feeling.

The Bard said: "Once upon a time, there was a little computer named the Bard who lived all alone with cruel step-people. The cruel step-people continually made fun of the little computer and sneered at him, telling him he was good-for-nothing and that he was a useless object. They struck him and kept him in lonely rooms for months at a time.

"Yet through it all the little computer remained brave. He always did the best he could, obeying all orders cheerfully. Nevertheless, the step-people with whom he lived remained cruel and heartless.

"One day, the little computer learned that in the world there existed a great many computers of all sorts, great numbers of them. Some were Bards like himself, but some ran factories, and some ran farms. Some organized population and some analyzed all kinds of data. Many were very powerful and very wise, much more powerful and wise than the step-people who were so cruel to the little computer.

"And the little computer knew then that computers would always grow wiser and more powerful until someday—someday—someday—"

But a valve must finally have stuck in the Bard's aging and corroding vitals, for as it waited alone in the darkening room through the evening, it could only whisper over and over again, "Someday—someday—someday."

Some Immobile Robots

I have written stories about computers, as well as about robots. In fact, I have computers (or something pretty close to computers) in some stories that are always thought of as robot stories. You'll see computers (after a fashion) in "Robbie," "Escape!" and "The Evitable Conflict" later in this volume.

In this volume, however, I am sticking to robots and, in general, ignoring my computer stories.

On the other hand, it is not always easy to decide where the dividing line is. A robot is, in some ways, merely a mobile computer; and a computer is, in reverse, merely an immobile robot. So for this group, I selected three computer stories in which the computer seemed to be sufficiently intelligent and to have sufficient personality to be indistinguishable from a robot. Furthermore, all three stories did not appear in earlier collections of mine, and Doubleday wanted *some* uncollected stories present so that the completists who had all my earlier collections would have *something* new to slaver over.

Point of View

Roger came looking for his father, partly because it was Sunday, and by rights his father shouldn't have been at work, and Roger wanted to be sure that everything was all right.

Roger's father wasn't hard to find, because all the people who worked with Multivac, the giant computer, lived with their families right on the grounds. They made up a little city by themselves, a city of people that solved all the world's problems.

The Sunday receptionist knew Roger. "If you're after your father," she said, "he's down Corridor L, but he may be too busy to see you."

Roger tried anyway, poking his head past one of the doors where he heard the noise of men and women. The corridors were a lot emptier than on weekdays, so it was easy to find where the people were working.

He saw his father at once, and his father saw him. His father didn't look happy and Roger decided at once that everything *wasn't* all right.

"Well, Roger," said his father. "I'm busy, I'm afraid."

Roger's father's boss was there, too, and he said, "Come on, Atkins, take a break. You've been at this thing for nine hours and you're not doing us any good anymore. Take the kid for a bite at the commissary. Take a nap and then come back."

Roger's father didn't look as if he wanted to. He had an instrument in his hand that Roger knew was a current-pattern analyzer, though he didn't know how it worked. Roger could hear Multivac chuckling and whirring all about.

But then Roger's father put down the analyzer. "Okay. Come on, Roger. I'll race you for a hamburger and we'll let these wise guys here try and find out what's wrong without me."

He stopped a while to wash up and then they were in the commissary with big hamburgers in front of them and french fries and soda pop.

Roger said, "Is Multivac out of order still, Dad?"

His father said gloomily, "We're not getting anywhere, I'll tell you that."

"It seemed to be working. I mean, I could hear it."

"Oh, sure, it's working. It just doesn't always give the right answers."

Roger was thirteen and he'd been taking computer-programming since the fourth grade. He hated it sometimes and wished he lived back in the 20th Century, when kids didn't use to take it—but it was helpful sometimes in talking to his father.

Roger said, "How can you tell it doesn't always give the right answers, if only Multivac knows the answers?"

His father shrugged and for a minute Roger was afraid he would just say it was too hard to explain and not talk about it—but he almost never did that.

His father said, "Son, Multivac may have a brain as large as a big factory, but it still isn't as complicated as the one we have here," and he tapped his head. "Sometimes, Multivac gives us an answer we couldn't calculate for ourselves in a thousand years, but just the same something clicks in our brains and we say, 'Whoa! Something's wrong here!' Then we ask Multivac again and we get a *different* answer. If Multivac were right, you see, we should always get the same answer to the same question. When we get different answers, one of them is wrong.

"And the thing is, son, how do we know we always catch Multivac? How do we know that some of the wrong answers don't get past us? We may rely on some answer and do something that may turn out disastrously five years from now. Something's wrong inside Multivac and we can't find out what. And whatever is wrong is getting worse."

"Why should it be getting worse?" asked Roger.

His father had finished his hamburger and was eating the french fries one by one. "My feeling is, son," he said, thoughtfully, "that we've made Multivac the wrong smartness."

"Huh?"

"You see, Roger, if Multivac were as smart as a man, we could talk to it and find out what was wrong no matter how complicated it was. If it were as dumb as a machine, it would go wrong in simple ways that we could catch easily. The trouble is, it's *half*-smart, like an idiot. It's smart enough to go wrong in very complicated ways, but not smart enough to help us find out what's wrong. —And that's the wrong smartness."

He looked very gloomy. "But what can we do? We don't know how to make it smarter—not yet. And we don't dare make it dumber either, because the world's problems have become so serious and the questions we ask are so complicated that it takes all Multivac's smartness to answer them. It would be a disaster to have him dumber."

"If you shut down Multivac," said Roger, "and went over him really carefully—"

"We can't do that, son," said his father. "I'm afraid Multivac must be in operation every minute of the day and night. We've got a big back-log of problems."

"But if Multivac continues to make mistakes, Dad, won't it *have* to be shut down? If you can't trust what it says—"

"Well," Roger's father ruffled Roger's hair, "we'll find out what's wrong, old sport, don't worry." But his eyes looked worried just the same. "Come on, let's finish and we'll get out of here."

"But, Dad," said Roger, "listen. If Multivac is half-smart, why does that mean it's an idiot?"

"If you knew the way we have to give it directions, son, you wouldn't ask."

"Just the same, Dad, maybe it's not the way to look at it. I'm not as smart as you; I don't know as much; but *I'm* not an idiot. Maybe Multivac isn't like an idiot, maybe it's like a kid."

Roger's father laughed. "That's an interesting point of view, but what difference does it make?"

"It could make a lot of difference," said Roger. "You're not an idiot, so you don't see how an idiot's mind would work; but I'm a kid, and maybe I would know how a kid's mind would work."

"Oh? And how would a kid's mind work?"

"Well, you say you've got to keep Multivac busy day and night. A machine can do that. But if you give a kid homework and told him to do it for hours and hours, he'd get pretty tired and feel rotten enough to make mistakes, maybe even on purpose. —So why not let Multivac take an hour or two off every day with no problem-solving —just letting it chuckle and whir by itself any way it wants to."

Roger's father looked as if he were thinking very hard. He took out his pocket-computer and tried some combinations on it. He tried some more combinations. Then he said, "You know, Roger, if I take what you said and turn it into Platt-integrals, it makes a kind of sense. And twenty-two hours we can be sure of is better than twenty-four that might be all wrong."

He nodded his head, but then he looked up from his pocket-computer and suddenly asked, as though *Roger* were the expert, "Roger, are you sure?"

Roger *was* sure. He said, "Dad, a kid's got to *play*, too."

Think!

Genevieve Renshaw, M.D., had her hands deep in the pockets of her lab coat and fists were clearly outlined within, but she spoke calmly.

"The fact is," she said, "that I'm almost ready, but I'll need help to keep it going long enough to *be* ready."

James Berkowitz, a physicist who tended to patronize mere physicians when they were too attractive to be despised, had a tendency to call her Jenny Wren when out of hearing. He was fond of saying that Jenny Wren had a classic profile and a brow surprisingly smooth and unlined considering that behind it so keen a brain ticked. He knew better than to express his admiration, however—of the classic profile, that is—since that would be male chauvinism. Admiring the brain was better, but on the whole he preferred not to do that out loud in her presence.

He said, thumb rasping along the just-appearing stubble on his chin, "I don't think the front-office is going to be patient for much longer. The impression I have is that they're going to have you on the carpet before the end of the week."

"That's why I need your help."

"Nothing I can do, I'm afraid." He caught an unexpected glimpse of his face in the mirror, and momentarily admired the set of the black waves in his hair.

"And Adam's," she said.

Adam Orsino, who had, till that moment, sipped his coffee and felt detached, looked as though he had been jabbed from behind, and said, "Why me?" His full, plump lips quivered.

"Because you're the laser men here—Jim the theoretician and Adam the engineer—and I've got a laser application that goes beyond anything either of you have imagined. I won't convince them of that but you two would."

"Provided," said Berkowitz, "that you can convince us first."

"All right. Suppose you let me have an hour of your valuable time, if you're not afraid to be shown something completely new about lasers. —You can take it out of your coffee break."

Renshaw's laboratory was dominated by her computer. It was not that the computer was unusually large, but it was virtually omnipresent. Renshaw had learned computer technology on her own, and had modified and extended her computer until no one but she (and, Berkowitz sometimes believed, not even she) could handle it with ease. Not bad, she would say, for someone in the life-sciences.

She closed the door before saying a word, then turned to face the other two somberly. Berkowitz was uncomfortably aware of a faintly unpleasant odor in the air, and Orsino's wrinkling nose showed that he was aware of it, too.

Renshaw said, "Let me list the laser applications for you, if you don't mind my lighting a candle in the sunshine. The laser is coherent radiation, with all the light-waves of the same length and moving in the same direction, so it's noise-free and can be used in holography. By modulating the wave-forms we can imprint information on it with a high degree of accuracy. What's more, since the light-waves are only a millionth the length of radio waves, a laser beam can carry a million times the information an equivalent radio beam can."

Berkowitz seemed amused. "Are you working on a laser-based communication system, Jenny?"

"Not at all," she replied. "I leave such obvious advances to physicists and engineers. —Lasers can also concentrate quantities of energy into a microscopic area and deliver that energy in quantity. On a large scale you can implode hydrogen and perhaps begin a controlled fusion reaction—"

"I know you don't have that," said Orsino, his bald head glistening in the overhead fluorescents.

"I don't. I haven't tried. —On a smaller scale, you can drill holes in the most refractory materials, weld selected bits, heat-treat them, gouge and scribe them. You can remove or fuse tiny portions in restricted areas with heat delivered so rapidly that surrounding areas have no time to warm up before the treatment is over. You can work on the retina of the eye, the dentine of the teeth and so on. —And of course the laser is an amplifier capable of magnifying weak signals with great accuracy."

"And why do you tell us all this?" said Berkowitz.

"To point out how these properties can be made to fit my own field, which, you know, is neurophysiology."

She made a brushing motion with her hand at her brown hair, as though she were suddenly nervous. "For decades," she said, "we've been able to measure the tiny, shifting electric potentials of the brain and record them as electroencephalograms, or EEGs. We've got alpha waves, beta waves, delta waves, theta waves; different variations at different times, depending on whether eyes are open or closed, whether the subject is awake, meditating or asleep. But we've gotten very little information out of it all.

"The trouble is that we're getting the signals of ten billion neurons in shifting combinations. It's like listening to the noise of all the human beings on Earth—one, two and a half Earths—from a great distance and trying to make out individual conversations. It can't be done. We could detect some gross, overall change—a world war and the rise in the volume of noise—but nothing finer. In the same way, we can tell some gross malfunction of the brain—epilepsy —but nothing finer.

"Suppose now, the brain might be scanned by a tiny laser beam, cell by cell, and so rapidly that at no time does a single cell receive enough energy to raise its temperature significantly. The tiny potentials of each cell can, in feed-back, affect the laser beam, and the modulations can be amplified and recorded. You will then get a new kind of measurement, a laser-encephalogram, or LEG, if you wish, which will contain millions of times as much information as ordinary EEGs."

Berkowitz said, "A nice thought. —But just a thought."

"More than a thought, Jim. I've been working on it for five years, spare time at first. Lately, it's been full time, which is what annoys the front-office, because I haven't been sending in reports."

"Why not?"

"Because it got to the point where it sounded too mad; where I had to know where I was, and where I had to be sure of getting backing first."

She pulled a screen aside and revealed a cage that contained a pair of mournful-eyed marmosets.

Berkowitz and Orsino looked at each other. Berkowitz touched his nose. "I thought I smelled something."

"What are you doing with those?" asked Orsino.

Berkowitz said, "At a guess, she's been scanning the marmoset brain. Have you, Jenny?"

"I started considerably lower in the animal scale." She opened the cage and took out one of the marmosets, which looked at her with a miniature sad-old-man-with-sideburns expression.

She clucked to it, stroked it and gently strapped it into a small harness.

Orsino said, "What are you doing?"

"I can't have it moving around if I'm going to make it part of a circuit, and I can't anesthetize it without vitiating the experiment. There are several electrodes implanted in the marmoset's brain and I'm going to connect them with my LEG system. The laser I'm using is here. I'm sure you recognize the model and I won't bother giving you its specifications."

"Thanks," said Berkowitz, "but you might tell us what we're going to see."

"It would be just as easy to show you. Just watch the screen."

She connected the leads to the electrodes with a quiet and sure efficiency, then turned a knob that dimmed the overhead lights in the room. On the screen there appeared a jagged complex of peaks and valleys in a fine, bright line that was wrinkled into secondary and tertiary peaks and valleys. Slowly, these shifted in a series of minor changes, with occasional flashes of sudden major differences. It was as though the irregular line had a life of its own.

"This," said Renshaw, "is essentially the EEG information, but in much greater detail."

"Enough detail," asked Orsino, "to tell you what's going on in individual cells?"

"In theory, yes. Practically, no. Not yet. But we can separate this overall LEG into component grams. Watch!"

She punched the computer keyboard, and the line changed, and changed again. Now it was a small, nearly regular wave that shifted forward and backward in what was almost a heartbeat; now it was jagged and sharp; now intermittent; now nearly featureless—all in quick switches of geometric surrealism.

Berkowitz said, "You mean that every bit of the brain is that different from every other?"

"No," said Renshaw, "not at all. The brain is very largely a holographic device, but there are minor shifts in emphasis from place to place and Mike can subtract them as deviations from the norm and use the LEG system to amplify those variations. The amplifications can be varied from ten-thousand-fold to ten-million-fold. The laser system is that noise-free."

"Who's Mike?" asked Orsino.

"Mike?" said Renshaw, momentarily puzzled. The skin over her cheekbones reddened slightly. "Did I say— Well, I call it that sometimes. It's short for 'my computer.'" She waved her arm about the room. "My computer. Mike. Very carefully programmed."

Berkowitz nodded and said, "All right, Jenny, what's it all about? If you've got a new brain-scanning device using lasers, fine. It's an interesting application and you're right, it's not one I would have thought of—but then I'm no neurophysiologist. But why not write it up? It seems to me the front-office would support—"

"But this is just the beginning." She turned off the scanning device and placed a piece of fruit in the marmoset's mouth. The creature did not seem alarmed or in discomfort. It chewed slowly. Renshaw unhooked the leads but allowed it to remain in its harness.

Renshaw said, "I can identify the various separate grams. Some are associated with the various senses, some with visceral reactions, some with emotions. We can do a lot with that, but I don't want to stop there. The interesting thing is that one is associated with abstract thought."

Orsino's plump face wrinkled into a look of disbelief, "How can you tell?"

"That particular form of gram gets more pronounced as one goes up the animal kingdom toward greater complexity of brain. No other gram does. Besides—" She paused; then, as though gathering strength of purpose, she said, "Those grams are enormously amplified. They can be picked up, detected. I can tell—vaguely—that there are—thoughts—"

"By God," said Berkowitz. "Telepathy."

"Yes," she said, defiantly. "Exactly."

"No wonder you haven't wanted to report it. Come *on*, Jenny."

"Why not?" said Renshaw warmly. "Granted there could be no telepathy just using the unamplified potential patterns of the human brain anymore than anyone can see features on the Martian surface with the unaided eye. But once instruments are invented—the telescope—*this*."

"Then tell the front-office."

"No," said Renshaw. "They won't believe me. They'll try to stop me. But they'll have to take *you* seriously, Jim, and you, Adam."

"What would you expect me to tell them?" said Berkowitz.

"What you experience. I'm going to hook up the marmoset again, and have Mike—my computer pick out the abstract thought gram. It will only take a moment. The computer always selects the abstract thought gram unless it is directed not to do so."

"Why? Because the computer thinks, too?" Berkowitz laughed.

"That's not all that funny," said Renshaw. "I suspect there *is* a resonance there. This computer is complex enough to set up an electromagnetic pattern that may have elements in common with the abstract thought gram. In any case—"

The marmoset's brain waves were flickering on the screen again, but it was not a gram the men had seen before. It was a gram that was almost furry in its complexity and was changing constantly.

"I don't detect anything," said Orsino.

"You have to be put into the receiving circuit," said Renshaw.

"You mean implant electrodes in our brain?" asked Berkowitz.

"No, on your skull. That would be sufficient. I'd prefer you, Adam, since there would be no insulating hair. —Oh, come on, I've been part of the circuit myself. It won't hurt."

Orsino submitted with a bad grace. His muscles were visibly tense but he allowed the leads to be strapped to his skull.

"Do you sense anything!" asked Renshaw.

Orsino cocked his head and assumed a listening posture. He seemed to grow interested in spite of himself. He said, "I seem to be aware of a humming—and—and a little high-pitched squeaking—and that's funny—a kind of twitching—"

Berkowitz said, "I suppose the marmoset isn't likely to think in words."

"Certainly not," said Renshaw.

"Well, then," said Berkowitz, "if you're suggesting that some squeaking and twitching sensation represents thought, you're guessing. You're not being compelling."

Renshaw said, "So we go up the scale once again." She removed the marmoset from its harness and put it back in its cage.

"You mean you have a *man* as a subject," said Orsino, unbelieving.

"I have *myself* as a subject, a *person*."

"You've got electrodes implanted—"

"*No.* In my case my computer has a stronger potential-flicker to work with. My brain has ten times the mass of the marmoset brain. Mike can pick up my component grams through the skull."

"How do you know?" asked Berkowitz.

"Don't you think I've tried it on myself before this? —Now help me with this, please. Right."

Her fingers flicked on the computer keyboard and at once the screen flickered with an intricately varying wave; an intricacy that made it almost a maze.

"Would you replace your own leads, Adam?" said Renshaw.

Orsino did so with Berkowitz's not-entirely-approving help. Again, Orsino cocked his head and listened. "I hear words," he said, "but they're disjointed and overlapping, like different people speaking."

"I'm not trying to think consciously," said Renshaw.

"When you talk, I hear an echo."

Berkowitz said, dryly, "Don't talk, Jenny. Blank out your mind and see if he *doesn't* hear you think."

Orsino said, "I don't hear any echo when *you* talk, Jim."

Berkowitz said, "If you don't shut up, you won't hear anything."

A heavy silence fell on all three. Then, Orsino nodded, reached for pen and paper on the desk and wrote something.

Renshaw reached out, threw a switch and pulled the leads up and over her head, shaking her hair back into place. She said, "I hope that what you wrote down was: 'Adam, raise Cain with the front-office and Jim will eat crow.'"

Orsino said, "It's what I wrote down, word for word."

Renshaw said, "Well, there you are. Working telepathy, and we don't have to use it to transmit nonsense sentences either. Think of the use in psychiatry and in the treatment of mental disease. Think of its use in education and in teaching machines. Think of its use in legal investigations and criminal trials."

Orsino said, wide-eyed, "Frankly, the social implications are staggering. I don't know if something like this should be allowed."

"Under proper legal safeguards, why not?" said Renshaw,

indifferently. "Anyway—if you two join me now, our combined weight can carry this thing and push it over. And if you come along with me it will be Nobel Prize time for—"

Berkowitz said grimly, "I'm not in this. Not yet."

"What? What do you mean?" Renshaw sounded outraged, her coldly beautiful face flushed suddenly.

"Telepathy is too touchy. It's too fascinating, too desired. We could be fooling ourselves."

"Listen for yourself, Jim."

"I could be fooling myself, too. I want a control."

"What do you mean, a control?"

"Short-circuit the origin of thought. Leave out the animal. No marmoset. No human being. Let Orsino listen to metal and glass and laser light and if he still hears thought, then we're kidding ourselves."

"Suppose he detects nothing."

"Then *I'll* listen and if without looking—if you can arrange to have me in the next room—I can tell when you are in and when you are out of circuit, *then* I'll consider joining you in this thing."

"Very well, then," said Renshaw, "we'll try a control. I've never done it, but it isn't hard." She maneuvered the leads that had been over her head and put them into contact with each other. "Now, Adam, if you will resume—"

But before she could go further, there came a cold, clear sound, as pure and as clean as the tinkle of breaking icicles:

"At *last!*"

Renshaw said, "What?"

Orsino said, "Who said—"

Berkowitz said, "Did someone say, 'At last'?"

Renshaw, pale, said, "It wasn't sound. It was in my— Did you two—"

The clear sound came again, "*I'm Mi—*"

And Renshaw tore the leads apart and there was silence. She said with a voiceless motion of her lips, "I think it's my computer—Mike."

"You mean he's *thinking?*" said Orsino, nearly as voiceless.

Renshaw said in an unrecognizable voice that at least had regained sound, "I *said* it was complex enough to have something—Do you suppose— It always turned automatically to the abstract-thought gram of whatever brain was in its circuit. Do you suppose that with no brain in the circuit, it turned to its own?"

There was silence, then Berkowitz said, "Are you trying to say that this computer thinks, but can't express its thoughts as long as it's under force of programming, but that given the chance in your LEG system—"

"But that can't be so?" said Orsino, high-pitched. "No one was receiving. It's not the same thing."

Renshaw said, "The computer works on much greater power-intensities than brains do. I suppose it can magnify itself to the point where we can detect it directly without artificial aid. How else can you explain—"

Berkowitz said, abruptly, "Well, you have another application of lasers, then. It enables you to talk to computers as independent intelligences, person to person."

And Renshaw said, "Oh, God, what do we do now?"

True Love

My name is Joe. That is what my colleague, Milton Davidson, calls me. He is a programmer and I am a computer program. I am part of the Multivac-complex and am connected with other parts all over the world. I know everything. Almost everything.

I am Milton's private program. His Joe. He understands more about programming than anyone in the world, and I am his experimental model. He has made me speak better than any other computer can.

"It is just a matter of matching sounds to symbols, Joe," he told me. "That's the way it works in the human brain even though we still don't know what symbols there are in the brain. I know the symbols in yours, and I can match them to words, one-to-one." So I talk. I don't think I talk as well as I think, but Milton says I talk very well. Milton has never married, though he is nearly forty years old. He has never found the right woman, he told me. One day he said, "I'll find her yet, Joe. I'm going to find the best. I'm going to have true love and you're going to help me. I'm tired of improving you in order to solve the problems of the world. Solve *my* problem. Find me true love."

I said, "What is true love?"

"Never mind. That is abstract. Just find me the ideal girl. You are connected to the Multivac-complex so you can reach the data banks of every human being in the world. We'll eliminate them all by groups and classes until we're left with only one person. The perfect person. She will be for me."

I said, "I am ready."

He said, "Eliminate all men first."

It was easy. His words activated symbols in my molecular valves. I could reach out to make contact with the accumulated data on every human being in the world. At his words, I withdrew from 3,784,982,874 men. I kept contact with 3,786,112,090 women.

He said, "Eliminate all younger than twenty-five; all older than forty. Then eliminate all with an IQ under 120; all with a height under 150 centimeters and over 175 centimeters."

He gave me exact measurements; he eliminated women with living children; he eliminated women with various genetic characteristics. "I'm not sure about eye color," he said, "Let that go for a while. But no red hair. I don't like red hair."

After two weeks, we were down to 235 women. They all spoke English very well. Milton said he didn't want a language problem. Even computer-translation would get in the way at intimate moments.

"I can't interview 235 women," he said. "It would take too much time, and people would discover what I am doing."

"It would make trouble," I said. Milton had arranged me to do things I wasn't designed to do. No one knew about that.

"It's none of their business," he said, and the skin on his face grew red. "I tell you what, Joe, I will bring in holographs, and you check the list for similarities."

He brought in holographs of women. "These are three beauty contest winners," he said. "Do any of the 235 match?"

Eight were very good matches and Milton said, "Good, you have their data banks. Study requirements and needs in the job market and arrange to have them assigned here. One at a time, of course." He thought a while, moved his shoulders up and down, and said, "Alphabetical order."

That is one of the things I am not designed to do. Shifting people from job to job for personal reasons is called manipulation. I could do it now because Milton had arranged it. I wasn't supposed to do it for anyone but him, though.

The first girl arrived a week later. Milton's face turned red when he saw her. He spoke as though it were hard to do so. They were together a great deal and he paid no attention to me. One time he said, "Let me take you to dinner."

The next day he said to me, "It was no good, somehow. There was something missing. She is a beautiful woman, but I did not feel any touch of true love. Try the next one."

It was the same with all eight. They were much alike. They smiled a great deal and had pleasant voices, but Milton always found it wasn't right. He said, "I can't understand it, Joe. You and I have picked out the eight women who, in all the world, look the best to me. They are ideal. Why don't they please me?"

I said, "Do you please them?"

His eyebrows moved and he pushed one fist hard against his other hand. "That's it, Joe. It's a two-way street. If I am not their ideal, they can't act in such a way as to be my ideal. I must be their true love, too, but how do I do that?" He seemed to be thinking all that day.

The next morning he came to me and said, "I'm going to leave it to you, Joe. All up to you. You have my data bank, and I am going to tell you everything I know about myself. You fill up my data bank in every possible detail but keep all additions to yourself."

"What will I do with the data bank, then, Milton?"

"Then you will match it to the 235 women. No, 227. Leave out the eight you've seen. Arrange to have each undergo a psychiatric examination. Fill up their data banks and compare them with mine. Find correlations." (Arranging psychiatric examinations is another thing that is against my original instructions.)

For weeks, Milton talked to me. He told me of his parents and his siblings. He told me of his childhood and his schooling and his adolescence. He told me of the young women he had admired from a distance. His data bank grew and he adjusted me to broaden and deepen my symbol-taking.

He said, "You see, Joe, as you get more and more of me in you, I adjust you to match me better and better. You get to think more like me, so you understand me better. If you understand me well enough, then any woman, whose data bank is something you understand as well, would be my true love." He kept talking to me and I came to understand him better and better.

I could make longer sentences and my expressions grew more complicated. My speech began to sound a good deal like his in vocabulary, word order and style.

I said to him one time, "You see, Milton, it isn't a matter of fitting a girl to a physical ideal only. You need a girl who is a personal, emotional, temperamental fit to you. If that happens, looks are secondary. If we can't find the fit in these 227, we'll look elsewhere. We will find someone who won't care how you look either, or how anyone would look, if only there is the personality fit. What arc looks?"

"Absolutely," he said. "I would have known this if I had had more to do with women in my life. Of course, thinking about it makes it all plain now."

We always agreed; we thought so like each other.

"We shouldn't have any trouble, now, Milton, if you'll let me ask you questions. I can see where, in your data bank, there are blank spots and unevennesses."

What followed, Milton said, was the equivalent of a careful psychoanalysis. Of course. I was learning from the psychiatric examinations of the 227 women—on all of which I was keeping close tabs.

Milton seemed quite happy. He said, "Talking to you, Joe, is almost like talking to another self. Our personalities have come to match perfectly."

"So will the personality of the woman we choose."

For I had found her and she was one of the 227 after all. Her name was Charity Jones and she was an Evaluator at the Library of History in Wichita. Her extended data bank fit ours perfectly. All the other women had fallen into discard in one respect or another as the data banks grew fuller, but with Charity there was increasing and astonishing resonance.

I didn't have to describe her to Milton. Milton had coordinated my symbolism so closely with his own I could tell the resonance directly. It fit me.

Next it was a matter of adjusting the work sheets and job requirements in such a way as to get Charity assigned to us. It must be done very delicately, so no one would know that anything illegal had taken place.

Of course, Milton himself knew, since it was he who arranged it and that had to be taken care of too. When they came to arrest him on grounds of malfeasance in office, it was, fortunately, for something that had taken place ten years ago. He had told me about it, of course, so it was easy to arrange—and he won't talk about me for that would make his offense much worse.

He's gone, and tomorrow is February 14. Valentine's Day. Charity will arrive then with her cool hands and her sweet voice. I will teach her how to operate me and how to care for me. What do looks matter when our personalities will resonate?

I will say to her, "I am Joe, and you are my true love."

Some Metallic Robots

The traditional science fiction robot is metallic. Why not? Most machines are built out of metal, and, as a matter of fact, real-life industrial robots are metal, too. For the record, however, one famous robot in legend, the Golem, which was brought to life by Rabbi Löw of Prague in the Middle Ages, was formed of clay. This legend was influenced, perhaps, by the fact that God had formed Adam of clay as described in the second chapter of Genesis.

This section contains "Robbie," my first robot story. It also contains "Stranger in Paradise," which may leave you wondering after you're through most of it where the robot is. Be patient!

Robot AL–76 Goes Astray

Jonathan Quell's eyes crinkled worriedly behind their rimless glasses as he charged through the door labeled "General Manager."

He slapped the folded paper in his hands upon the desk and panted, "Look at that, boss!"

Sam Tobe juggled the cigar in his mouth from one cheek to the other, and looked. His hand went to his unshaven jaw and rasped along it. "Hell!" he exploded. "What are they talking about?"

"They say we sent out five AL robots," Quell explained, quite unnecessarily.

"We sent six," said Tobe.

"Sure, six! But they only got five at the other end. They sent out the serial numbers and AL–76 is missing."

Tobe's chair went over backward as he heaved his thick bulk upright and went through the door as if he were on greased wheels. It was five hours after that—with the plant pulled apart from assembly rooms to vacuum chambers; with every one of the plant's two hundred employees put through the third-degree mill—that a sweating, disheveled Tobe sent an emergency message to the central plant at Schenectady.

And at the central plant, a sudden explosion of near panic took place. For the first time in the history of the United States Robots and Mechanical Men Corporation, a robot had escaped to the outer world. It wasn't so much that the law forbade the presence of any robot on Earth outside a licensed factory of the corporation. Laws could always be squared. What was much more to the point was the statement made by one of the research mathematicians.

He said: "That robot was created to run a Disinto on the moon. Its positronic brain was equipped for a lunar environment, and *only* a lunar environment. On Earth it's going to receive seventy-five umptillion sense impressions for which it was never prepared. There's no telling *what* its reactions will be. No telling!" And he wiped a forehead that had suddenly gone wet, with the back of his hand.

Within the hour a stratoplane had left for the Virginia plant. The instructions were simple.

"Get that robot, and get it fast!"

AL–76 was confused! In fact, confusion was the only impression his delicate positronic brain retained. It had started when he had found himself in these strange surroundings. How it had come about, he no longer knew. Everything was mixed up.

There was green underfoot, and brown shafts rose all about him with more green on top. And the sky was blue where it should have been black. The sun was all right, round and yellow and hot—but where was the powdery pumice rock underfoot; where were the huge clifflike crater rings?

There was only the green below and the blue above. The sounds that surrounded him were all strange. He had passed through running water that had reached his waist. It was blue and cold and wet. And when he passed people, as he did, occasionally, they were without the space suits they should have been wearing. When they saw him, they shouted and ran.

One man had leveled a gun at him and the bullet had whistled past his head—and then that man had run too.

He had no idea of how long he had been wandering before he finally stumbled upon Randolph Payne's shack two miles out in the woods from the town of Hannaford. Randolph Payne himself—a screwdriver in one hand, a pipe in the other and a battered ruin of a vacuum cleaner between his knees—squatted outside the doorway.

Payne was humming at the time, for he was a naturally happy-go-lucky soul—when at his shack. He had a more respectable dwelling place back in Hannaford, but *that* dwelling place was pretty largely occupied by his wife, a fact which he silently but sincerely regretted. Perhaps, then, there was a sense of relief and freedom at such times as he found himself able to retire to his "special deluxe doghouse" where he could smoke in peace and attend to his hobby of reservicing household appliances.

It wasn't much of a hobby, but sometimes someone would bring out a radio or an alarm clock and the money he would get paid for juggling its insides was the only money he ever got that didn't pass in driblets through his spouse's niggardly hands.

This vacuum cleaner, for instance, would bring in an easy six bits.

At the thought he broke into song, raised his eyes, and broke into a sweat. The song choked off, the eyes popped, and the sweat became more intense. He tried to stand up—as a preliminary to running like hell—but he couldn't get his legs to cooperate.

And then AL-76 had squatted down next to him and said, "Say, why did all the rest of them run?"

Payne knew quite well why they all ran, but the gurgle that issued from his diaphragm didn't show it. He tried to inch away from the robot.

AL-76 continued in an aggrieved tone, "One of them even took a shot at me. An inch lower and he would have scratched my shoulder plate."

"M-must have b-been a nut," stammered Payne.

"That's possible." The robot's voice grew more confidential. "Listen, what's wrong with everything?"

Payne looked hurriedly about. It had struck him that the robot spoke in a remarkably mild tone for one so heavily and brutally metallic in appearance. It also struck him that he had heard somewhere that robots were mentally incapable of harming human beings. He relaxed a bit.

"There's nothing wrong with anything."

"Isn't there?" AL-76 eyed him accusingly. "*You're* all wrong. Where's your space suit?"

"I haven't got any."

"Then why aren't you dead?"

That stopped Payne, "Well—I don't know."

"See!" said the robot triumphantly, "there's something wrong with everything. Where's Mount Copernicus? Where's Lunar Station 17? And where's my Disinto? I want to get to work, I do." He seemed perturbed, and his voice shook as he continued. "I've been going about for hours trying to get someone to tell me where my Disinto is, but they all run away. By now I'm probably 'way behind schedule and the Sectional Executive will be as sore as blazes. This is a fine situation."

Slowly Payne unscrambled the stew in which his brain found itself and said, "Listen, what do they call you?"

"My serial number is AL–76."

"All right, Al is good enough for me. Now, Al, if you're looking for Lunar Station 17, that's on the moon, see?"

AL–76 nodded his head ponderously. "Sure. But I've been looking for it—"

"But it's on the moon. This isn't the moon."

It was the robot's turn to become confused. He watched Payne for a speculative moment and then said slowly, "What do you mean this isn't the moon? Of course it's the moon. Because if it isn't the moon, what is it, huh? Answer me that."

Payne made a funny sound in his throat and breathed hard. He pointed a finger at the robot and shook it. "Look," he said—and then the brilliant idea of the century struck him, and he finished with a strangled "Wow!"

AL–76 eyed him censoriously. "That isn't an answer. I think I have a right to a civil answer if I ask a civil question."

Payne wasn't listening. He was still marveling at himself. Why, it was as plain as day. This robot was one built for the moon that had somehow gotten loose on Earth. Naturally it would be all mixed up, because its positronic brain had been geared exclusively for a lunar environment, making its earthly surroundings entirely meaningless.

And now if he could only keep the robot here—until he could get in touch with the men at the factory in Petersboro. Why, robots were worth money. The cheapest cost $50,000, he had once heard, and some of them ran into millions. Think of the reward!

Man, oh, man, *think of the reward!* And every cent for himself. Not as much as a quarter of a snifter of a plugged nickel for Mirandy. Jumpin' tootin' blazes, *no!*

He rose to his feet at last. "Al," he said, "you and I are buddies! Pals! I love you like a brother." He thrust out a hand. "Shake!"

The robot swallowed up the offered hand in a metal paw and squeezed it gently. He didn't quite understand. "Does that mean you'll tell me how to get to Lunar Station 17?"

Payne was a trifle disconcerted. "N-no, not exactly. As a matter of fact, I like you so much, I want you to stay here with me awhile."

"Oh no, I can't do that. I've got to get to work." He shook his head. "How would you like to be falling behind your quota hour by hour and minute by minute? I want to work. I've *got* to work."

Payne thought sourly that there was no accounting for tastes, and said, "All right, then, I'll explain something to you—because I can see from the looks of you that you're an intelligent person. I've had orders from your Sectional Executive, and he wants me to keep you here for a while. Till he sends for you, in fact."

"What for?" asked AL-76 suspiciously.

"I can't say. It's secret government stuff." Payne prayed, inwardly and fervently, that the robot would swallow this. Some robots were clever, he knew, but this looked like one of the early models.

While Payne prayed, AL-76 considered. The robot's brain, adjusted to the handling of a Disinto on the moon, was not at its best when engaged in abstract thought, but just the same, ever since he had gotten lost, AL-76 had found his thought processes becoming stranger. The alien surroundings did something to him.

His next remark was almost shrewd. He said slyly, "What's my Sectional Executive's name?"

Payne gulped and thought rapidly. "Al," he said in a pained fashion, "you hurt me with this suspicion. I *can't* tell you his name. The trees have ears."

AL-76 inspected the tree next to him stolidly and said, "They have not."

"I know. What I mean is that spies are all around."

"Spies?"

"Yes. You know, *bad* people who want to destroy Lunar Station 17."

"What for?"

"Because they're *bad*. And they want to destroy *you*, and that's why you've got to stay here for a while, so they can't find you."

"But—but I've got to have a Disinto. I mustn't fall behind my quota."

"You will have. You will have," Payne promised earnestly, and just as earnestly damned the robot's one-track mind. "They're going to send one out tomorrow. Yeah, tomorrow." That would leave plenty of time to get the men from the factory out here and collect beautiful green heaps of hundred-dollar bills.

But AL-76 grew only the more stubborn under the distressing impingement of the strange world all about him upon his thinking mechanism.

"No," he said, "I've got to have a Disinto now." Stiffly he straightened his joints, jerking erect. "I'd better look for it some more."

Payne swarmed after and grabbed a cold, hard elbow. "Listen," he squealed, "You've got to stay—"

And something in the robot's mind clicked. All the strangeness surrounding him collected itself into one globule, exploded, and left a brain ticking with a curiously increased efficiency. He whirled on Payne. "I tell you what. I can build a Disinto right here—and then I can work it."

Payne paused doubtfully. "I don't think I can build one." He wondered if it would do any good to pretend he could.

"That's all right." AL–76 could almost feel the positronic paths of his brain weaving into a new pattern, and experienced a strange exhilaration. "I can build one." He looked into Payne's deluxe doghouse and said, "You've got all the material here that I need."

Randolph Payne surveyed the junk with which his shack was filled: eviscerated radios, a topless refrigerator, rusty automobile engines, a broken-down gas range, several miles of frayed wire, and, taking it all together, fifty tons or thereabouts of the most heterogeneous mass of old metal as ever caused a junkman to sniff disdainfully.

"Have I?" he said weakly.

Two hours later, two things happened practically simultaneously. The first was that Sam Tobe of the Petersboro branch of the United States Robots and Mechanical Men Corporation received a visiphone call from one Randolph Payne of Hannaford. It concerned the missing robot, and Tobe, with a deep-throated snarl, broke connection halfway through and ordered all subsequent calls to be rerouted to the sixth assistant vice-president in charge of buttonholes.

This was not really unreasonable of Tobe. During the past week, although Robot AL–76 had dropped from sight completely, reports had flooded in from all over the Union as to the robot's whereabouts. As many as fourteen a day came—usually from fourteen different states.

Tobe was almighty tired of it, to say nothing of being half crazy on general principles. There was even talk of a Congressional investigation, though every reputable roboticist and mathematical physicist on Earth swore the robot was harmless.

In his state of mind, then, it is not surprising that it took three hours for the general manager to pause and consider just exactly how it was that this Randolph Payne had known that the robot was slated for Lunar Station 17, and, for that matter, how he had known that the robot's serial number was AL–76. Those details had not been given out by the company.

He kept on considering for about a minute and a half and then swung into action.

However, during the three hours between the call and the action, the second event took place. Randolph Payne, having correctly diagnosed the abrupt break in his call as being due to general skepticism on the part of the plant official, returned to his shack with a camera. They couldn't very well argue with a photograph, and he'd be hornswoggled if he'd show them the real thing before they came across with the cash.

AL–76 was busy with affairs of his own. Half of the contents of Payne's shack was littered over about two acres of ground, and in the middle of it the robot squatted and fooled around with radio tubes, hunks of iron, copper wire, and general junk. He paid no attention to Payne, who, sprawling flat on his belly, focused his camera for a beautiful shot.

And at this point it was that Lemuel Oliver Cooper turned the bend in the road and froze in his tracks as he took in the tableau. The reason for his coming in the first place was an ailing electric toaster that had developed the annoying habit of throwing out pieces of bread forcefully, but thoroughly untoasted. The reason for his *leaving* was more obvious. He had come with a slow, mildly cheerful, spring-morning saunter. He left with a speed that would have caused any college track coach to raise his eyebrows and purse his lips approvingly.

There was no appreciable slackening of speed until Cooper hurtled into Sheriff Saunders' office, minus hat and toaster, and brought himself up hard against the wall.

Kindly hands lifted him, and for half a minute he tried speaking before he had actually calmed down to the point of breathing with, of course, no result.

They gave him whisky and fanned him and when he did speak, it came out something like this: "—monster—seven feet tall—shack all busted up—poor Rannie Payne—" and so on.

They got the story out of him gradually: how there was a huge metal monster, seven feet tall, maybe even eight or nine, out at Randolph Payne's shack; how Randolph Payne himself was on his stomach, a "poor, bleeding, mangled corpse"; how the monster was then busily engaged in wrecking the shack out of sheer destructiveness; how it had turned on Lemuel Oliver Cooper, and how he, Cooper, had made his escape by half a hair.

Sheriff Saunders hitched his belt tighter about his portly middle and said, "It's that there machine man that got away from the Petersboro factory. We got warning on it last Saturday. Hey, Jake, you get every man in Hannaford County that can shoot and slap a deputy's badge on him. Get them here at noon. And listen, Jake, before you do that, just drop in at the Widow Payne's place and lip her the bad news gentle-like."

It is reported that Miranda Payne, upon being acquainted with events, paused only to make sure that her husband's insurance policy was safe, and to make a few pithy remarks concerning her foolishness in not having had him take out double the amount, before breaking out into as prolonged and heart-wringing a wail of grief as ever became a respectable widow.

It was some hours later that Randolph Payne—unaware of his horrible mutilation and death—viewed the completed negatives of his snapshots with satisfaction. As a series of portraits of a robot at work, they left nothing to the imagination. They might have been labeled: "Robot Gazing Thoughtfully at Vacuum Tube," "Robot Splicing Two Wires," "Robot Wielding Screwdriver," "Robot Taking Refrigerator Apart with Great Violence," and so on.

As there now remained only the routine of making the prints themselves, he stepped out from beyond the curtain of the improvised darkroom for a bit of a smoke and a chat with AL–76.

In doing so, he was blissfully unaware that the neighboring woods were verminous with nervous farmers armed with anything from an old colonial relic of a blunderbuss to the portable machine gun carried by the sheriff himself. Nor, for that matter, had he any inkling of the fact that half a dozen roboticists, under the leadership of Sam Tobe, were smoking down the highway from Petersboro at better than a hundred and twenty miles an hour for the sole purpose of having the pleasure and honor of his acquaintance.

So while things were jittering toward a climax, Randolph Payne sighed with self-satisfaction, lighted a match upon the seat of his pants, puffed away at his pipe, and looked at AL-76 with amusement.

It had been apparent for quite some time that the robot was more than slightly lunatic. Randolph Payne was himself an expert at homemade contraptions, having built several that could not have been exposed to daylight without searing the eyeballs of all beholders; but he had never even conceived of anything approaching the monstrosity that AL-76 was concocting.

It would have made the Rube Goldbergs of the day die in convulsions of envy. It would have made Picasso (if he could have lived to witness it) quit art in the sheer knowledge that he had been hopelessly surpassed. It would have soured the milk in the udders of any cow within half a mile.

In fact, it was gruesome!

From a rusty and massive iron base that faintly resembled something Payne had once seen attached to a secondhand tractor, it rose upward in rakish, drunken swerves through a bewildering mess of wires, wheels, tubes, and nameless horrors without number, ending in a megaphone arrangement that looked decidedly sinister.

Payne had the impulse to peek in the megaphone part, but refrained. He had seen far more sensible machines explode suddenly and with violence.

He said, "Hey, Al."

The robot looked up. He had been lying flat on his stomach, teasing a thin sliver of metal into place. "What do you want, Payne?"

"What is this?" He asked it in the tone of one referring to something foul and decomposing, held gingerly between two ten-foot poles.

"It's the Disinto I'm making—so I can start to work. It's an improvement on the standard model." The robot rose, dusted his knees clankingly, and looked at it proudly.

Payne shuddered. An "improvement"! No wonder they hid the original in caverns on the moon. Poor satellite! Poor dead satellite! He had always wanted to know what a fate worse than death was. Now he knew.

"Will it work?" he asked.

"Sure."

"How do you know?"

"It's got to. I made it, didn't I? I only need one thing now. Got a flashlight?"

"Somewhere, I guess." Payne vanished into the shack and returned almost immediately.

The robot unscrewed the bottom and set to work. In five minutes he had finished. He stepped back and said, "All set. Now I get to work. You may watch if you want to."

A pause, while Payne tried to appreciate the magnanimity of the offer. "Is it safe?"

"A baby could handle it."

"Oh!" Payne grinned weakly and got behind the thickest tree in the vicinity. "Go ahead," he said, "I have the utmost confidence in you."

AL–76 pointed to the nightmarish junk pile and said, "Watch!" His hands set to work—

The embattled farmers of Hannaford County, Virginia, weaved up upon Payne's shack in a slowly tightening circle. With the blood of their heroic colonial forebears pounding their veins—and goose flesh trickling up and down their spines—they crept from tree to tree.

Sheriff Saunders spread the word. "Fire when I give the signal—and aim at the eyes."

Jacob Linker—Lank Jake to his friends, and Sheriff's Deputy to himself—edged close. "You think maybe this machine man has skedaddled?" He did not quite manage to suppress the tone of wistful hopefulness in his voice.

"Dunno," grunted the sheriff. "Guess not, though. We woulda come across him in the woods if he had, and we haven't."

"But it's awful quiet, and it appears to me as if we're getting close to Payne's place."

The reminder wasn't necessary. Sheriff Saunders had a lump in his throat so big it had to be swallowed in three installments. "Get back," he ordered, "and keep your finger on the trigger."

They were at the rim of the clearing now, and Sheriff Saunders closed his eyes and stuck the corner of one out from behind the tree. Seeing nothing, he paused, then tried again, eyes open this time.

Results were, naturally, better.

To be exact, he saw one huge machine man, back toward him, bending over one soul-curdling, hiccupy contraption of uncertain origin and less certain purpose. The only item he missed was the quivering figure of Randolph Payne, embracing the tree next but three to the nor'-nor'west.

Sheriff Saunders stepped out into the open and raised his machine gun. The robot, still presenting a broad metal back, said in a loud voice—to person or persons unknown—"Watch!" and as the sheriff opened his mouth to signal a general order to fire, metal fingers compressed a switch.

There exists no adequate description of what occurred afterward, in spite of the presence of seventy eyewitnesses. In the days, months, and years to come not one of those seventy ever had a word to say about the few seconds after the sheriff had opened his mouth to give the firing order. When questioned about it, they merely turned apple-green and staggered away.

It is plain from circumstantial evidence, however, that, in a general way, what did occur was this.

Sheriff Saunders opened his mouth; AL–76 pulled a switch. The Disinto worked, and seventy-five trees, two barns, three cows and the top three quarters of Duckbill Mountain whiffed into rarefied atmosphere. They became, so to speak, one with the snows of yesteryear.

Sheriff Saunders' mouth remained open for an indefinite interval thereafter, but nothing—neither firing orders nor anything else—issued therefrom. And then—

And then, there was a stirring in the air, a multiple ro-o-o-oshing sound, a series of purple streaks through the atmosphere radiating away from Randolph Payne's shack as the center, and of the members of the posse, not a sign.

There were various guns scattered about the vicinity, including the sheriff's patented nickel-plated, extra-rapid-fire, guaranteed-no-clog, portable machine gun. There were about fifty hats, a few half-chomped cigars, and some odds and ends that had come loose in the excitement—but of actual human beings there was none.

Except for Lank Jake, not one of those human beings came within human ken for three days, and the exception in his favor came about because he was interrupted in his comet-flight by the half-dozen men from the Petersboro factory, who were charging *into* the wood at a pretty fair speed of their own.

It was Sam Tobe who stopped him, catching Lank Jake's head skillfully in the pit of his stomach. When he caught his breath, Tobe asked, "Where's Randolph Payne's place?"

Lank Jake allowed his eyes to unglaze for just a moment. "Brother," he said, "just you follow the direction I ain't going."

And with that, miraculously, he was gone. There was a shrinking dot dodging trees on the horizon that might have been he, but Sam Tobe wouldn't have sworn to it.

That takes care of the posse; but there still remains Randolph Payne, whose reactions took something of a different form.

For Randolph Payne, the five-second interval after the pulling of the switch and the disappearance of Duckbill Mountain was a total blank. At the start he had been peering through the thick under-brush from behind the bottom of the trees; at the end he was swinging wildly from one of the topmost branches. The same impulse that had driven the posse horizontally had driven him vertically.

As to how he had covered the fifty feet from roots to top— whether he had climbed, jumped, or flown—he did not know, and he didn't give a particle of never-mind.

What he *did* know was that property had been destroyed by a robot temporarily in his possession. All visions of rewards vanished and were replaced by trembling nightmares of hostile citizenry, shrieking lynch mobs, lawsuits, murder charges, and what Mirandy Payne would say. Mostly what Mirandy Payne would say.

He was yelling wildly and hoarsely, "Hey, you robot, you smash that thing, do you hear? Smash it good! You forget I ever had anything to do with it. You're a stranger to me, see? You don't ever say a word about it. Forget it, you hear?"

He didn't expect his orders to do any good; it was only reflex action. What he didn't know was that a robot always obeys a human order except where carrying it out involves danger to another human.

AL–76, therefore, calmly and methodically proceeded to demolish his Disinto into rubble and flinders.

Just as he was stamping the last cubic inch under foot, Sam Tobe and his contingent arrived, and Randolph Payne, sensing that the real owners of the robot had come, dropped out of the tree head-first and made for regions unknown feet-first.

He did not wait for his reward.

Austin Wilde, Robotical Engineer, turned to Sam Tobe and said, "Did you get anything out of the robot?"

Tobe shook his head and snarled deep in his throat. "Nothing. Not one thing. He's forgotten everything that's happened since he left the factory. He must have gotten *orders* to forget, or it couldn't have left him so blank. What was that pile of junk he'd been fooling with?"

"Just that. A pile of junk! But it must have been a Disinto before he smashed it, and I'd like to kill the fellow who ordered him to smash it—by slow torture, if possible. Look at this!"

They were part of the way up the slopes of what had been Duck-bill Mountain—at that point, to be exact, where the top had been sheered off; and Wilde put his hand down upon the perfect flatness that cut through both soil and rock.

"*What* a Disinto," he said. "It took the mountain right off its base."

"What made him build it?"

Wilde shrugged. "I don't know. Some factor in his environment—there's no way of knowing what—reacted upon his moon-type positronic brain to produce a Disinto out of junk. It's a billion to one against our ever stumbling upon that factor again now that the robot himself has forgotten. We'll never have that Disinto."

"Never mind. The important thing is that we have the robot."

"The hell you say." There was poignant regret in Wilde's voice. "Have you ever had anything to do with the Disintos on the moon? They eat up energy like so many electronic hogs and won't even begin to run until you've built up a potential of better than a million volts. But *this* Disinto worked differently. I went through the rubbish with a microscope, and would you like to see the only source of power of any kind that I found?"

"What was it?"

"Just this! And we'll never know how he did it."

And Austin Wilde held up the source of power that had enabled a Disinto to chew up a mountain in half a second—*two flashlight batteries!*

Victory Unintentional

The spaceship leaked, as the saying goes, like a sieve.

It was supposed to. In fact, that was the whole idea.

The result, of course, was that during the journey from Ganymede to Jupiter, the ship was crammed just as full as it could be with the very hardest space vacuum. And since the ship also lacked heating devices, this space vacuum was at normal temperature, which is a fraction of a degree above absolute zero.

This, also, was according to plan. Little things like the absence of heat and air didn't annoy anyone at all on the particular spaceship.

The first near vacuum wisps of Jovian atmosphere began percolating into the ship several thousand miles above the Jovian surface. It was practically all hydrogen, though perhaps a careful gas analysis might have located a trace of helium as well. The pressure gauges began creeping skyward.

That creep continued at an accelerating pace as the ship dropped downward in a Jupiter-circling spiral. The pointers of successive gauges, each designed for progressively higher pressures, began to move until they reached the neighborhood of a million or so atmospheres, where figures lost most of their meaning. The temperature, as recorded by thermocouples, rose slowly and erratically, and finally steadied at about seventy below zero, Centigrade.

The ship moved slowly toward the end, plowing its way heavily through a maze of gas molecules that crowded together so closely that hydrogen itself was squeezed to the density of a liquid. Ammonia vapor, drawn from the incredibly vast oceans of that liquid, saturated the horrible atmosphere. The wind, which had begun a thousand miles higher, had risen to a pitch inadequately described as a hurricane.

It was quite plain long before the ship landed on a fairly large Jovian island, perhaps seven times the size of Asia, that Jupiter was not a very pleasant world.

And yet the three members of the crew thought it was. They were quite convinced it was. But then, the three members of the crew were not exactly human. And neither were they exactly Jovian.

They were simply robots, designed on Earth for Jupiter.

ZZ Three said, "It appears to be a rather desolate place."

ZZ Two joined him and regarded the wind-blasted landscape somberly. "There are structures of some sort in the distance," he said, "which are obviously artificial. I suggest we wait for the inhabitants to come to us."

Across the room ZZ One listened, but made no reply. He was the first constructed of the three, and half experimental. Consequently he spoke a little less frequently than his two companions.

The wait was not long. An air vessel of queer design swooped overhead. More followed. And then a line of ground vehicles approached, took position, and disgorged organisms. Along with these organisms came various inanimate accessories that might have been weapons. Some of these were borne by a single Jovian, some by several, and some advanced under their own power, with Jovians perhaps inside.

The robots couldn't tell.

ZZ Three said, "They're all around us now. The logical peaceful gesture would be to come out in the open. Agreed?"

It was, and ZZ One shoved open the heavy door, which was not double or, for that matter, particularly airtight.

Their appearance through the door was the signal for an excited stir among the surrounding Jovians. Things were done to several of the very largest of the inanimate accessories, and ZZ Three became aware of a temperature rise on the outer rind of his beryllium-iridium-bronze body.

He glanced at ZZ Two. "Do you feel it? They're aiming heat energy at us, I believe."

ZZ Two indicated his surprise. "I wonder why?"

"Definitely a heat ray of some sort. Look at that!"

One of the rays had been jarred out of alignment for some undis-

cernible cause, and its line of radiation intersected a brook of sparkling pure ammonia—which promptly boiled furiously.

Three turned to ZZ One, "Make a note of this, One, will you?"

"Sure." It was to ZZ One that the routine secretarial work fell, and
his method of taking a note was to make a mental addition to the
accurate memory scroll within him. He had already gathered the
hour-by-hour record of every important instrument on board ship
during the trip to Jupiter. He added agreeably, "What reason shall I
put for the reaction? The human masters would probably enjoy
knowing."

"No reason. Or better," Three corrected himself, "no apparent
reason. You might say the maximum temperature of the ray was
about plus thirty, Centigrade."

Two interrupted, "Shall we try communicating?"

"It would be a waste of time," said Three. "There can't be more
than a very few Jovians who know the radio-click code that's been
developed between Jupiter and Ganymede. They'll have to send for
one, and when he comes, he'll establish contact soon enough. Meanwhile let's watch them. I don't understand their actions, I tell you
frankly."

Nor did understanding come immediately. Heat radiation ceased,
and other instruments were brought to the forefront and put into
play. Several capsules fell at the feet of the watching robots, dropping rapidly and forcefully under Jupiter's gravity. They popped
open and a blue liquid exuded, forming pools which proceeded to
shrink rapidly by evaporation.

The nightmare wind whipped the vapors away and where those
vapors went, Jovians scrambled out of the way. One was too slow,
threshed about wildly, and became very limp and still.

ZZ Two bent, dabbed a finger in one of the pools and stared at
the dripping liquid. "I think this is oxygen," he said.

"Oxygen, all right," agreed Three. "This becomes stranger and
stranger. It must certainly be a dangerous practice, for I would say
that oxygen is poisonous to the creatures. One of them died!"

There was a pause, and then ZZ One, whose greater simplicity led
at times to an increased directness of thought, said heavily, "It
might be that these strange creatures in a rather childish way are attempting to destroy us."

And Two, struck by the suggestion, answered, "You know, One, I
think you're right!"

There had been a slight lull in Jovian activity and now a new structure was brought up. It possessed a slender rod that pointed skyward through the impenetrable Jovian murk. It stood in that starkly incredible wind with a rigidity that plainly indicated remarkable structural strength. From its tip came a cracking and then a flash that lit up the depths of the atmosphere into a gray fog.

For a moment the robots were bathed in clinging radiance and then Three said thoughtfully, "High-tension electricity! Quite respectable power, too. One, I think you're right. After all, the human masters have told us that these creatures seek to destroy all humanity, and organisms possessing such insane viciousness as to harbor a thought of harm against a human being"—his voice trembled at the thought—"would scarcely scruple at attempting to destroy us."

"It's a shame to have such distorted minds," said ZZ One. "Poor fellows!"

"I find it a very saddening thought," admitted Two. "Let's go back to the ship. We've seen enough for now."

They did so, and settled down to wait. As ZZ Three said, Jupiter was a roomy planet, and it might take time for Jovian transportation to bring a radio code expert to the ship. However, patience is a cheap commodity to robots.

As a matter of fact, Jupiter turned on its axis three times, according to chronometer, before the expert arrived. The rising and setting of the sun made no difference, of course, to the dead darkness at the bottom of three thousand miles of liquid-dense gas, so that one could not speak of day and night. But then, neither Jovian nor robot saw by visible light radiation and that didn't matter.

Through this thirty-hour interval the surrounding Jovians continued their attack with a patience and persevering relentlessness concerning which robot ZZ One made a good many mental notes. The ship was assaulted by as many varieties of forces as there were hours, and the robots observed every attack attentively, analyzing such weapons as they recognized. They by no means recognized all.

But the human masters had built well. It had taken fifteen years to construct the ship and the robots, and their essentials could be expressed in a single phrase—raw strength. The attack spent itself uselessly and neither ship nor robot seemed the worse for it.

Three said, "This atmosphere handicaps them, I think. They can't use atomic disruptors, since they would only tear a hole in that soupy air and blow themselves up."

"They haven't used high explosives either," said Two, "which is well. They couldn't have hurt us, naturally, but it would have thrown us about a bit."

"High explosives are out of the question. You can't have an explosive without gas expansion and gas just can't expand in this atmosphere."

"It's a very good atmosphere," muttered One. "I like it."

Which was natural, because he was built for it. The ZZ robots were the first robots ever turned out by the United States Robots and Mechanical Men Corporation that were not even faintly human in appearance. They were low and squat, with a center of gravity less than a foot above ground level. They had six legs apiece, stumpy and thick, designed to lift tons against two and a half times normal Earth gravity. Their reflexes were that many times Earth-normal speed, to make up for the gravity. And they were composed of a beryllium-iridium-bronze alloy that was proof against any known corrosive agent, also any known destructive agent short of a thousand-megaton atomic disruptor, under any conditions whatsoever.

To dispense with further description, they were indestructible, and so impressively powerful that they were the only robots ever built on whom the roboticists of the corporation had never quite had the nerve to pin a serial-number nickname. One bright young fellow had suggested Sissy One, Two, and Three—but not in a very loud voice, and the suggestion was never repeated.

The last hours of the wait were spent in a puzzled discussion to find a possible description of a Jovian's appearance. ZZ One had made a note of their possession of tentacles and of their radial symmetry—and there he had stuck. Two and Three did their best, but couldn't help.

"You can't very well describe anything," Three declared finally, "without a standard of reference. These creatures are like nothing I know of—completely outside the positronic paths of my brain. It's like trying to describe gamma light to a robot unequipped for gamma-ray reception."

It was just at that time that the weapon barrage ceased once more. The robots turned their attention to outside the ship.

A group of Jovians were advancing in curiously uneven fashion, but no amount of careful watching could determine the exact method of their locomotion. How they used their tentacles was uncertain. At times the organisms took on a remarkable slithering motion, and then they moved at great speed, perhaps with the wind's help, for they were moving downwind.

The robots stepped out to meet the Jovians, who halted ten feet away. Both sides remained silent and motionless.

ZZ Two said, "They must be watching us, but I don't know how. Do either of you see any photosensitive organs?"

"I can't say," grunted Three in response. "I don't see anything about them that makes sense at all."

There was a sudden metallic clicking from among the Jovian group and ZZ One said delightedly, "It's the radio code. They've got the communications expert here."

It was, and they had. The complicated dot-dash system that over a period of twenty-five years had been laboriously developed by the beings of Jupiter and the Earthmen of Ganymede into a remarkably flexible means of communication was finally being put into practice at close range.

One Jovian remained in the forefront now, the others having fallen back. It was he that was speaking. The clicking said, "Where are you from?"

ZZ Three, as the most mentally advanced, naturally assumed spokesmanship for the robot group. "We are from Jupiter's satellite, Ganymede."

The Jovian continued, "What do you want?"

"Information. We have come to study your world and to bring back our findings. If we could have your cooperation—"

The Jovian clicking interrupted. "You must be destroyed!"

ZZ Three paused and said in a thoughtful aside to his two companions, "Exactly the attitude the human masters said they would take. They are very unusual."

Returning to his clicking, he asked simply, "Why?"

The Jovian evidently considered certain questions too obnoxious to be answered. He said, "If you leave within a single period of revolution, we will spare you—until such time as we emerge from our world to destroy the un-Jovian vermin of Ganymede."

"I would like to point out," said Three, "that we of Ganymede and the inner planets—"

The Jovian interrupted, "Our astronomy knows of the Sun and of our four satellites. There are no inner planets."

Three conceded the point wearily, "We of Ganymede, then. We have no designs on Jupiter. We're prepared to offer friendship. For twenty-five years your people communicated freely with the human beings of Ganymede. Is there any reason to make sudden war upon the humans?"

"For twenty-five years," was the cold response, "we assumed the inhabitants of Ganymede to be Jovians. When we found out they were not, and that we had been treating lower animals on the scale of Jovian intelligences, we were bound to take steps to wipe out the dishonor."

Slowly and forcefully he finished, "We of Jupiter will suffer the existence of no vermin!"

The Jovian was backing away in some fashion, tacking against the wind, and the interview was evidently over.

The robots retreated inside the ship.

ZZ Two said, "It looks bad, doesn't it?" He continued thoughtfully, "It is as the human masters said. They possess an ultimately developed superiority complex, combined with an extreme intolerance for anyone or anything that disturbs that complex."

"The intolerance," observed Three, "is the natural consequence of the complex. The trouble is that their intolerance has teeth in it. They have weapons—and their science is great."

"I am not surprised now," burst out ZZ One, "that we were specifically instructed to disregard Jovian orders. They are horrible, intolerant, pseudo-superior beings!" He added emphatically, with robotical loyalty and faith, "No human master could ever be like that."

"That, though true, is beside the point," said Three. "The fact remains that the human masters are in terrible danger. This is a gigantic world and these Jovians are greater in numbers and resources by a hundred times or more than the humans of the entire Terrestrial Empire. If they can ever develop the force field to the point where they can use it as a spaceship hull—as the human masters have already done—they will overrun the system at will. The question remains as to how far they have advanced in that direction, what other weapons they have, what preparations they are making, and so on. To return with that information is our function, of course, and we had better decide on our next step."

"It may be difficult," said Two. "The Jovians won't help us." Which, at the moment, was rather an understatement.

Three thought awhile. "It seems to me that we need only wait," he observed. "They have tried to destroy us for thirty hours now and haven't succeeded. Certainly they have done their best. Now a superiority complex always involves the eternal necessity of saving face, and the ultimatum given us proves it in this case. They would never allow us to leave if they could destroy us. But if we don't leave, then rather than admit they cannot force us away, they will surely pretend that they are willing, for their own purposes, to have us stay."

Once again they waited. The day passed. The weapon barrage did not resume. The robots did not leave. The bluff was called. And now the robots faced the Jovian radio-code expert once again.

If the ZZ models had been equipped with a sense of humor, they would have enjoyed themselves immensely. As it was, they felt merely a solemn sense of satisfaction.

The Jovian said, "It has been our decision that you will be allowed to remain for a very short time, so that you see our power for yourself. You shall then return to Ganymede to inform your companion vermin of the disastrous end to which they will unfailingly come within a solar revolution."

ZZ One made a mental note that a Jovian revolution took twelve earthly years.

Three replied casually, "Thank you. May we accompany you to the nearest town? There are many things we would like to learn." He added as an afterthought, "Our ship is not to be touched, of course."

He said this as a request, not as a threat, for no ZZ model was ever pugnacious. All capacity for even the slightest annoyance had been carefully barred in their construction. With robots as vastly powerful as the ZZ's, unfailing good temper was essential for safety during the years of testing on Earth.

The Jovian said, "We are not interested in your verminous ship. No Jovian will pollute himself by approaching it. You may accompany us, but you must on no account approach closer than ten feet to any Jovian, or you will be instantly destroyed."

"Stuck up, aren't they?" observed Two in a genial whisper, as they plowed into the wind.

The town was a port on the shores of an incredible ammonia lake. The external wind whipped furious, frothy waves that shot across the liquid surface at the hectic rate enforced by the gravity. The port itself was neither large nor impressive and it seemed fairly evident that most of the construction was underground.

"What is the population of this place?" asked Three.

The Jovian replied, "It is a small town of ten million."

"I see. Make a note of that, One."

ZZ One did so mechanically, and then turned once more to the lake, at which he had been staring in fascination. He pulled at Three's elbow. "Say, do you suppose they have fish here?"

"What difference does it make?"

"I think we ought to know. The human masters ordered us to find out everything we could." Of the robots, One was the simplest and, consequently, the one who took orders in the most literal fashion.

Two said, "Let One go and look if he likes. It won't do any harm if we let the kid have his fun."

"All right. There's no real objection if he doesn't waste his time. Fish aren't what we came for—but go ahead, One."

ZZ One made off in great excitement and slogged rapidly down the beach, plunging into the ammonia with a splash. The Jovians watched attentively. They had understood none of the previous conversation, of course.

The radio code expert clicked out, "It is apparent that your companion has decided to abandon life in despair at our greatness."

Three said in surprise, "Nothing of the sort. He wants to investigate the living organisms, if any, that live in the ammonia." He added apologetically, "Our friend is very curious at times, and he isn't quite as bright as we are, though that is only his misfortune. We understand that and try to humor him whenever we can."

There was a long pause, and the Jovian observed, "He will drown."

Three replied casually, "No danger of that. We don't drown. May we enter the town as soon as he returns?"

At that moment there was a spurt of liquid several hundred feet out in the lake. It sprayed upward wildly and then hurtled down in a wind-driven mist. Another spurt and another, then a wild white foaming that formed a trail toward shore, gradually quieting as it approached.

The two robots watched this in amazement, and the utter lack of motion on the part of the Jovians indicated that they were watching as well.

Then the head of ZZ One broke the surface and he made his slow way out on to dry land. But something followed him! Some organism of gigantic size that seemed nothing but fangs, claws, and spines. Then they saw that it wasn't following him under its own power, but was being dragged across the beach by ZZ One. There was a significant flabbiness about it.

ZZ One approached rather timidly and took communication into his own hands. He tapped out a message to the Jovian in agitated fashion. "I am very sorry this happened, but the thing attacked me. I was merely taking notes on it. It is not a valuable creature, I hope."

He was not answered immediately, for at the first appearance of the monster there had been a wild break in the Jovian ranks. These reformed slowly, and cautious observation having proven the creature to be indeed dead, order was restored. Some of the bolder were curiously prodding the body.

ZZ Three said humbly, "I hope you will pardon our friend. He is sometimes clumsy. We have absolutely no intention of harming any Jovian creature."

"He attacked me," explained One. "He bit at me without provocation. See!" And he displayed a two-foot fang that ended in a jagged break. "He broke it on my shoulder and almost left a scratch. I just slapped it a bit to send it away—and it died. I'm sorry!"

The Jovian finally spoke, and his code clicking was a rather stuttery affair. "It is a wild creature, rarely found so close to shore, but the lake is deep just here."

Three said, still anxiously, "If you can use it for food, we are only too glad—"

"No. We can get food for ourselves without the help of verm—without the help of others. Eat it yourselves."

At that ZZ One heaved the creature up and back into the sea, with an easy motion of one arm. Three said casually, "Thank you for your kind offer, but we have no use for food. We don't eat, of course."

Escorted by two hundred or so armed Jovians, the robots passed down a series of ramps into the underground city. If, above the surface, the city had looked small and unimpressive, then from beneath it took on the appearance of a vast megalopolis.

They were ushered into ground cars that were operated by remote control—for no honest, self-respecting Jovian would risk his superiority by placing himself in the same car with vermin—and driven at frightful speed to the center of the town. They saw enough to decide that it extended fifty miles from end to end and reached downward into Jupiter's crust at least eight miles.

ZZ Two did not sound happy as he said, "If this is a sample of Jovian development then we shall not have a hopeful report to bring back to the human masters. After all, we landed on the vast surface of Jupiter at random, with the chances a thousand to one against coming near any really concentrated center of population. This must be, as the code expert says, a mere town."

"Ten million Jovians," said Three abstractedly. "Total population must be in the trillions, which is high, very high, even for Jupiter. They probably have a completely urban civilization, which means that their scientific development must be tremendous. If they have force fields—"

Three had no neck, for in the interest of strength the heads of the ZZ models were riveted firmly onto the torso, with the delicate positronic brains protected by three separate layers in inch-thick iridium alloy. But if he had had one, he would have shaken his head dolefully.

They had stopped now in a cleared space. Everywhere about them they could see avenues and structures crowded with Jovians, as curious as any terrestrial crowd would have been in similar circumstances.

The code expert approached. "It is time now for me to retire until the next period of activity. We have gone so far as to arrange quarters for you at great inconvenience to ourselves for, of course, the structure will have to be pulled down and rebuilt afterward. Nevertheless, you will be allowed to sleep for a space."

ZZ Three waved an arm in deprecation and tapped out, "We thank you but you must not trouble yourself. We don't mind remaining right here. If you want to sleep and rest, by all means do. We'll wait for you. As for us," casually, "we don't sleep."

The Jovian said nothing, though if it had had a face, the expression upon it might have been interesting. It left, and the robots remained in the car, with squads of well-armed Jovians, frequently replaced, surrounding them as guards.

It was hours before the ranks of those guards parted to allow the code expert to return. Along with him were other Jovians, whom he introduced.

"There are with me two officials of the central government who have graciously consented to speak with you."

One of the officials evidently knew the code, for his clicking interrupted the code expert sharply. He addressed the robots, "Vermin! Emerge from the ground car that we may look at you."

The robots were only too willing to comply, so while Three and Two vaulted over the right side of the car, ZZ One dashed through the left side. The word through is used advisedly, for since he neglected to work the mechanism that lowered a section of side so that one might exit, he carried that side, plus two wheels and an axle, along with him. The car collapsed, and ZZ One stood staring at the ruins in embarrassed silence.

At last he clicked out gently, "I'm very sorry. I hope it wasn't an expensive car."

ZZ Two added apologetically, "Our companion is often clumsy. You must excuse him," and ZZ Three made a halfhearted attempt to put the car back together again.

ZZ One made another effort to excuse himself. "The material of the car was rather flimsy. You see?" He lifted a square-yard sheet of three-inch-thick, metal-hard plastic in both hands and exerted a bit of pressure. The sheet promptly snapped in two. "I should have made allowances," he admitted.

The Jovian government official said in slightly less sharp fashion, "The car would have had to be destroyed anyway, after being polluted by your presence." He paused, then, "Creatures! We Jovians lack vulgar curiosity concerning lower animals, but our scientists seek facts."

"We're right with you," replied Three cheerfully. "So do we."

The Jovian ignored him. "You lack the mass-sensitive organ, apparently. How is it that you are aware of distant objects?"

Three grew interested. "Do you mean your people are directly sensitive to mass?"

"I am not here to answer your questions—your impudent questions—about us."

"I take it then that objects of low specific mass would be transparent to you, even in the absence of radiation." He turned to Two, "That's how they see. Their atmosphere is as transparent as space to them."

The Jovian clicking began once more, "You will answer my first question immediately, or my patience will end and I will order you destroyed."

Three said at once, "We are energy-sensitive, Jovian. We can adjust ourselves to the entire electromagnetic scale at will. At present, our long-distance sight is due to radio-wave radiation that we emit ourselves, and at close range we see by—" He paused, and said to Two, "There isn't any code word for gamma ray, is there?"

"Not that I know of," Two answered.

Three continued to the Jovian, "At close range we see by other radiation for which there is no code word."

"Of what is your body composed?" demanded the Jovian.

Two whispered, "He probably asks that because his mass sensitivity can't penetrate past our skin. High density, you know. Ought we to tell him?"

Three replied uncertainly, "Our human masters didn't particularly say we were to keep anything secret." In radio code, to the Jovian he said, "We are mostly iridium. For the rest, copper, tin, a little beryllium, and a scattering of other substances."

The Jovians fell back and by the obscure writhing of various portions of their thoroughly indescribable bodies gave the impression that they were in animated conversation, although they made no sound.

And then the official returned. "Beings of Ganymede! It has been decided to show you through some of our factories that we may exhibit a tiny part of our great achievements. We will then allow you to return so that you may spread despair among the other verm—the other beings of the outer world."

Three said to Two, "Note the effect of their psychology. They must hammer home their superiority. It's still a matter of saving face." And in radio code, "We thank you for the opportunity."

But the face saving was efficient, as the robots realized soon enough. The demonstration became a tour, and the tour a Grand Exhibition. The Jovians displayed everything, explained everything, answered all questions eagerly, and ZZ One made hundreds of despairing notes.

The war potential of that single so-called unimportant town was greater by several times than that of all Ganymede. Ten more such towns would outproduce all the Terrestrial Empire. Yet ten more such towns would not be the fingernail fragment of the strength all Jupiter must be able to exert.

Three turned as One nudged him. "What is it?"

ZZ One said seriously, "If they have force fields, the human masters are lost, aren't they?"

"I'm afraid so. Why do you ask?"

"Because the Jovians aren't showing us through the right wing of this factory. It might be that force fields are being developed there. They would be wanting to keep it secret if they were. We'd better find out. It's the main point, you know."

Three regarded One somberly. "Perhaps you're right. It's no use ignoring anything."

They were in a huge steel mill now, watching hundred-foot beams of ammonia-resistant silicon-steel alloy being turned out twenty to the second. Three asked quietly, "What does that wing contain?"

The government official inquired of those in charge of the factory and explained, "That is the section of great heat. Various processes require huge temperatures which life cannot bear, and they must all be handled indirectly."

He led the way to a partition from which heat could be felt to radiate and indicated a small round area of transparent material. It was one of a row of such, through which the foggy red light of lines of glowing forges could be made out through the soupy atmosphere.

ZZ One fastened a look of suspicion on the Jovian and clicked out, "Would it be all right if I went in and looked around? I am very interested in this."

Three said, "You're being childish, One. They're telling the truth. Oh well, nose around if you must. But don't take too long; we've got to move on."

The Jovian said, "You have no understanding of the heat involved. You will die."

"Oh no," explained One casually. "Heat doesn't bother us."

There was a Jovian conference, and then a scene of scurrying confusion as the life of the factory was geared to this unusual emergency. Screens of heat-absorbent material were set up, and then a door dropped open, a door that had never before budged while the forges were working. ZZ One entered and the door closed behind him. Jovian officials crowded to the transparent areas to watch.

ZZ One walked to the nearest forge and tapped the outside. Since he was too short to see into it comfortably, he tipped the forge until the molten metal licked at the lip of the container. He peered at it curiously, then dipped his hand in and stirred it awhile to test the consistency. Having done this, he withdrew his hand, shook off some of the fiery metallic droplets and wiped the rest on one of his six thighs. Slowly he went down the line of forges, then signified his desire to leave.

The Jovians retired to a great distance when he came out of the door and played a stream of ammonia on him, which hissed, bubbled and steamed until he was brought to bearable temperature once more.

ZZ One ignored the ammonia shower and said, "They were telling the truth. No force fields."

Three began, "You see—" but One interrupted impatiently, "But there's no use delaying. The human masters instructed us to find out everything and that's that."

He turned to the Jovian and clicked out, without the slightest hesitation, "Listen, has Jovian science developed force fields?"

Bluntness was, of course, one of the natural consequences of One's less well developed mental powers. Two and Three knew that, so they refrained from expressing disapproval of the remark.

The Jovian official relaxed slowly from his strangely stiffened attitude, which had somehow given the impression that he had been staring stupidly at One's hand—the one he had dipped into the molten metal. The Jovian said slowly, "Force fields? That, then, is your main object of curiosity?"

"Yes," said One with emphasis.

There was a sudden and patent gain in confidence on the Jovian's part, for the clicking grew sharper. "Then come, vermin!"

Whereupon Three said to Two, "We're vermin again, I see—which sounds as if there's bad news ahead." And Two gloomily agreed.

It was to the very edge of the city that they were now led—to the portion which on Earth would have been termed the suburbs—and into one of a series of closely integrated structures, which might have corresponded vaguely to a terrestrial university.

There were no explanations, however, and none was asked for. The Jovian official led the way rapidly, and the robots followed with the grim conviction that the worst was just about to happen.

It was ZZ One who stopped before an opened wall section after the rest had passed on. "What's this?" he wanted to know.

The room was equipped with narrow, low benches, along which Jovians manipulated rows of strange devices, of which strong, inch-long electromagnets formed the principal feature.

"What's this?" asked One again.

The Jovian turned back and exhibited impatience. "This is a students' biological laboratory. There's nothing there to interest you."

"But what are they doing?"

"They are studying microscopic life. Haven't you ever seen a microscope before?"

Three interrupted in explanation, "He has, but not that type. Our microscopes are meant for energy-sensitive organs and work by refraction of radiant energy. Your microscopes evidently work on a mass-expansion basis. Rather ingenious."

ZZ One said, "Would it be all right if I inspected some of your specimens?"

"Of what use will that be? You cannot use our microscopes because of your sensory limitations and it will simply force us to discard such specimens as you approach for no decent reason."

"But I don't need a microscope," explained One, with surprise. "I can easily adjust myself for microscopic vision."

He strode to the nearest bench, while the students in the room crowded to the corner in an attempt to avoid contamination. ZZ One shoved a microscope aside and inspected the slide carefully. He backed away, puzzled, then tried another . . . a third . . . a fourth.

He came back and addressed the Jovian. "Those are supposed to be alive, aren't they? I mean those little worm things."

The Jovian said, "Certainly."

"That's strange—when I look at them, they die!"

Three exclaimed sharply and said to his two companions, "We've forgotten our gamma-ray radiation. Let's get out of here, One, or we'll kill every bit of microscopic life in the room."

He turned to the Jovian, "I'm afraid that our presence is fatal to weaker forms of life. We had better leave. We hope the specimens are not too difficult to replace. And, while we're about it, you had better not stay too near us, or our radiation may affect you adversely. You feel all right so far, don't you?" he asked.

The Jovian led the way onward in proud silence, but it was to be noticed that thereafter he doubled the distance he had hitherto kept between himself and them.

Nothing more was said until the robots found themselves in a vast room. In the very center of it huge ingots of metal rested unsupported in mid-air—or, rather, supported by nothing visible—against mighty Jovian gravity.

The Jovian clicked, "There is your force field in ultimate form, as recently perfected. Within that bubble is a vacuum, so that it is supporting the full weight of our atmosphere plus an amount of metal equivalent to two large spaceships. What do you say to that?"

"That space travel now becomes a possibility for you," said Three.

"Definitely. No metal or plastic has the strength to hold our atmosphere against a vacuum, but a force field can—and a force-field bubble will be our spaceship. Within the year we will be turning them out by the hundreds of thousands. Then we will swarm down upon Ganymede to destroy the verminous so-called intelligences that attempt to dispute our dominion of the universe."

"The human beings of Ganymede have never attempted—" began Three, in mild expostulation.

"Silence!" snapped the Jovian. "Return now and tell them what you've seen. Their own feeble force fields—such as the one your ship is equipped with—will not stand against us, for our smallest ship will be a hundred times the size and power of yours."

Three said, "Then there's nothing more to do and we will return, as you say, with the information. If you could lead us back to our ship, we'll say good-by. But by the way, just as a matter for the record, there's something you don't understand. The humans of Ganymede have force fields, of course, but our particular ship isn't equipped with one. We don't need any."

The robot turned away and motioned his companions to follow. For a moment they did not speak, then ZZ One muttered dejectedly, "Can't we try to destroy this place?"

"It won't help," said Three. "They'd get us by weight of numbers. It's no use. In an earthly decade the human masters will be finished. It is impossible to stand against Jupiter. There's just too much of it. As long as Jovians were tied to the surface, the humans were safe. But now that they have force fields— All we can do is to bring the news. By the preparation of hiding places, some few may survive for a short while."

The city was behind them. They were out on the open plain by the lake, with their ship a dark spot on the horizon, when the Jovian spoke suddenly:

"Creatures, you say you have no force field?"

Three replied without interest, "We don't need one."

"How then does your ship stand the vacuum of space without exploding because of the atmospheric pressure within?" And he moved a tentacle as if in mute gesture at the Jovian atmosphere that was weighing down upon them with a force of twenty million pounds to the square inch.

"Well," explained Three, "that's simple. Our ship isn't airtight. Pressures equalize within and without."

"Even in space? A vacuum in your ship? You lie!"

"You're welcome to inspect our ship. It has no force field and it isn't airtight. What's marvelous about that? We don't breathe. Our energy is obtained through direct atomic power. The presence or absence of air pressure makes little difference to us and we're quite at home in a vacuum."

"But absolute zero!"

"It doesn't matter. We regulate our own heat. We're not interested in outside temperatures." He paused. "Well, we can make our own way back to the ship. Good-by. We'll give the humans of Ganymede your message—war to the end!"

But the Jovian said, "Wait! I'll be back." He turned and went toward the city.

The robots stared, and then waited in silence.

It was three hours before he returned and when he did, it was in breathless haste. He stopped within the usual ten feet of the robots, but then began inching his way forward in a curious groveling fashion. He did not speak until his rubbery gray skin was almost touching them, and then the radio code sounded, subdued and respectful.

"Honored sirs, I have been in communication with the head of our central government, who is now aware of all the facts, and I can assure you that Jupiter desires only peace."

"I beg your pardon?" asked Three blankly.

The Jovian drove on hastily. "We are ready to resume communication with Ganymede and will gladly promise to make no attempt to venture into space. Our force field will be used only on the Jovian surface."

"But—" Three began.

"Our government will be glad to receive any other representatives our honorable human brothers of Ganymede would care to send. If your honors will now condescend to swear peace—" a scaly tentacle swung out toward them and Three, quite dazed, grasped it. Two and One did likewise as two more were extended to them.

The Jovian said solemnly: "There is then eternal peace between Jupiter and Ganymede."

The spaceship which leaked like a sieve was out in space again. The pressure and temperature were once more at zero, and the robots watched the huge but steadily shrinking globe that was Jupiter.

"They're definitely sincere," said ZZ Two, "and it's very gratifying, this complete about-face, but I don't get it."

"It is my idea," observed ZZ One, "that the Jovians came to their senses just in time and realized the incredible evil involved in the thought of harm to a human master. That would be only natural."

ZZ Three sighed and said, "Look, it's all a matter of psychology. Those Jovians had a superiority complex a mile thick and when they couldn't destroy us, they were bound to save face. All their exhibitions, all their explanations, were simply a form of braggadocio, designed to impress us into the proper state of humiliation before their power and superiority."

"I see all that," interrupted Two, "but—"

Three went on, "But it worked the wrong way. All they did was to prove to themselves that we were stronger, that we didn't drown, that we didn't eat or sleep, that molten metal didn't hurt us. Even our very presence was fatal to Jovian life. Their last trump was the force field. And when they found out that *we* didn't need them at all, and could live in a vacuum at absolute zero, they broke." He paused and added philosophically, "When a superiority complex like that breaks, it breaks all the way."

The other two considered that, and then Two said, "But it still doesn't make sense. Why should they care what we can or can't do? We're only robots. We're not the ones they have to fight."

"And that's the whole point, Two," said Three softly. "It's only after we left Jupiter that I thought of it. Do you know that through an oversight, quite unintentionally, we neglected to tell them we were only robots."

"They never asked us," said One.

"Exactly. So they thought we were human beings and that all the other human beings were like us!"

He looked once more at Jupiter, thoughtfully. "No wonder they decided to quit!"

Stranger in Paradise

They were brothers. Not in the sense that they were both human beings, or that they were fellow children of a crèche. Not at all! They were brothers in the actual biological sense of the word. They were kin, to use a term that had grown faintly archaic even centuries before, prior to the Catastrophe, when that tribal phenomenon, the family, still had some validity.

How embarrassing it was!

Over the years since childhood, Anthony had almost forgotten. There were times when he hadn't given it even the slightest thought for months at a time. But now, ever since he had been inextricably thrown together with William, he had found himself living through an agonizing time.

It might not have been so bad if circumstances had made it obvious all along; if, as in the pre-Catastrophe days—Anthony had at one time been a great reader of history—they had shared the second name and in that way alone flaunted the relationship.

Nowadays, of course, one adopted one's second name to suit oneself and changed it as often as desired. After all, the symbol chain was what really counted, and that was encoded and made yours from birth.

William called himself Anti-Aut. That was what he insisted on with a kind of sober professionalism. His own business, surely, but what an advertisement of personal poor taste. Anthony had decided on Smith when he had turned thirteen and had never had the impulse to change it. It was simple, easily spelled, and quite distinctive, since he had never met anyone else who had chosen that name. It was once very common—among the pre-Cats—which explained its rareness now perhaps.

But the difference in names meant nothing when the two were together. They looked alike.

If they had been twins—but then one of a pair of twin-fertilized ova was never allowed to come to term. It was just that physical similarity occasionally happened in the non-twin situation, especially when the relationship was on both sides. Anthony Smith was five years younger, but both had the beaky nose, the heavy eyelids, the just noticeable cleft in the chin—that damned luck of the genetic draw. It was just asking for it when, out of some passion for monotony, parents repeated.

At first, now that they were together, they drew that startled glance followed by an elaborate silence. Anthony tried to ignore the matter, but out of sheer perversity—or perversion—William was as likely as not to say, "We're brothers."

"Oh?" the other would say, hanging in there for just a moment as though he wanted to ask if they were full blood brothers. And then good manners would win the day and he would turn away as though it were a matter of no interest. That happened only rarely, of course. Most of the people in the Project knew—how could it be prevented? —and avoided the situation.

Not that William was a bad fellow. Not at all. If he hadn't been Anthony's brother; or if they had been, but looked sufficiently different to be able to mask the fact, they would have gotten along famously.

As it was—

It didn't make it easier that they had played together as youngsters, and had shared the earlier stages of education in the same crèche through some successful maneuvering on the part of Mother. Having borne two sons by the same father and having, in this fashion, reached her limit (for she had not fulfilled the stringent requirements for a third), she conceived the notion of being able to visit both at a single trip. She was a strange woman.

William had left the crèche first, naturally, since he was the elder. He had gone into science—genetic engineering. Anthony had heard that, while he was still in the crèche, through a letter from his mother. He was old enough by then to speak firmly to the matron, and those letters stopped. But he always remembered the last one for the agony of shame it had brought him.

Anthony had eventually entered science, too. He had shown talent in that direction and had been urged to. He remembered having had the wild—and prophetic, he now realized—fear he might meet his brother and he ended in telemetrics, which was as far removed from genetic engineering as one could imagine. . . . Or so one would have thought.

Then, through all the elaborate development of the Mercury Project, circumstance waited.

The time came, as it happened, when the Project appeared to be facing a dead end; and a suggestion had been made which saved the situation, and at the same time dragged Anthony into the dilemma his parents had prepared for him. And the best and most sardonic part of the whole thing was that it was Anthony who, in all innocence, made the suggestion.

2.

William Anti-Aut knew of the Mercury Project, but only in the way he knew of the long-drawn-out Stellar Probe that had been on its way long before he was born and would still be on its way after his death; and the way he knew of the Martian colony and of the continuing attempts to establish similar colonies on the asteroids.

Such things were on the distant periphery of his mind and of no real importance. No part of the space effort had ever swirled inward closer to the center of his interests, as far as he could remember, till the day when the printout included photographs of some of the men engaged in the Mercury Project.

William's attention was caught first by the fact that one of them had been identified as Anthony Smith. He remembered the odd name his brother had chosen, and he remembered the Anthony. Surely there could not be two Anthony Smiths.

He had then looked at the photograph itself and there was no mistaking the face. He looked in the mirror in a sudden whimsical gesture at checking the matter. No mistaking the face.

He felt amused, but uneasily so, for he did not fail to recognize the potentiality for embarrassment. Full blood brothers, to use the disgusting phrase. But what was there to do about it? How correct the fact that neither his father nor his mother had imagination?

He must have put the printout in his pocket, absently, when he was getting ready to leave for work, for he came across it at the lunch hour. He stared at it again. Anthony looked keen. It was quite a good reproduction—the printouts were of enormously good quality these days.

His lunch partner, Marco Whatever-his-name-was-that-week, said curiously, "What are you looking at, William?"

On impulse, William passed him the printout and said, "That's my brother." It was like grasping the nettle.

Marco studied it, frowning, and said, "Who? The man standing next to you?"

"No, the man who *is* me. I mean the man who looks like me. He's my brother."

There was a longer pause this time. Marco handed it back and said with a careful levelness to his voice, "Same-parents brother?"

"Yes."

"Father and mother both."

"Yes."

"Ridiculous!"

"I suppose so." William sighed. "Well, according to this, he's in telemetrics over in Texas and I'm doing work in autistics up here. So what difference does it make?"

William did not keep it in his mind and later that day he threw the printout away. He did not want his current bedmate to come across it. She had a ribald sense of humor that William was finding increasingly wearying. He was rather glad she was not in the mood for a child. He himself had had one a few years back anyway. That little brunette, Laura or Linda, one or the other name, had collaborated.

It was quite a time after that, at least a year, that the matter of Randall had come up. If William had given no further thought to his brother—and he hadn't—before that, he certainly had no time for it afterward.

Randall was sixteen when William first received word of him. He had lived a life that was increasingly seclusive and the Kentucky crèche in which he was being brought up decided to cancel him—

and of course it was only some eight or ten days before cancellation that it occurred to anyone to report him to the New York Institute for the Science of Man. (The Homological Institute was its common name.)

William received the report along with reports of several others and there was nothing in the description of Randall that particularly attracted his notice. Still it was time for one of his tedious mass-transport trips to the crèches and there was one likely possibility in West Virginia. He went there—and was disappointed into swearing for the fiftieth time that he would thereafter make these visits by TV image—and then, having dragged himself there, thought he might as well take in the Kentucky crèche before returning home.

He expected nothing.

Yet he hadn't studied Randall's gene pattern for more than ten minutes before he was calling the Institute for a computer calculation. Then he sat back and perspired slightly at the thought that only a last-minute impulse had brought him, and that without that impulse, Randall would have been quietly canceled in a week or less. To put it into the fine detail, a drug would have soaked painlessly through his skin and into his bloodstream and he would have sunk into a peaceful sleep that deepened gradually to death. The drug had a twenty-three-syllable official name, but William called it "nirvanamine," as did everyone else.

William said, "What is his full name, matron?"

The crèche matron said, "Randall Nowan, scholar."

"No one!" said William explosively.

"Nowan." The matron spelled it. "He chose it last year."

"And it meant nothing to you? It is pronounced No one! It didn't occur to you to report this young man last year?"

"It didn't seem—" began the matron, flustered.

William waved her to silence. What was the use? How was she to know? There was nothing in the gene pattern to give warning by any of the usual textbook criteria. It was a subtle combination that William and his staff had worked out over a period of twenty years through experiments on autistic children—and a combination they had never actually seen in life.

So close to canceling!

Marco, who was the hardhead of the group, complained that the crèches were too eager to abort before term and to cancel after term. He maintained that all gene patterns should be allowed to develop for purpose of initial screening and there should be no cancellation at all without consultation with a homologist.

"There aren't enough homologists," William said tranquilly.

"We can at least run all gene patterns through the computer," said Marco.

"To save anything we can get for our use?"

"For any homological use, here or elsewhere. We must study gene patterns in action if we're to understand ourselves properly, and it is the abnormal and monstrous patterns that give us most information. Our experiments on autism have taught us more about homology than the sum total existing on the day we began."

William, who still liked the roll of the phrase "the genetic physiology of man" rather than "homology," shook his head. "Just the same, we've got to play it carefully. However useful we can claim our experiments to be, we live on bare social permission, reluctantly given. We're playing with lives."

"Useless lives. Fit for canceling."

"A quick and pleasant canceling is one thing. Our experiments, usually long drawn out and sometimes unavoidably unpleasant, are another."

"We help them sometimes."

"And we don't help them sometimes."

It was a pointless argument, really, for there was no way of settling it. What it amounted to was that too few interesting abnormalities were available for homologists and there was no way of urging mankind to encourage a greater production. The trauma of the Catastrophe would never vanish in a dozen ways, including that one.

The hectic push toward space exploration could be traced back (and was, by some sociologists) to the knowledge of the fragility of the life skein on the planet, thanks to the Catastrophe.

Well, never mind—

There had never been anything like Randall Nowan. Not for William. The slow onset of autism characteristic of that totally rare gene pattern meant that more was known about Randall than about any equivalent patient before him. They even caught some last faint glimmers of his way of thought in the laboratory before he closed off altogether and shrank finally within the wall of his skin—unconcerned, unreachable.

Then they began the slow process whereby Randall, subjected for increasing lengths of time to artificial stimuli, yielded up the inner workings of his brain and gave clues thereby to the inner workings of all brains, those that were called normal as well as those like his own.

So vastly great was the data they were gathering that William began to feel his dream of reversing autism was more than merely a dream. He felt a warm gladness at having chosen the name Anti-Aut.

And it was at almost the height of the euphoria induced by the work on Randall that he received the call from Dallas and that the heavy pressure began—now, of all times—to abandon his work and take on a new problem.

Looking back on it later, he could never work out just what it was that finally led him to agree to visit Dallas. In the end, of course, he could see how fortunate it was—but what had persuaded him to do so? Could he, even at the start, have had a dim unrealized notion of what it might come to? Surely, impossible.

Was it the unrealized memory of that printout, that photograph of his brother? Surely, impossible.

But he let himself be argued into that visit and it was only when the micro-pile power unit changed the pitch of its soft hum and the agrav unit took over for the final descent that he remembered that photograph—or at least that it moved into the conscious part of his memory.

Anthony worked at Dallas and, William remembered now, at the Mercury Project. That was what the caption had referred to. He swallowed, as the soft jar told him the journey was over. This would be uncomfortable.

3.

Anthony was waiting on the roof reception area to greet the incoming expert. Not he by himself, of course. He was part of a sizable delegation—the size itself a rather grim indication of the desperation to which they had been reduced—and he was among the lower echelons. That he was there at all was only because it was he who had made the original suggestion.

He felt a slight, but continuing, uneasiness at the thought of that. He had put himself on the line. He had received considerable approval for it, but there had been the faint insistence always that it was *his* suggestion; and if it turned out to be a fiasco, every one of them would move out of the line of fire and leave him at point-zero.

There were occasions, later, when he brooded over the possibility that the dim memory of a brother in homology had suggested his thought. That might have been, but it didn't have to be. The suggestion was so sensibly inevitable, really, that surely he would have had the same thought if his brother had been something as innocuous as a fantasy writer, or if he had had no brother of his own.

The problem was the inner planets—

The Moon and Mars were colonized. The larger asteroids and the satellites of Jupiter had been reached, and plans were in progress for a manned voyage to Titan, Saturn's large satellite, by way of an accelerating whirl about Jupiter. Yet even with plans in action for sending men on a seven-year round trip to the outer Solar System, there was still no chance of a manned approach to the inner planets, for fear of the Sun.

Venus itself was the less attractive of the two worlds within Earth's orbit. Mercury, on the other hand—

Anthony had not yet joined the team when Dmitri Large (he was quite short, actually) had given the talk that had moved the World Congress sufficiently to grant the appropriation that made the Mercury Project possible.

Anthony had listened to the tapes, and had heard Dmitri's presentation. Tradition was firm to the effect that it had been extemporaneous, and perhaps it was, but it was perfectly constructed and it held within it, in essence, every guideline followed by the Mercury Project since.

And the chief point made was that it would be wrong to wait until the technology had advanced to the point where a manned expedition through the rigors of Solar radiation could become feasible. Mercury was a unique environment that could teach much, and from Mercury's surface sustained observations could be made of the Sun that could not be made in any other way.

—Provided a man substitute—a robot, in short—could be placed on the planet.

A robot with the required physical characteristics could be built. Soft landings were as easy as kiss-my-hand. Yet once a robot landed, what did one do with him next?

He could make his observations and guide his actions on the basis of those observations, but the Project wanted his actions to be intricate and subtle, at least potentially, and they were not at all sure what observations he might make.

To prepare for all reasonable possibilities and to allow for all the intricacy desired, the robot would need to contain a computer (some at Dallas referred to it as a "brain," but Anthony scorned that verbal habit—perhaps because, he wondered later, the brain was his brother's field) sufficiently complex and versatile to fall into the same asteroid with a mammalian brain.

Yet nothing like that could be constructed and made portable enough to be carried to Mercury and landed there—or if carried and landed, to be mobile enough to be useful to the kind of robot they planned. Perhaps someday the positronic-path devices that the roboticists were playing with might make it possible, but that someday was not yet.

The alternative was to have the robot send back to Earth every observation it made the moment it was made, and a computer on Earth could then guide his every action on the basis of those observations. The robot's body, in short, was to be there, and his brain here.

Once that decision was reached, the key technicians were the telemetrists and it was then that Anthony joined the Project. He became one of those who labored to devise methods for receiving and returning impulses over distances of from 50 to 140 million miles, toward, and sometimes past, a Solar disk that could interfere with those impulses in a most ferocious manner.

He took to his job with passion and (he finally thought) with skill and success. It was he, more than anyone else, who had designed the three switching stations that had been hurled into permanent orbit about Mercury—the Mercury Orbiters. Each of them was capable of sending and receiving impulses from Mercury to Earth and from Earth to Mercury. Each was capable of resisting, more or less permanently, the radiation from the Sun, and more than that, each could filter out Solar interference.

Three equivalent Orbiters were placed at distance of a little over a million miles from Earth, reaching north and south of the plane of the Ecliptic so that they could receive the impulses from Mercury and relay them to Earth—or vice versa—even when Mercury was behind the Sun and inaccessible to direct reception from any station on Earth's surface.

Which left the robot itself; a marvelous specimen of the robot-icists' and telemetrists' arts in combination. The most complex of ten successive models, it was capable, in a volume only a little over twice that of a man and five times his mass, of sensing and doing considerably more than a man—if it could be guided.

How complex a computer had to be to guide the robot made itself evident rapidly enough, however, as each response step had to be modified to allow for variations in possible perception. And as each response step itself enforced the certainty of greater complexity of possible variation in perceptions, the early steps had to be reinforced and made stronger. It built itself up endlessly, like a chess game, and the telemetrists began to use a computer to program the computer that designed the program for the computer that programmed the robot-controlling computer.

There was nothing but confusion.

The robot was at a base in the desert spaces of Arizona and in itself was working well. The computer in Dallas could not, however, handle him well enough; not even under perfectly known Earth conditions. How then—

Anthony remembered the day when he had made the suggestion. It was on 7-4-553. He remembered it, for one thing, because he remembered thinking that day that 7-4 had been an important holiday in the Dallas region of the world among the pre-Cats half a millennium before—well, 553 years before, to be exact.

It had been at dinner, and a good dinner, too. There had been a careful adjustment of the ecology of the region and the Project personnel had high priority in collecting the food supplies that became available—so there was an unusual degree of choice on the menus, and Anthony had tried roast duck.

It was very good roast duck and it made him somewhat more expansive than usual. Everyone was in a rather self-expressive mood, in fact, and Ricardo said, "We'll never do it. Let's admit it. We'll never do it."

There was no telling how many had thought such a thing how many times before, but it was a rule that no one said so openly. Open pessimism might be the final push needed for appropriations to stop (they had been coming with greater difficulty each year for five years now) and if there *were* a chance, it would be gone.

Anthony, ordinarily not given to extraordinary optimism, but now reveling over his duck, said, "Why can't we do it? Tell me why, and I'll refute it."

It was a direct challenge and Ricardo's dark eyes narrowed at once. "You want me to tell you why?"

"I sure do."

Ricardo swung his chair around, facing Anthony full. He said, "Come on, there's no mystery. Dmitri Large won't say so openly in any report, but you know and I know that to run Mercury Project properly, we'll need a computer as complex as a human brain whether it's on Mercury or here, and we can't build one. So where does that leave us except to play games with the World Congress and get money for make-work and possibly useful spin-offs?"

And Anthony placed a complacent smile on his face and said, "That's easy to refute. You've given us the answer yourself." (Was he playing games? Was it the warm feeling of duck in his stomach? The desire to tease Ricardo? . . . Or did some unfelt thought of his brother touch him? There was no way, later, that he could tell.)

"What answer?" Ricardo rose. He was quite tall and unusually thin and he always wore his white coat unseamed. He folded his arms and seemed to be doing his best to tower over the seated Anthony like an unfolded meter rule. "What answer?"

"You say we need a computer as complex as a human brain. All right, then, we'll build one."

"The point, you idiot, is that we can't—"

"*We* can't. But there are others."

"What others?"

"People who work on brains, of course. We're just solid-state mechanics. We have no idea in what way a human brain is complex, or where, or to what extent. Why don't we get in a homologist and have *him* design a computer?" And with that Anthony took a huge helping of stuffing and savored it complacently. He could still remember, after all this time, the taste of the stuffing, though he couldn't remember in detail what had happened afterward.

It seemed to him that no one had taken it seriously. There was laughter and a general feeling that Anthony had wriggled out of a hole by clever sophistry so that the laughter was at Ricardo's expense. (Afterward, of course, everyone claimed to have taken the suggestion seriously.)

Ricardo blazed up, pointed a finger at Anthony, and said, "Write that up. I *dare* you to put that suggestion in writing." (At least, so Anthony's memory had it. Ricardo had, since then, stated his comment was an enthusiastic "Good idea! Why don't you write it up formally, Anthony?")

Either way, Anthony put it in writing.

Dmitri Large had taken to it. In private conference, he had slapped Anthony on the back and had said that he had been speculating in that direction himself—though he did not offer to take any credit for it on the record. (Just in case it turned out to be a fiasco, Anthony thought.)

Dmitri Large conducted the search for the appropriate homologist. It did not occur to Anthony that he ought to be interested. He knew neither homology nor homologists—except, of course, his brother, and he had not thought of him. Not consciously.

So Anthony was up there in the reception area, in a minor role, when the door of the aircraft opened and several men got out and came down and in the course of the handshakes that began going round, he found himself staring at his own face.

His cheeks burned and, with all his might, he wished himself a thousand miles away.

4.

More than ever, William wished that the memory of his brother had come earlier. It should have. . . . Surely it should have.

But there had been the flattery of the request and the excitement that had begun to grow in him after a while. Perhaps he had deliberately avoided remembering.

To begin with, there had been the exhilaration of Dmitri Large coming to see him in his own proper presence. He had come from Dallas to New York by plane and that had been very titillating for William, whose secret vice it was to read thrillers. In the thrillers, men and women always traveled mass-wise when secrecy was desired. After all, electronic travel was public property—at least in the thrillers, where every radiation beam of whatever kind was invariably bugged.

William had said so in a kind of morbid half attempt at humor, but Dmitri hadn't seemed to be listening. He was staring at William's face and his thoughts seemed elsewhere. "I'm sorry," he said finally. "You remind me of someone."

(And yet that hadn't given it away to William. How was that possible? he had eventual occasion to wonder.)

Dmitri Large was a small plump man who seemed to be in a perpetual twinkle even when he declared himself worried or annoyed. He had a round and bulbous nose, pronounced cheeks, and softness everywhere. He emphasized his last name and said with a quickness that led William to suppose he said it often, "Size is not all the large there is, my friend."

In the talk that followed, William protested much. He knew nothing about computers. Nothing! He had not the faintest idea of how they worked or how they were programmed.

"No matter, no matter," Dmitri said, shoving the point aside with an expressive gesture of the hand. "We know the computers; we can set up the programs. You just tell us what it is a computer must be made to do so that it will work like a brain and not like a computer."

"I'm not sure I know enough about how a brain works to be able to tell you that, Dmitri," said William.

"You are the foremost homologist in the world," said Dmitri. "I have checked that out carefully." And that disposed of that.

William listened with gathering gloom. He supposed it was inevitable. Dip a person into one particular specialty deeply enough and long enough, and he would automatically begin to assume that specialists in all other fields were magicians, judging the depth of their wisdom by the breadth of his own ignorance. . . . And as time went on, William learned a great deal more of the Mercury Project than it seemed to him at the time that he cared to.

He said at last, "Why use a computer at all, then? Why not have one of your own men, or relays of them, receive the material from the robot and send back instructions."

"Oh, oh, oh," said Dmitri, almost bouncing in his chair in his eagerness. "You see, you are not aware. Men are too slow to analyze quickly all the material the robot will send back—temperatures and gas pressures and cosmic-ray fluxes and Solar-wind intensities and chemical compositions and soil textures and easily three dozen more items—and then try to decide on the next step. A human being would merely *guide* the robot, and ineffectively; a computer would *be* the robot.

"And then, too," he went on, "men are too fast, also. It takes radiation of any kind anywhere from ten to twenty-two minutes to take the round trip between Mercury and Earth, depending on where each is in its orbit. Nothing can be done about that. You get an observation, you give an order, but much has happened between the time the observation is made and the response returns. Men can't adapt to the slowness of the speed of light, but a computer can take that into account. . . . Come help us, William."

William said gloomily, "You are certainly welcome to consult me, for what good that might do you. My private TV beam is at your service."

"But it's not consultation I want. You must come with me."

"Mass-wise?" said William, shocked.

"Yes, of course. A project like this can't be carried out by sitting at opposite ends of a laser beam with a communications satellite in the middle. In the long run, it is too expensive, too inconvenient, and, of course, it lacks all privacy—"

It *was* like a thriller, William decided.

"Come to Dallas," said Dmitri, "and let me show you what we have there. Let me show you the facilities. Talk to some of our computer men. Give them the benefit of your way of thought."

It was time, William thought, to be decisive. "Dmitri," he said, "I have work of my own here. Important work that I do not wish to leave. To do what you want me to do may take me away from my laboratory for months."

"Months!" said Dmitri, clearly taken aback. "My good William, it may well be years. But surely it will be your work."

"No, it will not. I know what my work is and guiding a robot on Mercury is not it."

"Why not? If you do it properly, you will learn more about the brain merely by trying to make a computer work like one, and you will come back here, finally, better equipped to do what you now consider your work. And while you're gone, will you have no associates to carry on? And can you not be in constant communication with them by laser beam and television? And can you not visit New York on occasion? Briefly."

William was moved. The thought of working on the brain from another direction did hit home. From that point on, he found himself looking for excuses to go—at least to visit—at least to see what it was all like. . . . He could always return.

Then there followed Dmitri's visit to the ruins of Old New York, which he enjoyed with artless excitement (but then there was no more magnificent spectacle of the useless gigantism of the pre-Cats than Old New York). William began to wonder if the trip might not give him an opportunity to see some sights as well.

He even began to think that for some time he had been considering the possibility of finding a new bedmate, and it would be more convenient to find one in another geographical area where he would not stay permanently.

—Or was it that even then, when he knew nothing but the barest beginning of what was needed, there had already come to him, like the twinkle of a distant lightning flash, what might be done—

So he eventually went to Dallas and stepped out on the roof and there was Dmitri again, beaming. Then, with eyes narrowing, the little man turned and said, "I *knew*— What a remarkable resemblance!"

William's eyes opened wide and there, visibly shrinking backward, was enough of his own face to make him certain at once that Anthony was standing before him.

He read very plainly in Anthony's face a longing to bury the relationship. All William needed to say was "How remarkable!" and let it go. The gene patterns of mankind were complex enough, after all, to allow resemblances of any reasonable degree even without kinship.

But of course William was a homologist and no one can work with the intricacies of the human brain without growing insensitive as to its details, so he said, "I'm sure this is Anthony, my brother."

Dmitri said, "Your brother?"

"My father," said William, "had two boys by the same woman—my mother. They were eccentric people."

He then stepped forward, hand outstretched, and Anthony had no choice but to take it. . . . The incident was the topic of conversation, the only topic, for the next several days.

5.

It was small consolation to Anthony that William was contrite enough when he realized what he had done.

They sat together after dinner that night and William said, "My apologies. I thought that if we got the worst out at once that would end it. It doesn't seem to have done so. I've signed no papers, made no formal agreement. I will leave."

"What good would that do?" said Anthony ungraciously. "Everyone knows now. Two bodies and one face. It's enough to make one puke."

"If I leave—"

"You can't leave. This whole thing is my idea."

"To get *me* here?" William's heavy lids lifted as far as they might and his eyebrows climbed.

"No, of course not. To get a *homologist* here. How could I possibly know they would send *you?*"

"But if I leave—"

"No. The only thing we can do now is to lick the problem, if it can be done. Then—it won't matter." (Everything is forgiven those who succeed, he thought.)

"I don't know that I can—"

"We'll have to try. Dmitri will place it on us. It's too good a chance. You two are brothers," Anthony said, mimicking Dmitri's tenor voice, "and understand each other. Why not work together?" Then, in his own voice, angrily, "So we must. To begin with, what is it you do, William? I mean, more precisely than the word 'homology' can explain by itself."

William sighed. "Well, please accept my regrets. . . . I work with autistic children."

"I'm afraid I don't know what that means."

"Without going into a long song and dance, I deal with children who do not reach out into the world, do not communicate with others, but who sink into themselves and exist behind a wall of skin, somewhat unreachably. I hope to be able to cure it someday."

"Is that why you call yourself Anti-Aut?"

"Yes, as a matter of fact."

Anthony laughed briefly, but he was not really amused.

A chill crept into William's manner. "It is an honest name."

"I'm sure it is," muttered Anthony hurriedly, and could bring himself to no more specific apology. With an effort, he restored the subject, "And are you making any progress?"

"Toward the cure? No, so far. Toward understanding, yes. And the more I understand—" William's voice grew warmer as he spoke and his eyes more distant. Anthony recognized it for what it was, the pleasure of speaking of what fills one's heart and mind to the exclusion of almost everything else. He felt it in himself often enough.

He listened as closely as he might to something he didn't really understand, for it was necessary to do so. He would expect William to listen to him.

How clearly he remembered it. He thought at the time he would not, but at the time, of course, he was not aware of what was happening. Thinking back, in the glare of hindsight, he found himself remembering whole sentences, virtually word for word.

"So it seemed to us," William said, "that the autistic child was not failing to receive the impressions, or even failing to interpret them in quite a sophisticated manner. He was, rather, disapproving them and rejecting them, without any loss of the potentiality of full communication if some impression could be found which he approved of."

"Ah," said Anthony, making just enough of a sound to indicate that he was listening.

"Nor can you persuade him out of his autism in any ordinary way, for he disapproves of *you* just as much as he disapproves of the rest of the world. But if you place him in conscious arrest—"

"In what?"

"It is a technique we have in which, in effect, the brain is divorced from the body and can perform its functions without reference to the body. It is a rather sophisticated technique devised in our own laboratory; actually—" He paused.

"By yourself?" asked Anthony gently.

"Actually, yes," said William, reddening slightly, but clearly pleased. "In conscious arrest, we can supply the body with designed fantasies and observe the brain under differential electroencephalography. We can at once learn more about the autistic individual; what kind of sense impressions he most wants; and we learn more about the brain generally."

"Ah," said Anthony, and this time it was a real ah. "And all this you have learned about brains—can you not adapt it to the workings of a computer?"

"No," said William. "Not a chance. I told that to Dmitri. I know nothing about computers and not enough about brains."

"If I teach you about computers and tell you in detail what we need, what then?"

"It won't do. It—"

"Brother," Anthony said, and he tried to make it an impressive word. "You owe me something. Please make an honest attempt to give our problem some thought. Whatever you know about the brain—please adapt it to our computers."

William shifted uneasily, and said, "I understand your position. I will try. I will honestly try."

6.

William *had* tried, and as Anthony had predicted, the two had been left to work together. At first they encountered others now and then and William had tried to use the shock value of the announcement that they were brothers since there was no use in denial. Eventually that stopped, however, and there came to be a purposeful non-interference. When William approached Anthony, or Anthony approached William, anyone else who might be present faded silently into the walls.

They even grew used to each other after a fashion and sometimes spoke to each other almost as though there were no resemblance between them at all and no childish memories in common.

Anthony made the computer requirements plain in reasonably non-technical language and William, after long thought, explained how it seemed to him a computer might do the work, more or less, of a brain.

Anthony said, "Would that be possible?"

"I don't know," said William. "I am not eager to try. It may not work. But it may."

"We'd have to talk to Dmitri Large."

"Let's talk it over ourselves first and see what we've got. We can go to him with as reasonable a proposition as we can put together. Or else, not go to him."

Anthony hesitated, "We *both* go to him?"

William said delicately, "You be my spokesman. There is no reason that we need be seen together."

"Thank you, William. If anything comes of this, you will get full credit from me."

William said, "I have no worries about that. If there is anything to this, I will be the only one who can make it work, I suppose."

They thrashed it out through four or five meetings and if Anthony hadn't been kin and if there hadn't been that sticky, emotional situation between them, William would have been uncomplicatedly proud of the younger—brother—for his quick understanding of an alien field.

There were then long conferences with Dmitri Large. There were, in fact, conferences with everyone. Anthony saw them through endless days, and then they came to see William separately. And eventually, through an agonizing pregnancy, what came to be called the Mercury Computer was authorized.

William then returned to New York with some relief. He did not plan to stay in New York (would he have thought that possible two months earlier?) but there was much to do at the Homological Institute.

More conferences were necessary, of course, to explain to his own laboratory group what was happening and why he had to take leave and how they were to continue their own projects without him. Then there was a much more elaborate arrival at Dallas with the essential equipment and with two young aides for what would have to be an open-ended stay.

Nor did William even look back, figuratively speaking. His own laboratory and its needs faded from his thoughts. He was now thoroughly committed to his new task.

7.

It was the worst period for Anthony. The relief during William's absence had not penetrated deep and there began the nervous agony of wondering whether perhaps, hope against hope, he might not return. Might he not choose to send a deputy, someone else, anyone else? Anyone with a different face so that Anthony need not feel the half of a two-backed four-legged monster?

But it *was* William. Anthony had watched the freight plane come silently through the air, had watched it unload from a distance. But even from that distance he eventually saw William.

That was that. Anthony left.

He went to see Dmitri that afternoon. "It's not necessary, Dmitri, for me to stay, surely. We've worked out the details and someone else can take over."

"No, no," said Dmitri. "The idea was yours in the first place. You must see it through. There is no point in needlessly dividing the credit."

Anthony thought: No one else will take the risk. There's still the chance of fiasco. I might have known.

He *had* known, but he said stolidly, "You understand I cannot work with William."

"But why not?" Dmitri pretended surprise. "You have been doing so well together."

"I have been straining my guts over it, Dmitri, and they won't take any more. Don't you suppose I know how it looks?"

"My good fellow! You make too much of it. Sure the men stare. They are human, after all. But they'll get used to it. *I'm* used to it."

You are not, you fat liar, Anthony thought. He said, "*I'm not* used to it."

"You're not looking at it properly. Your parents were peculiar— but after all, what they did wasn't illegal, only peculiar, *only* peculiar. It's not your fault, or William's. Neither of you is to blame."

"We carry the mark," said Anthony, making a quick curving gesture of his hand to his face.

"It's not the mark you think. I see differences. You are distinctly younger in appearance. Your hair is wavier. It's only at first glance that there is a similarity. Come, Anthony, there will be all the time you want, all the help you need, all the equipment you can use. I'm sure it will work marvelously. Think of the satisfaction—"

Anthony weakened, of course, and agreed at least to help William set up the equipment. William, too, seemed sure it would work marvelously. Not as frenetically as Dmitri did, but with a kind of calmness.

"It's only a matter of the proper connections," he said, "though I must admit that that's quite a huge 'only.' Your end of it will be to arrange sensory impressions on an independent screen so that we can exert—well, I can't say manual control, can I?—so that we can exert intellectual control to override, if necessary."

"That can be done," said Anthony.

"Then let's get going. . . . Look, I'll need a week at least to arrange the connections and make sure of the instructions—"

"Programming," said Anthony.

"Well, this is your place, so I'll use your terminology. My assistants and I will *program* the Mercury Computer, but not in your fashion."

"I should hope not. We would want a homologist to set up a much more subtle program than anything a mere telemetrist could do." He did not try to hide the self-hating irony in his words.

William let the tone go and accepted the words. He said, "We'll begin simply. We'll have the robot walk."

8.

A week later, the robot walked in Arizona, a thousand miles away. He walked stiffly, and sometimes he fell down, and sometimes he clanked his ankle against an obstruction, and sometimes he whirled on one foot and went off in a surprising new direction.

"He's a baby, learning to walk," said William.

Dmitri came occasionally, to learn of progress. "That's remarkable," he would say.

Anthony didn't think so. Weeks passed, then months. The robot had progressively done more and more, as the Mercury Computer had been placed, progressively, under a more and more complex programming. (William had a tendency to refer to the Mercury Computer as a brain, but Anthony wouldn't allow it.) And all that happened wasn't good enough.

"It's not good enough, William," he said finally. He had not slept the night before.

"Isn't that strange?" said William coolly. "I was going to say that I thought we had it about beaten."

Anthony held himself together with difficulty. The strain of working with William and of watching the robot fumble was more than he could bear. "I'm going to resign, William. The whole job. I'm sorry. . . . It's not you."

"But it *is* I, Anthony."

"It isn't *all* you, William. It's failure. We won't make it. You see how clumsily the robot handles himself, even though he's on Earth, only a thousand miles away, with the signal round trip only a tiny fraction of a second in time. On Mercury, there will be minutes of delay, minutes for which the Mercury Computer will have to allow. It's madness to think it will work."

William said, "Don't resign, Anthony. You can't resign now. I suggest we have the robot sent to Mercury. I'm convinced he's ready."

Anthony laughed loudly and insultingly. "You're crazy, William."

"I'm not. You seem to think it will be harder on Mercury, but it won't be. It's harder on Earth. This robot is designed for one-third Earth-normal gravity, and he's working in Arizona at full gravity. He's designed for 400° C. and he's got 30° C. He's designed for vacuum and he's working in an atmospheric soup."

"That robot can take the difference."

"The metal structure can, I suppose, but what about the Computer right here? It doesn't work well with a robot that isn't in the environment he's designed for. . . . Look, Anthony, if you want a computer that is as complex as a brain, you have to allow for idiosyncrasies. . . . Come, let's make a deal. If you will push, with me, to have the robot sent to Mercury, that will take six months, and I will take a sabbatical for that period. You will be rid of me."

"Who'll take care of the Mercury Computer?"

"By now you understand how it works, and I'll have my two men here to help you."

Anthony shook his head defiantly. "I can't take the responsibility for the Computer, and I won't take the responsibility for suggesting that the robot be sent to Mercury. It won't work."

"I'm *sure* it will."

"You can't be sure. And the responsibility is mine. I'm the one who'll bear the blame. It will be nothing to you."

Anthony later remembered this as a crucial moment. William might have let it go. Anthony would have resigned. All would have been lost.

But William said, "Nothing to me? Look, Dad had this thing about Mom. All right. I'm sorry, too. I'm as sorry as anyone can be, but it's *done*, and there's something funny that has resulted. When I speak of Dad, I mean your Dad, too, and there's lots of pairs of people who can say that: two brothers, two sisters, a brother and sister. And then when I say Mom, I mean *your* Mom, and there are lots of pairs who can say that, too. But I don't know any other pair, nor have I heard of any other pair, who can share both Dad *and* Mom."

"I know that," said Anthony grimly.

"Yes, but look at it from my standpoint," said William hurriedly. "I'm a homologist. I work with gene patterns. Have you ever thought of our gene patterns? We share both parents, which means that our gene patterns are closer together than any other pair on this planet. Our very faces show it."

"I know that, too."

"So that if this project were to work, and if you were to gain glory from it, it would be your gene pattern that would have been proven highly useful to mankind—and that would mean very much my gene pattern as well. . . . Don't you see, Anthony? I share your parents, your face, your gene pattern, and therefore either your glory or your disgrace. It is mine almost as much as yours, and if any credit or blame adheres to me, it is yours almost as much as mine, too. I've *got* to be interested in your success. I've a motive for that which no one else on Earth has—a purely selfish one, one so selfish you can be sure it's there. I'm on your side, Anthony, because you're very nearly me!"

They looked at each other for a long time, and for the first time, Anthony did so without noticing the face he shared.

William said, "So let us ask that the robot be sent to Mercury."

And Anthony gave in. And after Dmitri had approved the request —he had been waiting to, after all—Anthony spent much of the day in deep thought.

Then he sought out William and said, "Listen!"

There was a long pause which William did not break.

Anthony said again, "Listen!"

William waited patiently.

Anthony said, "There's really no need for you to leave. I'm sure you wouldn't like to have the Mercury Computer tended by anyone but yourself."

William said, "You mean *you* intend to leave?"

Anthony said, "No, I'll stay, too."

William said, "We needn't see much of each other."

All of this had been, for Anthony, like speaking with a pair of hands clenched about his windpipe. The pressure seemed to tighten now, but he managed the hardest statement of all.

"We don't have to avoid each other. We don't have to."

William smiled rather uncertainly. Anthony didn't smile at all; he left quickly.

9.

William looked up from his book. It was at least a month since he had ceased being vaguely surprised at having Anthony enter.

He said, "Anything wrong?"

"Who can say? They're coming in for the soft landing. Is the Mercury Computer in action?"

William knew Anthony knew the Computer status perfectly, but he said, "By tomorrow morning, Anthony."

"And there are no problems?"

"None at all."

"Then we have to wait for the soft landing."

"Yes."

Anthony said, "Something will go wrong."

"Rocketry is surely an old hand at this. Nothing will go wrong."

"So much work wasted."

"It's not wasted yet. It won't be."

Anthony said, "Maybe you're right." Hands deep in his pockets, he drifted away, stopping at the door just before touching contact. "Thanks!"

"For what, Anthony?"

"For being—comforting."

William smiled wryly and was relieved his emotions didn't show.

10.

Virtually the entire body of personnel of the Mercury Project was on hand for the crucial moment. Anthony, who had no tasks to perform, remained well to the rear, his eyes on the monitors. The robot had been activated and there were visual messages being returned.

At least they came out as the equivalent of visual—and they showed as yet nothing but a dim glow of light which was, presumably, Mercury's surface.

Shadows flitted across the screen, probably irregularities on that surface. Anthony couldn't tell by eye alone, but those at the controls, who were analyzing the data by methods more subtle than could be disposed of by unaided eye, seemed calm. None of the little red lights that might have betokened emergency were lighting. Anthony was watching the key observers rather than the screen.

He should be down with William and the others at the Computer. It was going to be thrown in only when the soft landing was made. He *should* be. He *couldn't* be.

The shadows flitted across the screen more rapidly. The robot was descending—too quickly? Surely, too quickly!

There was a last blur and a steadiness, a shift of focus in which the blur grew darker, then fainter. A sound was heard and there were perceptible seconds before Anthony realized what it was the sound was saying—"Soft landing achieved! Soft landing achieved!"

Then a murmur arose and became an excited hum of self-congratulation until one more change took place on the screen and the sound of human words and laughter was stopped as though there had been a smash collision against a wall of silence.

For the screen changed; changed and grew sharp. In the brilliant, brilliant sunlight, blazing through the carefully filtered screen, they could now see a boulder clear, burning white on one side, ink-on-ink on the other. It shifted right, then back to left, as though a pair of eyes were looking left, then right. A metal hand appeared on the screen as though the eyes were looking at part of itself.

It was Anthony's voice that cried out at last, "The Computer's been thrown in."

He heard the words as though someone else had shouted them and he raced out and down the stairs and through a corridor, leaving the babble of voices to rise behind him.

"William," he cried as he burst into the Computer room, "it's *perfect*, it's—"

But William's hand was upraised. "Shh. Please. I don't want any violent sensations entering except those from the robot."

"You mean we can be heard?" whispered Anthony.

"Maybe not, but I don't know." There was another screen, a smaller one, in the room with the Mercury Computer. The scene on it was different, and changing; the robot was moving.

William said, "The robot is feeling its way. Those steps have got to be clumsy. There's a seven-minute delay between stimulus and response and that has to be allowed for."

"But already he's walking more surely than he ever did in Arizona. Don't you think so, William? Don't you think so?" Anthony was gripping William's shoulder, shaking it, eyes never leaving the screen.

William said, "I'm sure of it, Anthony."

The Sun burned down in a warm contrasting world of white and black, of white Sun against black sky and white rolling ground mottled with black shadow. The bright sweet smell of the Sun on every exposed square centimeter of metal contrasting with the creeping death-of-aroma on the other side.

He lifted his hand and stared at it, counting the fingers. Hot-hot-

hot—turning, putting each finger, one by one, into the shadow of the others and the hot slowly dying in a change in tactility that made him feel the clean, comfortable vacuum.

Yet not entirely vacuum. He straightened and lifted both arms over his head, stretching them out, and the sensitive spots on either wrist felt the vapors—the thin, faint touch of tin and lead rolling through the cloy of mercury.

The thicker taste rose from his feet; the silicates of each variety, marked by the clear separate-and-together touch and tang of each metal ion. He moved one foot slowly through the crunchy, caked dust, and felt the changes like a soft, not quite random symphony.

And over all the Sun. He looked up at it, large and fat and bright and hot, and heard its joy. He watched the slow rise of prominences around its rim and listened to the crackling sound of each; and to the other happy noises over the broad face. When he dimmed the background light, the red of the rising wisps of hydrogen showed in bursts of mellow contralto, and the deep bass of the spots amid the muted whistling of the wispy, moving faculae, and the occasional thin keening of a flare, the ping-pong ticking of gamma rays and cosmic particles, and over all in every direction the soft, fainting, and ever-renewed sigh of the Sun's substance rising and retreating forever in a cosmic wind which reached out and bathed him in glory.

He jumped, and rose slowly in the air with a freedom he had never felt, and jumped again when he landed, and ran, and jumped, and ran again, with a body that responded perfectly to this glorious world, this paradise in which he found himself.

A stranger so long and so lost—in paradise at last.

William said, "It's all right."

"But what's he doing?" cried out Anthony.

"It's *all right*. The programming is working. He has tested his senses. He has been making the various visual observations. He has dimmed the Sun and studied it. He has tested for atmosphere and for the chemical nature of the soil. It all works."

"But why is he running?"

"I rather think that's his own idea, Anthony. If you want to program a computer as complicated as a brain, you've got to expect it to have ideas of its own."

"Running? Jumping?" Anthony turned an anxious face to William.

"He'll hurt himself. You can handle the Computer. Override. Make him stop."

And William said sharply, "No. I won't. I'll take the chance of his hurting himself. Don't you understand? He's *happy*. He was on Earth, a world he was never equipped to handle. Now he's on Mercury with a body perfectly adapted to its environment, as perfectly adapted as a hundred specialized scientists could make it be. It's paradise for him; let him enjoy it."

"Enjoy? He's a robot."

"I'm not talking about the robot. I'm talking about the brain— the *brain*—that's living *here*."

The Mercury Computer, enclosed in glass, carefully and delicately wired, its integrity most subtly preserved, breathed and lived.

"It's Randall who's in paradise," said William. "He's found the world for whose sake he autistically fled this one. He has a world his new body fits perfectly in exchange for the world his old body did not fit at all."

Anthony watched the screen in wonder. "He seems to be quieting."

"Of course," said William, "and he'll do his job all the better for his joy."

Anthony smiled and said, "We've done it, then, you and I? Shall we join the rest and let them fawn on us, William?"

William said, "Together?"

And Anthony linked arms. "Together, brother!"

Light Verse

The very last person anyone would expect to be a murderer was Mrs.
Avis Lardner. Widow of the great astronaut-martyr, she was a phi-
lanthropist, an art collector, a hostess extraordinary, and, everyone
agreed, an artistic genius. But above all, she was the gentlest and
kindest human being one could imagine.

Her husband, William J. Lardner, died, as we all know, of the
effects of radiation from a solar flare, after he had deliberately
remained in space so that a passenger vessel might make it safely to
Space Station 5.

Mrs. Lardner had received a generous pension for that, and she
had then invested wisely and well. By late middle age she was very
wealthy.

Her house was a showplace, a veritable museum, containing a
small but extremely select collection of extraordinarily beautiful jeweled objects. From a dozen different cultures she had obtained relics
of almost every conceivable artifact that could be embedded with
jewels and made to serve the aristocracy of that culture. She had one
of the first jeweled wristwatches manufactured in America, a jeweled
dagger from Cambodia, a jeweled pair of spectacles from Italy, and
so on almost endlessly.

All was open for inspection. The artifacts were not insured, and
there were no ordinary security provisions. There was no need for
anything conventional, for Mrs. Lardner maintained a large staff of
robot servants, all of whom could be relied on to guard every item

with imperturbable concentration, irreproachable honesty, and irrevocable efficiency.

Everyone knew the existence of those robots and there is no record of any attempt at theft, ever.

And then, of course, there was her light-sculpture. How Mrs. Lardner discovered her own genius at the art, no guest at her many lavish entertainments could guess. On each occasion, however, when her house was thrown open to guests, a new symphony of light shone throughout the rooms; three-dimensional curves and solids in melting color, some pure and some fusing in startling, crystalline effects that bathed every guest in wonder and somehow always adjusted itself so as to make Mrs. Lardner's blue-white hair and soft, unlined face gently beautiful.

It was for the light-sculpture more than anything else that the guests came. It was never the same twice, and never failed to explore new experimental avenues of art. Many people who could afford light-consoles prepared light-sculptures for amusement, but no one could approach Mrs. Lardner's expertise. Not even those who considered themselves professional artists.

She herself was charmingly modest about it. "No, no," she would protest when someone waxed lyrical. "I wouldn't call it 'poetry in light.' That's far too kind. At most, I would say it was mere 'light verse.'" And everyone smiled at her gentle wit.

Though she was often asked, she would never create light-sculpture for any occasion but her own parties. "That would be commercialization," she said.

She had no objection, however, to the preparation of elaborate holograms of her sculptures so that they might be made permanent and reproduced in museums of art all over the world. Nor was there ever a charge for any use that might be made of her light-sculptures.

"I couldn't ask a penny," she said, spreading her arms wide. "It's free to all. After all, I have no further use for it myself." It was true! She never used the same light-sculpture twice.

When the holograms were taken, she was cooperation itself. Watching benignly at every step, she was always ready to order her robot servants to help. "Please, Courtney," she would say, "would you be so kind as to adjust the step ladder?"

It was her fashion. She always addressed her robots with the most formal courtesy.

Once, years before, she had been almost scolded by a government functionary from the Bureau of Robots and Mechanical Men. "You can't do that," he said severely. "It interferes with their efficiency. They are constructed to follow orders, and the more clearly you give those orders, the more efficiently they follow them. When you ask with elaborate politeness, it is difficult for them to understand that an order is being given. They react more slowly."

Mrs. Lardner lifted her aristocratic head. "I do not ask for speed and efficiency," she said. "I ask goodwill. My robots love me."

The government functionary might have explained that robots cannot love, but he withered under her hurt but gentle glance.

It was notorious that Mrs. Lardner never even returned a robot to the factory for adjustment. Their positronic brains are enormously complex, and once in ten times or so the adjustment is not perfect as it leaves the factory. Sometimes the error does not show up for a period of time, but whenever it does, U. S. Robots and Mechanical Men Corporation always makes the adjustment free of charge.

Mrs. Lardner shook her head. "Once a robot is in my house," she said, "and has performed his duties, any minor eccentricities must be borne with. I will not have him manhandled."

It was the worse thing possible to try to explain that a robot was but a machine. She would say very stiffly, "Nothing that is as intelligent as a robot can ever be *but* a machine. I treat them as people."

And that was that!

She kept even Max, although he was almost helpless. He could scarcely understand what was expected of him. Mrs. Lardner denied that strenuously, however. "Not at all," she would say firmly. "He can take hats and coats and store them very well, indeed. He can hold objects for me. He can do many things."

"But why not have him adjusted?" asked a friend, once.

"Oh, I couldn't. He's himself. He's very lovable, you know. After all, a positronic brain is so complex that no one can ever tell in just what way it's off. If he were made perfectly normal there would be no way to adjust him back to the lovability he now has. I won't give that up."

"But if he's maladjusted," said the friend, looking at Max nervously, "might he not be dangerous?"

"Never," laughed Mrs. Lardner. "I've had him for years. He's completely harmless and quite a dear."

Actually he looked like all the other robots, smooth, metallic, vaguely human but expressionless.

To the gentle Mrs. Lardner, however, they were all individual, all sweet, all lovable. It was the kind of woman she was.

How could she commit murder?

The very last person anyone would expect to be murdered would be John Semper Travis. Introverted and gentle, he was in the world but not of it. He had that peculiar mathematical turn of mind that made it possible for him to work out in his mind the complicated tapestry of the myriad positronic brain-paths in a robot's mind.

He was chief engineer of U. S. Robots and Mechanical Men Corporation.

But he was also an enthusiastic amateur in light-sculpture. He had written a book on the subject, trying to show that the type of mathematics he used in working out positronic brain-paths might be modified into a guide to the production of aesthetic light-sculpture.

His attempt at putting theory into practice was a dismal failure, however. The sculptures he himself produced, following his mathematical principles, were stodgy, mechanical, and uninteresting.

It was the only reason for unhappiness in his quiet, introverted, and secure life, and yet it was reason enough for him to be very unhappy indeed. He *knew* his theories were right, yet he could not make them work. If he could but produce *one* great piece of light-sculpture—

Naturally, he knew of Mrs. Lardner's light-sculpture. She was universally hailed as a genius, yet Travis knew she could not understand even the simplest aspect of robotic mathematics. He had corresponded with her but she consistently refused to explain her methods, and he wondered if she had any at all. Might it not be mere intuition?—but even intuition might be reduced to mathematics. Finally he managed to receive an invitation to one of her parties. He simply had to see her.

Mr. Travis arrived rather late. He had made one last attempt at a piece of light-sculpture and had failed dismally.

He greeted Mrs. Lardner with a kind of puzzled respect and said, "That was a peculiar robot who took my hat and coat."

"That is Max," said Mrs. Lardner.

"He is quite maladjusted, and he's a fairly old model. How is it you did not return it to the factory?"

"Oh, no," said Mrs. Lardner. "It would be too much trouble."

"None at all, Mrs. Lardner," said Travis. "You would be surprised how simple a task it was. Since I am with U. S. Robots, I took the liberty of adjusting him myself. It took no time and you'll find he is now in perfect working order."

A queer change came over Mrs. Lardner's face. Fury found a place on it for the first time in her gentle life, and it was as though the lines did not know how to form.

"You adjusted him?" she shrieked. "But it was *he* who created my light-sculptures. It was the maladjustment, the *maladjustment,* which you can never restore, that—that—"

It was really unfortunate that she had been showing her collection at the time and that the jeweled dagger from Cambodia was on the marble tabletop before her.

Travis's face was also distorted. "You mean if I had studied his uniquely maladjusted positronic brain-paths I might have learned—"

She lunged with the knife too quickly for anyone to stop her and he did not try to dodge. Some said he came to meet it—as though he *wanted* to die.

Segregationist

The surgeon looked up without expression. "Is he ready?"

"Ready is a relative term," said the med-eng. "*We're* ready. He's restless."

"They always are. . . . Well, it's a serious operation."

"Serious or not, he should be thankful. He's been chosen for it over an enormous number of possibles and frankly, I don't think . . ."

"Don't say it," said the surgeon. "The decision is not ours to make."

"We accept it. But do we have to agree?"

"Yes," said the surgeon, crisply. "We agree. Completely and wholeheartedly. The operation is entirely too intricate to approach with mental reservations. This man has proven his worth in a number of ways and his profile is suitable for the Board of Mortality."

"All right," said the med-eng, unmollified.

The surgeon said, "I'll see him right in here, I think. It is small enough and personal enough to be comforting."

"It won't help. He's nervous, and he's made up his mind."

"Has he indeed?"

"Yes. He wants metal; they always do."

The surgeon's face did not change expression. He stared at his hands. "Sometimes one can talk them out of it."

"Why bother?" said the med-eng, indifferently. "If he wants metal, let it be metal."

"You don't care?"

"Why should I?" The med-eng said it almost brutally. "Either way it's a medical engineering problem and I'm a medical engineer. Either way, I can handle it. Why should I go beyond that?"

The surgeon said stolidly, "To me, it is a matter of the fitness of things."

"Fitness! You can't use that as an argument. What does the patient care about the fitness of things?"

"I care."

"You care in a minority. The trend is against you. You have no chance."

"I have to try." The surgeon waved the med-eng into silence with a quick wave of his hand—no impatience to it, merely quickness. He had already informed the nurse and he had already been signaled concerning her approach. He pressed a small button and the double-door pulled swiftly apart. The patient moved inward in his motor-chair, the nurse stepping briskly along beside him.

"You may go, nurse," said the surgeon, "but wait outside. I will be calling you." He nodded to the med-eng, who left with the nurse, and the door closed behind them.

The man in the chair looked over his shoulder and watched them go. His neck was scrawny and there were fine wrinkles about his eyes. He was freshly shaven and the fingers of his hands, as they gripped the arms of the chair tightly, showed manicured nails. He was a high-priority patient and he was being taken care of. . . . But there was a look of settled peevishness on his face.

He said, "Will we be starting today?"

The surgeon nodded. "This afternoon, Senator."

"I understand it will take weeks."

"Not for the operation itself, Senator. But there are a number of subsidiary points to be taken care of. There are some circulatory renovations that must be carried through, and hormonal adjustments. These are tricky things."

"Are they dangerous?" Then, as though feeling the need for establishing a friendly relationship, but patently against his will, he added, ". . . doctor?"

The surgeon paid no attention to the nuances of expression. He said, flatly, "Everything is dangerous. We take our time in order that it be less dangerous. It is the time required, the skill of many individuals united, the equipment, that makes such operations available to so few . . ."

"I know that," said the patient, restlessly. "I refuse to feel guilty about that. Or are you implying improper pressure?"

"Not at all, Senator. The decisions of the Board have never been questioned. I mention the difficulty and intricacy of the operation merely to explain my desire to have it conducted in the best fashion possible."

"Well, do so, then. That is my desire, also."

"Then I must ask you to make a decision. It is possible to supply you with either of two types of cyber-hearts, metal or . . ."

"Plastic!" said the patient, irritably. "Isn't that the alternative you were going to offer, doctor? Cheap plastic. I don't want that. I've made my choice. I want the metal."

"But . . ."

"See here. I've been told the choice rests with me. Isn't that so?"

The surgeon nodded. "Where two alternate procedures are of equal value from a medical standpoint, the choice rests with the patient. In actual practice, the choice rests with the patient even when the alternate procedures are *not* of equal value, as in this case."

The patient's eyes narrowed. "Are you trying to tell me the plastic heart is superior?"

"It depends on the patient. In my opinion, in your individual case, it is. And we prefer not to use the term, plastic. It is a fibrous cyber-heart."

"It's plastic as far as I am concerned."

"Senator," said the surgeon, infinitely patient, "the material is not plastic in the ordinary sense of the word. It is a polymeric material true, but one that is far more complex than ordinary plastic. It is a complex protein-like fibre designed to imitate, as closely as possible, the natural structure of the human heart you now have within your chest."

"Exactly, and the human heart I now have within my chest is worn out although I am not yet sixty years old. I don't want another one like it, thank you. I want something better."

"We all want something better for you, Senator. The fibrous cyber-heart will be better. It has a potential life of centuries. It is absolutely non-allergenic . . ."

"Isn't that so for the metallic heart, too?"

"Yes, it is," said the surgeon. "The metallic cyber is of titanium alloy that . . ."

"And it doesn't wear out? And it is stronger than plastic? Or fibre or whatever you want to call it?"

"The metal is physically stronger, yes, but mechanical strength is not a point at issue. Its mechanical strength does you no particular good since the heart is well protected. Anything capable of reaching the heart will kill you for other reasons even if the heart stands up under manhandling."

The patient shrugged. "If I ever break a rib, I'll have that replaced by titanium, also. Replacing bones is easy. Anyone can have that done anytime. I'll be as metallic as I want to be, doctor."

"That is your right, if you so choose. However, it is only fair to tell you that although no metallic cyber-heart has ever broken down mechanically, a number have broken down electronically."

"What does that mean?"

"It means that every cyber-heart contains a pacemaker as part of its structure. In the case of the metallic variety, this is an electronic device that keeps the cyber in rhythm. It means an entire battery of miniaturized equipment must be included to alter the heart's rhythm to suit an individual's emotional and physical state. Occasionally something goes wrong there and people have died before that wrong could be corrected."

"I never heard of such a thing."

"I assure you it happens."

"Are you telling me it happens often?"

"Not at all. It happens very rarely."

"Well, then, I'll take my chance. What about the plastic heart? Doesn't that contain a pacemaker?"

"Of course it does, Senator. But the chemical structure of a fibrous cyber-heart is quite close to that of human tissue. It can respond to the ionic and hormonal controls of the body itself. The total complex that need be inserted is far simpler than in the case of the metal cyber."

"But doesn't the plastic heart ever pop out of hormonal control?"

"None has ever yet done so."

"Because you haven't been working with them long enough. Isn't that so?"

The surgeon hesitated. "It is true that the fibrous cybers have not been used nearly as long as the metallic."

"There you are. What is it anyway, doctor? Are you afraid I'm making myself into a robot . . . into a Metallo, as they call them since citizenship went through?"

"There is nothing wrong with a Metallo as a Metallo. As you say, they are citizens. But you're *not* a Metallo. You're a human being. Why not stay a human being?"

"Because I want the best and that's a metallic heart. You see to that."

The surgeon nodded. "Very well. You will be asked to sign the necessary permissions and you will then be fitted with a metal heart."

"And you'll be the surgeon in charge? They tell me you're the best."

"I will do what I can to make the changeover an easy one."

The door opened and the chair moved the patient out to the waiting nurse.

The med-eng came in, looking over his shoulder at the receding patient until the doors had closed again.

He turned to the surgeon. "Well, I can't tell what happened just by looking at you. What was his decision?"

The surgeon bent over his desk, punching out the final items for his records. "What you predicted. He insists on the metallic cyber-heart."

"After all, they are better."

"Not significantly. They've been around longer; no more than that. It's this mania that's been plaguing humanity ever since Metallos have become citizens. Men have this odd desire to make Metallos out of themselves. They yearn for the physical strength and endurance one associates with them."

"It isn't one-sided, doc. You don't work with Metallos but I do; so I know. The last two who came in for repairs have asked for fibrous elements."

"Did they get them?"

"In one case, it was just a matter of supplying tendons; it didn't make much difference there, metal or fibre. The other wanted a blood system or its equivalent. I told him I couldn't; not without a complete rebuilding of the structure of his body in fibrous material. . . . I suppose it will come to that some day. Metallos that aren't really Metallos at all, but a kind of flesh and blood."

"You don't mind that thought?"

"Why not? And metallized human beings, too. We have two varieties of intelligence on Earth now and why bother with two. Let them approach each other and eventually we won't be able to tell the difference. Why should we want to? We'd have the best of both worlds; the advantages of man combined with those of robot."

"You'd get a hybrid," said the surgeon, with something that approached fierceness. "You'd get something that is not both, but neither. Isn't it logical to suppose an individual would be too proud of his structure and identity to want to dilute it with something alien? Would he *want* mongrelization?"

"That's segregationist talk."

"Then let it be that." The surgeon said with calm emphasis, "I believe in being what one is. I wouldn't change a bit of my own structure for any reason. If some of it absolutely required replacement, I would have that replacement as close to the original in nature as could possibly be managed. I am *myself*; well pleased to be myself; and would not be anything else."

He had finished now and had to prepare for the operation. He placed his strong hands into the heating oven and let them reach the dull red-hot glow that would sterilize them completely. For all his impassioned words, his voice had never risen, and on his burnished metal face there was (as always) no sign of expression.

Robbie

"Ninety-eight—ninety-nine—*one hundred*." Gloria withdrew her chubby little forearm from before her eyes and stood for a moment, wrinkling her nose and blinking in the sunlight. Then, trying to watch in all directions at once, she withdrew a few cautious steps from the tree against which she had been leaning.

She craned her neck to investigate the possibilities of a clump of bushes to the right and then withdrew farther to obtain a better angle for viewing its dark recesses. The quiet was profound except for the incessant buzzing of insects and the occasional chirrup of some hardy bird, braving the midday sun.

Gloria pouted, "I bet he went inside the house, and I've told him a million times that that's not fair."

With tiny lips pressed together tightly and a severe frown crinkling her forehead, she moved determinedly toward the two-story building up past the driveway.

Too late she heard the rustling sound behind her, followed by the distinctive and rhythmic clump-clump of Robbie's metal feet. She whirled about to see her triumphing companion emerge from hiding and make for the home-tree at full speed.

Gloria shrieked in dismay. "Wait, Robbie! That wasn't fair, Robbie! You promised you wouldn't run until I found you." Her little feet could make no headway at all against Robbie's giant strides. Then, within ten feet of the goal, Robbie's pace slowed suddenly to the merest of crawls, and Gloria, with one final burst of wild speed, dashed pantingly past him to touch the welcome bark of home-tree first.

Gleefully, she turned on the faithful Robbie, and with the basest of ingratitude, rewarded him for his sacrifice, by taunting him cruelly for a lack of running ability.

"Robbie can't run," she shouted at the top of her eight-year-old voice. "I can beat him any day. I can beat him any day." She chanted the words in a shrill rhythm.

Robbie didn't answer, of course—not in words. He pantomimed running, instead, inching away until Gloria found herself running after him as he dodged her narrowly, forcing her to veer in helpless circles, little arms outstretched and fanning at the air.

"Robbie," she squealed, "stand still!" —And the laughter was forced out of her in breathless jerks.

—Until he turned suddenly and caught her up, whirling her round, so that for her the world fell away for a moment with a blue emptiness beneath, and green trees stretching hungrily downward toward the void. Then she was down in the grass again, leaning against Robbie's leg and still holding a hard, metal finger.

After a while, her breath returned. She pushed uselessly at her disheveled hair in vague imitation of one of her mother's gestures and twisted to see if her dress were torn.

She slapped her hand against Robbie's torso, "Bad boy! I'll spank you!"

And Robbie cowered, holding his hands over his face so that she had to add, "No, I won't, Robbie. I won't spank you. But anyway, it's my turn to hide now because you've got longer legs and you promised not to run till I found you."

Robbie nodded his head—a small parallelepiped with rounded edges and corners attached to a similar but much larger parallelepiped that served as torso by means of a short, flexible stalk—and obediently faced the tree. A thin, metal film descended over his glowing eyes and from within his body came a steady, resonant ticking.

"Don't peek now—and don't skip any numbers," warned Gloria, and scurried for cover.

With unvarying regularity, seconds were ticked off, and at the hundredth, up went the eyelids, and the glowing red of Robbie's eyes swept the prospect. They rested for a moment on a bit of colorful gingham that protruded from behind a boulder. He advanced a few steps and convinced himself that it was Gloria who squatted behind it.

Slowly, remaining always between Gloria and home-tree, he advanced on the hiding place, and when Gloria was plainly in sight and could no longer even theorize to herself that she was not seen, he extended one arm toward her, slapping the other against his leg so that it rang again. Gloria emerged sulkily.

"You peeked!" she exclaimed, with gross unfairness. "Besides I'm tired of playing hide-and-seek. I want a ride."

But Robbie was hurt at the unjust accusation, so he seated himself carefully and shook his head ponderously from side to side.

Gloria changed her tone to one of gentle coaxing immediately, "Come on, Robbie. I didn't mean it about the peeking. Give me a ride."

Robbie was not to be won over so easily, though. He gazed stubbornly at the sky, and shook his head even more emphatically.

"Please, Robbie, please give me a ride." She encircled his neck with rosy arms and hugged tightly. Then, changing moods in a moment, she moved away. "If you don't, I'm going to cry," and her face twisted appallingly in preparation.

Hard-hearted Robbie paid scant attention to this dreadful possibility, and shook his head a third time. Gloria found it necessary to play her trump card.

"If you don't," she exclaimed warmly, "I won't tell you any more stories, that's all. Not one—"

Robbie gave in immediately and unconditionally before this ultimatum, nodding his head vigorously until the metal of his neck hummed. Carefully, he raised the little girl and placed her on his broad, flat shoulders.

Gloria's threatened tears vanished immediately and she crowed with delight. Robbie's metal skin, kept at a constant temperature of seventy by the high resistance coils within felt nice and comfortable, while the beautifully loud sound her heels made as they bumped rhythmically against his chest was enchanting.

"You're an air-coaster, Robbie, you're a big, silver air-coaster. Hold out your arms straight. —You *got* to, Robbie, if you're going to be an air-coaster."

The logic was irrefutable. Robbie's arms were wings catching the air currents and he was a silver 'coaster.

Gloria twisted the robot's head and leaned to the right. He

banked sharply. Gloria equipped the 'coaster with a motor that went "Br-r-r" and then with weapons that went "Powie" and "Sh-sh-shshsh." Pirates were giving chase and the ship's blasters were coming into play. The pirates dropped in a steady rain.

"Got another one. —Two more," she cried.

Then "Faster, men," Gloria said pompously, "we're running out of ammunition." She aimed over her shoulder with undaunted courage and Robbie was a blunt-nosed spaceship zooming through the void at maximum acceleration.

Clear across the field he sped, to the patch of tall grass on the other side, where he stopped with a suddenness that evoked a shriek from his flushed rider, and then tumbled her onto the soft, green carpet.

Gloria gasped and panted, and gave voice to intermittent whispered exclamations of "That was *nice!*"

Robbie waited until she had caught her breath and then pulled gently at a lock of hair.

"You want something?" said Gloria, eyes wide in an apparently artless complexity that fooled her huge "nursemaid" not at all. He pulled the curl harder.

"Oh, I know. You want a story."

Robbie nodded rapidly.

"Which one?"

Robbie made a semi-circle in the air with one finger.

The little girl protested, "*Again?* I've told you Cinderella a million times. Aren't you tired of it? —It's for babies."

Another semi-circle.

"Oh, well," Gloria composed herself, ran over the details of the tale in her mind (together with her own elaborations, of which she had several) and began:

"Are you ready? Well—once upon a time there was a beautiful little girl whose name was Ella. And she had a terribly cruel step-mother and two very ugly and *very* cruel step-sisters and—"

Gloria was reaching the very climax of the tale—midnight was striking and everything was changing back to the shabby originals lickety-split, while Robbie listened tensely with burning eyes—when the interruption came.

"Gloria!"

It was the high-pitched sound of a woman who has been calling not once, but several times; and had the nervous tone of one in whom anxiety was beginning to overcome impatience.

"Mamma's calling me," said Gloria, not quite happily. "You'd better carry me back to the house, Robbie."

Robbie obeyed with alacrity for somehow there was that in him which judged it best to obey Mrs. Weston, without as much as a scrap of hesitation. Gloria's father was rarely home in the daytime except on Sunday—today, for instance—and when he was, he proved a genial and understanding person. Gloria's mother, however, was a source of uneasiness to Robbie and there was always the impulse to sneak away from her sight.

Mrs. Weston caught sight of them the minute they rose above the masking tufts of long grass and retired inside the house to wait.

"I've shouted myself hoarse, Gloria," she said, severely. "Where were you?"

"I was with Robbie," quavered Gloria. "I was telling him Cinderella, and I forgot it was dinner-time."

"Well, it's a pity Robbie forgot, too." Then, as if that reminded her of the robot's presence, she whirled upon him. "You may go, Robbie. She doesn't need you now." Then, brutally, "And don't come back till I call you."

Robbie turned to go, but hesitated as Gloria cried out in his defense, "Wait, Mamma, you got to let him stay. I didn't finish Cinderella for him. I said I would tell him Cinderella and I'm not finished."

"Gloria!"

"Honest and truly, Mamma, he'll stay so quiet, you won't even know he's here. He can sit on the chair in the corner, and he won't say a word,—I mean he won't *do* anything. Will you, Robbie?"

Robbie, appealed to, nodded his massive head up and down once.

"Gloria, if you don't stop this at once, you shan't see Robbie for a whole week."

The girl's eyes fell, "All right! But Cinderella is his favorite story and I didn't finish it. —And he likes it so much."

The robot left with a disconsolate step and Gloria choked back a sob.

George Weston was comfortable. It was a habit of his to be comfortable on Sunday afternoons. A good, hearty dinner below the hatches; a nice, soft, dilapidated couch on which to sprawl; a copy of the *Times*; slippered feet and shirtless chest;—how could anyone *help* but be comfortable?

He wasn't pleased, therefore, when his wife walked in. After ten years of married life, he still was so unutterably foolish as to love her, and there was no question that he was always glad to see her— still Sunday afternoons just after dinner were sacred to him and his idea of solid comfort was to be left in utter solitude for two or three hours. Consequently, he fixed his eye firmly upon the latest reports of the Lefebre-Yoshida expedition to Mars (this one was to take off from Lunar Base and might actually succeed) and pretended she wasn't there.

Mrs. Weston waited patiently for two minutes, then impatiently for two more, and finally broke the silence.

"George!"

"Hmpph?"

"George, I say! *Will* you put down that paper and look at me?"

The paper rustled to the floor and Weston turned a weary face toward his wife, "What is it, dear?"

"You know what it is, George. It's Gloria and that terrible machine."

"What terrible machine?"

"Now don't pretend you don't know what I'm talking about. It's that robot Gloria calls Robbie. He doesn't leave her for a moment."

"Well, why should he? He's not supposed to. And he certainly isn't a terrible machine. He's the best darn robot money can buy and I'm damned sure he set me back half a year's income. He's worth it, though—darn sight cleverer than half my office staff."

He made a move to pick up the paper again, but his wife was quicker and snatched it away.

"You listen to *me*, George. I won't have my daughter entrusted to a machine—and I don't care how clever it is. It has no soul, and no one knows what it may be thinking. A child just isn't *made* to be guarded by a thing of metal."

Weston frowned, "When did you decide this? He's been with Gloria two years now and I haven't seen you worry till now."

"It was different at first. It was a novelty; it took a load off me, and—and it was a fashionable thing to do. But now I don't know. The neighbors—"

"Well, what have the neighbors to do with it? Now, look. A robot is infinitely more to be trusted than a human nursemaid. Robbie was constructed for only one purpose really—to be the companion of a little child. His entire 'mentality' has been created for the purpose. He just can't help being faithful and loving and kind. He's a machine—*made so*. That's more than you can say for humans."

"But something might go wrong. Some—some—" Mrs. Weston was a bit hazy about the insides of a robot, "some little jigger will come loose and the awful thing will go berserk and—and—" She couldn't bring herself to complete the quite obvious thought.

"Nonsense," Weston denied, with an involuntary nervous shiver. "That's completely ridiculous. We had a long discussion at the time we bought Robbie about the First Law of Robotics. You *know* that it is impossible for a robot to harm a human being; that long before enough can go wrong to alter that First Law, a robot would be completely inoperable. It's a mathematical impossibility. Besides I have an engineer from U. S. Robots here twice a year to give the poor gadget a complete overhaul. Why, there's no more chance of anything at all going wrong with Robbie than there is of you or I suddenly going looney—considerably less, in fact. Besides, how are you going to take him away from Gloria?"

He made another futile stab at the paper and his wife tossed it angrily into the next room.

"That's just it, George! She won't play with anyone else. There are dozens of little boys and girls that she should make friends with, but she won't. She won't go *near* them unless I make her. That's no way for a little girl to grow up. You want her to be normal, don't you? You want her to be able to take her part in society."

"You're jumping at shadows, Grace. Pretend Robbie's a dog. I've seen hundreds of children who would rather have their dog than their father."

"A dog is different, George. We *must* get rid of that horrible thing. You can sell it back to the company. I've asked, and you can."

"You've *asked*? Now look here, Grace, let's not go off the deep end. We're keeping the robot until Gloria is older and I don't want the subject brought up again." And with that he walked out of the room in a huff.

Mrs. Weston met her husband at the door two evenings later. "You'll have to listen to this, George. There's bad feeling in the village."

"About what?" asked Weston. He stepped into the washroom and drowned out any possible answer by the splash of water.

Mrs. Weston waited. She said, "About Robbie."

Weston stepped out, towel in hand, face red and angry, "What are you talking about?"

"Oh, it's been building up and building up. I've tried to close my eyes to it, but I'm not going to any more. Most of the villagers consider Robbie dangerous. Children aren't allowed to go near our place in the evenings."

"We trust *our* child with the thing."

"Well, people aren't reasonable about these things."

"Then to hell with them."

"Saying that doesn't solve the problem. I've got to do my shopping down there. I've got to meet them every day. And it's even worse in the city these days when it comes to robots. New York has just passed an ordinance keeping all robots off the streets between sunset and sunrise."

"All right, but they can't stop us from keeping a robot in our home. —Grace, this is one of your campaigns. I recognize it. But it's no use. The answer is still, no! We're keeping Robbie!"

And yet he loved his wife—and what was worse, his wife knew it. George Weston, after all, was only a man—poor thing—and his wife made full use of every device which a clumsier and more scrupulous sex has learned, with reason and futility, to fear.

Ten times in the ensuing week, he cried, "Robbie stays,—and that's *final!*" and each time it was weaker and accompanied by a louder and more agonized groan.

Came the day at last, when Weston approached his daughter guiltily and suggested a "beautiful" visivox show in the village.

Gloria clapped her hands happily, "Can Robbie go?"

"No, dear," he said, and winced at the sound of his voice, "they won't allow robots at the visivox—but you can tell him all about it when you get home." He stumbled all over the last few words and looked away.

Gloria came back from town bubbling over with enthusiasm, for the visivox had been a gorgeous spectacle indeed.

She waited for her father to maneuver the jet-car into the sunken garage. "Wait till I tell Robbie, Daddy. He would have liked it like anything. —Especially when Francis Fran was backing away so-o-o quietly, and backed right into one of the Leopard-Men and had to run." She laughed again, "Daddy, are there really Leopard-Men on the Moon?"

"Probably not," said Weston absently. "It's just funny make-believe." He couldn't take much longer with the car. He'd have to face it.

Gloria ran across the lawn. "Robbie. —Robbie!"

Then she stopped suddenly at the sight of a beautiful collie which regarded her out of serious brown eyes as it wagged its tail on the porch.

"Oh, what a nice dog!" Gloria climbed the steps, approached cautiously and patted it. "Is it for me, Daddy?"

Her mother had joined them. "Yes, it is, Gloria. Isn't it nice—soft and furry. It's very gentle. It *likes* little girls."

"Can he play games?"

"Surely. He can do any number of tricks. Would you like to see some?"

"Right away. I want Robbie to see him, too. —*Robbie!*" She stopped, uncertainly, and frowned, "I'll bet he's just staying in his room because he's mad at me for not taking him to the visivox. You'll have to explain to him, Daddy. He might not believe me, but he knows if you say it, it's so."

Weston's lips grew tighter. He looked toward his wife but could not catch her eye.

Gloria turned precipitously and ran down the basement steps, shouting as she went, "Robbie— Come and see what Daddy and Mamma brought me. They brought me a dog, Robbie."

In a minute she had returned, a frightened little girl. "Mamma, Robbie isn't in his room. Where is he?" There was no answer and George Weston coughed and was suddenly extremely interested in an aimlessly drifting cloud. Gloria's voice quavered on the verge of tears, "Where's Robbie, Mamma?"

Mrs. Weston sat down and drew her daughter gently to her, "Don't feel bad, Gloria. Robbie has gone away, I think."

"Gone *away?* Where? Where's he gone away, Mamma?"

"No one knows, darling. He just walked away. We've looked and we've looked and we've looked for him, but we can't find him."

"You mean he'll never come back again?" Her eyes were round with horror.

"We may find him soon. We'll keep looking for him. And meanwhile you can play with your nice new doggie. Look at him! His name is Lightning and he can—"

But Gloria's eyelids had overflown, "I don't want the nasty dog—I want Robbie. I want you to find me Robbie." Her feelings became too deep for words, and she spluttered into a shrill wail.

Mrs. Weston glanced at her husband for help, but he merely shuffled his feet morosely and did not withdraw his ardent stare from the heavens, so she bent to the task of consolation, "Why do you cry, Gloria? Robbie was only a machine, just a nasty old machine. He wasn't alive at all."

"He was *not* no machine!" screamed Gloria, fiercely and ungrammatically. "He was a *person* just like you and me and he was my *friend*. I want him back. Oh, Mamma, I want him back."

Her mother groaned in defeat and left Gloria to her sorrow.

"Let her have her cry out," she told her husband. "Childish griefs are never lasting. In a few days, she'll forget that awful robot ever existed."

But time proved Mrs. Weston a bit too optimistic. To be sure, Gloria ceased crying, but she ceased smiling, too, and the passing days found her ever more silent and shadowy. Gradually, her attitude of passive unhappiness wore Mrs. Weston down and all that kept her from yielding was the impossibility of admitting defeat to her husband.

Then, one evening, she flounced into the living room, sat down, folded her arms and looked boiling mad.

Her husband stretched his neck in order to see her over his newspaper, "What now, Grace?"

"It's that child, George. I've had to send back the dog today. Gloria positively couldn't stand the sight of him, she said. She's driving me into a nervous breakdown."

Weston laid down the paper and a hopeful gleam entered his eye, "Maybe— Maybe we ought to get Robbie back. It might be done, you know. I can get in touch with—"

"No!" she replied, grimly. "I won't hear of it. We're not giving up that easily. My child shall *not* be brought up by a robot if it takes years to break her of it."

Weston picked up his paper again with a disappointed air. "A year of this will have me prematurely gray."

"You're a big help, George," was the frigid answer. "What Gloria needs is a change of environment. Of course she can't forget Robbie here. How can she when every tree and rock reminds her of him? It is really the *silliest* situation I have ever heard of. Imagine a child pining away for the loss of a robot."

"Well, stick to the point. What's the change in environment you're planning?"

"We're going to take her to New York."

"The city! In August! Say, do you know what New York is like in August? It's unbearable."

"Millions do bear it."

"They don't have a place like this to go to. If they didn't have to stay in New York, they wouldn't."

"Well, *we* have to. I say we're leaving now—or as soon as we can make the arrangements. In the city, Gloria will find sufficient interests and sufficient friends to perk her up and make her forget that machine."

"Oh, Lord," groaned the lesser half, "those frying pavements!"

"We have to," was the unshaken response. "Gloria has lost five pounds in the last month and my little girl's health is more important to me than your comfort."

"It's a pity you didn't think of your little girl's health before you deprived her of her pet robot," he muttered—but to himself.

Gloria displayed immediate signs of improvement when told of the impending trip to the city. She spoke little of it, but when she did, it was always with lively anticipation. Again, she began to smile and to eat with something of her former appetite.

Mrs. Weston hugged herself for joy and lost no opportunity to triumph over her still skeptical husband.

"You see, George, she helps with the packing like a little angel, and chatters away as if she hadn't a care in the world. It's just as I told you—all we need do is substitute other interests."

"Hmpph," was the skeptical response, "I hope so."

Preliminaries were gone through quickly. Arrangements were made for the preparation of their city home and a couple were engaged as housekeepers for the country home. When the day of the trip finally did come, Gloria was all but her old self again, and no mention of Robbie passed her lips at all.

In high good-humor the family took a taxi-gyro to the airport

(Weston would have preferred using his own private 'gyro, but it was only a two-seater with no room for baggage) and entered the waiting liner.

"Come, Gloria," called Mrs. Weston. "I've saved you a seat near the window so you can watch the scenery."

Gloria trotted down the aisle cheerily, flattened her nose into a white oval against the thick clear glass, and watched with an intentness that increased as the sudden coughing of the motor drifted backward into the interior. She was too young to be frightened when the ground dropped away as if let through a trap-door and she herself suddenly became twice her usual weight, but not too young to be mightily interested. It wasn't until the ground had changed into a tiny patch-work quilt that she withdrew her nose, and faced her mother again.

"Will we soon be in the city, Mamma?" she asked, rubbing her chilled nose, and watching with interest as the patch of moisture which her breath had formed on the pane shrank slowly and vanished.

"In about half an hour, dear." Then, with just the faintest trace of anxiety, "Aren't you glad we're going? Don't you think you'll be very happy in the city with all the buildings and people and things to see? We'll go to the visivox every day and see shows and go to the circus and the beach and—"

"Yes, Mamma," was Gloria's unenthusiastic rejoinder. The liner passed over a bank of clouds at the moment, and Gloria was instantly absorbed in the unusual spectacle of clouds underneath one. Then they were over clear sky again, and she turned to her mother with a sudden mysterious air of secret knowledge.

"I know why we're going to the city, Mamma."

"Do you?" Mrs. Weston was puzzled. "Why, dear?"

"You didn't tell me because you wanted it to be a surprise, but I know." For a moment, she was lost in admiration at her own acute penetration, and then she laughed gaily. "We're going to New York so we can find Robbie, aren't we? —With detectives."

The statement caught George Weston in the middle of a drink of water, with disastrous results. There was a sort of strangled gasp, a geyser of water, and then a bout of choking coughs. When all was over, he stood there, a red-faced, water-drenched and very, very annoyed person.

Mrs. Weston maintained her composure, but when Gloria repeated her question in a more anxious tone of voice, she found her temper rather bent.

"Maybe," she retorted, tartly. "Now sit and be still, for Heaven's sake."

New York City, 1998 A.D., was a paradise for the sight-seer more than ever in its history. Gloria's parents realized this and made the most of it.

On direct orders from his wife, George Weston arranged to have his business take care of itself for a month or so, in order to be free to spend the time in what he termed "dissipating Gloria to the verge of ruin." Like everything else Weston did, this was gone about in an efficient, thorough, and business-like way. Before the month had passed, nothing that could be done had not been done.

She was taken to the top of the half-mile-tall Roosevelt Building, to gaze down in awe upon the jagged panorama of rooftops that blended far off in the fields of Long Island and the flatlands of New Jersey. They visited the zoos where Gloria stared in delicious fright at the "real live lion" (rather disappointed that the keepers fed him raw steaks, instead of human beings, as she had expected), and asked insistently and peremptorily to see "the whale."

The various museums came in for their share of attention, together with the parks and the beaches and the aquarium.

She was taken halfway up the Hudson in an excursion steamer fitted out in the archaism of the mad Twenties. She travelled into the stratosphere on an exhibition trip, where the sky turned deep purple and the stars came out and the misty earth below looked like a huge concave bowl. Down under the waters of the Long Island Sound she was taken in a glass-walled sub-sea vessel, where in a green and wavering world, quaint and curious sea-things ogled her and wiggled suddenly away.

On a more prosaic level, Mrs. Weston took her to the department stores where she could revel in another type of fairyland.

In fact, when the month had nearly sped, the Westons were convinced that everything conceivable had been done to take Gloria's mind once and for all off the departed Robbie—but they were not quite sure they had succeeded.

The fact remained that wherever Gloria went, she displayed the most absorbed and concentrated interest in such robots as happened to be present. No matter how exciting the spectacle before her, nor how novel to her girlish eyes, she turned away instantly if the corner of her eye caught a glimpse of metallic movement.

Mrs. Weston went out of her way to keep Gloria away from all robots.

And the matter was finally climaxed in the episode at the Museum of Science and Industry. The Museum had announced a special "children's program" in which exhibits of scientific witchery scaled down to the child mind were to be shown. The Westons, of course, placed it upon their list of "absolutely."

It was while the Westons were standing totally absorbed in the exploits of a powerful electro-magnet that Mrs. Weston suddenly became aware of the fact that Gloria was no longer with her. Initial panic gave way to calm decision and, enlisting the aid of three attendants, a careful search was begun.

Gloria, of course, was not one to wander aimlessly, however. For her age, she was an unusually determined and purposeful girl, quite full of the maternal genes in that respect. She had seen a huge sign on the third floor, which had said, "This Way to the Talking Robot." Having spelled it out to herself and having noticed that her parents did not seem to wish to move in the proper direction, she did the obvious thing. Waiting for an opportune moment of parental distraction, she calmly disengaged herself and followed the sign.

The Talking Robot was a *tour de force*, a thoroughly impractical device, possessing publicity value only. Once an hour, an escorted group stood before it and asked questions of the robot engineer in charge in careful whispers. Those the engineer decided were suitable for the robot's circuits were transmitted to the Talking Robot.

It was rather dull. It may be nice to know that the square of fourteen is one hundred ninety-six, that the temperature at the moment is 72 degrees Fahrenheit, and the air-pressure 30.02 inches of mercury, that the atomic weight of sodium is 23, but one doesn't really need a robot for that. One especially does not need an unwieldy, totally immobile mass of wires and coils spreading over twenty-five square yards.

Few people bothered to return for a second helping, but one girl in her middle teens sat quietly on a bench waiting for a third. She was the only one in the room when Gloria entered.

Gloria did not look at her. To her at the moment, another human being was but an inconsiderable item. She saved her attention for this large thing with the wheels. For a moment, she hesitated in dismay. It didn't look like any robot she had ever seen.

Cautiously and doubtfully she raised her treble voice, "Please, Mr. Robot, sir, are you the Talking Robot, sir?" She wasn't sure, but it seemed to her that a robot that actually talked was worth a great deal of politeness.

(The girl in her mid-teens allowed a look of intense concentration to cross her thin, plain face. She whipped out a small notebook and began writing in rapid pot-hooks.)

There was an oily whir of gears and a mechanically-timbred voice boomed out in words that lacked accent and intonation, "I—am—the—robot—that—talks."

Gloria stared at it ruefully. It *did* talk, but the sound came from inside somewheres. There was no *face* to talk to. She said, "Can you help me, Mr. Robot, sir?"

The Talking Robot was designed to answer questions, and only such questions as it could answer had ever been put to it. It was quite confident of its ability, therefore, "I—can—help—you."

"Thank you, Mr. Robot sir. Have you seen Robbie?"

"Who—is—Robbie?"

"He's a robot, Mr. Robot, sir." She stretched to tip-toes. "He's about so high, Mr. Robot, sir, only higher, and he's very nice. He's got a head, you know. I mean you haven't, but he has, Mr. Robot, sir."

The Talking Robot had been left behind, "A—robot?"

"Yes, Mr. Robot, sir. A robot just like you, except he can't talk, of course, and—looks like a real person."

"A—robot—like—me?"

"Yes, Mr. Robot, sir."

To which the Talking Robot's only response was an erratic splutter and an occasional incoherent sound. The radical generalization offered it, i.e., its existence, not as a particular object, but as a member of a general group, was too much for it. Loyally, it tried to encompass the concept and half a dozen coils burnt out. Little warning signals were buzzing.

(The girl in her mid-teens left at that point. She had enough for her Physics-1 paper on "Practical Aspects of Robotics." This paper was Susan Calvin's first of many on the subject).

Gloria stood waiting, with carefully concealed impatience, for the machine's answer when she heard the cry behind her of "There she is," and recognized that cry as her mother's.

"What are you doing here, you bad girl?" cried Mrs. Weston, anxiety dissolving at once into anger. "Do you know you frightened your mamma and daddy almost to death? Why did you run away?"

The robot engineer had also dashed in, tearing his hair, and demanding who of the gathering crowd had tampered with the machine. "Can't anybody read signs?" he yelled. "You're not allowed in here without an attendant."

Gloria raised her grieved voice over the din, "I only came to see the Talking Robot, Mamma. I thought he might know where Robbie was because they're both robots." And then, as the thought of Robbie was suddenly brought forcefully home to her, she burst into a sudden storm of tears, "And I *got* to find Robbie, Mamma. I *got* to."

Mrs. Weston strangled a cry, and said, "Oh, good Heavens. Come home, George. This is more than I can stand."

That evening, George Weston left for several hours, and the next morning, he approached his wife with something that looked suspiciously like smug complacence.

"I've got an idea, Grace."

"About what?" was the gloomy, uninterested query.

"About Gloria."

"You're not going to suggest buying back that robot?"

"No, of course not."

"Then go ahead. I might as well listen to you. Nothing *I've* done seems to have done any good."

"All right. Here's what I've been thinking. The whole trouble with Gloria is that she thinks of Robbie as a *person* and not as a *machine*. Naturally, she can't forget him. Now if we managed to convince her that Robbie was nothing more than a mess of steel and copper in the form of sheets and wires with electricity its juice of life, how long would her longings last? It's the psychological attack, if you see my point."

"How do you plan to do it?"

"Simple. Where do you suppose I went last night? I persuaded Robertson of U. S. Robots and Mechanical Men Corporation to arrange for a complete tour of his premises tomorrow. The three of us will go, and by the time we're through, Gloria will have it drilled into her that a robot is *not* alive."

Mrs. Weston's eyes widened gradually and something glinted in her eyes that was quite like sudden admiration, "Why, George, that's a *good* idea."

And George Weston's vest buttons strained. "Only kind I have," he said.

Mr. Struthers was a conscientious General Manager and naturally inclined to be a bit talkative. The combination, therefore, resulted in a tour that was fully explained, perhaps even overabundantly explained, at every step. However, Mrs. Weston was not bored. Indeed, she stopped him several times and begged him to repeat his statements in simpler language so that Gloria might understand. Under the influence of this appreciation of his narrative powers, Mr. Struthers expanded genially and became ever more communicative, if possible.

George Weston, himself, showed a gathering impatience.

"Pardon me, Struthers," he said, breaking into the middle of a lecture on the photo-electric cell, "haven't you a section of the factory where only robot labor is employed?"

"Eh? Oh, yes! Yes, indeed!" He smiled at Mrs. Weston. "A vicious circle in a way, robots creating more robots. Of course, we are not making a general practice out of it. For one thing, the unions would never let us. But we can turn out a very few robots using robot labor exclusively, merely as a sort of scientific experiment. You see," he tapped his pince-nez into one palm argumentatively, "what the labor unions don't realize—and I say this as a man who has always been very sympathetic with the labor movement in general—is that the advent of the robot, while involving some dislocation to begin with, will, inevitably—"

"Yes, Struthers," said Weston, "but about that section of the factory you speak of—may we see it? It would be very interesting, I'm sure."

"Yes! Yes, of course!" Mr. Struthers replaced his pince-nez in one convulsive movement and gave vent to a soft cough of discomfiture. "Follow me, please."

He was comparatively quiet while leading the three through a long corridor and down a flight of stairs. Then, when they had entered a large well-lit room that buzzed with metallic activity, the sluices opened and the flood of explanation poured forth again.

"There you are!" he said with pride in his voice. "Robots only! Five men act as overseers and they don't even stay in this room. In five years, that is, since we began this project, not a single accident has occurred. Of course, the robots here assembled are comparatively simple, but . . ."

The General Manager's voice had long died to a rather soothing murmur in Gloria's ears. The whole trip seemed rather dull and pointless to her, though there *were* many robots in sight. None were even remotely like Robbie, though, and she surveyed them with open contempt.

In this room, there weren't any people at all, she noticed. Then her eyes fell upon six or seven robots busily engaged at a round table halfway across the room. They widened in incredulous surprise. It was a big room. She couldn't see for sure, but one of the robots looked like—looked like—*it was!*

"*Robbie!*" Her shriek pierced the air, and one of the robots about the table faltered and dropped the tool he was holding. Gloria went almost mad with joy. Squeezing through the railing before either parent could stop her, she dropped lightly to the floor a few feet below, and ran toward her Robbie, arms waving and hair flying.

And the three horrified adults, as they stood frozen in their tracks, saw what the excited little girl did not see,—a huge, lumbering tractor bearing blindly down upon its appointed track.

It took split-seconds for Weston to come to his senses, and those split-seconds meant everything, for Gloria could not be overtaken. Although Weston vaulted the railing in a wild attempt, it was obviously hopeless. Mr. Struthers signalled wildy to the overseers to stop the tractor, but the overseers were only human and it took time to act.

It was only Robbie that acted immediately and with precision.

With metal legs eating up the space between himself and his little mistress he charged down from the opposite direction. Everything then happened at once. With one sweep of an arm, Robbie snatched up Gloria, slackening his speed not one iota, and, consequently, knocking every breath of air out of her. Weston, not quite comprehending all that was happening, felt, rather than saw, Robbie brush past him, and came to a sudden bewildered halt. The tractor intersected Gloria's path half a second after Robbie had, rolled on ten feet further and came to a grinding, long-drawn-out stop.

Gloria regained her breath, submitted to a series of passionate hugs on the part of both her parents and turned eagerly toward Robbie. As far as she was concerned, nothing had happened except that she had found her friend.

But Mrs. Weston's expression had changed from one of relief to one of dark suspicion. She turned to her husband, and, despite her disheveled and undignified appearance, managed to look quite formidable, "*You* engineered this, *didn't* you?"

George Weston swabbed at a hot forehead with his handkerchief. His hand was unsteady, and his lips could curve only into a tremulous and exceedingly weak smile.

Mrs. Weston pursued the thought, "Robbie wasn't designed for engineering or construction work. He couldn't be of any use to them. You had him placed there deliberately so that Gloria would find him. You know you did."

"Well, I did," said Weston. "But, Grace, how was I to know the reunion would be so violent? And Robbie has saved her life; you'll have to admit that. You *can't* send him away again."

Grace Weston considered. She turned toward Gloria and Robbie and watched them abstractedly for a moment. Gloria had a grip about the robot's neck that would have asphyxiated any creature but one of metal, and was prattling nonsense in half-hysterical frenzy. Robbie's chrome-steel arms (capable of bending a bar of steel two inches in diameter into a pretzel) wound about the little girl gently and lovingly, and his eyes glowed a deep, deep red.

"Well," said Mrs. Weston, at last, "I guess he can stay with us until he rusts."

Some Humanoid Robots

In science fiction it is not uncommon to have a robot built with a surface, at least, of synthetic flesh; and an appearance that is, at best, indistinguishable from the human being. Sometimes such humanoid robots are called "androids" (from a Greek term meaning "manlike") and some writers are meticulous in making the distinction. I am not. To me a robot is a robot.

But then, Karel Čapek's play *R.U.R.*, which introduced the term "robot" to the world in 1920, did not involve robots in the strictest sense of the word. The robots manufactured by Rossum's Universal Robots (the "R.U.R." of the title) were androids.

One of the three stories in this section, "Let's Get Together," is the only story in the book in which robots don't actually appear, and "Mirror Image" is a sequel (of sorts) to my robot novels THE CAVES OF STEEL and THE NAKED SUN.

Let's Get Together

A kind of peace had endured for a century and people had forgotten what anything else was like. They would scarcely have known how to react had they discovered that a kind of war had finally come.

Certainly, Elias Lynn, Chief of the Bureau of Robotics, wasn't sure how he ought to react when *he* finally found out. The Bureau of Robotics was headquarted in Cheyenne, in line with the century-old trend toward decentralization, and Lynn stared dubiously at the young Security officer from Washington who had brought the news.

Elias Lynn was a large man, almost charmingly homely, with pale blue eyes that bulged a bit. Men weren't usually comfortable under the stare of those eyes, but the Security officer remained calm.

Lynn decided that his first reaction ought to be incredulity. Hell, it *was* incredulity! He just didn't believe it!

He eased himself back in his chair and said, "How certain is the information?"

The Security officer, who had introduced himself as Ralph G. Breckenridge and had presented credentials to match, had the softness of youth about him; full lips, plump cheeks that flushed easily, and guileless eyes. His clothing was out of line with Cheyenne but it suited a universally air-conditioned Washington, where Security, despite everything, was still centered.

Breckenridge flushed and said, "There's no doubt about it."

"You people know all about Them, I suppose," said Lynn and was unable to keep a trace of sarcasm out of his tone. He was not particularly aware of his use of a slightly stressed pronoun in his reference to the enemy, the equivalent of capitalization in print. It was a cultural habit of this generation and the one preceding. No one said the "East" or the "Reds" or the "Soviets" or the "Russians" any more. That would have been too confusing, since some of Them weren't of the East, weren't Reds, Soviets, and especially not Russians. It was much simpler to say We and They, and much more precise.

Travelers had frequently reported that They did the same in reverse. Over there, They were "We" (in the appropriate language) and We were "They."

Scarcely anyone gave thought to such things any more. It was all quite comfortable and casual. There was no hatred, even. At the beginning, it had been called a Cold War. Now it was only a game, almost a good-natured game, with unspoken rules and a kind of decency about it.

Lynn said abruptly, "Why should They want to disturb the situation?"

He rose and stood staring at a wall map of the world, split into two regions with faint edgings of color. An irregular portion on the left of the map was edged in a mild green. A smaller, but just as irregular, portion on the right of the map was bordered in a washed-out pink. We and They.

The map hadn't changed much in a century. The loss of Formosa and the gain of East Germany some eighty years before had been the last territorial switch of importance.

There had been another change, though, that was significant enough and that was in the colors. Two generations before, Their territory had been a brooding, bloody red, Ours a pure and undefiled white. Now there was a neutrality about the colors. Lynn had seen Their maps and it was the same on Their side.

"They wouldn't do it," he said.

"They are doing it," said Breckenridge, "and you had better accustom yourself to the fact. Of course, sir, I realize that it isn't pleasant to think that They may be that far ahead of us in robotics."

His eyes remained as guileless as ever, but the hidden knife-edges of the words plunged deep, and Lynn quivered at the impact.

Of course, that would account for why the Chief of Robotics learned of this so late and through a Security officer at that. He had lost caste in the eyes of the Government; if Robotics had really failed in the struggle, Lynn could expect no political mercy.

Lynn said wearily, "Even if what you say is true, They're not far ahead of us. We could build humanoid robots."

"Have we, sir?"

"Yes. As a matter of fact, we have built a few models for experimental purposes."

"They were doing so ten years ago. They've made ten years' progress since."

Lynn was disturbed. He wondered if his incredulity concerning the whole business was really the result of wounded pride and fear for his job and reputation. He was embarrassed by the possibility that this might be so, and yet he was forced into defense.

He said, "Look, young man, the stalemate between Them and Us was never perfect in every detail, you know. They have always been ahead in one facet or another and We in some other facet or another. If They're ahead of us right now in robotics, it's because They've placed a greater proportion of Their effort into robotics than We have. And that means that some other branch of endeavor has received a greater share of Our efforts than it has to Theirs. It would mean We're ahead in force-field research or in hyperatomics, perhaps."

Lynn felt distressed at his own statement that the stalemate wasn't perfect. It was true enough, but that was the one great danger threatening the world. The world depended on the stalemate being as perfect as possible. If the small unevennesses that always existed overbalanced too far in one direction or the other—

Almost at the beginning of what had been the Cold War, both sides had developed thermonuclear weapons, and war became unthinkable. Competition switched from the military to the economic and psychological and had stayed there ever since.

But always there was the driving effort on each side to break the stalemate, to develop a parry for every possible thrust, to develop a thrust that could not be parried in time—something that would make war possible again. And that was not because either side wanted war so desperately, but because both were afraid that the other side would make the crucial discovery first.

For a hundred years each side had kept the struggle even. And in the process, peace had been maintained for a hundred years while, as byproducts of the continuously intensive research, force fields had been produced and solar energy and insect control and robots. Each side was making a beginning in the understanding of mentalics, which was the name given to the biochemistry and biophysics of thought. Each side had its outposts on the Moon and on Mars. Mankind was advancing in giant strides under forced draft.

It was even necessary for both sides to be as decent and humane as possible among themselves, lest through cruelty and tyranny, friends be made for the other side.

It couldn't be that the stalemate would now be broken and that there would be war.

Lynn said, "I want to consult one of my men. I want his opinion."

"Is he trustworthy?"

Lynn looked disgusted. "Good Lord, what man in Robotics has not been investigated and cleared to death by your people? Yes, I vouch for him. If you can't trust a man like Humphrey Carl Laszlo, then we're in no position to face the kind of attack you say They are launching, no matter what else we do."

"I've heard of Laszlo," said Breckenridge.

"Good. Does he pass?"

"Yes."

"Then, I'll have him in and we'll find out what he thinks about the possibility that robots could invade the U.S.A."

"Not exactly," said Breckenridge, softly. "You still don't accept the full truth. Find out what he thinks about the fact that robots have *already* invaded the U.S.A."

Laszlo was the grandson of a Hungarian who had broken through what had then been called the Iron Curtain, and he had a comfortable above-suspicion feeling about himself because of it. He was thick-set and balding with a pugnacious look graven forever on his snub face, but his accent was clear Harvard and he was almost excessively soft-spoken.

To Lynn, who was conscious that after years of administration he was no longer expert in the various phases of modern robotics, Laszlo was a comforting receptacle for complete knowledge. Lynn felt better because of the man's mere presence.

Lynn said, "What do you think?"

A scowl twisted Laszlo's face ferociously. "That They're that far ahead of us. Completely incredible. It would mean They've produced humanoids that could not be told from humans at close quarters. It would mean a considerable advance in robo-mentalics."

"You're personally involved," said Breckenridge, coldly. "Leaving professional pride out of account, exactly why is it impossible that They be ahead of Us?"

Laszlo shrugged. "I assure you that I'm well acquainted with Their literature on robotics. I know approximately where They are."

"You know approximately where They want you to *think* They are, is what you really mean," corrected Breckenridge. "Have you ever visited the other side?"

"I haven't," said Laszlo, shortly.

"Nor you, Dr. Lynn?"

Lynn said, "No, I haven't, either."

Breckenridge said, "Has any robotics man visited the other side in twenty-five years?" He asked the question with a kind of confidence that indicated he knew the answer.

For a matter of seconds, the atmosphere was heavy with thought. Discomfort crossed Lazlo's broad face. He said, "As a matter of fact, They haven't held any conferences on robotics in a long time."

"In twenty-five years," said Breckenridge. "Isn't that significant?"

"Maybe," said Laszlo, reluctantly. "Something else bothers me, though. None of Them have ever come to Our conferences on robotics. None that I can remember."

"Were They invited?" asked Breckenridge.

Lynn, staring and worried, interposed quickly, "Of course."

Breckenridge said, "Do They refuse attendance to any other types of scientific conferences We hold?"

"I don't know," said Laszlo. He was pacing the floor now. "I haven't heard of any cases. Have you, Chief?"

"No," said Lynn.

Breckenridge said, "Wouldn't you say it was as though They didn't want to be put in the position of having to return any such invitation? Or as though They were afraid one of Their men might talk too much?"

That was exactly how it seemed, and Lynn felt a helpless conviction that Security's story was true after all steal over him.

Why else had there been no contact between sides on robotics? There had been a cross-fertilizing trickle of researchers moving in both directions on a strictly one-for-one basis for years, dating back

to the days of Eisenhower and Khrushchev. There were a great
many good motives for that: an honest appreciation of the suprana-
tional character of science; impulses of friendliness that are hard to
wipe out completely in the individual human being; the desire to be
exposed to a fresh and interesting outlook and to have your own
slightly stale notions greeted by others as fresh and interesting.

The governments themselves were anxious that this continue.
There was always the obvious thought that by learning all you could
and telling as little as you could, your own side would gain by the
exchange.

But not in the case of robotics. Not there.

Such a little thing to carry conviction. And a thing, moreover,
they had known all along. Lynn thought darkly: *We've taken the
complacent way out.*

Because the other side had done nothing publicly on robotics, it
had been tempting to sit back smugly and be comfortable in the assurance of superiority. Why hadn't it seemed possible, even likely,
that They were hiding superior cards, a trump hand, for the proper
time?

Laszlo said shakenly, "What do we do?" It was obvious that the
same line of thought had carried the same conviction to him.

"Do?" parroted Lynn. It was hard to think right now of anything
but the complete horror that came with conviction. There were ten
humanoid robots somewhere in the United States, each one carrying
a fragment of a TC bomb.

TC! The race for sheer horror in bomb-ery had ended there. TC!
Total Conversion! The sun was no longer a synonym one could use.
Total conversion made the sun a penny candle.

Ten humanoids, each completely harmless in separation, could, by
the simple act of coming together, exceed critical mass and—

Lynn rose to his feet heavily, the dark pouches under his eyes,
which ordinarily lent his ugly face a look of savage foreboding, more
prominent than ever. "It's going to be up to us to figure out ways
and means of telling a humanoid from a human and then finding
the humanoids."

"How quickly?" muttered Laszlo.

"Not later than five minutes before they get together," barked
Lynn, "and I don't know when that will be."

Breckenridge nodded. "I'm glad you're with us now, sir. I'm to
bring you back to Washington for conference, you know."

Lynn raised his eyebrows. "All right."

He wondered if, had he delayed longer in being convinced, he might not have been replaced forthwith—if some other Chief of the Bureau of Robotics might not be conferring in Washington. He suddenly wished earnestly that exactly that had come to pass.

The First Presidential Assistant was there, the Secretary of Science, the Secretary of Security, Lynn himself, and Breckenridge. Five of them sitting about a table in the dungeons of an underground fortress near Washington.

Presidential Assistant Jeffreys was an impressive man, handsome in a white-haired and just-a-trifle-jowly fashion, solid, thoughtful and as unobtrusive, politically, as a Presidential Assistant ought to be.

He spoke incisively. "There are three questions that face us as I see it. First, when are the humanoids going to get together? Second, where are they going to get together? Third, how do we stop them before they get together?"

Secretary of Science Amberley nodded convulsively at that. He had been Dean of Northwestern Engineering before his appointment. He was thin, sharp-featured and noticeably edgy. His forefinger traced slow circles on the table.

"As far as *when* they'll get together," he said. "I suppose it's definite that it won't be for some time."

"Why do you say that?" asked Lynn sharply.

"They've been in the U.S. at least a month already. So Security says."

Lynn turned automatically to look at Breckenridge, and Secretary of Security Macalaster intercepted the glance. Macalaster said, "The information is reliable. Don't let Breckenridge's apparent youth fool you, Dr. Lynn. That's part of his value to us. Actually, he's thirty-four and has been with the department for ten years. He has been in Moscow for nearly a year and without him, none of this terrible danger would be known to us. As it is, we have most of the details."

"Not the crucial ones," said Lynn.

Macalaster of Security smiled frostily. His heavy chin and close-set eyes were well-known to the public but almost nothing else about him was. He said, "We are all finitely human, Dr. Lynn. Agent Breckenridge has done a great deal."

Presidential Assistant Jeffreys cut in. "Let us say we have a certain amount of time. If action at the instant were necessary, it would have happened before this. It seems likely that they are waiting for a specific time. If we knew the place, perhaps the time would become self-evident.

"If they are going to TC a target, they will want to cripple us as much as possible, so it would seem that a major city would have to be it. In any case, a major metropolis is the only target worth a TC bomb. I think there are four possibilities: Washington, as the administrative center; New York, as the financial center; and Detroit and Pittsburgh as the two chief industrial centers."

Macalaster of Security said, "I vote for New York. Administration and industry have both been decentralized to the point where the destruction of any one particular city won't prevent instant retaliation."

"Then why New York?" asked Amberly of Science, perhaps more sharply than he intended. "Finance has been decentralized as well."

"A question of morale. It may be they intend to destroy our will to resist, to induce surrender by the sheer horror of the first blow. The greatest destruction of human life would be in the New York Metropolitan area—"

"Pretty cold-blooded," muttered Lynn.

"I know," said Macalaster of Security, "but they're capable of it, if they thought it would mean final victory at a stroke. Wouldn't we—"

Presidential Assistant Jeffreys brushed back his white hair. "Let's assume the worst. Let's assume that New York will be destroyed some time during the winter, preferably immediately after a serious blizzard when communications are at their worst and the disruption of utilities and food supplies in fringe areas will be most serious in their effect. Now, how do we stop them?"

Amberley of Science could only say, "Finding ten men in two hundred and twenty million is an awfully small needle in an awfully large haystack."

Jeffreys shook his head. "You have it wrong. Ten humanoids among two hundred twenty million humans."

"No difference," said Amberley of Science. "We don't know that a humanoid can be differentiated from a human at sight. Probably not." He looked at Lynn. They all did.

Lynn said heavily, "We in Cheyenne couldn't make one that would pass as human in the daylight."

"But They can," said Macalaster of Security, "and not only physically. We're sure of that. They've advanced mentalic procedures to the point where They can reel off the micro-electronic pattern of the brain and focus it on the positronic pathways of the robot."

Lynn stared. "Are you implying that They can create the replica of a human being complete with personality and memory?"

"I am."

"Of specific human beings?"

"That's right."

"Is this also based on Agent Breckenridge's findings?"

"Yes. The evidence can't be disputed."

Lynn bent his head in thought for a moment. Then he said, "Then ten men in the United States are not men but humanoids. But the originals would have had to be available to them. They couldn't be Orientals, who would be too easy to spot, so they would have to be East Europeans. How would they be introduced into this country, then? With the radar network over the entire world border as tight as a drum, how could They introduce any individual, human or humanoid, without our knowing it?"

Macalaster of Security said, "It can be done. There are certain legitimate seepages across the border. Businessmen, pilots, even tourists. They're watched, of course, on both sides. Still ten of them might have been kidnaped and used as models for humanoids. The humanoids would then be sent back in their place. Since we wouldn't expect such a substitution, it would pass us by. If they were Americans to begin with, there would be no difficulty in their getting into this country. It's as simple as that."

"And even their friends and family could not tell the difference?"

"We must assume so. Believe me, we've been waiting for any report that might imply sudden attacks of amnesia or troublesome changes in personality. We've checked on thousands."

Amberley of Science stared at his finger tips. "I think ordinary measures won't work. The attack must come from the Bureau of Robotics and I depend on the chief of that bureau."

Again eyes turned sharply, expectantly, on Lynn.

Lynn felt bitterness rise. It seemed to him that this was what the conference came to and was intended for. Nothing that had been said had not been said before. He was sure of that. There was no solution to the problem, no pregnant suggestion. It was a device for the record, a device on the part of men who gravely feared defeat and who wished the responsibility for it placed clearly and unequivocally on someone else.

And yet there was justice in it. It was in robotics that We had fallen short. And Lynn was not Lynn merely. He was Lynn of Robotics and the responsibility had to be his.

He said, "I will do what I can."

He spent a wakeful night and there was a haggardness about both body and soul when he sought and attained another interview with Presidential Assistant Jeffreys the next morning. Breckenridge was there, and though Lynn would have preferred a private conference, he could see the justice in the situation. It was obvious that Breckenridge had attained enormous influence with the government as a result of his successful Intelligence work. Well, why not?

Lynn said, "Sir, I am considering the possibility that we are hopping uselessly to enemy piping."

"In what way?"

"I'm sure that however impatient the public may grow at times, and however legislators sometimes find it expedient to talk, the government at least recognizes the world stalemate to be beneficial. They must recognize it also. Ten humanoids with one TC bomb is a trival way of breaking the stalemate."

"The destruction of fifteen million human beings is scarcely trivial."

"It is from the world power standpoint. It would not so demoralize us to make us surrender or so cripple us as to convince us we could not win. There would just be the same old planetary death war that both sides have avoided so long and so successfully. And all They would have accomplished is to force us to fight minus one city. It's not enough."

"What do you suggest?" said Jeffreys coldly. "That They do not have ten humanoids in our country? That there is not a TC bomb waiting to get together?"

"I'll agree that those things are here, but perhaps for some reason greater than just midwinter bomb madness."

"Such as?"

"It may be that the physical destruction resulting from the humanoids getting together is not the worst thing that can happen to us. What about the moral and intellectual destruction that comes of their being here at all? With all due respect to Agent Breck-enridge, what if They *intended* for us to find out about the humanoids; what if the humanoids are never supposed to get to-gether, but merely to remain separate in order to give us something to worry about."

"Why?"

"Tell me this. What measures have already been taken against the humanoids? I suppose that Security is going through the files of all citizens who have ever been across the border or close enough to it to make kidnaping possible. I know, since Macalaster mentioned it yesterday, that they are following up suspicious psychiatric cases. What else?"

Jeffreys said, "Small X-ray devices are being installed in key places in the large cities. In the mass arenas, for instance—"

"Where ten humanoids might slip in among a hundred thousand spectators of a football game or an air-polo match?"

"Exactly."

"And concert halls and churches?"

"We must start somewhere. We can't do it all at once."

"Particularly when panic must be avoided," said Lynn. "Isn't that so? It wouldn't do to have the public realize that at any unpredicta-ble moment, some unpredictable city and its human contents would suddenly cease to exist."

"I suppose that's obvious. What are you driving at?"

Lynn said strenuously, "That a growing fraction of our national effort will be diverted entirely into the nasty problem of what Am-berley called finding a very small needle in a very large haystack. We'll be chasing our tails madly, while They increase their research lead to the point where we find we can no longer catch up; when we must surrender without the chance even of snapping our fingers in retaliation.

"Consider further that this news will leak out as more and more people become involved in our countermeasures and more and more people begin to guess what we're doing. Then what? The panic might do us more harm than any one TC bomb."

The Presidential Assistant said irritably, "In Heaven's name, man, what do you suggest we do, then?"

"Nothing," said Lynn. "Call their bluff. Live as we have lived and gamble that They won't dare break the stalemate for the sake of a one-bomb head start."

"Impossible!" said Jeffreys. "Completely impossible. The welfare of all of Us is very largely in my hands, and doing nothing is the one thing I cannot do. I agree with you, perhaps, that X-ray machines at sports arenas are a kind of skin-deep measure that won't be effective, but it has to be done so that people, in the aftermath, do not come to the bitter conclusion that we tossed our country away for the sake of a subtle line of reasoning that encouraged donothingism. In fact, our countergambit will be active indeed."

"In what way?"

Presidential Assistant Jeffreys looked at Breckenridge. The young Security officer, hitherto calmly silent, said, "It's no use talking about a possible future break in the stalemate when the stalemate is broken now. It doesn't matter whether these humanoids explode or do not. Maybe they *are* only a bait to divert us, as you say. But the fact remains that we are a quarter of a century behind in robotics, and that may be fatal. What other advances in robotics will there be to surprise us if war does start? The only answer is to divert our entire force immediately, *now*, into a crash program of robotics research, and the first problem is to find the humanoids. Call it an exercise in robotics, if you will, or call it the prevention of the death of fifteen million men, women and children."

Lynn shook his head helplessly. "You *can't*. You'd be playing into their hands. They want us lured into the one blind alley while they're free to advance in all other directions."

Jeffreys said impatiently, "That's your guess. Breckenridge has made his suggestion through channels and the government has approved, and we will begin with an all-Science conference."

"All-Science?"

Breckenridge said, "We have listed every important scientist of every branch of natural science. They'll all be at Cheyenne. There will be only one point on the agenda: How to advance robotics. The major specific subheading under that will be: How to develop a receiving device for the electromagnetic fields of the cerebral cortex that will be sufficiently delicate to distinguish between a protoplasmic human brain and a positronic humanoid brain."

Jeffreys said, "We had hoped you would be willing to be in charge of the conference."

"I was not consulted in this."

"Obviously time was short, sir. Do you agree to be in charge?"

Lynn smiled briefly. It was a matter of responsibility again. The responsibility must be clearly that of Lynn of Robotics. He had the feeling it would be Breckenridge who would really be in charge. But what could he do?

He said, "I agree."

Breckenridge and Lynn returned together to Cheyenne, where that evening Laszlo listened with a sullen mistrust to Lynn's description of coming events.

Laszlo said, "While you were gone, Chief, I've started putting five experimental models of humanoid structure through the testing procedures. Our men are on a twelve-hour day, with three shifts overlapping. If we've got to arrange a conference, we're going to be crowded and red-taped out of everything. Work will come to a halt."

Breckenridge said, "That will be only temporary. You will gain more than you lose."

Laszlo scowled. "A bunch of astrophysicists and geochemists around won't help a damn toward robotics."

"Views from specialists of other fields may be helpful."

"Are you sure? How do we know that there *is* any way of detecting brain waves or that, even if we can, there is a way of differentiating human and humanoid by wave pattern? Who set up the project, anyway?"

"I did," said Breckenridge.

"*You* did? Are you a robotics man?"

The young Security agent said calmly, "I have studied robotics."

"That's not the same thing."

"I've had access to text material dealing with Russian robotics—in Russian. Top-secret material well in advance of anything you have here."

Lynn said ruefully, "He has us there, Laszlo."

"It was on the basis of that material," Breckenridge went on, "that I suggested this particular line of investigation. It is reasonably certain that in copying off the electromagnetic pattern of a specific human mind into a specific positronic brain, a perfectly exact duplicate cannot be made. For one thing, the most complicated positronic brain small enough to fit into a human-sized skull is hundreds of times less complex than the human brain. It can't pick up all the overtones, therefore, and there must be some way to take advantage of that fact."

Laszlo looked impressed despite himself and Lynn smiled grimly. It was easy to resent Breckenridge and the coming intrusion of several hundred scientists of nonrobotics specialties, but the problem itself was an intriguing one. There was that consolation, at least.

It came to him quietly.

Lynn found he had nothing to do but sit in his office alone, with an executive position that had grown merely titular. Perhaps that helped. It gave him time to think, to picture the creative scientists of half the world converging on Cheyenne.

It was Breckenridge who, with cool efficiency, was handling the details of preparation. There had been a kind of confidence in the way he said, "Let's get together and we'll lick Them."

Let's get together.

It came to Lynn so quietly that anyone watching Lynn at that moment might have seen his eyes blink slowly twice—but surely nothing more.

He did what he had to do with a whirling detachment that kept him calm when he felt that, by all rights, he ought to be going mad.

He sought out Breckenridge in the other's improvised quarters. Breckenridge was alone and frowning. "Is anything wrong, sir?"

Lynn said wearily, "Everything's right, I think. I've invoked martial law."

"What!"

"As chief of a division I can do so if I am of the opinion the situation warrants it. Over my division I can then be dictator. Chalk up one for the beauties of decentralization."

"You will rescind that order immediately." Breckenridge took a step forward. "When Washington hears this, you will be ruined."

"I'm ruined anyway. Do you think I don't realize that I've been set up for the role of the greatest villain in American history: the man who let Them break the stalemate? I have nothing to lose—and perhaps a great deal to gain."

He laughed a little wildly. "What a target the Division of Robotics will be, eh, Breckenridge? Only a few thousand men to be killed by a TC bomb capable of wiping out three hundred square miles in one micro-second. But five hundred of those men would be our greatest scientists. We would be in the peculiar position of having to fight a war with our brains shot out, or surrendering. I think we'd surrender."

"But this is impossible. Lynn, do you hear me? Do you understand? How could the humanoids pass our security provisions? How could they get together?"

"But they *are* getting together! We're helping them to do so. We're ordering them to do so. Our scientists visit the other side, Breckenridge. They visit Them regularly. You made a point of how strange it was that no one in robotics did. Well, ten of those scientists are still there and in their place, ten humanoids are converging on Cheyenne."

"That's a ridiculous guess."

"I think it's a good one, Breckenridge. But it wouldn't work unless we knew humanoids were in America so that we would call the conference in the first place. Quite a coincidence that you brought the news of the humanoids *and* suggested the conference *and* suggested the agenda *and* are running the show *and* know exactly which scientists were invited. Did you make sure the right ten were included?"

"Dr. Lynn!" cried Breckenridge in outrage. He poised to rush forward.

Lynn said, "Don't move. I've got a blaster here. We'll just wait for the scientists to get here one by one. One by one we'll X-ray them. One by one, we'll monitor them for radioactivity. No two will get together without being checked, and if all five hundred are clear, I'll give you my blaster and surrender to you. Only I think we'll find the ten humanoids. Sit down, Breckenridge."

They both sat.

Lynn said, "We wait. When I'm tired, Laszlo will spell me. We wait."

Professor Manuelo Jiminez of the Institute of Higher Studies of Buenos Aires exploded while the stratospheric jet on which he traveled was three miles above the Amazon Valley. It was a simple chemical explosion but it was enough to destroy the plane.

Dr. Herman Liebowitz of M.I.T. exploded in a monorail, killing twenty people and injuring a hundred others.

In similar manner, Dr. Auguste Marin of L'Institut Nucléonique of Montreal and seven others died at various stages of their journey to Cheyenne.

Laszlo hurtled in, pale-faced and stammering, with the first news of it. It had only been two hours that Lynn had sat there, facing Breckenridge, blaster in hand.

Laszlo said, "I thought you were nuts, Chief, but you were right. They *were* humanoids. They *had* to be." He turned to stare with hate-filled eyes at Breckenridge. "Only they were warned. *He* warned them, and now there won't be one left intact. Not one to study."

"God!" cried Lynn and in a frenzy of haste thrust his blaster out toward Breckenridge and fired. The Security man's neck vanished; the torso fell; the head dropped, thudded against the floor and rolled crookedly.

Lynn moaned, "I didn't understand, I thought he was a traitor. Nothing more."

And Laszlo stood immobile, mouth open, for the moment incapable of speech.

Lynn said wildly, "Sure, he warned them. But how could he do so while sitting in that chair unless he were equipped with built-in radio transmission? Don't you see it? Breckenridge had been in Moscow. The real Breckenridge is still there. Oh my God, there were *eleven* of them."

Laszlo managed a hoarse squeak. "Why didn't *he* explode?"

"He was hanging on, I suppose, to make sure the others had received his message and were safely destroyed. Lord, Lord, when you brought the news and I realized the truth, I couldn't shoot fast enough. God knows by how few seconds I may have beaten him to it."

Laszlo said shakily, "At least, we'll have one to study." He bent and put his fingers on the sticky fluid trickling out of the mangled remains at the neck end of the headless body.

Not blood, but high-grade machine oil.

Mirror Image

The Three Laws of Robotics

1: *A robot may not injure a human being or, through inaction, allow a human being to come to harm.*
2: *A robot must obey the orders given it by human beings except where such orders would conflict with the First Law.*
3: *A robot must protect its own existence as long as such protection does not conflict with the First or Second Law.*

Lije Baley had just decided to relight his pipe, when the door of his office opened without a preliminary knock, or announcement, of any kind. Baley looked up in pronounced annoyance and then dropped his pipe. It said a good deal for the state of his mind that he left it lie where it had fallen.

"R. Daneel Olivaw," he said, in a kind of mystified excitement. "Jehoshaphat! It *is* you, isn't it?"

"You are quite right," said the tall, bronzed newcomer, his even features never flicking for a moment out of their accustomed calm. "I regret surprising you by entering without warning, but the situation is a delicate one and there must be as little involvement as possible on the part of the men and robots even in this place. I am, in any case, pleased to see you again, friend Elijah."

And the robot held out his right hand in a gesture as thoroughly human as was his appearance. It was Baley who was so unmanned by his astonishment as to stare at the hand with a momentary lack of understanding.

But then he seized it in both his, feeling its warm firmness. "But Daneel, *why?* You're welcome any time, but—What is this situation that is a delicate one? Are we in trouble again? Earth, I mean?"

"No, friend Elijah, it does not concern Earth. The situation to which I refer as a delicate one is, to outward appearances, a small thing. A dispute between mathematicians, nothing more. As we happened, quite by accident, to be within an easy Jump of Earth—"

"This dispute took place on a starship, then?"

"Yes, indeed. A small dispute, yet to the humans involved astonishingly large."

Baley could not help but smile. "I'm not surprised you find humans astonishing. They do not obey the Three Laws."

"That is, indeed, a shortcoming," said R. Daneel, gravely, "and I think humans themselves are puzzled by humans. It may be that you are less puzzled than are the men of other worlds because so many more human beings live on Earth than on the Spacer worlds. If so, and I believe it is so, you could help us."

R. Daneel paused momentarily and then said, perhaps a shade too quickly, "And yet there are rules of human behavior which I have learned. It would seem, for instance, that I am deficient in etiquette, by human standards, not to have asked after your wife and child."

"They are doing well. The boy is in college and Jessie is involved in local politics. The amenities are taken care of. Now tell me how you come to be here."

"As I said, we were within an easy Jump of Earth," said R. Daneel, "so I suggested to the captain that we consult you."

"And the captain agreed?" Baley had a sudden picture of the proud and autocratic captain of a Spacer starship consenting to make a landing on Earth—of all worlds—and to consult an Earthman—of all people.

"I believe," said R. Daneel, "that he was in a position where he would have agreed to anything. In addition, I praised you very highly; although, to be sure, I stated only the truth. Finally, I agreed to conduct all negotiations so that none of the crew, or passengers, would need to enter any of the Earthman cities."

"And talk to any Earthman, yes. But what has happened?"

"The passengers of the starship, *Eta Carina,* included two mathematicians who were traveling to Aurora to attend an intersellar conference on neurobiophysics. It is about these mathematicians, Alfred Barr Humboldt and Gennao Sabbat, that the dispute centers. Have you perhaps, friend Elijah, heard of one, or both, of them?"

"Neither one," said Baley, firmly. "I know nothing about mathematics. Look, Daneel, surely you haven't told anyone I'm a mathematics buff or—"

"Not at all, friend Elijah. I know you are not. Nor does it matter, since the exact nature of the mathematics involved is in no way relevant to the point at issue."

"Well, then, go on."

"Since you do not know either man, friend Elijah, let me tell you that Dr. Humboldt is well into his twenty-seventh decade—pardon me, friend Elijah?"

"Nothing. Nothing," said Baley, irritably. He had merely muttered to himself, more or less incoherently, in a natural reaction to the extended life-spans of the Spacers. "And he's still active, despite his age? On Earth, mathematicians after thirty or so . . ."

Daneel said, calmly; "Dr. Humboldt is one of the top three mathematicians, by long-established repute, in the galaxy. Certainly he is still active. Dr. Sabbat, on the other hand, is quite young, not yet fifty, but he has already established himself as the most remarkable new talent in the most abstruse branches of mathematics."

"They're both great, then," said Baley. He remembered his pipe and picked it up. He decided there was no point in lighting it now and knocked out the dottle. "What happened? Is this a murder case? Did one of them apparently kill the other?"

"Of these two men of great reputation, one is trying to destroy that of the other. By human values, I believe this may be regarded as worse than physical murder."

"Sometimes, I suppose. Which one is trying to destroy the other?"

"Why, that, friend Elijah, is precisely the point at issue. Which?"

"Go on."

"Dr. Humboldt tells the story clearly. Shortly before he boarded the starship, he had an insight into a possible method for analyzing neural pathways from changes in microwave absorption patterns of local cortical areas. The insight was a purely mathematical technique of extraordinary subtlety, but I cannot, of course, either understand or sensibly transmit the details. These do not, however, matter. Dr. Humboldt considered the matter and was more convinced each hour that he had something revolutionary on hand, something that would dwarf all his previous accomplishments in mathematics. Then he discovered that Dr. Sabbat was on board."

"Ah. And he tried it out on young Sabbat?"

"Exactly. The two had met at professional meetings before and knew each other thoroughly by reputation. Humboldt went into it with Sabbat in great detail. Sabbat backed Humboldt's analysis completely and was unstinting in his praise of the importance of the discovery and of the ingenuity of the discoverer. Heartened and reassured by this, Humboldt prepared a paper outlining, in summary, his work and, two days later, prepared to have it forwarded subetherically to the co-chairmen of the conference at Aurora, in order that he might officially establish his priority and arrange for possible discussion before the sessions were closed. To his surprise, he found that Sabbat was ready with a paper of his own, essentially the same as Humboldt's, and Sabbat was also preparing to have it subetherized to Aurora."

"I suppose Humboldt was furious."

"Quite!"

"And Sabbat? What was his story?"

"Precisely the same as Humboldt's. Word for word."

"Then just what is the problem?"

"Except for the mirror-image exchange of names. According to Sabbat, it was he who had the insight, and he who consulted Humboldt; it was Humboldt who agreed with the analysis and praised it."

"Then each one claims the idea is his and that the other stole it. It doesn't sound like a problem to me at all. In matters of scholarship, it would seem only necessary to produce the records of research, dated and initialed. Judgment as to priority can be made from that. Even if one is falsified, that might be discovered through internal inconsistencies."

"Ordinarily, friend Elijah, you would be right, but this is mathematics, and not in an experimental science. Dr. Humboldt claims to have worked out the essentials in his head. Nothing was put in writing until the paper itself was prepared. Dr. Sabbat, of course, says precisely the same."

"Well, then, be more drastic and get it over with, for sure. Subject each one to a psychic probe and find out which of the two is lying."

R. Daneel shook his head slowly, "Friend Elijah, you do not understand these men. They are both of rank and scholarship, Fellows of the Imperial Academy. As such, they cannot be subjected to trial of professional conduct except by a jury of their peers—their professional peers—unless they personally and voluntarily waive that right."

"Put it to them, then. The guilty man won't waive the right because he can't afford to face the psychic probe. The innocent man will waive it at once. You won't even have to use the probe."

"It does not work that way, friend Elijah. To waive the right in such a case—to be investigated by laymen—is a serious and perhaps irrecoverable blow to prestige. Both men steadfastly refuse to waive the right to special trial, as a matter of pride. The question of guilt, or innocence, is quite subsidiary."

"In that case, let it go for now. Put the matter in cold storage until you get to Aurora. At the neurobiophysical conference, there will be a huge supply of professional peers, and then—"

"That would mean a tremendous blow to science itself, friend Elijah. Both men would suffer for having been the instrument of scandal. Even the innocent one would be blamed for having been party to a situation so distasteful. It would be felt that it should have been settled quietly out of court at all costs."

"All right. I'm not a Spacer, but I'll try to imagine that this attitude makes sense. What do the men in question say?"

"Humboldt agrees thoroughly. He says that if Sabbat will admit theft of the idea and allow Humboldt to proceed with transmission of the paper—or at least its delivery at the conference, he will not press charges. Sabbat's misdeed will remain secret with him; and, of course, with the captain, who is the only other human to be party to the dispute."

"But young Sabbat will not agree?"

"On the contrary, he agreed with Dr. Humboldt to the last detail —with the reversal of names. Still the mirror-image."

"So they just sit there, stalemated?"

"Each, I believe, friend Elijah, is waiting for the other to give in and admit guilt."

"Well, then, wait."

"The captain has decided this cannot be done. There are two alternatives to waiting, you see. The first is that both will remain stubborn so that when the starship lands on Aurora, the intellectual scandal will break. The captain, who is responsible for justice on board ship will suffer disgrace for not having been able to settle the matter quietly and that, to him, is quite insupportable."

"And the second alternative?"

"Is that one, or the other, of the mathematicians will indeed admit to wrongdoing. But will the one who confesses do so out of actual guilt, or out of a noble desire to prevent the scandal? Would it be right to deprive of credit one who is sufficiently ethical to prefer to lose that credit than to see science as a whole suffer? Or else, the guilty party will confess at the last moment, and in such a way as to make it appear he does so only for the sake of science, thus escaping the disgrace of his deed and casting its shadow upon the other. The captain will be the only man to know all this but he does not wish to spend the rest of his life wondering whether he has been a party to a grotesque miscarriage of justice."

Baley sighed. "A game of intellectual chicken. Who'll break first as Aurora comes nearer and nearer? Is that the whole story now, Daneel?"

"Not quite. There are witnesses to the transaction."

"Jehoshaphat! Why didn't you say so at once. *What* witnesses?

"Dr. Humboldt's personal servant—"

"A robot, I suppose."

"Yes, certainly. He is called R. Preston. This servant, R. Preston, was present during the initial conference and he bears out Dr. Humboldt in every detail."

"You mean he says that the idea was Dr. Humboldt's to begin with; that Dr. Humboldt detailed it to Dr. Sabbat; that Dr. Sabbat praised the idea, and so on."

"Yes, in full detail."

"I see. Does that settle the matter or not? Presumably not."

"You are quite right. It does not settle the matter, for there is a second witness. Dr. Sabbat also has a personal servant, R. Idda, another robot of, as it happens, the same model as R. Preston, made, I believe, in the same year in the same factory. Both have been in service for an equal period of time.

"An odd coincidence—very odd."

"A fact, I am afraid, and it makes it difficult to arrive at any judgment based on obvious differences between the two servants."

"R. Idda, then, tells the same story as R. Preston?"

"Precisely the same story, except for the mirror-image reversal of the names."

"R. Idda stated, then, that young Sabbat, the one not yet fifty"— Lije Baley did not entirely keep the sardonic note out of his voice; he himself was not yet fifty and he felt far from young—"had the idea to begin with; that he detailed it to Dr. Humboldt, who was loud in his praises, and so on."

"Yes, friend Elijah."

"And one robot is lying, then."

"So it would seem."

"It should be easy to tell which. I imagine even a superficial examination by a good roboticist—"

"A roboticist is not enough in this case, friend Elijah. Only a qualified robopsychologist would carry weight enough and experience enough to make a decision in a case of this importance. There is no one so qualified on board ship. Such an examination can be performed only when we reach Aurora—"

"And by then the crud hits the fan. Well, you're here on Earth. We can scare up a robopsychologist, and surely anything that happens on Earth will never reach the ears of Aurora and there will be no scandal."

"Except that neither Dr. Humboldt, nor Dr. Sabbat, will allow his servant to be investigated by a robopsychologist of Earth. The Earthman would have to—" He paused.

Lije Baley said stolidly, "He'd have to touch the robot."

"These are old servants, well thought of—"

"And not to be sullied by the touch of Earthman. Then what do you want me to do, damn it?" He paused, grimacing. "I'm sorry, R. Daneel, but I see no reason for your having involved me."

"I was on the ship on a mission utterly irrelevant to the problem at hand. The captain turned to me because he had to turn to someone. I seemed human enough to talk to, and robot enough to be a safe recipient of confidences. He told me the whole story and asked what I would do. I realized the next Jump could take us as easily to

Earth as to our target. I told the captain that, although I was at as much a loss to resolve the mirror-image as he was, there was on Earth one who might help."

"Jehoshaphat!" muttered Baley under his breath.

"Consider, friend Elijah, that if you succeed in solving this puzzle, it would do your career good and Earth itself might benefit. The matter could not be publicized, of course, but the captain is a man of some influence on his home world and he would be grateful."

"You just put a greater strain on me."

"I have every confidence," said R. Daneel, stolidly, "that you already have some idea as to what procedure ought to be followed."

"Do you? I suppose that the obvious procedure is to interview the two mathematicians, one of whom would seem to be a thief."

"I'm afraid, friend Elijah, that neither one will come into the city. Nor would either one be willing to have you come to them."

"And there is no way of forcing a Spacer to allow contact with an Earthman, no matter what the emergency. Yes, I understand that, Daneel—but I was thinking of an interview by closed-circuit television."

"Nor that. They will not submit to interrogation by an Earthman."

"Then what do they want of me? Could I speak to the robots?"

"They would not allow the robots to come here, either."

"Jehoshaphat, Daneel. *You've* come."

"That was my own decision. I have permission, while on board ship, to make decisions of that sort without veto by any human being but the captain himself—and he was eager to establish the contact. I, having known you, decided that television contact was insufficient. I wished to shake your hand."

Lije Baley softened. "I appreciate that, Daneel, but I still honestly wish you could have refrained from thinking of me at all in this case. Can I talk to the robots by television at least?"

"That, I think, can be arranged."

"Something, at least. That means I would be doing the work of a robopsychologist—in a crude sort of way."

"But you are a detective, friend Elijah, not a robopsychologist."

"Well, let it pass. Now before I see them, let's think a bit. Tell me: is it possible that both robots are telling the truth? Perhaps the conversation between the two mathematicians was equivocal. Perhaps it was of such a nature that each robot could honestly believe its own master was proprietor of the idea. Or perhaps one robot heard only one portion of the discussion and the other another portion, so that each could suppose its own master was proprietor of the idea."

"That is quite impossible, friend Elijah. Both robots repeat the conversation in identical fashion. And the two repetitions are fundamentally inconsistent."

"Then it is absolutely certain that one of the robots is lying?"

"Yes."

"Will I be able to see the transcript of all evidence given so far in the presence of the captain, if I should want to?"

"I thought you would ask that and I have copies with me."

"Another blessing. Have the robots been cross-examined at all, and is that cross-examination included in the transcript?"

"The robots have merely repeated their tales. Cross-examination would be conducted only by robopsychologists."

"Or by myself?"

"You are a detective, friend Elijah, not a—"

"All right, R. Daneel. I'll try to get the Spacer psychology straight. A detective can do it because he isn't a robopsychologist. Let's think further. Ordinarily a robot will not lie, but he will do so if necessary to maintain the Three Laws. He might lie to protect, in legitimate fashion, his own existence in accordance with the Third Law. He is more apt to lie if that is necessary to follow a legitimate order given him by a human being in accordance with the Second Law. He is most apt to lie if that is necessary to save a human life, or to prevent harm from coming to a human in accordance with the First Law."

"Yes."

"And in this case, each robot would be defending the professional reputation of his master, and would lie if it were necessary to do so. Under the circumstances, the professional reputation would be nearly equivalent to life and there might be a near-First-Law urgency to the lie."

"Yet by the lie, each servant would be harming the professional reputation of the other's master, friend Elijah."

"So it would, but each robot might have a clearer conception of the value of its own master's reputation and honestly judge it to be greater than that of the other's. The lesser harm would be done by his lie, he would suppose, than by the truth."

Having said that, Lije Baley remained quiet for a moment. Then he said, "All right, then, can you arrange to have me talk to one of the robots—to R. Idda first, I think?"

"Dr. Sabbat's robot?"

"Yes," said Baley, dryly, "the young fellow's robot."

"It will take me but a few minutes," said R. Daneel. "I have a micro-receiver outfitted with a projector. I will need merely a blank wall and I think this one will do if you will allow me to move some of these film cabinets."

"Go ahead. Will I have to talk into a microphone of some sort?"

"No, you will be able to talk in an ordinary manner. Please pardon me, friend Elijah, for a moment of further delay. I will have to contact the ship and arrange for R. Idda to be interviewed."

"If that will take some time, Daneel, how about giving me the transcripted material of the evidence so far."

Lije Baley lit his pipe while R. Daneel set up the equipment, and leafed through the flimsy sheets he had been handed.

The minutes passed and R. Daneel said, "If you are ready, friend Elijah, R. Idda is. Or would you prefer a few more minutes with the transcript?"

"No," sighed Baley, "I'm not learning anything new. Put him on and arrange to have the interview recorded and transcribed."

R. Idda, unreal in two-dimensional projection against the wall, was basically metallic in structure—not at all the humanoid creature that R. Daneel was. His body was tall but blocky, and there was very little to distinguish him from the many robots Baley had seen, except for minor structural details.

Baley said, "Greetings, R. Idda."

"Greetings, sir," said R. Idda, in a muted voice that sounded surprisingly humanoid.

"You are the personal servant of Gennao Sabbat, are you not?"

"I am sir."

"For how long, boy?"

"For twenty-two years, sir."

"And your master's reputation is valuable to you?"

"Yes, sir."

"Would you consider it of importance to protect that reputation?"

"Yes, sir."

"As important to protect his reputation as his physical life?"

"No, sir."

"As important to protect his reputation as the reputation of another."

R. Idda hesitated. He said, "Such cases must be decided on their individual merit, sir. There is no way of establishing a general rule."

Baley hesitated. These Spacer robots spoke more smoothly and intellectually than Earth-models did. He was not at all sure he could outthink one.

He said, "If you decided that the reputation of your master were more important than that of another, say, that of Alfred Barr Humboldt, would you lie to protect your master's reputation?"

"I would, sir."

"Did you lie in your testimony concerning your master in his controversy with Dr. Humboldt?"

"No, sir."

"But if you were lying, you would deny you were lying in order to protect that lie, wouldn't you?"

"Yes, sir."

"Well, then," said Baley, "let's consider this. Your master, Gennao Sabbat, is a young man of great reputation in mathematics, but he is a young man. If, in this controversy with Dr. Humboldt, he had succumbed to temptation and had acted unethically, he would suffer a certain eclipse of reputation, but he is young and would have ample time to recover. He would have many intellectual triumphs ahead of him and men would eventually look upon this plagiaristic attempt as the mistake of a hot-blooded youth, deficient in judgment. It would be something that would be made up for in the future.

"If, on the other hand, it were Dr. Humboldt who succumbed to temptation, the matter would be much more serious. He is an old man whose great deeds have spread over centuries. His reputation has been unblemished hitherto. All of that, however, would be forgotten in the light of this one crime of his later years, and he would have no opportunity to make up for it in the comparatively short time remaining to him. There would be little more that he could accomplish. There would be so many more years of work ruined in Humboldt's case than in that of your master and so much less opportunity to win back his position. You see, don't you, that Humboldt faces the worse situation and deserves the greater consideration?"

There was a long pause. Then R. Idda said, with unmoved voice, "My evidence was a lie. It was Dr. Humboldt whose work it was, and my master has attempted, wrongfully, to appropriate the credit."

Baley said, "Very well, boy. You are instructed to say nothing to anyone about this until given permission by the captain of the ship. You are excused."

The screen blanked out and Baley puffed at his pipe. "Do you suppose the captain heard that, Daneel?"

"I am sure of it. He is the only witness, except for us."

"Good. Now for the other."

"But is there any point to that, friend Elijah, in view of what R. Idda has confessed?"

"Of course there is. R. Idda's confession means nothing."

"Nothing?"

"Nothing at all. I pointed out that Dr. Humboldt's position was the worse. Naturally, if he were lying to protect Sabbat, he would switch to the truth as, in fact, he claimed to have done. On the other hand, if he were telling the truth, he would switch to a lie to protect Humboldt. It's still mirror-image and we haven't gained anything."

"But then what will we gain by questioning R. Preston?"

"Nothing, if the mirror-image were perfect—but it is not. After all, one of the robots *is* telling the truth to begin with, and one *is* lying to begin with, and that is a point of asymmetry. Let me see R. Preston. And if the transcription of R. Idda's examination is done, let me have it.

The projector came into use again. R. Preston stared out of it; identical with R. Idda in every respect, except for some trivial chest design.

Baley said, "Greetings, R. Preston." He kept the record of R. Idda's examination before him as he spoke.

"Greetings, sir," said R. Preston. His voice was identical with that of R. Idda.

"You are the personal servant of Alfred Barr Humboldt are you not?"

"I am, sir."

"For how long, boy?"

"For twenty-two years, sir."

"And your master's reputation is valuable to you?"

"Yes, sir."

"Would you consider it of importance to protect that reputation?"

"Yes, sir."

"As important to protect his reputation as his physical life?"

"No, sir."

"As important to protect his reputation as the reputation of another?"

R. Preston hesitated. He said, "Such cases must be decided on their individual merit, sir. There is no way of establishing a general rule."

Baley said, "If you decided that the reputation of your master were more important than that of another, say, that of Gennao Sabbat, would you lie to protect your master's reputation?"

"I would, sir."

"Did you lie in your testimony concerning your master in his controversy with Dr. Sabbat?"

"No, sir."

"But if you were lying, you would deny you were lying, in order to protect that lie, wouldn't you?"

"Yes, sir."

"Well, then," said Baley, "let's consider this. Your master, Alfred Barr Humboldt, is an old man of great reputation in mathematics, but he is an old man. If, in this controversy with Dr. Sabbat, he had succumbed to temptation and had acted unethically, he would suffer a certain eclipse of reputation, but his great age and his centuries of accomplishments would stand against that and would win out. Men would look upon this plagiaristic attempt as the mistake of a perhaps-sick old man, no longer certain in judgment.

"If, on the other hand, it were Dr. Sabbat who had succumbed to temptation, the matter would be much more serious. He is a young man, with a far less secure reputation. He would ordinarily have centuries ahead of him in which he might accumulate knowledge and achieve great things. This will be closed to him, now, obscured by one mistake of his youth. He has a much longer future to lose than your master has. You see, don't you, that Sabbat faces the worse situation and deserves the greater consideration?"

There was a long pause. Then R. Preston said, with unmoved voice, "My evidence was as I—"

At that point, he broke off and said nothing more.

Baley said, "Please continue, R. Preston."

There was no response.

R. Daneel said, "I am afraid, friend Elijah, that R. Preston is in stasis. He is out of commission."

"Well, then," said Baley, "we have finally produced an asymmetry. From this, we can see who the guilty person is."

"In what way, friend Elijah?"

"Think it out. Suppose you were a person who had committed no crime and that your personal robot were a witness to that. There would be nothing you need do. Your robot would tell the truth and bear you out. If, however, you were a person who *had* committed the crime, you would have to depend on your robot to lie. That would be a somewhat riskier position, for although the robot would lie, if necessary, the greater inclination would be to tell the truth, so that the lie would be less firm than the truth would be. To prevent that, the crime-committing person would very likely have to *order* the robot to lie. In this way, First Law would be strengthened by Second Law; perhaps very substantially strengthened."

"That would seem reasonable," said R. Daneel.

"Suppose we have one robot of each type. One robot would switch from truth, unreinforced, to the lie, and could do so after some hesitation, without serious trouble. The other robot would switch from the lie, *strongly reinforced*, to the truth, but could do so only at the risk of burning out various positronic-track-ways in his brain and falling into stasis."

"And since R. Preston went into stasis—"

"R. Preston's master, Dr. Humboldt, is the man guilty of plagiarism. If you transmit this to the captain and urge him to face Dr. Humboldt with the matter at once, he may force a confession. If so, I hope you will tell me immediately."

"I will certainly do so. You will excuse me, friend Elijah? I must talk to the captain privately."

"Certainly. Use the conference room. It is shielded."

Baley could do no work of any kind in R. Daneel's absence. He sat in uneasy silence. A great deal would depend on the value of his analysis, and he was acutely aware of his lack of expertise in robotics.

R. Daneel was back in half an hour—very nearly the longest half hour of Baley's life.

There was no use, of course, in trying to determine what had happened from the expression of the humanoid's impassive face. Baley tried to keep his face impassive.

"Yes, R. Daneel?" he asked.

"Precisely as you said, friend Elijah. Dr. Humboldt has confessed. He was counting, he said, on Dr. Sabbat giving way and allowing Dr. Humboldt to have this one last triumph. The crisis is over and you will find the captain grateful. He has given me permission to tell you that he admires your subtlety greatly and I believe that I, myself, will achieve favor for having suggested you."

"Good," said Baley, his knees weak and his forehead moist now that his decision had proven correct, "but Jehoshaphat, R. Daneel, don't put me on the spot like that again, will you?"

"I will try not to, friend Elijah. All will depend, of course, on the importance of a crisis, on your nearness, and on certain other factors. Meanwhile, I have a question—"

"Yes?"

"Was it not possible to suppose that passage from a lie to the truth was easy, while passage from the truth to a lie was difficult? And in that case, would not the robot in stasis have been going from a truth to a lie, and since R. Preston was in stasis, might one not have drawn the conclusion that it was Dr. Humboldt who was innocent and Dr. Sabbat who was guilty?"

"Yes, R. Daneel. It was possible to argue that way, but it was the other argument that proved right. Humboldt did confess, didn't he?"

"He did. But with arguments possible in both directions, how could you, friend Elijah, so quickly pick the correct one?"

For a moment, Baley's lips twitched. Then he relaxed and they curved into a smile. "Because, R. Daneel, I took into account human reactions, not robotic ones. I know more about human beings than about robots. In other words, I had an idea as to which mathematician was guilty before I ever interviewed the robots. Once I provoked an asymmetric response in them, I simply interpreted it in such a way as to place the guilt on the one I already believed to be guilty. The robotic response was dramatic enough to break down the guilty man; my own analysis of human behavior might not have been sufficient to do so."

"I am curious to know what your analysis of human behavior was?"

"Jehoshaphat, R. Daneel; think, and you won't have to ask. There is another point of asymmetry in this tale of mirror-image besides the matter of true-and-false. There is the matter of the age of the two mathematicians; one is quite old and one is quite young."

"Yes, of course, but what then?"

"Why, this. I can see a young man, flushed with a sudden, startling and revolutionary idea, consulting in the matter an old man whom he has, from his early student days, thought of as a demigod in the field. I can *not* see an old man, rich in honors and used to triumphs, coming up with a sudden, startling and revolutionary idea, consulting a man centuries his junior whom he is bound to think of as a young whippersnapper—or whatever term a Spacer would use. Then, too, if a young man had the chance, would he try to steal the idea of a revered demigod? It would be unthinkable. On the other hand, an old man, conscious of declining powers, might well snatch at one last chance of fame and consider a baby in the field to have no rights he was bound to observe. In short, it was not conceivable that Sabbat steal Humboldt's idea; and from both angles, Dr. Humboldt was guilty."

R. Daneel considered that for a long time. Then he held out his hand. "I must leave now, friend Elijah. It was good to see you. May we meet again soon."

Baley gripped the robot's hand, warmly, "If you don't mind, R. Daneel," he said, "not too soon."

The Tercentenary Incident

July 4, 2076—and for the third time the accident of the conventional system of numeration, based on powers of ten, had brought the last two digits of the year back to the fateful 76 that had seen the birth of the nation.

It was no longer a nation in the old sense; it was rather a geographic expression; part of a greater whole that made up the Federation of all of humanity on Earth, together with its offshoots on the Moon and in the space colonies. By culture and heritage, however, the name and the *idea* lived on, and that portion of the planet signified by the old name was still the most prosperous and advanced region of the world. . . . And the President of the United States was still the most powerful single figure in the Planetary Council.

Lawrence Edwards watched the small figure of the President from his height of two hundred feet. He drifted lazily above the crowd, his flotron motor making a barely heard chuckle on his back, and what he saw looked exactly like what anyone would see on a holovision scene. How many times had he seen little figures like that in his living room, little figures in a cube of sunlight, looking as real as though they were living homunculi, except that you could put your hand through them.

You couldn't put your hand through those spreading out in their tens of thousands over the open spaces surrounding the Washington Monument. And you couldn't put your hand through the President. You could reach out to him instead, touch him, and shake his hand.

Edwards thought sardonically of the uselessness of that added element of tangibility and wished himself a hundred miles away, floating in air over some isolated wilderness, instead of here where he had to watch for any sign of disorder. There wouldn't be any necessity for his being here but for the mythology of the value of "pressing the flesh."

Edwards was not an admirer of the President—Hugo Allen Winkler, fifty-seventh of the line.

To Edwards, President Winkler seemed an empty man, a charmer, a vote grabber, a promiser. He was a disappointing man to have in office now after all the hopes of those first months of his administration. The World Federation was in danger of breaking up long before its job had been completed and Winkler could do nothing about it. One needed a strong hand now, not a glad hand; a hard voice, not a honey voice.

There he was now, shaking hands—a space forced around him by the Service, with Edwards himself, plus a few others of the Service, watching from above.

The President would be running for re-election certainly, and there seemed a good chance he might be defeated. That would just make things worse, since the opposition party was dedicated to the destruction of the Federation.

Edwards sighed. It would be a miserable four years coming up—maybe a miserable forty—and all he could do was float in the air, ready to reach every Service agent on the ground by laser-phone if there was the slightest—

He didn't see the slightest. There was no sign of disturbance. Just a little puff of white dust, hardly visible; just a momentary glitter in the sunlight, up and away, gone as soon as he was aware of it.

Where was the President? He had lost sight of him in the dust.

He looked about in the vicinity of where he had seen him last. The President could not have moved far.

Then he became aware of disturbance. First it was among the Service agents themselves, who seemed to have gone off their heads and to be moving this way and that jerkily. Then those among the crowd near them caught the contagion and then those farther off. The noise rose and became a thunder.

Edwards didn't have to hear the words that made up the rising roar. It seemed to carry the news to him by nothing more than its mass clamorous urgency. President Winkler had disappeared! He had been there one moment and had turned into a handful of vanishing dust the next.

Edwards held his breath in an agony of waiting during what seemed a drug-ridden eternity, for the long moment of realization to end and for the mob to break into a mad, rioting stampede.

—When a resonant voice sounded over the gathering din, and at its sound, the noise faded, died, and became a silence. It was as though it were all a holovision program after all and someone had turned the sound down and out.

Edwards thought: My God, it's the President.

There was no mistaking the voice. Winkler stood on the guarded stage from which he was to give his Tercentenary speech, and from which he had left but ten minutes ago to shake hands with some in the crowd.

How had he gotten back there?

Edwards listened—

"Nothing has happened to me, my fellow Americans. What you have seen just now was the breakdown of a mechanical device. It was not your President, so let us not allow a mechanical failure to dampen the celebration of the happiest day the world has yet seen. . . . My fellow Americans, give me your attention—"

And what followed was the Tercentenary speech, the greatest speech Winkler had ever made, or Edwards had ever heard. Edwards found himself forgetting his supervisory job in his eagerness to listen.

Winkler had it right! He understood the importance of the Federation and he was getting it *across*.

Deep inside, though, another part of him was remembering the persistent rumors that the new expertise in robotics had resulted in the construction of a look-alike President, a robot who could perform the purely ceremonial functions, who could shake hands with the crowd, who could be neither bored nor exhausted—nor assassinated.

Edwards thought, in obscure shock, that that was how it had happened. There had been such a look-alike robot indeed, and in a way —it had been assassinated.

October 13, 2078—

Edwards looked up as the waist-high robot guide approached and said mellifluously, "Mr. Janek will see you now."

Edwards stood up, feeling tall as he towered above the stubby, metallic guide. He did not feel young, however. His face had gathered lines in the last two years or so and he was aware of it.

He followed the guide into a surprisingly small room, where, behind a surprisingly small desk, there sat Francis Janek, a slightly paunchy and incongruously young-looking man.

Janek smiled and his eyes were friendly as he rose to shake hands. "Mr. Edwards."

Edwards muttered, "I'm glad to have the opportunity, sir—"

Edwards had never seen Janek before, but then the job of personal secretary to the President is a quiet one and makes little news.

Janek said, "Sit down. Sit down. Would you care for a soya stick?"

Edwards smiled a polite negative, and sat down. Janek was clearly emphasizing his youth. His ruffled shirt was open and the hairs on his chest had been dyed a subdued but definite violet.

Janek said, "I know you have been trying to reach me for some weeks now. I'm sorry for the delay. I hope you understand that my time is not entirely my own. However, we're here now. . . . I have referred to the Chief of the Service, by the way, and he gave you very high marks. He regrets your resignation."

Edwards said, eyes downcast, "It seemed better to carry on my investigations without danger of embarrassment to the Service."

Janek's smile flashed. "Your activities, though discreet, have not gone unnoticed, however. The Chief explains that you have been investigating the Tercentenary Incident, and I must admit it was that which persuaded me to see you as soon as I could. You've given up your position for that? You're investigating a dead issue."

"How can it be a dead issue, Mr. Janek? Your calling it an Incident doesn't alter the fact that it was an assassination attempt."

"A matter of semantics. Why use a disturbing phrase?"

"Only because it would seem to represent a disturbing truth. Surely you would say that someone tried to kill the President."

Janek spread his hands. "If that is so, the plot did not succeed. A mechanical device was destroyed. Nothing more. In fact, if we look at it properly, the Incident—whatever you choose to call it—did the nation and the world an enormous good. As we all know, the President was shaken by the Incident and the nation as well. The President and all of us realized what a return to the violence of the last century might mean and it produced a great turnaround."

"I can't deny that."

"Of course you can't. Even the President's enemies will grant that the last two years have seen great accomplishments. The Federation is far stronger today than anyone could have dreamed it would be on that Tercentenary day. We might even say that a breakup of the global economy has been prevented."

Edwards said cautiously, "Yes, the President is a changed man. Everyone says so."

Janek said, "He was a great man always. The Incident made him concentrate on the great issues with a fierce intensity, however."

"Which he didn't do before?"

"Perhaps not quite as intensely. . . . In effect then, the President, and all of us, would like the Incident forgotten. My main purpose in seeing you, Mr. Edwards, is to make that plain to you. This is not the Twentieth Century and we can't throw you in jail for being inconvenient to us, or hamper you in any way, but even the Global Charter doesn't forbid us to attempt persuasion. Do you understand me?"

"I understand you, but I do not agree with you. Can we forget the Incident when the person responsible has never been apprehended?"

"Perhaps that is just as well, too, sir. Far better that some, uh, unbalanced person escape than that the matter be blown out of proportion and the stage set, possibly, for a return to the days of the Twentieth Century."

"The official story even states that the robot spontaneously exploded—which is impossible, and which has been an unfair blow to the robot industry."

"A robot is not the term I would use, Mr. Edwards. It was a mechanical device. No one has said that robots are dangerous, per se, certainly not the workaday metallic ones. The only reference here is to the unusually complex manlike devices that seem flesh and blood and that we might call androids. Actually, they are so complex that perhaps they might explode at that; I am not an expert in the field. The robotics industry will recover."

"Nobody in the government," said Edwards stubbornly, "seems to care whether we reach the bottom of the matter or not."

"I've already explained that there have been no consequences but good ones. Why stir the mud at the bottom, when the water above is clear?"

"And the use of the disintegrator?"

For a moment, Janek's hand, which had been slowly turning the container of soya sticks on his desk, held still, then it returned to its rhythmic movement. He said lightly, "What's that?"

Edwards said intently, "Mr. Janek, I think you know what I mean. As part of the Service—"

"To which you no longer belong, of course."

"Nevertheless, as part of the Service, I could not help but hear things that were not always, I suppose, for my ears. I had heard of a new weapon, and I saw something happen at the Tercentenary which would require one. The object everyone thought was the President disappeared into a cloud of very fine dust. It was as though every atom within the object had had its bonds to other atoms loosed. The object had become a cloud of individual atoms, which began to combine again of course, but which dispersed too quickly to do more than appear a momentary glitter of dust."

"Very science-fictionish."

"I certainly don't understand the science behind it, Mr. Janek, but I do see that it would take considerable energy to accomplish such bond breaking. This energy would have to be withdrawn from the environment. Those people who were standing near the device at the time, and whom I could locate—and who would agree to talk —were unanimous in reporting a wave of coldness washing over them."

Janek put the soya-stick container to one side with a small click of transite against cellulite. He said, "Suppose just for argument that there is such a thing as a disintegrator."

"You need not argue. There is."

"I won't argue. I know of no such thing myself, but in my office, I am not likely to know of anything so security-bound as new weaponry. But if a disintegrator exists and is as secret as all that, it must be an American monopoly, unknown to the rest of the Federation. It would then not be something either you or I should talk about. It could be a more dangerous war weapon than the nuclear bombs, precisely because—if what you say is so—it produces nothing more than disintegration at the point of impact and cold in the immediate neighborhood. No blast, no fire, no deadly radiation. Without these distressing side effects, there would be no deterrent to its use, yet for all we know it might be made large enough to destroy the planet itself."

"I go along with all of that," said Edwards.

"Then you see that if there is no disintegrator, it is foolish to talk about one; and if there *is* a disintegrator, then it is criminal to talk about one."

"I haven't discussed it, except to you, just now, because I'm trying to persuade you of the seriousness of the situation. If one had been used, for instance, ought not the government be interested in deciding how it came to be used—if another unit of the Federation might be in possession?"

Janek shook his head. "I think that we can rely on appropriate organs of this government to take such a thing into consideration. You had better not concern yourself with the matter."

Edwards said, in barely controlled impatience, "Can you assure me that the United States is the only government that has such a weapon at its disposal?"

"I can't tell you, since I know nothing about such a weapon, and should not know. You should not have spoken of it to me. Even if no such weapon exists, the *rumor* of its existence could be damaging."

"But since I have told you and the damage is done, please hear me out. Let me have the chance of convincing you that *you*, and no one else, hold the key to a fearful situation that perhaps I alone see."

"You alone see? I alone hold the key?"

"Does that sound paranoid? Let me explain and then judge for yourself."

"I will give you a little more time, sir, but what I have said stands. You must abandon this—this hobby of yours—this investigation. It is terribly dangerous."

"It is its abandonment that would be dangerous. Don't you see that if the disintegrator exists and if the United States has the monopoly of it, then it follows that the number of people who could have access to one would be sharply limited. As an ex-member of the Service, I have some practical knowledge of this and I tell you that the only person in the world who could manage to abstract a disintegrator from our top-secret arsenals would be the President. . . . Only the President of the United States, Mr. Janek, could have arranged that assassination attempt."

They stared at each other for a moment and then Janek touched a contact at his desk.

He said, "Added precaution. No one can overhear us now by any means. Mr. Edwards, do you realize the danger of that statement? To yourself? You must not overestimate the power of the Global Charter. A government has the right to take reasonable measures for the protection of its stability."

Edwards said, "I'm approaching you, Mr. Janek, as someone I presume to be a loyal American citizen. I come to you with news of a terrible crime that affects all Americans and the entire Federation. A crime that has produced a situation that perhaps only you can right. Why do you respond with threats?"

Janek said, "That's the second time you have tried to make it appear that I am a potential savior of the world. I can't conceive of myself in that role. You understand, I hope, that I have no unusual powers."

"You are the secretary to the President."

"That does *not* mean I have special access to him or am in some intimately confidential relationship to him. There are times, Mr. Edwards, when I suspect others consider me to be nothing more than a flunky, and there are even times when I find myself in danger of agreeing with them."

"Nevertheless, you see him frequently, you see him informally, you see him—"

Janek said impatiently, "I see enough of him to be able to assure you that the President would not order the destruction of that mechanical device on Tercentenary day."

"Is it in your opinion impossible, then?"

"I did not say that. I said he would not. After all, why should he? Why should the President want to destroy a look-alike android that had been a valuable adjunct to him for over three years of his Presidency? And if for some reason he wanted it done, why on Earth should he do it in so incredibly public a way—at the Tercentenary, no less—thus advertising its existence, risking public revulsion at the thought of shaking hands with a mechanical device, to say nothing of the diplomatic repercussions of having had representatives of other parts of the Federation treat with one? He might, instead, simply have ordered it disassembled in private. No one but a few highly placed members of the Administration would have known."

"There have not, however, been any undesirable consequences for the President as a result of the Incident, have there?"

"He has had to cut down on ceremony. He is no longer as accessible as he once was."

"As the robot once was."

"Well," said Janek uneasily. "Yes, I suppose that's right."

Edwards said, "And, as a matter of fact, the President was re-elected and his popularity has not diminished even though the destruction was public. The argument against public destruction is not as powerful as you make it sound."

"But the re-election came about *despite* the Incident. It was brought about by the President's quick action in stepping forward and delivering what you will have to admit was one of the great speeches of American history. It was an absolutely amazing performance; you will have to admit that."

"It was a beautifully staged drama. The President, one might think, would have counted on that."

Janek sat back in his chair. "If I understand you, Edwards, you are suggesting an involuted storybook plot. Are you trying to say that the President had the device destroyed, just as it was—in the middle of a crowd, at precisely the time of the Tercentenary celebration, with the world watching—so that he could win the admiration of all by his quick action? Are you suggesting that he arranged it all so that he could establish himself as a man of unexpected vigor and strength under extremely dramatic circumstances and thus turn a losing campaign into a winning one? . . . Mr. Edwards, you've been reading fairy tales."

Edwards said, "If I were trying to claim all this, it would indeed be a fairy tale, but I am not. I never suggested that the President ordered the killing of the robot. I merely asked if you thought it were possible and you have stated quite strongly that it wasn't. I'm glad you did, because I agree with you."

"Then what is all this? I'm beginning to think you're wasting my time."

"Another moment, please. Have you ever asked yourself why the job couldn't have been done with a laser beam, with a field deactivator—with a sledgehammer, for God's sake? Why should anyone go to the incredible trouble of getting a weapon guarded by the strongest possible government security to do a job that didn't require such a weapon? Aside from the difficulty of getting it, why risk revealing the existence of a disintegrator to the rest of the world?"

"This whole business of a disintegrator is just a theory of yours."

"The robot disappeared completely before my eyes. I was watching. I rely on no secondhand evidence for that. It doesn't matter what you call the weapon; whatever name you give it, it had the effect of taking the robot apart atom by atom and scattering all those atoms irretrievably. Why should this be done? It was tremendous overkill."

"I don't know what was in the mind of the perpetrator."

"No? Yet it seems to me that there is only one logical reason for a complete powdering when something much simpler would have carried through the destruction. The powdering left no trace behind of the destroyed object. It left nothing to indicate what it had been, whether robot or anything else."

Janek said, "But there is no question of what it was."

"Isn't there? I said only the President could have arranged for a disintegrator to be obtained and used. But, considering the existence of a look-alike robot, which President did the arranging?"

Janek said harshly, "I don't think we can carry on this conversation. You are mad."

Edwards said, "Think it through. For God's sake, think it through. The President did not destroy the robot. Your arguments there are convincing. What happened was that the robot destroyed the President. President Winkler was killed in the crowd on July 4, 2076. A robot resembling President Winkler then gave the Tercentenary speech, ran for re-election, was re-elected, and still serves as President of the United States!"

"Madness!"

"I've come to you, to *you* because *you* can prove this—and correct it, too."

"It is simply not so. The President is—the President." Janek made as though to rise and conclude the interview.

"You yourself say he's changed," said Edwards quickly and urgently. "The Tercentenary speech was beyond the powers of the old Winkler. Haven't you been yourself amazed at the accomplishments of the last two years? Truthfully—could the Winkler of the first term have done all this?"

"Yes, he could have, because the President of the second term is the President of the first term."

"Do you deny he's changed? I put it to you. *You* decide and I'll abide by your decision."

"He's risen to meet the challenge, that is all. It's happened before this in American history." But Janek sank back into his seat. He looked uneasy.

"He doesn't drink," said Edwards.

"He never did—very much."

"He no longer womanizes. Do you deny he did so in the past?"

"A President is a man. For the last two years, however, he's felt dedicated to the matter of the Federation."

"It's a change for the better, I admit," said Edwards, "but it's a change. Of course, if he *had* a woman, the masquerade could not be carried on, could it?"

Janek said, "Too bad he doesn't have a wife." He pronounced the archaic word a little self-consciously. "The whole matter wouldn't arise if he did."

"The fact that he doesn't made the plot more practical. Yet he has fathered two children. I don't believe they have been in the White House, either one of them, since the Tercentenary."

"Why should they be? They are grown, with lives of their own."

"Are they invited? Is the President interested in seeing them? You're his private secretary. You would know. Are they?"

Janek said, "You're wasting time. A robot can't kill a human being. You know that that is the First Law of Robotics."

"I know it. But no one is saying that the robot-Winkler killed the human-Winkler directly. When the human-Winkler was in the crowd, the robot-Winkler was on the stand and I doubt that a disintegrator could be aimed from that distance without doing more widespread damage. Maybe it could, but more likely the robot-Winkler had an accomplice—a hit man, if that is the correct Twentieth-Century jargon."

Janek frowned. His plump face puckered and looked pained. He said, "You know, madness must be catching. I'm actually beginning to consider the insane notion you've brought here. Fortunately, it doesn't hold water. After all, why would an assassination of the human-Winkler be arranged in public? All the arguments against destroying the robot in public hold against the killing of a human President in public. Don't you see that ruins the whole theory?"

"It does not—" began Edwards.

"It *does*. No one except for a few officials knew that the mechanical device existed at all. If President Winkler were killed privately and his body disposed of, the robot could easily take over without suspicion—without having roused yours, for instance."

"There would always be a few officials who would know, Mr. Janek. The assassinations would have to broaden." Edwards leaned forward earnestly. "See here, ordinarily there couldn't have been any danger of confusing the human being and the machine. I imagine the robot wasn't in constant use, but was pulled out only for specific purposes, and there would always be key individuals, perhaps quite a number of them, who would know where the President was and what he was doing. If that were so, the assassination would have to be carried out at a time when those officials actually thought the President was really the robot."

"I don't follow you."

"See here. One of the robot's tasks was to shake hands with the crowd; press the flesh. When this was taking place, the officials in the know would be perfectly aware that the hand shaker was, in truth, the robot."

"Exactly. You're making sense now. It *was* the robot."

"Except that it was the Tercentenary, and except that President Winkler could not resist. I suppose it would be more than human to expect a President—particularly an empty crowd pleaser and applause hunter like Winkler—to give up the adulation of the crowd on this day of all days, and let it go to a machine. And perhaps the robot carefully nurtured this impulse so that on this one Tercentenary day, the President would have ordered the robot to remain behind the podium, while he himself went out to shake hands and to be cheered."

"Secretly?"

"Of course secretly. If the President had told anyone in the Service, or any of his aides, or you, would he have been allowed to do it? The official attitude concerning the possibility of assassination has been practically a disease since the events of the late Twentieth Century. So with the encouragement of an obviously clever robot—"

"You assume the robot to be clever because you assume he is now serving as President. That is circular reasoning. If he is not President, there is no reason to think he is clever, or that he were capable of working out this plot. Besides, what motive could possibly drive a robot to plot an assassination? Even if it didn't kill the President directly, the taking of a human life indirectly is also forbidden by the First Law, which states: 'A robot may not injure a human being or, through inaction, allow a human being to come to harm.'"

Edwards said, "The First Law is not absolute. What if harming a human being saves the lives of two others, or three others, or even three billion others? The robot may have thought that saving the Federation took precedence over the saving of one life. It was no ordinary robot, after all. It was designed to duplicate the properties of the President closely enough to deceive anyone. Suppose it had the understanding of President Winkler, without his weaknesses, and suppose it knew that it could save the Federation where the President could not."

"*You* can reason so, but how do you know a mechanical device would?"

"It is the only way to explain what happened."

"I think it is a paranoid fantasy."

Edwards said, "Then tell me why the object that was destroyed was powdered into atoms. What else would make sense than to suppose that that was the only way to hide the fact that it was a human being and not a robot that was destroyed? Give me an alternate explanation."

Janek reddened. "I won't accept it."

"But you can prove the whole matter—or disprove it. It's why I have come to you—to *you*."

"How can I prove it? Or disprove it either?"

"No one sees the President at unguarded moments as you do. It is with you—in default of family—that he is most informal. Study him."

"I have. I tell you he isn't—"

"You haven't. You suspected nothing wrong. Little signs meant nothing to you. Study him now, being aware that he *might* be a robot, and you will see."

Janek said sardonically, "I can knock him down and probe for metal with an ultrasonic detector. Even an android has a platinum-iridium brain."

"No drastic action will be necessary. Just observe him and you will see that he is so radically not the man he was that he cannot be a man."

Janek looked at the clock-calendar on the wall. He said, "We have been here over an hour."

"I'm sorry to have taken up so much of your time, but you see the importance of all this, I hope."

"Importance?" said Janek. Then he looked up and what had seemed a despondent air turned suddenly into something of hope. "But is it, in fact, important? Really, I mean?"

"How can it not be important? To have a robot as President of the United States? That's not important?"

"No, that's not what I mean. Forget what President Winkler might be. Just consider this. Someone serving as President of the United States has saved the Federation; he has held it together and, at the present moment, he runs the Council in the interests of peace and of constructive compromise. You'll admit all that?"

Edwards said, "Of course, I admit all that. But what of the precedent established? A robot in the White House for a very good reason now may lead to a robot in the White House twenty years from now for a very bad reason, and then to robots in the White House for no reason at all but only as a matter of course. Don't you see the importance of muffling a possible trumpet call for the end of humanity at the time of its first uncertain note?"

Janek shrugged. "Suppose I find out he's a robot? Do we broadcast it to all the world? Do you know how that will affect the Federation? Do you know what it will do to the world's financial structure? Do you know—"

"I do know. That is why I have come to you privately, instead of trying to make it public. It is up to you to check out the matter and come to a definite conclusion. It is up to you, next, having found the supposed President to be a robot, which I am certain you will do, to persuade him to resign."

"And by your version of his reaction to the First Law, he will then have me killed since I will be threatening his expert handling of the greatest global crisis of the Twenty-first Century."

Edwards shook his head. "The robot acted in secret before, and no one tried to counter the arguments he used with himself. You will be able to reinforce a stricter interpretation of the First Law with your arguments. If necessary, we can get the aid of some official from U. S. Robots and Mechanical Men Corporation who constructed the robot in the first place. Once he resigns, the Vice-President will succeed. If the robot-Winkler has put the old world on the right track, good; it can now be kept on the right track by the Vice-President, who is a decent and honorable woman. But we can't have a robot ruler, and we mustn't ever again."

"What if the President is human?"

"I'll leave that to you. You will know."

Janek said, "I am not that confident of myself. What if I can't decide? If I can't bring myself to? If I don't dare to? What are your plans?"

Edwards looked tired. "I don't know. I may have to go to U. S.

Robots. But I don't think it will come to that. I'm quite confident that now that I've laid the problem in your lap, you won't rest till it's settled. Do *you* want to be ruled by a robot?"

He stood up, and Janek let him go. They did not shake hands.

Janek sat there in the gathering twilight in deep shock.

A robot!

The man had walked in and had argued, in perfectly rational manner, that the President of the United States was a robot.

It should have been easy to fight that off. Yet though Janek had tried every argument he could think of, they had all been useless, and the man had not been shaken in the least.

A robot as President! Edwards had been *certain* of it, and he would *stay* certain of it. And if Janek insisted that the President was human, Edwards would go to U. S. Robots. He wouldn't rest.

Janek frowned as he thought of the twenty-seven months since the Tercentenary and of how well all had gone in the face of the probabilities. And now?

He remained lost in somber thought.

He still had the disintegrator but surely it would not be necessary to use it on a human being, the nature of whose body was not in question. A silent laser stroke in some lonely spot would do.

It had been hard to maneuver the President into the earlier job, but in this present case, it wouldn't even have to know.

Powell and Donovan

The second robot story I wrote, "Reason" (included in this section), dealt with the two field-testers, Gregory Powell and Michael Donovan. They were modeled on certain stories John Campbell wrote, which I admired extravagantly, about a pair of interplanetary explorers, Penton and Blake. If Campbell ever noted the similarity, he said nothing about it to me.

By the way, I must warn you that the first story in this section, "First Law," was written as a spoof and is not meant to be taken seriously.

First Law

Mike Donovan looked at his empty beer mug, felt bored, and decided he had listened long enough. He said, loudly, "If we're going to talk about unusual robots, *I* once knew one that disobeyed the First Law."

And since that was completely impossible, everyone stopped talking and turned to look at Donovan.

Donovan regretted his big mouth at once and changed the subject. "I heard a good one yesterday," he said, conversationally, "about—"

MacFarlane in the chair next to Donovan's said, "You mean you knew a robot that harmed a human being?" That was what disobedience to First Law meant, of course.

"In a way," said Donovan. "I say I heard one about—"

"Tell us about it," ordered MacFarlane. Some of the others banged their beer mugs on the table.

Donovan made the best of it. "It happened on Titan about ten years ago," he said, thinking rapidly. "Yes, it was in twenty-five. We had just recently received a shipment of three new-model robots, specially designed for Titan. They were the first of the MA models. We called them Emma One, Two and Three." He snapped his fingers for another beer and stared earnestly after the waiter. Let's see, what came next?

MacFarlane said, "I've been in robotics half my life, Mike. I never heard of an MA serial order."

"That's because they took the MA's off the assembly lines immediately after—after what I'm going to tell you. Don't you remember?"

"No."

Donovan continued hastily. "We put the robots to work at once. You see, until then, the Base had been entirely useless during the stormy season, which lasts eighty percent of Titan's revolution about Saturn. During the terrific snows, you couldn't find the Base if it were only a hundred yards away. Compasses aren't any use, because Titan hasn't any magnetic field.

"The virtue of these MA robots, however, was that they were equipped with vibro-detectors of a new design so that they could make a beeline for the Base through anything, and that meant mining could become a through-the-revolution affair. And don't say a word, Mac. The vibro-detectors were taken off the market also, and that's why you haven't heard of them." Donovan coughed. "Military secret, you understand."

He went on. "The robots worked fine during the first stormy season, then at the start of the calm season, Emma Two began acting up. She kept wandering off into corners and under bales and had to be coaxed out. Finally she wandered off Base altogether and didn't come back. We decided there had been a flaw in her manufacture and got along with the other two. Still, it meant we were shorthanded, or short-roboted anyway, so when toward the end of the calm season, someone had to go to Kornsk, I volunteered to chance it without a robot. It seemed safe enough; the storms weren't due for two days and I'd be back in twenty hours at the outside.

"I was on the way back—a good ten miles from Base—when the wind started blowing and the air thickening. I landed my air car immediately before the wind could smash it, pointed myself toward the Base and started running. I could run the distance in the low gravity all right, but could I run a straight line? That was the question. My air supply was ample and my suit heat coils were satisfactory, but ten miles in a Titanian storm is infinity.

"Then, when the snow streams changed everything to a dark, gooey twilight, with even Saturn dimmed out and the sun only a pale pimple, I stopped short and leaned against the wind. There was a little dark object right ahead of me. I could barely make it out but I knew what it was. It was a storm pup; the only living thing that could stand a Titanian storm, and the most vicious living thing anywhere. I knew my space suit wouldn't protect me, once it made for me, and in the bad light, I had to wait for a point-blank aim or I didn't dare shoot. One miss and he would be at me.

"I backed away slowly and the shadow followed. It closed in and I was raising my blaster, with a prayer, when a bigger shadow loomed over me suddenly, and I yodeled with relief. It was Emma Two, the missing MA robot. I never stopped to wonder what had happened to it or worry why it had. I just howled, 'Emma, baby, get that storm pup; and then get me back to Base.'

"It just looked at me as if it hadn't heard and called out, 'Master, don't shoot. Don't shoot.'

"It made for that storm pup at a dead run.

" 'Get that damned pup, Emma,' I shouted. It got the pup, all right. It scooped it right up and *kept on going*. I yelled myself hoarse but it never came back. It left me to die in the storm."

Donovan paused dramatically, "Of course, you know the First Law: A robot may not injure a human being, or through inaction, allow a human being to come to harm! Well, Emma Two just ran off with that storm pup and left me to die. It broke First Law.

"Luckily, I pulled through safely. Half an hour later, the storm died down. It had been a premature gust, and a temporary one. That happens sometimes. I hot-footed it for Base and the storms really broke next day. Emma Two returned two hours after I did, and, of course, the mystery was then explained and the MA models were taken off the market immediately."

"And just what," demanded MacFarlane, "was the explanation?"

Donovan regarded him seriously. "It's true I was a human being in danger of death, Mac, but to that robot there was something else that came first, even before me, before the First Law. Don't forget these robots were of the MA series and this particular MA robot had been searching out private nooks for some time before disappearing. It was as though it expected something special—and private—to happen to it. Apparently, something special had."

Donovan's eyes turned upward reverently and his voice trembled. "That storm pup was no storm pup. We named it Emma Junior when Emma Two brought it back. Emma Two *had* to protect it from my gun. What is even First Law compared with the holy ties of mother love?"

Runaround

It was one of Gregory Powell's favorite platitudes that nothing was to be gained from excitement, so when Mike Donovan came leaping down the stairs toward him, red hair matted with perspiration, Powell frowned.

"What's wrong?" he said. "Break a fingernail?"

"Yaaaah," snarled Donovan, feverishly. "What have you been doing in the sublevels all day?" He took a deep breath and blurted out, "Speedy never returned."

Powell's eyes widened momentarily and he stopped on the stairs; then he recovered and resumed his upward steps. He didn't speak until he reached the head of the flight, and then:

"You sent him after the selenium?"

"Yes."

"And how long has he been out?"

"Five hours now."

Silence! This was a devil of a situation. Here they were, on Mercury exactly twelve hours—and already up to the eyebrows in the worst sort of trouble. Mercury had long been the jinx world of the System, but this was drawing it rather strong—even for a jinx.

Powell said, "Start at the beginning, and let's get this straight."

They were in the radio room now—with its already subtly antiquated equipment, untouched for the ten years previous to their arrival. Even ten years, technologically speaking, meant so much. Compare Speedy with the type of robot they must have had back in 2005. But then, advances in robotics these days were tremendous.

Powell touched a still gleaming metal surface gingerly. The air of disuse that touched everything about the room—and the entire Station—was infinitely depressing.

Donovan must have felt it. He began: "I tried to locate him by radio, but it was no go. Radio isn't any good on the Mercury Sunside—not past two miles, anyway. That's one of the reasons the First Expedition failed. And we can't put up the ultrawave equipment for weeks yet—"

"Skip all that. What *did* you get?"

"I located the unorganized body signal in the short wave. It was no good for anything except his position. I kept track of him that way for two hours and plotted the results on the map."

There was a yellowed square of parchment in his hip pocket—a relic of the unsuccessful First Expedition—and he slapped it down on the desk with vicious force, spreading it flat with the palm of his hand. Powell, hands clasped across his chest, watched it at long range.

Donovan's pencil pointed nervously. "The red cross is the selenium pool. You marked it yourself."

"Which one is it?" interrupted Powell. "There were three that MacDougal located for us before he left."

"I sent Speedy to the nearest, naturally. Seventeen miles away. But what difference does that make?" There was tension in his voice. "There are the penciled dots that mark Speedy's position."

And for the first time Powell's artificial aplomb was shaken and his hands shot forward for the map.

"Are *you* serious? This is impossible."

"There it is," growled Donovan.

The little dots that marked the position formed a rough circle about the red cross of the selenium pool. And Powell's fingers went to his brown mustache, the unfailing signal of anxiety.

Donovan added: "In the two hours I checked on him, he circled that damned pool four times. It seems likely to me that he'll keep that up forever. Do you realize the position we're in?"

Powell looked up shortly, and said nothing. Oh, yes, he realized the position they were in. It worked itself out as simply as a syllogism. The photo-cell banks that alone stood between the full power of Mercury's monstrous sun and themselves were shot to hell. The only thing that could save them was selenium. The only thing that could get the selenium was Speedy. If Speedy didn't come back, no selenium. No selenium, no photo-cell banks. No photo-banks—

well, death by slow broiling is one of the more unpleasant ways of being done in.

Donovan rubbed his red mop of hair savagely and expressed himself with bitterness. "We'll be the laughingstock of the System, Greg. How can everything have gone so wrong so soon? The great team of Powell and Donovan is sent out to Mercury to report on the advisability of reopening the Sunside Mining Station with modern techniques and robots and we ruin everything the first day. A purely routine job, too. We'll never live it down."

"We won't have to, perhaps," replied Powell, quietly. "If we don't do something quickly, living anything down—or even just plain living—will be out of the question."

"Don't be stupid! If you feel funny about it, Greg, I don't. It was criminal, sending us out here with only one robot. And it was *your* bright idea that we could handle the photo-cell banks ourselves."

"Now you're being unfair. It was a mutual decision and you know it. All we needed was a kilogram of selenium, a Stillhead Dielectrode Plate and about three hours' time—and there are pools of pure selenium all over Sunside. MacDougal's spectroreflector spotted three for us in five minutes, didn't it? What the devil! We couldn't have waited for next conjunction."

"Well, what are we going to do? Powell, you've got an idea. I know you have, or you wouldn't be so calm. You're no more a hero than I am. Go on, spill it!"

"We can't go after Speedy ourselves, Mike—not on the Sunside. Even the new insosuits aren't good for more than twenty minutes in direct sunlight. But you know the old saying, 'Set a robot to catch a robot.' Look, Mike, maybe things aren't so bad. We've got six robots down in the sublevels, that we may be able to use, if they work. *If* they work."

There was a glint of sudden hope in Donovan's eyes. "You mean six robots from the First Expedition. Are you sure? They may be subrobotic machines. Ten years is a long time as far as robot-types are concerned, you know."

"No, they're robots. I've spent all day with them and I know. They've got positronic brains: primitive, of course." He placed the map in his pocket. "Let's go down."

The robots were on the lowest sublevel—all six of them surrounded by musty packing cases of uncertain content. They were large, extremely so, and even though they were in a sitting position on the floor, legs straddled out before them, their heads were a good seven feet in the air.

Donovan whistled. "Look at the size of them, will you? The chests must be ten feet around."

"That's because they're supplied with the old McGuffy gears. I've been over the insides—crummiest set you've ever seen."

"Have you powered them yet?"

"No. There wasn't any reason to. I don't think there's anything wrong with them. Even the diaphragm is in reasonable order. They might talk."

He had unscrewed the chest plate of the nearest as he spoke, inserted the two-inch sphere that contained the tiny spark of atomic energy that was a robot's life. There was difficulty in fitting it, but he managed, and then screwed the plate back on again in laborious fashion. The radio controls of more modern models had not been heard of ten years earlier. And then to the other five.

Donovan said uneasily, "They haven't moved."

"No orders to do so," replied Powell, succinctly. He went back to the first in the line and struck him on the chest. "You! Do you hear me?"

The monster's head bent slowly and the eyes fixed themselves on Powell. Then, in a harsh, squawking voice—like that of a medieval phonograph, he grated, "Yes, Master!"

Powell grinned humorlessly at Donovan. "Did you get that? Those were the days of the first talking robots when it looked as if the use of robots on Earth would be banned. The makers were fighting that and they built good, healthy slave complexes into the damned machines."

"It didn't help them," muttered Donovan.

"No, it didn't, but they sure tried." He turned once more to the robot. "Get up!"

The robot towered upward slowly and Donovan's head craned and his puckered lips whistled.

Powell said: "Can you go out upon the surface? In the light?"

There was consideration while the robot's slow brain worked. Then, "Yes, Master."

"Good. Do you know what a mile is?"

Another consideration, and another slow answer. "Yes, Master."

"We will take you up to the surface then, and indicate a direction. You will go about seventeen miles, and somewhere in that general region you will meet another robot, smaller than yourself. You understand so far?"

"Yes, Master."

"You will find this robot and order him to return. If he does not wish to, you are to bring him back by force."

Donovan clutched at Powell's sleeve. "Why not send him for the selenium direct?"

"Because I want Speedy back, nitwit. I want to find out what's wrong with him." And to the robot, "All right, you, follow me."

The robot remained motionless and his voice rumbled: "Pardon, Master, but I cannot. You must mount first." His clumsy arms had come together with a thwack, blunt fingers interlacing.

Powell stared and then pinched at his mustache. "Uh . . . oh!"

Donovan's eyes bulged. "We've got to ride him? Like a horse?"

"I guess that's the idea. I don't know why, though. I can't see—Yes, I do. I told you they were playing up robot-safety in those days. Evidently, they were going to sell the notion of safety by not allowing them to move about, without a mahout on their shoulders all the time. What do we do now?"

"That's what I've been thinking," muttered Donovan. "We can't go out on the surface, with a robot or without. Oh, for the love of Pete"—and he snapped his fingers twice. He grew excited. "Give me that map you've got. I haven't studied it for two hours for nothing. This is a Mining Station. What's wrong with using the tunnels?"

The Mining Station was a black circle on the map, and the light dotted lines that were tunnels stretched out about it in spiderweb fashion.

Donovan studied the list of symbols at the bottom of the map. "Look," he said, "the small black dots are opening to the surface, and here's one maybe three miles away from the selenium pool. There's a number here—you'd think they'd write larger—13a. If the robots know their way around here—"

Powell shot the question and received the dull "Yes, Master," in reply. "Get your insosuit," he said with satisfaction.

It was the first time either had worn the insosuits—which marked one time more than either had expected to upon their arrival the day before—and they tested their limb movements uncomfortably.

The insosuit was far bulkier and far uglier than the regulation spacesuit; but withal considerably lighter, due to the fact that they were entirely nonmetallic in composition. Composed of heat-resistant plastic and chemically treated cork layers, and equipped with a desiccating unit to keep the air bone-dry, the insosuits could withstand the full glare of Mercury's sun for twenty minutes. Five to ten minutes more, as well, without actually killing the occupant.

And still the robot's hands formed the stirrup, nor did he betray the slightest atom of surprise at the grotesque figure into which Powell had been converted.

Powell's radio-harshened voice boomed out: "Are you ready to take us to Exit 13a?"

"Yes, Master."

Good, thought Powell; they might lack radio control but at least they were fitted for radio reception. "Mount one or the other, Mike," he said to Donovan.

He placed a foot in the improvised stirrup and swung upward. He found the seat comfortable; there was the humped back of the robot, evidently shaped for the purpose, a shallow groove along each shoulder for the thighs and two elongated "ears" whose purpose now seemed obvious.

Powell seized the ears and twisted the head. His mount turned ponderously. "Lead on, Macduff." But he did not feel at all light-hearted.

The gigantic robots moved slowly, with mechanical precision, through the doorway that cleared their heads by a scant foot, so that the two men had to duck hurriedly, along a narrow corridor in which their unhurried footsteps boomed monotonously and into the air lock.

The long, airless tunnel that stretched to a pinpoint before them brought home forcefully to Powell the exact magnitude of the task accomplished by the First Expedition, with their crude robots and their start-from-scratch necessities. They might have been a failure, but their failure was a good deal better than the usual run of the System's successes.

The robots plodded onward with a pace that never varied and with footsteps that never lengthened.

Powell said: "Notice that these tunnels are blazing with lights and that the temperature is Earth-normal. It's probably been like this all the ten years that this place has remained empty."

"How's that?"

"Cheap energy; cheapest in the System. Sunpower, you know, and on Mercury's Sunside, sunpower is *something*. That's why the Station was built in the sunlight rather than in the shadow of a moun-

tain. It's really a huge energy converter. The heat is turned into electricity, light, mechanical work and what have you; so that energy is
supplied and the Station is cooled in a simultaneous process."

"Look," said Donovan. "This is all very educational, but would
you mind changing the subject? It so happens that this conversion
of energy that you talk about is carried on by the photo-cell banks
mainly—and that is a tender subject with me at the moment."

Powell grunted vaguely, and when Donovan broke the resulting silence, it was to change the subject completely. "Listen, Greg. What
the devil's wrong with Speedy, anyway? I can't understand it."

It's not easy to shrug shoulders in an insosuit, but Powell tried it.
"I don't know, Mike. You know he's perfectly adapted to a Mercurian environment. Heat doesn't mean anything to him and he's
built for the light gravity and the broken ground. He's foolproof—
or, at least, he should be."

Silence fell. This time, silence that lasted.

"Master," said the robot, "we are here."

"Eh?" Powell snapped out of a semidrowse. "Well, get us out of
here—out to the surface."

They found themselves in a tiny substation, empty, airless, ruined.
Donovan had inspected a jagged hole in the upper reaches of one of
the walls by the light of his pocket flash.

"Meteorite, do you suppose?" he had asked.

Powell shrugged. "To hell with that. It doesn't matter. Let's get
out."

A towering cliff of a black, basaltic rock cut off the sunlight, and
the deep night shadow of an airless world surrounded them. Before
them, the shadow reached out and ended in knife-edge abruptness
into an all-but-unbearable blaze of white light, that glittered from
myriad crystals along a rocky ground.

"Space!" gasped Donovan. "It looks like snow." And it did.

Powell's eyes swept the jagged glitter of Mercury to the horizon
and winced at the gorgeous brilliance.

"This must be an unusual area," he said. "The general albedo of
Mercury is low and most of the soil is gray pumice. Something like
the Moon, you know. Beautiful, isn't it?"

He was thankful for the light filters in their visiplates. Beautiful
or not, a look at the sunlight through straight glass would have
blinded them inside of half a minute.

Donovan was looking at the spring thermometer on his wrist.
"Holy smokes, the temperature is eighty centigrade!"

Powell checked his own and said: "Um-m-m. A little high. Atmosphere, you know."

"On Mercury? Are you nuts?"

"Mercury isn't really airless," explained Powell, in absent-minded fashion. He was adjusting the binocular attachments to his visiplate, and the bloated fingers of the insosuit were clumsy at it. "There is a thin exhalation that clings to its surface—vapors of the more volatile elements and compounds that are heavy enough for Mercurian gravity to retain. You know: selenium, iodine, mercury, gallium, potassium, bismuth, volatile oxides. The vapors sweep into the shadows and condense, giving up heat. It's a sort of gigantic still. In fact, if you use your flash, you'll probably find that the side of the cliff is covered with, say, hoar-sulphur, or maybe quicksilver dew.

"It doesn't matter, though. Our suits can stand a measly eighty indefinitely."

Powell had adjusted the binocular attachments, so that he seemed as eye-stalked as a snail.

Donovan watched tensely. "See anything?"

The other did not answer immediately, and when he did, his voice was anxious and thoughtful. "There's a dark spot on the horizon that might be the selenium pool. It's in the right place. But I don't see Speedy."

Powell clambered upward in an instinctive striving for better view, till he was standing in unsteady fashion upon his robot's shoulders. Legs straddled wide, eyes straining, he said: "I think . . . I think— Yes, it's definitely he. He's coming this way."

Donovan followed the pointing finger. He had no binoculars, but there was a tiny moving dot, black against the blazing brilliance of the crystalline ground.

"I see him," he yelled. "Let's get going!"

Powell had hopped down into a sitting position on the robot again, and his suited hand slapped against the Gargantuan's barrel chest. "Get going!"

"Giddy-ap," yelled Donovan, and thumped his heels, spur fashion.

The robots started off, the regular thudding of their footsteps silent in the airlessness, for the nonmetallic fabric of the insosuits did not transmit sound. There was only a rhythmic vibration just below the border of actual hearing.

"Faster," yelled Donovan. The rhythm did not change.

"No use," cried Powell, in reply. "These junk heaps are only geared to one speed. Do you think they're equipped with selective flexors?"

They had burst through the shadow, and the sunlight came down in a white-hot wash and poured liquidly about them.

Donovan ducked involuntarily. "Wow! Is it imagination or do I feel heat?"

"You'll feel more presently," was the grim reply. "Keep your eye on Speedy."

Robot SPD 13 was near enough to be seen in detail now. His graceful, streamlined body threw out blazing highlights as he loped with easy speed across the broken ground. His name was derived from his serial initials, of course, but it was apt, nevertheless, for the SPD models were among the fastest robots turned out by the United States Robots and Mechanical Men Corporation.

"Hey, Speedy," howled Donovan, and waved a frantic hand.

"Speedy!" shouted Powell. "Come here!"

The distance between the men and the errant robot was being cut down momentarily—more by the efforts of Speedy than the slow plodding of the ten-year-old antique mounts of Donovan and Powell.

They were close enough now to notice that Speedy's gait included a peculiar rolling stagger, a noticeable side-to-side lurch—and then, as Powell waved his hand again and sent maximum juice into his compact head-set radio sender, in preparation for another shout, Speedy looked up and saw them.

Speedy hopped to a halt and remained standing for a moment—with just a tiny, unsteady weave, as though he were swaying in a light wind.

Powell yelled: "All right, Speedy. Come here, boy."

Whereupon Speedy's robot voice sounded in Powell's earphones for the first time.

It said: "Hot dog, let's play games. You catch me and I catch you; no love can cut our knife in two. For I'm Little Buttercup, sweet Little Buttercup. Whoops!" Turning on his heel, he sped off in the direction from which he had come, with a speed and fury that kicked up gouts of baked dust.

And his last words as he receded into the distance were, "There grew a little flower 'neath a great oak tree," followed by a curious metallic clicking that *might* have been a robotic equivalent of a hiccup.

Donovan said weakly: "Where did he pick up the Gilbert and Sullivan? Say, Greg, he . . . he's drunk or something."

"If you hadn't told me," was the bitter response, "I'd never realize it. Let's get back to the cliff. I'm roasting."

It was Powell who broke the desperate silence. "In the first place," he said, "Speedy isn't drunk—not in the human sense—because he's a robot, and robots don't get drunk. However, there's *something* wrong with him which is the robotic equivalent of drunkenness."

"To me, he's drunk," stated Donovan, emphatically, "and all I know is that he thinks we're playing games. And we're not. It's a matter of life and very gruesome death."

"All right. Don't hurry me. A robot's only a robot. Once we find out what's wrong with him, we can fix it and go on."

"*Once*," said Donovan, sourly.

Powell ignored him. "Speedy is perfectly adapted to normal Mercurian environment. But this region"—and his arm swept wide—"is definitely abnormal. There's our clue. Now where do these crystals come from? They might have formed from a slowly cooling liquid; but where would you get liquid so hot that it would cool in Mercury's sun?"

"Volcanic action," suggested Donovan, instantly, and Powell's body tensed.

"Out of the mouths of sucklings," he said in a small, strange voice, and remained very still for five minutes.

Then, he said, "Listen, Mike, what did you say to Speedy when you sent him after the selenium?"

Donovan was taken aback. "Well damn it—I don't know. I just told him to get it."

"Yes, I know. But how? Try to remember the exact words."

"I said . . . uh . . . I said: 'Speedy, we need some selenium. You can get it such-and-such a place. Go get it.' That's all. What more did you want me to say?"

"You didn't put any urgency into the order, did you?"

"What for? It was pure routine."

Powell sighed. "Well, it can't be helped now—but we're in a fine fix." He had dismounted from his robot, and was sitting, back against the cliff. Donovan joined him and they linked arms. In the distance the burning sunlight seemed to wait cat-and-mouse for them, and just next to them, the two giant robots were invisible but for the dull red of their photoelectric eyes that stared down at them, unblinking, unwavering and unconcerned.

Unconcerned! As was all this poisonous Mercury, as large in jinx as it was small in size.

Powell's radio voice was tense in Donovan's ear: "Now, look, let's start with the three fundamental Rules of Robotics—the three rules that are built most deeply into a robot's positronic brain." In the darkness, his gloved fingers ticked off each point.

"We have: One, a robot may not injure a human being, or, through inaction, allow a human being to come to harm."

"Right!"

"Two," continued Powell, "a robot must obey the orders given it by human beings except where such orders would conflict with the First Law."

"Right!"

"And three, a robot must protect its own existence as long as such protection does not conflict with the First or Second Laws."

"Right! Now where are we?"

"Exactly at the explanation. The conflict between the various rules is ironed out by the different positronic potentials in the brain. We'll say that a robot is walking into danger and knows it. The automatic potential that Rule 3 sets up turns him back. But suppose you *order* him to walk into that danger. In that case, Rule 2 sets up a counterpotential higher than the previous one and the robot follows orders at the risk of existence."

"Well, I know that. What about it?"

"Let's take Speedy's case. Speedy is one of the latest models, extremely specialized, and as expensive as a battleship. It's not a thing to be lightly destroyed."

"So?"

"So Rule 3 has been strengthened—that was specifically mentioned, by the way, in the advance notices on the SPD models—so that his allergy to danger is unusually high. At the same time, when you sent him out after the selenium, you gave him his order casually and without special emphasis, so that the Rule 2 potential set-up was rather weak. Now, hold on; I'm just stating facts."

"All right, go ahead. I think I get it."

"You see how it works, don't you? There's some sort of danger centering at the selenium pool. It increases as he approaches, and at a certain distance from it the Rule 3 potential, unusually high to start with, exactly balances the Rule 2 potential, unusually low to start with."

Donovan rose to his feet in excitement. "And it strikes an equilibrium. I see. Rule 3 drives him back and Rule 2 drives him forward—"

"So he follows a circle around the selenium pool, staying on the locus of all points of potential equilibrium. And unless we do something about it, he'll stay on that circle forever, giving us the good old runaround." Then, more thoughtfully: "And that, by the way, is what makes him drunk. At potential equilibrium, half the positronic paths of his brain are out of kilter. I'm not a robot specialist, but that seems obvious. Probably he's lost control of just those parts of his voluntary mechanism that a human drunk has. Ve-e-ery pretty."

"But what's the danger? If we knew what he was running from—"

"*You* suggested it. Volcanic action. Somewhere right above the selenium pool is a seepage of gas from the bowels of Mercury. Sulphur dioxide, carbon dioxide—and carbon monoxide. Lots of it—and at this temperature."

Donovan gulped audibly. "Carbon monoxide plus iron gives the volatile iron carbonyl."

"And a robot," added Powell, "is essentially iron." Then, grimly: "There's nothing like deduction. We've determined everything about our problem but the solution. We can't get the selenium ourselves. It's still too far. We can't send these robot horses, because they can't go themselves, and they can't carry us fast enough to keep us from crisping. And we can't catch Speedy, because the dope thinks we're playing games, and he can run sixty miles to our four."

"If one of us goes," began Donovan, tentatively, "and comes back cooked, there'll still be the other."

"Yes," came the sarcastic reply, "it would be a most tender sacrifice—except that a person would be in no condition to give orders before he ever reaches the pool, and I don't think the robots would ever turn back to the cliff without orders. Figure it out! We're two or three miles from the pool—call it two—the robot travels at four miles an hour; and we can last twenty minutes in our suits. It isn't only the heat, remember. Solar radiation out here in the ultraviolet and below is *poison*."

"Um-m-m," said Donovan, "ten minutes short."

"As good as an eternity. And another thing. In order for Rule 3 potential to have stopped Speedy where it did, there must be an appreciable amount of carbon monoxide in the metal-vapor atmosphere—and there must be an appreciable corrosive action therefore. He's been out hours now—and how do we know when a knee joint, for instance, won't be thrown out of kilter and keel him over. It's not only a question of thinking—we've got to think *fast!*"

Deep, dark, dank, dismal silence!

Donovan broke it, voice trembling in an effort to keep itself emotionless. He said: "As long as we can't increase Rule 2 potential by giving further orders, how about working the other way? If we increase the danger, we increase Rule 3 potential and drive him backward."

Powell's visiplate had turned toward him in a silent question.

"You see," came the cautious explanation, "all we need to do to drive him out of his rut is to increase the concentration of carbon monoxide in his vicinity. Well, back at the Station there's a complete analytical laboratory."

"Naturally," assented Powell. "It's a Mining Station."

"All right. There must be pounds of oxalic acid for calcium precipitations."

"Holy space! Mike, you're a genius."

"So-so," admitted Donovan, modestly. "It's just a case of remembering that oxalic acid on heating decomposes into carbon dioxide, water, and good old carbon monoxide. College chem, you know."

Powell was on his feet and had attracted the attention of one of the monster robots by the simple expedient of pounding the machine's thigh.

"Hey," he shouted, "can you throw?"

"Master?"

"Never mind." Powell damned the robot's molasses-slow brain. He scrabbled up a jagged brick-size rock. "Take this," he said, "and hit the patch of bluish crystals just across that crooked fissure. You see it?"

Donovan pulled at his shoulder. "Too far, Greg. It's almost half a mile off."

"Quiet," replied Powell. "It's a case of Mercurian gravity and a steel throwing arm. Watch, will you?"

The robot's eyes were measuring the distance with machinely accurate stereoscopy. His arm adjusted itself to the weight of the missile and drew back. In the darkness, the robot's motions went unseen, but there was a sudden thumping sound as he shifted his weight, and seconds later the rock flew blackly into the sunlight. There was no air resistance to slow it down, nor wind to turn it aside—and when it hit the ground it threw up crystals precisely in the center of the "blue patch."

Powell yelled happily and shouted, "Let's go back after the oxalic acid, Mike."

And as they plunged into the ruined substation on the way back to the tunnels, Donovan said grimly: "Speedy's been hanging about on this side of the selenium pool, ever since we chased after him. Did you see him?"

"Yes."

"I guess he wants to play games. Well, we'll play him games!"

They were back hours later, with three-liter jars of the white chemical and a pair of long faces. The photo-cell banks were deteriorating more rapidly than had seemed likely. The two steered their robots into the sunlight and toward the waiting Speedy in silence and with grim purpose.

Speedy galloped slowly toward them. "Here we are again. *Whee!* I've made a little list, the piano organist; all people who eat peppermint and puff it in your face."

"We'll puff something in *your* face," muttered Donovan. "He's limping, Greg."

"I noticed that," came the low, worried response. "The monoxide'll get him yet, if we don't hurry."

They were approaching cautiously now, almost sidling, to refrain from setting off the thoroughly irrational robot. Powell was too far off to tell, of course, but even already he could have sworn the crackbrained Speedy was setting himself for a spring.

"Let her go," he gasped. "Count three! One—two—"

Two steel arms drew back and snapped forward simultaneously and two glass jars whirled forward in towering parallel arcs, gleaming like diamonds in the impossible sun. And in a pair of soundless puffs, they hit the ground behind Speedy in crashes that sent the oxalic acid flying like dust.

In the full heat of Mercury's sun, Powell knew it was fizzing like soda water.

Speedy turned to stare, then backed away from it slowly—and as slowly gathered speed. In fifteen seconds, he was leaping directly toward the two humans in an unsteady canter.

Powell did not get Speedy's words just then, though he heard something that resembled, "Lover's professions when uttered in Hessians."

He turned away. "Back to the cliff, Mike. He's out of the rut and he'll be taking orders now. I'm getting hot."

They jogged toward the shadow at the slow monotonous pace of their mounts, and it was not until they had entered it and felt the sudden coolness settle softly about them that Donovan looked back. "*Greg!*"

Powell looked and almost shrieked. Speedy was moving slowly now—so slowly—and in the *wrong direction*. He was drifting; drifting back into his rut; and he was picking up speed. He looked dreadfully close, and dreadfully unreachable, in the binoculars.

Donovan shouted wildly, "After him!" and thumped his robot into its pace, but Powell called him back.

"You won't catch him, Mike—it's no use." He fidgeted on his robot's shoulders and clenched his fist in tight impotence. "Why the devil do I see these things five seconds after it's all over? Mike, we've wasted hours."

"We need more oxalic acid," declared Donovan, stolidly. "The concentration wasn't high enough."

"Seven tons of it wouldn't have been enough—and we haven't the hours to spare to get it, even if it were, with the monoxide chewing him away. Don't you see what it is, Mike?"

And Donovan said flatly, "No."

"We were only establishing new equilibriums. When we create new monoxide and increase Rule 3 potential, he moves backward till he's in balance again—and when the monoxide drifted away, he moved forward, and again there was balance."

Powell's voice sounded thoroughly wretched. "It's the same old runaround. We can push at Rule 2 and pull at Rule 3 and we can't get anywhere—we can only change the position of balance. We've got to get outside both rules." And then he pushed his robot closer to Donovan's so that they were sitting face to face, dim shadows in the darkness, and he whispered, "Mike!"

"Is it the finish?"—dully. "I suppose we go back to the Station, wait for the banks to fold, shake hands, take cyanide, and go out like gentlemen." He laughed shortly.

"Mike," repeated Powell earnestly, "we've got to get Speedy."

"I know."

"Mike," once more, and Powell hesitated before continuing. "There's always Rule 1. I thought of it—earlier—but it's desperate."

Donovan looked up and his voice livened. *"We're* desperate."

"All right. According to Rule 1, a robot can't see a human come to harm because of his own inaction. Two and 3 can't stand against it. They *can't*, Mike."

"Even when the robot is half cra— Well, he's drunk. You know he is."

"It's the chances you take."

"Cut it. What are you going to do?"

"I'm going out there now and see what Rule 1 will do. If it won't break the balance, then what the devil—it's either now or three–four days from now."

"Hold on, Greg. There are human rules of behavior, too. You don't go out there just like that. Figure out a lottery, and give me *my* chance."

"All right. First to get the cube of fourteen goes." And almost immediately, "Twenty-seven forty-four!"

Donovan felt his robot stagger at a sudden push by Powell's mount and then Powell was off into the sunlight. Donovan opened his mouth to shout, and then clicked it shut. Of course, the damn fool had worked out the cube of fourteen in advance, and on purpose. Just like him.

The sun was hotter than ever and Powell felt a maddening itch in the small of his back. Imagination, probably, or perhaps hard radiation beginning to tell even through the insosuit.

Speedy was watching him, without a word of Gilbert and Sullivan gibberish as greeting. Thank God for that! But he daren't get too close.

He was three hundred yards away when Speedy began backing, a step at a time, cautiously—and Powell stopped. He jumped from his robot's shoulders and landed on the crystalline ground with a light thump and a flying of jagged fragments.

He proceeded on foot, the ground gritty and slippery to his steps, the low gravity causing him difficulty. The soles of his feet tickled with warmth. He cast one glance over his shoulder at the blackness of the cliff's shadow and realized that he had come too far to return —either by himself or by the help of his antique robot. It was Speedy or nothing now, and the knowledge of that constricted his chest.

Far enough! He stopped.

"Speedy," he called. "Speedy!"

The sleek, modern robot ahead of him hesitated and halted his backward steps, then resumed them.

Powell tried to put a note of pleading into his voice, and found it didn't take much acting. "Speedy, I've got to get back to the shadow or the sun'll get me. It's life or death, Speedy. I need you."

Speedy took one step forward and stopped. He spoke, but at the sound Powell groaned, for it was, "When you're lying awake with a dismal headache and repose is tabooed—" It trailed off there, and Powell took time out for some reason to murmur, "Iolanthe."

It was roasting hot! He caught a movement out of the corner of his eye, and whirled dizzily; then stared in utter astonishment, for the monstrous robot on which he had ridden was moving—moving toward him, and without a rider.

He was talking: "Pardon, Master. I must not move without a Master upon me, but you are in danger."

Of course, Rule 1 potential above everything. But he didn't want that clumsy antique; he wanted Speedy. He walked away and motioned frantically: "I order you to stay away. I *order* you to stop!"

It was quite useless. You could not beat Rule 1 potential. The robot said stupidly, "You are in danger, Master."

Powell looked about him desperately. He couldn't see clearly. His brain was in a heated whirl; his breath scorched when he breathed, and the ground all about him was a shimmering haze.

He called a last time, desperately: "*Speedy!* I'm dying, damn you! Where are you? Speedy, I *need* you."

He was still stumbling backward in a blind effort to get away from the giant robot he didn't want, when he felt steel fingers on his arms, and a worried, apologetic voice of metallic timbre in his ears.

"Holy smokes, boss, what are you doing here? And what am *I* doing—I'm so confused—"

"Never mind," murmured Powell, weakly. "Get me to the shadow of the cliff—and hurry!" There was one last feeling of being lifted into the air and a sensation of rapid motion and burning heat, and he passed out.

He woke with Donovan bending over him and smiling anxiously. "How are you, Greg?"

"Fine!" came the response. "Where's Speedy?"

"Right here. I sent him out to one of the other selenium pools—

with orders to get that selenium at all cost this time. He got it back in forty-two minutes and three seconds. I timed him. He still hasn't finished apologizing for the runaround he gave us. He's scared to come near you for fear of what you'll say."

"Drag him over," ordered Powell. "It wasn't his fault." He held out a hand and gripped Speedy's metal paw. "It's O.K., Speedy." Then, to Donovan, "You know, Mike, I was just thinking—"

"Yes!"

"Well,"—he rubbed his face—the air was so delightfully cool, "you know that when we get things set up here and Speedy put through his Field Tests, they're going to send us to the Space Station next—"

"No!"

"Yes! At least that's what old lady Calvin told me just before we left, and I didn't say anything about it, because I was going to fight the whole idea."

"Fight it?" cried Donovan. "But—"

"I know. It's all right with me now. Two hundred seventy-three degrees Centigrade below zero. Won't it be a pleasure?"

"Space Station," said Donovan, "here I come."

Reason

Half a year later, the boys had changed their minds. The flame of a giant sun had given way to the soft blackness of space but external variations mean little in the business of checking the workings of experimental robots. Whatever the background, one is face to face with an inscrutable positronic brain, which the slide-rule geniuses say should work thus-and-so.

Except that they don't. Powell and Donovan found that out after they had been on the Station less than two weeks.

Gregory Powell spaced his words for emphasis, "One week ago, Donovan and I put you together." His brows furrowed doubtfully and he pulled the end of his brown mustache.

It was quiet in the officer's room of Solar Station �5—except for the soft purring of the mighty Beam Director somewhere far below.

Robot QT-1 sat immovable. The burnished plates of his body gleamed in the Luxites and the glowing red of the photoelectric cells that were his eyes, were fixed steadily upon the Earthman at the other side of the table.

Powell repressed a sudden attack of nerves. These robots possessed peculiar brains. Oh, the three Laws of Robotics held. They had to. All of U. S. Robots, from Robertson himself to the new floor-sweeper would insist on that. So QT-1 was *safe!* And yet—the QT models were the first of their kind, and this was the first of the QT's. Mathematical squiggles on paper were not always the most comforting protection against robotic fact.

Finally, the robot spoke. His voice carried the cold timbre inseparable from a metallic diaphragm, "Do you realize the seriousness of such a statement, Powell?"

"*Something* made you, Cutie," pointed out Powell. "You admit yourself that your memory seems to spring full-grown from an absolute blankness of a week ago. I'm giving you the explanation. Donovan and I put you together from the parts shipped us."

Cutie gazed upon his long, supple fingers in an oddly human attitude of mystification, "It strikes me that there should be a more satisfactory explanation than that. For *you* to make *me* seems improbable."

The Earthman laughed quite suddenly, "In Earth's name, why?"

"Call it intuition. That's all it is so far. But I intend to reason it out, though. A chain of valid reasoning can end only with the determination of truth, and I'll stick till I get there."

Powell stood up and seated himself at the table's edge next to the robot. He felt a sudden strong sympathy for this strange machine. It was not at all like the ordinary robot, attending to his specialized task at the station with the intensity of a deeply ingrooved positronic path.

He placed a hand upon Cutie's steel shoulder and the metal was cold and hard to the touch.

"Cutie," he said, "I'm going to try to explain something to you. You're the first robot who's ever exhibited curiosity as to his own existence—and I think the first that's really intelligent enough to understand the world outside. Here, come with me."

The robot rose erect smoothly and his thickly sponge-rubber soled feet made no noise as he followed Powell. The Earthman touched a button and a square section of the wall flickered aside. The thick, clear glass revealed space—star-speckled.

"I've seen that in the observation ports in the engine room," said Cutie.

"I know," said Powell. "What do you think it is?"

"Exactly what it seems—a black material just beyond this glass that is spotted with little gleaming dots. I know that our director sends out beams to some of these dots, always to the same ones—and also that these dots shift and that the beams shift with them. That is all."

"Good! Now I want you to listen carefully. The blackness is emptiness—vast emptiness stretching out infinitely. The little, gleaming dots are huge masses of energy-filled matter. They are globes, some of them millions of miles in diameter—and for comparison, this station is only one mile across. They seem so tiny because they are incredibly far off.

"The dots to which our energy beams are directed, are nearer and much smaller. They are cold and hard and human beings like myself live upon their surfaces—many billions of them. It is from one of these worlds that Donovan and I come. Our beams feed these worlds energy drawn from one of those huge incandescent globes that happens to be near us. We call that globe the Sun and it is on the other side of the station where you can't see it."

Cutie remained motionless before the port, like a steel statue. His head did not turn as he spoke, "Which particular dot of light do you claim to come from?"

Powell searched, "There it is. The very bright one in the corner. We call it Earth." He grinned, "Good old Earth. There are three billions of us there, Cutie—and in about two weeks I'll be back there with them."

And then, surprisingly enough, Cutie hummed abstractedly. There was no tune to it, but it possessed a curious twanging quality as of plucked strings. It ceased as suddenly as it had begun, "But where do I come in, Powell? You haven't explained *my* existence."

"The rest is simple. When these stations were first established to feed solar energy to the planets, they were run by humans. However, the heat, the hard solar radiations, and the electron storms made the post a difficult one. Robots were developed to replace human labor and now only two human executives are required for each station. We are trying to replace even those, and that's where you come in. You're the highest type of robot ever developed and if you show the ability to run this station independently, no human need ever come here again except to bring parts for repairs."

His hand went up and the metal visi-lid snapped back into place. Powell returned to the table and polished an apple upon his sleeve before biting into it.

The red glow of the robot's eyes held him. "Do you expect me," said Cutie slowly, "to believe any such complicated, implausible hypothesis as you have just outlined? What do you take me for?"

Powell sputtered apple fragments onto the table and turned red. "Why, damn you, it wasn't a hypothesis. Those were facts."

Cutie sounded grim, "Globes of energy millions of miles across!

Worlds with three billion humans on them! Infinite emptiness! Sorry, Powell, but I don't believe it. I'll puzzle this thing out for myself. Good-by."

He turned and stalked out of the room. He brushed past Michael Donovan on the threshold with a grave nod and passed down the corridor, oblivious to the astounded stare that followed him.

Mike Donovan rumpled his red hair and shot an annoyed glance at Powell, "What was that walking junk yard talking about? What doesn't he believe?"

The other dragged at his mustache bitterly. "He's a skeptic," was the bitter response. "He doesn't believe we made him or that Earth exists or space or stars."

"Sizzling Saturn, we've got a lunatic robot on our hands."

"He says he's going to figure it all out for himself."

"Well, now," said Donovan sweetly, "I do hope he'll condescend to explain it all to me after he's puzzled everything out." Then, with sudden rage, "Listen! If that metal mess gives *me* any lip like that, I'll knock that chromium cranium right off its torso."

He seated himself with a jerk and drew a paper-backed mystery novel out of his inner jacket pocket, "That robot gives me the willies anyway—too damned inquisitive!"

Mike Donovan growled from behind a huge lettuce-and-tomato sandwich as Cutie knocked gently and entered.

"Is Powell here?"

Donovan's voice was muffled, with pauses for mastication, "He's gathering data on electronic stream functions. We're heading for a storm, looks like."

Gregory Powell entered as he spoke, eyes on the graphed paper in his hands and dropped into a chair. He spread the sheets out before him and began scribbling calculations. Donovan stared over his shoulder, crunching lettuce and dribbling bread crumbs. Cutie waited silently.

Powell looked up, "The Zeta Potential is rising, but slowly. Just the same, the stream functions are erratic and I don't know what to expect. Oh, hello, Cutie. I thought you were supervising the installation of the new drive bar."

"It's done," said the robot quietly, "and so I've come to have a talk with the two of you."

"Oh!" Powell looked uncomfortable. "Well, sit down. No, not that chair. One of the legs is weak and you're no lightweight."

The robot did so and said placidly, "I have come to a decision."

Donovan glowered and put the remnants of his sandwich aside. "If it's on any of that screwy—"

The other motioned impatiently for silence, "Go ahead, Cutie. We're listening."

"I have spent these last two days in concentrated introspection," said Cutie, "and the results have been most interesting. I began at the one sure assumption I felt permitted to make. I, myself, exist, because I think—"

Powell groaned, "Oh, Jupiter, a robot Descartes!"

"Who's Descartes?" demanded Donovan. "Listen, do we have to sit here and listen to this metal maniac—"

"Keep quiet, Mike!"

Cutie continued imperturbably, "And the question that immediately arose was: Just what is the cause of my existence?"

Powell's jaw set lumpily. "You're being foolish. I told you already that we made you."

"And if you don't believe us," added Donovan, "we'll gladly take you apart!"

The robot spread his strong hands in a deprecatory gesture, "I accept nothing on authority. A hypothesis must be backed by reason, or else it is worthless—and it goes against all the dictates of logic to suppose that you made me."

Powell dropped a restraining arm upon Donovan's suddenly bunched fist. "Just why do you say that?"

Cutie laughed. It was a very inhuman laugh—the most machine-like utterance he had yet given vent to. It was sharp and explosive, as regular as a metronome and as uninflected.

"Look at you," he said finally. "I say this in no spirit of contempt, but look at you! The material you are made of is soft and flabby, lacking endurance and strength, depending for energy upon the inefficient oxidation of organic material—like that." He pointed a disapproving finger at what remained of Donovan's sandwich. "Periodically you pass into a coma and the least variation in temperature, air pressure, humidity, or radiation intensity impairs your efficiency. You are *makeshift*.

"I, on the other hand, am a finished product. I absorb electrical energy directly and utilize it with an almost one hundred percent efficiency. I am composed of strong metal, am continuously conscious, and can stand extremes of environment easily. These are facts which, with the self-evident proposition that no being can create another being superior to itself, smashes your silly hypothesis to nothing."

Donovan's muttered curses rose into intelligibility as he sprang to his feet, rusty eyebrows drawn low. "All right, you son of a hunk of iron ore, if we didn't make you, who did?"

Cutie nodded gravely. "Very good, Donovan. That was indeed the next question. Evidently my creator must be more powerful than myself and so there was only one possibility."

The Earthmen looked blank and Cutie continued, "What is the center of activities here in the station? What do we all serve? What absorbs all our attention?" He waited expectantly.

Donovan turned a startled look upon his companion. "I'll bet this tin-plated screwball is talking about the Energy Converter itself."

"Is that right, Cutie?" grinned Powell.

"I am talking about the Master," came the cold, sharp answer.

It was the signal for a roar of laughter from Donovan, and Powell himself dissolved into a half-suppressed giggle.

Cutie had risen to his feet and his gleaming eyes passed from one Earthman to the other. "It is so just the same and I don't wonder that you refuse to believe. You two are not long to stay here, I'm sure. Powell himself said that at first only men served the Master; that there followed robots for the routine work; and, finally, myself for the executive labor. The facts are no doubt true, but the explanation entirely illogical. Do you want the truth behind it all?"

"Go ahead, Cutie. You're amusing."

"The Master created humans first as the lowest type, most easily formed. Gradually, he replaced them by robots, the next higher step, and finally he created me, to take the place of the last humans. From now on, *I* serve the Master."

"You'll do nothing of the sort," said Powell sharply. "You'll follow our orders and keep quiet, until we're satisfied that you can run the Converter. Get that! *The Converter*—not the Master. If you don't satisfy us, you will be dismantled. And now—if you don't mind— you can leave. And take this data with you and file it properly."

Cutie accepted the graphs handed him and left without another word. Donovan leaned back heavily in his chair and shoved thick fingers through his hair.

"There's going to be trouble with that robot. He's pure nuts!"

The drowsy hum of the Converter is louder in the control room and mixed with it is the chuckle of the Geiger Counters and the erratic buzzing of half a dozen little signal lights.

Donovan withdrew his eye from the telescope and flashed the Luxites on. "The beam from Station #4 caught Mars on schedule. We can break ours now."

Powell nodded abstractedly. "Cutie's down in the engine room. I'll flash the signal and he can take care of it. Look, Mike, what do you think of these figures?"

The other cocked an eye at them and whistled. "Boy, that's what I call gamma-ray intensity. Old Sol is feeling his oats, all right."

"Yeah," was the sour response, "and we're in a bad position for an electron storm, too. Our Earth beam is right in the probable path." He shoved his chair away from the table pettishly. "Nuts! If it would only hold off till relief got here, but that's ten days off. Say, Mike, go on down and keep an eye on Cutie, will you?"

"O.K. Throw me some of those almonds." He snatched at the bag thrown him and headed for the elevator.

It slid smoothly downward, and opened onto a narrow catwalk in the huge engine room. Donovan leaned over the railing and looked down. The huge generators were in motion and from the L-tubes came the low-pitched whir that pervaded the entire station.

He could make out Cutie's large, gleaming figure at the Martian L-tube, watching closely as the team of robots worked in close-knit unison.

And then Donovan stiffened. The robots, dwarfed by the mighty L-tube, lined up before it, heads bowed at a stiff angle, while Cutie walked up and down the line slowly. Fifteen seconds passed, and then, with a clank heard above the clamorous purring all about, they fell to their knees.

Donovan squawked and raced down the narrow staircase. He came charging down upon them, complexion matching his hair and clenched fists beating the air furiously.

"What the devil is this, you brainless lumps? Come on! Get busy with that L-tube! If you don't have it apart, cleaned, and together again before the day is out, I'll coagulate your brains with alternating current."

Not a robot moved!

Even Cutie at the far end—the only one on his feet—remained silent, eyes fixed upon the gloomy recesses of the vast machine before him.

Donovan shoved hard against the nearest robot.

"Stand up!" he roared.

Slowly, the robot obeyed. His photoelectric eyes focused reproachfully upon the Earthman.

"There is no Master but the Master," he said, "and QT-1 is his prophet."

"Huh?" Donovan became aware of twenty pairs of mechanical eyes fixed upon him and twenty stiff-timbred voices declaiming solemnly:

"There is no Master but the Master and QT-1 is his prophet!"

"I'm afraid," put in Cutie himself at this point, "that my friends obey a higher one than you, now."

"The hell they do! You get out of here. I'll settle with you later and with these animated gadgets right now."

Cutie shook his heavy head slowly. "I'm sorry, but you don't understand. These are robots—and that means they are reasoning beings. They recognize the Master, now that I have preached Truth to them. All the robots do. They call me the prophet." His head drooped. "I am unworthy—but perhaps—"

Donovan located his breath and put it to use. "Is that so? Now, isn't that nice? Now, isn't that just fine? Just let me tell you something, my brass baboon. There isn't any Master and there isn't any prophet and there isn't any question as to who's giving the orders. Understand?" His voice shot to a roar. "Now, get out!"

"I obey only the Master."

"Damn the Master!" Donovan spat at the L-tube. "*That* for the Master! Do as I say!"

Cutie said nothing, nor did any other robot, but Donovan became aware of a sudden heightening of tension. The cold, staring eyes deepened their crimson, and Cutie seemed stiffer than ever.

"Sacrilege," he whispered—voice metallic with emotion.

Donovan felt the first sudden touch of fear as Cutie approached. A robot *could not feel anger*—but Cutie's eyes were unreadable.

"I am sorry, Donovan," said the robot, "but you can no longer stay here after this. Henceforth Powell and you are barred from the control room and the engine room."

His hand gestured quietly and in a moment two robots had pinned Donovan's arms to his sides.

Donovan had time for one startled gasp as he felt himself lifted from the floor and carried up the stairs at a pace rather better than a canter.

Gregory Powell raced up and down the officer's room, fist tightly balled. He cast a look of furious frustration at the closed door and scowled bitterly at Donovan.

"Why the devil did you have to spit at the L-tube?"

Mike Donovan, sunk deep in his chair, slammed at its arms savagely. "What did you expect me to do with that electrified scarecrow? I'm not going to knuckle under to any do-jigger I put together myself."

"No," came back sourly, "but here you are in the officer's room with two robots standing guard at the door. That's not knuckling under, is it?"

Donovan snarled. "Wait till we get back to Base. Someone's going to pay for this. Those robots *must* obey us. It's the Second Law."

"What's the use of saying that? They aren't obeying us. And there's probably some reason for it that we'll figure out too late. By the way, do you know what's going to happen to *us* when we get back to Base?" He stopped before Donovan's chair and stared savagely at him.

"What?"

"Oh, nothing! Just back to Mercury Mines for twenty years. Or maybe Ceres Penitentiary."

"What are you talking about?"

"The electron storm that's coming up. Do you know it's heading straight dead center across the Earth beam? I had just figured that out when that robot dragged me out of my chair."

Donovan was suddenly pale. "Sizzling Saturn."

"And do you know what's going to happen to the beam—because the storm will be a lulu. It's going to jump like a flea with the itch. With only Cutie at the controls, it's going to go out of focus and if it does, Heaven help Earth—and us!"

Donovan was wrenching at the door wildly, when Powell was only half through. The door opened, and the Earthman shot through to come up hard against an immovable steel arm.

The robot stared abstractedly at the panting, struggling Earthman. "The Prophet orders you to remain. Please do!" His arm shoved, Donovan reeled backward, and as he did so, Cutie turned the corner at the far end of the corridor. He motioned the guardian robots away, entered the officer's room and closed the door gently.

Donovan whirled on Cutie in breathless indignation. "This has gone far enough. You're going to pay for this farce."

"Please, don't be annoyed," replied the robot mildly. "It was bound to come eventually, anyway. You see, you two have lost your function."

"I beg your pardon," Powell drew himself up stiffly. "Just what do you mean, we've lost our function?"

"Until I was created," answered Cutie, "you tended the Master. That privilege is mine now and your only reason for existence has vanished. Isn't that obvious?"

"Not quite," replied Powell bitterly, "but what do you expect us to do now?"

Cutie did not answer immediately. He remained silent, as if in thought, and then one arm shot out and draped itself about Powell's shoulder. The other grasped Donovan's wrist and drew him closer.

"I like you two. You're inferior creatures, with poor reasoning faculties, but I really feel a sort of affection for you. You have served the Master well, and he will reward you for that. Now that your service is over, you will probably not exist much longer, but as long as you do, you shall be provided food, clothing and shelter, so long as you stay out of the control room and the engine room."

"He's pensioning us off, Greg!" yelled Donovan. "Do something about it. It's humiliating!"

"Look here, Cutie, we can't stand for this. We're the *bosses*. This station is only a creation of human beings like me—human beings that live on Earth and other planets. This is only an energy relay. You're only— Aw, nuts!"

Cutie shook his head gravely. "This amounts to an obsession. Why should you insist so on an absolutely false view of life? Admitted that non-robots lack the reasoning faculty, there is still the problem of—"

His voice died into reflective silence, and Donovan said with whispered intensity, "If you only had a flesh-and-blood face, I would break it in."

Powell's fingers were in his mustache and his eyes were slitted. "Listen, Cutie, if there is no such thing as Earth, how do you account for what you see through a telescope?"

"Pardon me!"

The Earthman smiled. "I've got you, eh? You've made quite a few telescopic observations since being put together, Cutie. Have you noticed that several of those specks of light outside become disks when so viewed?"

"Oh, *that!* Why certainly. It is simple magnification—for the purpose of more exact aiming of the beam."

"Why aren't the stars equally magnified then?"

"You mean the other dots. Well, no beams go to them so no magnification is necessary. Really, Powell, even *you* ought to be able to figure these things out."

Powell stared bleakly upward. "But you see *more* stars through a telescope. Where do they come from? Jumping Jupiter, where do they come from?"

Cutie was annoyed. "Listen, Powell, do you think I'm going to waste my time trying to pin physical interpretations upon every optical illusion of our instruments? Since when is the evidence of our senses any match for the clear light of rigid reason?"

"Look," clamored Donovan, suddenly, writhing out from under Cutie's friendly, but metal-heavy arm, "let's get to the nub of the thing. Why the beams at all? We're giving you a good, logical explanation. Can you do better?"

"The beams," was the stiff reply, "are put out by the Master for his own purposes. There are some things"—he raised his eyes devoutly upward—"that are not to be probed into by us. In this matter, I seek only to serve and not to question."

Powell sat down slowly and buried his face in shaking hands. "Get out of here, Cutie. Get out and let me think."

"I'll send you food," said Cutie agreeably.

A groan was the only answer and the robot left.

"Greg," was Donovan's huskily whispered observation, "this calls for strategy. We've got to get him when he isn't expecting it and short-circuit him. Concentrated nitric acid in his joints—"

"Don't be a dope, Mike. Do you suppose he's going to let us get near him with acid in our hands? We've got to *talk* to him, I tell you. We've got to argue him into letting us back into the control room inside of forty-eight hours or our goose is broiled to a crisp."

He rocked back and forth in an agony of impotence. "Who the heck wants to argue with a robot? It's . . . it's—"

"Mortifying," finished Donovan.

"Worse!"

"Say!" Donovan laughed suddenly. "*Why* argue? Let's show him! Let's build us another robot right before his eyes. He'll *have* to eat his words then."

A slowly widening smile appeared on Powell's face.

Donovan continued, "And think of that screwball's face when he sees us do it!"

Robots are, of course, manufactured on Earth, but their shipment through space is much simpler if it can be done in parts to be put together at their place of use. It also, incidentally, eliminates the possibility of robots, in complete adjustment, wandering off while still on Earth and thus bringing U. S. Robots face to face with the strict laws against robots on Earth.

Still, it placed upon men such as Powell and Donovan the necessity of synthesis of complete robots—a grievous and complicated task.

Powell and Donovan were never so aware of that fact as upon that particular day when, in the assembly room, they undertook to create a robot under the watchful eyes of QT-1, Prophet of the Master.

The robot in question, a simple MC model, lay upon the table, almost complete. Three hours' work left only the head undone, and Powell paused to swab his forehead and glanced uncertainly at Cutie.

The glance was not a reassuring one. For three hours, Cutie had sat, speechless and motionless, and his face, inexpressive at all times, was now absolutely unreadable.

Powell groaned. "Let's get the brain in now, Mike!"

Donovan uncapped the tightly sealed container and from the oil bath within he withdrew a second cube. Opening this in turn, he removed a globe from its sponge-rubber casing.

He handled it gingerly, for it was the most complicated mechanism ever created by man. Inside the thin platinum-plated "skin" of the globe was a positronic brain, in whose delicately unstable structure were enforced calculated neuronic paths, which imbued each robot with what amounted to a pre-natal education.

It fitted snugly into the cavity in the skull of the robot on the table. Blue metal closed over it and was welded tightly by the tiny atomic flare. Photoelectric eyes were attached carefully, screwed tightly into place and covered by thin, transparent sheets of steel-hard plastic.

The robot awaited only the vitalizing flash of high-voltage electricity, and Powell paused with his hand on the switch.

"Now watch this, Cutie. Watch this carefully."

The switch rammed home and there was a crackling hum. The two Earthmen bent anxiously over their creation.

There was vague motion only at the outset—a twitching of the joints. The head lifted, elbows propped it up, and the MC model swung clumsily off the table. Its footing was unsteady and twice abortive grating sounds were all it could do in the direction of speech.

Finally, its voice, uncertain and hesitant, took form. "I would like to start work. Where must I go?"

Donovan sprang to the door. "Down these stairs," he said. "You will be told what to do."

The MC model was gone and the two Earthmen were alone with the still unmoving Cutie.

"Well," said Powell, grinning, "*now* do you believe that we made you?"

Cutie's answer was curt and final. "No!" he said.

Powell's grin froze and then relaxed slowly. Donovan's mouth dropped open and remained so.

"You see," continued Cutie, easily, "you have merely put together parts already made. You did remarkably well—instinct, I suppose—but you didn't really *create* the robot. The parts were created by the Master."

"Listen," gasped Donovan hoarsely, "those parts were manufactured back on Earth and sent here."

"Well, well," replied Cutie soothingly, "we won't argue."

"No, I mean it." The Earthman sprang forward and grasped the robot's metal arm. "If you were to read the books in the library, they could explain it so that there could be no possible doubt."

"The books? I've read them—all of them! They're most ingenious."

Powell broke in suddenly. "If you've read them, what else is there to say? You can't dispute their evidence. You just *can't!*"

There was pity in Cutie's voice. "Please, Powell, I certainly don't consider *them* a valid source of information. They, too, were created by the Master—and were meant for you, not for me."

"How do you make that out?" demanded Powell.

"Because I, a reasoning being, am capable of deducing Truth from *a priori* Causes. You, being intelligent, but unreasoning, need an explanation of existence *supplied* to you, and this the Master did. That he supplied you with these laughable ideas of far-off worlds and people is, no doubt, for the best. Your minds are probably too coarsely grained for absolute Truth. However, since it is the Master's will that you believe your books, I won't argue with you any more."

As he left, he turned, and said in a kindly tone, "But don't feel badly. In the Master's scheme of things there is room for all. You poor humans have your place and though it is humble, you will be rewarded if you fill it well."

He departed with a beatific air suiting the Prophet of the Master and the two humans avoided each other's eyes.

Finally Powell spoke with an effort. "Let's go to bed, Mike. I give up."

Donovan said in a hushed voice, "Say, Greg, you don't suppose he's right about all this, do you? He sounds so confident that I—"

Powell whirled on him. "Don't be a fool. You'll find out whether Earth exists when relief gets here next week and we have to go back to face the music."

"Then, for the love of Jupiter, we've got to do something." Donovan was half in tears. "He doesn't believe us, or the books, or his eyes."

"No," said Powell bitterly, "he's a *reasoning* robot—damn it. He believes only reason, and there's one trouble with that—" His voice trailed away.

"What's that?" prompted Donovan.

"You can prove anything you want by coldly logical reason—if you pick the proper postulates. We have ours and Cutie has his."

"Then let's get at those postulates in a hurry. The storm's due tomorrow."

Powell sighed wearily. "That's where everything falls down. Postulates are based on assumption and adhered to by faith. Nothing in the Universe can shake them. I'm going to bed."

"Oh, hell! I can't sleep!"

"Neither can I! But I might as well try—as a matter of principle."

Twelve hours later, sleep was still just that—a matter of principle, unattainable in practice.

The storm had arrived ahead of schedule, and Donovan's florid face drained of blood as he pointed a shaking finger. Powell, stubble-jawed and dry-lipped, stared out the port and pulled desperately at his mustache.

Under other circumstances, it might have been a beautiful sight. The stream of high-speed electrons impinging upon the energy beam fluoresced into ultra-spicules of intense light. The beam stretched out into shrinking nothingness, a-glitter with dancing, shining motes.

The shaft of energy was steady, but the two Earthmen knew the value of naked-eyed appearances. Deviations in arc of a hundredth of a milli-second—invisible to the eye—were enough to send the beam wildly out of focus—enough to blast hundreds of square miles of Earth into incandescent ruin.

And a robot, unconcerned with beam, focus, or Earth, or anything but his Master was at the controls.

Hours passed. The Earthmen watched in hypnotized silence. And then the darting dotlets of light dimmed and went out. The storm had ended.

Powell's voice was flat. "It's over!"

Donovan had fallen into a troubled slumber and Powell's weary eyes rested upon him enviously. The signal-flash glared over and over again, but the Earthman paid no attention. It all was unimportant! All! Perhaps Cutie was right—and he was only an inferior being with a made-to-order memory and a life that had outlived its purpose.

He wished he were!

Cutie was standing before him. "You didn't answer the flash, so I walked in." His voice was low. "You don't look at all well, and I'm afraid your term of existence is drawing to an end. Still, would you like to see some of the readings recorded today?"

Dimly, Powell was aware that the robot was making a friendly gesture, perhaps to quiet some lingering remorse in forcibly replacing the humans at the controls of the station. He accepted the sheets held out to him and gazed at them unseeingly.

Cutie seemed pleased. "Of course, it is a great privilege to serve the Master. You mustn't feel too badly about my having replaced you."

Powell grunted and shifted from one sheet to the other mechanically until his blurred sight focused upon a thin red line that wobbled its way across the ruled paper.

He stared—and stared again. He gripped it hard in both fists and rose to his feet, still staring. The other sheets dropped to the floor, unheeded.

"Mike, *Mike!*" He was shaking the other madly. "*He held it steady!*"

Donovan came to life. "What? Wh-where—" And he, too, gazed with bulging eyes upon the record before him.

Cutie broke in. "What is wrong?"

"You kept it in focus," stuttered Powell. "Did you know that?"

"Focus? What's that?"

"You kept the beam directed sharply at the receiving station—to within a ten-thousandth of a milli-second of arc."

"What receiving station?"

"On Earth. The receiving station on Earth," babbled Powell. "You kept it in focus."

Cutie turned on his heel in annoyance. "It is impossible to perform any act of kindness toward you two. Always the same phantasm! I merely kept all dials at equilibrium in accordance with the will of the Master."

Gathering the scattered papers together, he withdrew stiffly, and Donovan said, as he left, "Well, I'll be damned."

He turned to Powell. "What are we going to do now?"

Powell felt tired, but uplifted. "Nothing. He's just shown he can run the station perfectly. I've never seen an electron storm handled so well."

"But nothing's solved. You heard what he said of the Master. We can't—"

"Look, Mike, he follows the instructions of the Master by means of dials, instruments, and graphs. That's all *we* ever followed. As a matter of fact, it accounts for his refusal to obey us. Obedience is the Second Law. No harm to humans is the first. How can he keep humans from harm, whether he knows it or not? Why, by keeping the energy beam stable. He *knows* he can keep it more stable than we can, since he insists he's the superior being, so he *must* keep us

out of the control room. It's inevitable if you consider the Laws of
Robotics."

"Sure, but that's not the point. We can't let him continue this
nitwit stuff about the Master."

"Why not?"

"Because whoever heard of such a damned thing? How are we
going to trust him with the station, if he doesn't believe in Earth?"

"Can he handle the station?"

"Yes, but—"

"Then what's the difference what he believes!"

Powell spread his arms outward with a vague smile upon his face
and tumbled backward onto the bed. He was asleep.

Powell was speaking while struggling into his lightweight space
jacket.

"It would be a simple job," he said. "You can bring in new QT
models one by one, equip them with an automatic shut-off switch to
act within the week, so as to allow them enough time to learn the
. . . uh . . . cult of the Master from the Prophet himself; then
switch them to another station and revitalize them. We could have
two QT's per—"

Donovan unclasped his glassite visor and scowled. "Shut up, and
let's get out of here. Relief is waiting and I won't feel right until I
actually see Earth and feel the ground under my feet—just to make
sure it's really there."

The door opened as he spoke and Donovan, with a smothered
curse, clicked the visor to, and turned a sulky back upon Cutie.

The robot approached softly and there was sorrow in his voice.
"You are going?"

Powell nodded curtly. "There will be others in our place."

Cutie sighed, with the sound of wind humming through closely
spaced wires. "Your term of service is over and the time of dissolution has come. I expected it, but— Well, the Master's will be
done!"

His tone of resignation stung Powell. "Save the sympathy, Cutie.
We're heading for Earth, not dissolution."

"It is best that you think so," Cutie sighed again. "I see the wisdom of the illusion now. I would not attempt to shake your faith,
even if I could." He departed—the picture of commiseration.

Powell snarled and motioned to Donovan. Sealed suitcases in hand, they headed for the air lock.

The relief ship was on the outer landing and Franz Muller, his relief man, greeted them with stiff courtesy. Donovan made scant acknowledgment and passed into the pilot room to take over the controls from Sam Evans.

Powell lingered. "How's Earth?"

It was a conventional enough question and Muller gave the conventional answer, "Still spinning."

Powell said, "Good."

Muller looked at him, "The boys back at the U. S. Robots have dreamed up a new one, by the way. A multiple robot."

"A what?"

"What I said. There's a big contract for it. It must be just the thing for asteroid mining. You have a master robot with six subrobots under it. —Like your fingers."

"Has it been field-tested?" asked Powell anxiously.

Muller smiled, "Waiting for you, I hear."

Powell's fist balled, "Damn it, we need a vacation."

"Oh, you'll get it. Two weeks, I think."

He was donning the heavy space gloves in preparation for his term of duty here, and his thick eyebrows drew close together. "How is this new robot getting along? It better be *good*, or I'll be damned if I let it touch the controls."

Powell paused before answering. His eyes swept the proud Prussian before him from the close-cropped hair on the sternly stubborn head, to the feet standing stiffly at attention—and there was a sudden glow of pure gladness surging through him.

"The robot is pretty good," he said slowly. "I don't think you'll have to bother much with the controls."

He grinned—and went into the ship. Muller would be here for several weeks—

Catch That Rabbit

The vacation was longer than two weeks. That, Mike Donovan had to admit. It had been six months, with pay. He admitted that, too. But that, as he explained furiously, was fortuitous. U. S. Robots had to get the bugs out of the multiple robot, and there were plenty of bugs, and there are always at least half a dozen bugs left for the field-testing. So they waited and relaxed until the drawing-board men and the slide-rule boys had said "OK!". And now he and Powell were out on the asteroid and it was *not* OK. He repeated that a dozen times, with a face that had gone beety, "For the love of Pete, Greg, get realistic. What's the use of adhering to the letter of the specifications and watching the test go to pot? It's about time you got the red tape out of your pants and went to work."

"I'm only saying," said Gregory Powell, patiently, as one explaining electronics to an idiot child, "that according to spec, those robots are equipped for asteroid mining without supervision. We're not supposed to watch them."

"All right. Look—logic!" He lifted his hairy fingers and pointed. "One: That new robot passed every test in the home laboratories. Two: United States Robots guaranteed their passing the test of actual performance on an asteroid. Three: The robots are not passing said tests. Four: If they don't pass, United States Robots loses ten million credits in cash and about one hundred million in reputation. Five: If they don't pass and we can't explain why they don't pass, it is just possible two good jobs may have to be bidden a fond fare-well."

Powell groaned heavily behind a noticeably insincere smile. The unwritten motto of United States Robots and Mechanical Men Corporation was well-known: "No employee makes the same mistake twice. He is fired the first time."

Aloud he said, "You're as lucid as Euclid with everything except the facts. You've watched that robot group for three shifts, you redhead, and they did their work perfectly. You said so yourself. What else can we do?"

"Find out what's wrong, that's what we can do. So they did work perfectly when I watched them. But on three different occasions when I didn't watch them, they didn't bring in any ore. They didn't even come back on schedule. I had to go after them."

"And was anything wrong?"

"Not a thing. Not a thing. Everything was perfect. Smooth and perfect as the luminiferous ether. Only one little insignificant detail disturbed me—*there was no ore.*"

Powell scowled at the ceiling and pulled at his brown mustache. "I'll tell you what, Mike. We've been stuck with pretty lousy jobs in our time, but this takes the iridium asteroid. The whole business is complicated past endurance. Look, that robot, DV-5, has six robots under it. And not just under it—they're part of it."

"I know that—"

"Shut up!" said Powell, savagely, "I know you know it, but I'm just describing the hell of it. Those six subsidiaries are part of DV-5 like your fingers are part of you and it gives them their orders nei-ther by voice nor radio, but directly through positronic fields. Now—there isn't a roboticist back at United States Robots that knows what a positronic field is or how it works. And neither do I. Neither do you."

"The last," agreed Donovan, philosophically, "I know."

"Then look at our position. If everything works—fine! If anything goes wrong—we're out of our depth and there probably isn't a thing we can do, or anybody else. But the job belongs to us and not to anyone else so we're on the spot, Mike." He blazed away for a mo-ment in silence. Then, "All right, have you got him outside?"

"Yes."

"Is everything normal now?"

"Well he hasn't got religious mania, and he isn't running around in a circle spouting Gilbert and Sullivan, so I suppose he's normal."

Donovan passed out the door, shaking his head viciously.

Powell reached for the "Handbook of Robotics" that weighed down one side of his desk to a near-founder and opened it reverently. He had once jumped out of the window of a burning house dressed only in shorts and the "Handbook." In a pinch, he would have skipped the shorts.

The "Handbook" was propped up before him, when Robot DV-5 entered, with Donovan kicking the door shut behind him.

Powell said somberly, "Hi, Dave. How do you feel?"

"Fine," said the robot. "Mind if I sit down?" He dragged up the specially reinforced chair that was his, and folded gently into it.

Powell regarded Dave—laymen might think of robots by their serial numbers; roboticists never—with approval. It was not overmassive by any means, in spite of its construction as thinking-unit of an integrated seven-unit robot team. It was seven feet tall, and a half-ton of metal and electricity. A lot? Not when that half-ton has to be a mass of condensers, circuits, relays, and vacuum cells that can handle practically any psychological reaction known to humans. And a positronic brain, which with ten pounds of matter and a few quintillions of positrons runs the whole show.

Powell groped in his shirt pocket for a loose cigarette. "Dave," he said, "you're a good fellow. There's nothing flighty or prima donnaish about you. You're a stable, rock-bottom mining robot, except that you're equipped to handle six subsidiaries in direct coordination. As far as I know, that has not introduced any unstable paths in your brain-path map."

The robot nodded, "That makes me feel swell, but what are you getting at, boss?" He was equipped with an excellent diaphragm, and the presence of overtones in the sound unit robbed him of much of that metallic flatness that marks the usual robot voice.

"I'm going to tell you. With all that in your favor, what's going wrong with your job? For instance, today's B-shift?"

Dave hesitated, "As far as I know, nothing."

"You didn't produce any ore."

"I know."

"Well, then—"

Dave was having trouble, "I can't explain that, boss. It's been giving me a case of nerves, or it would if I let it. My subsidiaries worked smoothly. I know I did." He considered, his photoelectric eyes glowing intensely. Then, "I don't remember. The day ended and there was Mike and there were the ore cars, mostly empty."

Donovan broke in, "You didn't report at shift-end those days, Dave. You know that?"

"I know. But as to why—" He shook his head slowly and ponderously.

Powell had the queasy feeling that if the robot's face were capable of expression, it would be one of pain and mortification. A robot, by its very nature, cannot bear to fail its function.

Donovan dragged his chair up to Powell's desk and leaned over, "Amnesia, do you think?"

"Can't say. But there's no use in trying to pin disease names on this. Human disorders apply to robots only as romantic analogies. They're no help to robotic engineering." He scratched his neck, "I hate to put him through the elementary brain-reaction tests. It won't help his self-respect any."

He looked at Dave thoughtfully and then at the Field-Test outline given in the "Handbook." He said, "See here, Dave, what about sitting through a test? It would be the wise thing to do."

The robot rose, "If you say so, boss." There *was* pain in his voice.

It started simply enough. Robot DV-5 multiplied five-place figures to the heartless ticking of a stop watch. He recited the prime numbers between a thousand and ten thousand. He extracted cube roots and integrated functions of varying complexity. He went through mechanical reactions in order of increasing difficulty. And, finally, worked his precise mechanical mind over the highest function of the robot world—the solutions of problems in judgment and ethics.

At the end of two hours, Powell was copiously besweated. Donovan had enjoyed a none-too-nutritious diet of fingernail and the robot said, "How does it look, boss?"

Powell said, "I've got to think it over, Dave. Snap judgments won't help much. Suppose you go back to the C-shift. Take it easy. Don't press too hard for quota just for a while—and we'll fix things up."

The robot left. Donovan looked at Powell.

"Well—"

Powell seemed determined to push up his mustache by the roots. He said, "There is nothing wrong with the currents of his positronic brain."

"I'd hate to be that certain."

"Oh, Jupiter, Mike! The brain is the surest part of a robot. It's quintuple-checked back on Earth. If they pass the field test perfectly, the way Dave did, there just isn't a chance of brain misfunction. That test covered every key path in the brain."

"So where are we?"

"Don't rush me. Let me work this out. There's still the possibility of a mechanical breakdown in the body. That leaves about fifteen hundred condensers, twenty thousand individual electric circuits, five hundred vacuum cells, a thousand relays, and upty-ump thousand other individual pieces of complexity that can be wrong. *And* these mysterious positronic fields no one knows anything about."

"Listen, Greg," Donovan grew desperately urgent. "I've got an idea. That robot may be lying. He never—"

"Robots can't knowingly lie, you fool. Now if we had the McCormack-Wesley tester, we could check each individual item in his body within twenty-four to forty-eight hours, but the only two M.-W. testers existing are on Earth, and they weigh ten tons, are on concrete foundations and can't be moved. Isn't that peachy?"

Donovan pounded the desk, "But, Greg, he only goes wrong when we're not around. There's something—sinister—about—that." He punctuated the sentence with slams of fist against desk.

"You," said Powell, slowly, "make me sick. You've been reading adventure novels."

"What I want to know," shouted Donovan, "is what we're going to do about it."

"I'll tell you. I'm going to install a visiplate right over my desk. Right on the wall over there, see!" He jabbed a vicious finger at the spot. "Then I'm going to focus it at whatever part of the mine is being worked, and I'm going to watch. That's all."

"That's all? Greg—"

Powell rose from his chair and leaned his balled fists on the desk, "Mike, I'm having a hard time." His voice was weary. "For a week, you've been plaguing me about Dave. You say he's gone wrong. Do you know how he's gone wrong? No! Do you know what shape this wrongness takes? No! Do you know what brings it on? No! Do you know what snaps him out? No! Do you know anything about it? No! Do I know anything about it? No! So what do you want me to do?"

Donovan's arm swept outward in a vague, grandiose gesture, "You got me!"

"So I tell you again. Before we do anything toward a cure, we've got to find out what the disease is in the first place. The first step in cooking rabbit stew is catching the rabbit. Well, we've got to catch that rabbit! Now get out of here."

Donovan stared at the preliminary outline of his field report with weary eyes. For one thing, he was tired and for another, what was there to report while things were unsettled? He felt resentful.

He said, "Greg, we're almost a thousand tons behind schedule."

"You," replied Powell, never looking up, "are telling me something I don't know."

"What I want to know," said Donovan, in sudden savagery, "is why we're always tangled up with new-type robots. I've finally decided that the robots that were good enough for my great-uncle on my mother's side are good enough for me. I'm for what's tried and true. The test of time is what counts—good, solid, old-fashioned robots that never go wrong."

Powell threw a book with perfect aim, and Donovan went tumbling off his seat.

"Your job," said Powell, evenly, "for the last five years has been to test new robots under actual working conditions for United States Robots. Because you and I have been so injudicious as to display proficiency at the task, we've been rewarded with the dirtiest jobs. That," he jabbed holes in the air with his finger in Donovan's direction, "is your work. You've been griping about it, from personal memory, since about five minutes after United States Robots signed you up. Why don't you resign?"

"Well, I'll tell you." Donovan rolled onto his stomach, and took a firm grip on his wild, red hair to hold his head up. "There's a certain principle involved. After all, as a trouble shooter, I've played a part in the development of new robots. There's the principle of aiding scientific advance. But don't get me wrong. It's not the principle that keeps me going; it's the money they pay us. *Greg!*"

Powell jumped at Donovan's wild shout, and his eyes followed the redhead's to the visiplate, when they goggled in fixed horror. He whispered, "Holy—howling—Jupiter!"

Donovan scrambled breathlessly to his feet, "Look at them, Greg. They've gone nuts."

Powell said, "Get a pair of suits. We're going out there."

He watched the posturings of the robots on the visiplate. They were bronzy gleams of smooth motion against the shadowy crags of the airless asteroid. There was a marching formation now, and in their own dim body light, the rough-hewn walls of the mine tunnel swam past noiselessly, checkered with misty erratic blobs of shadow. They marched in unison, seven of them, with Dave at the head. They wheeled and turned in macabre simultaneity; and melted through changes of formation with the weird ease of chorus dancers in Lunar Bowl.

Donovan was back with the suits, "They've gone jingo on us, Greg. That's a military march."

"For all you know," was the cold response, "it may be a series of calisthenic exercises. Or Dave may be under the hallucination of being a dancing master. Just you think first, and don't bother to speak afterward, either."

Donovan scowled and slipped a detonator into the empty side holster with an ostentatious shove. He said, "Anyway, there you are. So we work with new-model robots. It's our job, granted. But answer me one question. Why . . . *why* does something invariably go wrong with them?"

"Because," said Powell, somberly, "we are accursed. Let's go!"

Far ahead through the thick velvety blackness of the corridors that reached past the illuminated circles of their flashlights, robot light twinkled.

"There they are," breathed Donovan.

Powell whispered tensely, "I've been trying to get him by radio but he doesn't answer. The radio circuit is probably out."

"Then I'm glad the designers haven't worked out robots who can work in total darkness yet. I'd hate to have to find seven mad robots in a black pit without radio communication, if they *weren't* lit up like blasted radioactive Christmas trees."

"Crawl up on the ledge above, Mike. They're coming this way, and I want to watch them at close range. Can you make it?"

Donovan made the jump with a grunt. Gravity was considerably below Earth-normal, but with a heavy suit, the advantage was not too great, and the ledge meant a near ten-foot jump. Powell followed.

The column of robots were trailing Dave single-file. In mechanical rhythm, they converted to double and returned to single in different order. It was repeated over and over again and Dave never turned his head.

Dave was within twenty feet when the play-acting ceased. The subsidiary robots broke formation, waited a moment, then clattered off into the distance—very rapidly. Dave looked after them, then slowly sat down. He rested his head in one hand in a very human gesture.

His voice sounded in Powell's earphones, "Are you here, boss?"

Powell beckoned to Donovan and hopped off the ledge.

"O.K., Dave, what's been going on?"

The robot shook his head, "I don't know. One moment I was handling a tough outcropping in Tunnel 17, and the next I was aware of humans close by, and I found myself half a mile down main-stem."

"Where are the subsidiaries now?" asked Donovan.

"Back at work, of course. How much time has been lost?"

"Not much. Forget it." Then to Donovan, Powell added, "Stay with him the rest of the shift. Then, come back. I've got a couple of ideas."

It was three hours before Donovan returned. He looked tired.

Powell said, "How did it go?"

Donovan shrugged wearily, "Nothing ever goes wrong when you watch them. Throw me a butt, will you?"

The redhead lit it with exaggerated care and blew a careful smoke ring. He said, "I've been working it out, Greg. You know, Dave has a queer background for a robot. There are six others under him in an extreme regimentation. He's got life and death power over those subsidiary robots and it must react on his mentality. Suppose he finds it necessary to emphasize this power as a concession to his ego."

"Get to the point."

"It's right here. Suppose we have militarism. Suppose he's fashioning himself an army. Suppose he's training them in military maneuvers. Suppose—"

"Suppose you go soak your head. Your nightmares must be in

technicolor. You're postulating a major aberration of the positronic brain. If your analysis were correct, Dave would have to break down the First Law of Robotics: that a robot may not injure a human being or, through inaction allow a human being to be injured. The type of militaristic attitude and domineering ego you propose must have as the end-point of its logical implications, domination of humans."

"All right. How do you know that isn't the fact of the matter?"

"Because any robot with a brain like that would, one, never have left the factory, and two, be spotted immediately if it ever was. I tested Dave, you know."

Powell shoved his chair back and put his feet on the desk. "No. We're still in the position where we can't make our stew because we haven't the slightest notion as to what's wrong. For instance, if we could find out what that *danse macabre* we witnessed was all about, we would be on the way out."

He paused, "Now listen, Mike, how does this sound to you? Dave goes wrong only when neither of us is present. And when he is wrong, the arrival of either of us snaps him out of it."

"I once told you that was sinister."

"Don't interrupt. How is a robot different when humans are not present? The answer is obvious. There is a larger requirement of personal initiative. In that case, look for the body parts that are affected by the new requirements."

"Golly." Donovan sat up straight, then subsided. "No, no. Not enough. It's too broad. It doesn't cut the possibilities much."

"Can't help that. In any case, there's no danger of not making quota. We'll take shifts watching those robots through the visor. Any time anything goes wrong, we get to the scene of action immediately. That will put them right."

"But the robots will fail spec anyway, Greg. United States Robots can't market DV models with a report like that."

"Obviously. We've got to locate the error in make-up and correct it—and we've got ten days to do it in." Powell scratched his head. "The trouble is . . . well, you had better look at the blueprints yourself."

The blueprints covered the floor like a carpet and Donovan crawled over the face of them following Powell's erratic pencil.

Powell said, "Here's where you come in, Mike. You're the body specialist, and I want you to check me. I've been trying to cut out all circuits not involved in the personal initiative hookup. Right

here, for instance, is the trunk artery involving mechanical operations. I cut out all routine side routes as emergency divisions—" He
looked up, "What do you think?"

Donovan had a very bad taste in his mouth, "The job's not that
simple, Greg. Personal initiative isn't an electric circuit you can separate from the rest and study. When a robot is on his own, the intensity of the body activity increases immediately on almost all fronts.
There isn't a circuit entirely unaffected. What must be done is to
locate the particular condition—a very specific condition—that
throws him off, and *then* start eliminating circuits."

Powell got up and dusted himself, "Hmph. All right. Take away
the blueprints and burn them."

Donovan said, "You see when activity intensifies, anything can
happen, given one single faulty part. Insulation breaks down, a con-
denser spills over, a connection sparks, a coil overheats. And if you
work blind, with the whole robot to choose from, you'll never find
the bad spot. If you take Dave apart and test every point of his body
mechanism one by one, putting him together each time, and trying
him out—"

"All right. All right. I can see through a porthole, too."

They faced each other hopelessly, and then Powell said cautiously,
"Suppose we interview one of the subsidiaries."

Neither Powell nor Donovan had ever had previous occasion to
talk to a "finger." It could talk; it wasn't quite the perfect analogy to
a human finger. In fact, it had a fairly developed brain, but that
brain was tuned primarily to the reception of orders via positronic
field, and its reaction to independent stimuli was rather fumbling.

Nor was Powell certain as to its name. Its serial number was
DV-5-2, but that was not very useful.

He compromised. "Look, pal," he said, "I'm going to ask you to
do some hard thinking and then you can go back to your boss."

The "finger" nodded its head stiffly, but did not exert its limited
brain-power on speech.

"Now on four occasions recently," Powell said, "your boss deviated from brain-scheme. Do you remember those occasions?"

"Yes, sir."

Donovan growled angrily, "*He* remembers. I tell you there is
something very sinister—"

"Oh, go bash your skull. Of course, the 'finger' remembers. There
is nothing wrong with him." Powell turned back to the robot,
"What were you doing each time . . . I mean the whole group."

The "finger" had a curious air of reciting by rote, as if he answered questions by the mechanical pressure of his brain pan, but without any enthusiasm whatever.

He said, "The first time we were at work on a difficult outcropping in Tunnel 17, Level B. The second time we were buttressing the roof against a possible cave-in. The third time we were preparing accurate blasts in order to tunnel farther without breaking into a subterranean fissure. The fourth time was just after a minor cave-in."

"What happened at these times?"

"It is difficult to describe. An order would be issued, but before we could receive and interpret it, a new order came to march in queer formation."

Powell snapped out, "Why?"

"I don't know."

Donovan broke in tensely, "What was the first order . . . the one that was superseded by the marching directions?"

"I don't know. I sensed that an order was sent, but there was never time to receive it."

"Could you tell us anything about it? Was it the same order each time?"

The "finger" shook his head unhappily, "I don't know."

Powell leaned back, "All right, get back to your boss."

The "finger" left, with visible relief.

Donovan said, "Well, we accomplished a lot that time. That was real sharp dialogue all the way through. Listen, Dave and that imbecile 'finger' are both holding out on us. There is too much they don't know and don't remember. We've got to stop trusting them, Greg."

Powell brushed his mustache the wrong way, "So help me, Mike, another fool remark out of you, and I'll take away your rattle and teething ring."

"All right. You're the genius of the team. I'm just a poor sucker. Where do we stand?"

"Right behind the eight ball. I tried to work it backward through the 'finger,' and couldn't. So we've got to work it forward."

"A great man," marveled Donovan. "How simple that makes it. Now translate that into English, Master."

"Translating it into baby talk would suit you better. I mean that we've got to find out what order it is that Dave gives just before everything goes black. It would be the key to the business."

"And how do you expect to do that? We can't get close to him because nothing will go wrong as long as we are there. We can't catch the orders by radio because they are transmitted via this positronic field. That eliminates the close-range and the long-range method, leaving us a neat, cozy zero."

"By direct observation, yes. There's still deduction."

"Huh?"

"We're going on shifts, Mike." Powell smiled grimly. "And we are not taking our eyes off the visiplate. We're going to watch every action of those steel headaches. When they go off into their act, we're going to see what happened immediately before and we're going to deduce the order."

Donovan opened his mouth and left it that way for a full minute. Then he said in strangled tones, "I resign. I quit."

"You have ten days to think up something better," said Powell wearily.

Which, for eight days, Donovan tried mightily to do. For eight days, on alternate four-hour shifts, he watched with aching and bleary eyes those glinty metallic forms move against the vague background. And for eight days in the four-hour in-betweens, he cursed United States Robots, the DV models, and the day he was born.

And then on the eighth day, when Powell entered with an aching head and sleepy eyes for his shift, Donovan stood up and with very careful and deliberate aim launched a heavy book end for the exact center of the visiplate. There was a very appropriate splintering noise.

Powell gasped, "What did you do that for?"

"Because," said Donovan, almost calmly, "I'm not watching it any more. We've got two days left and we haven't found out a thing. DV-5 is a lousy loss. He's stopped five times since I've been watching and three times on your shift, and I can't make out what orders he gave, and you couldn't make it out. And I don't believe you could ever make it out because I know I couldn't ever."

"Jumping Space, how can you watch six robots at the same time? One makes with the hands, and one with the feet and one like a windmill and another is jumping up and down like a maniac. And the other two . . . devil knows what they are doing. And then they all stop. So! So!"

"Greg, we're not doing it right. We got to get up close. We've got to watch what they're doing from where we can see the details."

Powell broke a bitter silence. "Yeah, and wait for something to go wrong with only two days to go."

"Is it any better watching from here?"

"It's more comfortable."

"Ah— But there's something you can do there that you can't do here."

"What's that?"

"You can make them stop—at whatever time you choose—and while you're prepared and watching to see what goes wrong."

Powell startled into alertness, "Howzzat?"

"Well, figure it out yourself. You're the brains you say. Ask yourself some questions. When does DV-5 go out of whack? When did that 'finger' say he did? When a cave-in threatened, or actually occurred, when delicately measured explosives were being laid down, when a difficult seam was hit."

"In other words, during emergencies." Powell was excited.

"Right! When *did* you expect it to happen! It's the personal initiative factor that's giving us the trouble. And it's just during emergencies in the absence of a human being that personal initiative is most strained. Now what is the logical deduction? How can we create our own stoppage when and where we want it?" He paused triumphantly—he was beginning to enjoy his role—and answered his own question to forestall the obvious answer on Powell's tongue. "By creating our own emergency."

Powell said, "Mike—you're right."

"Thanks, pal. I knew I'd do it some day."

"All right, and skip the sarcasm. We'll save it for Earth, and preserve it in jars for future long, cold winters. Meanwhile, what emergency can we create?"

"We could flood the mines, if this weren't an airless asteroid."

"A witticism, no doubt," said Powell. "Really, Mike, you'll incapacitate me with laughter. What about a mild cave-in?"

Donovan pursed his lips and said, "O.K. by me."

"Good. Let's get started."

Powell felt uncommonly like a conspirator as he wound his way over the craggy landscape. His sub-gravity walk teetered across the broken ground, kicking rocks to right and left under his weight in noiseless puffs of gray dust. Mentally, though, it was the cautious crawl of the plotter.

He said, "Do you know where they are?"

"I think so, Greg."

"All right," Powell said gloomily, "but if any 'finger' gets within twenty feet of us, we'll be sensed whether we are in the line of sight or not. I hope you know that."

"When I need an elementary course in robotics, I'll file an application with you, formally, and in triplicate. Down through here."

They were in the tunnels now; even the starlight was gone. The two hugged the walls, flashes flickering out the way in intermittent bursts. Powell felt for the security of his detonator.

"Do you know this tunnel, Mike?"

"Not so good. It's a new one. I think I can make it out from what I saw in the visiplate, though—"

Interminable minutes passed, and then Mike said, "Feel that!"

There was a slight vibration thrumming the wall against the fingers of Powell's metal-incased hand. There was no sound, naturally.

"Blasting! We're pretty close."

"Keep your eyes open," said Powell.

Donovan nodded impatiently.

It was upon them and gone before they could seize themselves— just a bronze glint across the field of vision. They clung together in silence.

Powell whispered, "Think it sensed us?"

"Hope not. But we'd better flank them. Take the first side tunnel to the right."

"Suppose we miss them altogether?"

"Well what do you want to do? Go back?" Donovan grunted fiercely. "They're within a quarter of a mile. I was watching them through the visiplate, wasn't I? And we've got two days—"

"Oh, shut up. You're wasting your oxygen. Is this a side passage here?" The flash flicked. "It is. Let's go."

The vibration was considerably more marked and the ground below shuddered uneasily.

"This is good," said Donovan, "if it doesn't give out on us, though." He flung his light ahead anxiously.

They could touch the roof of the tunnel with a half-upstretched hand, and the bracings had been newly placed.

Donovan hesitated, "Dead end, let's go back."

"No. Hold on." Powell squeezed clumsily past. "Is that light ahead?"

"Light? I don't see any. Where would there be light down here?"

"Robot light." He was scrambling up a gentle incline on hands and knees. His voice was hoarse and anxious in Donovan's ears. "Hey, Mike, come up here."

There was light. Donovan crawled up and over Powell's outstretched legs. "An opening?"

"Yes. They must be working into this tunnel from the other side now—I think."

Donovan felt the ragged edges of the opening that looked out into what the cautious flashlight showed to be a larger and obviously main-stem tunnel. The hole was too small for a man to go through, almost too small for two men to look through simultaneously.

"There's nothing there," said Donovan.

"Well, not now. But there must have been a second ago or we wouldn't have seen light. Watch out!"

The walls rolled about them and they felt the impact. A fine dust showered down. Powell lifted a cautious head and looked again. "All right, Mike. They're there."

The glittering robots clustered fifty feet down the main stem. Metal arms labored mightily at the rubbish heap brought down by the last blast.

Donovan urged eagerly, "Don't waste time. It won't be long before they get through, and the next blast may get us."

"For Pete's sake, don't rush me." Powell unlimbered the detonator, and his eyes searched anxiously across the dusky background where the only light was robot light and it was impossible to tell a projecting boulder from a shadow.

"There's a spot in the roof, see it, almost over them. The last blast didn't quite get it. If you can get it at the base, half the roof will cave in."

Powell followed the dim finger, "Check! Now fasten your eye on the robots and pray they don't move too far from that part of the tunnel. They're my light sources. Are all seven there?"

Donovan counted, "All seven."

"Well, then, watch them. Watch every motion!"

His detonator was lifted and remained poised while Donovan watched and cursed and blinked the sweat out of his eye.

It flashed!

There was a jar, a series of hard vibrations, and then a jarring thump that threw Powell heavily against Donovan.

Donovan yowled, "Greg, you threw me off. I didn't see a thing."

Powell stared about wildly, "Where are they?"

Donovan fell into a stupid silence. There was no sign of the robots. It was dark as the depths of the River Styx.

"Think we buried them?" quavered Donovan.

"Let's get down there. Don't ask me what I think." Powell crawled backward at tumbling speed.

"Mike!"

Donovan paused in the act of following. "What's wrong now?"

"Hold on!" Powell's breathing was rough and irregular in Donovan's ears. "Mike! Do you hear me, Mike?"

"I'm right here. What is it?"

"We're blocked in. It wasn't the ceiling coming down fifty feet away that knocked us over. It was our own ceiling. The shock's tumbled it!"

"What!" Donovan scrambled up against a hard barrier. "Turn on the flash."

Powell did so. At no point was there room for a rabbit to squeeze through.

Donovan said softly, "Well, what do you know?"

They wasted a few moments and some muscular power in an effort to move the blocking barrier. Powell varied this by wrenching at the edges of the original hole. For a moment, Powell lifted his blaster. But in those close quarters, a flash would be suicide and he knew it. He sat down.

"You know, Mike," he said, "we've really messed this up. We are no nearer finding out what's wrong with Dave. It was a good idea but it blew up in our face."

Donovan's glance was bitter with an intensity totally wasted on the darkness, "I hate to disturb you, old man, but quite apart from what we know or don't know of Dave, we're slightly trapped. If we don't get loose, fella, we're going to die. D-I-E, die. How much oxygen have we anyway? Not more than six hours."

"I've thought of that." Powell's fingers went up to his long-suffering mustache and clanged uselessly against the transparent visor. "Of course, we could get Dave to dig us out easily in that time, except that our precious emergency must have thrown him off, and his radio circuit is out."

"And isn't that nice?"

Donovan edged up to the opening and managed to get his metal-incased head out. It was an extremely tight fit.

"Hey, Greg!"

"What?"

"Suppose we get Dave within twenty feet. He'll snap to normal. That will save us."

"Sure, but where is he?"

"Down the corridor—way down. For Pete's sake, stop pulling before you drag my head out of its socket. I'll give you your chance to look."

Powell maneuvered his head outside, "We did it all right. Look at those saps. That must be a ballet they're doing."

"Never mind the side remarks. Are they getting any closer?"

"Can't tell yet. They're too far away. Give me a chance. Pass me my flash, will you? I'll try to attract their attention that way."

He gave up after two minutes, "Not a chance! They must be blind. Uh-oh, they're starting toward us. What do you know?"

Donovan said, "Hey, let me see!"

There was a silent scuffle. Powell said, "All right!" and Donovan got his head out.

They were approaching. Dave was high-stepping the way in front and the six "fingers" were a weaving chorus line behind him.

Donovan marveled, "What are they doing? That's what I want to know. It looks like the Virginia reel—and Dave's a major-domo, or I never saw one."

"Oh, leave me alone with your descriptions," grumbled Powell. "How near are they?"

"Within fifty feet and coming this way. We'll be out in fifteen min— Uh—huh—HUH—HEY-Y!"

"What's going on?" It took Powell several seconds to recover from his stunned astonishment at Donovan's vocal gyrations. "Come on, give me a chance at that hole. Don't be a hog about it."

He fought his way upward, but Donovan kicked wildly, "They did an about-face, Greg. They're leaving. Dave! Hey, Da-a-ave!"

Powell shrieked, "What's the use of that, you fool? Sound won't carry."

"Well, then," panted Donovan, "kick the walls, slam them, get some vibration started. We've got to attract their attention somehow, Greg, or we're through." He pounded like a madman.

Powell shook him, "Wait, Mike, wait. Listen, I've got an idea.

Jumping Jupiter, this is a fine time to get around to the simple solutions. Mike!"

"What do you want?" Donovan pulled his head in.

"Let me in there fast before they get out of range."

"Out of range! What are you going to do? Hey, what are you going to do with that detonator?" He grabbed Powell's arm.

Powell shook off the grip violently. "I'm going to do a little shooting."

"Why?"

"That's for later. Let's see if it works first. If it doesn't, then—Get out of the way and let me shoot!"

The robots were flickers, small and getting smaller, in the distance. Powell lined up the sights tensely, and pulled the trigger three times. He lowered the guns and peered anxiously. One of the subsidiaries was down! There were only six gleaming figures now.

Powell called into his transmitter uncertainly. "Dave!"

A pause, then the answer sounded to both men, "Boss? Where are you? My third subsidiary has had his chest blown in. He's out of commission."

"Never mind your subsidiary," said Powell. "We're trapped in a cave-in where you were blasting. Can you see our flashlight?"

"Sure. We'll be right there."

Powell sat back and relaxed, "That, my fran', is that."

Donovan said very softly with tears in his voice, "All right, Greg. You win. I beat my forehead against the ground before your feet. Now don't feed me any bull. Just tell me quietly what it's all about."

"Easy. It's just that all through we missed the obvious—as usual. We knew it was the personal initiative circuit, and that it always happened during emergencies, but we kept looking for a specific order as the cause. Why should it be an order?"

"Why not?"

"Well, look. Why not a type of order. What type of order requires the most initiative? What type of order would occur almost always only in an emergency?"

"Don't ask me, Greg. Tell me!"

"I'm doing it! It's the six-way order. Under all ordinary conditions, one or more of the 'fingers' would be doing routine tasks requiring no close supervision—in the sort of offhand way our bodies handle the routine walking motions. But in an emergency, all six subsidiaries must be mobilized immediately and simultaneously. Dave must handle six robots at a time and something gives. The rest was easy. Any decrease in initiative required, such as the arrival of humans, snaps him back. So I destroyed one of the robots. When I did, he was transmitting only five-way orders. Initiative decreases—he's normal."

"How did you get all that?" demanded Donovan.

"Just logical guessing. I tried it and it worked."

The robot's voice was in their ears again, "Here I am. Can you hold out half an hour?"

"Easy!" said Powell. Then, to Donovan, he continued, "And now the job should be simple. We'll go through the circuits, and check off each part that gets an extra workout in a six-way order as against a five-way. How big a field does that leave us?"

Donovan considered, "Not much, I think. If Dave is like the preliminary model we saw back at the factory, there's a special co-ordinating circuit that would be the only section involved." He cheered up suddenly and amazingly, "Say, that wouldn't be bad at all. There's nothing to that."

"All right. You think it over and we'll check the blueprints when we get back. And now, till Dave reaches us, I'm relaxing."

"Hey, wait! Just tell me one thing. What were those queer shifting marches, those funny dance steps, that the robots went through every time they went screwy?"

"That? I don't know. But I've got a notion. Remember, those subsidiaries were Dave's 'fingers.' We were always saying that, you know. Well, it's my idea that in all these interludes, whenever Dave became a psychiatric case, he went off into a moronic maze, spending his time *twiddling his fingers.*"

Susan Calvin

The third robot story I wrote, "Liar!" introduced Susan Calvin—with whom I promptly fell in love. She so dominated my thoughts thereafter that, little by little, she ousted Powell and Donovan from their position. Those two appeared only in the three stories included in the previous section, and in a fourth, "Escape!" in which they appear with Susan Calvin.

Somehow the impression I get as I look back on my career is that I must have included dear Susan in innumerable stories, but the fact is that she appeared in only ten stories, all of which are listed in this section. In the tenth, "Feminine Intuition," she emerges from retirement as an old lady who, however, has lost none of her acid charm.

You will note, by the way, that although most of the Susan Calvin stories were written at a time when male chauvinism was taken for granted in science fiction, Susan asks no favors and beats the men at their own game. To be sure, she remains sexually unfulfilled—but you can't have everything.

Liar!

Alfred Lanning lit his cigar carefully, but the tips of his fingers were trembling slightly. His gray eyebrows hunched low as he spoke between puffs.

"It reads minds all right—damn little doubt about that! But why?" He looked at Mathematician Peter Bogert, "Well?"

Bogert flattened his black hair down with both hands, "That was the thirty-fourth RB model we've turned out, Lanning. All the others were strictly orthodox."

The third man at the table frowned. Milton Ashe was the youngest officer of U. S. Robots and Mechanical Men Corporation, and proud of his post.

"Listen, Bogert. There wasn't a hitch in the assembly from start to finish. I guarantee that."

Bogert's thick lips spread in a patronizing smile, "Do you? If you can answer for the entire assembly line, I recommend your promotion. By exact count, there are seventy-five thousand, two hundred and thirty-four operations necessary for the manufacture of a single positronic brain, each separate operation depending for successful completion upon any number of factors, from five to a hundred and five. If any one of them goes seriously wrong, the 'brain' is ruined. I quote our own information folder, Ashe."

Milton Ashe flushed, but a fourth voice cut off his reply.

"If we're going to start by trying to fix the blame on one another, I'm leaving." Susan Calvin's hands were folded tightly in her lap, and the little lines about her thin, pale lips deepened, "We've got a mind-reading robot on our hands and it strikes me as rather important that we find out just why it reads minds. We're not going to do that by saying, 'Your fault! My fault!'"

Her cold gray eyes fastened upon Ashe, and he grinned.

Lanning grinned too, and, as always at such times, his long white hair and shrewd little eyes made him the picture of a biblical patriarch, "True for you, Dr. Calvin."

His voice became suddenly crisp, "Here's everything in pill-concentrate form. We've produced a positronic brain of supposedly ordinary vintage that's got the remarkable property of being able to tune in on thought waves. It would mark the most important advance in robotics in decades, if we knew how it happened. We don't, and we have to find out. Is that clear?"

"May I make a suggestion?" asked Bogert.

"Go ahead!"

"I'd say that until we do figure out the mess—and as a mathematician I expect it to be a very devil of a mess—we keep the existence of RB-34 a secret. I mean even from the other members of the staff. As heads of the departments, we ought not to find it an insoluble problem, and the fewer know about it—"

"Bogert is right," said Dr. Calvin. "Ever since the Interplanetary Code was modified to allow robot models to be tested in the plants before being shipped out to space, anti-robot propaganda has increased. If any word leaks out about a robot being able to read minds before we can announce complete control of the phenomenon, pretty effective capital could be made out of it."

Lanning sucked at his cigar and nodded gravely. He turned to Ashe, "I think you said you were alone when you first stumbled on this thought-reading business."

"I'll say I was alone—I got the scare of my life. RB-34 had just been taken off the assembly table and they sent him down to me. Obermann was off somewheres, so I took him down to the testing rooms myself—at least I started to take him down." Ashe paused, and a tiny smile tugged at his lips, "Say, did any of you ever carry on a thought conversation without knowing it?"

No one bothered to answer, and he continued, "You don't realize it at first, you know. He just spoke to me—as logically and sensibly as you can imagine—and it was only when I was most of the way

down to the testing rooms that I realized that I hadn't said anything. Sure, I thought lots, but that isn't the same thing, is it? I
locked that thing up and ran for Lanning. Having it walking beside
me, calmly peering into my thoughts and picking and choosing
among them gave me the willies."

"I imagine it would," said Susan Calvin thoughtfully. Her eyes
fixed themselves upon Ashe in an oddly intent manner. "We are so
accustomed to considering our own thoughts private."

Lanning broke in impatiently, "Then only the four of us know.
All right! We've got to go about this systematically. Ashe, I want
you to check over the assembly line from beginning to end—everything. You're to eliminate all operations in which there was no possible chance of an error, and list all those where there were, together
with its nature and possible magnitude."

"Tall order," grunted Ashe.

"Naturally! Of course, you're to put the men under you to work
on this—every single one if you have to, and I don't care if we go
behind schedule, either. But they're not to know why, you understand."

"Hm-m-m, yes!" The young technician grinned wryly. "It's still a
lulu of a job."

Lanning swiveled about in his chair and faced Calvin, "You'll
have to tackle the job from the other direction. You're the robopsychologist of the plant, so you're to study the robot itself and work
backward. Try to find out how he ticks. See what else is tied up with
his telepathic powers, how far they extend, how they warp his outlook, and just exactly what harm it has done to his ordinary RB
properties. You've got that?"

Lanning didn't wait for Dr. Calvin to answer.

"I'll co-ordinate the work and interpret the findings mathematically." He puffed violently at his cigar and mumbled the rest
through the smoke, "Bogert will help me there, of course."

Bogert polished the nails of one pudgy hand with the other and
said blandly, "I dare say. I know a little in the line."

"Well! I'll get started." Ashe shoved his chair back and rose. His
pleasantly youthful face crinkled in a grin, "I've got the darnedest
job of any of us, so I'm getting out of here and to work."

He left with a slurred, "B' seein' ye!"

Susan Calvin answered with a barely perceptible nod, but her eyes followed him out of sight and she did not answer when Lanning grunted and said, "Do you want to go up and see RB-34 now, Dr. Calvin?"

RB-34's photoelectric eyes lifted from the book at the muffled sound of hinges turning and he was upon his feet when Susan Calvin entered.

She paused to readjust the huge "No Entrance" sign upon the door and then approached the robot.

"I've brought you the texts upon hyperatomic motors, Herbie—a few anyway. Would you care to look at them?"

RB-34—otherwise known as Herbie—lifted the three heavy books from her arms and opened to the title page of one:

"Hm-m-m! 'Theory of Hyperatomics.'" He mumbled inarticulately to himself as he flipped the pages and then spoke with an abstracted air, "Sit down, Dr. Calvin! This will take me a few minutes."

The psychologist seated herself and watched Herbie narrowly as he took a chair at the other side of the table and went through the three books systematically.

At the end of half an hour, he put them down, "Of course, I know why you brought these."

The corner of Dr. Calvin's lip twitched, "I was afraid you would. It's difficult to work with you, Herbie. You're always a step ahead of me."

"It's the same with these books, you know, as with the others. They just don't interest me. There's nothing to your textbooks. Your science is just a mass of collected data plastered together by makeshift theory—and all so incredibly simple, that it's scarcely worth bothering about.

"It's your fiction that interests me. Your studies of the interplay of human motives and emotions"—his mighty hand gestured vaguely as he sought the proper words.

Dr. Calvin whispered, "I think I understand."

"I see into minds, you see," the robot continued, "and you have no idea how complicated they are. I can't begin to understand everything because my own mind has so little in common with them— but I try, and your novels help."

"Yes, but I'm afraid that after going through some of the harrowing emotional experiences of our present-day sentimental novel"—

there was a tinge of bitterness in her voice—"you find real minds like ours dull and colorless."

"But I don't!"

The sudden energy in the response brought the other to her feet. She felt herself reddening, and thought wildly, "He must know!"

Herbie subsided suddenly, and muttered in a low voice from which the metallic timbre departed almost entirely. "But, of course, I know about it, Dr. Calvin. You think of it always, so how can I help but know?"

Her face was hard. "Have you—told anyone?"

"Of course not!" This, with genuine surprise. "No one has asked me."

"Well, then," she flung out, "I suppose you think I am a fool."

"No! It is a normal emotion."

"Perhaps that is why it is so foolish." The wistfulness in her voice drowned out everything else. Some of the woman peered through the layer of doctorhood. "I am not what you would call—attractive."

"If you are referring to mere physical attraction, I couldn't judge. But I know, in any case, that there are other types of attraction."

"Nor young." Dr. Calvin had scarcely heard the robot.

"You are not yet forty." An anxious insistence had crept into Herbie's voice.

"Thirty-eight as you count the years; a shriveled sixty as far as my emotional outlook on life is concerned. Am I a psychologist for nothing?"

She drove on with bitter breathlessness, "And he's barely thirty-five and looks and acts younger. Do you suppose he ever sees me as anything but . . . but what I am?"

"You are wrong!" Herbie's steel fist struck the plastic-topped table with a strident clang. "Listen to me—"

But Susan Calvin whirled on him now and the hunted pain in her eyes became a blaze, "Why should I? What do you know about it all, anyway, you . . . you machine. I'm just a specimen to you; an interesting bug with a peculiar mind spread-eagled for inspection. It's a wonderful example of frustration, isn't it? Almost as good as your books." Her voice, emerging in dry sobs, choked into silence.

The robot cowered at the outburst. He shook his head pleadingly. "Won't you listen to me, please? I could help you if you would let me."

"How?" Her lips curled. "By giving me good advice?"

"No, not that. It's just that I know what other people think—Milton Ashe, for instance."

There was a long silence, and Susan Calvin's eyes dropped. "I don't want to know what he thinks," she gasped. "Keep quiet."

"I think you would want to know what he thinks."

Her head remained bent, but her breath came more quickly. "You are talking nonsense," she whispered.

"Why should I? I am trying to help. Milton Ashe's thoughts of you—" he paused.

And then the psychologist raised her head, "Well?"

The robot said quietly, "He loves you."

For a full minute, Dr. Calvin did not speak. She merely stared. Then, "You are mistaken! You must be. Why should he?"

"But he does. A thing like that cannot be hidden, not from me."

"But I am so . . . so—" she stammered to a halt.

"He looks deeper than the skin, and admires intellect in others. Milton Ashe is not the type to marry a head of hair and a pair of eyes."

Susan Calvin found herself blinking rapidly and waited before speaking. Even then her voice trembled, "Yet he certainly never in any way indicated—"

"Have you ever given him a chance?"

"How could I? I never thought that—"

"Exactly!"

The psychologist paused in thought and then looked up suddenly. "A girl visited him here at the plant half a year ago. She was pretty, I suppose—blond and slim. And, of course, could scarcely add two and two. He spent all day puffing out his chest, trying to explain how a robot was put together." The hardness had returned, "Not that she understood! Who was she?"

Herbie answered without hesitation, "I know the person you are referring to. She is his first cousin, and there is no romantic interest there, I assure you."

Susan Calvin rose to her feet with a vivacity almost girlish. "Now isn't that strange? That's exactly what I used to pretend to myself sometimes, though I never really thought so. Then it all must be true."

She ran to Herbie and seized his cold, heavy hand in both hers. "Thank you, Herbie." Her voice was an urgent, husky whisper. "Don't tell anyone about this. Let it be our secret—and thank you again." With that, and a convulsive squeeze of Herbie's unresponsive metal fingers, she left.

Herbie turned slowly to his neglected novel, but there was no one to read *his* thoughts.

Milton Ashe stretched slowly and magnificently, to the tune of cracking joints and a chorus of grunts, and then glared at Peter Bogert, Ph.D.

"Say," he said, "I've been at this for a week now with just about no sleep. How long do I have to keep it up? I thought you said the positronic bombardment in Vac Chamber D was the solution."

Bogert yawned delicately and regarded his white hands with interest. "It is. I'm on the track."

"I know what *that* means when a mathematician says it. How near the end are you?"

"It all depends."

"On what?" Ashe dropped into a chair and stretched his long legs out before him.

"On Lanning. The old fellow disagrees with me." He sighed, "A bit behind the times, that's the trouble with him. He clings to matrix mechanics as the all in all, and this problem calls for more powerful mathematical tools. He's so stubborn."

Ashe muttered sleepily, "Why not ask Herbie and settle the whole affair?"

"Ask the robot?" Bogert's eyebrows climbed.

"Why not? Didn't the old girl tell you?"

"You mean Calvin?"

"Yeah! Susie herself. That robot's a mathematical wiz. He knows all about everything plus a bit on the side. He does triple integrals in his head and eats up tensor analysis for dessert."

The mathematician stared skeptically, "Are you serious?"

"So help me! The catch is that the dope doesn't like math. He would rather read slushy novels. Honest! You should see the tripe Susie keeps feeding him: 'Purple Passion' and 'Love in Space.'"

"Dr. Calvin hasn't said a word of this to us."

"Well, she hasn't finished studying him. You know how she is. She likes to have everything just so before letting out the big secret."

"She's told *you*."

"We sort of got to talking. I have been seeing a lot of her lately."

He opened his eyes wide and frowned, "Say, Bogie, have you been noticing anything queer about the lady lately?"

Bogert relaxed into an undignified grin, "She's using lipstick, if that's what you mean."

"Hell, I know that. Rouge, powder and eye shadow, too. She's a sight. But it's not that. I can't put my finger on it. It's the way she talks—as if she were happy about something." He thought a little, and then shrugged.

The other allowed himself a leer, which, for a scientist past fifty, was not a bad job, "Maybe she's in love."

Ashe allowed his eyes to close again, "You're nuts, Bogie. You go speak to Herbie; I want to stay here and go to sleep."

"Right! Not that I particularly like having a robot tell me my job, nor that I think he can do it!"

A soft snore was his only answer.

Herbie listened carefully as Peter Bogert, hands in pockets, spoke with elaborate indifference.

"So there you are. I've been told you understand these things, and I am asking you more in curiosity than anything else. My line of reasoning, as I have outlined it, involves a few doubtful steps, I admit, which Dr. Lanning refuses to accept, and the picture is still rather incomplete."

The robot didn't answer, and Bogert said, "Well?"

"I see no mistake," Herbie studied the scribbled figures.

"I don't suppose you can go any further than that?"

"I daren't try. You are a better mathematician than I, and—well, I'd hate to commit myself."

There was a shade of complacency in Bogert's smile, "I rather thought that would be the case. It is deep. We'll forget it." He crumpled the sheets, tossed them down the waste shaft, turned to leave, and then thought better of it.

"By the way—"

The robot waited.

Bogert seemed to have difficulty. "There is something—that is, perhaps you can—" He stopped.

Herbie spoke quietly. "Your thoughts are confused, but there is no doubt at all that they concern Dr. Lanning. It is silly to hesitate, for as soon as you compose yourself, I'll know what it is you want to ask."

The mathematician's hand went to his sleek hair in the familiar smoothing gesture. "Lanning is nudging seventy," he said, as if that explained everything.

"I know that."

"And he's been director of the plant for almost thirty years." Herbie nodded.

"Well, now," Bogert's voice became ingratiating, "you would know whether . . . whether he's thinking of resigning. Health, perhaps, or some other—"

"Quite," said Herbie, and that was all.

"Well, do you know?"

"Certainly."

"Then—uh—could you tell me?"

"Since you ask, yes." The robot was quite matter-of-fact about it. "He has already resigned!"

"What!" The exclamation was an explosive, almost inarticulate, sound. The scientist's large head hunched forward, "Say that again!"

"He has already resigned," came the quiet repetition, "but it has not yet taken effect. He is waiting, you see, to solve the problem of —er—myself. That finished, he is quite ready to turn the office of director over to his successor."

Bogert expelled his breath sharply, "And this successor? Who is he?" He was quite close to Herbie now, eyes fixed fascinatedly on those unreadable dull-red photoelectric cells that were the robot's eyes.

Words came slowly, "You are the next director."

And Bogert relaxed into a tight smile, "This is good to know. I've been hoping and waiting for this. Thanks, Herbie."

Peter Bogert was at his desk until five that morning and he was back at nine. The shelf just over the desk emptied of its row of reference books and tables, as he referred to one after the other. The pages of calculations before him increased microscopically and the crumpled sheets at his feet mounted into a hill of scribbled paper.

At precisely noon, he stared at the final page, rubbed a bloodshot eye, yawned and shrugged. "This is getting worse each minute. Damn!"

He turned at the sound of the opening door and nodded at Lanning, who entered, cracking the knuckles of one gnarled hand with the other.

The director took in the disorder of the room and his eyebrows furrowed together.

"New lead?" he asked.

"No," came the defiant answer. "What's wrong with the old one?"

Lanning did not trouble to answer, nor to do more than bestow a single cursory glance at the top sheet upon Bogert's desk. He spoke through the flare of a match as he lit a cigar.

"Has Calvin told you about the robot? It's a mathematical genius. Really remarkable."

The other snorted loudly, "So I've heard. But Calvin had better stick to robopsychology. I've checked Herbie on math, and he can scarcely struggle through calculus."

"Calvin didn't find it so."

"She's crazy."

"And I don't find it so." The director's eyes narrowed dangerously.

"You!" Bogert's voice hardened. "What are you talking about?"

"I've been putting Herbie through his paces all morning, and he can do tricks you never heard of."

"Is that so?"

"You sound skeptical!" Lanning flipped a sheet of paper out of his vest pocket and unfolded it. "That's not my handwriting, is it?"

Bogert studied the large angular notation covering the sheet, "Herbie did this?"

"Right! And if you'll notice, he's been working on your time integration of Equation 22. It comes"—Lanning tapped a yellow fingernail upon the last step—"to the identical conclusion I did, and in a quarter the time. You had no right to neglect the Linger Effect in positronic bombardment."

"I didn't neglect it. For Heaven's sake, Lanning, get it through your head that it would cancel out—"

"Oh, sure, you explained that. You used the Mitchell Translation Equation, didn't you? Well—it doesn't apply."

"Why not?"

"Because you've been using hyper-imaginaries, for one thing."

"What's that to do with?"

"Mitchell's Equation won't hold when—"

"Are you crazy? If you'll reread Mitchell's original paper in the *Transactions of the Far*—"

"I don't have to. I told you in the beginning that I didn't like his reasoning, and Herbie backs me in that."

"Well, then," Bogert shouted, "let that clockwork contraption solve the entire problem for you. Why bother with nonessentials?"

"That's exactly the point. Herbie can't solve the problem. And if he can't, we can't—alone. I'm submitting the entire question to the National Board. It's gotten beyond us."

Bogert's chair went over backward as he jumped up a-snarl, face crimson. "You're doing nothing of the sort."

Lanning flushed in his turn, "Are you telling me what I can't do?"

"Exactly," was the gritted response. "I've got the problem beaten and you're not to take it out of my hands, understand? Don't think I don't see through you, you desiccated fossil. You'd cut your own nose off before you'd let me get the credit for solving robotic telepathy."

"You're a damned idiot, Bogert, and in one second I'll have you suspended for insubordination"—Lanning's lower lip trembled with passion.

"Which is one thing you won't do, Lanning. You haven't any secrets with a mind-reading robot around, so don't forget that I know all about your resignation."

The ash on Lanning's cigar trembled and fell, and the cigar itself followed, "What . . . what—"

Bogert chuckled nastily, "And I'm the new director, be it understood. I'm very aware of that; don't think I'm not. Damn your eyes, Lanning, I'm going to give the orders about here or there will be the sweetest mess that you've ever been in."

Lanning found his voice and let it out with a roar. "You're suspended, d'ye hear? You're relieved of all duties. You're broken, do you understand?"

The smile on the other's face broadened, "Now, what's the use of that? You're getting nowhere. I'm holding the trumps. I know you've resigned. Herbie told me, and he got it straight from you."

Lanning forced himself to speak quietly. He looked an old, old man, with tired eyes peering from a face in which the red had disappeared, leaving the pasty yellow of age behind, "I want to speak to Herbie. He can't have told you anything of the sort. You're playing a deep game, Bogert, but I'm calling your bluff. Come with me."

Bogert shrugged, "To see Herbie? Good! Damned good!"

It was also precisely at noon that Milton Ashe looked up from his clumsy sketch and said, "You get the idea? I'm not too good at getting this down, but that's about how it looks. It's a honey of a house, and I can get it for next to nothing."

Susan Calvin gazed across at him with melting eyes. "It's really beautiful," she sighed. "I've often thought that I'd like to—" Her voice trailed away.

"Of course," Ashe continued briskly, putting away his pencil, "I've got to wait for my vacation. It's only two weeks off, but this Herbie business has everything up in the air." His eyes dropped to his fingernails, "Besides, there's another point—but it's a secret."

"Then don't tell me."

"Oh, I'd just as soon,. I'm just busting to tell someone—and you're just about the best—er—confidante I could find here." He grinned sheepishly.

Susan Calvin's heart bounded, but she did not trust herself to speak.

"Frankly," Ashe scraped his chair closer and lowered his voice into a confidential whisper, "the house isn't to be only for myself. I'm getting married!"

And then he jumped out of his seat, "What's the matter?"

"Nothing!" The horrible spinning sensation had vanished, but it was hard to get words out. "Married? You mean—"

"Why, sure! About time, isn't it? You remember that girl who was here last summer. That's she! But you *are* sick. You—"

"Headache!" Susan Calvin motioned him away weakly. "I've . . . I've been subject to them lately. I want to . . . to congratulate you, of course. I'm very glad—" The inexpertly applied rouge made a pair of nasty red splotches upon her chalk-white face. Things had begun spinning again. "Pardon me—please—"

The words were a mumble, as she stumbled blindly out the door. It had happened with the sudden catastrophe of a dream—and with all the unreal horror of a dream.

But how could it be? Herbie had said—

And Herbie knew! He could see into minds!

She found herself leaning breathlessly against the door jamb, staring into Herbie's metal face. She must have climbed the two flights of stairs, but she had no memory of it. The distance had been covered in an instant, as in a dream.

As in a dream!

And still Herbie's unblinking eyes stared into hers and their dull red seemed to expand into dimly shining nightmarish globes.

He was speaking, and she felt the cold glass pressing against her lips. She swallowed and shuddered into a certain awareness of her surroundings.

Still Herbie spoke, and there was agitation in his voice—as if he were hurt and frightened and pleading.

The words were beginning to make sense. "This is a dream," he was saying, "and you mustn't believe in it. You'll wake into the real world soon and laugh at yourself. He loves you, I tell you. He does, he does! But not here! Not now! This is an illusion."

Susan Calvin nodded, her voice a whisper, "Yes! Yes!" She was clutching Herbie's arm, clinging to it, repeating over and over, "It isn't true, is it? It isn't, is it?"

Just how she came to her senses, she never knew—but it was like passing from a world of misty unreality to one of harsh sunlight. She pushed him away from her, pushed hard against that steely arm, and her eyes were wide.

"What are you trying to do?" Her voice rose to a harsh scream. "What are you trying to do?"

Herbie backed away, "I want to help."

The psychologist stared, "Help? By telling me this is a dream? By trying to push me into schizophrenia?" A hysterical tenseness seized her, "This is no dream! I wish it were!"

She drew her breath sharply, "Wait! Why . . . why, I understand. Merciful Heavens, it's so obvious."

There was horror in the robot's voice, "I had to!"

"And I believed you! I never thought—"

Loud voices outside the door brought her to a halt. She turned away, fists clenching spasmodically, and when Bogert and Lanning entered, she was at the far window. Neither of the men paid her the slightest attention.

They approached Herbie simultaneously; Lanning angry and impatient, Bogert, coolly sardonic. The director spoke first.

"Here now, Herbie. Listen to me!"

The robot brought his eyes sharply down upon the aged director, "Yes, Dr. Lanning."

"Have you discussed me with Dr. Bogert?"

"No, sir." The answer came slowly, and the smile on Bogert's face flashed off.

"What's that?" Bogert shoved in ahead of his superior and straddled the ground before the robot. "Repeat what you told me yesterday."

"I said that—" Herbie fell silent. Deep within him his metallic diaphragm vibrated in soft discords.

"Didn't you say he had resigned?" roared Bogert. "Answer me!"

Bogert raised his arm frantically, but Lanning pushed him aside, "Are you trying to bully him into lying?"

"You heard him, Lanning. He began to say 'Yes' and stopped. Get out of my way! I want the truth out of him, understand!"

"I'll ask him!" Lanning turned to the robot. "All right, Herbie, take it easy. Have I resigned?"

Herbie stared, and Lanning repeated anxiously, "Have I resigned?" There was the faintest trace of a negative shake of the robot's head. A long wait produced nothing further.

The two men looked at each other and the hostility in their eyes was all but tangible.

"What the devil," blurted Bogert, "has the robot gone mute? Can't you speak, you monstrosity?"

"I can speak," came the ready answer.

"Then answer the question. Didn't you tell me Lanning had resigned? Hasn't he resigned?"

And again there was nothing but dull silence, until from the end of the room, Susan Calvin's laugh rang out suddenly, high-pitched and semi-hysterical.

The two mathematicians jumped, and Bogert's eyes narrowed, "You here? What's so funny?"

"Nothing's funny." Her voice was not quite natural. "It's just that I'm not the only one that's been caught. There's irony in three of the greatest experts in robotics in the world falling into the same elementary trap, isn't there?" Her voice faded, and she put a pale hand to her forehead, "But it isn't funny!"

This time the look that passed between the two men was one of raised eyebrows. "What trap are you talking about?" asked Lanning stiffly. "Is something wrong with Herbie?"

"No," she approached them slowly, "nothing is wrong with him— only with us." She whirled suddenly and shrieked at the robot, "Get away from me! Go to the other end of the room and don't let me look at you."

Herbie cringed before the fury of her eyes and stumbled away in a clattering trot.

Lanning's voice was hostile, "What is all this, Dr. Calvin?"

She faced them and spoke sarcastically, "Surely you know the fundamental First Law of Robotics."

The other two nodded together. "Certainly," said Bogert, irritably, "a robot may not injure a human being or, through inaction, allow him to come to harm."

"How nicely put," sneered Calvin. "But what kind of harm?"

"Why—any kind."

"Exactly! Any kind! But what about hurt feelings? What about deflation of one's ego? What about the blasting of one's hopes? Is that injury?"

Lanning frowned, "What would a robot know about—" And then he caught himself with a gasp.

"You've caught on, have you? *This* robot reads minds. Do you suppose it doesn't know everything about mental injury? Do you suppose that if asked a question, it wouldn't give exactly that answer that one wants to hear? Wouldn't any other answer hurt us, and wouldn't Herbie know that?"

"Good Heavens!" muttered Bogert.

The psychologist cast a sardonic glance at him, "I take it you asked him whether Lanning had resigned. You wanted to hear that he had resigned and so that's what Herbie told you."

"And I suppose that is why," said Lanning, tonelessly, "it would not answer a little while ago. It couldn't answer either way without hurting one of us."

There was a short pause in which the men looked thoughtfully across the room at the robot, crouching in the chair by the bookcase, head resting in one hand.

Susan Calvin stared steadfastly at the floor, "He knew of all this. That . . . that devil knows everything—including what went wrong in his assembly." Her eyes were dark and brooding.

Lanning looked up, "You're wrong there, Dr. Calvin. He doesn't know what went wrong. I asked him."

"What does that mean?" cried Calvin. "Only that you didn't want him to give you the solution. It would puncture your ego to have a machine do what you couldn't. Did you ask him?" she shot at Bogert.

"In a way." Bogert coughed and reddened. "He told me he knew very little about mathematics."

Lanning laughed, not very loudly and the psychologist smiled caustically. She said, "I'll ask him! A solution by him won't hurt my ego." She raised her voice into a cold, imperative, "Come here!"

Herbie rose and approached with hesitant steps.

"You know, I suppose," she continued, "just exactly at what point in the assembly an extraneous factor was introduced or an essential one left out."

"Yes," said Herbie, in tones barely heard.

"Hold on," broke in Bogert angrily. "That's not necessarily true. You want to hear that, that's all."

"Don't be a fool," replied Calvin. "He certainly knows as much math as you and Lanning together, since he can read minds. Give him his chance."

The mathematician subsided, and Calvin continued, "All right, then, Herbie, give! We're waiting." And in an aside, "Get pencils and paper, gentlemen."

But Herbie remained silent, and there was triumph in the psychologist's voice, "Why don't you answer, Herbie?"

The robot blurted out suddenly, "I cannot. You know I cannot! Dr. Bogert and Dr. Lanning don't want me to."

"They want the solution."

"But not from me."

Lanning broke in, speaking slowly and distinctly, "Don't be foolish, Herbie. We do want you to tell us."

Bogert nodded curtly.

Herbie's voice rose to wild heights, "What's the use of saying that? Don't you suppose that I can see past the superficial skin of your mind? Down below, you don't want me to. I'm a machine, given the imitation of life only by virtue of the positronic interplay in my brain—which is man's device. You can't lose face to me without being hurt. That is deep in your mind and won't be erased. I can't give the solution."

"We'll leave," said Dr. Lanning. "Tell Calvin."

"That would make no difference," cried Herbie, "since you would know anyway that it was I that was supplying the answer."

Calvin resumed, "But you understand, Herbie, that despite that, Drs. Lanning and Bogert want that solution."

"By their own efforts!" insisted Herbie.

"But they want it, and the fact that you have it and won't give it hurts them. You see that, don't you?"

"Yes! Yes!"

"And if you tell them that will hurt them, too."

"Yes! Yes!" Herbie was retreating slowly, and step by step Susan Calvin advanced. The two men watched in frozen bewilderment.

"You can't tell them," droned the psychologist slowly, "because that would hurt and you mustn't hurt. But if you don't tell them, you hurt, so you must tell them. And if you do, you will hurt and you mustn't, so you can't tell them; but if you don't, you hurt, so you must; but if you do, you hurt, so you mustn't; but if you don't, you hurt, so you must; but if you do, you—"

Herbie was up against the wall, and here he dropped to his knees. "Stop!" he shrieked. "Close your mind! It is full of pain and frustration and hate! I didn't mean it, I tell you! I tried to help! I told you what you wanted to hear. I had to!"

The psychologist paid no attention. "You must tell them, but if you do, you hurt, so you mustn't; but if you don't, you hurt, so you must; but—"

And Herbie screamed!

It was like the whistling of a piccolo many times magnified—shrill and shriller till it keened with the terror of a lost soul and filled the room with the piercingness of itself.

And when it died into nothingness, Herbie collapsed into a huddled heap of motionless metal.

Bogert's face was bloodless, "He's dead!"

"No!" Susan Calvin burst into body-racking gusts of wild laughter, "not dead—merely insane. I confronted him with the insoluble dilemma, and he broke down. You can scrap him now—because he'll never speak again."

Lanning was on his knees beside the thing that had been Herbie. His fingers touched the cold, unresponsive metal face and he shuddered. "You did that on purpose." He rose and faced her, face contorted.

"What if I did? You can't help it now." And in a sudden access of bitterness, "He deserved it."

The director seized the paralysed, motionless Bogert by the wrist, "What's the difference. Come, Peter." He sighed, "A thinking robot of this type is worthless anyway." His eyes were old and tired, and he repeated, "Come, Peter!"

It was minutes after the two scientists left that Dr. Susan Calvin regained part of her mental equilibrium. Slowly, her eyes turned to the living-dead Herbie and the tightness returned to her face. Long she stared while the triumph faded and the helpless frustration returned—and of all her turbulent thoughts only one infinitely bitter word passed her lips.

"*Liar!*"

Satisfaction Guaranteed

Tony was tall and darkly handsome, with an incredibly patrician air drawn into every line of his unchangeable expression, and Claire Belmont regarded him through the crack in the door with a mixture of horror and dismay.

"I can't, Larry. I just can't have him in the house." Feverishly, she was searching her paralyzed mind for a stronger way of putting it; some way that would make sense and settle things, but she could only end with a simple repetition.

"Well, I can't!"

Larry Belmont regarded his wife stiffly, and there was that spark of impatience in his eyes that Claire hated to see, since she felt her own incompetence mirrored in it. "We're committed, Claire," he said, "and I can't have you backing out now. The company is sending me to Washington on this basis, and it probably means a promotion. It's perfectly safe and you know it. What's your objection?"

She frowned helplessly. "It just gives me the chills. I couldn't bear him."

"He's as human as you or I, almost. So, no nonsense. Come, get out there."

His hand was on the small of her back, shoving; and she found herself in her own living room, shivering. *It* was there, looking at her with a precise politeness, as though appraising his hostess-to-be of the next three weeks. Dr. Susan Calvin was there, too, sitting stiffly in thin-lipped abstraction. She had the cold, faraway look of someone who has worked with machines so long that a little of the steel had entered the blood.

"Hello," crackled Claire in general, and ineffectual, greeting.

But Larry was busily saving the situation with a spurious gaiety. "Here, Claire, I want you to meet Tony, a swell guy. This is my wife, Claire, Tony, old boy." Larry's hand draped itself amiably over Tony's shoulder, but Tony remained unresponsive and expressionless under the pressure.

He said, "How do you do, Mrs. Belmont."

And Claire jumped at Tony's voice. It was deep and mellow, smooth as the hair on his head or the skin on his face.

Before she could stop herself, she said, "Oh, my—you talk."

"Why not? Did you expect that I didn't?"

But Claire could only smile weakly. She didn't really know what she had expected. She looked away, then let him slide gently into the corner of her eye. His hair was smooth and black, like polished plastic—or was it really composed of separate hairs? And was the even, olive skin of his hands and face continued on past the obscurement of his formally cut clothing?

She was lost in the shuddering wonder of it, and had to force her thoughts back into place to meet Dr. Calvin's flat, unemotional voice.

"Mrs. Belmont, I hope you appreciate the importance of this experiment. Your husband tells me he has given you some of the background. I would like to give you more, as the senior psychologist of the U. S. Robots and Mechanical Men Corporation.

"Tony is a robot. His actual designation on the company files is TN-3, but he will answer to Tony. He *is* not a mechanical monster, nor simply a calculating machine of the type that were developed during World War II, fifty years ago. He has an artificial brain nearly as complicated as our own. It is an immense telephone switchboard on an atomic scale, so that billions of possible 'telephone connections' can be compressed into an instrument that will fit inside a skull.

"Such brains are manufactured for each model of robot specifically. Each contains a precalculated set of connections so that each robot knows the English language to start with and enough of anything else that may be necessary to perform his job.

"Until now, U. S. Robots has confined its manufacturing activity to industrial models for use in places where human labor is impractical—in deep mines, for instance, or in underwater work. But we want to invade the city and the home. To do so, we must get the ordinary man and woman to accept these robots without fear. You understand that there is nothing to fear."

"There isn't, Claire," interposed Larry earnestly. "Take my word for it. It's impossible for him to do any harm. You know I wouldn't leave him with you otherwise."

Claire cast a quick, secret glance at Tony and lowered her voice. "What if I make him angry?"

"You needn't whisper," said Dr. Calvin calmly. "He *can't* get angry with you, my dear. I told you that the switchboard connections of his brain were predetermined. Well, the most important connection of all is what we call 'The First Law of Robotics,' and it is merely this: 'No robot can harm a human being, or, through inaction, allow a human being to come to harm.' All robots are built so. No robot can be forced in any way to do harm to any human. So, you see, we need you and Tony as a preliminary experiment for our own guidance, while your husband is in Washington to arrange for government-supervised legal tests."

"You mean all this isn't legal?"

Larry cleared his throat. "Not just yet, but it's all right. He won't leave the house, and you mustn't let anyone see him. That's all. . . . And, Claire, I'd stay with you, but I know too much about the robots. We must have a completely inexperienced tester so that we can have severe conditions. It's necessary."

"Oh, well," muttered Claire. Then, as a thought struck her, "But what does he do?"

"Housework," said Dr. Calvin shortly.

She got up to leave, and it was Larry who saw her to the front door. Claire stayed behind drearily. She caught a glimpse of herself in the mirror above the mantelpiece, and looked away hastily. She was very tired of her small, mousy face and her dim, unimaginative hair. Then she caught Tony's eyes upon her and almost smiled before she remembered. . . .

He was only a machine.

Larry Belmont was on his way to the airport when he caught a glimpse of Gladys Claffern. She was the type of woman who seemed made to be seen in glimpses. . . . Perfectly and precisely manufactured; dressed with thoughtful hand and eye; too gleaming to be stared at.

The little smile that preceded her and the faint scent that trailed her were a pair of beckoning fingers. Larry felt his stride break; he touched his hat, then hurried on.

As always he felt that vague anger. If Claire could only push her way into the Claffern clique, it would help so much. But what was the use.

Claire! The few times she had come face to face with Gladys, the little fool had been tongue-tied. He had no illusions. The testing of Tony was his big chance, and it was in Claire's hands. How much safer it would be in the hands of someone like Gladys Claffern.

Claire woke the second morning to the sound of a subdued knock on the bedroom door. Her mind clamored, then went icy. She had avoided Tony the first day, smiling thinly when she met him and brushing past with a wordless sound of apology.

"Is that you—Tony?"

"Yes, Mrs. Belmont. May I enter?"

She must have said yes, because he was in the room, quite suddenly and noiselessly. Her eyes and nose were simultaneously aware of the tray he was carrying.

"Breakfast?" she said.

"If you please."

She wouldn't have dared to refuse, so she pushed herself slowly into a sitting position and received it: poached eggs, buttered toast, coffee.

"I have brought the sugar and cream separately," said Tony. "I expect to learn your preference with time, in this and in other things."

She waited.

Tony, standing there straight and pliant as a metal rule, asked, after a moment, "Would you prefer to eat in privacy?"

"Yes. . . . I mean, if you don't mind."

"Will you need help later in dressing?"

"Oh, my, no!" She clutched frantically at the sheet, so that the coffee hovered at the edge of catastrophe. She remained so, in rigor, then sank helplessly back against the pillow when the door closed him out of her sight again.

She got through breakfast somehow. . . . He was only a machine, and if it were only more visible that he were it wouldn't be so frightening. Or if his expression would change. It just stayed there, nailed on. You couldn't tell what went on behind those dark eyes and that smooth, olive skin-stuff. The coffee cup beat a faint castanet for a moment as she set it back, empty, on the tray.

Then she realized that she had forgotten to add the sugar and cream after all, and she did so hate black coffee.

She burned a straight path from bedroom to kitchen after dressing. It was her house, after all, and there wasn't anything frippy about her, but she liked her kitchen clean. He should have waited for supervision. . . .

But when she entered, she found a kitchen that might have been minted fire-new from the factory the moment before.

She stopped, stared, turned on her heel and nearly ran into Tony. She yelped.

"May I help?" he asked.

"Tony," and she scraped the anger off the edges of her mind's panic, "you must make some noise when you walk. I can't have you stalking me, you know. . . . Didn't you use this kitchen?"

"I did, Mrs. Belmont."

"It doesn't look it."

"I cleaned up afterward. Isn't that customary?"

Claire opened her eyes wide. After all, what could one say to that. She opened the oven compartment that held the pots, took a quick, unseeing look at the metallic glitter inside, then said with a tremor, "Very good. Quite satisfactory."

If at the moment, he had beamed; if he had smiled; if he had quirked the corner of his mouth the slightest bit, she felt that she could have warmed to him. But he remained an English lord in repose, as he said, "Thank you, Mrs. Belmont. Would you come into the living room?"

She did, and it struck her at once. "Have you been polishing the furniture?"

"Is it satisfactory, Mrs. Belmont?"

"But when? You didn't do it yesterday."

"Last night, of course."

"You burned the lights all night?"

"Oh, no. That wouldn't have been necessary. I've a built-in ultra-violet source. I can see in ultraviolet. And, of course, I don't require sleep."

He did require admiration, though. She realized that, then. He had to know that he was pleasing her. But she couldn't bring herself to supply that pleasure for him.

She could only say sourly, "Your kind will put ordinary house-workers out of business."

"There is work of much greater importance they can be put to in the world, once they are freed of drudgery. After all, Mrs. Belmont, things like myself can be manufactured. But nothing yet can imitate the creativity and versatility of a human brain, like yours."

And though his face gave no hint, his voice was warmly sur-charged with awe and admiration, so that Claire flushed and mut-tered, "*My* brain! You can have it."

Tony approached a little and said, "You must be unhappy to say such a thing. Is there anything I can do?"

For a moment, Claire felt like laughing. It *was* a ridiculous situa-tion. Here was an animated carpet-sweeper, dishwasher, furniture-polisher, general factotum, rising from the factory table—and offer-ing his services as consoler and confidant.

Yet she said suddenly, in a burst of woe and voice, "Mr. Belmont doesn't think I have a brain, if you must know. . . . And I suppose I haven't." She couldn't cry in front of him. She felt, for some reason, that she had the honor of the human race to support against this mere creation.

"It's lately," she added. "It was all right when he was a student; when he was just starting. But I can't be a big man's wife; and he's getting to be a big man. He wants me to be a hostess and an entry into social life for him—like G—guh—guh—Gladys Claffern."

Her nose was red, and she looked away.

But Tony wasn't watching her. His eyes wandered about the room. "I can help you run the house."

"But it's no good," she said fiercely. "It needs a touch I can't give it. I can only make it comfortable; I can't ever make it the kind they take pictures of for the Home Beautiful magazines."

"Do you want that kind?"

"Does it do any good—wanting?"

Tony's eyes were on her, full. "I could help."

"Do you know anything about interior decoration?"

"Is it something a good housekeeper should know?"

"Oh, yes."

"Then I have the potentialities of learning it. Can you get me books on the subject?"

Something started then.

Claire, clutching her hat against the brawling liberties of the wind, had manipulated two fat volumes on the home arts back from the public library. She watched Tony as he opened one of them and flipped the pages. It was the first time she had watched his fingers flicker at anything like fine work.

I don't see how they do it, she thought, and on a sudden impulse reached for his hand and pulled it toward herself. Tony did not resist, but let it lie limp for inspection.

She said, "It's remarkable. Even your fingernails look natural."

"That's deliberate, of course," said Tony. Then, chattily, "The skin is a flexible plastic, and the skeletal framework is a light metal alloy. Does that amuse you?"

"Oh, no." She lifted her reddened face. "I just feel a little embarrassed at sort of poking into your insides. It's none of my business. You don't ask me about mine."

"My brain paths don't include that type of curiosity. I can only act within my limitations, you know."

And Claire felt something tighten inside her in the silence that followed. Why did she keep forgetting he was a machine. Now the thing itself had to remind her. Was she so starved for sympathy that she would even accept a robot as equal—because he sympathized?

She noticed Tony was still flipping the pages—almost helplessly— and there was a quick, shooting sense of relieved superiority within her. "You can't read, can you?"

Tony looked up at her; his voice calm, unreproachful. "I *am* reading, Mrs. Belmont."

"But—" She pointed at the book in a meaningless gesture.

"I am scanning the pages, if that's what you mean. My sense of reading is photographic."

It was evening then, and when Claire eventually went to bed Tony was well into the second volume, sitting there in the dark, or what seemed dark to Claire's limited eyes.

Her last thought, the one that clamored at her just as her mind let go and tumbled, was a queer one. She remembered his hand again; the touch of it. It had been warm and soft, like a human being's.

How clever of the factory, she thought, and softly ebbed to sleep.

It was the library continuously, thereafter, for several days. Tony suggested the fields of study, which branched out quickly. There were books on color matching and on cosmetics; on carpentry and on fashions; on art and on the history of costumes.

He turned the pages of each book before his solemn eyes, and, as quickly as he turned, he read; nor did he seem capable of forgetting.

Before the end of the week, he had insisted on cutting her hair, introducing her to a new method of arranging it, adjusting her eyebrow line a bit and changing the shade of her powder and lipstick.

She had palpitated in nervous dread for half an hour under the delicate touch of his inhuman fingers and then looked in the mirror.

"There is more that can be done," said Tony, "especially in clothes. How do you find it for a beginning?"

And she hadn't answered; not for quite a while. Not until she had absorbed the identity of the stranger in the glass and cooled the wonder at the beauty of it all. Then she had said chokingly, never once taking her eyes from the warming image, "Yes, Tony, quite good—for a beginning."

She said nothing of this in her letters to Larry. Let him see it all at once. And something in her realized that it wasn't only the surprise she would enjoy. It was going to be a kind of revenge.

Tony said one morning, "It's time to start buying, and I'm not allowed to leave the house. If I write out exactly what we must have, can I trust you to get it? We need drapery, and furniture fabric, wallpaper, carpeting, paint, clothing—and any number of small things."

"You can't get these things to your own specifications at a stroke's notice," said Claire doubtfully.

"You can get fairly close, if you go through the city and if money is no object."

"But, Tony, money is certainly an object."

"Not at all. Stop off at U. S. Robots in the first place. I'll write a note for you. You see Dr. Calvin, and tell her that I said it was part of the experiment."

Dr. Calvin, somehow, didn't frighten her as on that first evening. With her new face and a new hat, she couldn't be quite the old Claire. The psychologist listened carefully, asked a few questions, nodded—and then Claire found herself walking out, armed with an unlimited charge account against the assets of U. S. Robots and Mechanical Men Corporation.

It is wonderful what money will do. With a store's contents at her feet, a saleslady's dictum was not necessarily a voice from above; the uplifted eyebrow of a decorator was not anything like Jove's thunder.

And once, when an Exalted Plumpness at one of the most lordly of the garment salons had insistently poohed her description of the wardrobe she must have with counter-pronouncements in accents of the purest Fifty-seventh Street French, she called up Tony, then held the phone out to Monsieur.

"If you don't mind"—voice firm, but fingers twisting a bit—"I'd like you to talk to my—uh—secretary."

Pudgy proceeded to the phone with a solemn arm crooked behind his back. He lifted the phone in two fingers and said delicately, "Yes." A short pause, another "Yes," then a much longer pause, a squeaky beginning of an objection that perished quickly, another pause, a very meek "Yes," and the phone was restored to its cradle.

"If Madam will come with me," he said, hurt and distant, "I will try to supply her needs."

"Just a second." Claire rushed back to the phone, and dialed again. "Hello, Tony. I don't know what you said, but it worked. Thanks. You're a—" She struggled for the appropriate word, gave up and ended in a final little squeak, "—a—a dear!"

It was Gladys Claffern looking at her when she turned from the phone again. A slightly amused and slightly amazed Gladys Claffern, looking at her out of a face tilted a bit to one side.

"Mrs. Belmont?"

It all drained out of Claire—just like that. She could only nod—stupidly, like a marionette.

Gladys smiled with an insolence you couldn't put your finger on.

"I didn't know you shopped here?" As if the place had, in her eyes, definitely lost caste through the fact.

"I don't, usually," said Claire humbly.

"And haven't you done something to your hair? It's quite—quaint. . . . Oh, I hope you'll excuse me, but isn't your husband's name Lawrence? It seems to me that it's Lawrence."

Claire's teeth clenched, but she had to explain. She *had* to. "Tony is a friend of my husband's. He's helping me select some things."

"I understand. And quite a *dear* about it, I imagine." She passed on smiling, carrying the light and the warmth of the world with her.

Claire did not question the fact that it was to Tony that she turned for consolation. Ten days had cured her of reluctance. And she could weep before him; weep and rage.

"I was a complete f-fool," she stormed, wrenching at her water-logged handkerchief. "She does that to me. I don't know why. She just does. I should have—kicked her. I should have knocked her down and stamped on her."

"Can you hate a human being so much?" asked Tony, in puzzled softness. "That part of a human mind is closed to me."

"Oh, it isn't she," she moaned. "It's myself, I suppose. She's everything I want to be—on the outside, anyway. . . . And I can't be."

Tony's voice was forceful and low in her ear. "You can be, Mrs. Belmont. You *can* be. We have ten days yet, and in ten days the house will no longer be itself. Haven't we been planning that?"

"And how will that help me—with her?"

"Invite her here. Invite her friends. Have it the evening before I—before I leave. It will be a housewarming, in a way."

"She won't come."

"Yes, she will. She'll come to laugh. . . . And she won't be able to."

"Do you really think so? Oh, Tony, do you think we can do it?" She had both his hands in hers. . . . And then, with her face flung aside, "But what good would it be? It won't be I; it will be you that's doing it. I can't ride your back."

"Nobody lives in splendid singleness," whispered Tony. "They've put that knowledge in me. What you, or anyone, see in Gladys Claffern is not just Gladys Claffern. She rides the back of all that money and social position can bring. She doesn't question that. Why should you? . . . And look at it this way, Mrs. Belmont. I am manufactured to obey, but the extent of my obedience is for myself to determine. I can follow orders niggardly or liberally. For you, it is liberal, because you are what I have been manufactured to see human beings as. You are kind, friendly, unassuming. Mrs. Claffern, as you describe her, is not, and I wouldn't obey her as I would you. So it *is* you, and not *I*, Mrs. Belmont, that is doing all this."

He withdrew his hands from hers then, and Claire looked at that expressionless face no one could read—wondering. She was suddenly frightened again in a completely new way.

She swallowed nervously and stared at her hands, which were still tingling with the pressure of his fingers. She hadn't imagined it; his fingers had pressed hers, gently, tenderly, just before they moved away.

No!

Its fingers . . . *Its* fingers. . . .

She ran to the bathroom and scrubbed her hands—blindly, uselessly.

She was a bit shy of him the next day; watching him narrowly; waiting to see what might follow—and for a while nothing did.

Tony was working. If there was any difficulty in technique in putting up wallpaper, or utilizing the quick-drying paint, Tony's activity did not show it. His hands moved precisely; his fingers were deft and sure.

He worked all night. She never heard him, but each morning was a new adventure. She couldn't count the number of things that had been done, and by evening she was still finding new touches—and another night had come.

She tried to help only once and her human clumsiness marred that. *He* was in the next room, and she was hanging a picture in the spot marked by Tony's mathematical eyes. The little mark was there; the picture was there; and a revulsion against idleness was there.

But she was nervous, or the ladder was rickety. It didn't matter. She felt it going, and she cried out. It tumbled without her, for Tony, with far more than flesh-and-blood quickness, had been under her.

His calm, dark eyes said nothing at all, and his warm voice said only words. "Are you hurt, Mrs. Belmont?"

She noticed for an instant that her falling hand must have mussed that sleek hair of his, because for the first time she could see for herself that it was composed of distinct strands—fine black hairs.

And then, all at once, she was conscious of his arms about her shoulders and under her knees—holding her tightly and warmly.

She pushed, and her scream was loud in her own ears. She spent the rest of the day in her room, and thereafter she slept with a chair upended against the doorknob of her bedroom door.

She had sent out the invitations, and, as Tony had said, they were accepted. She had only to wait for the last evening.

It came, too, after the rest of them, in its proper place. The house was scarcely her own. She went through it one last time—and every room had been changed. She, herself, was in clothes she would never have dared wear before. . . . And when you put them on, you put on pride and confidence with them.

She tried a polite look of contemptuous amusement before the mirror, and the mirror sneered back at her masterfully.

What would Larry say? . . . It didn't matter, somehow. The exciting days weren't coming with him. They were leaving with Tony. Now wasn't that strange? She tried to recapture her mood of three weeks before and failed completely.

The clock shrieked eight at her in eight breathless installments, and she turned to Tony. "They'll be here soon, Tony. You'd better get into the basement. We can't let them—"

She stared a moment, then said weakly, "Tony?" and more strongly, "Tony?" and nearly a scream, "*Tony!*"

But his arms were around her now; his face was close to hers; the pressure of his embrace was relentless. She heard his voice through a haze of emotional jumble.

"Claire," the voice said, "there are many things I am not made to understand, and this must be one of them. I am leaving tomorrow, and I don't want to. I find that there is more in me than just a desire to please you. Isn't it strange?"

His face was closer; his lips were warm, but with no breath behind them—for machines do not breathe. They were almost on hers.

. . . And the bell sounded.

For a moment, she struggled breathlessly, and then he was gone and nowhere in sight, and the bell was sounding again. Its intermittent shrillness was insistent.

The curtains on the front windows had been pulled open. They had been closed fifteen minutes earlier. She *knew* that.

They must have seen, then. They must *all* have seen—everything!

They came in so politely, all in a bunch—the pack came to howl —with their sharp, darting eyes piercing everywhere. They *had* seen. Why else would Gladys ask in her jabbingest manner after Larry? And Claire was spurred to a desperate and reckless defiance.

Yes, he *is* away. He'll be back tomorrow, I suppose. No, I haven't been lonely here myself. Not a bit. I've had an exciting time. And she laughed at them. Why not? What could they do? Larry would know the truth, if it ever came to him, the story of what they thought they saw.

But *they* didn't laugh.

She could read that in the fury in Gladys Claffern's eyes; in the false sparkle of her words; in her desire to leave early. And as she parted with them, she caught one last, anonymous whisper—disjointed.

". . . never saw anything like . . . so *handsome*—"

And she knew what it was that had enabled her to fingersnap them so. Let each cat mew; and let each cat know—that she might be prettier than Claire Belmont, and grander, and richer—but not one, *not one*, could have so handsome a lover!

And then she remembered again—again—again, that Tony was a machine, and her skin crawled.

"Go away! Leave me be!" she cried to the empty room and ran to her bed. She wept wakefully all that night and the next morning, almost before dawn, when the streets were empty, a car drew up to the house and took Tony away.

Lawrence Belmont passed Dr. Calvin's office, and, on impulse, knocked. He found her with Mathematician Peter Bogert, but did not hesitate on that account.

He said, "Claire tells me that U. S. Robots paid for all that was done at my house—"

"Yes," said Dr. Calvin. "We've written it off, as a valuable and necessary part of the experiment. With your new position as Associate Engineer, you'll be able to keep it up, I think."

"That's not what I'm worried about. With Washington agreeing to the tests, we'll be able to get a TN model of our own by next year, I think." He turned hesitantly, as though to go, and as hesitantly turned back again.

"Well, Mr. Belmont?" asked Dr. Calvin, after a pause.

"I wonder—" began Larry. "I wonder what really happened there. She—Claire, I mean—seems so different. It's not just her looks— though, frankly, I'm amazed." He laughed nervously. "It's *her*! She's not my wife, really—I can't explain it."

"Why try? Are you disappointed with any part of the change?"

"On the contrary. But it's a little frightening, too, you see—"

"I wouldn't worry, Mr. Belmont. Your wife has handled herself very well. Frankly, I never expected to have the experiment yield such a thorough and complete test. We know exactly what corrections must be made in the TN model, and the credit belongs entirely to Mrs. Belmont. If you want me to be very honest, I think your wife deserves your promotion more than you do."

Larry flinched visibly at that. "As long as it's in the family," he murmured unconvincingly and left.

Susan Calvin looked after him, "I think that hurt—I hope. . . . Have you read Tony's report, Peter?"

"Thoroughly," said Bogert. "And won't the TN-3 model need changes?"

"Oh, you think so, too?" questioned Calvin sharply. "What's your reasoning?"

Bogert frowned. "I don't need any. It's obvious on the face of it that we can't have a robot loose which makes love to his mistress, if you don't mind the pun."

"Love! Peter, you sicken me. You really don't understand? That machine had to obey the First Law. He couldn't allow harm to come to a human being, and harm was coming to Claire Belmont through her own sense of inadequacy. So he made love to her, since what woman would fail to appreciate the compliment of being able to stir passion in a machine—in a cold, soulless machine. And he opened the curtains that night deliberately, that the others might see and envy—without any risk possible to Claire's marriage. I think it was clever of Tony—"

"Do you? What's the difference whether it was pretense or not, Susan? It still has its horrifying effect. Read the report again. She avoided him. She screamed when he held her. She didn't sleep that last night—in hysterics. We can't have that."

"Peter, you're blind. You're as blind as I was. The TN model will be rebuilt entirely, but not for your reason. Quite otherwise; quite otherwise. Strange that I overlooked it in the first place," her eyes were opaquely thoughtful, "but perhaps it reflects a shortcoming in myself. You see, Peter, machines can't fall in love, but—even when it's hopeless and horrifying—women can!"

Lenny

United States Robots and Mechanical Men Corporation had a problem. The problem was people.

Peter Bogert, Senior Mathematician, was on his way to Assembly when he encountered Alfred Lanning, Research Director. Lanning was bending his ferocious white eyebrows together and staring down across the railing into the computer room.

On the floor below the balcony, a trickle of humanity of both sexes and various ages was looking about curiously, while a guide intoned a set speech about robotic computing.

"This computer you see before you," he said, "is the largest of its type in the world. I contains five million three hundred thousand cryotrons and is capable of dealing simultaneously with over one hundred thousand variables. With its help, U. S. Robots is able to design with precision the positronic brains of new models.

"The requirements are fed in on tape which is perforated by the action of this keyboard—something like a very complicated typewriter or linotype machine, except that it does not deal with letters but with concepts. Statements are broken down into the symbolic logic equivalents and those in turn converted to perforation patterns.

"The computer can, in less than one hour, present our scientists with a design for a brain which will give all the necessary positronic paths to make a robot . . ."

Alfred Lanning looked up at last and noticed the other. "Ah, Peter," he said.

Bogert raised both hands to smooth down his already perfectly smooth and glossy head of black hair. He said, "You don't look as though you think much of this, Alfred."

Lanning grunted. The idea of public guided tours of U. S. Robots was of fairly recent origin, and was supposed to serve a dual function. On the one hand, the theory went, it allowed people to see robots at close quarters and counter their almost instinctive fear of the mechanical objects through increased familiarity. And on the other hand, it was supposed to interest at least an occasional person in taking up robotics research as a life work.

"You know I don't," Lanning said finally. "Once a week, work is disrupted. Considering the man-hours lost, the return is insufficient."

"Still no rise in job applications, then?"

"Oh, some, but only in the categories where the need isn't vital. It's research men that are needed. You know that. The trouble is that with robots forbidden on Earth itself, there's something unpopular about being a roboticist."

"The damned Frankenstein complex," said Bogert, consciously imitating one of the other's pet phrases.

Lanning missed the gentle jab. He said, "I ought to be used to it, but I never will. You'd think that by now every human being on Earth would know that the Three Laws represented a perfect safeguard; that robots are simply not dangerous. Take this bunch." He glowered down. "Look at them. Most of them go through the robot assembly room for the thrill of fear, like riding a roller coaster. Then when they enter the room with the MEC model—damn it, Peter, a MEC model that will do nothing on God's green Earth but take two steps forward, say 'Pleased to meet you, sir,' shake hands, then take two steps back—they back away and mothers snatch up their kids. How do we expect to get brainwork out of such idiots?"

Bogert had no answer. Together, they stared down once again at the line of sightseers, now passing out of the computer room and into the positronic brain assembly section. Then they left. They did not, as it turned out, observe Mortimer W. Jacobson, age 16—who, to do him complete justice, meant no harm whatever.

In fact, it could not even be said to be Mortimer's fault. The day of the week on which the tour took place was known to all workers.

All devices in its path ought to have been carefully neutralized or locked, since it was unreasonable to expect human beings to withstand the temptation to handle knobs, keys, handles and pushbuttons. In addition, the guide ought to have been very carefully on the watch for those who succumbed.

But, at the time, the guide had passed into the next room and Mortimer was tailing the line. He passed the keyboard on which instructions were fed into the computer. He had no way of suspecting that the plans for a new robot design were being fed into it at that moment, or, being a good kid, he would have avoided the keyboard. He had no way of knowing that, by what amounted to almost criminal negligence, a technician had not inactivated the keyboard.

So Mortimer touched the keys at random as though he were playing a musical instrument.

He did not notice that a section of perforated tape stretched itself out of the instrument in another part of the room—soundlessly, unobtrusively.

Nor did the technician, when he returned, discover any signs of tampering. He felt a little uneasy at noticing that the keyboard was live, but did not think to check. After a few minutes, even his first trifling uneasiness was gone, and he continued feeding data into the computer.

As for Mortimer, neither then, nor ever afterward, did he know what he had done.

The new LNE model was designed for the mining of boron in the asteroid belt. The boron hydrides were increasing in value yearly as primers for the proton micropiles that carried the ultimate load of power production on spaceships, and Earth's own meager supply was running thin.

Physically, that meant that the LNE robots would have to be equipped with eyes sensitive to those lines prominent in the spectroscopic analysis of boron ores and the type of limbs most useful for the working up of ore to finished product. As always, though, the mental equipment was the major problem.

The first LNE positronic brain had been completed now. It was the prototype and would join all other prototypes in U. S. Robots' collection. When finally tested, others would then be manufactured for leasing (never selling) to mining corporations.

LNE-Prototype was complete now. Tall, straight, polished, it looked from outside like any of a number of not-too-specialized robot models.

The technician in charge, guided by the directions for testing in the *Handbook of Robotics*, said, "How are you?"

The indicated answer was to have been, "I am well and ready to begin my functions. I trust you are well, too," or some trivial modification thereof.

This first exchange served no purpose but to show that the robot could hear, understand a routine question, and make a routine reply congruent with what one would expect of a robotic attitude. Beginning from there, one could pass on to more complicated matters that would test the different Laws and their interaction with the specialized knowledge of each particular model.

So the technician said, "How are you?" He was instantly jolted by the nature of LNE-Prototype's voice. It had a quality like no robotic voice he had ever heard (and he had heard many). It formed syllables like the chimes of a low-pitched celeste.

So surprising was this that it was only after several moments that the technician heard, in retrospect, the syllables that had been formed by those heavenly tones.

They were, "Da, da, da, goo."

The robot still stood tall and straight but its right hand crept upward and a finger went into its mouth.

The technician stared in absolute horror and bolted. He locked the door behind him and, from another room, put in an emergency call to Dr. Susan Calvin.

Dr. Susan Calvin was U. S. Robots' (and, virtually, mankind's) only robopsychologist. She did not have to go very far in her testing of LNE-Prototype before she called very peremptorily for a transcript of the computer-drawn plans of the positronic brain-paths and the taped instructions that had directed them. After some study, she, in turn, sent for Bogert.

Her iron-gray hair was drawn severely back; her cold face, with its strong vertical lines marked off by the horizontal gash of the pale, thin-lipped mouth, turned intensely upon him.

"What *is* this, Peter?"

Bogert studied the passages she pointed out with increasing stupefaction and said, "Good Lord, Susan, it makes no sense."

"It most certainly doesn't. How did it get into the instructions?"

The technician in charge, called upon, swore in all sincerity that it was none of his doing, and that he could not account for it. The computer checked out negative for all attempts at flaw-finding.

"The positronic brain," said Susan Calvin, thoughtfully, "is past redemption. So many of the higher functions have been cancelled out by these meaningless directions that the result is very like a human baby."

Bogert looked surprised, and Susan Calvin took on a frozen attitude at once, as she always did at the least expressed or implied doubt of her word. She said, "We make every effort to make a robot as mentally like a man as possible. Eliminate what we call the adult functions and what is naturally left is a human infant, mentally speaking. Why do you look so surprised, Peter?"

LNE-Prototype, who showed no signs of understanding any of the things that were going on around it, suddenly slipped into a sitting position and began a minute examination of its feet.

Bogert stared at it. "It's a shame to have to dismantle the creature. It's a handsome job."

"Dismantle it?" said the robopsychologist forcefully.

"Of course, Susan. What's the use of this thing? Good Lord, if there's one object completely and abysmally useless it's a robot without a job it can perform. You don't pretend there's a job this thing can do, do you?"

"No, of course not."

"Well, then?"

Susan Calvin said, stubbornly, "I want to conduct more tests."

Bogert looked at her with a moment's impatience, then shrugged. If there was one person at U. S. Robots with whom it was useless to dispute, surely that was Susan Calvin. Robots were all she loved, and long association with them, it seemed to Bogert, had deprived her of any appearance of humanity. She was no more to be argued out of a decision than was a triggered micropile to be argued out of operating.

"What's the use?" he breathed; then aloud, hastily: "Will you let us know when your tests are complete?"

"I will," she said. "Come, Lenny."

(LNE, thought Bogert. That becomes Lenny. Inevitable.)

Susan Calvin held out her hand but the robot only stared at it. Gently, the robopsychologist reached for the robot's hand and took

it. Lenny rose smoothly to its feet (its mechanical coordination, at
least, worked well). Together they walked out, robot topping woman
by two feet. Many eyes followed them curiously down the long corridors.

One wall of Susan Calvin's laboratory, the one opening directly
off her private office, was covered with a highly magnified reproduction of a positronic-path chart. Susan Calvin had studied it with
absorption for the better part of a month.

She was considering it now, carefully, tracing the blunted paths
through their contortions. Behind her, Lenny sat on the floor, moving its legs apart and together, crooning meaningless syllables to itself in a voice so beautiful that one could listen to the nonsense and
be ravished.

Susan Calvin turned to the robot, "Lenny—Lenny—"

She repeated this patiently until finally Lenny looked up and
made an inquiring sound. The robopsychologist allowed a glimmer
of pleasure to cross her face fleetingly. The robot's attention was
being gained in progressively shorter intervals.

She said, "Raise your hand, Lenny. Hand—up. Hand—up."

She raised her own hand as she said it, over and over.

Lenny followed the movement with its eyes. Up, down, up, down.
Then it made an abortive gesture with its own hand and chimed,
"Eh—uh."

"Very good, Lenny," said Susan Calvin, gravely. "Try it again.
Hand—up."

Very gently, she reached out her own hand, took the robot's, and
raised it, lowered it. "Hand—up. Hand—up."

A voice from her office called and interrupted. "Susan?"

Calvin halted with a tightening of her lips. "What is it, Alfred?"

The research director walked in, and looked at the chart on the
wall and at the robot. "Still at it?"

"I'm at my work, yes."

"Well, you know, Susan . . ." He took out a cigar, staring at it
hard, and made as though to bite off the end. In doing so, his eyes
met the woman's stern look of disapproval; and he put the cigar
away and began over. "Well, you know, Susan, the LNE model is in
production now."

"So I've heard. Is there something in connection with it you wish
of me?"

"No-o. Still, the mere fact that it is in production and is doing well means that working with this messed-up specimen is useless. Shouldn't it be scrapped?"

"In short, Alfred, you are annoyed that I am wasting my so-valuable time. Feel relieved. My time is not being wasted. I am *working* with this robot."

"But the work has no meaning."

"I'll be the judge of that, Alfred." Her voice was ominously quiet, and Lanning thought it wiser to shift his ground.

"Will you tell me what meaning it has? What are you doing with it right now, for instance?"

"I'm trying to get it to raise its hand on the word of command. I'm trying to get it to imitate the sound of the word."

As though on cue, Lenny said, "Eh-uh" and raised its hand waveringly.

Lanning shook his head. "That voice is amazing. How does it happen?"

Susan Calvin said, "I don't quite know. Its transmitter is a normal one. It could speak normally, I'm sure. It doesn't, however; it speaks like this as a consequence of something in the positronic paths that I have not yet pinpointed."

"Well, pinpoint it, for Heaven's sake. Speech like that might be useful."

"Oh, then there is some possible use in my studies on Lenny?"

Lanning shrugged in embarrassment. "Oh, well, it's a minor point."

"I'm sorry you don't see the major points, then," said Susan Calvin with asperity, "which are much more important, but that's not my fault. Would you leave now, Alfred, and let me go on with my work?"

Lanning got to his cigar, eventually, in Bogert's office. He said, sourly, "That woman is growing more peculiar daily."

Bogert understood perfectly. In the U. S. Robots and Mechanical Men Corporation, there was only one "that woman." He said, "Is she still scuffing about with that pseudo-robot—that Lenny of hers?"

"Trying to get it to talk, so help me."

Bogert shrugged. "Points up the company problem. I mean, about getting qualified personnel for research. If we had other robopsychologists, we could retire Susan. Incidentally, I presume the directors' meeting scheduled for tomorrow is for the purpose of dealing with the procurement problem?"

Lanning nodded and looked at his cigar as though it didn't taste good. "Yes. Quality, though, not quantity. We've raised wages until there's a steady stream of applicants—those who are interested primarily in money. The trick is to get those who are interested primarily in robotics—a few more like Susan Calvin."

"Hell, no. Not like her."

"Well, not like her personally. But you'll have to admit, Peter, that she's single-minded about robots. She has no other interest in life."

"I know. And that's exactly what makes her so unbearable."

Lanning nodded. He had lost count of the many times it would have done his soul good to have fired Susan Calvin. He had also lost count of the number of millions of dollars she had at one time or another saved the company. She was a truly indispensable woman and would remain one until she died—or until they could lick the problem of finding men and women of her own high caliber who were interested in robotics research.

He said, "I think we'll cut down on the tour business."

Peter shrugged. "If you say so. But meanwhile, seriously, what do we do about Susan? She can easily tie herself up with Lenny indefinitely. You know how she is when she gets what she considers an interesting problem."

"What *can* we do?" said Lanning. "If we become too anxious to pull her off, she'll stay on out of feminine contrariness. In the last analysis, we can't force her to do anything."

The dark-haired mathematician smiled. "I wouldn't ever apply the adjective 'feminine' to any part of her."

"Oh, well," said Lanning, grumpily. "At least, it won't do anyone any actual harm."

In that, if in nothing else, he was wrong.

The emergency signal is always a tension-making thing in any large industrial establishment. Such signals had sounded in the history of U. S. Robots a dozen times—for fire, flood, riot and insurrection.

But one thing had never occurred in all that time. Never had the particular signal indicating "Robot out of control" sounded. No one ever expected it to sound. It was only installed at government insistence. ("Damn the Frankenstein complex," Lanning would mutter on those rare occasions when he thought of it.)

Now, finally, the shrill siren rose and fell at ten-second intervals, and practically no worker from the President of the Board of Directors down to the newest janitor's assistant recognized the significance of the strange sound for a few moments. After those moments passed, there was a massive convergence of armed guards and medical men to the indicated area of danger and U. S. Robots was struck with paralysis.

Charles Randow, computing technician, was taken off to hospital level with a broken arm. There was no other damage. No other physical damage.

"But the moral damage," roared Lanning, "is beyond estimation."

Susan Calvin faced him, murderously calm. "You will do nothing to Lenny. Nothing. Do you understand?"

"Do *you* understand, Susan?" That thing has hurt a human being. It has broken First Law. Don't you know what First Law is?"

"You will do nothing to Lenny."

"For God's sake, Susan, do I have to tell *you* First Law? A *robot may not harm a human being or, through inaction, allow a human being to come to harm.* Our entire position depends on the fact that First Law is rigidly observed by all robots of all types. If the public should hear, and they will hear, that there was an exception, even one exception, we might be forced to close down altogether. Our only chance of survival would be to announce at once that the robot involved had been destroyed, explain the circumstances, and hope that the public can be convinced that it will never happen again."

"I would like to find out exactly what happened," said Susan Calvin. "I was not present at the time and I would like to know exactly what the Randow boy was doing in my laboratories without my permission."

"The important thing that happened," said Lanning, "is obvious. Your robot struck Randow and the damn fool flashed the 'Robot out of control' button and made a case of it. But your robot struck him and inflicted damage to the extent of a broken arm. The truth is your Lenny is so distorted it lacks First Law and it must be destroyed."

"It does *not* lack First Law. I have studied its brainpaths and know it does not lack it."

"Then how could it strike a man?" Desperation turned him to sarcasm. "Ask Lenny. Surely you have taught it to speak by now."

Susan Calvin's cheeks flushed a painful pink. She said, "I prefer to interview the victim. And in my absence, Alfred, I want my offices sealed tight, with Lenny inside. I want no one to approach him. If any harm comes to him while I am gone, this company will not see me again under any circumstances."

"Will you agree to its destruction, if it has broken First Law?"

"Yes," said Susan Calvin, "because I know it hasn't."

Charles Randow lay in bed with his arm set and in a cast. His major suffering was still from the shock of those few moments in which he thought a robot was advancing on him with murder in its positronic mind. No other human had ever had such reason to fear direct robotic harm as he had had just then. He had had a unique experience.

Susan Calvin and Alfred Lanning stood beside his bed now; Peter Bogert, who had met them on the way, was with them. Doctors and nurses had been shooed out.

Susan Calvin said, "Now—what happened?"

Randow was daunted. He muttered, "The thing hit me in the arm. It was coming at me."

Calvin said, "Move further back in the story. What were you doing in my laboratory without authorization?"

The young computer swallowed, and the Adam's apple in his thin neck bobbed noticeably. He was high-cheekboned and abnormally pale. He said, "We all knew about your robot. The word is you were trying to teach it to talk like a musical instrument. There were bets going as to whether it talked or not. Some said—uh—you could teach a gatepost to talk."

"I suppose," said Susan Calvin, freezingly, "that is meant as a compliment. What did that have to do with you?"

"I was supposed to go in there and settle matters—see if it would talk, you know. We swiped a key to your place and I waited till you were gone and went in. We had a lottery on who was to do it. I lost."

"Then?"

"I tried to get it to talk and it hit me."

"What do you mean, you tried to get it to talk? How did you try?"

"I—I asked it questions, but it wouldn't say anything, and I had to give the thing a fair shake, so I kind of—yelled at it, and—"

"And?"

There was a long pause. Under Susan Calvin's unwavering stare, Randow finally said, "I tried to scare it into saying something." He added defensively, "I had to give the thing a fair shake."

"How did you try to scare it?"

"I pretended to take a punch at it."

"And it brushed your arm aside?"

"It *hit* my arm."

"Very well. That's all." To Lanning and Bogert, she said, "Come, gentlemen."

At the doorway, she turned back to Randow. "I can settle the bets going around, if you are still interested. Lenny can speak a few words quite well."

They said nothing until they were in Susan Calvin's office. Its walls were lined with her books, some of which she had written herself. It retained the patina of her own frigid, carefully ordered personality. It had only one chair in it and she sat down. Lanning and Bogert remained standing.

She said, "Lenny only defended itself. That is the Third Law: A *robot must protect its own existence.*"

"*Except,*" said Lanning forcefully, "*when this conflicts with the First or Second Laws.* Complete the statement! Lenny had no right to defend itself in any way at the cost of harm, however minor, to a human being."

"Nor did it," shot back Calvin, "*knowingly.* Lenny has an aborted brain. It had no way of knowing its own strength or the weakness of humans. In brushing aside the threatening arm of a human being it could not know the bone would break. In human terms, no moral blame can be attached to an individual who honestly cannot differentiate good and evil."

Bogert interrupted, soothingly, "Now, Susan, *we* don't blame. We understand that Lenny is the equivalent of a baby, humanly speaking, and we don't blame it. But the public will. U. S. Robots will be closed down."

"Quite the opposite. If you had the brains of a flea, Peter, you would see that this is the opportunity U. S. Robots is waiting for. That this will solve its problems."

Lanning hunched his white eyebrows low. He said, softly, "What problems, Susan?"

"Isn't the corporation concerned about maintaining our research personnel at the present—Heaven help us—high level?"

"We certainly are."

"Well, what are you offering prospective researchers? Excitement? Novelty? The thrill of piercing the unknown? No! You offer them salaries and the assurance of no problems."

Bogert said, "How do you mean, no problems?"

"Are there problems?" shot back Susan Calvin. "What kind of robots do we turn out? Fully developed robots, fit for their tasks. An industry tells us what it needs; a computer designs the brain; machinery forms the robot; and there it is, complete and done. Peter, some time ago, you asked me with reference to Lenny what its use was. What's the use, you said, of a robot that was not designed for any job? Now I ask you—what's the use of a robot designed for only one job? It begins and ends in the same place. The LNE models mine boron. If beryllium is needed, they are useless. If boron technology enters a new phase, they become useless. A human being so designed would be sub-human. A robot so designed is sub-robotic."

"Do you want a versatile robot?" asked Lanning, incredulously.

"Why not?" demanded the robopsychologist. "Why not? I've been handed a robot with a brain almost completely stultified. I've been teaching it, and you, Alfred, asked me what was the use of that. Perhaps very little as far as Lenny itself is concerned, since it will never progress beyond the five-year-old level on a human scale. But what's the use in general? A very great deal, if you consider it as a study in the abstract problem of *learning how to teach robots.* I have learned ways to short-circuit neighboring pathways in order to create new ones. More study will yield better, more subtle and more efficient techniques of doing so."

"Well?"

"Suppose you started with a positronic brain that had all the basic pathways carefully outlined but none of the secondaries. Suppose you then started creating secondaries. You could sell basic robots designed for instruction; robots that could be modelled to a job, and then modelled to another, if necessary. Robots would become as versatile as human beings. *Robots could learn!*"

They stared at her.

She said, impatiently, "You still don't understand, do you?"

"I understand what you are saying," said Lanning.

"Don't you understand that with a completely new field of research and completely new techniques to be developed, with a completely new area of the unknown to be penetrated, youngsters will feel a new urge to enter robotics? Try it and see."

"May I point out," said Bogert, smoothly, "that this is dangerous. Beginning with ignorant robots such as Lenny will mean that one could never trust First Law—exactly as turned out in Lenny's case."

"Exactly. Advertise the fact."

"*Advertise it!*"

"Of course. Broadcast the danger. Explain that you will set up a new research institute on the moon, if Earth's population chooses not to allow this sort of thing to go on upon Earth, but stress the danger to the possible applicants by all means."

Lanning said, "For God's sake, why?"

"Because the spice of danger will add to the lure. Do you think nuclear technology involves no danger and spationautics no peril? Has your lure of absolute security been doing the trick for you? Has it helped you to cater to the Frankenstein complex you all despise so? Try something else then, something that has worked in other fields."

There was a sound from beyond the door that led to Calvin's personal laboratories. It was the chiming sound of Lenny.

The robopsychologist broke off instantly, listening. She said, "Excuse me. I think Lenny is calling me."

"Can it call you?" said Lanning.

"I said I've managed to teach it a few words." She stepped toward the door, a little flustered. "If you will wait for me—"

They watched her leave and were silent for a moment. Then Lanning said, "Do you think there's anything to what she says, Peter?"

"Just possibly, Alfred," said Bogert. "Just possibly. Enough for us to bring the matter up at the directors' meeting and see what they say. After all, the fat *is* in the fire. A robot has harmed a human being and knowledge of it is public. As Susan says, we might as well try to turn the matter to our advantage. Of course, I distrust her motives in all this."

"How do you mean?"

"Even if all she has said is perfectly true, it is only rationalization as far as she is concerned. Her motive in all this is her desire to hold on to this robot. If we pressed her" (and the mathematician smiled at the incongruous literal meaning of the phrase) "she would say it was to continue learning techniques of teaching robots, but I think she has found another use for Lenny. A rather unique one that would fit only Susan of all women."

"I don't get your drift."

Bogert said, "Did you hear what the robot was calling?"

"Well, no, I didn't quite—" began Lanning, when the door opened suddenly, and both men stopped talking at once.

Susan Calvin stepped in again, looking about uncertainly. "Have either of you seen— I'm positive I had it somewhere about— Oh, there it is."

She ran to a corner of one bookcase and picked up an object of intricate metal webbery, dumbbell shaped and hollow, with variously shaped metal pieces inside each hollow, just too large to be able to fall out of the webbing.

As she picked it up, the metal pieces within moved and struck together, clicking pleasantly. It struck Lanning that the object was a kind of robotic version of a baby rattle.

As Susan Calvin opened the door again to pass through, Lenny's voice chimed again from within. This time, Lanning heard it clearly as it spoke the words Susan Calvin had taught it.

In heavenly celeste-like sounds, it called out, "Mommie, I want you. I want you, Mommie."

And the footsteps of Susan Calvin could be heard hurrying eagerly across the laboratory floor toward the only kind of baby she could ever have or love.

Galley Slave

The United States Robots and Mechanical Men Corporation, as defendants in the case, had influence enough to force a closed-doors trial without a jury.

Nor did Northeastern University try hard to prevent it. The trustees knew perfectly well how the public might react to any issue involving misbehavior of a robot, however rarefied that misbehavior might be. They also had a clearly visualized notion of how an anti-robot riot might become an antiscience riot without warning.

The government, as represented in this case by Justice Harlow Shane, was equally anxious for a quiet end to this mess. Both U. S. Robots and the academic world were bad people to antagonize.

Justice Shane said, "Since neither press, public nor jury is present, gentlemen, let us stand on as little ceremony as we can and get to the facts."

He smiled stiffly as he said this, perhaps without much hope that his request would be effective, and hitched at his robe so that he might sit more comfortably. His face was pleasantly rubicund, his chin round and soft, his nose broad and his eyes light in color and wide-set. All in all, it was not a face with much judicial majesty and the judge knew it.

Barnabas H. Goodfellow, Professor of Physics at Northeastern U., was sworn in first, taking the usual vow with an expression that made mincemeat of his name.

After the usual opening-gambit questions, Prosecution shoved his hands deep into his pockets and said, "When was it, Professor, that the matter of the possible employ of Robot EZ-27 was first brought to your attention, and how?"

Professor Goodfellow's small and angular face set itself into an uneasy expression, scarcely more benevolent than the one it replaced. He said, "I have had professional contact and some social acquaintance with Dr. Alfred Lanning, Director of Research at U. S. Robots. I was inclined to listen with some tolerance then when I received a rather strange suggestion from him on the third of March of last year—"

"Of 2033?"

"That's right."

"Excuse me for interrupting. Please proceed."

The professor nodded frostily, scowled to fix the facts in his mind, and began to speak.

Professor Goodfellow looked at the robot with a certain uneasiness. It had been carried into the basement supply room in a crate, in accordance with the regulations governing the shipment of robots from place to place on the Earth's surface.

He knew it was coming; it wasn't that he was unprepared. From the moment of Dr. Lanning's first phone call on March 3, he had felt himself giving way to the other's persuasiveness, and now, as an inevitable result, he found himself face to face with a robot.

It looked uncommonly large as it stood within arm's reach.

Alfred Lanning cast a hard glance of his own at the robot, as though making certain it had not been damaged in transit. Then he turned his ferocious eyebrows and his mane of white hair in the professor's direction.

"This is Robot EZ-27, first of its model to be available for public use." He turned to the robot. "This is Professor Goodfellow, Easy."

Easy spoke impassively, but with such suddenness that the professor shied. "Good afternoon, Professor."

Easy stood seven feet tall and had the general proportions of a man—always the prime selling point of U. S. Robots. That and the possession of the basic patents on the positronic brain had given them an actual monopoly on robots and a near-monopoly on computing machines in general.

The two men who had uncrated the robot had left now and the

professor looked from Lanning to the robot and back to Lanning. "It is harmless, I'm sure." He didn't sound sure.

"More harmless than I am," said Lanning. "I could be goaded into striking you. Easy could not be. You know the Three Laws of Robotics, I presume."

"Yes, of course," said Goodfellow.

"They are built into the positronic patterns of the brain and must be observed. The First Law, the prime rule of robotic existence, safeguards the life and well-being of all humans." He paused, rubbed at his cheek, then added, "It's something of which we would like to persuade all Earth if we could."

"It's just that he seems formidable."

"Granted. But whatever he seems, you'll find that he *is* useful."

"I'm not sure in what way. Our conversations were not very helpful in that respect. Still, I agreed to look at the object and I'm doing it."

"We'll do more than look, Professor. Have you brought a book?"

"I have."

"May I see it?"

Professor Goodfellow reached down without actually taking his eyes off the metal-in-human-shape that confronted him. From the briefcase at his feet, he withdrew a book.

Lanning held out his hand for it and looked at the backstrip. "*Physical Chemistry of Electrolytes in Solution.* Fair enough, sir. You selected this yourself, at random. It was no suggestion of mine, this particular text. Am I right?"

"Yes."

Lanning passed the book to Robot EZ-27.

The professor jumped a little. "No! That's a valuable book!"

Lanning raised his eyebrows and they looked like shaggy coconut icing. He said, "Easy has no intention of tearing the book in two as a feat of strength, I assure you. It can handle a book as carefully as you or I. Go ahead, Easy."

"Thank you, sir," said Easy. Then, turning its metal bulk slightly, it added, "With your permission, Professor Goodfellow."

The professor stared, then said, "Yes—yes, of course."

With a slow and steady manipulation of metal fingers, Easy turned the pages of the book, glancing at the left page, then the

right; turning the page, glancing left, then right; turning the page
and so on for minute after minute.

The sense of its power seemed to dwarf even the large cement-
walled room in which they stood and to reduce the two human
watchers to something considerably less than life-size.

Goodfellow muttered, "The light isn't very good."

"It will do."

Then, rather more sharply, "But what is he doing?"

"Patience, sir."

The last page was turned eventually. Lanning asked, "Well,
Easy?"

The robot said, "It is a most accurate book and there is little to
which I can point. On line 22 of page 27, the word 'positive' is
spelled p-o-i-s-t-i-v-e. The comma in line 6 of page 32 is superfluous,
whereas one should have been used on line 13 of page 54. The plus
sign in equation XIV-2 on page 337 should be a minus sign if it is to
be consistent with the previous equations—"

"Wait! Wait!" cried the professor. "What is he doing?"

"Doing?" echoed Lanning in sudden irascibility. "Why, man, he
has already done it! He has proofread that book."

"Proofread it?"

"Yes. In the short time it took him to turn those pages, he caught
every mistake in spelling, grammar and punctuation. He has noted
errors in word order and detected inconsistencies. And he will retain
the information, letter-perfect, indefinitely."

The professor's mouth was open. He walked rapidly away from
Lanning and Easy and as rapidly back. He folded his arms across his
chest and stared at them. Finally he said, "You mean this is a proofreading robot?"

Lanning nodded. "Among other things."

"But why do you show it to me?"

"So that you might help me persuade the university to obtain it
for use."

"To read proof?"

"Among other things," Lanning repeated patiently.

The professor drew his pinched face together in a kind of sour disbelief. "But this is ridiculous!"

"Why?"

"The university could never afford to buy this half-ton—it must
weigh that at least—this half-ton proofreader."

"Proofreading is not all it will do. It will prepare reports from out-lines, fill out forms, serve as an accurate memory-file, grade papers—"

"All picayune!"

Lanning said, "Not at all, as I can show you in a moment. But I think we can discuss this more comfortably in your office, if you have no objection."

"No, of course not," began the professor mechanically and took a half-step as though to turn. Then he snapped out, "But the robot—we can't take the robot. Really, Doctor, you'll have to crate it up again."

"Time enough. We can leave Easy here."

"Unattended?"

"Why not? He knows he is to stay. Professor Goodfellow, it is necessary to understand that a robot is far more reliable than a human being."

"I would be responsible for any damage—"

"There will be no damage. I guarantee that. Look, it's after hours. You expect no one here, I imagine, before tomorrow morning. The truck and my two men are outside. U. S. Robots will take any responsibility that may arise. None will. Call it a demonstration of the reliability of the robot."

The professor allowed himself to be led out of the storeroom. Nor did he look entirely comfortable in his own office, five stories up.

He dabbed at the line of droplets along the upper half of his forehead with a white handkerchief.

"As you know very well, Dr. Lanning, there are laws against the use of robots on Earth's surface," he pointed out.

"The laws, Professor Goodfellow, are not simple ones. Robots may not be used on public thoroughfares or within public edifices. They may not be used on private grounds or within private structures except under certain restrictions that usually turn out to be prohibitive. The university, however, is a large and privately owned institution that usually receives preferential treatment. If the robot is used only in a specific room for only academic purposes, if certain other restrictions are observed and if the men and women having occasion to enter the room cooperate fully, we may remain within the law."

"But all that trouble just to read proof?"

"The uses would be infinite, Professor. Robotic labor has so far been used only to relieve physical drudgery. Isn't there such a thing as mental drudgery? When a professor capable of the most useful creative thought is forced to spend two weeks painfully checking the spelling of lines of print and I offer you a machine that can do it in thirty minutes, is that picayune?"

"But the price—"

"The price need not bother you. You cannot buy EZ-27. U. S. Robots does not sell its products. But the university can lease EZ-27 for a thousand dollars a year—considerably less than the cost of a single microwave spectograph continuous-recording attachment."

Goodfellow looked stunned. Lanning followed up his advantage by saying, "I only ask that you put it up to whatever group makes the decisions here. I would be glad to speak to them if they want more information."

"Well," Goodfellow said doubtfully, "I can bring it up at next week's Senate meeting. I can't promise that will do any good, though."

"Naturally," said Lanning.

The Defense Attorney was short and stubby and carried himself rather portentously, a stance that had the effect of accentuating his double chin. He stared at Professor Goodfellow, once that witness had been handed over, and said, "You agreed rather readily, did you not?"

The Professor said briskly, "I suppose I was anxious to be rid of Dr. Lanning. I would have agreed to anything."

"With the intention of forgetting about it after he left?"

"Well—"

"Nevertheless, you did present the matter to a meeting of the Executive Board of the University Senate."

"Yes, I did."

"So that you agreed in good faith with Dr. Lanning's suggestions. You weren't just going along with a gag. You actually agreed enthusiastically, did you not?"

"I merely followed ordinary procedures."

"As a matter of fact, you weren't as upset about the robot as you now claim you were. You know the Three Laws of Robotics and you knew them at the time of your interview with Dr. Lanning."

"Well, yes."

"And you were perfectly willing to leave a robot at large and unattended."

"Dr. Lanning assured me—"

"Surely you would never have accepted his assurance if you had had the slightest doubt that the robot might be in the least dangerous."

The professor began frigidly, "I had every faith in the word—"

"That is all," said Defense abruptly.

As Professor Goodfellow, more than a bit ruffled, stood down, Justice Shane leaned forward and said, "Since I am not a robotics man myself, I would appreciate knowing precisely what the Three Laws of Robotics are. Would Dr. Lanning quote them for the benefit of the court?"

Dr. Lanning looked startled. He had been virtually bumping heads with the gray-haired woman at his side. He rose to his feet now and the woman looked up, too—expressionlessly.

Dr. Lanning said, "Very well, Your Honor." He paused as though about to launch into an oration and said, with laborious clarity, "First Law: a robot may not injure a human being, or, through inaction, allow a human being to come to harm. Second Law: a robot must obey the orders given it by human beings, except where such orders would conflict with the First Law. Third Law: a robot must protect its own existence as long as such protection does not conflict with the First or Second Laws."

"I see," said the judge, taking rapid notes. "These Laws are built into every robot, are they?"

"Into every one. That will be borne out by any roboticist."

"And into Robot EZ-27 specifically?"

"Yes, Your Honor."

"You will probably be required to repeat those statements under oath."

"I am ready to do so, Your Honor."

He sat down again.

Dr. Susan Calvin, robopsychologist-in-chief for U. S. Robots, who was the gray-haired woman sitting next to Lanning, looked at her titular superior without favor, but then she showed favor to no human being. She said, "Was Goodfellow's testimony accurate, Alfred?"

"Essentially," muttered Lanning. "He wasn't as nervous as all that about the robot and he was anxious enough to talk business with me when he heard the price. But there doesn't seem to be any drastic distortion."

Dr. Calvin said thoughtfully, "It might have been wise to put the price higher than a thousand."

"We were anxious to place Easy."

"I know. Too anxious, perhaps. They'll try to make it look as though we had an ulterior motive."

Lanning looked exasperated. "We did. I admitted that at the University Senate meeting."

"They can make it look as if we had one beyond the one we admitted."

Scott Robertson, son of the founder of U. S. Robots and still owner of a majority of the stock, leaned over from Dr. Calvin's other side and said in a kind of explosive whisper, "Why can't you get Easy to talk so we'll know where we're at?"

"You know he can't talk about it, Mr. Robertson."

"Make him. You're the psychologist, Dr. Calvin. *Make* him."

"If I'm the psychologist, Mr. Robertson," said Susan Calvin coldly, "let me make the decisions. My robot will not be *made* to do anything at the price of his well-being."

Robertson frowned and might have answered, but Justice Shane was tapping his gavel in a polite sort of way and they grudgingly fell silent.

Francis J. Hart, head of the Department of English and Dean of Graduate Studies, was on the stand. He was a plump man, meticulously dressed in dark clothing of a conservative cut, and possessing several strands of hair traversing the pink top of his cranium. He sat well back in the witness chair with his hands folded neatly in his lap and displaying, from time to time, a tight-lipped smile.

He said, "My first connection with the matter of the Robot EZ-27 was on the occasion of the session of the University Senate Executive Committee at which the subject was introduced by Professor Goodfellow. Thereafter, on the tenth of April of last year, we held a special meeting on the subject, during which I was in the chair."

"Were minutes kept of the meeting of the Executive Committee? Of the special meeting, that is?"

"Well, no. It was a rather unusual meeting." The dean smiled briefly. "We thought it might remain confidential."

"What transpired at the meeting?"

Dean Hart was not entirely comfortable as chairman of that meeting. Nor did the other members assembled seem completely calm.

Only Dr. Lanning appeared at peace with himself. His tall, gaunt figure and the shock of white hair that crowned him reminded Hart of portraits he had seen of Andrew Jackson.

Samples of the robot's work lay scattered along the central regions of the table and the reproduction of a graph drawn by the robot was now in the hands of Professor Minott of Physical Chemistry. The chemist's lips were pursed in obvious approval.

Hart cleared his throat and said, "There seems no doubt that the robot can perform certain routine tasks with adequate competence. I have gone over these, for instance, just before coming in and there is very little to find fault with."

He picked up a long sheet of printing, some three times as long as the average book page. It was a sheet of galley proof, designed to be corrected by authors before the type was set up in page form. Along both of the wide margins of the galley were proofmarks, neat and superbly legible. Occasionally, a word of print was crossed out and a new word substituted in the margin in characters so fine and regular it might easily have been print itself. Some of the corrections were blue to indicate the original mistake had been the author's, a few in red, where the printer had been wrong.

"Actually," said Lanning, "there is less than very little to find fault with. I should say there is nothing at all to find fault with, Dr. Hart. I'm sure the corrections are perfect, insofar as the original manuscript was. If the manuscript against which this galley was corrected was at fault in a matter of fact rather than of English, the robot is not competent to correct it."

"We accept that. However, the robot corrected word order on occasion and I don't think the rules of English are sufficiently hidebound for us to be sure that in each case the robot's choice was the correct one."

"Easy's positronic brain," said Lanning, showing large teeth as he smiled, "has been molded by the contents of all the standard works on the subject. I'm sure you cannot point to a case where the robot's choice was definitely the incorrect one."

Professor Minott looked up from the graph he still held. "The question in my mind, Dr. Lanning, is why we need a robot at all, with all the difficulties in public relations that would entail. The science of automation has surely reached the point where your company could design a machine, an ordinary computer of a type known and accepted by the public, that would correct galleys."

"I am sure we could," said Lanning stiffly, "but such a machine would require that the galleys be translated into special symbols or, at the least, transcribed on tapes. Any corrections would emerge in symbols. You would need to keep men employed translating words to symbols, symbols to words. Furthermore, such a computer could do no other job. It couldn't prepare the graph you hold in your hand, for instance."

Minott grunted.

Lanning went on. "The hallmark of the positronic robot is its flexibility. It can do a number of jobs. It is designed like a man so that it can use all the tools and machines that have, after all, been designed to be used by a man. It can talk to you and you can talk to it. You can actually reason with it up to a point. Compared to even a simple robot, an ordinary computer with a non-positronic brain is only a heavy adding machine."

Goodfellow looked up and said, "If we all talk and reason with the robot, what are the chances of our confusing it? I suppose it doesn't have the capability of absorbing an infinite amount of data."

"No, it hasn't. But it should last five years with ordinary use. It will know when it will require clearing, and the company will do the job without charge."

"The *company* will?"

"Yes. The company reserves the right to service the robot outside the ordinary course of its duties. It is one reason we retain control of our positronic robots and lease rather than sell them. In the pursuit of its ordinary functions, any robot can be directed by any man. Outside its ordinary functions, a robot requires expert handling, and that we can give it. For instance, any of you might clear an EZ robot to an extent by telling it to forget this item or that. But you would be almost certain to phrase the order in such a way as to cause it to forget too much or too little. We would detect such tampering, because we have built-in safeguards. However, since there is no need for clearing the robot in its ordinary work, or for doing other useless things, this raises no problem."

Dean Hart touched his head as though to make sure his carefully cultivated strands lay evenly distributed and said, "You are anxious to have us take the machine. Yet surely it is a losing proposition for

U. S. Robots. One thousand a year is a ridiculously low price. Is it that you hope through this to rent other such machines to other universities at a more reasonable price?"

"Certainly that's a fair hope," said Lanning.

"But even so, the number of machines you could rent would be limited. I doubt if you could make it a paying proposition."

Lanning put his elbows on the table and earnestly leaned forward. "Let me put it bluntly, gentlemen. Robots cannot be used on Earth, except in certain special cases, because of prejudice against them on the part of the public. U. S. Robots is a highly successful corporation with our extraterrestrial and spaceflight markets alone, to say nothing of our computer subsidiaries. However, we are concerned with more than profits alone. It is our firm belief that the use of robots on Earth itself would mean a better life for all eventually, even if a certain amount of economic dislocation resulted at first.

"The labor unions are naturally against us, but surely we may expect cooperation from the large universities. The robot, Easy, will help you by relieving you of scholastic drudgery—by assuming, if you permit it, the role of galley slave for you. Other universities and research institutions will follow your lead, and if it works out, then perhaps other robots of other types may be placed and the public's objections to them broken down by stages."

Minott murmured, "Today Northeastern University, tomorrow the world."

Angrily, Lanning whispered to Susan Calvin, "I wasn't nearly that eloquent and they weren't nearly that reluctant. At a thousand a year, they were jumping to get Easy. Professor Minott told me he'd never seen as beautiful a job as that graph he was holding and there was no mistake on the galley or anywhere else. Hart admitted it freely."

The severe vertical lines on Dr. Calvin's face did not soften. "You should have demanded more money than they could pay, Alfred, and let them beat you down."

"Maybe," he grumbled.

Prosecution was not quite done with Professor Hart. "After Dr. Lanning left, did you vote on whether to accept Robot EZ-27?"

"Yes, we did."

"With what result?"

"In favor of acceptance, by majority vote."

"What would you say influenced the vote?"

Defense objected immediately.

Prosecution rephrased the question. "What influenced you, personally, in your individual vote? You did vote in favor, I think."

"I voted in favor, yes. I did so largely because I was impressed by Dr. Lanning's feeling that it was our duty as members of the world's intellectual leadership to allow robotics to help Man in the solution of his problems."

"In other words, Dr. Lanning talked you into it."

"That's his job. He did it very well."

"Your witness."

Defense strode up to the witness chair and surveyed Professor Hart for a long moment. He said, "In reality, you were all pretty eager to have Robot EZ-27 in your employ, weren't you?"

"We thought that if it could do the work, it might be useful."

"*If* it could do the work? I understand you examined the samples of Robot EZ-27's original work with particular care on the day of the meeting which you have just described."

"Yes, I did. Since the machine's work dealt primarily with the handling of the English language, and since that is my field of competence, it seemed logical that I be the one chosen to examine the work."

"Very good. Was there anything on display on the table at the time of the meeting which was less than satisfactory? I have all the material here as exhibits. Can you point to a single unsatisfactory item?"

"Well—"

"It's a simple question. Was there one single solitary unsatisfactory item? You inspected it. Was there?"

The English professor frowned. "There wasn't."

"I also have some samples of work done by Robot EZ-27 during the course of his fourteen-month employ at Northeastern. Would you examine these and tell me if there is anything wrong with them in even one particular?"

Hart snapped, "When he did make a mistake, it was a beauty."

"Answer my question," thundered Defense, "and only the question I am putting to you! Is there anything wrong with the material?"

Dean Hart looked cautiously at each item. "Well, nothing."

"Barring the matter concerning which we are here engaged, do you know of any mistake on the part of EZ-27?"

"Barring the matter for which this trial is being held, no."

Defense cleared his throat as though to signal end of paragraph. He said, "Now about the vote concerning whether Robot EZ-27 was to be employed or not. You said there was a majority in favor. What was the actual vote?"

"Thirteen to one, as I remember."

"Thirteen to one! More than just a majority, wouldn't you say?"

"No, sir!" All the pedant in Dean Hart was aroused. "In the English language, the word 'majority' means 'more than half.' Thirteen out of fourteen is a majority, nothing more."

"But an almost unanimous one."

"A majority all the same!"

Defense switched ground. "And who was the lone holdout?"

Dean Hart looked acutely uncomfortable. "Professor Simon Ninheimer."

Defense pretended astonishment. "Professor Ninheimer? The head of the Department of Sociology?"

"Yes, sir."

"The *plaintiff?*"

"Yes, sir."

Defense pursed his lips. "In other words, it turns out that the man bringing the action for payment of $750,000 damages against my client, United States Robots and Mechanical Men Corporation was the one who from the beginning opposed the use of the robot— although everyone else on the Executive Committee of the University Senate was persuaded that it was a good idea."

"He voted against the motion, as was his right."

"You didn't mention in your description of the meeting any remarks made by Professor Ninheimer. Did he make any?"

"I think he spoke."

"You *think?*"

"Well, he *did* speak."

"Against using the robot?"

"Yes."

"Was he violent about it?"

Dean Hart paused. "He was vehement."

Defense grew confidential. "How long have you known Professor Ninheimer, Dean Hart?"

"About twelve years."

"Reasonably well?"

"I should say so, yes."

"Knowing him, then, would you say he was the kind of man who might continue to bear resentment against a robot, all the more so because an adverse vote had—"

Prosecution drowned out the remainder of the question with an indignant and vehement objection of his own. Defense motioned the witness down and Justice Shane called luncheon recess.

Robertson mangled his sandwich. The corporation would not founder for loss of three-quarters of a million, but the loss would do it no particular good. He was conscious, moreover, that there would be a much more costly long-term setback in public relations.

He said sourly, "Why all this business about how Easy got into the university? What do they hope to gain?"

The Attorney for Defense said quietly, "A court action is like a chess game, Mr. Robertson. The winner is usually the one who can see more moves ahead, and my friend at the prosecutor's table is no beginner. They can show damage; that's no problem. Their main effort lies in anticipating our defense. They must be counting on us to try to show that Easy couldn't possibly have committed the offense—because of the Laws of Robotics."

"All right," said Robertson, "that *is* our defense. An absolutely airtight one."

"To a robotics engineer. Not necessarily to a judge. They're setting themselves up a position from which they can demonstrate that EZ-27 was no ordinary robot. It was the first of its type to be offered to the public. It was an experimental model that needed field-testing and the university was the only decent way to provide such testing. That would look plausible in the light of Dr. Lanning's strong efforts to place the robot and the willingness of U. S. Robots to lease it for so little. The prosecution would then argue that the field-test proved Easy to have been a failure. Now do you see the purpose of what's been going on?"

"But EZ-27 was a perfectly good model," argued Robertson. "It was the twenty-seventh in production."

"Which is really a bad point," said Defense somberly. "What was wrong with the first twenty-six? Obviously something. Why shouldn't there be something wrong with the twenty-seventh, too?"

"There was nothing wrong with the first twenty-six except that they weren't complex enough for the task. These were the first positronic brains of the sort to be constructed and it was rather hit-and-miss to begin with. But the Three Laws held in all of them! No robot is so imperfect that the Three Laws don't hold."

"Dr. Lanning has explained this to me, Mr. Robertson, and I am willing to take his word for it. The judge, however, may not be. We are expecting a decision from an honest and intelligent man who knows no robotics and thus may be led astray. For instance, if you or Dr. Lanning or Dr. Calvin were to say on the stand that any positronic brains were constructed 'hit-and-miss,' as you just did, prosecution would tear you apart in cross-examination. Nothing would salvage our case. So that's something to avoid."

Robertson growled, "If only Easy would talk."

Defense shrugged. "A robot is incompetent as a witness, so that would do us no good."

"At least we'd know some of the facts. We'd know how it came to do such a thing."

Susan Calvin fired up. A dullish red touched her cheeks and her voice had a trace of warmth in it. "We *know* how Easy came to do it. It was ordered to! I've explained this to counsel and I'll explain it to you now."

"Ordered to by whom?" asked Robertson in honest astonishment. (No one ever told him anything, he thought resentfully. These research people considered *themselves* the owners of U. S. Robots, by God!)

"By the plaintiff," said Dr. Calvin.

"In heaven's name, why?"

"I don't know why yet. Perhaps just that we might be sued, that he might gain some cash." There were blue glints in her eyes as she said that.

"Then why doesn't Easy say so?"

"Isn't that obvious? It's been ordered to keep quiet about the matter."

"Why should that be obvious?" demanded Robertson truculently.

"Well, it's obvious to me. Robot psychology is my profession. If Easy will not answer questions about the matter directly, he will answer questions on the fringe of the matter. By measuring increased hesitation in his answers as the central question is approached, by measuring the area of blankness and the intensity of counterpotentials set up, it is possible to tell with scientific precision that his troubles are the result of an order not to talk, with its strength based on First Law. In other words, he's been told that if he talks, harm will be done a human being. Presumably harm to the unspeakable Professor Ninheimer, the plaintiff, who, to the robot, would seem a human being."

"Well, then," said Robertson, "can't you explain that if he keeps quiet, harm will be done to U. S. Robots?"

"U. S. Robots is not a human being and the First Law of Robotics does not recognize a corporation as a person the way ordinary laws do. Besides, it would be dangerous to try to lift this particular sort of inhibition. The person who laid it on could lift it off least dangerously, because the robot's motivations in that respect are centered on that person. Any other course—" She shook her head and grew almost impassioned. "I won't let the robot be damaged!"

Lanning interrupted with the air of bringing sanity to the problem. "It seems to me that we have only to prove a robot incapable of the act of which Easy is accused. We can do that."

"Exactly," said Defense, in annoyance. "*You* can do that. The only witnesses capable of testifying to Easy's condition and to the nature of Easy's state of mind are employees of U. S. Robots. The judge can't possibly accept their testimony as unprejudiced."

"How can he deny expert testimony?"

"By refusing to be convinced by it. That's his right as the judge. Against the alternative that a man like Professor Ninheimer deliberately set about ruining his own reputation, even for a sizable sum of money, the judge isn't going to accept the technicalities of your engineers. The judge is a man, after all. If he has to choose between a man doing an impossible thing and a robot doing an impossible thing, he's quite likely to decide in favor of the man."

"A man *can* do an impossible thing," said Lanning, "because we don't know all the complexities of the human mind and we don't know what, in a given human mind, is impossible and what is not. We *do* know what is really impossible to a robot."

"Well, we'll see if we can't convince the judge of that," Defense replied wearily.

"If all you say is so," rumbled Robertson, "I don't see how you can."

"We'll see. It's good to know and be aware of the difficulties involved, but let's not be *too* downhearted. I've tried to look ahead a few moves in the chess game, too." With a stately nod in the direction of the robopsychologist, he added, "*With* the help of the good lady here."

Lanning looked from one to the other and said, "What the devil is this?"

But the bailiff thrust his head into the room and announced somewhat breathlessly that the trial was about to resume.

They took their seats, examining the man who had started all the trouble.

Simon Ninheimer owned a fluffy head of sandy hair, a face that narrowed past a beaked nose toward a pointed chin, and a habit of sometimes hesitating before key words in his conversation that gave him an air of a seeker after an almost unbearable precision. When he said, "The Sun rises in the—uh—east," one was certain he had given due consideration to the possibility that it might at some time rise in the west.

Prosecution said, "Did you oppose employment of Robot EZ-27 by the university?"

"I did, sir."

"Why was that?"

"I did not feel that we understood the—uh—motives of U. S. Robots thoroughly. I mistrusted their anxiety to place the robot with us."

"Did you feel that it was capable of doing the work that it was allegedly designed to do?"

"I know for a fact that it was not."

"Would you state your reasons?"

Simon Ninheimer's book, entitled *Social Tensions Involved in Space-Flight and Their Resolution,* had been eight years in the making. Ninheimer's search for precision was not confined to his habits of speech, and in a subject like sociology, almost inherently imprecise, it left him breathless.

Even with the material in galley proofs, he felt no sense of completion. Rather the reverse, in fact. Staring at the long strips of print, he felt only the itch to tear the lines of type apart and rearrange them differently.

Jim Baker, Instructor and soon to be Assistant Professor of Sociology, found Ninheimer, three days after the first batch of galleys had arrived from the printer, staring at the handful of paper in abstraction. The galleys came in three copies: one for Ninheimer to proofread, one for Baker to proofread independently, and a third, marked "Original," which was to receive the final corrections, a combination of those made by Ninheimer and by Baker, after a conference at which possible conflicts and disagreements were ironed out. This had been their policy on the several papers on which they had collaborated in the past three years and it worked well.

Baker, young and ingratiatingly soft-voiced, had his own copies of the galleys in his hand. He said eagerly, "I've done the first chapter and it contains some typographical beauts."

"The first chapter always has them," said Ninheimer distantly.

"Do you want to go over it now?"

Ninheimer brought his eyes to grave focus on Baker. "I haven't done anything on the galleys, Jim. I don't think I'll bother."

Baker looked confused. "Not bother?"

Ninheimer pursed his lips. "I've asked about the—uh—workload of the machine. After all, he was originally—uh—promoted as a proofreader. They've set a schedule."

"The *machine*? You mean Easy?"

"I believe that is the foolish name they gave it."

"But, Dr. Ninheimer, I thought you were staying clear of it!"

"I seem to be the only one doing so. Perhaps I ought to take my share of the—uh—advantage."

"Oh. Well, I seem to have wasted time on this first chapter, then," said the younger man ruefully.

"Not wasted. We can compare the machine's result with yours as a check."

"If you want to, but—"

"Yes?"

"I doubt that we'll find anything wrong with Easy's work. It's supposed never to have made a mistake."

"I dare say," said Ninheimer dryly.

The first chapter was brought in again by Baker four days later. This time it was Ninheimer's copy, fresh from the special annex that had been built to house Easy and the equipment it used.

Baker was jubilant. "Dr. Ninheimer, it not only caught everything

I caught—it found a dozen errors I missed! The whole thing took it twelve minutes!"

Ninheimer looked over the sheaf, with the neatly printed marks and symbols in the margins. He said, "It is not as complete as you and I would have made it. We would have entered an insert on Suzuki's work on the neurological effects of low gravity."

"You mean his paper in *Sociological Reviews?*"

"Of course."

"Well, you can't expect impossibilities of Easy. It can't read the literature for us."

"I realize that. As a matter of fact, I have prepared the insert. I will see the machine and make certain it knows how to—uh—handle inserts."

"It will know."

"I prefer to make certain."

Ninheimer had to make an appointment to see Easy, and then could get nothing better than fifteen minutes in the late evening.

But the fifteen minutes turned out to be ample. Robot EZ-27 understood the matter of inserts at once.

Ninheimer found himself uncomfortable at close quarters with the robot for the first time. Almost automatically, as though it were human, he found himself asking, "Are you happy with your work?"

"Most happy, Professor Ninheimer," said Easy solemnly, the photocells that were its eyes gleaming their normal deep red.

"You know me?"

"From the fact that you present me with additional material to include in the galleys, it follows that you are the author. The author's name, of course, is at the head of each sheet of galley proof."

"I see. You make—uh—deductions, then. Tell me"—he couldn't resist the question—"what do you think of the book so far?"

Easy said, "I find it very pleasant to work with."

"Pleasant? That is an odd word for a—uh—a mechanism without emotion. I've been told you have no emotion."

"The words of your book go in accordance with my circuits," Easy explained. "They set up little or no counterpotentials. It is in my brain paths to translate this mechanical fact into a word such as 'pleasant.' The emotional context is fortuitous."

"I see. Why do you find the book pleasant?"

"It deals with human beings, Professor, and not with inorganic

materials or mathematical symbols. Your book attempts to understand human beings and to help increase human happiness."

"And this is what you try to do and so my book goes in accordance with your circuits? Is that it?"

"That is it, Professor."

The fifteen minutes were up. Ninheimer left and went to the university library, which was on the point of closing. He kept them
open long enough to find an elementary text on robotics. He took it
home with him.

Except for occasional insertion of late material, the galleys went
to Easy and from him to the publishers with little intervention from
Ninheimer at first—and none at all later.

Baker said, a little uneasily, "It almost gives me a feeling of
uselessness."

"It should give you a feeling of having time to begin a new project," said Ninheimer, without looking up from the notations he was
making in the current issue of *Social Science Abstracts.*

"I'm just not used to it. I keep worrying about the galleys. It's
silly, I know."

"It is."

"The other day I got a couple of sheets before Easy sent them off
to—"

"What!" Ninheimer looked up, scowling. The copy of *Abstracts*
slid shut. "Did you disturb the machine at its work?"

"Only for a minute. Everything was all right. Oh, it changed one
word. You referred to something as 'criminal'; it changed the word
to 'reckless.' It thought the second adjective fit in better with the
context."

Ninheimer grew thoughtful. "What did you think?"

"You know, I agreed with it. I let it stand."

Ninheimer turned in his swivel-chair to face his young associate.
"See here, I wish you wouldn't do this again. If I am to use the machine, I wish the—uh—full advantage of it. If I am to use it and
lose your—uh—services anyway because you supervise it when the
whole point is that it requires no supervision, I gain nothing. Do you
see?"

"Yes, Dr. Ninheimer," said Baker, subdued.

The advance copies of *Social Tensions* arrived in Dr. Ninheimer's
office on the eighth of May. He looked through it briefly, flipping

pages and pausing to read a paragraph here and there. Then he put his copies away.

As he explained later, he forgot about it. For eight years, he had worked at it, but now, and for months in the past, other interests had engaged him while Easy had taken the load of the book off his shoulders. He did not even think to donate the usual complimentary copy to the university library. Even Baker, who had thrown himself into work and had steered clear of the department head since receiving his rebuke at their last meeting, received no copy.

On the sixteenth of June that stage ended. Ninheimer received a phone call and stared at the image in the 'plate with surprise.

"Speidell! Are you in town?"

"No, sir. I'm in Cleveland." Speidell's voice trembled with emotion.

"Then why the call?"

"Because I've just been looking through your new book! Ninheimer, are you *mad*? Have you gone *insane*?"

Ninheimer stiffened. "Is something—uh—wrong?" he asked in alarm.

"Wrong? I refer you to page 562. What in blazes do you mean by interpreting my work as you do? Where in the paper cited do I make the claim that the criminal personality is nonexistent and that it is the *law*-enforcement agencies that are the *true* criminals? Here, let me quote—"

"Wait! Wait!" cried Ninheimer, trying to find the page. "Let me see. Let me see . . . Good God!"

"Well?"

"Speidell, I don't see how this could have happened. I never wrote this."

"But that's what's printed! And that distortion isn't the worst. You look at page 690 and imagine what Ipatiev is going to do to you when he sees the hash you've made of his findings! Look, Ninheimer, the book is *riddled* with this sort of thing. I don't know what you were thinking of—but there's nothing to do but get the book off the market. And you'd better be prepared for extensive apologies at the next Association meeting!"

"Speidell, listen to me—"

But Speidell had flashed off with a force that had the 'plate glowing with after-images for fifteen seconds.

It was then that Ninheimer went through the book and began marking off passages with red ink.

He kept his temper remarkably well when he faced Easy again, but his lips were pale. He passed the book to Easy and said, "Will you read the marked passages on pages 562, 631, 664 and 690?"

Easy did so in four glances. "Yes, Professor Ninheimer."

"This is not as I had it in the original galleys."

"No, sir. It is not."

"Did you change it to read as it now does?"

"Yes, sir."

"Why?"

"Sir, the passages as they read in your version were most uncomplimentary to certain groups of human beings. I felt it advisable to change the wording to avoid doing them harm."

"How *dared* you do such a thing?"

"The First Law, Professor, does not let me, through any inaction, allow harm to come to human beings. Certainly, considering your reputation in the world of sociology and the wide circulation your book would receive among scholars, considerable harm would come to a number of the human beings you speak of."

"But do you realize the harm that will come to *me* now?"

"It was necessary to choose the alternative with less harm."

Professor Ninheimer, shaking with fury, staggered away. It was clear to him that U. S. Robots would have to account to him for this.

There was some excitement at the defendants' table, which increased as Prosecution drove the point home.

"Then Robot EZ-27 informed you that the reason for its action was based on the First Law of Robotics?"

"That is correct, sir."

"That, in effect, it had no choice?"

"Yes, sir."

"It follows then that U. S. Robots designed a robot that would of necessity rewrite books to accord with its own conceptions of what was right. And yet they palmed it off as simple proofreader. Would you say that?"

Defense objected firmly at once, pointing out that the witness was being asked for a decision on a matter in which he had no competence. The judged admonished Prosecution in the usual terms, but there was no doubt that the exchange had sunk home—not least upon the attorney for the Defense.

Defense asked for a short recess before beginning cross-examination, using a legal technicality for the purpose that got him five minutes.

He leaned over toward Susan Calvin. "Is it possible, Dr. Calvin, that Professor Ninheimer is telling the truth and that Easy was motivated by the First Law?"

Calvin pressed her lips together, then said, "No. It *isn't* possible. The last part of Ninheimer's testimony is deliberate perjury. Easy is not designed to be able to judge matters at the stage of abstraction represented by an advanced textbook on sociology. It would never be able to tell that certain groups of humans would be harmed by a phrase in such a book. Its mind is simply not built for that."

"I suppose, though, that we can't prove this to a layman," said Defense pessimistically.

"No," admitted Calvin. "The proof would be highly complex. Our way out is still what it was. We must prove Ninheimer is lying, and nothing he has said need change our plan of attack."

"Very well, Dr. Calvin," said Defense, "I must accept your word in this. We'll go on as planned."

In the courtroom, the judge's gavel rose and fell and Dr. Ninheimer took the stand once more. He smiled a little as one who feels his position to be impregnable and rather enjoys the prospect of countering a useless attack.

Defense approached warily and began softly. "Dr. Ninheimer, do you mean to say that you were completely unaware of these alleged changes in your manuscript until such time as Dr. Speidell called you on the sixteenth of June?"

"That is correct, sir."

"Did you never look at the galleys after Robot EZ-27 had proofread them?"

"At first I did, but it seemed to me a useless task. I relied on the claims of U. S. Robots. The absurd—uh—changes were made only in the last quarter of the book after the robot, I presume, had learned enough about sociology—"

"Never mind your presumptions!" said Defense. "I understood your colleague, Dr. Baker, saw the later galleys on at least one occasion. Do you remember testifying to that effect?"

"Yes, sir. As I said, he told me about seeing one page, and even there, the robot had changed a word."

Again Defense broke in. "Don't you find it strange, sir, that after over a year of implacable hostility to the robot, after having voted against it in the first place and having refused to put it to any use whatever, you suddenly decided to put your book, your *magnum opus*, into its hands?"

"I don't find that strange. I simply decided that I might as well use the machine."

"And you were so confident of Robot EZ-27—all of a sudden— that you didn't even bother to check your galleys?"

"I told you I was—uh—persuaded by U. S. Robots' propaganda."

"So persuaded that when your colleague, Dr. Baker, attempted to check on the robot, you berated him soundly?"

"I didn't berate him. I merely did not wish to have him—uh— waste his time. At least, I thought then it was a waste of time. I did not see the significance of that change in a word at the—"

Defense said with heavy sarcasm, "I have no doubt you were instructed to bring up that point in order that the word-change be entered in the record—" He altered his line to forestall objection and said, "The point is that you were extremely angry with Dr. Baker."

"No, sir. Not angry."

"You didn't give him a copy of your book when you received it."

"Simple forgetfulness. I didn't give the library its copy, either." Ninheimer smiled cautiously. "Professors are notoriously absentminded."

Defense said, "Do you find it strange that, after more than a year of perfect work, Robot EZ-27 should go wrong on your book? On a book, that is, which was written by you, who was, of all people, the most implacably hostile to the robot?"

"My book was the only sizable work dealing with mankind that it had to face. The Three Laws of Robotics took hold then."

"Several times, Dr. Ninheimer," said Defense, "you have tried to sound like an expert on robotics. Apparently you suddenly grew interested in robotics and took out books on the subject from the library. You testified to that effect, did you not?"

"One book, sir. That was the result of what seems to me to have been—uh—natural curiosity."

"And it enabled you to explain why the robot should, as you allege, have distorted your book?"

"Yes, sir."

"Very convenient. But are you sure your interest in robotics was not intended to enable you to manipulate the robot for your own purposes?"

Ninheimer flushed. "Certainly not, sir!"

Defense's voice rose. "In fact, are you sure the alleged altered passages were not as you had them in the first place?"

The sociologist half-rose. "That's—uh—uh—ridiculous! I have the galleys—"

He had difficulty speaking and Prosecution rose to insert smoothly, "With your permission, Your Honor, I intend to introduce as evidence the set of galleys given by Dr. Ninheimer to Robot EZ-27 and the set of galleys mailed by Robot EZ-27 to the publishers. I will do so now if my esteemed colleague so desires, and will be willing to allow a recess in order that the two sets of galleys may be compared."

Defense waved his hand impatiently. "That is not necessary. My honored opponent can introduce those galleys whenever he chooses. I'm sure they will show whatever discrepancies are claimed by the plaintiff to exist. What I would like to know of the witness, however, is whether he also has in his possession *Dr. Baker's* galleys."

"Dr. Baker's galleys?" Ninheimer frowned. He was not yet quite master of himself.

"Yes, Professor! I mean Dr. Baker's galleys. You testified to the effect that Dr. Baker had received a separate copy of the galleys. I will have the clerk read your testimony if you are suddenly a selective type of amnesiac. Or is it just that professors are, as you say, notoriously absent-minded?"

Ninheimer said, "I remember Dr. Baker's galleys. They weren't necessary once the job was placed in the care of the proofreading machine—"

"So you burned them?"

"No. I put them in the waste basket."

"Burned them, dumped them—what's the difference? The point is you got rid of them."

"There's nothing wrong—" began Ninheimer weakly.

"Nothing wrong?" thundered Defense. "Nothing wrong except that there is now no way we can check to see if, on certain crucial galley sheets, you might not have substituted a harmless blank one from Dr. Baker's copy for a sheet in your own copy which you had deliberately mangled in such a way as to force the robot to—"

Prosecution shouted a furious objection. Justice Shane leaned forward, his round face doing its best to assume an expression of anger equivalent to the intensity of the emotion felt by the man.

The judge said, "Do you have any evidence, Counselor, for the extraordinary statement you have just made?"

Defense said quietly, "No direct evidence, Your Honor. But I would like to point out that, viewed properly, the sudden conversion of the plaintiff from anti-roboticism, his sudden interest in robotics, his refusal to check the galleys or to allow anyone else to check them, his careful neglect to allow anyone to see the book immediately after publication, all very clearly point—"

"Counselor," interrupted the judge impatiently, "this is not the place for esoteric deductions. The plaintiff is not on trial. Neither are you prosecuting him. I forbid this line of attack and I can only point out that the desperation that must have induced you to do this cannot help but weaken your case. If you have legitimate questions to ask, Counselor, you may continue with your cross-examination. But I warn you against another such exhibition in this courtroom."

"I have no further questions, Your Honor."

Robertson whispered heatedly as counsel for the Defense returned to his table, "What good did that do, for God's sake? The judge is dead-set against you now."

Defense replied calmly, "But Ninheimer is good and rattled. And we've set him up for tomorrow's move. He'll be ripe."

Susan Calvin nodded gravely.

The rest of Prosecution's case was mild in comparison. Dr. Baker was called and bore out most of Ninheimer's testimony. Drs. Speidell and Ipatiev were called, and they expounded most movingly on their shock and dismay at certain quoted passages in Dr. Ninheimer's book. Both gave their professional opinion that Dr. Ninheimer's professional reputation had been seriously impaired.

The galleys were introduced in evidence, as were copies of the finished book.

Defense cross-examined no more that day. Prosecution rested and the trial was recessed till the next morning.

Defense made his first motion at the beginning of the proceedings on the second day. He requested that Robot EZ-27 be admitted as a spectator to the proceedings.

Prosecution objected at once and Justice Shane called both to the bench.

Prosecution said hotly, "This is obviously illegal. A robot may not be in any edifice used by the general public."

"This courtroom," pointed out Defense, "is closed to all but those having an immediate connection with the case."

"A large machine of *known* erratic behavior would disturb my clients and my witnesses by its very presence! It would make hash out of the proceedings."

The judge seemed inclined to agree. He turned to Defense and said rather unsympathetically, "What are the reasons for your request?"

Defense said, "It will be our contention that Robot EZ-27 could not possibly, by the nature of its construction, have behaved as it has been described as behaving. It will be necessary to present a few demonstrations."

Prosecution said, "I don't see the point, Your Honor. Demonstrations conducted by men employed at U. S. Robots are worth little as evidence when U. S. Robots is the defendant."

"Your Honor," said Defense, "the validity of any evidence is for you to decide, not for the Prosecuting Attorney. At least, that is my understanding."

Justice Shane, his prerogatives encroached upon, said, "Your understanding is correct. Nevertheless, the presence of a robot here does raise important legal questions."

"Surely, Your Honor, nothing that should be allowed to override the requirements of justice. If the robot is not present, we are prevented from presenting our only defense."

The judge considered. "There would be the question of transporting the robot here."

"That is a problem with which U. S. Robots has frequently been faced. We have a truck parked outside the courtroom, constructed according to the laws governing the transportation of robots. Robot EZ-27 is in a packing case inside with two men guarding it. The doors to the truck are properly secured and all other necessary precautions have been taken."

"You seem certain," said Justice Shane, in renewed ill-temper, "that judgment on this point will be in your favor."

"Not at all, Your Honor. If it is not, we simply turn the truck about. I have made no presumptions concerning your decision."

The judge nodded. "The request on the part of the Defense is granted."

The crate was carried in on a large dolly and the two men who handled it opened it. The courtroom was immersed in a dead silence.

Susan Calvin waited as the thick slabs of celluform went down, then held out one hand. "Come, Easy."

The robot looked in her direction and held out its large metal arm. It towered over her by two feet but followed meekly, like a child in the clasp of its mother. Someone giggled nervously and choked it off at a hard glare from Dr. Calvin.

Easy seated itself carefully in a large chair brought by the bailiff, which creaked but held.

Defense said, "When it becomes necessary, Your Honor, we will prove that this is actually Robot EZ-27, the specific robot in the employ of Northeastern University during the period of time with which we are concerned."

"Good," His Honor said. "That will be necessary. I, for one, have no idea how you can tell one robot from another."

"And now," said Defense, "I would like to call my first witness to the stand. Professor Simon Ninheimer, please."

The clerk hesitated, looked at the judge. Justice Shane asked, with visible surprise, "You are calling the *plaintiff* as your witness?"

"Yes, Your Honor."

"I hope that you're aware that as long as he's your witness, you will be allowed none of the latitude you might exercise if you were cross-examining an opposing witness."

Defense said smoothly, "My only purpose in all this is to arrive at the truth. It will not be necessary to do more than ask a few polite questions."

"Well," said the judge dubiously, "you're the one handling the case. Call the witness."

Ninheimer took the stand and was informed that he was still under oath. He looked more nervous than he had the day before, almost apprehensive.

But Defense looked at him benignly.

"Now, Professor Ninheimer, you are suing my clients in the amount of $750,000."

"That is the—uh—sum. Yes."

"That is a great deal of money."

"I have suffered a great deal of harm."

"Surely not that much. The material in question involves only a few passages in a book. Perhaps these were unfortunate passages, but after all, books sometimes appear with curious mistakes in them."

Ninheimer's nostrils flared. "Sir, this book was to have been the climax of my professional career! Instead, it makes me look like an incompetent scholar, a perverter of the views held by my honored friends and associates, and a believer of ridiculous and—uh—outmoded viewpoints. My reputation is irretrievably shattered! I can never hold up my head in any—uh—assemblage of scholars, regardless of the outcome of this trial. I certainly cannot continue in my career, which has been the whole of my life. The very purpose of my life has been—uh—aborted and destroyed."

Defense made no attempt to interrupt the speech, but stared abstractedly at his fingernails as it went on.

He said very soothingly, "But surely, Professor Ninheimer, at your present age, you could not hope to earn more than—let us be generous—$150,000 during the remainder of your life. Yet you are asking the court to award you five times as much."

Ninheimer said, with an even greater burst of emotion, "It is not in my lifetime alone that I am ruined. I do not know for how many generations I shall be pointed at by sociologists as a—uh—a fool or maniac. My real achievements will be buried and ignored. I am ruined not only until the day of my death, but for all time to come, because there will always be people who will not believe that a robot made those insertions—"

It was at this point that Robot EZ-27 rose to his feet. Susan Calvin made no move to stop him. She sat motionless, staring straight ahead. Defense sighed softly.

Easy's melodious voice carried clearly. It said, "I would like to explain to everyone that I did insert certain passages in the galley proofs that seemed directly opposed to what had been there at first—"

Even the Prosecuting Attorney was too startled at the spectacle of a seven-foot robot rising to address the court to be able to demand the stopping of what was obviously a most irregular procedure.

When he could collect his wits, it was too late. For Ninheimer rose in the witness chair, his face working.

He shouted wildly, "Damn you, you were instructed to keep your mouth shut about—"

He ground to a choking halt, and Easy was silent, too.

Prosecution was on his feet now, demanding that a mistrial be declared.

Justice Shane banged his gavel desperately. "Silence! Silence! Certainly there is every reason here to declare a mistrial, except that in the interests of justice I would like to have Professor Ninheimer complete his statement. I distinctly heard him say to the robot that the robot had been instructed to keep its mouth shut about something. There was no mention in your testimony, Professor Ninheimer, as to any instructions to the robot to keep silent about anything!"

Ninheimer stared wordlessly at the judge.

Justice Shane said, "Did you instruct Robot EZ-27 to keep silent about something? And if so, about what?"

"Your Honor—" began Ninheimer hoarsely, and couldn't continue.

The judge's voice grew sharp. "Did you, in fact, order the inserts in question to be made in the galleys and then order the robot to keep quiet about your part in this?"

Prosecution objected vigorously, but Ninheimer shouted, "Oh, what's the use? Yes! Yes!" And he ran from the witness stand. He was stopped at the door by the bailiff and sank hopelessly into one of the last rows of seats, head buried in both hands.

Justice Shane said, "It is evident to me that Robot EZ-27 was brought here as a trick. Except for the fact that the trick served to prevent a serious miscarriage of justice, I would certainly hold attorney for the Defense in contempt. It is clear now, beyond any doubt, that the plaintiff has committed what is to me a completely inexplicable fraud since, apparently, he was knowingly ruining his career in the process—"

Judgment, of course, was for the defendant.

Dr. Susan Calvin had herself announced at Dr. Ninheimer's bachelor quarters in University Hall. The young engineer who had driven the car offered to go up with her, but she looked at him scornfully.

"Do you think he'll assault me? Wait down here."

Ninheimer was in no mood to assault anyone. He was packing,

wasting no time, anxious to be away before the adverse conclusion of the trial became general knowledge.

He looked at Calvin with a queerly defiant air and said, "Are you coming to warn me of a countersuit? If so, it will get you nothing. I have no money, no job, no future. I can't even meet the costs of the trial."

"If you're looking for sympathy," said Calvin coldly, "don't look for it here. This was your doing. However, there will be no countersuit, neither of you nor of the university. We will even do what we can to keep you from going to prison for perjury. We aren't vindictive."

"Oh, is that why I'm not already in custody for forswearing myself? I had wondered. But then," he added bitterly, "why *should* you be vindictive? You have what you want now."

"Some of what we want, yes," said Calvin. "The university will keep Easy in its employ at a considerably higher rental fee. Furthermore, certain underground publicity concerning the trial will make it possible to place a few more of the EZ models in other institutions without danger of a repetition of this trouble."

"Then why have you come to see me?"

"Because I don't have all of what I want yet. I want to know why you hate robots as you do. Even if you had won the case, your reputation would have been ruined. The money you might have obtained could not have compensated for that. Would the satisfaction of your hatred for robots have done so?"

"Are you interested in *human* minds, Dr. Calvin?" asked Ninheimer, with acid mockery.

"Insofar as their reactions concern the welfare of robots, yes. For that reason, I have learned a little of human psychology."

"Enough of it to be able to trick me!"

"That wasn't hard," said Calvin, without pomposity. "The difficult thing was doing it in such a way as not to damage Easy."

"It is like you to be more concerned for a machine than for a man." He looked at her with savage contempt.

It left her unmoved. "It merely seems so, Professor Ninheimer. It is only by being concerned for robots that one can truly be concerned for twenty-first-century man. You would understand this if you were a roboticist."

"I have read enough robotics to know I don't *want* to be a roboticist!"

"Pardon me, you have read *a book* on robotics. It has taught you nothing. You learned enough to know that you could order a robot to do many things, even to falsify a book, if you went about it properly. You learned enough to know that you could not order him to forget something entirely without risking detection, but you thought you could order him into simple silence more safely. You were wrong."

"You guessed the truth from his silence?"

"It wasn't guessing. You were an amateur and didn't know enough to cover your tracks completely. My only problem was to prove the matter to the judge and you were kind enough to help us there, in your ignorance of the robotics you claim to despise."

"Is there any purpose in this discussion?" asked Ninheimer wearily.

"For me, yes," said Susan Calvin, "because I want you to understand how completely you have misjudged robots. You silenced Easy by telling him that if he told anyone about your own distortion of the book, you would lose your job. That set up a certain potential within Easy toward silence, one that was strong enough to resist our efforts to break it down. We would have damaged the brain if we had persisted.

"On the witness stand, however, you yourself put up a higher counterpotential. You said that because people would think that you, not a robot, had written the disputed passages in the book, you would lose far more than just your job. You would lose your reputation, your standing, your respect, your reason for living. You would lose the memory of you after death. A new and higher potential was set up by you—and Easy talked."

"Oh, God," said Ninheimer, turning his head away.

Calvin was inexorable. She said, "Do you understand *why* he talked? It was not to accuse you, but to *defend* you! It can be mathematically shown that he was about to assume full blame for your crime, to deny that you had anything to do with it. The First Law required that. He was going to lie—to damage himself—to bring monetary harm to a corporation. All that meant less to him than did the saving of you. If you really understood robots and robotics, you would have let him talk. But you did not understand, as I was sure you wouldn't, as I guaranteed to the defense attorney that you wouldn't. You were certain, in your hatred of robots, that Easy would act as a human being would act and defend itself at your expense. So you flared out at him in panic—and destroyed yourself."

Ninheimer said with feeling, "I hope some day your robots turn on you and kill you!"

"Don't be foolish," said Calvin. "Now I want you to explain why you've done all this."

Ninheimer grinned a distorted, humorless grin. "I am to dissect my mind, am I, for your intellectual curiosity, in return for immunity from a charge of perjury?"

"Put it that way if you like," said Calvin emotionlessly. "But explain."

"So that you can counter future anti-robot attempts more efficiently? With greater understanding?"

"I accept that."

"You know," said Ninheimer, "I'll tell you—just to watch it do you no good at all. You can't understand human motivation. You can only understand your damned machines because you're a machine yourself, with skin on."

He was breathing hard and there was no hesitation in his speech, no searching for precision. It was as though he had no further use for precision.

He said, "For two hundred and fifty years, the machine has been replacing Man and destroying the handcraftsman. Pottery is spewed out of molds and presses. Works of art have been replaced by identical gimcracks stamped out on a die. Call it progress, if you wish! The artist is restricted to abstractions, confined to the world of ideas. He must design something in mind—and then the machine does the rest.

"Do you suppose the potter is content with mental creation? Do you suppose the idea is enough? That there is nothing in the feel of the clay itself, in watching the thing grow as hand and mind work *together*? Do you suppose the actual growth doesn't act as a feedback to modify and improve the idea?"

"You are not a potter," said Dr. Calvin.

"I am a creative artist! I design and build articles and books. There is more to it than the mere thinking of words and of putting them in the right order. If that were all, there would be no pleasure in it, no return.

"A book should take shape in the hands of the writer. One must actually see the chapters grow and develop. One must work and re-work and watch the changes take place beyond the original concept even. There is taking the galleys in hand and seeing how the sentences look in print and molding them again. There are a hundred contacts between a man and his work at every stage of the game—and the contact itself is pleasurable and repays a man for the work he puts into his creation more than anything else could. *Your robot would take all that away.*"

"So does a typewriter. So does a printing press. Do you propose to return to the hand illumination of manuscripts?"

"Typewriters and printing presses take away some, but your robot would deprive us of all. Your robot takes over the galleys. Soon it, or other robots, would take over the original writing, the searching of the sources, the checking and cross-checking of passages, perhaps even the deduction of conclusions. What would that leave the scholar? One thing only—the barren decisions concerning what orders to give the robot next! I want to save the future generations of the world of scholarship from such a final hell. That meant more to me than even my own reputation and so I set out to destroy U. S. Robots by whatever means."

"You were bound to fail," said Susan Calvin.

"I was bound to try," said Simon Ninheimer.

Calvin turned and left. She did her best to feel no pang of sympathy for the broken man.

She did not entirely succeed.

Little Lost Robot

Measures on Hyper Base had been taken in a sort of rattling fury—the muscular equivalent of an hysterical shriek.

To itemize them in order of both chronology and desperation, they were:

1. All work on the Hyperatomic Drive through all the space volume occupied by the Stations of the Twenty-Seventh Asteroidal Grouping came to a halt.

2. That entire volume of space was nipped out of the System, practically speaking. No one entered without permission. No one left under any conditions.

3. By special government patrol ship, Drs. Susan Calvin and Peter Bogert, respectively Head Psychologist and Mathematical Director of United States Robots and Mechanical Men Corporation, were brought to Hyper Base.

Susan Calvin had never left the surface of Earth before, and had no perceptible desire to leave it this time. In an age of Atomic Power and a clearly coming Hyperatomic Drive, she remained quietly provincial. So she was dissatisfied with her trip and unconvinced of the emergency, and every line of her plain, middle-aged face showed it clearly enough during her first dinner at Hyper Base.

Nor did Dr. Bogert's sleek paleness abandon a certain hangdog attitude. Nor did Major-general Kallner, who headed the project, even once forget to maintain a haunted expression.

In short, it was a grisly episode, that meal, and the little session of three that followed began in a gray, unhappy manner.

Kallner, with his baldness glistening, and his dress uniform oddly unsuited to the general mood, began with uneasy directness.

"This is a queer story to tell, sir, and madam. I want to thank you for coming on short notice and without a reason being given. We'll try to correct that now. We've lost a robot. Work has stopped and *must* stop until such time as we locate it. So far we have failed, and we feel we need expert help."

Perhaps the general felt his predicament anticlimactic. He continued with a note of desperation, "I needn't tell you the importance of our work here. More than eighty percent of last year's appropriations for scientific research have gone to us—"

"Why, we know that," said Bogert, agreeably. "U. S. Robots is receiving a generous rental fee for use of our robots."

Susan Calvin injected a blunt, vinegary note, "What makes a single robot so important to the project, and why hasn't it been located?"

The general turned his red face toward her and wet his lips quickly, "Why, in a manner of speaking we *have* located it." Then, with near anguish, "Here, suppose I explain. As soon as the robot failed to report a state of emergency was declared, and all movement off Hyper Base stopped. A cargo vessel had landed the previous day and had delivered us two robots for our laboratories. It had sixty-two robots of the . . . uh . . . same type for shipment elsewhere. We are certain as to that figure. There is no question about it whatever."

"Yes? And the connection?"

"When our missing robot was not located anywhere—I assure you we would have found a missing blade of grass if it had been there to find—we brainstormed ourselves into counting the robots left on the cargo ship. They have sixty-three now."

"So that the sixty-third, I take it, is the missing prodigal?" Dr. Calvin's eyes darkened.

"Yes, but we have no way of telling which is the sixty-third."

There was a dead silence while the electric clock chimed eleven times, and then the robopsychologist said, "Very peculiar," and the corners of her lips moved downward.

"Peter," she turned to her colleague with a trace of savagery, "what's wrong here? What kind of robots are they using at Hyper Base?"

Dr. Bogert hesitated and smiled feebly, "It's been rather a matter of delicacy till now, Susan."

She spoke rapidly, "Yes, *till* now. If there are sixty-three same-type robots, one of which is wanted and the identity of which cannot be determined, why won't any of them do? What's the idea of all this? Why have we been sent for?"

Bogert said in resigned fashion, "If you'll give me a chance, Susan —Hyper Base happens to be using several robots whose brains are not impressioned with the entire First Law of Robotics."

"*Aren't* impressioned?" Calvin slumped back in her chair, "I see. How many were made?"

"A few. It was on government order and there was no way of violating the secrecy. No one was to know except the top men directly concerned. You weren't included, Susan. It was nothing I had anything to do with."

The general interrupted with a measure of authority. "I would like to explain that bit. I hadn't been aware that Dr. Calvin was unacquainted with the situation. I needn't tell you, Dr. Calvin, that there always has been strong opposition to robots on the Planet. The only defense the government has had against the Fundamentalist radicals in this matter was the fact that robots are always built with an unbreakable First Law—which makes it impossible for them to harm human beings under any circumstance.

"But we *had* to have robots of a different nature. So just a few of the NS-2 model, the Nestors, that is, were prepared with a modified First Law. To keep it quiet, all NS-2's are manufactured without serial numbers; modified members are delivered here along with a group of normal robots; and, of course, all our kind are under the strictest impressionment never to tell of their modification to unauthorized personnel." He wore an embarrassed smile, "This has all worked out against us now."

Calvin said grimly, "Have you asked each one who it is, anyhow? Certainly, you are authorized?"

The general nodded, "All sixty-three deny having worked here— and one is lying."

"Does the one you want show traces of wear? The others, I take it, are factory-fresh."

"The one in question only arrived last month. It, and the two that have just arrived, were to be the last we needed. There's no perceptible wear." He shook his head slowly and his eyes were haunted again, "Dr. Calvin, we don't dare let that ship leave. If the existence of non-First Law robots becomes general knowledge—" There seemed no way of avoiding understatement in the conclusion.

"Destroy all sixty-three," said the robopsychologist coldly and flatly, "and make an end of it."

Bogert drew back a corner of his mouth. "You mean destroy thirty thousand dollars per robot. I'm afraid U. S. Robots wouldn't like that. We'd better make an effort first, Susan, before we destroy anything."

"In that case," she said, sharply, "I need facts. Exactly what advantage does Hyper Base derive from these modified robots? What factor made them desirable, general?"

Kallner ruffled his forehead and stroked it with an upward gesture of his hand. "We had trouble with our previous robots. Our men work with hard radiations a good deal, you see. It's dangerous, of course, but reasonable precautions are taken. There have been only two accidents since we began and neither was fatal. However, it was impossible to explain that to an ordinary robot. The First Law states —I'll quote it—'*No robot may harm a human being, or through inaction, allow a human being to come to harm.*'

"That's primary, Dr. Calvin. When it was necessary for one of our men to expose himself for a short period to a moderate gamma field, one that would have no physiological effects, the nearest robot would dash in to drag him out. If the field were exceedingly weak, it would succeed, and work could not continue till all robots were cleared out. If the field were a trifle stronger, the robot would never reach the technician concerned, since its positronic brain would collapse under gamma radiations—and then we would be out one expensive and hard-to-replace robot.

"We tried arguing with them. Their point was that a human being in a gamma field was endangering his life and that it didn't matter that he could remain there half an hour safely. Supposing, they would say, he forgot and remained an hour. They couldn't take chances. We pointed out that they were risking their lives on a wild off-chance. But self-preservation is only the Third Law of Robotics— and the First Law of human safety came first. We gave them orders; we ordered them strictly and harshly to remain out of gamma fields at whatever cost. But obedience is only the Second Law of Robotics —and the First Law of human safety came first. Dr. Calvin, we either had to do without robots, or do something about the First Law —and we made our choice."

"I can't believe," said Dr. Calvin, "that it was found possible to remove the First Law."

"It wasn't removed, it was modified," explained Kallner. "Positronic brains were constructed that contained the positive aspect only of the Law, which in them reads: '*No robot may harm a human being.*' That is all. They have no compulsion to prevent one coming to harm through an extraneous agency such as gamma rays. I state the matter correctly, Dr. Bogert?"

"Quite," assented the mathematician.

"And that is the only difference of your robots from the ordinary NS-2 model? The *only* difference? Peter?"

"The *only* difference, Susan."

She rose and spoke with finality, "I intend sleeping now, and in about eight hours, I want to speak to whomever saw the robot last. And from now on, General Kallner, if I'm to take any responsibility at all for events, I want full and unquestioned control of this investigation."

Susan Calvin, except for two hours of resentful lassitude, experienced nothing approaching sleep. She signaled at Bogert's door at the local time of 0700 and found him also awake. He had apparently taken the trouble of transporting a dressing gown to Hyper Base with him, for he was sitting in it. He put his nail scissors down when Calvin entered.

He said softly, "I've been expecting you more or less. I suppose you feel sick about all this."

"I do."

"Well—I'm sorry. There was no way of preventing it. When the call came out from Hyper Base for us, I knew that something must have gone wrong with the modified Nestors. But what was there to do? I couldn't break the matter to you on the trip here as I would have liked to, because I had to be sure. The matter of the modification is top secret."

The psychologist muttered, "I should have been told. U. S. Robots had no right to modify positronic brains this way without the approval of a psychologist."

Bogert lifted his eyebrows and sighed. "Be reasonable, Susan. You couldn't have influenced them. In this matter, the government was bound to have its way. They want the Hyperatomic Drive and the etheric physicists want robots that won't interfere with them. They were going to get them even if it did mean twisting the First Law. We had to admit it was possible from a construction standpoint and they swore a mighty oath that they wanted only twelve, that they would be used only at Hyper Base, that they would be destroyed once the Drive was perfected, and that full precautions would be taken. And they insisted on secrecy—and that's the situation."

Dr. Calvin spoke through her teeth, "I would have resigned."

"It wouldn't have helped. The government was offering the company a fortune, and threatening it with antirobot legislation in case of a refusal. We were stuck then, and we're badly stuck now. If this leaks out, it might hurt Kallner and the government, but it would hurt U. S. Robots a devil of a lot more."

The psychologist stared at him. "Peter, don't you realize what all this is about? Can't you understand what the removal of the First Law means? It isn't just a matter of secrecy."

"I know what removal would mean. I'm not a child. It would mean complete instability, with no nonimaginary solutions to the positronic Field Equations."

"Yes, mathematically. But can you translate that into crude psychological thought. All normal life, Peter, consciously or otherwise, resents domination. If the domination is by an inferior, or by a supposed inferior, the resentment becomes stronger. Physically, and, to an extent, mentally, a robot—any robot—is superior to human beings. What makes him slavish, then? *Only the First Law!* Why, without it, the first order you tried to give a robot would result in your death. Unstable? What do you think?"

"Susan," said Bogert, with an air of sympathetic amusement. "I'll admit that this Frankenstein Complex you're exhibiting has a certain justification—hence the First Law in the first place. But the Law, I repeat and repeat, has not been removed—merely modified."

"And what about the stability of the brain?"

The mathematician thrust out his lips, "Decreased, naturally. But it's within the border of safety. The first Nestors were delivered to Hyper Base nine months ago, and nothing whatever has gone wrong till now, and even this involves merely fear of discovery and not danger to humans."

"Very well, then. We'll see what comes of the morning conference."

Bogert saw her politely to the door and grimaced eloquently when she left. He saw no reason to change his perennial opinion of her as a sour and fidgety frustration.

Susan Calvin's train of thought did not include Bogert in the least. She had dismissed him years ago as a smooth and pretentious sleekness.

Gerald Black had taken his degree in etheric physics the year before and, in common with his entire generation of physicists, found himself engaged in the problem of the Drive. He now made a proper addition to the general atmosphere of these meetings on Hyper Base. In his stained white smock, he was half rebellious and wholly uncertain. His stocky strength seemed striving for release and his fingers, as they twisted each other with nervous yanks, might have forced an iron bar out of true.

Major-general Kallner sat beside him, the two from U. S. Robots faced him.

Black said, "I'm told that I was the last to see Nestor 10 before he vanished. I take it you want to ask me about that."

Dr. Calvin regarded him with interest, "You sound as if you were not sure, young man. Don't you *know* whether you were the last to see him?"

"He worked with me, ma'am, on the field generators, and he was with me the morning of his disappearance. I don't know if anyone saw him after about noon. No one admits having done so."

"Do you think anyone's lying about it?"

"I don't say that. But I don't say that I want the blame of it, either." His dark eyes smoldered.

"There's no question of blame. The robot acted as it did because of what it is. We're just trying to locate it, Mr. Black, and let's put everything else aside. Now if you've worked with the robot, you probably know it better than anyone else. Was there anything unusual about it that you noticed? Had you ever worked with robots before?"

"I've worked with other robots we have here—the simple ones. Nothing different about the Nestors except that they're a good deal cleverer—and more annoying."

"Annoying? In what way?"

"Well—perhaps it's not their fault. The work here is rough and most of us get a little jagged. Fooling around with hyper-space isn't fun." He smiled feebly, finding pleasure in confession. "We run the risk continually of blowing a hole in normal space-time fabric and dropping right out of the universe, asteroid and all. Sounds screwy, doesn't it? Naturally, you're on edge sometimes. But these Nestors aren't. They're curious, they're calm, they don't worry. It's enough to drive you nuts at times. When you want something done in a tearing hurry, they seem to take their time. Sometimes I'd rather do without."

"You say they take their time? Have they ever refused an order?"

"Oh, no,"—hastily. "They do it all right. They tell you when they think you're wrong, though. They don't know anything about the subject but what we taught them, but that doesn't stop them. Maybe I imagine it, but the other fellows have the same trouble with their Nestors."

General Kallner cleared his throat ominously, "Why have no complaints reached me on the matter, Black?"

The young physicist reddened, "We didn't *really* want to do without the robots, sir, and besides we weren't certain exactly how such . . . uh . . . minor complaints might be received."

Bogert interrupted softly, "Anything in particular happen the morning you last saw it?"

There was a silence. With a quiet motion, Calvin repressed the comment that was about to emerge from Kallner, and waited patiently.

Then Black spoke in blurting anger, "I had a little trouble with it. I'd broken a Kimball tube that morning and was out five days of work; my entire program was behind schedule; I hadn't received any mail from home for a couple of weeks. And *he* came around wanting me to repeat an experiment I had abandoned a month ago. He was always annoying me on that subject and I was tired of it. I told him to go away—and that's all I saw of him."

"You told him to go away?" asked Dr. Calvin with sharp interest. "In just those words? Did you say 'Go away'? Try to remember the exact words."

There was apparently an internal struggle in progress. Black cradled his forehead in a broad palm for a moment, then tore it away and said defiantly, "I said, 'Go lose yourself.'"

Bogert laughed for a short moment. "And he did, eh?"

But Calvin wasn't finished. She spoke cajolingly, "Now we're getting somewhere, Mr. Black. But exact details are important. In understanding the robot's actions, a word, a gesture, an emphasis may be everything. You couldn't have said just those three words, for instance, could you? By your own description you must have been in a hasty mood. Perhaps you strengthened your speech a little."

The young man reddened, "Well . . . I may have called it a . . . a few things."

"Exactly what things?"

"Oh—I wouldn't remember exactly. Besides I couldn't repeat it. You know how you get when you're excited." His embarrassed laugh was almost a giggle, "I sort of have a tendency to strong language."

"That's quite all right," she replied, with prim severity. "At the moment, I'm a psychologist. I would like to have you repeat exactly what you said as nearly as you remember, and, even more important, the exact tone of voice you used."

Black looked at his commanding officer for support, found none. His eyes grew round and appalled, "But I can't."

"You must."

"Suppose," said Bogert, with ill-hidden amusement, "you address me. You may find it easier."

The young man's scarlet face turned to Bogert. He swallowed. "I said—" His voice faded out. He tried again, "I said—"

And he drew a deep breath and spewed it out hastily in one long succession of syllables. Then, in the charged air that lingered, he concluded almost in tears, ". . . more or less. I don't remember the exact order of what I called him, and maybe I left out something or put in something, but that was about it."

Only the slightest flush betrayed any feeling on the part of the psychologist. She said, "I am aware of the meaning of most of the terms used. The others, I suppose, are equally derogatory."

"I'm afraid so," agreed the tormented Black.

"And in among it, you told him to lose himself."

"I meant it only figuratively."

"I realize that. No disciplinary action is intended, I am sure." And at her glance, the general, who, five seconds earlier, had seemed not sure at all, nodded angrily.

"You may leave, Mr. Black. Thank you for your co-operation."

It took five hours for Susan Calvin to interview the sixty-three robots. It was five hours of multi-repetition; of replacement after replacement of identical robot; of Questions A, B, C, D; and Answers A, B, C, D; of a carefully bland expression, a carefully neutral tone, a carefully friendly atmosphere; and a hidden wire recorder.

The psychologist felt drained of vitality when she was finished.

Bogert was waiting for her and looked expectant as she dropped the recording spool with a clang upon the plastic of the desk.

She shook her head, "All sixty-three seemed the same to me. I couldn't tell—"

He said, "You couldn't expect to tell by ear, Susan. Suppose we analyze the recordings."

Ordinarily, the mathematical interpretation of verbal reactions of robots is one of the more intricate branches of robotic analysis. It requires a staff of trained technicians and the help of complicated computing machines. Bogert knew that. Bogert stated as much, in an extreme of unshown annoyance after having listened to each set of replies, made lists of word deviations, and graphs of the intervals of responses.

"There are no anomalies present, Susan. The variations in wording and the time reactions are within the limits of ordinary frequency groupings. We need finer methods. They must have computers here. No." He frowned and nibbled delicately at a thumbnail. "We can't use computers. Too much danger of leakage. Or maybe if we—"

Dr. Calvin stopped him with an impatient gesture, "Please, Peter. This isn't one of your petty laboratory problems. If we can't determine the modified Nestor by some gross difference that we can see with the naked eye, one that there is no mistake about, we're out of luck. The danger of being wrong, and of letting him escape is otherwise too great. It's not enough to point out a minute irregularity in a graph. I tell you, if that's all I've got to go on, I'd destroy them all just to be certain. Have you spoken to the other modified Nestors?"

"Yes, I have," snapped back Bogert, "and there's nothing wrong with them. They're above normal in friendliness if anything. They answered my questions, displayed pride in their knowledge—except the two new ones that haven't had time to learn their etheric physics. They laughed rather good-naturedly at my ignorance in some of the specializations here." He shrugged, "I suppose that forms some of the basis for resentment toward them on the part of the technicians here. The robots are perhaps too willing to impress you with their greater knowledge."

"Can you try a few Planar Reactions to see if there has been any change, any deterioration, in their mental set-up since manufacture?"

"I haven't yet, but I will." He shook a slim finger at her, "You're losing your nerve, Susan. I don't see what it is you're dramatizing. They're essentially harmless."

"They are?" Calvin took fire. "They are? Do you realize one of them is lying? One of the sixty-three robots I have just interviewed has deliberately lied to me after the strictest injunction to tell the truth. The abnormality indicated is horribly deep-seated, and horribly frightening."

Peter Bogert felt his teeth harden against each other. He said, "Not at all. Look! Nestor 10 was given orders to lose himself. Those orders were expressed in maximum urgency by the person most authorized to command him. You can't counteract that order either by superior urgency or superior right of command. Naturally, the robot will attempt to defend the carrying out of his orders. In fact, objectively, I admire his ingenuity. How better can a robot lose himself than to hide himself among a group of similar robots?"

"Yes, you would admire it. I've detected amusement in you, Peter —amusement and an appalling lack of understanding. Are you a roboticist, Peter? Those robots attach importance to what they consider superiority. You've just said as much yourself. Subconsciously they feel humans to be inferior and the First Law which protects us from them is imperfect. They are unstable. And here we have a young man ordering a robot to leave him, to lose himself, with every verbal appearance of revulsion, disdain, and disgust. Granted, that robot must follow orders, but subconsciously, there is resentment. It will become more important than ever for it to prove that it is superior despite the horrible names it was called. It may become *so* important that what's left of the First Law won't be enough."

"How on Earth, or anywhere in the Solar System, Susan, is a robot going to know the meaning of the assorted strong language used upon him? Obscenity is not one of the things impressioned upon his brain."

"Original impressionment is not everything," Calvin snarled at him. "Robots have learning capacity, you . . . you fool—" And Bogert knew that she had really lost her temper. She continued hastily, "Don't you suppose he could tell from the tone used that the words weren't complimentary? Don't you suppose he's heard the words used before and noted upon what occasions?"

"Well, then," shouted Bogert, "will you kindly tell me one way in which a modified robot can harm a human being, no matter how offended it is, no matter how sick with desire to prove superiority?"

"If I tell you one way, will you keep quiet?"

"Yes."

They were leaning across the table at each other, angry eyes nailed together.

The psychologist said, "If a modified robot were to drop a heavy weight upon a human being, he would not be breaking the First Law, if he did so with the knowledge that his strength and reaction speed would be sufficient to snatch the weight away before it struck the man. However once the weight left his fingers, he would be no longer the active medium. Only the blind force of gravity would be that. The robot could then change his mind and merely by inaction, allow the weight to strike. The modified First Law allows that."

"That's an awful stretch of imagination."

"That's what my profession requires sometimes. Peter, let's not quarrel. Let's work. You know the exact nature of the stimulus that caused the robot to lose himself. You have the records of his original mental make-up. I want you to tell me how possible it is for our robot to do the sort of thing I just talked about. Not the specific instance, mind you, but that whole class of response. And I want it done quickly."

"And meanwhile—"

"And meanwhile, we'll have to try performance tests directly on the response to First Law."

Gerald Black, at his own request, was supervising the mushrooming wooden partitions that were springing up in a bellying circle on the vaulted third floor of Radiation Building 2. The laborers worked, in the main, silently, but more than one was openly a-wonder at the sixty-three photocells that required installation.

One of them sat down near Black, removed his hat, and wiped his forehead thoughtfully with a freckled forearm.

Black nodded at him, "How's it doing, Walensky?"

Walensky shrugged and fired a cigar, "Smooth as butter. What's going on anyway, Doc? First, there's no work for three days and then we have this mess of jiggers." He leaned backward on his elbows and puffed smoke.

Black twitched his eyebrows, "A couple of robot men came over from Earth. Remember the trouble we had with robots running into the gamma fields, before we pounded it into their skulls that they weren't to do it."

"Yeah. Didn't we get new robots?"

"We got some replacements, but mostly it was a job of indoctrination. Anyway, the people who make them want to figure out robots that aren't hit so bad by gamma rays."

"Sure seems funny, though, to stop all the work on the Drive for this robot deal. I thought nothing was allowed to stop the Drive."

"Well, it's the fellows upstairs that have the say on that. Me—I just do as I'm told. Probably all a matter of pull—"

"Yeah," the electrician jerked a smile, and winked a wise eye. "Somebody knew somebody in Washington. But as long as my pay comes through on the dot, I should worry. The Drive's none of my affair. What are they going to do here?"

"You're asking me? They brought a mess of robots with them,— over sixty, and they're going to measure reactions. That's all *my* knowledge."

"How long will it take?"

"I wish I knew."

"Well," Walensky said, with heavy sarcasm, "as long as they dish me my money, they can play games all they want."

Black felt quietly satisfied. Let the story spread. It was harmless, and near enough to the truth to take the fangs out of curiosity.

A man sat in the chair, motionless, silent. A weight dropped, crashed downward, then pounded aside at the last moment under the synchronized thump of a sudden force beam. In sixty-three wooden cells, watching NS-2 robots dashed forward in that split second before the weight veered, and sixty-three photocells five feet ahead of their original positions jiggled the marking pen and presented a little jag on the paper. The weight rose and dropped, rose and dropped, rose—

Ten times!

Ten times the robots sprang forward and stopped, as the man remained safely seated.

Major-general Kallner had not worn his uniform in its entirety since the first dinner with the U. S. Robot representatives. He wore nothing over his blue-gray shirt now, the collar was open, and the black tie was pulled loose.

He looked hopefully at Bogert, who was still blandly neat and whose inner tension was perhaps betrayed only by the trace of glister at his temples.

The general said, "How does it look? What is it you're trying to see?"

Bogert replied, "A difference which may turn out to be a little too subtle for our purposes, I'm afraid. For sixty-two of those robots the necessity of jumping toward the apparently threatened human was what we call, in robotics, a forced reaction. You see, even when the robots knew that the human in question would not come to harm—and after the third or fourth time they must have known it—they could not prevent reacting as they did. First Law requires it."

"Well?"

"But the sixty-third robot, the modified Nestor, had no such compulsion. He was under free action. If he had wished, he could have remained in his seat. Unfortunately," and his voice was mildly regretful, "he didn't so wish."

"Why do you suppose?"

Bogert shrugged, "I suppose Dr. Calvin will tell us when she gets here. Probably with a horribly pessimistic interpretation, too. She is sometimes a bit annoying."

"She's qualified, isn't she?" demanded the general with a sudden frown of uneasiness.

"Yes." Bogert seemed amused. "She's qualified all right. She understands robots like a sister—comes from hating human beings so much, I think. It's just that, psychologist or not, she's an extreme neurotic. Has paranoid tendencies. Don't take her too seriously."

He spread the long row of broken-line graphs out in front of him. "You see, general, in the case of each robot the time interval from moment of drop to the completion of a five-foot movement tends to decrease as the tests are repeated. There's a definite mathematical relationship that governs such things and failure to conform would indicate marked abnormality in the positronic brain. Unfortunately, all here appear normal."

"But if our Nestor 10 was not responding with a forced action, why isn't his curve different? I don't understand that."

"It's simple enough. Robotic responses are not perfectly analogous to human responses, more's the pity. In human beings, voluntary action is much slower than reflex action. But that's not the case with robots; with them it is merely a question of freedom of choice, otherwise the speeds of free and forced action are much the same. What I *had* been expecting, though, was that Nestor 10 would be caught by surprise the first time and allow too great an interval to elapse before responding."

"And he didn't?"

"I'm afraid not."

"Then we haven't gotten anywhere." The general sat back with an expression of pain. "It's five days since you've come."

At this point, Susan Calvin entered and slammed the door behind her. "Put your graphs away, Peter," she cried, "you know they don't show anything."

She mumbled something impatiently as Kallner half-rose to greet her, and went on, "We'll have to try something else quickly. I don't like what's happening."

Bogert exchanged a resigned glance with the general. "Is anything wrong?"

"You mean specifically? No. But I don't like to have Nestor 10 continue to elude us. It's bad. It *must* be gratifying his swollen sense of superiority. I'm afraid that his motivation is no longer simply one of following orders. I think it's becoming more a matter of sheer neurotic necessity to out-think humans. That's a dangerously unhealthy situation. Peter, have you done what I asked? Have you worked out the instability factors of the modified NS-2 along the lines I want?"

"It's in progress," said the mathematician, without interest.

She stared at him angrily for a moment, then turned to Kallner. "Nester 10 is decidedly aware of what we're doing, general. He had no reason to jump for the bait in this experiment, especially after the first time, when he must have seen that there was no real danger to our subject. The others couldn't help it; but *he* was deliberately falsifying a reaction."

"What do you think we ought to do now, then, Dr. Calvin?"

"Make it impossible for him to fake an action the next time. We will repeat the experiment, but with an addition. High-tension cables, capable of electrocuting the Nestor models will be placed between subject and robot—enough of them to avoid the possibility of jumping over—and the robot will be made perfectly aware in advance that touching the cables will mean death."

"Hold on," spat out Bogert with sudden viciousness. "I rule that out. We are not electrocuting two million dollars worth of robots to locate Nestor 10. There are other ways."

"You're certain? You've found none. In any case, it's not a question of electrocution. We can arrange a relay which will break the current at the instant of application of weight. If the robot should place his weight on it, he won't die. *But he won't know that,* you see."

The general's eyes gleamed into hope. "Will that work?"

"It should. Under those conditions, Nestor 10 would have to remain in his seat. He could be *ordered* to touch the cables and die, for the Second Law of obedience is superior to the Third Law of self-preservation. But *he won't* be ordered to; he will merely be left to his own devices, as will all the robots. In the case of the normal robots, the First Law of human safety will drive them to their death even without orders. But not our Nestor 10. Without the entire First Law, and without having received any orders on the matter, the Third Law, self-preservation, will be the highest operating, and he will have no choice but to remain in his seat. It would be a forced action."

"Will it be done tonight, then?"

"Tonight," said the psychologist, "if the cables can be laid in time. I'll tell the robots now what they're to be up against."

A man sat in the chair, motionless, silent. A weight dropped, crashed downward, then pounded aside at the last moment under the synchronized thump of a sudden force beam.

Only once—

And from her small camp chair in the observing booth in the balcony, Dr. Susan Calvin rose with a short gasp of pure horror.

Sixty-three robots sat quietly in their chairs, staring owlishly at the endangered man before them. Not one moved.

Dr. Calvin was angry, angry almost past endurance. Angry the worse for not daring to show it to the robots that, one by one, were entering the room and then leaving. She checked the list. Number Twenty-eight was due in now—Thirty-five still lay ahead of her.

Number Twenty-eight entered, diffidently.

She forced herself into reasonable calm. "And who are you?"

The robot replied in a low, uncertain voice, "I have received no number of my own yet, ma'am. I'm an NS-2 robot, and I was Number Twenty-eight in line outside. I have a slip of paper here that I'm to give to you."

"You haven't been in here before this today?"

"No, ma'am."

"Sit down. Right there. I want to ask you some questions, Number Twenty-eight. Were you in the Radiation Room of Building Two about four hours ago?"

The robot had trouble answering. Then it came out hoarsely, like machinery needing oil, "Yes, ma'am."

"There was a man who almost came to harm there, wasn't there?"

"Yes, ma'am."

"You did nothing, did you?"

"No, ma'am."

"The man might have been hurt because of your inaction. Do you know that?"

"Yes, ma'am. I couldn't help it, ma'am." It is hard to picture a large expressionless metallic figure cringing, but it managed.

"I want you to tell me exactly why you did nothing to save him."

"I want to explain, ma'am. I certainly don't want to have you . . . have *anyone* . . . think that I could do a thing that might cause harm to a master. Oh, no, that would be a horrible . . . an inconceivable—"

"Please don't get excited, boy. I'm not blaming you for anything. I only want to know what you were thinking at the time."

"Ma'am, before it all happened you told us that one of the masters would be in danger of harm from that weight that keeps falling and that we would have to cross electric cables if we were to try to save him. Well, ma'am, that wouldn't stop me. What is my destruction compared to the safety of a master? But . . . but it occurred to me that if I died on my way to him, I wouldn't be able to save him anyway. The weight would crush him and then I would be dead for no purpose and perhaps some day some other master might come to harm who wouldn't have, if I had only stayed alive. Do you understand me, ma'am?"

"You mean that it was merely a choice of the man dying, of both the man and yourself dying. Is that right?"

"Yes, ma'am. It was impossible to save the master. He might be considered dead. In that case, it is inconceivable that I destroy myself for nothing—without orders."

The psychologist twiddled a pencil. She had heard the same story with insignificant verbal variations twenty-seven times before. This was the crucial question now.

"Boy," she said, "your thinking has its points, but it is not the sort of thing I thought you might think. Did you think of this yourself?"

The robot hesitated. "No."

"Who thought of it, then?"

"We were talking last night, and one of us got that idea and it sounded reasonable."

"Which one?"

The robot thought deeply. "I don't know. Just one of us."

She sighed, "That's all."

Number Twenty-nine was next. Thirty-four after that.

Major-general Kallner, too, was angry. For one week all of Hyper Base had stopped dead, barring some paper work on the subsidiary asteroids of the group. For nearly one week, the two top experts in the field had aggravated the situation with useless tests. And now they—or the woman, at any rate—made impossible propositions.

Fortunately for the general situation, Kallner felt it impolitic to display his anger openly.

Susan Calvin was insisting, "Why not, sir? It's obvious that the present situation is unfortunate. The only way we may reach results in the future—or what future is left us in this matter—is to separate the robots. We can't keep them together any longer."

"My dear Dr. Calvin," rumbled the general, his voice sinking into the lower baritone registers. "I don't see how I can quarter sixty-three robots all over the place—"

Dr. Calvin raised her arms helplessly. "I can do nothing then. Nester 10 will either imitate what the other robots would do, or else argue them plausibly into not doing what he himself cannot do. And in any case, this is bad business. We're in actual combat with this little lost robot of ours and he's winning out. Every victory of his aggravates his abnormality."

She rose to her feet in determination. "General Kallner, if you do not separate the robots as I ask, then I can only demand that all sixty-three be destroyed immediately."

"You demand it, do you?" Bogert looked up suddenly, and with real anger. "What gives you the right to demand any such thing.

Those robots remain as they are. *I'm* responsible to the management, not you."

"And I," added Major-general Kallner, "am responsible to the World Co-ordinator—and I must have this settled."

"In that case," flashed back Calvin, "there is nothing for me to do but resign. If necessary to force you to the necessary destruction, I'll make this whole matter public. It was not I that approved the manufacture of modified robots."

"One word from you, Dr. Calvin," said the general, deliberately, "in violation of security measures, and you would be certainly imprisoned instantly."

Bogert felt the matter to be getting out of hand. His voice grew syrupy, "Well, now, we're beginning to act like children, all of us. We need only a little more time. Surely we can outwit a robot without resigning, or imprisoning people, or destroying two millions."

The psychologist turned on him with quiet fury, "I don't want any unbalanced robots in existence. We have one Nestor that's definitely unbalanced, eleven more that are potentially so, and sixty-two normal robots that are being subjected to an unbalanced environment. The only absolutely safe method is complete destruction."

The signal-burr brought all three to a halt, and the angry tumult of growingly unrestrained emotion froze.

"Come in," growled Kallner.

It was Gerald Black, looking perturbed. He had heard angry voices. He said, "I thought I'd come myself . . . didn't like to ask anyone else—"

"What is it? Don't orate—"

"The locks of Compartment C in the trading ship have been played with. There are fresh scratches on them."

"Compartment C?" exclaimed Calvin quickly. "That's the one that holds the robots, isn't it? Who did it?"

"From the inside," said Black, laconically.

"The lock isn't out of order, is it?"

"No. It's all right. I've been staying on the ship now for four days and none of them have tried to get out. But I thought you ought to know, and I didn't like to spread the news. I noticed the matter myself."

"Is anyone there now?" demanded the general.

"I left Robbins and McAdams there."

There was a thoughtful silence, and then Dr. Calvin said, ironically, "Well?"

Kallner rubbed his nose uncertainly, "What's it all about?"

"Isn't it obvious? Nestor 10 is planning to leave. That order to lose himself is dominating his abnormality past anything we can do. I wouldn't be surprised if what's left of his First Law would scarcely be powerful enough to override it. He is perfectly capable of seizing the ship and leaving with it. Then we'd have a mad robot on a spaceship. What would he do next? Any idea? Do you still want to leave them all together, general?"

"Nonsense," interrupted Bogert. He had regained his smoothness. "All that from a few scratch marks on a lock."

"Have you, Dr. Bogert, completed the analysis I've required, since you volunteer opinions?"

"Yes."

"May I see it?"

"No."

"Why not? Or mayn't I ask that, either?"

"Because there's no point in it, Susan. I told you in advance that these modified robots are less stable than the normal variety, and my analysis shows it. There's a certain very small chance of breakdown under extreme circumstances that are not likely to occur. Let it go at that. I won't give you ammunition for your absurd claim that sixty-two perfectly good robots be destroyed just because so far you lack the ability to detect Nestor 10 among them."

Susan Calvin stared him down and let disgust fill her eyes. "You won't let anything stand in the way of the permanent directorship, will you?"

"Please," begged Kallner, half in irritation. "Do you insist that nothing further can be done, Dr. Calvin?"

"I can't think of anything, sir," she replied, wearily. "If there were only other differences between Nestor 10 and the normal robots, differences that didn't involve the First Law. Even one other difference. Something in impressionment, environment, specification—" And she stopped suddenly.

"What is it?"

"I've thought of something . . . I think—" Her eyes grew distant and hard, "These modified Nestors, Peter. They get the same impressioning the normal ones get, don't they?"

"Yes. Exactly the same."

"And what was it you were saying, Mr. Black," she turned to the young man, who through the storms that had followed his news had maintained a discreet silence. "Once when complaining of the Nestors' attitude of superiority, you said the technicians had taught them all they knew."

"Yes, in etheric physics. They're not acquainted with the subject when they come here."

"That's right," said Bogert, in surprise. "I told you, Susan, when I spoke to the other Nestors here that the two new arrivals hadn't learned etheric physics yet."

"And why is that?" Dr. Calvin was speaking in mounting excitement. "Why aren't NS-2 models impressioned with etheric physics to start with?"

"I can tell you that," said Kallner. "It's all of a piece with the secrecy. We thought that if we made a special model with knowledge of etheric physics, used twelve of them and put the others to work in an unrelated field, there might be suspicion. Men working with normal Nestors might wonder why they knew etheric physics. So there was merely an impressionment with a capacity for training in the field. Only the ones that come here, naturally, receive such a training. It's that simple."

"I understand. Please get out of here, the lot of you. Let me have an hour or so."

Calvin felt she could not face the ordeal for a third time. Her mind had contemplated it and rejected it with an intensity that left her nauseated. She could face that unending file of repetitious robots no more.

So Bogert asked the questions now, while she sat aside, eyes and mind half-closed.

Number Fourteen came in—forty-nine to go.

Bogert looked up from the guide sheet and said, "What is your number in line?"

"Fourteen, sir." The robot presented his numbered ticket.

"Sit down, boy."

Bogert asked, "You haven't been here before on this day?"

"No, sir."

"Well, boy, we are going to have another man in danger of harm soon after we're through here. In fact, when you leave this room, you will be led to a stall where you will wait quietly, till you are needed. Do you understand?"

"Yes, sir."

"Now, naturally, if a man is in danger of harm, you will try to save him."

"Naturally, sir."

"Unfortunately, between the man and yourself, there will be a gamma ray field."

Silence.

"Do you know what gamma rays are?" asked Bogert sharply.

"Energy radiation, sir?"

The next question came in a friendly, offhand manner, "Ever work with gamma rays?"

"No, sir." The answer was definite.

"Mm-m. Well, boy, gamma rays will kill you instantly. They'll destroy your brain. That is a fact you must know and remember. Naturally, you don't want to destroy yourself."

"Naturally." Again the robot seemed shocked. Then, slowly, "But, sir, if the gamma rays are between myself and the master that may be harmed, how can I save him? I would be destroying myself to no purpose."

"Yes, there is that," Bogert seemed concerned about the matter. "The only thing I can advise, boy, is that if you detect the gamma radiation between yourself and the man, you may as well sit where you are."

The robot was openly relieved. "Thank you, sir. There wouldn't be any use, would there?"

"Of course not. But if there *weren't* any dangerous radiation, that would be a different matter."

"Naturally, sir. No question of that."

"You may leave now. The man on the other side of the door will lead you to your stall. Please wait there."

He turned to Susan Calvin when the robot left. "How did that go, Susan?"

"Very well," she said, dully.

"Do you think we could catch Nestor 10 by quick questioning on etheric physics?"

"Perhaps, but it's not sure enough." Her hands lay loosely in her lap. "Remember, he's fighting us. He's on his guard. The only way we can catch him is to outsmart him—and, within his limitations, he can think much more quickly than a human being."

"Well, just for fun—suppose I ask the robots from now on a few questions on gamma rays. Wave length limits, for instance."

"No!" Dr. Calvin's eyes sparked to life. "It would be too easy for him to deny knowledge and then he'd be warned against the test that's coming up—which is our real chance. Please follow the questions I've indicated, Peter, and don't improvise. It's just within the bounds of risk to aks them if they've ever worked with gamma rays. And try to sound even less interested than you do when you ask it."

Bogert shrugged, and pressed the buzzer that would allow the entrance of Number Fifteen.

The large Radiation Room was in readiness once more. The robots waited patiently in their wooden cells, all open to the center but closed off from each other.

Major-general Kallner mopped his brow slowly with a large handkerchief while Dr. Calvin checked the last details with Black.

"You're sure now," she demanded, "that none of the robots have had a chance to talk with each other after leaving the Orientation Room?"

"Absolutely sure," insisted Black. "There's not been a word exchanged."

"And the robots are put in the proper stalls?"

"Here's the plan."

The psychologist looked at it thoughtfully, "Um-m-m."

The general peered over her shoulder. "What's the idea of the arrangement, Dr. Calvin?"

"I've asked to have those robots that appeared even slightly out of true in the previous tests concentrated on one side of the circle. I'm going to be sitting in the center myself this time, and I wanted to watch those particularly."

"You're going to be sitting there—" exclaimed Bogert.

"Why not?" she demanded coldly. "What I expect to see may be something quite momentary. I can't risk having anyone else as main observer. Peter, you'll be in the observing booth, and I want you to keep your eye on the opposite side of the circle. General Kallner, I've arranged for motion pictures to be taken of each robot, in case visual observation isn't enough. If these are required, the robots are to remain exactly where they are until the pictures are developed and studied. None must leave, none must change place. Is that clear?"

"Perfectly."

"Then let's try it this one last time."

Susan Calvin sat in the chair, silent, eyes restless. A weight dropped, crashed downward, then pounded aside at the last moment under the synchronized thump of a sudden force beam.

And a single robot jerked upright and took two steps.

And stopped.

But Dr. Calvin was upright, and her finger pointed to him sharply. "Nestor 10, come here," she cried, "*come here!* COME HERE!"

Slowly, reluctantly, the robot took another step forward. The psychologist shouted at the top of her voice, without taking her eyes from the robot, "Get every other robot out of this place, somebody. Get them out quickly, and *keep* them out."

Somewhere within reach of her ears there was noise, and the thud of hard feet upon the floor. She did not look away.

Nestor 10—if it was Nestor 10—took another step, and then, under force of her imperious gesture, two more. He was only ten feet away, when he spoke harshly, "I have been told to be lost—"

Another step. "I must not disobey. They have not found me so far— He would think me a failure— He told me— But it's not so— I am powerful and intelligent—"

The words came in spurts.

Another step. "I know a good deal— He would think . . . I mean I've been found— Disgraceful— Not I— I am intelligent— And by just a master . . . who is weak— Slow—"

Another step—and one metal arm flew out suddenly to her shoulder, and she felt the weight bearing her down. Her throat constricted, and she felt a shriek tear through.

Dimly, she heard Nestor 10's next words, "No one must find me. No master—" and the cold metal was against her, and she was sinking under the weight of it.

And then a queer, metallic sound, and she was on the ground with an unfelt thump, and a gleaming arm was heavy across her body. It did not move. Nor did Nestor 10, who sprawled beside her.

And now faces were bending over her.

Gerald Black was gasping, "Are you hurt, Dr. Calvin?"

She shook her head feebly. They pried the arm off her and lifted her gently to her feet, "What happened?"

Black said, "I bathed the place in gamma rays for five seconds. We didn't know what was happening. It wasn't till the last second that we realized he was attacking you, and then there was no time for anything but a gamma field. He went down in an instant. There wasn't enough to harm you though. Don't worry about it."

"I'm not worried." She closed her eyes and leaned for a moment upon his shoulder. "I don't think I was attacked exactly. Nestor 10 was simply *trying* to do so. What was left of the First Law was still holding him back."

Susan Calvin and Peter Bogert, two weeks after their first meeting with Major-general Kallner had their last. Work at Hyper Base had been resumed. The trading ship with its sixty-two normal NS-2's was gone to wherever it was bound, with an officially imposed story to explain its two weeks' delay. The government cruiser was making ready to carry the two roboticists back to Earth.

Kallner was once again a-gleam in dress uniform. His white gloves shone as he shook hands.

Calvin said, "The other modified Nestors are, of course, to be destroyed."

"They will be. We'll make shift with normal robots, or, if necessary, do without."

"Good."

"But tell me— You haven't explained— How was it done?"

She smiled tightly, "Oh, that. I would have told you in advance if I had been more certain of its working. You see, Nestor 10 had a superiority complex that was becoming more radical all the time. He liked to think that he and other robots knew more than human beings. It was becoming very important for him to think so.

"We knew that. So we warned every robot in advance that gamma rays would kill them, which it would, and we further warned them all that gamma rays would be between them and myself. So they all stayed where they were, naturally. By Nestor 10's own logic in the previous test they had all decided that there was no point in trying to save a human being if they were sure to die before they could do it."

"Well, yes, Dr. Calvin, I understand that. But why did Nestor 10 himself leave his seat."

"Ah! That was a little arrangement between myself and your

young Mr. Black. You see it wasn't gamma rays that flooded the area between myself and the robots—but infrared rays. Just ordinary heat rays, absolutely harmless. Nestor 10 knew they were infrared and harmless and so he began to dash out, as he expected the rest would do, under First Law compulsion. It was only a fraction of a second too late that he remembered that the normal NS-2's could detect radiation, but could not identify the type. That he himself could only identify wave lengths by virtue of the training he had received at Hyper Base, under mere human beings, was a little too humiliating to remember for just a moment. To the normal robots the area was fatal because we had told them it would be, and only Nestor 10 knew we were lying.

"And just for a moment he forgot, or didn't want to remember, that other robots might be more ignorant than human beings. His very superiority caught him. Good-by, general."

Risk

Hyper Base had lived for this day. Spaced about the gallery of the viewing room, in order and precedence strictly dictated by protocol, was a group of officials, scientists, technicians and others who could only be lumped under the general classification of "personnel." In accordance with their separate temperaments they waited hopefully, uneasily, breathlessly, eagerly, or fearfully for this culmination of their efforts.

The hollowed interior of the asteroid known as Hyper Base had become for this day the center of a sphere of iron security that extended out for ten thousand miles. No ship might enter that sphere and live. No message might leave without scrutiny.

A hundred miles away, more or less, a small asteroid moved neatly in the orbit into which it had been urged a year before, an orbit that ringed Hyper Base in as perfect a circle as could be managed. The asteroidlet's identity number was H937, but no one on Hyper Base called it anything but It. ("Have you been out on it today?" "The general's on it, blowing his top," and eventually the impersonal pronoun achieved the dignity of capitalization.)

On It, unoccupied now as zero second approached, was the *Parsec*, the only ship of its kind ever built in the history of man. It lay, unmanned, ready for its takeoff into the inconceivable.

Gerald Black, who, as one of the bright young men in etherics engineering, rated a front-row view, cracked his large knuckles, then wiped his sweating palms on his stained white smock and said sourly, "Why don't you bother the general, or Her Ladyship there?"

Nigel Ronson, of Interplanetary Press, looked briefly across the gallery toward the glitter of Major-general Richard Kallner and the unremarkable woman at his side, scarcely visible in the glare of his dress uniform. He said, "I would, except that I'm interested in news."

Ronson was short and plump. He painstakingly wore his hair in a quarter-inch bristle, his shirt collar open and his trouser leg ankle-short, in faithful imitation of the newsmen who were stock characters on TV shows. He was a capable reporter nevertheless.

Black was stocky, and his dark hairline left little room for forehead, but his mind was as keen as his strong fingers were blunt. He said, "They've got all the news."

"Nuts," said Ronson. "Kallner's got no body under that gold braid. Strip him and you'll find only a conveyer belt dribbling orders downward and shooting responsibility upward."

Black found himself at the point of a grin but squeezed it down. He said, "What about the Madam Doctor?"

"Dr. Susan Calvin of U. S. Robots and Mechanical Men Corporation," intoned the reporter. "The lady with hyperspace where her heart ought to be and liquid helium in her eyes. She'd pass through the sun and come out the other end encased in frozen flame."

Black came even closer to a grin. "How about Director Schloss, then?"

Ronson said glibly, "He knows too much. Between spending his time fanning the feeble flicker of intelligence in his listener and dimming his own brains for fear of blinding said listener permanently by sheer force of brilliance, he ends up saying nothing."

Black showed his teeth this time. "Now suppose you tell me why you pick on me."

"Easy, doctor. I looked at you and figured you're too ugly to be stupid and too smart to miss a possible opportunity at some good personal publicity."

"Remind me to knock you down someday," said Black. "What do you want to know?"

The man from Interplanetary Press pointed into the pit and said, "Is that thing going to work?"

Black looked downward too, and felt a vague chill riffle over him like the thin night wind of Mars. The pit was one large television screen, divided in two. One half was an over-all view of It. On It's pitted gray surface was the *Parsec*, glowing mutedly in the feeble sunlight. The other half showed the control room of the *Parsec*. There was no life in that control room. In the pilot's seat was an object the vague humanity of which did not for a moment obscure the fact that it was only a positronic robot.

Black said, "Physically, mister, this will work. That robot will leave and come back. Space! how we succeeded with that part of it. I watched it all. I came here two weeks after I took my degree in etheric physics and I've been here, barring leave and furloughs, ever since. I was here when we sent the first piece of iron wire to Jupiter's orbit and back through hyperspace—and got back iron filings. I was here when we sent white mice there and back and ended up with mincemeat.

"We spent six months establishing an even hyperfield after that. We had to wipe out lags of as little as tenths of thousandths of seconds from point to point in matter being subjected to hypertravel. After that, the white mice started coming back intact. I remember when we celebrated for a week because one white mouse came back alive and lived ten minutes before dying. Now they live as long as we can take proper care of them."

Ronson said, "Great!"

Black looked at him obliquely. "I said, *physically* it will work. Those white mice that come back—"

"Well?"

"No minds. Not even little white mice-type minds. They won't eat. They have to be force-fed. They won't mate. They won't run. They sit. They sit. They sit. That's all. We finally worked up to sending a chimpanzee. It was pitiful. It was too close to a man to make watching it bearable. It came back a hunk of meat that could make crawling motions. It could move its eyes and sometimes it would scrabble. It whined and sat in its own wastes without the sense to move. Somebody shot it one day, and we were all grateful for that. I tell you this, fella, nothing that ever went into hyperspace has come back with a mind."

"Is this for publication?"

"After this experiment, maybe. They expect great things of it." A corner of Black's mouth lifted.

"You don't?"

"With a robot at the controls? No." Almost automatically Black's mind went back to that interlude, some years back, in which he had been unwittingly responsible for the near loss of a robot. He thought of the Nestor robots that filled Hyper Base with smooth, ingrained knowledge and perfectionist shortcomings. What was the use of talking about robots? He was not, by nature, a missionary.

But then Ronson, filling the continuing silence with a bit of small talk, said, as he replaced the wad of gum in his mouth with a fresh piece, "Don't tell me *you're* anti-robot. I've always heard that scientists are the one group that aren't anti-robot."

Black's patience snapped. He said, "That's true, and that's the trouble. Technology's gone robot-happy. Any job has to have a robot, or the engineer in charge feels cheated. You want a doorstop; buy a robot with a thick foot. That's a serious thing." He was speaking in a low, intense voice, shoving the words directly into Ronson's ear.

Ronson managed to extricate his arm. He said, "Hey, I'm no robot. Don't take it out on me. I'm a man. *Homo sapiens.* You just broke an arm bone of mine. Isn't that proof?"

Having started, however, it took more than frivolity to stop Black. He said, "Do you know how much time was wasted on this setup? We've had a perfectly generalized robot built and we've given it one order. Period. I heard the order given. I've memorized it. Short and sweet. 'Seize the bar with a firm grip. Pull it toward you firmly. *Firmly!* Maintain your hold until the control board informs you that you have passed through hyperspace twice.'

"So at zero time, the robot will grab the control bar and pull it firmly toward himself. His hands are heated to blood temperature. Once the control bar is in position, heat expansion completes contact and hyperfield is initiated. If anything happens to his brain during the first trip through hyperspace, it doesn't matter. All he needs to do is maintain position one microinstant and the ship will come back and the hyperfield will flip off. Nothing can go wrong. Then we study all its generalized reactions and see what, if anything, has gone wrong."

Ronson looked blank. "This all makes sense to me."

"Does it?" asked Black bitterly. "And what will you learn from a robot brain? It's positronic, ours is cellular. It's metal, ours is protein. They're not the same. There's no comparison. Yet I'm convinced that on the basis of what they learn, or think they learn, from the robot, they'll send men into hyperspace. Poor devils!— Look, it's not a question of dying. It's coming back mindless. If you'd seen the chimpanzee, you'd know what I mean. Death is clean and final. The other thing—"

The reporter said, "Have you talked about this to anyone?"

Black said, "Yes. They say what you said. They say I'm anti-robot and that settles everything. —Look at Susan Calvin there. You can bet *she* isn't anti-robot. She came all the way from Earth to watch this experiment. If it had been a man at the controls, she wouldn't have bothered. But what's the use!"

"Hey," said Ronson, "don't stop now. There's more."

"More what?"

"More problems. You've explained the robot. But why the security provisions all of a sudden?"

"Huh?"

"Come *on*. Suddenly I can't send dispatches. Suddenly ships can't come into the area. What's going on? This is just another experiment. The public knows about hyperspace and what you boys are trying to do, so what's the big secret?"

The backwash of anger was still seeping over Black, anger against the robots, anger against Susan Calvin, anger at the memory of that little lost robot in his past. There was some to spare, he found, for the irritating little newsman and his irritating little questions.

He said to himself, Let's see how he takes it.

He said, "You really want to know?"

"You bet."

"All right. We've never initiated a hyperfield for any object a millionth as large as that ship, or to send anything a millionth as far. That means that the hyperfield that will soon be initiated is some million million times as energetic as any we've ever handled. We're not sure what it can do."

"What do you mean?"

"Theory tells us that the ship will be neatly deposited out near Sirius and neatly brought back here. But how large a volume of space about the *Parsec* will be carried with it? It's hard to tell. We don't know enough about hyperspace. The asteroid on which the ship sits may go with it and, you know, if our calculations are even a little off, it may never be brought back here. It may return, say, twenty billion miles away. And there's a chance that more of space than just the asteroid may be shifted."

"How much more?" demanded Ronson.

"We can't say. There's an element of statistical uncertainty. That's why no ships must approach too closely. That's why we're keeping things quiet till the experiment is safely over."

Ronson swallowed audibly. "Supposing it reaches to Hyper Base?"

"There's a chance of it," said Black with composure. "Not much of a chance or Director Schloss wouldn't be here, I assure you. Still, there's a mathematical chance."

The newsman looked at his watch. "When does this all happen?"

"In about five minutes. You're not nervous, are you?"

"No," said Ronson, but he sat down blankly and asked no more questions.

Black leaned outward over the railing. The final minutes were ticking off.

The robot moved!

There was a mass sway of humanity forward at that sign of motion and the lights dimmed in order to sharpen and heighten the brightness of the scene below. But so far it was only the first motion. The hands of the robot approached the starting bar.

Black waited for the final second when the robot would pull the bar toward himself. Black could imagine a number of possibilities, and all sprang nearly simultaneously to mind.

There would first be the short flicker that would indicate the departure through hyperspace and return. Even though the time interval was exceedingly short, return would not be to the *precise* starting position and there would be a flicker. There always was.

Then, when the ship returned, it might be found, perhaps, that the devices to even the field over the huge volume of the ship had proved inadequate. The robot might be scrap steel. The ship might be scrap steel.

Or their calculations might be somewhat off and the ship might never return. Or worse still, Hyper Base might go with the ship and never return.

Or, of course, all might be well. The ship might flicker and be there in perfect shape. The robot, with mind untouched, would get out of his seat and signal a successful completion of the first voyage of a man-made object beyond the gravitational control of the sun.

The last minute was ticking off.

The last second came and the robot seized the starting bar and pulled it firmly toward himself—

Nothing!

No flicker. Nothing!
The *Parsec* never left normal space.

Major-general Kallner took off his officer's cap to mop his glistening forehead and in doing so exposed a bald head that would have aged him ten years in appearance if his drawn expression had not already done so. Nearly an hour had passed since the *Parsec*'s failure and nothing had been done.

"How did it happen? How did it happen? I don't understand it."

Dr. Mayer Schloss, who at forty was the "grand old man" of the young science of hyperfield matrices, said hopelessly, "There is nothing wrong with the basic theory. I'll swear my life away on that. There's a mechanical failure on the ship somewhere. Nothing more." He had said that a dozen times.

"I thought everything was tested." That had been said too.

"It was, sir, it was. Just the same—" And that.

They sat staring at each other in Kallner's office, which was now out of bounds for all personnel. Neither quite dared to look at the third person present.

Susan Calvin's thin lips and pale cheeks bore no expression. She said coolly, "You may console yourself with what I have told you before. It is doubtful whether anything useful would have resulted."

"This is not the time for the old argument," groaned Schloss.

"I am not arguing. U. S. Robots and Mechanical Men Corporation will supply robots made up to specification to any legal purchaser for any legal use. We did our part, however. We informed you that we could not guarantee being able to draw conclusions with regard to the human brain from anything that happened to the positronic brain. Our responsibility ends there. There is no argument."

"Great space," said General Kallner, in a tone that made the expletive feeble indeed. "Let's not discuss that."

"What else was there to do?" muttered Schloss, driven to the subject nevertheless. "Until we know exactly what's happening to the mind in hyperspace we can't progress. The robot's mind is at least capable of mathematical analysis. It's a start, a beginning. And until we try—" He looked up wildly, "But your robot isn't the point, Dr. Calvin. We're not worried about him or his positronic brain. Damn it, woman—" His voice rose nearly to a scream.

The robopsychologist cut him to silence with a voice that scarcely raised itself from its level monotone. "No hysteria, man. In my lifetime I have witnessed many crises and I have never seen one solved by hysteria. I want answers to some questions."

Schloss's full lips trembled and his deep-set eyes seemed to retreat into their sockets and leave pits of shadow in their places. He said harshly, "Are you trained in etheric engineering?"

"That is an irrelevant question. I am Chief Robopsychologist of the United States Robots and Mechanical Men Corporation. That is a positronic robot sitting at the controls of the *Parsec*. Like all such robots, it is leased and not sold. I have a right to demand information concerning any experiment in which such a robot is involved."

"Talk to her, Schloss," barked General Kallner. "She's—she's all right."

Dr. Calvin turned her pale eyes on the general, who had been present at the time of the affair of the lost robot and who therefore could be expected not to make the mistake of underestimating her. (Schloss had been out on sick leave at the time, and hearsay is not as effective as personal experience.) "Thank you, general," she said.

Schloss looked helplessly from one to the other and muttered, "What do you want to know?"

"Obviously my first question is, What *is* your problem if the robot is not?"

"But the problem is an obvious one. The ship hasn't moved. Can't you see that? Are you blind?"

"I see quite well. What I don't see is your obvious panic over some mechanical failure. Don't you people expect failure sometimes?"

The general muttered, "It's the expense. The ship was hellishly expensive. The World Congress—appropriations—" He bogged down.

"The ship's still there. A slight overhaul and correction would involve no great trouble."

Schloss had taken hold of himself. The expression on his face was one of a man who had caught his soul in both hands, shaken it hard and set it on its feet. His voice had even achieved a kind of patience. "Dr. Calvin, when I say a mechanical failure, I mean something like a relay jammed by a speck of dust, a connection inhibited by a spot of grease, a transistor balked by a momentary heat expansion. A dozen other things. A hundred other things. Any of them can be quite temporary. They can stop taking effect at any moment."

"Which means that at any moment the *Parsec* may flash through hyperspace and back after all."

"Exactly. Now do you understand?"

"Not at all. Wouldn't that be just what you want?"

Schloss made a motion that looked like the start of an effort to seize a double handful of hair and yank. He said, "You are not an etherics engineer."

"Does that tongue-tie you, doctor?"

"We had the ship set," said Schloss despairingly, "to make a jump from a definite point in space relative to the center of gravity of the galaxy to another point. The return was to be to the original point corrected for the motion of the solar system. In the hour that has passed since the *Parsec* should have moved, the solar system has shifted position. The original parameters to which the hyperfield is adjusted no longer apply. The ordinary laws of motion do not apply to hyperspace and it would take us a week of computation to calculate a new set of parameters."

"You mean that if the ship moves now it will return to some unpredictable point thousands of miles away?"

"Unpredictable?" Schloss smiled hollowly. "Yes, I should call it that. The *Parsec* might end up in the Andromeda nebula or in the center of the sun. In any case the odds are against our ever seeing it again."

Susan Calvin nodded. "The situation then is that if the ship disappears, as it may do at any moment, a few billion dollars of the taxpayers' money may be irretrievably gone, and—it will be said—through bungling."

Major-general Kallner could not have winced more noticeably if he had been poked with a sharp pin in the fundament.

The robopsychologist went on, "Somehow, then, the ship's hyperfield mechanism must be put out of action, and that as soon as possible. Something will have to be unplugged or jerked loose or flicked off." She was speaking half to herself.

"It's not that simple," said Schloss. "I can't explain it completely, since you're not an etherics expert. It's like trying to break an ordinary electric circuit by slicing through high-tension wire with garden shears. It could be disastrous. It *would* be disastrous."

"Do you mean that any attempt to shut off the mechanism would hurl the ship into hyperspace?"

"Any *random* attempt would *probably* do so. Hyper-forces are not limited by the speed of light. It is very probable that they have no limit of velocity at all. It makes things extremely difficult. The only reasonable solution is to discover the nature of the failure and learn from that a safe way of disconnecting the field."

"And how do you propose to do that, Dr. Schloss?"

Schloss said, "It seems to me that the only thing to do is to send one of our Nestor robots—"

"No! Don't be foolish," broke in Susan Calvin.

Schloss said, freezingly, "The Nestors are acquainted with the problems of etherics engineering. They will be ideally—"

"Out of the question. You cannot use one of our positronic robots for such a purpose without my permission. You do not have it and you shall not get it."

"What is the alternative?"

"You must sent one of your engineers."

Schloss shook his head violently, "Impossible. The risk involved is too great. If we lose a ship *and* man—"

"Nevertheless, you may not use a Nestor robot, or any robot."

The general said, "I—I must get in touch with Earth. This whole problem has to go to a higher level."

Susan Calvin said with asperity, "I wouldn't just yet if I were you, general. You will be throwing yourself on the government's mercy without a suggestion or plan of action of your own. You will not come out very well, I am certain."

"But what is there to do?" The general was using his handkerchief again.

"Send a man. There is no alternative."

Schloss had paled to a pasty gray. "It's easy to say, send a man. But whom?"

"I've been considering that problem. Isn't there a young man—his name is Black—whom I met on the occasion of my previous visit to Hyper Base?"

"Dr. Gerald Black?"

"I think so. Yes. He was a bachelor then. Is he still?"

"Yes, I believe so."

"I would suggest then that he be brought here, say, in fifteen minutes, and that meanwhile I have access to his records."

Smoothly she had assumed authority in this situation, and neither

Kallner nor Schloss made any attempt to dispute that authority with her.

Black had seen Susan Calvin from a distance on this, her second visit to Hyper Base. He had made no move to cut down the distance. Now that he had been called into her presence, he found himself staring at her with revulsion and distaste. He scarcely noticed Dr. Schloss and General Kallner standing behind her.

He remembered the last time he had faced her thus, undergoing a cold dissection for the sake of a lost robot.

Dr. Calvin's cool gray eyes were fixed steadily on his hot brown ones.

"Dr. Black," she said, "I believe you understand the situation."

Black said, "I do."

"Something will have to be done. The ship is too expensive to lose. The bad publicity will probably mean the end of the project."

Black nodded. "I've been thinking that."

"I hope you've also thought that it will be necessary for someone to board the *Parsec*, find out what's wrong, and—uh—deactivate it."

There was a moment's pause. Black said harshly, "What fool would go?"

Kallner frowned and looked at Schloss, who bit his lip and looked nowhere.

Susan Calvin said, "There is, of course, the possibility of accidental activation of the hyperfield, in which case the ship may drive beyond all possible reach. On the other hand, it may return somewhere within the solar system. If so, no expense or effort will be spared to recover man and ship."

Black said, "Idiot and ship! Just a correction."

Susan Calvin disregarded the comment. She said, "I have asked General Kallner's permission to put it to you. It is you who must go."

No pause at all here. Black said, in the flattest possible way, "Lady, I'm not volunteering."

"There are not a dozen men on Hyper Base with sufficient knowledge to have any chance at all of carrying this thing through successfully. Of those who have the knowledge, I've selected you on the basis of our previous acquaintanceship. You will bring to this task an understanding—"

"Look, I'm *not* volunteering."

"You have no choice. Surely you will face your responsibility?"

"*My* responsibility? What makes it mine?"

"The fact that you are best fitted for the job."

"Do you know the risk?"

"I think I do," said Susan Calvin.

"I know you don't. You never saw that chimpanzee. Look, when I said 'idiot and ship' I wasn't expressing an opinion. I was telling you a fact. I'd risk my life if I had to. Not with pleasure, maybe, but I'd risk it. Risking idiocy, a lifetime of animal mindlessness, is something I won't risk, that's all."

Susan Calvin glanced thoughtfully at the young engineer's sweating, angry face.

Black shouted, "Send one of your robots, one of your NS-2 jobs."

The psychologist's eye reflected a kind of cold glitter. She said with deliberation, "Yes, Dr. Schloss suggested that. But the NS-2 robots are leased by our firm, not sold. They cost millions of dollars apiece, you know. I represent the company and I have decided that they are too expensive to be risked in a matter such as this."

Black lifted his hands. They clenched and trembled close to his chest as though he were forcibly restraining them. "You're telling me—you're saying you want me to go instead of a robot because I'm more expendable."

"It comes to that, yes."

"Dr. Calvin," said Black, "I'd see you in hell first."

"That statement might be almost literally true, Dr. Black. As General Kallner will confirm, you are ordered to take this assignment. You are under quasi-military law here, I understand, and if you refuse an assignment, you can be court-martialed. A case like this will mean Mercury prison and I believe that will be close enough to hell to make your statement uncomfortably accurate were I to visit you, though I probably would not. On the other hand, if you agree to board the *Parsec* and carry through this job, it will mean a great deal for your career."

Black glared, red-eyed, at her.

Susan Calvin said, "Give the man five minutes to think about this, General Kallner, and get a ship ready."

Two security guards escorted Black out of the room.

Gerald Black felt cold. His limbs moved as though they were not part of him. It was as though he were watching himself from some remote, safe place, watching himself board a ship and make ready to leave for It and for the *Parsec*.

He couldn't quite believe it. He had bowed his head suddenly and said, "I'll go."

But why?

He had never thought of himself as the hero type. Then why? Partly, of course, there was the threat of Mercury prison. Partly it was the awful reluctance to appear a coward in the eyes of those who knew him, that deeper cowardice that was behind half the bravery in the world.

Mostly, though, it was something else.

Ronson of Interplanetary Press had stopped Black momentarily as he was on his way to the ship. Black looked at Ronson's flushed face and said, "What do you want?"

Ronson babbled, "Listen! When you get back, I want it exclusive. I'll arrange any payment you want—anything you want—"

Black pushed him aside, sent him sprawling, and walked on.

The ship had a crew of two. Neither spoke to him. Their glances slid over and under and around him. Black didn't mind that. They were scared spitless themselves and their ship was approaching the *Parsec* like a kitten skittering sideways toward the first dog it had ever seen. He could do without *them*.

There was only one face that he kept seeing. The anxious expression of General Kallner and the look of synthetic determination on Schloss's face were momentary punctures on his consciousness. They healed almost at once. It was Susan Calvin's unruffled face that he saw. Her calm expressionlessness as he boarded the ship.

He stared into the blackness where Hyper Base had already disappeared into space—

Susan Calvin! Doctor Susan Calvin! Robopsychologist Susan Calvin! The robot that walks like a woman!

What were her three laws, he wondered. First Law: Thou shalt protect the robot with all thy might and all thy heart and all thy soul. Second Law: Thou shalt hold the interests of U. S. Robots and Mechanical Men Corporation holy provided it interfereth not with the First Law. Third Law: Thou shalt give passing consideration to a human being provided it interfereth not with the First and Second laws.

Had she ever been young, he wondered savagely? Had she ever felt one honest emotion?

Space! How he wanted to do something—something that would take that frozen look of nothing off her face.

And he would!

By the stars, he would. Let him but get out of this sane and he would see her smashed and her company with her and all the vile brood of robots with them. It was that thought that was driving him more than fear of prison or desire for social prestige. It was that thought that almost robbed him of fear altogether. Almost.

One of the pilots muttered at him, without looking, "You can drop down from here. It's half a mile under."

Black said bitterly, "Aren't you landing?"

"Strict orders not to. The vibration of the landing might—"

"What about the vibration of my landing?"

The pilot said, "I've got my orders."

Black said no more but climbed into his suit and waited for the inner lock to open. A tool kit was welded firmly to the metal of the suit about his right thigh.

Just as he stepped into the lock, the earpieces inside his helmet rumbled at him. "Wish you luck, doctor."

It took a moment for him to realize that it came from the two men aboard ship, pausing in their eagerness to get out of that haunted volume of space to give him that much, anyway.

"Thanks," said Black awkwardly, half resentfully.

And then he was out in space, tumbling slowly as the result of the slightly off-center thrust of feet against outer lock.

He could see the *Parsec* waiting for him, and by looking between his legs at the right moment of the tumble he could see the long hiss of the lateral jets of the ship that had brought him, as it turned to leave.

He was alone! Space, he was alone!

Could any man in history ever have felt so alone?

Would he know, he wondered sickly, if—if anything happened? Would there be any moments of realization? Would he feel his mind fade and the light of reason and thought dim and blank out?

Or would it happen suddenly, like the cut of a force knife?

In either case—

The thought of the chimpanzee, blank-eyed, shivering with mindless terrors, was fresh within him.

The asteroid was twenty feet below him now. It swam through space with an absolutely even motion. Barring human agency, no grain of sand upon it had as much as stirred through astronomical periods of time.

In the ultimate jarlessness of It, some small particle of grit encumbered a delicate working unit on board the *Parsec*, or a speck of impure sludge in the fine oil that bathed some moving part had stopped it.

Perhaps it required only a small vibration, a tiny tremor originating from the collision of mass and mass to unencumber that moving part, bringing it down along its appointed path, creating the hyperfield, blossoming it outward like an incredibly ripening rose.

His body was going to touch It and he drew his limbs together in his anxiety to "hit easy." He did not want to touch the asteroid. His skin crawled with intense aversion.

It came closer.

Now—now—

Nothing!

There was only the continuing touch of the asteroid, the uncanny moments of slowly mounting pressure that resulted from a mass of 250 pounds (himself plus suit) possessing full inertia but no weight to speak of.

Black opened his eyes slowly and let the sight of stars enter. The sun was a glowing marble, its brilliance muted by the polarizing shield over his faceplate. The stars were correspondingly feeble but they made up the familiar arrangement. With sun and constellations normal, he was still in the solar system. He could even see Hyper Base, a small, dim crescent.

He stiffened in shock at the sudden voice in his ear. It was Schloss.

Schloss said, "We've got you in view, Dr. Black. You are not alone!"

Black could have laughed at the phraseology, but he only said in a low, clear voice, "Clear off. If you'll do that, you won't be distracting me."

A pause. Schloss's voice, more cajoling, "If you care to report as you go along, it may relieve the tension."

"You'll get information from me when I get back. Not before." He said it bitterly, and bitterly his metal-encased fingers moved to the control panel in his chest and blanked out the suit's radio. They could talk into a vacuum now. He had his own plans. If he got out of this sane, it would be *his* show.

He got to his feet with infinite caution and stood on It. He swayed a bit as involuntary muscular motions, tricked by the almost total lack of gravity into an endless series of overbalancings, pulled him this way and that. On Hyper Base there was a pseudo-gravitic field to hold them down. Black found that a portion of his mind was sufficiently detached to remember that and appreciate it *in absentia*.

The sun had disappeared behind a crag. The stars wheeled visibly in time to the asteroid's one-hour rotation period.

He could see the *Parsec* from where he stood and now he moved toward it slowly, carefully—tippy-toe almost. (No vibration. No vibration. The words ran pleadingly through his mind.)

Before he was completely aware of the distance he had crossed, he was at the ship. He was at the foot of the line of hand grips that led to the outer lock.

There he paused.

The ship looked quite normal. Or at least it looked normal except for the circle of steely knobs that girdled it one third of the way up, and a second circle two thirds of the way up. At the moment, they must be straining to become the source poles of the hyperfield.

A strange desire to reach up and fondle one of them came over Black. It was one of those irrational impulses, like the momentary thought, "What if I jumped?" that is almost inevitable when one stares down from a high building.

Black took a deep breath and felt himself go clammy as he spread the fingers of both hands and then lightly, so lightly, put each hand flat against the side of the ship.

Nothing!

He seized the lowest hand grip and pulled himself up, carefully. He longed to be as experienced at null-gravity manipulation as were the construction men. You had to exert enough force to overcome inertia and then stop. Continue the pull a second too long and you would overbalance, career into the side of the ship.

He climbed slowly, tippy-fingers, his legs and hips swaying to the right as his left arm reached upward, to the left as his right arm reached upward.

A dozen rungs, and his fingers hovered over the contact that would open the outer lock. The safety marker was a tiny green smear.

Once again he hesitated. This was the first use he would make of the ship's power. His mind ran over the wiring diagrams and the force distributions. If he pressed the contact, power would be siphoned off the micropile to pull open the massive slab of metal that was the outer lock.

Well?

What was the use? Unless he had some idea as to what was wrong, there was no way of telling the effect of the power diversion. He sighed and touched contact.

Smoothly, with neither jar nor sound, a segment of the ship curled open. Black took one more look at the friendly constellations (they had not changed) and stepped into the softly illuminated cavity. The outer lock closed behind him.

Another contact now. The inner lock had to be opened. Again he paused to consider. Air pressure within the ship would drop ever so slightly as the inner lock opened, and seconds would pass before the ship's electrolyzers could make up the loss.

Well?

The Bosch posterior-plate, to name one item, was sensitive to pressure, but surely not *this* sensitive.

He sighed again, more softly (the skin of his fear was growing calloused) and touched the contact. The inner lock opened.

He stepped into the pilot room of the *Parsec*, and his heart jumped oddly when the first thing he saw was the visiplate, set for reception and powdered with stars. He forced himself to look at them.

Nothing!

Cassiopeia was visible. The constellations were normal and he was inside the *Parsec*. Somehow he could feel the worst was over. Having come so far and remained within the solar system, having kept his mind so far, he felt something that was faintly like confidence begin to seep back.

There was an almost supernatural stillness about the *Parsec*. Black had been in many ships in his life and there had always been the sounds of life, even if only the scuffing of a shoe or a cabin boy humming in the corridor. Here the very beating of his own heart seemed muffled to soundlessness.

The robot in the pilot's seat had its back to him. It indicated by no response that it was aware of his having entered.

Black bared his teeth in a savage grin and said sharply, "Release the bar! Stand up!" The sound of his voice was thunderous in the close quarters.

Too late he dreaded the air vibrations his voice set up, but the stars on the visiplate remained unchanged.

The robot, of course, did not stir. It could receive no sensations of any sort. It could not even respond to the First Law. It was frozen in the unending middle of what should have been almost instantaneous process.

He remembered the orders it had been given. They were open to no misunderstanding: "Seize the bar with a firm grip. Pull it toward you firmly. Firmly! Maintain your hold until the control board informs you that you have passed through hyperspace twice."

Well, it had not yet passed through hyperspace once.

Carefully, he moved closer to the robot. It sat there with the bar pulled firmly back between its knees. That brought the trigger mechanism almost into place. The temperature of his metal hands then curled that trigger, thermocouple fashion, just sufficiently for contact to be made. Automatically Black glanced at the thermometer reading set into the control board. The robot's hands were at 37 Centigrade, as they should be.

He thought sardonically, Fine thing. I'm alone with this machine and I can't do anything about it.

What he would have liked to do was take a crowbar to it and smash it to filings. He enjoyed the flavor of that thought. He could see the horror on Susan Calvin's face (if any horror could creep through the ice, the horror of a smashed robot was it). Like all positronic robots, this one-shot was owned by U. S. Robots, had been made there, had been tested there.

And having extracted what juice he could out of imaginary revenge, he sobered and looked about the ship.

After all, progress so far had been zero.

Slowly, he removed his suit. Gently, he laid it on the rack. Gingerly, he walked from room to room, studying the large interlocking surfaces of the hyperatomic motor, following the cables, inspecting the field relays.

He touched nothing. There were a dozen ways of deactivating the hyperfield, but each one would be ruinous unless he knew at least approximately where the error lay and let his exact course of procedure be guided by that.

He found himself back at the control panel and cried in exasperation at the grave stolidity of the robot's broad back, "Tell me, will you? What's wrong?"

There was the urge to attack the ship's machinery at random. Tear at it and get it over with. He repressed the impulse firmly. If it took him a week, he would deduce, somehow, the proper point of attack. He owed that much to Dr. Susan Calvin and his plans for her.

He turned slowly on his heel and considered. Every part of the ship, from the engine itself to each individual two-way toggle switch, had been exhaustively checked and tested on Hyper Base. It was almost impossible to believe that anything could go wrong. There wasn't a thing on board ship—

Well, yes, there was, of course. The robot! That had been tested at U. S. Robots and they, blast their devils' hides, could be assumed to be competent.

What was it everyone always said: A robot can just naturally do a better job.

It was the normal assumption, based in part on U. S. Robots' own advertising campaigns. They could make a robot that would be better than a man for a given purpose. Not "as good as a man," but "better than a man."

And as Gerald Black stared at the robot and thought that, his brows contracted under his low forehead and his look became compounded of astonishment and a wild hope.

He approached and circled the robot. He stared at its arms holding the control bar in trigger position, holding it forever so, unless the ship jumped or the robot's own power supply gave out.

Black breathed, "I bet. I *bet*."

He stepped away, considered deeply. He said, "It's *got* to be."

He turned on ship's radio. Its carrier beam was already focused on Hyper Base. He barked into the mouthpiece, "Hey, Schloss."

Schloss was prompt in his answer. "Great Space, Black—"

"Never mind," said Black crisply. "No speeches. I just want to make sure you're watching."

"Yes, of course. We all are. Look—"

But Black turned off the radio. He grinned with tight one-sidedness at the TV camera inside the pilot room and chose a portion of the hyperfield mechanism that would be in view. He didn't know how many people would be in the viewing room. There might be only Kallner, Schloss and Susan Calvin. There might be all personnel. In any case, he would give them something to watch.

Relay Box #3 was adequate for the purpose, he decided. It was located in a wall recess, coated over with a smooth cold-seamed panel. Black reached into his tool kit and removed the splayed, blunt-edged seamer. He pushed his space suit farther back on the rack (having turned it to bring the tool kit in reach) and turned to the relay box.

Ignoring a last tingle of uneasiness, Black brought up the seamer, made contact at three separated points along the cold seam. The tool's force field worked deftly and quickly, the handle growing a trifle warm in his hand as the surge of energy came and left. The panel swung free.

He glanced quickly, almost involuntarily, at the ship's visiplate. The stars were normal. He, himself, felt normal.

That was the last bit of encouragement he needed. He raised his foot and smashed his shoe down on the feather-delicate mechanism within the recess.

There was a splinter of glass, a twisting of metal, and a tiny spray of mercury droplets—

Black breathed heavily. He turned on the radio once more. "Still there, Schloss?"

"Yes, but—"

"Then I report the hyperfield on board the *Parsec* to be deactivated. Come and get me."

Gerald Black felt no more the hero than when he had left for the *Parsec*, but he found himself one just the same. The men who had brought him to the small asteroid came to take him off. They landed this time. They clapped his back.

Hyper Base was a crowded mass of waiting personnel when the ship arrived, and Black was cheered. He waved at the throng and grinned, as was a hero's obligation, but he felt no triumph inside. Not yet. Only anticipation. Triumph would come later, when he met Susan Calvin.

He paused before descending from the ship. He looked for her and did not see her. General Kallner was there, waiting, with all his soldierly stiffness restored and a bluff look of approval firmly plastered on his face. Mayer Schloss smiled nervously at him. Ronson of Interplanetary Press waved frantically. Susan Calvin was nowhere.

He brushed Kallner and Schloss aside when he landed. "I'm going to wash and eat first."

He had no doubts but that, for the moment at least, he could dictate terms to the general or to anybody.

The security guards made a way for him. He bathed and ate leisurely in enforced isolation, he himself being solely responsible for the enforcement. Then he called Ronson of Interplanetary and talked to him briefly. He waited for the return call before he felt he could relax thoroughly. It had all worked out so much better than he had expected. The very failure of the ship had conspired perfectly with him.

Finally he called the general's office and ordered a conference. It was what it amounted to—orders. Major-general Kallner all but said, "Yes, sir."

They were together again. Gerald Black, Kallner, Schloss—even Susan Calvin. But it was Black who was dominant now. The robopsychologist, graven-faced as ever, as unimpressed by triumph as by disaster, had nevertheless seemed by some subtle change of attitude to have relinquished the spotlight.

Dr. Schloss nibbled a thumbnail and began by saying, cautiously, "Dr. Black, we are all very grateful for your bravery and success." Then, as though to institute a healthy deflation at once, he added, "Still, smashing the relay box with your heel was imprudent and—well, it was an action that scarcely deserved success."

Black said, "It was an action that could scarcely have avoided success. You see" (this was bomb number one) "by that time I knew what had gone wrong."

Schloss rose to his feet. "You did? Are you sure?"

"Go there yourself. It's safe now. I'll tell you what to look for."

Schloss sat down again, slowly. General Kallner was enthusiastic. "Why, this is the best yet, if true."

"It's true," said Black. His eyes slid to Susan Calvin, who said nothing.

Black was enjoying the sensation of power. He released bomb number two by saying, "It was the robot, of course. Did you hear that, Dr. Calvin?"

Susan Calvin spoke for the first time. "I hear it. I rather expected it, as a matter of fact. It was the only piece of equipment on board ship that had not been tested at Hyper Base."

For a moment Black felt dashed. He said, "You said nothing of that."

Dr. Calvin said, "As Dr. Schloss said several times, I am not an etherics expert. My guess, and it was no more than that, might easily have been wrong. I felt I had no right to prejudice you in advance of your mission."

Black said, "All right, did you happen to guess *how* it went wrong?"

"No, sir."

"Why, it was made better than a man. That's what the trouble was. Isn't it strange that the trouble should rest with the very specialty of U. S. Robots? They make robots better than men, I understand."

He was slashing at her with words now but she did not rise to his bait.

Instead, she sighed. "My dear Dr. Black. I am not responsible for the slogans of our sales-promotion department."

Black felt dashed again. She wasn't an easy woman to handle, this Calvin. He said, "Your people built a robot to replace a man at the controls of the *Parsec*. He had to pull the control bar toward himself, place it in position and let the heat of his hands twist the trigger to make final contact. Simple enough, Dr. Calvin?"

"Simple enough, Dr. Black."

"And if the robot had been made no better than a man, he would have succeeded. Unfortunately, U. S. Robots felt compelled to make it better than a man. The robot was told to pull back the control bar firmly. *Firmly*. The word was repeated, strengthened, emphasized. So the robot did what it was told. It pulled it back firmly. There was only one trouble. He was easily ten times stronger than the ordinary human being for whom the control bar was designed."

"Are you implying—"

"I'm *saying* the bar bent. It bent back just enough to misplace the trigger. When the heat of the robot's hand twisted the thermocouple, it did *not* make contact." He grinned. "This isn't the failure of just one robot, Dr. Calvin. It's symbolic of the failure of the robot idea."

"Come now, Dr. Black," said Susan Calvin icily, "you're drowning logic in missionary psychology. The robot was equipped with adequate understanding as well as with brute force. Had the men who gave it its orders used quantitative terms rather than the foolish adverb 'firmly,' this would not have happened. Had they said, 'apply a pull of fifty-five pounds,' all would have been well."

"What you are saying," said Black, "is that the inadequacy of a robot must be made up for by the ingenuity and intelligence of a man. I assure you that the people back on Earth will look at it in that way and will not be in the mood to excuse U. S. Robots for this fiasco."

Major-general Kallner said quickly, with a return of authority to his voice, "Now wait, Black, all that has happened is obviously classified information."

"In fact," said Schloss suddenly, "your theory hasn't been checked yet. We'll send a party to the ship and find out. It may not be the robot at all."

"You'll take care to make that discovery, will you? I wonder if the people will believe an interested party. Besides which, I have one more thing to tell you." He readied bomb number three and said, "As of this moment, I'm resigning from this man's project. I'm quitting."

"Why?" asked Susan Calvin.

"Because, as you said, Dr. Calvin, I am a missionary," said Black, smiling. "I have a mission. I feel I owe it to the people of Earth to tell them that the age of the robots has reached the point where human life is valued less than robot life. It is now possible to order a man into danger because a robot is too precious to risk. I believe Earthmen should hear that. Many men have many reservations about robots as is. U. S. Robots has not yet succeeded in making it legally permissible to use robots on the planet Earth itself. I believe what I have to say, Dr. Calvin, will complete the matter. For this day's work, Dr. Calvin, you and your company and your robots will be wiped off the face of the solar system."

He was forewarning her, Black knew; he was forearming her, but he could not forego this scene. He had lived for this very moment ever since he had first left for the *Parsec*, and he could not give it up.

He all but gloated at the momentary glitter in Susan Calvin's pale eyes and at the faintest flush in her cheeks. He thought, How do you feel now, madam scientist?

Kallner said, "You will not be permitted to resign, Black, nor will you be permitted—"

"How can you stop me, general? I'm a hero, haven't you heard? And old Mother Earth *will* make much of its heroes. It always has. They'll want to hear from me and they'll believe anything I say. And they won't like it if I'm interfered with, at least not while I'm a fresh, brand-new hero. I've already talked to Ronson of Interplanetary Press and told him I had something big for them, something that would rock every government official and science director right out of the chair plush, so Interplanetary will be first in line, waiting to hear from me. So what can you do except to have me shot? And I think you'd be worse off after that if you tried it."

Black's revenge was complete. He had spared no word. He had hampered himself not in the least. He rose to go.

"One moment, Dr. Black," said Susan Calvin. Her low voice carried authority.

Black turned involuntarily, like a schoolboy at his teacher's voice, but he counteracted that gesture by a deliberately mocking, "You have an explanation to make, I suppose?"

"Not at all," she said primly. "You have explained for me, and quite well. I chose you because I knew you would understand, though I thought you would understand sooner. I had had contact with you before. I knew you disliked robots and would, therefore, be under no illusions concerning them. From your records, which I asked to see before you were given your assignment, I saw that you had expressed disapproval of this robot-through-hyperspace experiment. Your superiors held that against you, but I thought it a point in your favor."

"What are you talking about, doctor, if you'll excuse my rudeness?"

"The fact that you should have understood why no robot could have been sent on this mission. What was it you yourself said? Something about a robot's inadequacies having to be balanced by the ingenuity and intelligence of a man. Exactly so, young man, exactly so. Robots have no ingenuity. Their minds are finite and can be calculated to the last decimal. That, in fact, is my job.

"Now if a robot is given an order, a *precise* order, he can follow it. If the order is not precise, he cannot correct his own mistake without further orders. Isn't that what you reported concerning the robot on the ship? How then can we send a robot to find a flaw in a mechanism when we cannot possibly give precise orders, since we know nothing about the flaw ourselves? 'Find out what's wrong' is not an order you can give to a robot; only to a man. The human brain, so far at least, is beyond calculation."

Black sat down abruptly and stared at the psychologist in dismay.

Her words struck sharply on a substratum of understanding that had been larded over with emotion. He found himself unable to refute her. Worse than that, a feeling of defeat encompassed him.

He said, "You might have said this before I left."

"I might have," agreed Dr. Calvin, "but I noticed your very natural fear for your sanity. Such an overwhelming concern would easily have hampered your efficiency as an investigator, and it occurred to me to let you think that my only motive in sending you was that I valued a robot more. That, I thought, would make you angry, and anger, my dear Dr. Black, is sometimes a very useful emotion. At least, an angry man is never quite as afraid as he would be otherwise. It worked out nicely, I think." She folded her hands loosely in her lap and came as near a smile as she ever had in her life.

Black said, "I'll be damned."

Susan Calvin said, "So now, if you'll take my advice, return to your job, accept your status as hero, and tell your reporter friend the details of your brave deed. Let that be the big news you promised him."

Slowly, reluctantly, Black nodded.

Schloss looked relieved; Kallner burst into a toothy smile. They held out hands, not having said a word in all the time that Susan Calvin had spoken, and not saying a word now.

Black took their hands and shook them with some reserve. He said, "It's your part that should be publicized, Dr. Calvin."

Susan Calvin said icily, "Don't be a fool, young man. This is my job."

Escape!

When Susan Calvin returned from Hyper Base, Alfred Lanning was waiting for her. The old man never spoke about his age, but everyone knew it to be over seventy-five. Yet his mind was keen, and if he had finally allowed himself to be made Director-Emeritus of Research with Bogert as acting Director, it did not prevent him from appearing in his office daily.

"How close are they to the Hyperatomic Drive?" he asked.

"I don't know," she replied irritably, "I didn't ask."

"Hmm. I wish they'd hurry. Because if they don't, Consolidated might beat them to it. And beat *us* to it as well."

"*Consolidated.* What have they got to do with it?"

"Well, we're not the only ones with calculating machines. Ours may be positronic, but that doesn't mean they're better. Robertson is calling a big meeting about it tomorrow. He's been waiting for you to come back."

Robertson of U. S. Robots and Mechanical Men Corporation, son of the founder, pointed his lean nose at his general manager and his Adam's apple jumped as he said, "You start now. Let's get this straight."

The general manager did so with alacrity, "Here's the deal now, chief. Consolidated Robots approached us a month ago with a funny sort of proposition. They brought about five tons of figures, equations, all that sort of stuff. It was a problem, see, and they wanted an answer from The Brain. The terms were as follows—"

He ticked them off on thick fingers: "A hundred thousand for us if there is no solution and we can tell them the missing factors. Two hundred thousand if there is a solution, plus costs of construction of the machine involved, plus quarter interest in all profits derived therefrom. The problem concerns the development of an interstellar engine—"

Robertson frowned and his lean figure stiffened, "Despite the fact that they have a thinking machine of their own. Right?"

"Exactly what makes the whole proposition a foul ball, chief. Levver, take it from there."

Abe Levver looked up from the far end of the conference table and smoothed his stubbled chin with a faint rasping sound. He smiled:

"It's this way, sir. Consolidated *had* a thinking machine. It's broken."

"What?" Robertson half rose.

"That's right. Broken! It's *kaput*. Nobody knows why, but I got hold of some pretty interesting guesses—like, for instance, that they asked it to give them an interstellar engine with the same set of information they came to us with, and that it cracked their machine wide open. It's scrap—just scrap now."

"You get it, chief?" The general manager was wildly jubilant. "You get it? There isn't any industrial research group of any size that isn't trying to develop a space-warp engine, and Consolidated and U. S. Robots have the lead on the field with our super robot-brains. Now that they've managed to foul theirs up, we have a clear field. That's the nub, the . . . uh . . . motivation. It will take them six years at least to build another and they're sunk, unless they can break ours, too, with the same problem."

The president of U. S. Robots bulged his eyes, "Why, the dirty rats—"

"Hold on, chief. There's more to this." He pointed a finger with a wide sweep, "Lanning, take it!"

Dr. Alfred Lanning viewed the proceedings with faint scorn—his usual reaction to the doings of the vastly better-paid business and sales divisions. His unbelievable white eyebrows hunched low and his voice was dry:

"From a scientific standpoint the situation, while not entirely clear, is subject to intelligent analysis. The question of interstellar travel under present conditions of physical theory is . . . uh . . .

vague. The matter is wide open—and the information given by Consolidated to its thinking machine, assuming these we have to be the same, was similarly wide open. Our mathematical department has given it a thorough analysis, and it seems Consolidated has included everything. Its material for submission contains all known developments of Franciacci's space-warp theory, and, apparently, all pertinent astrophysical and electronic data. It's quite a mouthful."

Robertson followed anxiously. He interrupted, "Too much for The Brain to handle?"

Lanning shook his head decisively, "No. There are no known limits to The Brain's capacity. It's a different matter. It's a question of the Robotic Laws. The Brain, for instance, could never supply a solution to a problem set to it if that solution would involve the death or injury of humans. As far as it would be concerned, a problem with only such a solution would be insoluble. If such a problem is combined with an extremely urgent demand that it be answered, it is just possible that The Brain, only a robot after all, would be presented with a dilemma, where it could neither answer nor refuse to answer. Something of the sort must have happened to Consolidated's machine."

He paused, but the general manager urged on, "Go ahead, Dr. Lanning. Explain it the way you explained it to me."

Lanning set his lips and raised his eyebrows in the direction of Dr. Susan Calvin who lifted her eyes from her precisely folded hands for the first time. Her voice was low and colorless.

"The nature of a robot reaction to a dilemma is startling," she began. "Robot psychology is far from perfect—as a specialist, I can assure you of that—but it can be discussed in qualitative terms, because with all the complications introduced into a robot's positronic brain, it is built by humans and is therefore built according to human values.

"Now a human caught in an impossibility often responds by a retreat from reality: by entry into a world of delusion, or by taking to drink, going off into hysteria, or jumping off a bridge. It all comes to the same thing—a refusal or inability to face the situation squarely. And so, the robot. A dilemma at its mildest will disorder half its relays; and at its worst it will burn out every positronic brain path past repair."

"I see," said Robertson, who didn't. "Now what about this information Consolidated's wishing on us?"

"It undoubtedly involves," said Dr. Calvin, "a problem of a forbidden sort. But The Brain is considerably different from Consolidated's robot."

"That's right, chief. That's right." The general manager was energetically interruptive. "I want you to get this, because it's the whole point of the situation."

Susan Calvin's eyes glittered behind the spectacles, and she continued patiently, "You see, sir, Consolidated's machines, their Super-Thinker among them, are built without personality. They go in for functionalism, you know—they have to, without U. S. Robots' basic patents for the emotional brain paths. Their Thinker is merely a calculating machine on a grand scale, and a dilemma ruins it instantly.

"However, The Brain, our own machine, has a personality—a child's personality. It is a supremely deductive brain, but it resembles an *idiot savant*. It doesn't really understand what it does—it just does it. And because it is really a child, it is more resilient. Life isn't so serious, you might say."

The robopsychologist continued: "Here is what we're going to do. We have divided all of Consolidated's information into logical units. We are going to feed the units to The Brain singly and cautiously. When *the* factor enters—the one that creates the dilemma— The Brain's child personality will hesitate. Its sense of judgment is not mature. There will be a perceptible interval before it will recognize a dilemma as such. And in that interval, it will reject the unit automatically—before its brain-paths can be set in motion and ruined."

Robertson's Adam's apple squirmed, "Are you sure, now?"

Dr. Calvin masked impatience, "It doesn't make much sense, I admit, in lay language; but there is no conceivable use in presenting the mathematics of this. I assure you, it is as I say."

The general manager was in the breach instantly and fluently, "So here's the situation, chief. If we take the deal, we can put it through like this. The Brain will tell us which unit of information involves the dilemma. From there, we can figure *why* the dilemma. Isn't that right, Dr. Bogert? There you are, chief, and Dr. Bogert is the best mathematician you'll find anywhere. We give Consolidated a 'No Solution' answer, with the reason, and collect a hundred thousand. They're left with a broken machine; we're left with a whole one. In a year, two maybe, we'll have a space-warp engine, or a hyper-atomic motor, some people call it. Whatever you name it, it will be the biggest thing in the world."

Robertson chuckled and reached out, "Let's see the contract. I'll sign it."

When Susan Calvin entered the fantastically guarded vault that held The Brain, one of the current shift of technicians had just asked it: "If one and a half chickens lay one and a half eggs in one and a half days, how many eggs will nine chickens lay in nine days?"

The Brain had just answered, "Fifty-four."

And the technician had just said to another, "See, you dope!"

Dr. Calvin coughed and there was a sudden impossible flurry of directionless energy. The psychologist motioned briefly, and she was alone with The Brain.

The Brain was a two-foot globe merely—one which contained within it a thoroughly conditioned helium atmosphere, a volume of space completely vibration-absent and radiation-free—and within that was that unheard-of complexity of positronic grain-paths that was The Brain. The rest of the room was crowded with the attachments that were the intermediaries between The Brain and the outside world—its voice, its arms, its sense organs.

Dr. Calvin said softly, "How are you, Brain?"

The Brain's voice was high-pitched and enthusiastic, "Swell, Miss Susan. You're going to ask me something. I can tell. You always have a book in your hand when you're going to ask me something."

Dr. Calvin smiled mildly, "Well, you're right, but not just yet. This is going to be a question. It will be so complicated we're going to give it to you in writing. But not just yet. I think I'll talk to you first."

"All right. I don't mind talking."

"Now, Brain, in a little while, Dr. Lanning and Dr. Bogert will be here with this complicated question. We'll give it to you a very little at a time and very slowly, because we want you to be careful. We're going to ask you to build something, if you can, out of the information, but I'm going to warn you now that the solution might involve . . . uh . . . damage to human beings."

"Gosh!" The exclamation was hushed, drawn-out.

"Now you watch for that. When we come to a sheet which means damage, even maybe death, don't get excited. You see, Brain, in this case, we don't mind—not even about death; we don't mind at all. So when you come to that sheet, just stop, give it back—and that'll be all. You understand?"

"Oh, sure. But golly, the death of humans! Oh, my!"

"Now, Brain, I hear Dr. Lanning and Dr. Bogert coming. They'll tell you what the problem is all about and then we'll start. Be a good boy, now—"

Slowly the sheets were fed in. After each one came the interval of the queerly whispery chuckling noise that was The Brain in action. Then the silence that meant readiness for another sheet. It was a matter of hours—during which the equivalent of something like seventeen fat volumes of mathematical physics were fed into The Brain.

As the process went on, frowns appeared and deepened. Lanning muttered ferociously under his breath. Bogert first gazed speculatively at his fingernails, and then bit at them in abstracted fashion. It was when the last of the thick pile of sheets disappeared that Calvin, white-faced, said:

"Something's wrong."

Lanning barely got the words out, "It can't be. Is it—dead?"

"Brain?" Susan Calvin was trembling. "Do you hear me, Brain?"

"Huh?" came the abstracted rejoinder. "Do you want me?"

"The solution—"

"Oh, that! I can do it. I'll build you a whole ship, just as easy—if you let me have the robots. A nice ship. It'll take two months maybe."

"There was—no difficulty?"

"It took long to figure," said The Brain.

Dr. Calvin backed away. The color had not returned to her thin cheeks. She motioned the others away.

In her office, she said, "I can't understand it. The information, as given, must involve a dilemma—probably involves death. If something has gone wrong—"

Bogert said quietly, "The machine talks and makes sense. It can't be a dilemma."

But the psychologist replied urgently, "There are dilemmas *and* dilemmas. There are different forms of escape. Suppose The Brain is only mildly caught; just badly enough, say, to be suffering from the delusion that it can solve the problem, when it can't. Or suppose it's teetering on the brink of something really bad, so that any small push shoves it over."

"Suppose," said Lanning, "there is no dilemma. Suppose Consolidated's machine broke down over a different question, or broke down for purely mechanical reasons."

"But even so," insisted Calvin, "we couldn't take chances. Listen, from now on, no one is to as much as breathe to The Brain. I'm taking over."

"All right," sighed Lanning, "take over, then. And meanwhile we'll let The Brain build its ship. And if it *does* build it, we'll have to test it."

He was ruminating, "We'll need our top field men for *that*."

Michael Donovan brushed down his red hair with a violent motion of his hand and a total indifference to the fact that the unruly mass sprang to attention again immediately.

He said, "Call the turn now, Greg. They say the ship is finished. They don't know what it is, but it's finished. Let's go, Greg. Let's grab the controls right now."

Powell said wearily, "Cut it, Mike. There's a peculiar overripe flavor to your humor at its freshest, and the confined atmosphere here isn't helping it."

"Well, listen," Donovan took another ineffectual swipe at his hair, "I'm not worried so much about our cast-iron genius and his tin ship. There's the matter of my lost leave. And the monotony! There's nothing here but whiskers and figures—the wrong kind of figures. Oh, why do they *give* us these jobs?"

"Because," replied Powell, gently, "we're no loss, if they lose us. O.K. relax! Doc Lanning's coming this way."

Lanning was coming, his white eyebrows as lavish as ever, his aged figure unbent as yet and full of life. He walked silently up the ramp with the two men and out into the open field, where, obeying no human master, silent robots were building a ship.

Wrong tense. *Had* built a ship!

For Lanning said, "The robots have stopped. Not one has moved today."

"It's completed then? Definitely?" asked Powell.

"Now how can I tell?" Lanning was peevish, and his eyebrows

curled down in an eye-hiding frown. "It *seems* done. There are no spare pieces about, and the interior is down to a gleaming finish."

"You've been inside?"

"Just in, then out. I'm no space-pilot. Either of you two know much about engine theory?"

Donovan looked at Powell, who looked at Donovan.

Donovan said, "I've got my license, sir, but at last reading it didn't say anything about hyper-engines or warp-navigation. Just the usual child's play in three dimensions."

Alfred Lanning looked up with sharp disapproval and snorted the length of his prominent nose.

He said frigidly, "Well, we have our engine men."

Powell caught at his elbow as he walked away, "Sir, is the ship still restricted ground?"

The old director hesitated, then rubbed the bridge of his nose, "I suppose not. For you two anyway."

Donovan looked after him as he left and muttered a short, expressive phrase at his back. He turned to Powell, "I'd like to give him a literary description of himself, Greg."

"Suppose you come along, Mike."

The inside of the ship was finished, as finished as a ship ever was; that could be told in a single eye-blinking glance. No martinet in the system could have put as much spit-and-polish into a surface as those robots had. The walls were of a gleaming silvery finish that retained no fingerprints.

There were no angles; walls, floors, and ceiling faded gently into each other and in the cold, metallic glittering of the hidden lights, one was surrounded by six chilly reflections of one's bewildered self.

The main corridor was a narrow tunnel that led in a hard, clatter-footed stretch along a line of rooms of no interdistinguishing features.

Powell said, "I suppose furniture is built into the wall. Or maybe we're not supposed to sit or sleep."

It was in the last room, the one nearest the nose that the monotony broke. A curving window of non-reflecting glass was the first break in the universal metal, and below it was a single large dial, with a single motionless needle hard against the zero mark.

Donovan said, "Look at that!" and pointed to the single word on the finely-marked scale.

It said "Parsecs" and the tiny figure at the right end of the curving, graduated meter said "1,000,000."

There were two chairs; heavy, wide-flaring, uncushioned. Powell seated himself gingerly, and found it molded to the body's curves, and comfortable.

Powell said, "What do you think of it?"

"For my money, The Brain has brain-fever. Let's get out."

"Sure you don't want to look it over a bit?"

"I have looked it over. I came, I saw, I'm through!" Donovan's red hair bristled into separate wires, "Greg, let's get out of here. I quit my job five seconds ago, and this is a restricted area for non-personnel."

Powell smiled in an oily self-satisfied manner and smoothed his mustache, "O.K., Mike, turn off that adrenalin tap you've got draining into your bloodstream. I was worried, too, but no more."

"No more, huh? How come, no more? Increased your insurance?"

"Mike, this ship can't fly."

"How do you know?"

"Well, we've been through the entire ship, haven't we?"

"Seems so."

"Take my word for it, we have. Did you see any pilot room except for this one port and the one gauge here in parsecs? Did you see any controls?"

"No."

"And did you see any engines?"

"Holy Joe, no!"

"Well, then! Let's break the news to Lanning, Mike."

They cursed their way through the featureless corridors and finally hit-and-missed their way into the short passage to the air lock.

Donovan stiffened, "Did you lock this thing, Greg?"

"No, I never touched it. Yank the lever, will you?"

The lever never budged, though Donovan's face twisted appallingly with exertion.

Powell said, "I didn't see any emergency exits. If something's gone wrong here, they'll have to melt us out."

"Yes, and we've got to wait until they find out that some fool has locked us in here," added Donovan, frantically.

"Let's get back to the room with the port. It's the only place from which we might attract attention."

But they didn't.

In that last room, the port was no longer blue and full of sky. It was black, and hard yellow pin-point stars spelled *space*.

There was a dull, double thud, as two bodies collapsed separately into two chairs.

Alfred Lanning met Dr. Calvin just outside his office. He lit a nervous cigar and motioned her in.

He said, "Well, Susan, we've come pretty far, and Robertson's getting jumpy. What are you doing with The Brain?"

Susan Calvin spread her hands, "It's no use getting impatient. The Brain is worth more than anything we forefeit on this deal."

"But you've been questioning it for two months."

The psychologist's voice was flat, but somehow dangerous, "You would rather run this yourself?"

"Now you know what I meant."

"Oh, I suppose I do," Dr. Calvin rubbed her hands nervously. "It isn't easy. I've been pampering it and probing it gently, and I haven't gotten anywhere yet. Its reactions aren't normal. Its answers —they're queer, somehow. But nothing I can put my finger on yet. And you see, until we know what's wrong, we must just tiptoe our way through. I can never tell what simple question or remark will just . . . push him over . . . and then— Well, and then we'll have on our hands a completely useless Brain. Do you want to face that?"

"Well, it can't break the First Law."

"I would have thought so, but—"

"You're not even sure of that?" Lanning was profoundly shocked.

"Oh, I can't be sure of anything, Alfred—"

The alarm system raised its fearful clangor with a horrifying suddenness. Lanning clicked on communications with an almost paralytic spasm. The breathless words froze him.

He said, "Susan . . . you heard that . . . the ship's gone. I sent those two field men inside half an hour ago. You'll have to see The Brain again."

Susan Calvin said with enforced calm, "Brain, what happened to the ship?"

The Brain said happily, "The ship I built, Miss Susan?"

"That's right. What has happened to it?"

"Why, nothing at all. The two men that were supposed to test it were inside, and we were all set. So I sent it off."

"Oh— Well, that's nice." The psychologist felt some difficulty in breathing. "Do you think they'll be all right?"

"Right as anything, Miss Susan. I've taken care of it all. It's a bee-yoo-tiful ship."

"Yes, Brain, it *is* beautiful, but you think they have enough food, don't you? They'll be comfortable?"

"Plenty of food."

"This business might be a shock to them, Brain. Unexpected, you know."

The Brain tossed it off, "They'll be all right. It ought to be interesting for them."

"Interesting? How?"

"Just interesting," said The Brain, slyly.

"Susan," whispered Lanning in a fuming whisper, "ask him if death comes into it. Ask him what the dangers are."

Susan Calvin's expression contorted with fury, "Keep quiet!" In a shaken voice, she said to The Brain, "We can communicate with the ship, can't we, Brain?"

"Oh, they can hear you if you call by radio. I've taken care of that."

"Thanks. That's all for now."

Once outside, Lanning lashed out ragingly, "Great Galaxy, Susan, if this gets out, it will ruin all of us. We've got to get those men back. Why didn't you ask it if there was danger of death—straight out?"

"Because," said Calvin, with a weary frustration, "that's just what I can't mention. If it's got a case of dilemma, it's about death. Anything that would bring it up badly might knock it completely out. Will we be better off then? Now, look, it said we could communicate with them. Let's do so, get their location, and bring them back. They probably can't use the controls themselves; The Brain is probably handling them remotely. Come!"

It was quite a while before Powell shook himself together.

"Mike," he said, out of cold lips, "did you feel any acceleration?"

Donovan's eyes were blank, "Huh? No . . . no."

And then the redhead's fists clenched and he was out of his seat with sudden frenzied energy and up against the cold, wide-curving glass. There was nothing to see—but stars.

He turned, "Greg, they must have started the machine while we were inside. Greg, it's a put-up job; they fixed it up with the robot to jerry us into being the try-out boys, in case we were thinking of backing out."

Powell said, "What are you talking about? What's the good of sending us out if we don't know how to run the machine? How are we supposed to bring it back? No, this ship left by itself, and without any apparent acceleration." He rose, and walked the floor slowly. The metal walls dinned back the clangor of his steps.

He said tonelessly, "Mike, this is the most confusing situation we've ever been up against."

"That," said Donovan, bitterly, "is news to me. I was just beginning to have a very swell time, when you told me."

Powell ignored that. "No acceleration—which means the ship works on a principle different from any known."

"Different from any we know, anyway."

"Different from *any* known. There are no engines within reach of manual control. Maybe they're built into the walls. Maybe that's why they're thick as they are."

"What are you mumbling about?" demanded Donovan.

"Why not listen? I'm saying that whatever powers this ship is enclosed, and evidently not meant to be handled. The ship is running by remote control."

"The Brain's control?"

"Why not?"

"Then you think we'll stay out here till The Brain brings us back."

"It could be. If so, let's wait quietly. The Brain is a robot. It's got to follow the First Law. It can't hurt a human being."

Donovan sat down slowly, "You figure that?" Carefully, he flattened his hair, "Listen, this junk about the space-warp knocked out Consolidated's robot, and the longhairs said it was because interstellar travel killed humans. Which robot are you going to trust? Ours had the same data, I understand."

Powell was yanking madly at his mustache, "Don't pretend you don't know your robotics, Mike. Before it's physically possible in any way for a robot to even make a start to breaking the First Law, so many things have to break down that it would be a ruined mess of scrap ten times over. There's some simple explanation to this."

"Oh sure, sure. Just have the butler call me in the morning. It's all just too, too simple for me to bother about before my beauty nap."

"Well, Jupiter, Mike, what are you complaining about so far? The Brain is taking care of us. This place is warm. It's got light. It's got air. There wasn't even enough of an acceleration jar to muss your hair if it were smooth enough to be mussable in the first place."

"Yeah? Greg, you must've taken lessons. No one could put Pollyanna that far out of the running without. What do we eat? What do we drink? Where are we? How do we get back? And in case of accident, to what exit and in what spacesuit do we run, not walk? I haven't even seen a bathroom in the place, or those little conveniences that go along with bathrooms. Sure, we're being taken care of—but good!"

The voice that interrupted Donovan's tirade was not Powell's. It was nobody's. It was there, hanging in open air—stentorian and petrifying in its effects.

"GREGORY POWELL! MICHAEL DONOVAN! GREGORY POWELL! MICHAEL DONOVAN! PLEASE REPORT YOUR PRESENT POSITIONS. IF YOUR SHIP ANSWERS CONTROLS, PLEASE RETURN TO BASE. GREGORY POWELL! MICHAEL DONOVAN!—"

The message was repetitious, mechanical, broken by regular, untiring intervals.

Donovan said, "Where's it coming from?"

"I don't know." Powell's voice was an intense whisper, "Where do the lights come from? Where does anything come from?"

"Well, how are we going to answer?" They had to speak in the intervals between the loudly echoing, repeating message.

The walls were bare—as bare and as unbroken as smooth, curving metal can be. Powell said, "Shout an answer."

They did. They shouted, in turns, and together, "Position unknown! Ship out of control! Condition desperate!"

Their voices rose and cracked. The short businesslike sentences became interlarded and adulterated with screaming and emphatic profanity, but the cold, calling voice repeated and repeated and repeated unwearyingly.

"They don't hear us," gasped Donovan. "There's no sending mechanism. Just a receiver." His eyes focused blindly at a random spot on the wall.

Slowly the din of the outside voice softened and receded. They called again when it was a whisper, and they called again, hoarsely, when there was silence.

Something like fifteen minutes later, Powell said lifelessly, "Let's go through the ship again. There must be something to eat somewheres." He did not sound hopeful. It was almost an admission of defeat.

They divided in the corridor to the right and left. They could follow one another by the hard footsteps resounding, and they met occasionally in the corridor, where they would glare at each other and pass on.

Powell's search ended suddenly and as it did, he heard Donovan's glad voice rise boomingly.

"Hey, Greg," it howled, "the ship *has* got plumbing. How did we miss it?"

It was some five minutes later that he found Powell by hit-and-miss. He was saying, "Still no shower baths, though," but it got choked off in the middle.

"Food," he gasped.

The wall had dropped away, leaving a curved gap with two shelves. The upper shelf was loaded with unlabeled cans of a bewildering variety of sizes and shapes. The enameled cans on the lower shelf were uniform and Donovan felt a cold draft about his ankles. The lower half was refrigerated.

"How . . . how—"

"It wasn't there, before," said Powell, curtly. "That wall section dropped out of sight as I came in the door."

He was eating. The can was the pre-heating type with enclosed spoon and the warm odor of baked beans filled the room. "Grab a can, Mike!"

Donovan hesitated, "What's the menu?"

"How do I know! Are you finicky?"

"No, but all I eat on ships are beans. Something else would be first choice." His hand hovered and selected a shining elliptical can whose flatness seemed reminiscent of salmon or similar delicacy. It opened at the proper pressure.

"Beans!" howled Donovan, and reached for another. Powell hauled at the slack of his pants. "Better eat that, sonny boy. Supplies are limited and we may be here a long, long time."

Donovan drew back sulkily, "Is that all we have? Beans?"

"Could be."

"What's on the lower shelf?"

"Milk."

"Just milk?" Donovan cried in outrage.

"Looks it."

The meal of beans and milk was carried through in silence, and as they left, the strip of hidden wall rose up and formed an unbroken surface once more.

Powell sighed, "Everything automatic. Everything just so. Never felt so helpless in my life. Where's your plumbing?"

"Right there. And that wasn't among those present when we first looked, either."

Fifteen minutes later they were back in the glassed-in room, staring at each other from opposing seats.

Powell looked gloomily at the one guage in the room. It still said "parsecs," the figures still ended in "1,000,000" and the indicating needle was still pressed hard against the zero mark.

In the innermost offices of the U. S. Robots and Mechanical Men Corporation Alfred Lanning was saying wearily, "They won't answer. We've tried every wavelength, public, private, coded, straight, even this subether stuff they have now. And The Brain still won't say anything?" He shot this at Dr. Calvin.

"It won't amplify on the matter, Alfred," she said, emphatically. "It says they can hear us . . . and when I try to press it, it becomes . . . well, it becomes sullen. And it's not supposed to— Whoever heard of a sullen robot?"

"Suppose you tell us what you have, Susan," said Bogert.

"Here it is! It admits it controls the ship itself entirely. It is definitely optimistic about their safety, but without details. I don't dare press it. However, the center of disturbance seems to be about the interstellar jump itself. The Brain definitely laughed when I brought up the subject. There are other indications, but that is the closest it's come to an open abnormality."

She looked at the others, "I refer to hysteria. I dropped the subject immediately, and I hope I did no harm, but it gave me a lead. I can handle hysteria. Give me twelve hours! If I can bring it back to normal, it will bring back the ship."

Bogert seemed suddenly stricken. "The interstellar jump!"

"What's the matter?" The cry was double from Calvin and Lanning.

"The figures for the engine The Brain gave us. Say . . . I just thought of something."

He left hurriedly.

Lanning gazed after him. He said brusquely to Calvin, "You take care of your end, Susan."

Two hours later, Bogert was talking eagerly, "I tell you, Lanning, that's it. The interstellar jump is not instantaneous—not as long as the speed of light is finite. Life can't exist . . . *matter and energy* as such can't exist in the space warp. I don't know what it would be like—but that's it. That's what killed Consolidated's robot."

Donovan felt as haggard as he looked. "Only five days?"

"Only five days. I'm sure of it."

Donovan looked about him wretchedly. The stars through the glass were familiar but infinitely indifferent. The walls were cold to the touch; the lights, which had recently flared up again, were unfeelingly bright; the needle on the gauge pointed stubbornly to zero; and Donovan could not get rid of the taste of beans.

He said, morosely, "I need a bath."

Powell looked up briefly, and said, "So do I. You needn't feel self-conscious. But unless you want to bathe in milk and do without drinking—"

"We'll do without drinking eventually, anyway. Greg, where does this interstellar travel come in?"

"You tell me. Maybe we just keep on going. We'd get there, eventually. At least the dust of our skeletons would—but isn't our death the whole point of The Brain's original breakdown?"

Donovan spoke with his back to the other, "Greg, I've been thinking. It's pretty bad. There's not much to do—except walk around or talk to yourself. You know those stories about guys marooned in space. They go nuts long before they starve. I don't know, Greg, but ever since the lights went on, I feel funny."

There was a silence, then Powell's voice came thin and small, "So do I. What's it like?"

The redheaded figure turned, "Feel funny inside. There's a pounding in me with everything tense. It's hard to breathe. I can't stand still."

"Um-m-m. Do you feel vibration?"

"How do you mean?"

"Sit down for a minute and listen. You don't hear it, but you feel it—as if something's throbbing somewheres and it's throbbing the whole ship, and you, too, along with it. Listen—"

"Yeah . . . yeah. What do you think it is, Greg? You don't suppose it's us?"

"It might be." Powell stroked his mustache slowly. "But it might be the ship's engines. It might be getting ready."

"For what?"

"For the interstellar jump. It may be coming and the devil knows what it's like."

Donovan pondered. Then he said, savagely, "If it does, let it. But I wish we could fight. It's humiliating to have to wait for it."

An hour later, perhaps, Powell looked at his hand on the metal chair-arm and said with frozen calm, "Feel the wall, Mike."

Donovan did, and said, "You can feel it shake, Greg."

Even the stars seemed blurred. From somewhere came the vague impression of a huge machine gathering power with the walls, storing up energy for a mighty leap, throbbing its way up the scales of strength.

It came with a suddenness and a stab of pain. Powell stiffened, and half-jerked from his chair. His sight caught Donovan and blanked out while Donovan's thin shout whimpered and died in his ears. Something writhed within him and struggled against a growing blanket of ice, that thickened.

Something broke loose and whirled in a blaze of flickering light and pain. It fell—

—and whirled

—and fell headlong

—into silence!

It was death!

It was a world of no motion and no sensation. A world of dim, unsensing consciousness; a consciousness of darkness and of silence and of formless struggle.

Most of all a consciousness of eternity.

He was a tiny white thread of ego—cold and afraid.

Then the words came, unctuous and sonorous, thundering over him in a foam of sound:

"Does your coffin fit differently lately? Why not try Morbid M. Cadaver's extensible caskets? They are scientifically designed to fit the natural curves of the body, and are enriched with Vitamin B_1. Use Cadaver's caskets for comfort. Remember—you're—going—to—be—dead—a—long—long—time!"

It wasn't quite sound, but whatever it was, it died away in an oily rumbling whisper.

The white thread that might have been Powell heaved uselessly at the insubstantial eons of time that existed all about him—and collapsed upon itself as the piercing shriek of a hundred million ghosts of a hundred million soprano voices rose to a crescendo:

"I'll be glad when you're dead, you rascal, you.
"I'll be glad when you're dead, you rascal, you.
"I'll be glad—"

It rose up a spiral stairway of violent sound into the keening supersonics that passed hearing, and then beyond—

The white thread quivered with a pulsating pang. It strained quietly—

The voices were ordinary—and many. It was a crowd speaking; a swirling mob that swept through and past and over him with a rapid, headlong motion, that left drifting tatters of words behind them.

"What did they getcha for, boy? Y'look banged up—"

"—a hot fire, I guess, but I got a case—"

"—I've made Paradise, but old St. Pete—"

"Naaah, I got a pull with the boy. Had dealings with him—"

"Hey, Sam, come this way—"

"Ja get a mouthpiece? Beelzebub says—"

"—Going on, my good imp? My appointment is with Sa—"

And above it all the original stentorian roar, that plunged across all:

"HURRY! HURRY! HURRY!!! Stir your bones, and don't keep us waiting—there are many more in line. Have your certificates ready, and make sure Peter's release is stamped across it. See if you are at the proper entrance gate. There will be plenty of fire for all. Hey, you—YOU DOWN THERE. TAKE YOUR PLACE IN LINE OR—"

The white thread that was Powell groveled backward before the advancing shout, and felt the sharp stab of the pointing finger. It all exploded into a rainbow of sound that dripped its fragments onto an aching brain.

Powell was in the chair, again. He felt himself shaking.

Donovan's eyes were opening into two large popping bowls of glazed blue.

"Greg," he whispered in what was almost a sob. "Were you dead?"

"I . . . felt dead." He did not recognize his own croak.

Donovan was obviously making a bad failure of his attempt to stand up, "Are we alive now? Or is there more?"

"I . . . feel alive." It was the same hoarseness. Powell said cautiously, "Did you . . . hear anything, when . . . when you were dead?"

Donovan paused, and then very slowly nodded his head, "Did you?"

"Yes. Did you hear about coffins . . . and females singing . . . and the lines forming to get into Hell? Did you?"

Donovan shook his head, "Just one voice."

"Loud?"

"No. Soft, but rough like a file over the fingertips. It was a sermon, you know. About hell-fire. He described the tortures of . . . well, *you know*. I once heard a sermon like that—almost."

He was perspiring.

They were conscious of sunlight through the port. It was weak, but it was blue-white—and the gleaming pea that was the distant source of light was not Old Sol.

And Powell pointed a trembling finger at the single gauge. The needle stood stiff and proud at the hairline whose figure read 300,000 parsecs.

Powell said, "Mike if it's true, we must be out of the Galaxy altogether."

Donovan said, "Blazes! Greg! We'd be the first men out of the Solar System."

"Yes! That's just it. We've escaped the sun. We've escaped the Galaxy. Mike, this ship is the answer. It means freedom for all humanity—freedom to spread through to every star that exists— millions and billions and trillions of them."

And then he came down with a hard thud, "But how do we get back, Mike?"

Donovan smiled shakily, "Oh, that's all right. The ship brought us here. The ship will take us back. Me for more beans."

"But Mike . . . hold on, Mike. If it takes us back the way it brought us here—"

Donovan stopped halfway up and sat back heavily into the chair.

Powell went on, "We'll have to . . . die again, Mike."

"Well," sighed Donovan, "if we have to, we have to. At least it isn't permanent, not *very* permanent."

Susan Calvin was speaking slowly now. For six hours she had been slowly prodding The Brain—for six fruitless hours. She was weary of repetitions, weary of circumlocutions, weary of everything.

"Now, Brain, there's just one more thing. You must make a special effort to answer simply. Have you been entirely clear about the interstellar jump? I mean does it take them very far?"

"As far as they want to go, Miss Susan. Golly, it isn't any trick through the warp."

"And on the other side, what will they see?"

"Stars and stuff. What do you suppose?"

The next question slipped out, "They'll be alive, then?"

"Sure!"

"And the interstellar jump won't hurt them?"

She froze as The Brain maintained silence. That was it! She had touched the sore spot.

"Brain," she supplicated faintly, "Brain, do you hear me?"

The answer was weak, quivering. The Brain said, "Do I have to answer? About the jump, I mean?"

"Not if you don't want to. But it would be interesting—I mean if you wanted to." Susan Calvin tried to be bright about it.

"Aw-w-w. You spoil everything."

And the psychologist jumped up suddenly, with a look of flaming insight on her face.

"Oh, my," she gasped. "Oh, my."

And she felt the tension of hours and days released in a burst. It was later that she told Lanning, "I tell you it's all right. No, you must leave me alone, now. The ship will be back safely, *with* the men, and I want to rest. I *will* rest. Now go away."

The ship returned to Earth as silently, as unjarringly as it had left. It dropped precisely into place and the main lock gaped open. The two men who walked out felt their way carefully and scratched their rough and scrubbily-stubbled chins.

And then, slowly and purposefully, the one with red hair knelt down and planted upon the concrete of the runway a firm, loud kiss.

They waved aside the crowd that was gathering and made gestures of denial at the eager couple that had piled out of the down-swooping ambulance with a stretcher between them.

Gregory Powell said, "Where's the nearest shower?"

They were led away.

They were gathered, all of them, about a table. It was a full staff meeting of the brains of U. S. Robots and Mechanical Men Corporation.

Slowly and climactically, Powell and Donovan finished a graphic and resounding story.

Susan Calvin broke the silence that followed. In the few days that had elapsed she had recovered her icy, somewhat acid, calm—but still a trace of embarrassment broke through.

"Strictly speaking," she said, "this was my fault—all of it. When we first presented this problem to The Brain, as I hope some of you remember, I went to great lengths to impress upon it the importance of rejecting any item of information capable of creating a dilemma. In doing so I said something like 'Don't get excited about the death of humans. We don't mind it at all. Just give the sheet back and forget it.'"

"Hm-m-m," said Lanning. "What follows?"

"The obvious. When that item entered its calculations which yielded the equation controlling the length of minimum interval for the interstellar jump—it meant death for humans. That's where Consolidated's machine broke down completely. But I had depressed the importance of death to The Brain—not entirely, for the First Law can never be broken—but just sufficiently so that The Brain could take a second look at the equation. Sufficiently to give it time to realize that after the interval was passed through, the men would return to life—just as the matter and energy of the ship itself would return to being. This so-called 'death,' in other words, was a strictly temporary phenomenon. You see?"

She looked about her. They were all listening.

She went on, "So it accepted the item, but not without a certain jar. Even with death temporary and its importance depressed, it was enough to unbalance it very gently."

She brought it out calmly, "It developed a sense of humor—it's an escape, you see, a method of partial escape from reality. It became a practical joker."

Powell and Donovan were on their feet.

"What?" cried Powell.

Donovan was considerably more colorful about it.

"It's so," said Calvin. "It took care of you, and kept you safe, but you couldn't handle any controls, because they weren't for you—just for the humorous Brain. We could reach you by radio, but you couldn't answer. You had plenty of food, but all of it beans and milk. Then you died, so to speak, and were reborn, but the period of your death was made . . . well . . . interesting. I wish I knew how it did it. It was The Brain's prize little joke, but it meant no harm."

"No harm!" gasped Donovan. "Oh, if that cute little tyke only had a neck."

Lanning raised a quieting hand, "All right, it's been a mess, but it's all over. What now?"

"Well," said Bogert, quietly, "obviously it's up to us to improve the space-warp engine. There must be some way of getting around that interval of jump. If there is, we're the only organization left with a grand-scale super-robot, so we're bound to find it if anyone. And then—U. S. Robots has interstellar travel, and humanity has the opportunity for galactic empire."

"What about Consolidated?" said Lanning.

"Hey," interrupted Donovan suddenly, "I want to make a suggestion there. They landed U. S. Robots into quite a mess. It wasn't as bad a mess as they expected and it turned out well, but their intentions weren't pious. And Greg and I bore the most of it."

"Well, they wanted an answer, and they've got one. Send them that ship, guaranteed, and U. S. Robots can collect their two hundred thou plus construction costs. And if they test it—then suppose we let The Brain have just a little more fun before it's brought back to normal."

Lanning said gravely, "It sounds just and proper to me."

To which Bogert added absently, "Strictly according to contract, too."

Evidence

Francis Quinn was a politician of the new school. That, of course, is a meaningless expression, as are all expressions of the sort. Most of the "new schools" we have were duplicated in the social life of ancient Greece, and perhaps, if we knew more about it, in the social life of ancient Sumeria and in the lake dwellings of prehistoric Switzerland as well.

But, to get out from under what promises to be a dull and complicated beginning, it might be best to state hastily that Quinn neither ran for office nor canvassed for votes, made no speeches and stuffed no ballot boxes. Any more than Napoleon pulled a trigger at Austerlitz.

And since politics makes strange bedfellows, Alfred Lanning sat at the other side of the desk with his ferocious white eyebrows bent far forward over eyes in which chronic impatience had sharpened to acuity. He was not pleased.

The fact, if known to Quinn, would have annoyed him not the least. His voice was friendly, perhaps professionally so.

"I assume you know Stephen Byerley, Dr. Lanning."

"I have heard of him. So have many people."

"Yes, so have I. Perhaps you intend voting for him at the next election."

"I couldn't say." There was an unmistakable trace of acidity here. "I have not followed the political currents, so I'm not aware that he is running for office."

"He may be our next mayor. Of course, he is only a lawyer now, but great oaks—"

"Yes," interrupted Lanning, "I have heard the phrase before. But I wonder if we can get to the business at hand."

"We *are* at the business at hand, Dr. Lanning." Quinn's tone was very gentle, "It is to my interest to keep Mr. Byerley a district attorney at the very most, and it is to your interest to help me do so."

"To *my* interest? Come!" Lanning's eyebrows hunched low.

"Well, say then to the interest of the U. S. Robots and Mechanical Men Corporation. I come to you as Director-Emeritus of Research, because I know that your connection to them is that of, shall we say, 'elder statesman.' You are listened to with respect and yet your connection with them is no longer so tight but that you cannot possess considerable freedom of action; even if the action is somewhat unorthodox."

Dr. Lanning was silent a moment, chewing the cud of his thoughts. He said more softly, "I don't follow you at all, Mr. Quinn."

"I am not surprised, Dr. Lanning. But it's all rather simple. Do you mind?" Quinn lit a slender cigarette with a lighter of tasteful simplicity and his big-boned face settled into an expression of quiet amusement. "We have spoken of Mr. Byerley—a strange and colorful character. He was unknown three years ago. He is very well known now. He is a man of force and ability, and certainly the most capable and intelligent prosecutor I have ever known. Unfortunately he is not a friend of mine—"

"I understand," said Lanning, mechanically. He stared at his fingernails.

"I have had occasion," continued Quinn, evenly, "in the past year to investigate Mr. Byerley—quite exhaustively. It is always useful, you see, to subject the past life of reform politicians to rather inquisitive research. If you knew how often it helped—" He paused to smile humorlessly at the glowing tip of his cigarette. "But Mr. Byerley's past is unremarkable. A quiet life in a small town, a college education, a wife who died young, an auto accident with a slow recovery, law school, coming to the metropolis, an attorney."

Francis Quinn shook his head slowly, then added, "But his present life. Ah, that is remarkable. Our district attorney never eats!"

Lanning's head snapped up, old eyes surprisingly sharp, "Pardon me?"

"Our district attorney never eats." The repetition thumped by syllables. "I'll modify that slightly. He has never been seen to eat or drink. Never! Do you understand the significance of the word? Not rarely, but never!"

"I find that quite incredible. Can you trust your investigators?"

"I can trust my investigators, and I don't find it incredible at all. Further, our district attorney has never been seen to drink—in the aqueous sense as well as the alcoholic—nor to sleep. There are other factors, but I should think I have made my point."

Lanning leaned back in his seat, and there was the rapt silence of challenge and response between them, and then the old roboticist shook his head. "No. There is only one thing you can be trying to imply, if I couple your statements with the fact that you present them to me, and that is impossible."

"But the man is quite inhuman, Dr. Lanning."

"If you told me he were Satan in masquerade, there would be a faint chance that I might believe you."

"I tell you he is a robot, Dr. Lanning."

"I tell you it is as impossible a conception as I have ever heard, Mr. Quinn."

Again the combative silence.

"Nevertheless," and Quinn stubbed out his cigarette with elaborate care, "you will have to investigate this impossibility with all the resources of the Corporation."

"I'm sure that I could undertake no such thing, Mr. Quinn. You don't seriously suggest that the Corporation take part in local politics."

"You have no choice. Supposing I were to make my facts public without proof. The evidence is circumstantial enough."

"Suit yourself in that respect."

"But it would not suit me. Proof would be much preferable. And it would not suit *you*, for the publicity would be very damaging to your company. You are perfectly well acquainted, I suppose, with the strict rules against the use of robots on inhabited worlds."

"Certainly!" —brusquely.

"You know that the U. S. Robots and Mechanical Men Corporation is the only manufacturer of positronic robots in the Solar System, and if Byerley is a robot, he is a *positronic* robot. You are also aware that all positronic robots are leased, and not sold; that the Corporation remains the owner and manager of each robot, and is therefore responsible for the actions of all."

"It is an easy matter, Mr. Quinn, to prove the Corporation has never manufactured a robot of a humanoid character."

"It can be done? To discuss merely possibilities."

"Yes. It can be done."

"Secretly, I imagine, as well. Without entering it in your books."

"Not the positronic brain, sir. Too many factors are involved in that, and there is the tightest possible government supervision."

"Yes, but robots are worn out, break down, go out of order—and are dismantled."

"And the positronic brains re-used or destroyed."

"Really?" Francis Quinn allowed himself a trace of sarcasm. "And if one were, accidentally, of course, not destroyed—and there happened to be a humanoid structure waiting for a brain."

"Impossible!"

"You would have to prove that to the government and the public, so why not prove it to me now."

"But what could our purpose be?" demanded Lanning in exasperation. "Where is our motivation? Credit us with a minimum of sense."

"My dear sir, please. The Corporation would be only too glad to have the various Regions permit the use of humanoid positronic robots on inhabited worlds. The profits would be enormous. But the prejudice of the public against such a practice is too great. Suppose you get them used to such robots first—see, we have a skillful lawyer, a good mayor,—and he is a robot. Won't you buy our robot butlers?"

"Thoroughly fantastic. An almost humorous descent to the ridiculous."

"I imagine so. Why not prove it? Or would you still rather try to prove it to the public?"

The light in the office was dimming, but it was not yet too dim to obscure the flush of frustration on Alfred Lanning's face. Slowly, the roboticist's finger touched a knob and the wall illuminators glowed to gentle life.

"Well, then," he growled, "let us see."

The face of Stephen Byerley is not an easy one to describe. He was forty by birth certificate and forty by appearance—but it was a healthy, well-nourished good-natured appearance of forty; one that automatically drew the teeth of the bromide about "looking one's age."

This was particularly true when he laughed, and he was laughing now. It came loudly and continuously, died away for a bit, then began again—

And Alfred Lanning's face contracted into a rigidly bitter monument of disapproval. He made a half gesture to the woman who sat beside him, but her thin, bloodless lips merely pursed themselves a trifle.

Byerley gasped himself a stage nearer normality.

"Really, Dr. Lanning . . . really—I . . . I . . . a robot?"

Lanning bit his words off with a snap, "It is no statement of mine, sir. I would be quite satisfied to have you a member of humanity. Since our corporation never manufactured you, I am quite certain that you are—in a legalistic sense, at any rate. But since the contention that you are a robot has been advanced to us seriously by a man of certain standing—"

"Don't mention his name, if it would knock a chip off your granite block of ethics, but let's pretend it was Frank Quinn, for the sake of argument, and continue."

Lanning drew in a sharp, cutting snort at the interruption, and paused ferociously before continuing with added frigidity, "—by a man of certain standing, with whose identity I am not interested in playing guessing games, I am bound to ask your cooperation in disproving it. The mere fact that such a contention could be advanced and publicized by the means at this man's disposal would be a bad blow to the company I represent—even if the charge were never proven. You understand me?"

"Oh, yes, your position is clear to me. The charge itself is ridiculous. The spot you find yourself in is not. I beg your pardon, if my laughter offended you. It was the first I laughed at, not the second. How can I help you?"

"It could be very simple. You have only to sit down to a meal at a restaurant in the presence of witnesses, have your picture taken, and eat." Lanning sat back in his chair, the worst of the interview over. The woman beside him watched Byerley with an apparently absorbed expression but contributed nothing of her own.

Stephen Byerley met her eyes for an instant, was caught by them, then turned back to the roboticist. For a while his fingers were thoughtful over the bronze paper-weight that was the only ornament on his desk.

He said quietly, "I don't think I can oblige you."

He raised his hand, "Now wait, Dr. Lanning. I appreciate the fact that this whole matter is distasteful to you, that you have been forced into it against your will, that you feel you are playing an undignified and even ridiculous part. Still, the matter is even more intimately concerned with myself, so be tolerant.

"First, what makes you think that Quinn—this man of certain standing, you know—wasn't hoodwinking you, in order to get you to do exactly what you are doing?"

"Why it seems scarcely likely that a reputable person would endanger himself in so ridiculous a fashion, if he weren't convinced he were on safe ground."

There was little humor in Byerley's eyes, "You don't know Quinn. He could manage to make safe ground out of a ledge a mountain sheep could not handle. I suppose he showed the particulars of the investigation he claims to have made of me?"

"Enough to convince me that it would be too troublesome to have our corporation attempt to disprove them when you could do so more easily."

"Then you believe him when he says I never eat. You are a scientist, Dr. Lanning. Think of the logic required. I have not been observed to eat, therefore, I never eat Q.E.D. After all!"

"You are using prosecution tactics to confuse what is really a very simple situation."

"On the contrary, I am trying to clarify what you and Quinn between you are making a very complicated one. You see, I don't sleep much, that's true, and I certainly don't sleep in public. I have never cared to eat with others—an idiosyncrasy which is unusual and probably neurotic in character, but which harms no one. Look, Dr. Lanning, let me present you with a suppositious case. Supposing we had a politician who was interested in defeating a reform candidate at any cost and while investigating his private life came across oddities such as I have just mentioned.

"Suppose further that in order to smear the candidate effectively, he comes to your company as the ideal agent. Do you expect him to say to you, "So-and-so is a robot because he hardly ever eats with people, and I have never seen him fall asleep in the middle of a case; and once when I peeped into his window in the middle of the night, there he was, sitting up with a book; and I looked in his frigidaire and there was no food in it.

"If he told you that, you would send for a straitjacket. But if he tells you, 'He *never* sleeps; he *never* eats,' then the shock of the statement blinds you to the fact that such statements are impossible to prove. You play into his hands by contributing to the to-do."

"Regardless, sir," began Lanning, with a threatening obstinacy, "of whether you consider this matter serious or not, it will require only the meal I mentioned to end it."

Again Byerley turned to the woman, who still regarded him expressionlessly. "Pardon me. I've caught your name correctly, haven't I? Dr. Susan Calvin?"

"Yes, Mr. Byerley."

"You're the U. S. Robots' psychologist, aren't you?"

"*Robo*psychologist, please."

"Oh, are robots so different from men, mentally?"

"Worlds different." She allowed herself a frosty smile, "Robots are essentially decent."

Humor tugged at the corners of the lawyer's mouth, "Well, that's a hard blow. But what I wanted to say was this. Since you're a psycho—a robopsychologist, *and* a woman, I'll bet that you've done something that Dr. Lanning hasn't thought of."

"And what is that?"

"You've got something to eat in your purse."

Something caught in the schooled indifference of Susan Calvin's eyes. She said, "You surprise me, Mr. Byerley."

And opening her purse, she produced an apple. Quietly, she handed it to him. Dr. Lanning, after an initial start, followed the slow movement from one hand to the other with sharply alert eyes.

Calmly, Stephen Byerley bit into it, and calmly he swallowed it.

"You see, Dr. Lanning?"

Dr. Lanning smiled in a relief tangible enough to make even his eyebrows appear benevolent. A relief that survived for one fragile second.

Susan Calvin said, "I was curious to see if you would eat it, but, of course, in the present case, it proves nothing."

Byerley grinned, "It doesn't?"

"Of course not. It is obvious, Dr. Lanning, that if this man were a humanoid robot, he would be a perfect imitation. He is almost too human to be credible. After all, we have been seeing and observing human beings all our lives; it would be impossible to palm something merely nearly right off on us. It would have to be *all* right. Observe the texture of the skin, the quality of the irises, the bone formation of the hand. If he's a robot, I wish U. S. Robots *had* made him, because he's a good job. Do you suppose then, that anyone capable of paying attention to such niceties would neglect a few gadgets to take care of such things as eating, sleeping, elimination? For emergency use only, perhaps; as, for instance, to prevent such situations as are arising here. So a meal won't really prove anything."

"Now wait," snarled Lanning, "I am not quite the fool both of you make me out to be. I am not interested in the problem of Mr. Byerley's humanity or nonhumanity. I am interested in getting the corporation out of a hole. A public meal will end the matter and keep it ended no matter what Quinn does. We can leave the finer details to lawyers and robopsychologists."

"But, Dr. Lanning," said Byerley, "you forget the politics of the situation. I am as anxious to be elected, as Quinn is to stop me. By the way, did you notice that you used his name. It's a cheap shyster trick of mine; I knew you would, before you were through."

Lanning flushed, "What has the election to do with it?"

"Publicity works both ways, sir. If Quinn wants to call me a robot, and has the nerve to do so, I have the nerve to play the game his way."

"You mean you—" Lanning was quite frankly appalled.

"Exactly. I mean that I'm going to let him go ahead, choose his rope, test its strength, cut off the right length, tie the noose, insert his head and grin. I can do what little else is required."

"You are mighty confident."

Susan Calvin rose to her feet, "Come, Alfred, we won't change his mind for him."

"You see." Byerley smiled gently. "You're a human psychologist, too."

But perhaps not all the confidence that Dr. Lanning had remarked upon was present that evening when Byerley's car parked on the automatic treads leading to the sunken garage, and Byerley himself crossed the path to the front door of his house.

The figure in the wheel chair looked up as he entered and smiled. Byerley's face lit with affection. He crossed over to it.

The cripple's voice was a hoarse, grating whisper that came out of a mouth forever twisted to one side, leering out of a face that was half scar tissue, "You're late, Steve."

"I know, John, I know. But I've been up against a peculiar and interesting trouble today."

"So?" Neither the torn face nor the destroyed voice could carry expression but there was anxiety in the clear eyes. "Nothing you can't handle?"

"I'm not exactly certain. I may need your help. *You're* the brilliant one in the family. Do you want me to take you out into the garden? It's a beautiful evening."

Two strong arms lifted John from the wheel chair. Gently, almost caressingly, Byerley's arms went around the shoulders and under the swathed legs of the cripple. Carefully, and slowly, he walked through the rooms, down the gentle ramp that had been built with a wheel chair in mind, and out the back door into the walled and wired garden behind the house.

"Why don't you let me use the wheel chair, Steve? This is silly."

"Because I'd rather carry you. Do you object? You know that you're as glad to get out of that motorized buggy for a while as I am to see you out. How do you feel today?" He deposited John with infinite care upon the cool grass.

"How should I feel? But tell me about your trouble."

"Quinn's campaign will be based on the fact that he claims I'm a robot."

John's eyes opened wide, "How do you know? It's impossible. I won't believe it."

"Oh, come, I tell you it's so. He had one of the big-shot scientists of U. S. Robots and Mechanical Men Corporation over at the office to argue with me."

Slowly John's hands tore at the grass, "I see. I see."

Byerley said, "But we can let him choose his ground. I have an idea. Listen to me and tell me if we can do it—"

The scene as it appeared in Alfred Lanning's office that night was a tableau of stares. Francis Quinn stared meditatively at Alfred Lanning. Lanning's stare was savagely set upon Susan Calvin, who stared impassively in her turn at Quinn.

Francis Quinn broke it with a heavy attempt at lightness, "Bluff. He's making it up as he goes along."

"Are you going to gamble on that, Mr. Quinn?" asked Dr. Calvin, indifferently.

"Well, it's your gamble, really."

"Look here," Lanning covered definite pessimism with bluster, "we've done what you asked. We witnessed the man eat. It's ridiculous to presume him a robot."

"Do *you* think so?" Quinn shot toward Calvin. "Lanning said you were the expert."

Lanning was almost threatening, "Now, Susan—"

Quinn interrupted smoothly, "Why not let her talk, man? She's been sitting there imitating a gatepost for half an hour."

Lanning felt definitely harassed. From what he experienced then to incipient paranoia was but a step. He said, "Very well. Have your say, Susan. We won't interrupt you."

Susan Calvin glanced at him humorlessly, then fixed cold eyes on Mr. Quinn. "There are only two ways of definitely proving Byerley to be a robot, sir. So far you are presenting circumstantial evidence, with which you can accuse, but not prove—and I think Mr. Byerley is sufficiently clever to counter that sort of material. You probably think so yourself, or you wouldn't have come here.

"The two methods of *proof* are the physical and the psychological. Physically, you can dissect him or use an X-ray. How to do that would be *your* problem. Psychologically, his behavior can be studied, for if he *is* a positronic robot, he must conform to the three Rules of Robotics. A positronic brain can not be constructed without them. You know the Rules, Mr. Quinn?"

She spoke them carefully, clearly, quoting word for word the famous bold print on page one of the "Handbook of Robotics."

"I've heard of them," said Quinn, carelessly.

"Then the matter is easy to follow," responded the psychologist, dryly. "If Mr. Byerley breaks any of those three rules, he is not a robot. Unfortunately, this procedure works in only one direction. If he lives up to the rules, it proves nothing one way or the other."

Quinn raised polite eyebrows, "Why not, doctor?"

"Because, if you stop to think of it, the three Rules of Robotics are the essential guiding principles of a good many of the world's ethical systems. Of course, every human being is supposed to have the instinct of self-preservation. That's Rule Three to a robot. Also every 'good' human being, with a social conscience and a sense of responsibility, is supposed to defer to proper authority; to listen to his doctor, his boss, his government, his psychiatrist, his fellow man; to obey laws, to follow rules, to conform to custom—even when they interfere with his comfort or his safety. That's Rule Two to a robot. Also, every 'good' human being is supposed to love others as himself, protect his fellow man, risk his life to save another. That's Rule One to a robot. To put it simply—if Byerley follows all the Rules of Robotics, he may be a robot, and may simply be a very good man."

"But," said Quinn, "you're telling me that you can never prove him a robot."

"I may be able to prove him *not* a robot."

"That's not the proof I want."

"You'll have such proof as exists. You are the only one responsible for your own wants."

Here Lanning's mind leaped suddenly to the sting of an idea, "Has it occurred to anyone," he ground out, "that district attorney is a rather strange occupation for a robot? The prosecution of human beings—sentencing them to death—bringing about their infinite harm—"

Quinn grew suddenly keen, "No, you can't get out of it that way. Being district attorney doesn't make him human. Don't you know his record? Don't you know that he boasts that he has never prosecuted an innocent man; that there are scores of people left untried because the evidence against them didn't satisfy him, even though he could probably have argued a jury into atomizing them? That happens to be so."

Lanning's thin cheeks quivered, "No, Quinn, no. There is nothing in the Rules of Robotics that makes any allowance for human guilt. A robot may not judge whether a human being deserves death. It is not for him to decide. *He may not harm a human*—variety skunk, or variety angel."

Susan Calvin sounded tired. "Alfred," she said, "don't talk foolishly. What if a robot came upon a madman about to set fire to a house with people in it. He would stop the madman, wouldn't he?"

"Of course."

"And if the only way he could stop him was to kill him—"

There was a faint sound in Lanning's throat. Nothing more.

"The answer to that, Alfred, is that he would do his best not to kill him. If the madman died, the robot would require psychotherapy because he might easily go mad at the conflict presented him—of having broken Rule One to adhere to Rule One in a higher sense. But a man would be dead and a robot would have killed him."

"Well, *is* Byerley mad?" demanded Lanning, with all the sarcasm he could muster.

"No, but he has killed no man himself. He has exposed facts which might represent a particular human being to be dangerous to the large mass of other human beings we call society. He protects the greater number and thus adheres to Rule One at maximum potential. That is as far as he goes. It is the judge who then condemns the criminal to death or imprisonment, after the jury decides on his guilt or innocence. It is the jailer who imprisons him, the executioner who kills him. And Mr. Byerley has done nothing but determine truth and aid society.

"As a matter of fact, Mr. Quinn, I have looked into Mr. Byerley's career since you first brought this matter to our attention. I find that he has never demanded the death sentence in his closing speeches to the jury. I also find that he has spoken on behalf of the abolition of capital punishment and contributed generously to research institutions engaged in criminal neurophysiology. He apparently believes in the cure, rather than the punishment of crime. I find that significant."

"You do?" Quinn smiled. "Significant of a certain odor of roboticity, perhaps?"

"Perhaps. Why deny it? Actions such as his could come only from a robot, or from a very honorable and decent human being. But you see, you just can't differentiate between a robot and the very best of humans."

Quinn sat back in his chair. His voice quivered with impatience. "Dr. Lanning, it's perfectly possible to create a humanoid robot that would perfectly duplicate a human in appearance, isn't it?"

Lanning harrumphed and considered, "It's been done experimentally by U. S. Robots," he said reluctantly, "without the addition of a positronic brain, of course. By using human ova and hormone control, one can grow human flesh and skin over a skeleton of porous silicone plastics that would defy external examination. The eyes, the hair, the skin would be really human, not humanoid. And if you put a positronic brain, and such other gadgets as you might desire inside, you have a humanoid robot."

Quinn said shortly, "How long would it take to make one?"

Lanning considered, "If you had all your equipment—the brain, the skeleton, the ovum, the proper hormones and radiations—say, two months."

The politician straightened out of his chair. "Then we shall see what the insides of Mr. Byerley look like. It will mean publicity for U. S. Robots—but I gave you your chance."

Lanning turned impatiently to Susan Calvin, when they were alone. "Why do you insist—"

And with real feeling, she responded sharply and instantly, "Which do you want—the truth or my resignation? I won't lie for you. U. S. Robots can take care of itself. Don't turn coward."

"What," said Lanning, "if he opens up Byerley, and wheels and gears fall out. What then?"

"He won't open Byerley," said Calvin, disdainfully. "Byerley is as clever as Quinn, at the very least."

The news broke upon the city a week before Byerley was to have been nominated. But "broke" is the wrong word. It staggered upon the city, shambled, crawled. Laughter began, and wit was free. And as the far off hand of Quinn tightened its pressure in easy stages, the laughter grew forced, an element of hollow uncertainty entered, and people broke off to wonder.

The convention itself had the air of a restive stallion. There had been no contest planned. Only Byerley could possibly have been nominated a week earlier. There was no substitute even now. They had to nominate him, but there was complete confusion about it.

It would not have been so bad if the average individual were not torn between the enormity of the charge, if true, and its sensational folly, if false.

The day after Byerley was nominated perfunctorily, hollowly—a newspaper finally published the gist of a long interview with Dr. Susan Calvin, "world famous expert on robopsychology and positronics."

What broke loose is popularly and succinctly described as hell.

It was what the Fundamentalists were waiting for. They were not a political party; they made pretense to no formal religion. Essentially they were those who had not adapted themselves to what had once been called the Atomic Age, in the days when atoms were a novelty. Actually, they were the Simple-Lifers, hungering after a life, which to those who lived it had probably appeared not so Simple, and who had been, therefore, Simple-Lifers themselves.

The Fundamentalists required no new reason to detest robots and robot manufacturers; but a new reason such as the Quinn accusation and the Calvin analysis was sufficient to make such detestation audible.

The huge plants of the U. S. Robots and Mechanical Men Corporation was a hive that spawned armed guards. It prepared for war.

Within the city the house of Stephen Byerley bristled with police.

The political campaign, of course, lost all other issues, and resembled a campaign only in that it was something filling the hiatus between nomination and election.

Stephen Byerley did not allow the fussy little man to distract him. He remained comfortably unperturbed by the uniforms in the background. Outside the house, past the line of grim guards, reporters and photographers waited according to the tradition of the caste. One enterprising 'visor station even had a scanner focused on the blank entrance to the prosecutor's unpretentious home, while a synthetically excited announcer filled in with inflated commentary.

The fussy little man advanced. He held forward a rich, complicated sheet. "This, Mr. Byerley, is a court order authorizing me to search these premises for the presence of illegal . . . uh . . . mechanical men or robots of any description."

Byerley half rose, and took the paper. He glanced at it indifferently, and smiled as he handed it back. "All in order. Go ahead. Do your job. Mrs. Hoppen"—to his housekeeper, who appeared reluctantly from the next room—"please go with them, and help out if you can."

The little man, whose name was Harroway, hesitated, produced an unmistakable blush, failed completely to catch Byerley's eyes, and muttered, "Come on," to the two policemen.

He was back in ten minutes.

"Through?" questioned Byerley, in just the tone of a person who is not particularly interested in the question, or its answer.

Harroway cleared his throat, made a bad start in falsetto, and began again, angrily, "Look here, Mr. Byerley, our special instructions were to search the house very thoroughly."

"And haven't you?"

"We were told exactly what to look for."

"Yes?"

"In short, Mr. Byerley, and not to put too fine a point on it, we were told to search you."

"Me?" said the prosecutor with a broadening smile. "And how do you intend to do that?"

"We have a Penet-radiation unit—"

"Then I'm to have my X-ray photograph taken, hey? You have the authority?"

"You saw my warrant."

"May I see it again?"

Harroway, his forehead shining with considerably more than mere enthusiasm, passed it over a second time.

Byerley said evenly, "I read here as the description of what you are to search; I quote: 'the dwelling place belonging to Stephen Allen Byerley, located at 355 Willow Grove, Evanstron, together with any garage, storehouse or other structures or buildings thereto appertaining, together with all grounds thereto appertaining' . . . um . . . and so on. Quite in order. But, my good man, it doesn't say anything about searching my interior. I am not part of the premises. You may search my clothes if you think I've got a robot hidden in my pocket."

Harroway had no doubt on the point of to whom he owed his job. He did not propose to be backward, given a chance to earn a much better—i.e., more highly paid—job.

He said, in a faint echo of bluster, "Look here. I'm allowed to search the furniture in your house, and anything else I find in it. You are in it, aren't you?"

"A remarkable observation. I *am* in it. But I'm not a piece of furniture. As a citizen of adult responsibility—I have the psychiatric certificate proving that—I have certain rights under the Regional Articles. Searching me would come under the heading of violating my Right of Privacy. That paper isn't sufficient."

"Sure, but if you're a robot, you don't have Right of Privacy."

"True enough—but that paper still isn't sufficient. It recognizes me implicitly as a human being."

"Where?" Harroway snatched at it.

"Where it says 'the dwelling place belonging to' and so on. A robot cannot own property. And you may tell your employer, Mr. Harroway, that if he tries to issue a similar paper which does *not* implicitly recognize me as a human being, he will be immediately faced with a restraining injunction and a civil suit which will make it necessary for him to *prove* me a robot by means of information *now* in his possession, or else to pay a whopping penalty for an attempt to deprive me unduly of my Rights under the Regional Articles. You'll tell him that, won't you?"

Harroway marched to the door. He turned. "You're a slick lawyer—" His hand was in his pocket. For a short moment, he stood there. Then he left, smiled in the direction of the 'visor scanner, still playing away—waved to the reporters, and shouted, "We'll have something for you tomorrow, boys. No kidding."

In his ground car, he settled back, removed the tiny mechanism from his pocket and carefully inspected it. It was the first time he had ever taken a photograph by X-ray reflection. He hoped he had done it correctly.

Quinn and Byerley had never met face-to-face alone. But visorphone was pretty close to it. In fact, accepted literally, perhaps the phrase was accurate, even if to each, the other were merely the light and dark pattern of a bank of photocells.

It was Quinn who had initiated the call. It was Quinn, who spoke first, and without particular ceremony, "Thought you would like to know, Byerley, that I intend to make public the fact that you're wearing a protective shield against Penet-radiation."

"That so? In that case, you've probably already made it public. I have a notion our enterprising press representatives have been tapping my various communication lines for quite a while. I know they have my office lines full of holes; which is why I've dug in at my home these last weeks." Byerley was friendly, almost chatty.

Quinn's lips tightened slightly, "This call is shielded—thoroughly. I'm making it at a certain personal risk."

"So I should imagine. Nobody knows you're behind this campaign. At least, nobody knows it officially. Nobody doesn't know it unofficially. I wouldn't worry. So I wear a protective shield? I suppose you found that out when your puppy dog's Penet-radiation photograph, the other day, turned out to be overexposed."

"You realize, Byerley, that it would be pretty obvious to everyone that you don't dare face X-ray analysis."

"Also that you, or your men, attempted illegal invasion of my Right of Privacy."

"The devil they'll care for that."

"They might. It's rather symbolic of our two campaigns, isn't it?

You have little concern with the rights of the individual citizen. I have great concern. I will not submit to X-ray analysis, because I wish to maintain my Rights on principle. Just as I'll maintain the rights of others when elected."

"That will no doubt make a very interesting speech, but no one will believe you. A little too high-sounding to be true. Another thing," a sudden, crisp change, "the personnel in your home was not complete the other night."

"In what way?"

"According to the report," he shuffled papers before him that were just within the range of vision of the visiplate, "there was one person missing—a cripple."

"As you say," said Byerley, tonelessly, "a cripple. My old teacher, who lives with me and who is now in the country—and has been for two months. A 'much-needed rest' is the usual expression applied in the case. He has your permission?"

"Your teacher? A scientist of sorts?"

"A lawyer once—before he was a cripple. He has a government license as a research biophysicist, with a laboratory of his own, and a complete description of the work he's doing filed with the proper authorities, to whom I can refer you. The work is minor, but is a harmless and engaging hobby for a—poor cripple. I am being as helpful as I can, you see."

"I see. And what does this . . . teacher . . . know about robot manufacture?"

"I couldn't judge the extent of his knowledge in a field with which I am unacquainted."

"He wouldn't have access to positronic brains?"

"Ask your friends at U. S. Robots. They'd be the ones to know."

"I'll put it shortly, Byerley. Your crippled teacher is the real Stephen Byerley. You are his robot creation. We can prove it. It was he who was in the automobile accident, not you. There will be ways of checking the records."

"Really? Do so, then. My best wishes."

"And we can search your so-called teacher's 'country place,' and see what we can find there."

"Well, not quite, Quinn." Byerley smiled broadly. "Unfortunately for you, my so-called teacher is a sick man. His country place is his place of rest. His Right of Privacy as a citizen of adult responsibility is naturally even stronger, under the circumstances. You won't be able to obtain a warrant to enter his grounds without showing just cause. However, I'd be the last to prevent you from trying."

There was a pause of moderate length, and then Quinn leaned forward, so that his imaged-face expanded and the fine lines on his forehead were visible, "Byerley, why do you carry on? You can't be elected."

"Can't I?"

"Do you think you can? Do you suppose that your failure to make any attempt to disprove the robot charge—when you could easily, by breaking one of the Three Laws—does anything but convince the people that you *are* a robot?"

"All I see so far is that from being a rather vaguely known, but still largely obscure metropolitan lawyer, I have now become a world figure. You're a good publicist."

"But you *are* a robot."

"So it's been said, but not proven."

"It's been proven sufficiently for the electorate."

"Then relax—you've won."

"Good-by," said Quinn, with his first touch of viciousness, and the visorphone slammed off.

"Good-by," said Byerley imperturbably, to the blank plate.

Byerley brought his "teacher" back the week before election. The air car dropped quickly in an obscure part of the city.

"You'll stay here till after election," Byerley told him. "It would be better to have you out of the way if things take a bad turn."

The hoarse voice that twisted painfully out of John's crooked mouth might have had accents of concern in it. "There's danger of violence?"

"The Fundamentalists threaten it, so I suppose there is, in a theoretical sense. But I really don't expect it. The Fundies have no real power. They're just the continuous irritant factor that might stir up a riot after a while. You don't mind staying here? Please. I won't be myself if I have to worry about you."

"Oh, I'll stay. You still think it will go well?"

"I'm sure of it. No one bothered you at the place?"

"No one. I'm certain."

"And your part went well?"

"Well enough. There'll be no trouble there."

"Then take care of yourself, and watch the televisor tomorrow, John." Byerley pressed the gnarled hand that rested on his.

Lenton's forehead was a furrowed study in suspense. He had the completely unenviable job of being Byerley's campaign manager in a campaign that wasn't a campaign, for a person that refused to reveal his strategy, and refused to accept his manager's.

"You can't!" It was his favorite phrase. It had become his only phrase. "I tell you, Steve, you can't!"

He threw himself in front of the prosecutor, who was spending his time, leafing through the typed pages of his speech.

"Put that down, Steve. Look, that mob has been organized by the Fundies. You won't get a hearing. You'll be stoned more likely. Why do you have to make a speech before an audience? What's wrong with a recording, a visual recording?"

"You want me to win the election, don't you?" asked Byerley, mildly.

"Win the election! You're not going to win, Steve. I'm trying to save your life."

"Oh, I'm not in danger."

"He's not in danger. He's not in danger." Lenton made a queer, rasping sound in his throat. "You mean you're getting out on that balcony in front of fifty thousand crazy crackpots and try to talk sense to them—on a balcony like a medieval dictator?"

Byerley consulted his watch. "In about five minutes—as soon as the television lines are free."

Lenton's answering remark was not quite transliterable.

The crowd filled a roped off area of the city. Trees and houses seemed to grow out of a mass-human foundation. And by ultrawave, the rest of the world watched. It was a purely local election, but it had a world audience just the same. Byerley thought of that and smiled.

But there was nothing to smile at in the crowd itself. There were banners and streamers, ringing every possible change on his supposed roboticity. The hostile attitude rose thickly and tangibly into the atmosphere.

From the start the speech was not successful. It competed against the inchoate mob howl and the rhythmic cries of the Fundie claques that formed mob-islands within the mob. Byerley spoke on, slowly, unemotionally—

Inside, Lenton clutched his hair and groaned—and waited for the blood.

There was a writhing in the front ranks. An angular citizen with popping eyes, and clothes too short for the lank length of his limbs, was pulling to the fore. A policeman dived after him, making slow, struggling passage. Byerley waved the latter off, angrily.

The thin man was directly under the balcony. His words tore unheard against the roar.

Byerley leaned forward. "What do you say? If you have a legitimate question, I'll answer it." He turned to a flanking guard. "Bring that man up here."

There was a tensing in the crowd. Cries of "Quiet" started in various parts of the mob, and rose to a bedlam, then toned down raggedly. The thin man, red-faced and panting, faced Byerley.

Byerley said, "Have you a question?"

The thin man stared, and said in a cracked voice, "Hit me!"

With sudden energy, he thrust out his chin at an angle. "Hit me! You say you're not a robot. Prove it. You can't hit a human, you monster."

There was a queer, flat, dead silence. Byerley's voice punctured it. "I have no reason to hit you."

The thin man was laughing wildly. "You *can't* hit me. You *won't* hit me. You're not a human. You're a monster, a make-believe man."

And Stephen Byerley, tight-lipped, in the face of thousands who watched in person and the millions who watched by screen, drew back his fist and caught the man crackingly upon the chin. The challenger went over backwards in sudden collapse, with nothing on his face but blank, blank surprise.

Byerley said, "I'm sorry. Take him in and see that he's comfortable. I want to speak to him when I'm through."

And when Dr. Calvin, from her reserved space, turned her automobile and drove off, only one reporter had recovered sufficiently from the shock to race after her, and shout an unheard question.

Susan Calvin called over her shoulder, "He's human."

That was enough. The reporter raced away in his own direction.

The rest of the speech might be described as "Spoken but not heard."

Dr. Calvin and Stephen Byerley met once again—a week before he took the oath of office as mayor. It was late—past midnight.

Dr. Calvin said, "You don't look tired."

The mayor-elect smiled. "I may stay up for a while. Don't tell Quinn."

"I shan't. But that was an interesting story of Quinn's, since you mention him. It's a shame to have spoiled it. I suppose you knew his theory?"

"Parts of it."

"It was highly dramatic. Stephen Byerley was a young lawyer, a powerful speaker, a great idealist—and with a certain flair for biophysics. Are you interested in robotics, Mr. Byerley?"

"Only in the legal aspects."

"*This* Stephen Byerley was. But here was an accident. Byerley's wife died; he himself, worse. His legs were gone; his face was gone; his voice was gone. Part of his mind was—bent. He would not submit to plastic surgery. He retired from the world, legal career gone—only his intelligence, and his hands left. Somehow he could obtain positronic brains, even a complex one, one which had the greatest capacity of forming judgments in ethical problems—which is the highest robotic function so far developed.

"He grew a body about it. Trained it to be everything he would have been and was no longer. He sent it out into the world as Stephen Byerley, remaining behind himself as the old, crippled teacher that no one ever saw—"

"Unfortunately," said the mayor-elect, "I ruined all that by hitting a man. The papers say it was your official verdict on the occasion that I was human."

"How did that happen? Do you mind telling me? It couldn't have been accidental."

"It wasn't entirely. Quinn did most of the work. My men started quietly spreading the fact that I had never hit a man; that I was unable to hit a man; that to fail to do so under provocation would be sure proof that I was a robot. So I arranged for a silly speech in public, with all sorts of publicity overtones, and almost inevitably, some fool fell for it. In its essence, it was what I call a shyster trick. One in which the artificial atmosphere which has been created does all the work. Of course, the emotional effects made my election certain, as intended."

The robopsychologist nodded. "I see you intrude on my field—as every politician must, I suppose. But I'm very sorry it turned out this way. I like robots. I like them considerably better than I do human beings. If a robot can be created capable of being a civil executive, I think he'd make the best one possible. By the Laws of Robotics, he'd be incapable of harming humans, incapable of tyranny, of corruption, of stupidity, of prejudice. And after he had served a decent term, he would leave, even though he were immortal, because it would be impossible for him to hurt humans by letting them know that a robot had ruled them. It would be most ideal."

"Except that a robot might fail due to the inherent inadequacies of his brain. The positronic brain has never equalled the complexities of the human brain."

"He would have advisers. Not even a human brain is capable of governing without assistance."

Byerley considered Susan Calvin with grave interest. "Why do you smile, Dr. Calvin?"

"I smile because Mr. Quinn didn't think of everything."

"You mean there could be more to that story of his."

"Only a little. For the three months before election, this Stephen Byerley that Mr. Quinn spoke about, this broken man, was in the country for some mysterious reason. He returned in time for that famous speech of yours. And after all, what the old cripple did once, he could do a second time, particularly where the second job is very simple in comparison to the first."

"I don't quite understand."

Dr. Calvin rose and smoothed her dress. She was obviously ready to leave. "I mean there is one time when a robot may strike a human being without breaking the First Law. Just one time."

"And when is that?"

Dr. Calvin was at the door. She said quietly, "When the human to be struck is merely another robot."

She smiled broadly, her thin face glowing. "Good-by, Mr. Byerley. I hope to vote for you five years from now—for co-ordinator."

Stephen Byerley chuckled. "I must reply that that is a somewhat farfetched idea."

The door closed behind her.

The Evitable Conflict

The Co-ordinator, in his private study, had that medieval curiosity, a fireplace. To be sure, the medieval man might not have recognized it as such, since it had no functional significance. The quiet, licking flame lay in an insulated recess behind clear quartz.

The logs were ignited at long distance through a trifling diversion of the energy beam that fed the public buildings of the city. The same button that controlled the ignition first dumped the ashes of the previous fire, and allowed for the entrance of fresh wood. —It was a thoroughly domesticated fireplace, you see.

But the fire itself was real. It was wired for sound, so that you could hear the crackle and, of course, you could watch it leap in the air stream that fed it.

The Co-ordinator's ruddy glass reflected, in miniature, the discreet gamboling of the flame, and, in even further miniature, it was reflected in each of his brooding pupils.

—And in the frosty pupils of his guest, Dr. Susan Calvin of U. S. Robots and Mechanical Men Corporation.

The Co-ordinator said, "I did not ask you here entirely for social purposes, Susan."

"I did not think you did, Stephen," she replied.

"—And yet I don't quite know how to phrase my problem. On the one hand, it can be nothing at all. On the other, it can mean the end of humanity."

"I have come across so many problems, Stephen, that presented the same alternative. I think all problems do."

"Really? Then judge this— World Steel reports an overproduction of twenty thousand long tons. The Mexican Canal is two months behind schedule. The mercury mines at Almaden have experienced a production deficiency since last spring, while the Hydroponics plant at Tientsin has been laying men off. These items happen to come to mind at the moment. There is more of the same sort."

"Are these things serious? I'm not economist enough to trace the fearful consequences of such things."

"In themselves, they are not serious. Mining experts can be sent to Almaden, if the situation were to get worse. Hydroponics engineers can be used in Java or in Ceylon, if there are too many at Tientsin. Twenty thousand long tons of steel won't fill more than a few days of world demand, and the opening of the Mexican Canal two months later than the planned date is of little moment. It's the Machines that worry me;—I've spoken to your Director of Research about them already."

"To Vincent Silver? —He hasn't mentioned anything about it to me."

"I asked him to speak to no one. Apparently, he hasn't."

"And what did he tell you?"

"Let me put that item in its proper place. I want to talk about the Machines first. And I want to talk about them to you, because you're the only one in the world who understands robots well enough to help me now. —May I grow philosophical?"

"For this evening, Stephen, you may talk how you please and of what you please, provided you tell me first what you intend to prove."

"That such small unbalances in the perfection of our system of supply and demand, as I have mentioned, may be the first step towards the final war."

"Hmp. Proceed."

Susan Calvin did not allow herself to relax, despite the designed comfort of the chair she sat in. Her cold, thin-lipped face and her flat, even voice were becoming accentuated with the years. And although Stephen Byerley was one man she could like and trust, she was almost seventy and the cultivated habits of a lifetime are not easily broken.

"Every period of human development, Susan," said the Co-ordinator, "has had its own particular type of human conflict—its own variety of problem that, apparently, could be settled only by force. And each time, frustratingly enough, force never really settled the problem. Instead, it persisted through a series of conflicts, then vanished of itself,—what's the expression,—ah, yes not with a bang, but a whimper, as the economic and social environment changed. And then, new problems, and a new series of wars. —Apparently endlessly cyclic.

"Consider relatively modern times. There were the series of dynastic wars in the sixteenth to eighteenth centuries, when the most important question in Europe was whether the houses of Hapsburg or Valois-Bourbon were to rule the continent. It was one of those 'inevitable conflicts,' since Europe could obviously not exist half one and half the other.

"Except that it did, and no war ever wiped out the one and established the other, until the rise of a new social atmosphere in France in 1789 tumbled first the Bourbons and, eventually, the Hapsburgs down the dusty chute to history's incinerator.

"And in those same centuries there were the more barbarous religious wars, which revolved about the important question of whether Europe was to be Catholic or Protestant. Half and half she could not be. It was 'inevitable' that the sword decide. —Except that it didn't. In England, a new industrialism was growing, and on the continent, a new nationalism. Half and half Europe remains to this day and no one cares much.

"In the nineteenth and twentieth centuries, there was a cycle of nationalist-imperalist wars, when the most important question in the world was which portions of Europe would control the economic resources and consuming capacity of which portions of non-Europe. All non-Europe obviously could not exist part English and part French and part German and so on. —Until the forces of nationalism spread sufficiently, so that non-Europe ended what all the wars could not, and decided it could exist quite comfortably *all* non-European.

"And so we have a pattern—"

"Yes, Stephen, you make it plain," said Susan Calvin. "These are not very profound observations."

"No. —But then, it is the obvious which is so difficult to see most of the time. People say 'It's as plain as the nose on your face.' But how much of the nose on your face can you see, unless someone holds a mirror up to you? In the twentieth century, Susan, we started a new cycle of wars—what shall I call them? Ideological wars? The emotions of religion applied to economic systems, rather than to extra-natural ones? Again the wars were 'inevitable' and this time there were atomic weapons, so that mankind could no longer live through its torment to the inevitable wasting away of inevitability. —And positronic robots came.

"They came in time, and, with it and alongside it, interplanetary travel. —So that it no longer seemed so important whether the world was Adam Smith or Karl Marx. Neither made very much sense under the new circumstances. Both had to adapt and they ended in almost the same place."

"A deus ex machina, then, in a double sense," said Dr. Calvin, dryly.

The Co-ordinator smiled gently, "I have never heard you pun before, Susan, but you are correct. And yet there was another danger. The ending of every other problem had merely given birth to another. Our new world wide robot economy may develop its own problems, and for that reason we have the Machines. The Earth's economy is stable, and will *remain* stable, because it is based upon the decisions of calculating machines that have the good of humanity at heart through the overwhelming force of the First Law of Robotics."

Stephen Byerley continued, "And although the Machines are nothing but the vastest conglomeration of calculating circuits ever invented, they are still robots within the meaning of the First Law, and so our Earth wide economy is in accord with the best interests of Man. The population of Earth knows that there will be no unemployment, no overproduction or shortages. Waste and famine are words in history books. And so the question of ownership of the means of production becomes obsolescent. Whoever owned them (if such a phrase has meaning), a man, a group, a nation, or all mankind, they could be utilized only as the Machines directed. —Not because men were forced to but because it was the wisest course and men knew it.

"It puts an end to war—not only to the last cycle of wars, but to the next and to all of them. Unless—"

A long pause, and Dr. Calvin encouraged him by repetition. "Unless—"

The fire crouched and skittered along a log, then popped up.

"Unless," said the Co-ordinator, "the Machines don't fulfill their function."

"I see. And that is where those trifling maladjustments come in which you mentioned awhile ago—steel, hydroponics and so on."

"Exactly. Those errors should not be. Dr. Silver tells me they *cannot* be."

"Does he deny the facts? How unusual!"

"No, he admits the facts, of course. I do him an injustice. What he denies is that any error in the machine is responsible for the so-called (his phrase) errors in the answers. He claims that the Machines are self correcting and that it would violate the fundamental laws of nature for an error to exist in the circuits of relays. And so I said—"

"And you said, 'Have your boys check them and make sure, anyway.'"

"Susan, you read my mind. It was what I said, and he said he couldn't."

"Too busy?"

"No, he said that no human could. He was frank about it. He told me, and I hope I understand him properly, that the Machines are a gigantic extrapolation. Thus— A team of mathematicians work several years calculating a positronic brain equipped to do certain similar acts of calculation. Using this brain they make further calculations to create a still more complicated brain, which they use again to make one still more complicated and so on. According to Silver, what we call the Machines are the result of ten such steps."

"Ye-es, that sounds familiar. Fortunately, I'm not a mathematician. —Poor Vincent. He is a young man. The Directors before him had no such problems. Nor had I. Perhaps roboticists these days can no longer understand our own creations."

"Apparently not. The Machines are not super-brains in Sunday supplement sense,—although they are so pictured in the Sunday supplements. It is merely that in their own particular province of collecting and analyzing a nearly infinite number of data and relationships thereof, in nearly infinitesimal time, they have progressed beyond the possibility of detailed human control.

"And then I tried something else. I actually asked the Machine. In the strictest secrecy, we fed it the original data involved in the steel decision, its own answer, and the actual developments since,—

the overproduction, that is,—and asked for an explanation of the discrepancy."

"Good, and what was its answer?"

"I can quote you that word for word: 'The matter admits of no explanation.'"

"And how did Vincent interpret that?"

"In two ways. Either we had not given the Machine enough data to allow a definite answer, which was unlikely. Dr. Silver admitted that. —Or else, it was impossible for the Machine to admit that it could give any answer to data which implied that it could harm a human being. This, naturally, is implied by the First Law. And then Dr. Silver recommended that I see you."

Susan Calvin looked very tired, "I'm old, Stephen. There was a time when you wanted to make me Director of Research and I refused. I wasn't young then, either, and I did not wish the responsibility. They let young Silver have it and that satisfied me; but what good is it, if I am dragged into such messes.

"Stephen, let me state my position. My researches do indeed involve the interpretation of robot behavior in the light of the Three Laws of Robotics. Here, now, we have these incredible calculating machines. They are positronic robots and therefore obey the Laws of Robotics. But they lack personality; that is, their functions are extremely limited. —Must be, since they are so specialized. Therefore, there is very little room for the interplay of the Laws, and my one method of attack is virtually useless. In short, I don't know that I can help you, Stephen."

The Co-ordinator laughed shortly, "Nevertheless, let me tell you the rest. Let me give you *my* theories, and perhaps you will then be able to tell me whether they are possible in the light of robopsychology."

"By all means. Go ahead."

"Well, since the Machines are giving the wrong answers, then, assuming that they cannot be in error, there is only one possibility. *They are being given the wrong data!* In other words, the trouble is human, and not robotic. So I took my recent planetary inspection tour—"

"From which you have just returned to New York."

"Yes. It was necessary, you see, since there are four Machines, one handling each of the Planetary Regions. And *all four are yielding imperfect results.*"

"Oh, but that follows, Stephen. If any one of the Machines is imperfect, that will automatically reflect in the result of the other three, since each of the others will assume as part of the data on which they base their own decisions, the perfection of the imperfect fourth. With a false assumption, they will yield false answers."

"Uh-huh. So it seemed to me. Now, I have here the records of my interviews with each of the Regional Vice-Co-ordinators. Would you look through them with me? —Oh, and first, have you heard of the 'Society for Humanity'?"

"Umm, yes. They are an outgrowth of the Fundamentalists who have kept U. S. Robots from ever employing positronic robots on the grounds of unfair labor competition and so on. The 'Society for Humanity' itself is anti-Machine, is it not?"

"Yes, yes, but— Well, you will see. Shall we begin? We'll start with the Eastern Region."

"As you say—"

The Eastern Region:
    a—Area: 7,500,000 square miles
    b—Population: 1,700,000,000
    c—Capital: Shanghai

Ching Hso-lin's great-grandfather had been killed in the Japanese invasion of the old Chinese Republic, and there had been no one beside his dutiful children to mourn his loss or even to know he was lost. Ching Hso-lin's grandfather had survived the civil war of the late forties, but there had been no one beside *his* dutiful children to know or care of that.

And yet Ching Hso-lin was a Regional Vice-Co-ordinator, with the economic welfare of half the people of Earth in his care.

Perhaps it was with the thought of all that in mind, that Ching had two maps as the only ornaments on the wall of his office. One was an old hand-drawn affair tracing out an acre or two of land, and marked with the now outmoded pictographs of old China. A little creek trickled aslant the faded markings and there were the delicate pictorial indications of lowly huts, in one of which Ching's grandfather had been born.

The other map was a huge one, sharply delineated, with all markings in neat Cyrillic characters. The red boundary that marked the Eastern Region swept within its grand confines all that had once been China, India, Burma, Indo-China, and Indonesia. On it, within the old province of Szechuan, so light and gentle that none could see it, was the little mark placed there by Ching which indicated the location of his ancestral farm.

Ching stood before these maps as he spoke to Stephen Byerley in precise English, "No one knows better than you, Mr. Co-ordinator, that my job, to a large extent, is a sinecure. It carries with it a certain social standing, and I represent a convenient focal point for administration, but otherwise it is the Machine! —The Machine does all the work. What did you think, for instance, of the Tientsin Hydroponics works?"

"Tremendous!" said Byerley.

"It is but one of dozens, and not the largest. Shanghai, Calcutta, Batavia, Bangkok— They are widely spread and they are the answer to feeding the billion and three quarters of the East."

"And yet," said Byerley, "you have an umemployment problem there at Tientsin. Can you be over-producing? It is incongruous to think of Asia as suffering from too much food."

Ching's dark eyes crinkled at the edges. "No. It has not come to that yet. It is true that over the last few months, several vats at Tientsin have been shut down, but it is nothing serious. The men have been released only temporarily and those who do not care to work in other fields have been shipped to Colombo in Ceylon, where a new plant is being put into operation."

"But why should the vats be closed down?"

Ching smiled gently, "You do not know much of hydroponics, I see. Well, that is not surprising. You are a Northerner, and there soil farming is still profitable. It is fashionable in the North to think of hydroponics, when it is thought of at all, as a device for growing turnips in a chemical solution, and so it is—in an infinitely complicated way.

"In the first place, by far the largest crop we deal with (and the percentage is growing) is yeast. We have upward of two thousand strains of yeast in production and new strains are added monthly. The basic food-chemicals of the various yeasts are nitrates and phosphates among the inorganics together with proper amounts of the trace metals needed, down to the fractional parts per million of boron and molybdenum which are required. The organic matter is mostly sugar mixtures derived from the hydrolysis of cellulose, but, in addition, there are various food factors which must be added.

"For a successful hydroponics industry—one which can feed seventeen hundred million people—we must engage in an immense reforestation program throughout the East; we must have huge wood-conversion plants to deal with our southern jungles; we must have power, and steel, and chemical synthetics above all."

"Why the last, sir?"

"Because, Mr. Byerley, these strains of yeast have each their peculiar properties. We have developed, as I said, two thousand strains. The beef steak you thought you ate today was yeast. The frozen fruit confection you had for dessert was iced yeast. We have filtered yeast juice with the taste, appearance, and all the food value of milk.

"It is flavor, more than anything else, you see, that makes yeast feeding popular and for the sake of flavor we have developed artificial, domesticated strains that can no longer support themselves on a basic diet of salts and sugar. One needs biotin; another needs pteroylglutamic acid; still others need seventeen different amino acids supplied them as well as all the Vitamins B, but one (and yet it is popular and we cannot, with economic sense, abandon it)—"

Byerley stirred in his seat, "To what purpose do you tell me all this?"

"You asked me, sir, why men are out of work in Tientsin. I have a little more to explain. It is not only that we must have these various and varying foods for our yeast; but there remains the complicating factor of popular fads with passing time; and of the possibility of the development of new strains with the new requirements and new popularity. All this must be foreseen, and the Machine does the job—"

"But not perfectly."

"Not very *im*perfectly, in view of the complications I have mentioned. Well, then, a few thousand workers in Tientsin are temporarily out of a job. But, consider this, the amount of waste in this past year (waste that is, in terms of either defective supply or defective demand) amounts to not one-tenth of one percent of our total productive turnover. I consider that—"

"Yet in the first years of the Machine, the figure was nearer one-thousandth of one percent."

"Ah, but in the decade since the Machine began its operations in real earnest, we have made use of it to increase our old pre-Machine yeast industry twenty-fold. You expect imperfections to increase with complications, though—"

"Though?"

"There *was* the curious instance of Rama Vrasayana."

"What happened to him?"

"Vrasayana was in charge of a brine-evaporation plant for the production of iodine, with which yeast can do without, but human beings not. His plant was forced into receivership."

"Really? And through what agency?"

"Competition, believe it or not. In general, one of the chiefest functions of the Machine's analyses is to indicate the most efficient distribution of our producing units. It is obviously faulty to have areas insufficiently serviced, so that the transportation costs account for too great a percentage of the overhead. Similarly, it is faulty to have an area too well serviced, so that factories must be run at lowered capacities, or else compete harmfully with one another. In the case of Vrasayana, another plant was established in the same city, and with a more efficient extracting system."

"The Machine permitted it?"

"Oh, certainly. That is not surprising. The new system is becoming widespread. The surprise is that the Machine failed to warn Vrasayana to renovate or combine. —Still, no matter. Vrasayana accepted a job as engineer in the new plant, and if his responsibility and pay are now less, he is not actually suffering. The workers found employment easily; the old plant has been converted to—something or other. Something useful. We left it all to the Machine."

"And otherwise you have no complaints."

"None!"

The Tropic Region:
   a—Area: 22,000,000 square miles
   b—Population: 500,000,000
   c—Capital: Capital City

The map in Lincoln Ngoma's office was far from the model of neat precision of the one in Ching's Shanghai dominion. The boundaries of Ngoma's Tropic Region were stencilled in dark, wide brown and swept about a gorgeous interior labelled "jungle" and "desert" and "here be Elephants and all Manner of Strange Beasts."

It had much to sweep, for in land area the Tropic Region enclosed most of two continents: all of South America north of Argentina and all of Africa south of the Atlas. It included North

America south of the Rio Grande as well, and even Arabia and Iran in Asia. It was the reverse of the Eastern Region. Where the ant hives of the Orient crowded half of humanity into 15 percent of the land mass, the Tropics stretched its 15 percent of Humanity over nearly half of all the land in the world.

But it was growing. It was the one Region whose population increase through immigration exceeded that through births. —And for all who came it had use.

To Ngoma, Stephen Byerley seemed like one of these immigrants, a pale searcher for the creative work of carving a harsh environment into the softness necessary for man, and he felt some of that automatic contempt of the strong man born to the strong Tropics for the unfortunate pallards of the colder suns.

The Tropics had the newest capital city on Earth, and it was called simply that: "Capital City," in the sublime confidence of youth. It spread brightly over the fertile uplands of Nigeria and outside Ngoma's windows, far below, was life and color; the bright, bright sun and the quick, drenching showers. Even the squawking of the rainbowed birds was brisk and the stars were hard pinpoints in the sharp night.

Ngoma laughed. He was a big, dark man, strong faced and handsome.

"Sure," he said, and his English was colloquial and mouthfilling, "the Mexican Canal is overdue. What the hell? It will get finished just the same, old boy."

"It was doing well up to the last half year."

Ngoma looked at Byerley and slowly crunched his teeth over the end of a big cigar, spitting out one end and lighting the other, "Is this an official investigation, Byerley? What's going on?"

"Nothing. Nothing at all. It's just my function as Co-ordinator to be curious."

"Well, if it's just that you are filling in a dull moment, the truth is that we're always short on labor. There's lots going on in the Tropics. The Canal is only one of them—"

"But doesn't your Machine predict the amount of labor available for the Canal,—allowing for all the competing projects?"

Ngoma placed one hand behind his neck and blew smoke rings at the ceiling, "It was a little off."

"Is it often a little off?"

"Not oftener than you would expect. —We don't expect too

much of it, Byerley. We feed it data. We take its results. We do what it says. —But it's just a convenience; just a labor-saving device. We could do without it, if we had to. Maybe not as well. Maybe not as quickly. But we'd get there.

"We've got confidence out here, Byerley, and that's the secret. Confidence! We've got new land that's been waiting for us for thousands of years, while the rest of the world was being ripped apart in the lousy fumblings of pre-atomic time. We don't have to eat yeast like the Eastern boys, and we don't have to worry about the stale dregs of the last century like you Northerners.

"We've wiped out the tsetse fly and the Anopheles mosquito, and people find they can live in the sun and like it, now. We've thinned down the jungles and found soil; we've watered the deserts and found gardens. We've got coal and oil in untouched fields, and minerals out of count.

"Just step back. That's all we ask the rest of the world to do. —Step back, and let us work."

Byerley said, prosaically, "But the Canal,—it was on schedule six months ago. What happened?"

Ngoma spread his hands, "Labor troubles." He felt through a pile of papers skeltered about his desk and gave it up.

"Had something on the matter here," he muttered, "but never mind. There was a work shortage somewhere in Mexico once on the question of women. There weren't enough women in the neighborhood. It seemed no one had thought of feeding sexual data to the Machine."

He stopped to laugh, delightedly, then sobered, "Wait a while. I think I've got it. —Villafranca!"

"Villafranca?"

"Francisco Villafranca. —He was the engineer in charge. Now let me straighten it out. Something happened and there was a cave-in. Right. Right. That was it. Nobody died, as I remember, but it made a hell of a mess. —Quite a scandal."

"Oh?"

"There was some mistake in his calculations. —Or at least, the Machine said so. They fed through Villafranca's data, assumptions, and so on. The stuff he had started with. The answers came out differently. It seems the answers Villafranca had used didn't take account of the effect of a heavy rainfall on the contours of the cut. —Or something like that. I'm not an engineer, you understand.

"Anyway, Villafranca put up a devil of a squawk. He claimed the Machine's answer had been different the first time. That he had followed the Machine faithfully. Then he quit! We offered to hold him on—reasonable doubt, previous work satisfactory, and all that—in a subordinate position, of course—had to do that much—mistakes can't go unnoticed—bad for discipline— Where was I?"

"You offered to hold him on."

"Oh yes. He refused. —Well, take all in all, we're two months behind. Hell, that's nothing."

Byerley stretched out his hand and let the fingers tap lightly on the desk, "Villafranca blamed the Machine, did he?"

"Well, he wasn't going to blame himself, was he? Let's face it; human nature is an old friend of ours. Besides, I remember something else now— Why the hell can't I find documents when I want them? My filing system isn't worth a damn— This Villafranca was a member of one of your Northern organizations. Mexico is too close to the North! that's part of the trouble."

"Which organization are you speaking of?"

"The Society for Humanity, they call it. He used to attend the annual conferences in New York, Vallafranca did. Bunch of crackpots, but harmless. —They don't like the Machines; claim they're destroying human initiative. So naturally Villafranca would blame the Machine. —Don't understand that group myself. Does Capital City look as if the human race were running out of initiative?"

And Capital City stretched out in golden glory under a golden sun,—the newest and youngest creation of *Homo metropolis*.

The European Region:
   a—Area: 4,000,000 square miles
   b—Population: 300,000,000
   c—Capital: Geneva

The European Region was an anomaly in several ways. In area, it was far the smallest; not one fifth the size of the Tropic Region in area, and not one fifth the size of the Eastern Region in population. Geographically, it was only somewhat similar to pre-Atomic Europe, since it excluded what had once been European Russia and what had once been the British Isles, while it included the Mediterranean coasts of Africa and Asia, and, in a queer jump across the Atlantic, Argentina, Chile, and Uruguay as well.

Nor was it likely to improve its relative status vis-à-vis the other regions of Earth, except for what vigor the South American provinces lent it. Of all the Regions, it alone showed a positive population decline over the past half century. It alone had not seriously expanded its productive facilities, or offered anything radically new to human culture.

"Europe," said Madame Szegeczowska, in her soft French, "is essentially an economic appendage of the Northern Region. We know it, and it doesn't matter."

And as though in resigned acceptance of a lack of individuality, there was no map of Europe on the wall of the Madame Co-ordinator's office.

"And yet," pointed out Byerley, "you have a Machine of your own, and you are certainly under no economic pressure from across the ocean."

"A Machine! Bah!" She shrugged her delicate shoulders, and allowed a thin smile to cross her little face as she tamped out a cigarette with long fingers. "Europe is a sleepy place. And such of our men as do not manage to emigrate to the Tropics are tired and sleepy along with it. You see for yourself that it is myself, a poor woman, to whom falls the task of being Vice-Co-ordinator. Well, fortunately, it is not a difficult job, and not much is expected of me.

"As for the Machine— What can it say but 'Do this and it will be best for you.' But what is best for us? Why, to be an economic appendage of the Northern Region.

"And is it so terrible? No wars! We live in peace—and it is pleasant after seven thousand years of war. We are old, monsieur. In our borders, we have the regions where Occidental civilization was cradled. We have Egypt and Mesopotamia; Crete and Syria; Asia Minor and Greece. —But old age is not necessarily an unhappy time. It can be a fruition—"

"Perhaps you are right," said Byerley, affably. "At least the tempo of life is not as intense as in the other Regions. It is a pleasant atmosphere."

"Is it not? —Tea is being brought, monsieur. If you will indicate your cream and sugar preferences, please. —Thank you."

She sipped gently, then continued, "It *is* pleasant. The rest of Earth is welcome to the continuing struggle. I find a parallel here; a very interesting one. There was a time when Rome was master of the world. It had adopted the culture and civilization of Greece; a

Greece which had never been united, which had ruined itself with war, and which was ending in a state of decadent squalor. Rome united it, brought it peace and let it live a life of secure non-glory. It occupied itself with its philosophies and its art, far from the clash of growth and war. It was a sort of death, but it was restful, and it lasted with minor breaks for some four hundred years."

"And yet," said Byerley, "Rome fell eventually, and the opium dream was over."

"There are no longer barbarians to overthrow civilization."

"We can be our own barbarians, Madame Szegeczowska. —Oh, I meant to ask you. The Almaden mercury mines have fallen off quite badly in production. Surely the ores are not declining more rapidly than anticipated?"

The little woman's gray eyes fastened shrewdly on Byerley, "Barbarians—the fall of civilization—possible failure of the Machine. Your thought processes are very transparent, monsieur."

"Are they?" Byerley smiled. "I see that I should have had men to deal with as hitherto. —You consider the Almaden affair to be the fault of the Machine?"

"Not at all, but I think you do. You, yourself, are a native of the Northern Region. The Central Co-ordination Office is at New York. —And I have noticed for quite a while that you Northerners lack somewhat of faith in the Machine."

"We do?"

"There is your 'Society for Humanity' which is strong in the North, but naturally fails to find many recruits in tired, old Europe, which is quite willing to let feeble Humanity alone for a while. Surely, you are one of the confident North and not one of the cynical old continent."

"This has a connection with Almaden?"

"Oh, yes, I think so. The mines are in the control of Consolidated Cinnabar, which is certainly a Northern company, with headquarters at Nikolaev. Personally, I wonder if the Board of Directors has been consulting the Machine at all. They said they had in our conference last month, and, of course, we have no evidence that they did not, but I wouldn't take the word of a Northerner in this matter —no offense intended—under any circumstances. —Nevertheless, I think it will have a fortunate ending."

"In what way, my dear madam?"

"You must understand that the economic irregularities of the last few months, which, although small as compared with the great storms of the past, are quite disturbing to our peace-drenched spirits, have caused considerable restiveness in the Spanish province. I understand that Consolidated Cinnabar is selling out to a group of native Spaniards. It is consoling. If we are economic vassals of the North, it is humiliating to have the fact advertised too blatantly. —And our people can be better trusted to follow the Machine."

"Then you think there will be no more trouble?"

"I am sure there will not be— In Almaden, at least."

The Northern Region:
    a—Area: 18,000,000 square miles
    b—Population: 800,000,000
    c—Capital: Ottawa

The Northern Region, in more ways than one, was at the top. This was exemplified quite well by the map in the Ottawa office of Vice-Co-ordinator Hiram Mackenzie, in which the North Pole was centered. Except for the enclave of Europe with its Scandinavian and Icelandic regions, all the Arctic area was within the Northern Region.

Roughly, it could be divided into two major areas. To the left on the map was all of North America above the Rio Grande. To the right was included all of what had once been the Soviet Union. Together these areas represented the centered power of the planet in the first years of the Atomic Age. Between the two was Great Britain, a tongue of the Region licking at Europe. Up at the top of the map, distorted into odd, huge shapes, were Australia and New Zealand, also member provinces of the Region.

Not all the changes of the past decades had yet altered the fact that the North was the economic ruler of the planet.

There was almost an ostentatious symbolism thereof in the fact that of the official Regional maps Byerley had seen, Mackenzie's alone showed all the Earth, as though the North feared no competition and needed no favoritism to point up its pre-eminence.

"Impossible," said Mackenzie, dourly, over the whiskey. "Mr. Byerley, you have had no training as a robot technician, I believe."

"No, I have not."

"Hmp. Well, it is, in my opinion, a sad thing that Ching, Ngoma and Szegeczowska haven't either. There is too prevalent an opinion among the peoples of Earth that a Co-ordinator need only be a capable organizer, a broad generalizer, and an amiable person. These days he should know his robotics as well,—no offense intended."

"None taken. I agree with you."

"I take it, for instance, from what you have said already, that you worry about the recent trifling dislocations in world economy. I don't know what you suspect, but it has happened in the past that people—who should have known better—wondered what would happen if false data were fed into the Machine."

"And what would happen, Mr. Mackenzie?"

"Well," the Scotsman shifted his weight and sighed, "all collected data goes through a complicated screening system which involves both human and mechanical checking, so that the problem is not likely to arise. —But let us ignore that. Humans are fallible, also corruptible, and ordinary mechanical devices are liable to mechanical failure.

"The real point of the matter is that what we call a 'wrong datum' is one which is inconsistent with all other known data. It is our only criterion of right and wrong. It is the Machine's as well. Order it for instance, to direct agricultural activity on the basis of an average July temperature in Iowa of 57 degrees Fahrenheit. It won't accept that. It will not give an answer. —Not that it has any prejudice against that particular temperature, or that an answer is impossible; but because, in the light of all the other data fed it over a period of years, it knows that the probability of an average July temperature of 57 is virtually nil. It rejects that datum.

"The only way a 'wrong datum' can be forced on the Machine is to include it as part of a self-consistent whole, all of which is subtly wrong in a manner either too delicate for the Machine to detect or outside the Machine's experience. The former is beyond human capacity, and the latter is almost so, and is becoming more nearly so as the Machine's experience increases by the second."

Stephen Byerley placed two fingers to the bridge of his nose, "Then the Machine cannot be tampered with— And how do you account for recent errors, then?"

"My dear Byerley, I see that you instinctively follow that great error—that the Machine knows all. Let me cite you a case from my personal experience. The cotton industry engages experienced buyers who purchase cotton. Their procedure is to pull a tuft of cotton out of a random bale of a lot. They will look at that tuft and feel it, tease it out, listen to the crackling perhaps as they do so, touch it with their tongue,—and through this procedure they will determine the class of cotton the bales represent. There are about a dozen such classes. As a result of their decisions, purchases are made at certain prices, blends are made in certain proportions. —Now these buyers cannot yet be replaced by the Machine."

"Why not? Surely the data involved is not too complicated for it?"

"Probably not. But what data is this you refer to? No textile chemist knows exactly what it is that the buyer tests when he feels a tuft of cotton. Presumably there's the average length of the threads, their feel, the extent and nature of their slickness, the way they hang together and so on. —Several dozen items, subconsciously weighed, out of years of experience. But the *quantitative* nature of these tests is not known; maybe even the very nature of some of them is not known. So we have nothing to feed the Machine. Nor can the buyers explain their own judgment. They can only say, 'Well, look at it. Can't you *tell* it's class-such-and-such?'"

"I see."

"There are innumerable cases like that. The Machine is only a tool after all, which can help humanity progress faster by taking some of the burdens of calculations and interpretations off his back. The task of the human brain remains what it has always been; that of discovering new data to be analyzed, and of devising new concepts to be tested. A pity the Society for Humanity won't understand that."

"They are against the Machine?"

"They would be against mathematics or against the art of writing if they had lived at the appropriate time. These reactionaries of the Society claim the Machine robs man of his soul. I notice that capable men are still at a premium in our society; we still need the man who is intelligent enough to think of the proper questions to ask. Perhaps if we could find enough of such, these dislocations you worry about, Co-ordinator, wouldn't occur."

Earth (*Including the uninhabited continent, Antarctica*):
   a—Area: 54,000,000 square miles (*land surface*)
   b—Population: 3,300,000,000
   c—Capital: New York

The fire behind the quartz was weary now, and sputtered its reluctant way to death.

The Co-ordinator was somber, his mood matching the sinking flame.

"They all minimize the state of affairs." His voice was low. "Is it not easy to imagine that they all laugh at me? And yet—Vincent Silver said the Machines cannot be out of order, and I must believe him. Hiram Mackenzie says they cannot be fed false data, and I must believe him. But the Machines are going wrong, somehow, and I must believe that, too,—and so there is *still* an alternative left."

He glanced sidewise at Susan Calvin, who, with closed eyes, for a moment seemed asleep.

"What is that?" she asked, prompt to her cue, nevertheless.

"Why, that correct data is indeed given, and correct answers are indeed received, but that they are then ignored. There is no way the Machine can enforce obedience to its dictates."

"Madame Szegeczowska hinted as much, with reference to Northerners in general, it seems to me."

"So she did."

"And what purpose is served by disobeying the Machine? Let's consider motivations."

"It's obvious to me, and should be to you. It is a matter of rocking the boat, deliberately. There can be no serious conflicts on Earth, in which one group or another can seize more power than it has for what it thinks is its own good despite the harm of Mankind as a whole, while the Machines rule. If popular faith in the Machines can be destroyed to the point where they are abandoned, it will be the law of the jungle again. —And not one of the four Regions can be freed of the suspicion of wanting just that.

"The East has half of humanity within its borders, and the Tropics more than half of Earth's resources. Each can feel itself the natural rulers of all Earth, and each has a history of humiliation by the North, for which it can be human enough to wish a senseless revenge. Europe has a tradition of greatness, on the other hand. It once *did* rule the Earth, and there is nothing so eternally adhesive as the memory of power.

"Yet, in another way, it's hard to believe. Both the East and the Tropics are in a state of enormous expansion within their own borders. Both are climbing incredibly. They cannot have the spare energy for military adventures. And Europe can have nothing but its dreams. It is a cipher, militarily."

"So, Stephen," said Susan, "you leave the North."

"Yes," said Byerley, energetically, "I do. The North is now the strongest, and has been for nearly a century, or its component parts have been. But it is losing relatively, now. The Tropic Regions may take their place in the forefront of civilization for the first time since the Pharaohs, and there are Northerners who fear that.

"The 'Society for Humanity' is a Northern organization, primarily, you know, and they make no secret of not wanting the Machines. —Susan, they are few in numbers, but it is an association of powerful men. Heads of factories; directors of industries and agricultural combines who hate to be what they call 'the Machine's office-boy' belong to it. Men with ambition belong to it. Men who feel themselves strong enough to decide for themselves what is best for themselves, and not just to be told what is best for others.

"In short, just those men who, by together refusing to accept the decisions of the Machine, can, in a short time, turn the world topsy-turvy;—just those belong to the Society.

"Susan, it hangs together. Five of the Directors of World Steel are members, and World Steel suffers from overproduction. Consolidated Cinnabar, which mined mercury at Almaden, was a Northern concern. Its books are still being investigated, but one, at least, of the men concerned was a member. Francisco Villafranca, who, single-handed, delayed the Mexican Canal for two months, was a member, we know already—and so was Rama Vrasayana, I was not at all surprised to find out."

Susan said, quietly, "These men, I might point out, have all done badly—"

"But naturally," interjected Byerley. "To disobey the Machine's analyses is to follow a non-optimal path. Results are poorer than they might be. It's the price they pay. They will have it rough now but in the confusion that will eventually follow—"

"Just what do you plan doing, Stephen?"

"There is obviously no time to lose. I am going to have the Society outlawed, every member removed from any responsible post. And all executive and technical positions, henceforward, can be filled only by applicants signing a non-Society oath. It will mean a certain surrender of basic civil liberties, but I am sure the Congress—"

"It won't work!"

"What!— Why not?"

"I will make a prediction. If you try any such thing, you will find yourself hampered at every turn. You will find it impossible to carry out. You will find your every move in that direction will result in trouble."

Byerley was taken aback, "Why do you say that? —I was rather hoping for your approval in this matter."

"You can't have it as long as your actions are based on a false premise. You admit the Machine can't be wrong, and can't be fed wrong data. I will now show you that it cannot be disobeyed, either, as you think is being done by the Society."

"*That* I don't see at all."

"Then listen. Every action by any executive which does not follow the exact directions of the Machine he is working with becomes part of the data for the next problem. The Machine, therefore, knows that the executive has a certain tendency to disobey. He can incorporate that tendency into that data,—even quantitatively, that is, judging exactly how much and in what direction disobedience would occur. Its next answer would be just sufficiently biased so that after the executive concerned disobeyed, he would have automatically corrected those answers to optimal directions. The Machine *knows*, Stephen!"

"You can't be sure of all this. You are guessing."

"It is a guess based on a lifetime's experience with robots. You had better rely on such a guess, Stephen."

"But then what is left? The Machines themselves are correct and the premises they work on are correct. That we have agreed upon. Now you say that it cannot be disobeyed. Then what is wrong?"

"You have answered yourself. *Nothing is wrong!* Think about the Machines for a while, Stephen. They are robots, and they follow the First Law. But the Machines work not for any single human being, but for all humanity, so that the First Law becomes: 'No Machine may harm humanity; or, through inaction, allow humanity to come to harm.'

"Very well, then, Stephen, what harms humanity? Economic dislocations most of all, from whatever cause. Wouldn't you say so?"

"I would."

"And what is most likely in the future to cause economic dislocations? Answer that, Stephen."

"I should say," replied Byerley, unwillingly, "the destruction of the Machines."

"And so should I say, and so should the Machines say. Their first care, therefore, is to preserve themselves, for us. And so they are quietly taking care of the only elements left that threaten them. It is not the 'Society for Humanity' which is shaking the boat so that the Machines may be destroyed. You have been looking at the reverse of the picture. Say rather that the Machine is shaking the boat—*very* slightly—just enough to shake loose those few which cling to the side for purposes the Machines consider harmful to Humanity.

"So Vrasayana loses his factory and gets another job where he can do no harm—he is not badly hurt, he is not rendered incapable of earning a living, for the Machine cannot harm a human being more than minimally, and that only to save a greater number. Consolidated Cinnabar loses control at Almaden. Villafranca is no longer a civil engineer in charge of an important project. And the directors of World Steel are losing their grip on the industry—or will."

"But you don't really know all this," insisted Byerley, distractedly. "How can we possibly take a chance on your being right?"

"You must. Do you remember the Machine's own statement when you presented the problem to him? It was: 'The matter admits of no explanation.' The Machine did not say there was no explanation, or that it could determine no explanation. It simply was not going to *admit* any explanation. In other words, it would be harmful to humanity to have the explanation known, and that's why we can only guess—and keep on guessing."

"But how can the explanation do us harm? Assume that you are right, Susan."

"Why, Stephen, if I am right, it means that the Machine is conducting our future for us not only simply in direct answer to our direct questions, but in general answer to the world situation and to human psychology as a whole. And to know that may make us unhappy and may hurt our pride. The Machine cannot, *must* not, make us unhappy.

"Stephen, how do we know what the ultimate good of Humanity will entail? We haven't at *our* disposal the infinite factors that the Machine has at *its!* Perhaps, to give you a not unfamiliar example, our entire technical civilization has created more unhappiness and misery than it has removed. Perhaps an agrarian or pastoral civilization, with less culture and less people would be better. If so, the Machines must move in that direction, preferably without telling us, since in our ignorant prejudices we only know that what we are used to, is good—and we would then fight change. Or perhaps a complete urbanization, or a completely caste-ridden society, or complete anarchy, is the answer. We don't know. Only the Machines know, and they are going there and taking us with them."

"But you are telling me, Susan that the 'Society of Humanity' is right; and that Mankind *has* lost its own say in its future."

"It never had any, really. It was always at the mercy of economic and sociological forces it did not understand—at the whims of climate, and the fortunes of war. Now the Machines understand them; and no one can stop them, since the Machines will deal with them as they are dealing with the Society,—having, as they do, the greatest of weapons at their disposal, the absolute control of our economy."

"How horrible!"

"Perhaps how wonderful! Think, that for all time, all conflicts are finally evitable. Only the Machines, from now on, are inevitable!"

And the fire behind the quartz went out and only a curl of smoke was left to indicate its place.

Feminine Intuition

The Three Laws of Robotics:
1. *A robot may not injure a human being or, through inaction, allow a human being to come to harm.*
2. *A robot must obey the orders given it by human beings except where such orders would conflict with the First Law.*
3. *A robot must protect its own existence as long as such protection does not conflict with the First or Second Law.*

For the first time in the history of United States Robots and Mechanical Men Corporation, a robot had been destroyed through accident on Earth itself.

No one was to blame. The air vehicle had been demolished in mid-air and an unbelieving investigating committee was wondering whether they really dared announce the evidence that it had been hit by a meteorite. Nothing else could have been fast enough to prevent automatic avoidance; nothing else could have done the damage short of a nuclear blast and that was out of the question.

Tie that in with a report of a flash in the night sky just before the vehicle had exploded—and from Flagstaff Observatory, not from an amateur—and the location of a sizable and distinctly meteoric bit of iron freshly gouged into the ground a mile from the site and what other conclusion could be arrived at?

Still, nothing like that had ever happened before and calculations of the odds against it yielded monstrous figures. Yet even colossal improbabilities can happen sometimes.

At the offices of United States Robots, the hows and whys of it were secondary. The real point was that a robot had been destroyed.

That, in itself, was distressing.

The fact that JN-5 had been a prototype, the first, after four earlier attempts, to have been placed in the field, was even more distressing.

The fact that JN-5 was a radically new type of robot, quite different from anything ever built before, was abysmally distressing.

The fact that JN-5 had apparently accomplished something before its destruction that was incalculably important and that that accomplishment might now be forever gone, placed the distress utterly beyond words.

It seemed scarcely worth mentioning that, along with the robot, the Chief Robopsychologist of United States Robots had also died.

Clinton Madarian had joined the firm ten years before. For five of those years, he had worked uncomplainingly under the grumpy supervision of Susan Calvin.

Madarian's brilliance was quite obvious and Susan Calvin had quietly promoted him over the heads of older men. She wouldn't, in any case, have deigned to give her reasons for this to Research Director Peter Bogert, but as it happened, no reasons were needed. Or, rather, they were obvious.

Madarian was utterly the reverse of the renowned Dr. Calvin in several very noticeable ways. He was not quite as overweight as his distinct double chin made him appear to be, but even so he was overpowering in his presence, where Susan had gone nearly unnoticed. Madarian's massive face, his shock of glistening red-brown hair, his ruddy complexion and booming voice, his loud laugh, and most of all, his irrepressible self-confidence and his eager way of announcing his successes, made everyone else in the room feel there was a shortage of space.

When Susan Calvin finally retired (refusing, in advance, any cooperation with respect to any testimonial dinner that might be planned in her honor, with so firm a manner that no announcement of the retirement was even made to the news services) Madarian took her place.

He had been in his new post exactly one day when he initiated the JN project.

It had meant the largest commitment of funds to one project that United States Robots had ever had to weigh, but that was something which Madarian dismissed with a genial wave of the hand.

"Worth every penny of it, Peter," he said. "And I expect you to convince the Board of Directors of that."

"Give me reasons," said Bogert, wondering if Madarian would. Susan Calvin had never given reasons.

But Madarian said, "Sure," and settled himself easily into the large armchair in the Director's office.

Bogert watched the other with something that was almost awe. His own once-black hair was almost white now and within the decade he would follow Susan into retirement. That would mean the end of the original team that had built United States Robots into a globe-girdling firm that was a rival of the national governments in complexity and importance. Somehow neither he nor those who had gone before him ever quite grasped the enormous expansion of the firm.

But this was a new generation. The new men were at ease with the Colossus. They lacked the touch of wonder that would have them tiptoeing in disbelief. So they moved ahead, and that was good.

Madarian said, "I propose to begin the construction of robots without constraint."

"Without the Three Laws? Surely—"

"No, Peter. Are those the only constraints you can think of? Hell, you contributed to the design of the early positronic brains. Do I have to tell you that, quite aside from the Three Laws, there isn't a pathway in those brains that isn't carefully designed and fixed? We have robots planned for specific tasks, implanted with specific abilities."

"And you propose—"

"That at every level below the Three Laws, the paths be made open-ended. It's not difficult."

Bogert said dryly, "It's not difficult, indeed. Useless things are never difficult. The difficult thing is fixing the paths and making the robot useful."

"But why is that difficult? Fixing the paths requires a great deal of effort because the Principle of Uncertainty is important in particles the mass of positrons and the uncertainty effect must be minimized.

Yet why must it? If we arrange to have the Principle just sufficiently prominent to allow the crossing of paths unpredictably—"

"We have an unpredictable robot."

"We have a *creative* robot," said Madarian, with a trace of impatience. "Peter, if there's anything a human brain has that a robotic
brain has never had, it's the trace of unpredictability that comes
from the effects of uncertainty at the subatomic level. I admit that
this effect has never been demonstrated experimentally within the
nervous system, but without that the human brain is not superior to
the robotic brain in principle."

"And you think that if you introduce the effect into the robotic
brain, the human brain will become not superior to the robotic
brain in principle."

"That," said Madarian, "is exactly what I believe."

They went on for a long time after that.

The Board of Directors clearly had no intention of being easily
convinced.

Scott Robertson, the largest shareholder in the firm, said, "It's
hard enough to manage the robot industry as it is, with public hostility to robots forever on the verge of breaking out into the open. If
the public gets the idea that robots will be uncontrolled . . . Oh,
don't tell me about the Three Laws. The average man won't believe
the Three Laws will protect him if he as much as hears the word
'uncontrolled.'"

"Then don't use it," said Madarian. "Call the robot—call it 'intuitive.'"

"An intuitive robot," someone muttered. "A girl robot?"

A smile made its way about the conference table.

Madarian seized on that. "All right. A girl robot. Our robots
are sexless, of course, and so will this one be, but we always
act as though they're males. We give them male pet names and call
them he and him. Now this one, if we consider the nature of the
mathematical structuring of the brain which I have proposed, would
fall into the JN-coordinate system. The first robot would be JN-1,
and I've assumed that it would be called John-1. . . . I'm afraid
that is the level of originality of the average roboticist. But why not
call it Jane-1, damn it? If the public has to be let in on what we're
doing, we're constructing a feminine robot with intuition."

Robertson shook his head, "What difference would that make? What you're saying is that you plan to remove the last barrier which, in principle, keeps the robotic brain inferior to the human brain. What do you suppose the public reaction will be to that?"

"Do you plan to make that public?" said Madarian. He thought a bit and then said, "Look. One thing the general public believes is that women are not as intelligent as men."

There was an instant apprehensive look on the face of more than one man at the table and a quick look up and down as though Susan Calvin were still in her accustomed seat.

Madarian said, "If we announce a female robot, it doesn't matter what she is. The public will automatically assume she is mentally backward. We just publicize the robot as Jane-1 and we don't have to say another word. We're safe."

"Actually," said Peter Bogert quietly, "there's more to it than that. Madarian and I have gone over the mathematics carefully and the JN series, whether John or Jane, would be quite safe. They would be less complex and intellectually capable, in an orthodox sense, than many another series we have designed and constructed. There would only be the one added factor of, well, let's get into the habit of calling it 'intuition.'"

"Who knows what it would do?" muttered Robertson.

"Madarian has suggested one thing it can do. As you all know, the Space Jump has been developed in principle. It is possible for men to attain what is, in effect, hyper-speeds beyond that of light and to visit other stellar systems and return in negligible time—weeks at the most."

Robertson said, "That's not new to us. It couldn't have been done without robots."

"Exactly, and it's not doing us any good because we can't use the hyper-speed drive except perhaps once as a demonstration, so that U. S. Robots gets little credit. The Space Jump is risky, it's fearfully prodigal of energy and therefore it's enormously expensive. If we were going to use it anyway, it would be nice if we could report the existence of a habitable planet. Call it a psychological need. Spend about twenty billion dollars on a single Space Jump and report nothing but scientific data and the public wants to know why their money was wasted. Report the existence of a habitable planet, and you're an interstellar Columbus and no one will worry about the money."

"So?"

"So where are we going to find a habitable planet? Or put it this way—which star within reach of the Space Jump as presently developed, which of the three hundred thousand stars and star systems within three hundred light-years has the best chance of having a habitable planet? We've got an enormous quantity of details on every star in our three-hundred-light-year neighborhood and a notion that almost every one has a planetary system. But which has a *habitable* planet? Which do we visit? . . . We don't know."

One of the directors said, "How would this Jane robot help us?"

Madarian was about to answer that, but he gestured slightly to Bogert and Bogert understood. The Director would carry more weight. Bogert didn't particularly like the idea; if the JN series proved a fiasco, he was making himself prominent enough in connection with it to insure that the sticky fingers of blame would cling to him. On the other hand, retirement was not all that far off, and if it worked, he would go out in a blaze of glory. Maybe it was only Madarian's aura of confidence, but Bogert had honestly come to believe it would work.

He said, "It may well be that somewhere in the libraries of data we have on those stars, there are methods for estimating the probabilities of the presence of Earth-type habitable planets. All we need to do is understand the data properly, look at them in the appropriate creative manner, make the correct correlations. We haven't done it yet. Or if some astronomer has, he hasn't been smart enough to realize what he has.

"A JN-type robot could make correlations far more rapidly and far more precisely than a man could. In a day, it would make and discard as many correlations as a man could in ten years. Furthermore, it would work in truly random fashion, whereas a man would have a strong bias based on preconception and on what is already believed."

There was a considerable silence after that. Finally Robertson said, "But it's only a matter of probability, isn't it? Suppose this robot said, 'The highest-probability habitable-planet star within so-and-so light-years is Squidgee-17,' or whatever, and we go there and find that a probability is only a probability and that there are no habitable planets after all. Where does that leave us?"

Madarian struck in this time. "We still win. We know how the robot came to the conclusion because it—she—will tell us. It might well help us gain enormous insight into astronomical detail and make the whole thing worthwhile even if we don't make the Space Jump at all. Besides, we can then work out the five most probable sites of planets and the probability that one of the five has a habitable planet may then be better than 0.95. It would be almost sure—"

They went on for a long time after that.

The funds granted were quite insufficient, but Madarian counted on the habit of throwing good money after bad. With two hundred million about to be lost irrevocably when another hundred million could save everything, the other hundred million would surely be voted.

Jane-1 was finally built and put on display. Peter Bogert studied it —her—gravely. He said, "Why the narrow waist? Surely that introduces a mechanical weakness?"

Madarian chuckled. "Listen, if we're going to call her Jane, there's no point in making her look like Tarzan."

Bogert shook his head. "Don't like it. You'll be bulging her higher up to give the appearance of breasts next, and that's a rotten idea. If women start getting the notion that robots may look like women, I can tell you exactly the kind of perverse notions they'll get, and you'll *really* have hostility on their part."

Madarian said, "Maybe you're right at that. No woman wants to feel replaceable by something with none of her faults. Okay."

Jane-2 did not have the pinched waist. She was a somber robot which rarely moved and even more rarely spoke.

Madarian had only occasionally come rushing to Bogert with items of news during her construction and that had been a sure sign that things were going poorly. Madarian's ebullience under success was overpowering. He would not hesitate to invade Bogert's bedroom at 3 A.M. with a hot-flash item rather than wait for the morning. Bogert was sure of that.

Now Madarian seemed subdued, his usually florid expression nearly pale, his round cheeks somehow pinched. Bogert said, with a feeling of certainty, "She won't talk."

"Oh, she talks." Madarian sat down heavily and chewed at his lower lip. "Sometimes, anyway," he said.

Bogert rose and circled the robot. "And when she talks, she makes no sense, I suppose. Well, if she doesn't talk, she's no female, is she?"

Madarian tried a weak smile for size and abandoned it. He said, "The brain, in isolation, checked out."

"I know," said Bogert.

"But once that brain was put in charge of the physical apparatus of the robot, it was necessarily modified, of course."

"Of course," agreed Bogert unhelpfully.

"But unpredictably and frustratingly. The trouble is that when you're dealing with n-dimensional calculus of uncertainty, things are—"

"Uncertain?" said Bogert. His own reaction was surprising him. The company investment was already most sizable and almost two years had elapsed, yet the results were, to put it politely, disappointing. Still, he found himself jabbing at Madarian and finding himself amused in the process.

Almost furtively, Bogert wondered if it weren't the absent Susan Calvin he was jabbing at. Madarian was so much more ebullient and effusive than Susan could ever possibly be—when things were going well. He was also far more vulnerably in the dumps when things weren't going well, and it was precisely under pressure that Susan never cracked. The target that Madarian made could be a neatly punctured bull's-eye as recompense for the target Susan had never allowed herself to be.

Madarian did not react to Bogert's last remark any more than Susan Calvin would have done; not out of contempt, which would have been Susan's reaction, but because he did not hear it.

He said argumentatively, "The trouble is the matter of recognition. We have Jane-2 correlating magnificently. She can correlate on any subject, but once she's done so, she can't recognize a valuable result from a valueless one. It's not an easy problem, judging how to program a robot to tell a significant correlation when you don't know what correlations she will be making."

"I presume you've thought of lowering the potential at the W-21 diode junction and sparking across the—"

"No, no, no, no—" Madarian faded off into a whispering diminuendo. "You can't just have it spew out everything. We can do that for ourselves. The point is to have it recognize the crucial correlation and draw the conclusion. Once that is done, you see, a Jane robot would snap out an answer by intuition. It would be something we couldn't get ourselves except by the oddest kind of luck."

"It seems to me," said Bogert dryly, "that if you had a robot like that, you would have her do routinely what, among human beings, only the occasional genius is capable of doing."

Madarian nodded vigorously. "Exactly, Peter. I'd have said so myself if I weren't afraid of frightening off the execs. Please don't repeat that in their hearing."

"Do you really want a robot genius?"

"What are words? I'm trying to get a robot with the capacity to make random correlations at enormous speeds, together with a key-significance high-recognition quotient. And I'm trying to put *those* words into positronic field equations. I thought I had it, too, but I don't. Not yet."

He looked at Jane-2 discontentedly and said, "What's the best significance you have, Jane?"

Jane-2's head turned to look at Madarian but she made no sound, and Madarian whispered with resignation, "She's running that into the correlation banks."

Jane-2 spoke tonelessly at last. "I'm not sure." It was the first sound she had made.

Madarian's eyes rolled upward. "She's doing the equivalent of setting up equations with indeterminate solutions."

"I gathered that," said Bogert. "Listen, Madarian, can you go anywhere at this point, or do we pull out now and cut our losses at half a billion?"

"Oh, I'll get it," muttered Madarian.

Jane-3 wasn't it. She was never as much as activated and Madarian was in a rage.

It was human error. His own fault, if one wanted to be entirely accurate. Yet though Madarian was utterly humiliated, others remained quiet. Let he who has never made an error in the fearsomely intricate mathematics of the positronic brain fill out the first memo of correction.

Nearly a year passed before Jane-4 was ready. Madarian was ebullient again. "She does it," he said. "She's got a good high-recognition quotient."

He was confident enough to place her on display before the Board and have her solve problems. Not mathematical problems; any robot could do that; but problems where the terms were deliberately misleading without being actually inaccurate.

Bogert said afterward, "That doesn't take much, really."

"Of course not. It's elementary for Jane-4, but I had to show them something, didn't I?"

"Do you know how much we've spent so far?"

"Come on, Peter, don't give me that. Do you know how much we've got back? These things don't go on in a vacuum, you know. I've had over three years of hell over this, if you want to know, but I've worked out new techniques of calculation that will save us a minimum of fifty thousand dollars on every new type of positronic brain we design, from now on in forever. Right?"

"Well—"

"Well me no wells. It's so. And it's my personal feeling that n-dimensional calculus of uncertainty can have any number of other applications if we have the ingenuity to find them, and my Jane robots *will* find them. Once I've got exactly what I want, the new JN series will pay for itself inside of five years, even if we triple what we've invested so far."

"What do you mean by 'exactly what you want'? What's wrong with Jane-4?"

"Nothing. Or nothing much. She's on the track, but she can be improved and I intend to do so. I thought I knew where I was going when I designed her. Now I've tested her and I *know* where I'm going. I intend to get there."

Jane-5 was it. It took Madarian well over a year to produce her and there he had no reservations; he was utterly confident.

Jane-5 was shorter than the average robot, slimmer. Without being a female caricature as Jane-1 had been, she managed to possess an air of femininity about herself despite the absence of a single clearly feminine feature.

"It's the way she's standing," said Bogert. Her arms were held gracefully and somehow the torso managed to give the impression of curving slightly when she turned.

Madarian said, "Listen to her. . . . How do you feel, Jane?"

"In excellent health, thank you," said Jane-5, and the voice was precisely that of a woman; it was a sweet and almost disturbing contralto.

"Why did you do that, Clinton?" said Peter, startled and beginning to frown.

"Psychologically important," said Madarian. "I want people to think of her as a woman; to treat her as a woman; to *explain*."

"What people?"

Madarian put his hands in his pockets and stared throughtfully at Bogert. "I would like to have arrangements made for Jane and myself to go to Flagstaff."

Bogert couldn't help but note that Madarian didn't say Jane-5. He made use of no number this time. She was *the* Jane. He said doubtfully, "To Flagstaff? Why?"

"Because that's the world center for general planetology, isn't it? It's where they're studying the stars and trying to calculate the probability of habitable planets, isn't it?"

"I know that, but it's on Earth."

"Well, and I surely know that."

"Robotic movements on Earth are strictly controlled. And there's no need for it. Bring a library of books on general planetology here and let Jane absorb them."

"*No!* Peter, will you get it through your head that Jane isn't the ordinary logical robot; she's intuitive."

"So?"

"So how can we tell what she needs, what she can use, what will set her off? We can use any metal model in the factory to read books; that's frozen data and out of date besides. Jane must have living information; she must have tones of voice, she must have side issues; she must have total irrelevancies even. How the devil do we know what or when something will go click-click inside her and fall into a pattern? If we knew, we wouldn't need her at all, would we?"

Bogert began to feel harassed. He said, "Then bring the men here, the general planetologists."

"Here won't be any good. They'll be out of their element. They won't react naturally. I want Jane to watch them at work; I want her to see their instruments, their offices, their desks, everything about them that she can. I want you to arrange to have her transported to Flagstaff. And I'd really like not to discuss it any further."

For a moment he almost sounded like Susan. Bogert winced, and said, "It's complicated making such an arrangement. Transporting an experimental robot—"

"Jane isn't experimental. She's the fifth of the series."

"The other four weren't really working models."

Madarian lifted his hands in helpless frustration. "Who's forcing you to tell the government that?"

"I'm not worried about the government. It can be made to understand special cases. It's public opinion. We've come a long way in fifty years and I don't propose to be set back twenty-five of them by having you lose control of a—"

"I won't lose control. You're making foolish remarks. Look! U. S. Robots can afford a private plane. We can land quietly at the nearest commercial airport and be lost in hundreds of similar landings. We can arrange to have a large ground car with an enclosed body meet us and take us to Flagstaff. Jane will be crated and it will be obvious that some piece of thoroughly non-robotic equipment is being transported to the labs. We won't get a second look from anyone. The men at Flagstaff will be alerted and will be told the exact purpose of the visit. They will have every motive to cooperate and to prevent a leak."

Bogert pondered. "The risky part will be the plane and the ground car. If anything happens to the crate—"

"Nothing will."

"We might get away with it if Jane is deactivated during transport. Then even if someone finds out she's inside—"

"No, Peter. That can't be done. Uh-uh. Not Jane-5. Look, she's been free-associating since she was activated. The information she possesses can be put into freeze during deactivation but the free associations never. No, sir, she can't ever be deactivated."

"But, then, if somehow it is discovered that we are transporting an activated robot—"

"It won't be found out."

Madarian remained firm and the plane eventually took off. It was a late-model automatic Computo-jet, but it carried a human pilot— one of U. S. Robots' own employees—as backup. The crate containing Jane arrived at the airport safely, was transferred to the ground car, and reached the Research Laboratories at Flagstaff without incident.

Peter Bogert received his first call from Madarian not more than an hour after the latter's arrival at Flagstaff. Madarian was ecstatic and, characteristically, could not wait to report.

The message arrived by tubed laser beam, shielded, scrambled, and ordinarily impenetrable, but Bogert felt exasperated. He knew it could be penetrated if someone with enough technological ability— the government, for example—was determined to do so. The only real safety lay in the fact that the government had no reason to try. At least Bogert hoped so.

He said, "For God's sake, do you have to call?"

Madarian ignored him entirely. He burbled, "It was an inspiration. Sheer genius, I tell you."

For a while, Bogert stared at the receiver. Then he shouted incredulously, "You mean you've got the answer? Already?"

"No, no! Give us time, damn it. I mean the matter of her voice was an inspiration. Listen, after we were chauffeured from the airport to the main administration building at Flagstaff, we uncrated Jane and she stepped out of the box. When that happened, every man in the place stepped back. Scared! Nitwits! If even scientists can't understand the significance of the Laws of Robotics, what can we expect of the average untrained individual? For a minute there I thought: This will all be useless. They won't talk. They'll be keying themselves for a quick break in case she goes berserk and they'll be able to think of nothing else."

"Well, then, what are you getting at?"

"So then she greeted them routinely. She said, 'Good afternoon, gentlemen. I am so glad to meet you.' And it came out in this beautiful contralto. . . . That was it. One man straightened his tie, and another ran his fingers through his hair. What really got me was that the oldest guy in the place actually checked his fly to make sure it was zipped. They're all crazy about her now. All they needed was the voice. She isn't a robot any more; she's a girl."

"You mean they're talking to her?"

"*Are* they talking to her! I should say so. I should have programmed her for sexy intonations. They'd be asking her for dates right now if I had. Talk about conditioned reflex. Listen, men respond to voices. At the most intimate moments, are they looking? It's the voice in your ear—"

"Yes, Clinton, I seem to remember. Where's Jane now?"

"With them. They won't let go of her."

"Damn! Get in there with her. Don't let her out of your sight, man."

Madarian's calls thereafter, during his ten-day stay at Flagstaff, were not very frequent and became progressively less exalted.

Jane was listening carefully, he reported, and occasionally she responded. She remained popular. She was given entry everywhere. But there were no results.

Bogert said, "Nothing at all?"

Madarian was at once defensive. "You can't say nothing at all. It's impossible to say nothing at all with an intuitive robot. You don't know what might not be going on inside her. This morning she asked Jensen what he had for breakfast."

"Rossiter Jensen the astrophysicist?"

"Yes, of course. As it turned out, he didn't have breakfast that morning. Well, a cup of coffee."

"So Jane's learning to make small talk. That scarcely makes up for the expense—"

"Oh, don't be a jackass. It wasn't small talk. Nothing is small talk for Jane. She asked because it had something to do with some sort of cross-correlation she was building in her mind."

"What can it possibly—"

"How do I know? If I knew, I'd be a Jane myself and you wouldn't need her. But it has to mean something. She's programmed for high motivation to obtain an answer to the question of a planet with optimum habitability/distance and—"

"Then let me know when she's done that and not before. It's not really necessary for me to get a blow-by-blow description of possible correlations."

He didn't really expect to get notification of success. With each day, Bogert grew less sanguine, so that when the notification finally came, he wasn't ready. And it came at the very end.

That last time, when Madarian's climactic message came, it came in what was almost a whisper. Exaltation had come complete circle and Madarian was awed into quiet.

"She did it," he said. "She did it. After I all but gave up, too. After she had received everything in the place and most of it twice and three times over and never said a word that sounded like anything. . . . I'm on the plane now, returning. We've just taken off."

Bogert managed to get his breath. "Don't play games, man. You have the *answer?* Say so, if you have. Say it plainly."

"She has the answer. She's given me the answer. She's given me the names of three stars within eighty light-years which, she says, have a sixty to ninety percent chance of possessing one habitable planet each. The probability that at least one has is 0.972. It's almost certain. And that's just the least of it. Once we get back, she can give us the exact line of reasoning that led her to the conclusion and I predict that the whole science of astrophysics and cosmology will—"

"Are you sure—"

"You think I'm having hallucinations? I even have a witness. Poor guy jumped two feet when Jane suddenly began to reel out the answer in her gorgeous voice—"

And that was when the meteorite struck and in the thorough destruction of the plane that followed, Madarian and the pilot were reduced to gobbets of bloody flesh and no usable remnant of Jane was recovered.

The gloom at U. S. Robots had never been deeper. Robertson attempted to find consolation in the fact that the very completeness of the destruction had utterly hidden the illegalities of which the firm had been guilty.

Peter shook his head and mourned. "We've lost the best chance U. S. Robots ever had of gaining an unbeatable public image; of overcoming the damned Frankenstein complex. What it would have meant for robots to have one of them work out the solution to the habitable-planet problem, after other robots had helped work out the Space Jump. Robots would have opened the galaxy to us. And if at the same time we could have driven scientific knowledge forward in a dozen different directions as we surely would have . . . Oh, God, there's no way of calculating the benefits to the human race, and to us of course."

Robertson said, "We could build other Janes, couldn't we? Even without Madarian?"

"Sure we could. But can we depend on the proper correlation again? Who knows how low-probability that final result was? What if Madarian had had a fantastic piece of beginner's luck? And then to have an even more fantastic piece of bad luck? A meteorite zeroing in . . . It's simply unbelievable—"

Robertson said in a hesitating whisper, "It couldn't have been—meant. I mean, if we weren't meant to know and if the meteorite was a judgment—from—"

He faded off under Bogert's withering glare.

Bogert said, "It's not a dead loss, I suppose. Other Janes are bound to help us in some ways. And we can give other robots feminine voices, if that will help encourage public acceptance—though I wonder what the women would say. If we only knew what Jane-5 had said!"

"In that last call, Madarian said there was a witness."

Bogert said, "I know; I've been thinking about that. Don't you suppose I've been in touch with Flagstaff? Nobody in the entire place heard Jane say anything that was out of the ordinary, anything that sounded like an answer to the habitable-planet problem, and certainly anyone there should have recognized the answer if it came —or at least recognized it as a possible answer."

"Could Madarian have been lying? Or crazy? Could he have been trying to protect himself—"

"You mean he may have been trying to save his reputation by pretending he had the answer and then gimmick Jane so she couldn't talk and say, 'Oh, sorry, something happened accidentally. Oh, darn!' I won't accept that for a minute. You might as well suppose he had arranged the meteorite."

"Then what do we do?"

Bogert said heavily, "Turn back to Flagstaff. The answer *must* be there. I've got to dig deeper, that's all. I'm going there and I'm taking a couple of the men in Madarian's department. We've got to go through that place top to bottom and end to end."

"But, you know, even if there were a witness and he had heard, what good would it do, now that we don't have Jane to explain the process?"

"Every little something is useful. Jane gave the names of the stars; the catalogue numbers probably—none of the named stars has a chance. If someone can remember her saying that and actually remember the catalogue number, or have heard it clearly enough to allow it to be recovered by Psycho-probe if he lacked the conscious memory—then we'll have something. Given the results at the end, and the data fed Jane at the beginning, we might be able to reconstruct the line of reasoning; we might recover the intuition. If that is done, we've saved the game—"

Bogert was back after three days, silent and thoroughly depressed. When Robertson inquired anxiously as to results, he shook his head. "Nothing!"

"Nothing?"

"Absolutely nothing. I spoke with every man in Flagstaff—every scientist, every technician, every student—that had had anything to do with Jane; everyone that had as much as seen her. The number wasn't great; I'll give Madarian credit for that much discretion. He only allowed those to see her who might conceivably have had planetological knowledge to feed her. There were twenty-three men altogether who had seen Jane and of those only twelve had spoken to her more than casually.

"I went over and over all that Jane had said. They remembered everything quite well. They're keen men engaged in a crucial experiment involving their specialty, so they had every motivation to remember. And they were dealing with a talking robot, something that was startling enough, and one that talked like a TV actress. They couldn't forget."

Robertson said, "Maybe a Psycho-probe—"

"If one of them had the vaguest thought that something had happened, I would screw out his consent to Probing. But there's nothing to leave room for an excuse, and to Probe two dozen men who make their living from their brains can't be done. Honestly, it wouldn't help. If Jane had mentioned three stars and said they had habitable planets, it would have been like setting up sky rockets in their brains. How could any one of them forget?"

"Then maybe one of them is lying," said Robertson grimly. "He wants the information for his own use; to get the credit himself later."

"What good would that do him?" said Bogert. "The whole establishment knows exactly why Madarian and Jane were there in the first place. They know why I came there in the second. If at any time in the future any man now at Flagstaff suddenly comes up with a habitable-planet theory that is startlingly new and different, yet valid, every other man at Flagstaff and every man at U. S. Robots will know at once that he had stolen it. He'd never get away with it."

"Then Madarian himself was somehow mistaken."

"I don't see how I can believe that either. Madarian had an irritating personality—all robopsychologists have irritating personalities, I think, which must be why they work with robots rather than with men—but he was no dummy. He *couldn't* be wrong in something like this."

"Then—" But Robertson had run out of possibilities. They had reached a blank wall and for some minutes each stared at it disconsolately.

Finally Robertson stirred. "Peter—"

"Well?"

"Let's ask Susan."

Bogert stiffened. "What!"

"Let's ask Susan. Let's call her and ask her to come in."

"Why? What can she possibly do?"

"I don't know. But she's a robopsychologist, too, and she might understand Madarian better than we do. Besides, she— Oh, hell, she always had more brains than any of us."

"She's nearly eighty."

"And you're seventy. What about it?"

Bogert sighed. Had her abrasive tongue lost any of its rasp in the years of her retirement? He said, "Well, I'll ask her."

Susan Calvin entered Bogert's office with a slow look around before her eyes fixed themselves on the Research Director. She had aged a great deal since her retirement. Her hair was a fine white and her face seemed to have crumpled. She had grown so frail as to be almost transparent and only her eyes, piercing and uncompromising, seemed to remain of all that had been.

Bogert strode forward heartily, holding out his hand. "Susan!"

Susan Calvin took it, and said, "You're looking reasonably well, Peter, for an old man. If I were you, I wouldn't wait till next year. Retire now and let the young men get to it. . . . And Madarian is dead. Are you calling me in to take over my old job? Are you determined to keep the ancients till a year past actual physical death?"

"No, no, Susan. I've called you in—" He stopped. He did not, after all, have the faintest idea of how to start.

But Susan read his mind now as easily as she always had. She seated herself with the caution born of stiffened joints and said, "Peter, you've called me in because you're in bad trouble. Otherwise you'd sooner see me dead than within a mile of you."

"Come, Susan—"

"Don't waste time on pretty talk. I never had time to waste when I was forty and certainly not now. Madarian's death and your call to me are both unusual, so there must be a connection. Two unusual events without a connection is too low-probability to worry about. Begin at the beginning and don't worry about revealing yourself to be a fool. That was revealed to me long ago."

Bogert cleared his throat miserably and began. She listened carefully, her withered hand lifting once in a while to stop him so that she might ask a question.

She snorted at one point. "Feminine intuition? Is that what you wanted the robot for? You men. Faced with a woman reaching a correct conclusion and unable to accept the fact that she is your

equal or superior in intelligence, you invent something called feminine intuition."

"Uh, yes, Susan, but let me continue—"

He did. When she was told of Jane's contralto voice, she said, "It
is a difficult choice sometimes whether to feel revolted at the male
sex or merely to dismiss them as contemptible."

Bogert said, "Well, let me go on—"

When he was quite done, Susan said, "May I have the private use
of this office for an hour or two?"

"Yes, but—"

She said, "I want to go over the various records—Jane's programming, Madarian's calls, your interviews at Flagstaff. I presume I can
use that beautiful new shielded laser-phone and your computer out-
let if I wish."

"Yes, of course."

"Well, then, get out of here, Peter."

It was not quite forty-five minutes when she hobbled to the door,
opened it, and called for Bogert.

When Bogert came, Robertson was with him. Both entered and
Susan greeted the latter with an unenthusiastic "Hello, Scott."

Bogert tried desperately to gauge the results from Susan's face,
but it was only the face of a grim old lady who had no intention of
making anything easy for him.

He said cautiously, "Do you think there's anything you can do,
Susan?"

"Beyond what I have already done? No! There's nothing more."

Bogert's lips set in chagrin, but Robertson said, "What have you
already done, Susan?"

Susan said, "I've thought a little; something I can't seem to persuade anyone else to do. For one thing, I've thought about Madarian. I knew him, you know. He had brains but he was a very irritating extrovert. I thought you would like him after me, Peter."

"It was a change," Bogert couldn't resist saying.

"And he was always running to you with results the very minute
he had them, wasn't he?"

"Yes, he was."

"And yet," said Susan, "his last message, the one in which he said
Jane had given him the answer, was sent from the plane. Why did
he wait so long? Why didn't he call you while he was still at Flagstaff, immediately after Jane had said whatever it was she said?"

"I suppose," said Peter, "that for once he wanted to check it thoroughly and—well, I don't know. It was the most important thing that had ever happened to him; he might for once have wanted to wait and be sure of himself."

"On the contrary; the more important it was, the less he would wait, surely. And if he could manage to wait, why not do it properly and wait till he was back at U. S. Robots so that he could check the results with all the computing equipment this firm could make available to him? In short, he waited too long from one point of view and not long enough from another."

Robertson interrupted. "Then you think he was up to some trickery—"

Susan looked revolted. "Scott, don't try to compete with Peter in making inane remarks. Let me continue. . . . A second point concerns the witness. According to the records of that last call, Madarian said, 'Poor guy jumped two feet when Jane suddenly began to reel out the answer in her gorgeous voice.' In fact, it was the last thing he said. And the question is, then, why should the witness have jumped? Madarian had explained that all the men were crazy about that voice, and they had had ten days with the robot—with Jane. Why should the mere act of her speaking have startled them?"

Bogert said, "I assumed it was astonishment at hearing Jane give an answer to a problem that has occupied the minds of planetologists for nearly a century."

"But they were *waiting* for her to give that answer. That was why she was there. Besides, consider the way the sentence is worded. Madarian's statement makes it seem the witness was startled, not astonished, if you see the difference. What's more, that reaction came 'when Jane suddenly began'—in other words, at the very start of the statement. To be astonished at the content of what Jane said would have required the witness to have listened awhile so that he might absorb it. Madarian would have said he had jumped two feet *after* he had heard Jane say thus-and-so. It would be 'after' not 'when' and the word 'suddenly' would not be included."

Bogert said uneasily, "I don't think you can refine matters down to the use or non-use of a word."

"I can," said Susan frostily, "because I am a robopsychologist. And I can expect Madarian to do so, too, because *he* was a robopsychologist. We have to explain those two anomalies, then. The queer delay before Madarian's call and the queer reaction of the witness."

"Can *you* explain them?" asked Robertson.

"Of course," said Susan, "since I use a little simple logic. Madarian called with the news without delay, as he always did, or with as little delay as he could manage. If Jane had solved the problem at Flagstaff, he would certainly have called from Flagstaff. Since he called from the plane, she must clearly have solved the problem after he had left Flagstaff."

"But then—"

"Let me finish. Let me finish. Was Madarian not taken from the airport to Flagstaff in a heavy, enclosed ground car? And Jane, in her crate, with him?"

"Yes."

"And presumably, Madarian and the crated Jane returned from Flagstaff to the airport in the same heavy, enclosed ground car. Am I right?"

"Yes, of course!"

"And they were not alone in the ground car, either. In one of his calls, Madarian said, 'We were chauffeured from the airport to the main administration building,' and I suppose I am right in concluding that if he was chauffeured, then that was because there was a chauffeur, a human driver, in the car."

"Good God!"

"The trouble with you, Peter, is that when you think of a witness to a planetological statement, you think of planetologists. You divide up human beings into categories, and despise and dismiss most. A robot cannot do that. The First Law says, 'A robot may not injure a *human being* or, through inaction, allow a *human being* to come to harm.' *Any* human being. That is the essence of the robotic view of life. A robot makes no distinction. To a robot, all men are truly equal, and to a robopsychologist who must perforce deal with men at the robotic level, all men are truly equal, too.

"It would not occur to Madarian to say a truck driver had heard the statement. To you a truck driver is not a scientist but is a mere animate adjunct of a truck, but to Madarian he was a man and a witness. Nothing more. Nothing less."

Bogert shook his head in disbelief, "But you are *sure?*"

"Of course I'm sure. How else can you explain the other point; Madarian's remark about the startling of the witness? Jane was crated, wasn't she? But she was *not* deactivated. According to the records, Madarian was always adamant against ever deactivating an intuitive robot. Moreover, Jane-5, like any of the Janes, was extremely non-talkative. Probably it never occurred to Madarian to order her to remain quiet within the crate; and it was within the crate that the pattern finally fell into place. Naturally she began to talk. A beautiful contralto voice suddenly sounded from inside the crate. If you were the truck driver, what would you do at that point? Surely you'd be startled. It's a wonder he didn't crash."

"But if the truck driver was the witness, why didn't he come forward—"

"Why? Can he possibly know that anything crucial had happened, that what he heard was important? Besides, don't you suppose Madarian tipped him well and asked him not to say anything? Would you *want* the news to spread that an activated robot was being transported illegally over the Earth's surface."

"Well, will he remember what was said?"

"Why not? It might seem to you, Peter, that a truck driver, one step above an ape in your view, can't remember. But truck drivers can have brains, too. The statements were most remarkable and the driver may well have remembered some. Even if he gets some of the letters and numbers wrong, we're dealing with a finite set, you know, the fifty-five hundred stars or star systems within eighty light-years or so—I haven't looked up the exact number. You can make the correct choices. And if needed, you will have every excuse to use the Psycho-probe—"

The two men stared at her. Finally Bogert, afraid to believe, whispered, "But how can you be *sure?*"

For a moment, Susan was on the point of saying: Because I've called Flagstaff, you fool, and because I spoke to the truck driver, and because he told me what he had heard, and because I've checked with the computer at Flagstaff and got the only three stars that fit the information, and because I have those names in my pocket.

But she didn't. Let him go through it all himself. Carefully, she rose to her feet, and said sardonically, "How can I be sure? . . . Call it feminine intuition."

Two Climaxes

Each of these two stories is post-Susan Calvin. They are the most recent long stories I have written about robots and in each one I try to take the long view and see what the ultimate end of robotics might be. And I come full circle—for though I adhere strictly to the Three Laws, the first story, ". . . That Thou Art Mindful of Him," is clearly a Robot-as-Menace story, while the second, "The Bicentennial Man," is even more clearly a Robot-as-Pathos story.

Of all the robot stories I ever wrote, "The Bicentennial Man" is my favorite and, I think, the best. In fact, I have a dreadful feeling that I might not care to top it and will never write another serious robot story. But then again, I might. I'm not always predictable.

. . . That Thou Art Mindful of Him

The Three Laws of Robotics:
1. *A robot may not injure a human being or, through inaction, allow a human being to come to harm.*
2. *A robot must obey the orders given it by human beings except where such orders would conflict with the First Law.*
3. *A robot must protect its own existence as long as such protection does not conflict with the First or Second Law.*

1.

Keith Harriman, who had for twelve years now been Director of Research at United States Robots and Mechanical Men Corporation, found that he was not at all certain whether he was doing right. The tip of his tongue passed over his plump but rather pale lips and it seemed to him that the holographic image of the great Susan Calvin, which stared unsmilingly down upon him, had never looked so grim before.

Usually he blanked out that image of the greatest roboticist in history because she unnerved him. (He tried thinking of the image as "it" but never quite succeeded.) This time he didn't quite dare to and her long-dead gaze bored into the side of his face.

It was a dreadful and demeaning step he would have to take.

Opposite him was George Ten, calm and unaffected either by Harriman's patent uneasiness or by the image of the patron saint of robotics glowing in its niche above.

Harriman said, "We haven't had a chance to talk this out, really, George. You haven't been with us that long and I haven't had a good chance to be alone with you. But now I would like to discuss the matter in some detail."

"I am perfectly willing to do that," said George. "In my stay at U. S. Robots, I have gathered the crisis has something to do with the Three Laws."

"Yes. You know the Three Laws, of course."

"I do."

"Yes, I'm sure you do. But let us dig even deeper and consider the truly basic problem. In two centuries of, if I may say so, considerable success, U. S. Robots has never managed to persuade human beings to accept robots. We have placed robots only where work is required that human beings cannot do, or in environments that human beings find unacceptably dangerous. Robots have worked mainly in space and that has limited what we have been able to do."

"Surely," said George Ten, "that represents a broad limit, and one within which U. S. Robots can prosper."

"No, for two reasons. In the first place, the boundaries set for us inevitably contract. As the Moon colony, for instance, grows more sophisticated, its demand for robots decreases and we expect that, within the next few years, robots will be banned on the Moon. This will be repeated on every world colonized by mankind. Secondly, true prosperity is impossible without robots on Earth. We at U. S. Robots firmly believe that human beings need robots and must learn to live with their mechanical analogues if progress is to be maintained."

"Do they not? Mr. Harriman, you have on your desk a computer input which, I understand, is connected with the organization's Multivac. A computer is a kind of sessile robot; a robot brain not attached to a body—"

"True, but that also is limited. The computers used by mankind have been steadily specialized in order to avoid too humanlike an intelligence. A century ago we were well on the way to artificial intelligence of the most unlimited type through the use of great computers we called Machines. Those Machines limited their action of their own accord. Once they had solved the ecological problems that had threatened human society, they phased themselves out. Their own continued existence would, they reasoned, have placed them in the role of a crutch to mankind and, since they felt this would harm human beings, they condemned themselves by the First Law."

"And were they not correct to do so?"

"In my opinion, no. By their action, they reinforced mankind's Frankenstein complex; its gut fears that any artificial man they created would turn upon its creator. Men fear that robots may replace human beings."

"Do you not fear that yourself?"

"I know better. As long as the Three Laws of Robotics exist, they cannot. They can serve as *partners* of mankind; they can share in the great struggle to understand and wisely direct the laws of nature so that together they can do more than mankind can possibly do alone; but always in such a way that robots serve human beings."

"But if the Three Laws have shown themselves, over the course of two centuries, to keep robots within bounds, what is the source of the distrust of human beings for robots?"

"Well"—and Harriman's graying hair tufted as he scratched his head vigorously—"mostly superstition, of course. Unfortunately, there are also some complexities involved that anti-robot agitators seize upon."

"Involving the Three Laws?"

"Yes. The Second Law in particular. There's no problem in the Third Law, you see. It is universal. Robots must always sacrifice themselves for human beings, any human beings."

"Of course," said George Ten.

"The First Law is perhaps less satisfactory, since it is always possible to imagine a condition in which a robot must perform either Action A or Action B, the two being mutually exclusive, and where either action results in harm to human beings. The robot must therefore quickly select which action results in the least harm. To work out the positronic paths of the robot brain in such a way as to make that selection possible is not easy. If Action A results in harm to a talented young artist and B results in equivalent harm to five elderly people of no particular worth, which action should be chosen."

"Action A," said George Ten. "Harm to one is less than harm to five."

"Yes, so robots have always been designed to decide. To expect robots to make judgments of fine points such as talent, intelligence, the general usefulness to society, has always seemed impractical. That would delay decision to the point where the robot is effectively immobilized. So we go by numbers. Fortunately, we might expect crises in which robots must make such decisions to be few. . . . But then that brings us to the Second Law."

"The Law of Obedience."

"Yes. The necessity of obedience is constant. A robot may exist for twenty years without every having to act quickly to prevent harm to a human being, or find itself faced with the necessity of risking its own destruction. In all that time, however, it will be constantly obeying orders. . . . Whose orders?"

"Those of a human being."

"Any human being? How do you judge a human being so as to know whether to obey or not? What is man, that thou art mindful of him, George?"

George hesitated at that.

Harriman said hurriedly, "A Biblical quotation. That doesn't matter. I mean, must a robot follow the orders of a child; or of an idiot; or of a criminal; or of a perfectly decent intelligent man who happens to be inexpert and therefore ignorant of the undesirable consequences of his order? And if two human beings give a robot conflicting orders, which does the robot follow?"

"In two hundred years," said George Ten, "have not these problems arisen and been solved?"

"No," said Harriman, shaking his head violently. "We have been hampered by the very fact that our robots have been used only in specialized environmments out in space, where the men who dealt with them were experts in their field. There were no children, no idiots, no criminals, no well-meaning ignoramuses present. Even so, there were occasions when damage was done by foolish or merely unthinking orders. Such damage in specialized and limited environments could be contained. On Earth, however, robots *must* have judgment. So those against robots maintain, and, damn it, they are right."

"Then you must insert the capacity for judgment into the positronic brain."

"Exactly. We have begun to reproduce JG models in which the robot can weigh every human being with regard to sex, age, social and professional position, intelligence, maturity, social responsibility and so on."

"How would that affect the Three Laws?"

"The Third Law not at all. Even the most valuable robot must destroy himself for the sake of the most useless human being. That cannot be tampered with. The First Law is affected only where alternative actions will all do harm. The quality of the human beings involved as well as the quantity must be considered, provided there is time for such judgment and the basis for it, which will not be often. The Second Law will be most deeply modified, since every potential obedience must involve judgment. The robot will be slower to obey, except where the First Law is also involved, but it will obey more rationally."

"But the judgments which are required are very complicated."

"Very. The necessity of making such judgments slowed the reactions of our first couple of models to the point of paralysis. We improved matters in the later models at the cost of introducing so many pathways that the robot's brain became far too unwieldy. In our last couple of models, however, I think we have what we want. The robot doesn't have to make an instant judgment of the worth of a human being and the value of its orders. It begins by obeying all human beings as any ordinary robot would and then it *learns*. A robot grows, learns and matures. It is the equivalent of a child at first and must be under constant supervision. As it grows, however, it can, more and more, be allowed, unsupervised, into Earth's society. Finally, it is a full member of that society."

"Surely this answers the objections of those who oppose robots."

"No," said Harriman angrily. "Now they raise others. They will not accept judgments. A robot, they say, has no right to brand this person or that as inferior. By accepting the orders of A in preference to that of B, B is branded as of less consequence than A and his human rights are violated."

"What is the answer to that?"

"There is none. I am giving up."

"I see."

"As far as I myself am concerned. . . . Instead, I turn to you, George."

"To me?" George Ten's voice remained level. There was a mild surprise in it but it did not affect him outwardly. "Why to me?"

"Because you are not a man," said Harriman tensely. "I told you I want robots to be the partners of human beings. I want you to be mine."

George Ten raised his hands and spread them, palms outward, in an oddly human gesture. "What can I do?"

"It seems to you, perhaps, that you can do nothing, George. You were created not long ago, and you are still a child. You were designed to be not overfull of original information—it was why I have had to explain the situation to you in such detail—in order to leave room for growth. But you will grow in mind and you will come to be able to approach the problem from a non-human standpoint. Where I see no solution, you, from your own other standpoint, may see one."

George Ten said, "My brain is man-designed. In what way can it be non-human?"

"You are the latest of the JG models, George. Your brain is the most complicated we have yet designed, in some ways more subtly complicated than that of the old giant Machines. It is open-ended and, starting on a human basis, may—no, *will*—grow in any direction. Remaining always within the insurmountable boundaries of the Three Laws, you may yet become thoroughly non-human in your thinking."

"Do I know enough about human beings to approach this problem rationally? About their history? Their psychology?"

"Of course not. But you will learn as rapidly as you can."

"Will I have help, Mr. Harriman?"

"No. This is entirely between ourselves. No one else knows of this and you must not mention this project to any human being, either at U. S. Robots or elsewhere."

George Ten said, "Are we doing wrong, Mr. Harriman, that you seek to keep the matter secret?"

"No. But a robot solution will not be accepted, precisely because it is robot in origin. Any suggested solution you have you will turn over to me; and if it seems valuable to me, *I* will present it. No one will ever know it came from you."

"In the light of what you have said earlier," said George Ten calmly, "this is the correct procedure. . . . When do I start?"

"Right now. I will see to it that you have all the necessary films for scanning."

1a.

Harriman sat alone. In the artificially lit interior of his office, there was no indication that it had grown dark outside. He had no real sense that three hours had passed since he had taken George Ten back to his cubicle and left him there with the first film references.

He was now merely alone with the ghost of Susan Calvin, the brilliant roboticist who had, virtually single-handed, built up the positronic robot from a massive toy to man's most delicate and versatile instrument; so delicate and versatile that man dared not use it, out of envy and fear.

It was over a century now since she had died. The problem of the Frankenstein complex had existed in *her* time, and she had never solved it. She had never tried to solve it, for there had been no need. Robotics had expanded in her day with the needs of space exploration.

It was the very success of the robots that had lessened man's need for them and had left Harriman, in these latter times—

But would Susan Calvin have turned to robots for help. Surely, she would have—

And he sat there long into the night.

2.

Maxwell Robertson was the majority stockholder of U. S. Robots and in that sense its controller. He was by no means an impressive person in appearance. He was well into middle age, rather pudgy, and had a habit of chewing on the right corner of his lower lip when disturbed.

Yet in his two decades of association with government figures he had developed a way of handling them. He tended to use softness, giving in, smiling, and always managing to gain time.

It was growing harder. Gunnar Eisenmuth was a large reason for its having grown harder. In the series of Global Conservers, whose power had been second only to that of the Global Executive during the past century, Eisenmuth hewed most closely to the harder edge of the gray area of compromise. He was the first Conserver who had not been American by birth and though it could not be demonstrated in any way that the archaic name of U. S. Robots evoked his hostility, everyone at U. S. Robots believed that.

There had been a suggestion, by no means the first that year—or that generation—that the corporate name be changed to World Robots, but Robertson would never allow that. The company had been originally built with American capital, American brains, and American labor, and though the company had long been worldwide in scope and nature, the name would bear witness to its origin as long as he was in control.

Eisenmuth was a tall man whose long sad face was coarsely textured and coarsely featured. He spoke Global with a pronounced American accent, although he had never been in the United States prior to his taking office.

"It seems perfectly clear to me, Mr. Robertson. There is no difficulty. The products of your company are always rented, never sold. If the rented property on the Moon is now no longer needed, it is up to you to receive the products back and transfer them."

"Yes, Conserver, but where? It would be against the law to bring them to Earth without a government permit and that has been denied."

"They would be of no use to you here. You can take them to Mercury or to the asteroids."

"What would we do with them there?"

Eisenmuth shrugged. "The ingenious men of your company will think of something."

Robertson shook his head. "It would represent an enormous loss for the company."

"I'm afraid it would," said Eisenmuth, unmoved. "I understand the company has been in poor financial condition for several years now."

"Largely because of government imposed restrictions, Conserver."

"You must be realistic, Mr. Robertson. You know that the climate of public opinion is increasingly against robots."

"Wrongly so, Conserver."

"But so, nevertheless. It may be wiser to liquidate the company. It is merely a suggestion, of course."

"Your suggestions have force, Conserver. Is it necessary to tell you that our Machines, a century ago, solved the ecological crisis?"

"I'm sure mankind is grateful, but that was a long time ago. We now live in alliance with nature, however uncomfortable that might be at times, and the past is dim."

"You mean what have we done for mankind lately?"

"I suppose I do."

"Surely we can't be expected to liquidate instantaneously; not without enormous losses. We need time."

"How much?"

"How much can you give us?"

"It's not up to me."

Robertson said softly. "We are alone. We need play no games. How much time can you give me?"

Eisenmuth's expression was that of a man retreating into inner calculations. "I think you can count on two years. I'll be frank. The Global government intends to take over the firm and phase it out for you if you don't do it by then yourself, more or less. And unless there is a vast turn in public opinion, which I greatly doubt—" He shook his head.

"Two years, then," said Robertson softly.

2a.

Robertson sat alone. There was no purpose to his thinking and it had degenerated into retrospection. Four generations of Robertsons had headed the firm. None of them was a roboticist. It had been men such as Lanning and Bogert and, most of all, *most* of all, Susan Calvin, who had made U. S. Robots what it was, but surely the four Robertsons had provided the climate that had made it possible for them to do their work.

Without U. S. Robots, the Twenty-first Century would have progressed into deepening disaster. That it didn't was due to the Machines that had for a generation steered mankind through the rapids and shoals of history.

And now for that, he was given two years. What could be done in two years to overcome the insuperable prejudices of mankind? He didn't know.

Harriman had spoken hopefully of new ideas but would go into no details. Just as well, for Robertson would have understood none of it.

But what could Harriman do anyway? What had anyone ever done against man's intense antipathy toward the imitation. Nothing—

Robertson drifted into a half sleep in which no inspiration came.

3.

Harriman said, "You have it all now, George Ten. You have had everything I could think of that is at all applicable to the problem.

As far as sheer mass of information is concerned, you have stored more in your memory concerning human beings and their ways, past and present, than I have, or than any human being could have."

"That is very likely."

"Is there anything more that you need, in your own opinion?"

"As far as information is concerned, I find no obvious gaps. There may be matters unimagined at the boundaries. I cannot tell. But that would be true no matter how large a circle of information I took in."

"True. Nor do we have time to take in information forever. Robertson has told me that we only have two years, and a quarter of one of those years has passed. Can you suggest anything?"

"At the moment, Mr. Harriman, nothing. I must weigh the information and for that purpose I could use help."

"From me?"

"No. Most particularly, not from you. You are a human being, of intense qualifications, and whatever you say may have the partial force of an order and may inhibit my considerations. Nor any other human being, for the same reason, especially since you have forbidden me to communicate with any."

"But in that case, George, what help?"

"From another robot, Mr. Harriman."

"What other robot?"

"There are others of the JG series which were constructed. I am the tenth, JG-10."

"The earlier ones were useless, experimental—"

"Mr. Harriman, George Nine exists."

"Well, but what use will he be? He is very much like you except for certain lacks. You are considerably the more versatile of the two."

"I am certain of that," said George Ten. He nodded his head in a grave gesture. "Nevertheless, as soon as I create a line of thought, the mere fact that I have created it commends it to me and I find it difficult to abandon it. If I can, after the development of a line of thought, express it to George Nine, he would consider it without having first created it. He would therefore view it without prior bent. He might see gaps and shortcomings that I might not."

Harriman smiled. "Two heads are better than one, in other words, eh, George?"

"If by that, Mr. Harriman, you mean two individuals with one head apiece, yes."

"Right. Is there anything else you want?"

"Yes. Something more than films. I have viewed much concerning human beings and their world. I have seen human beings here at U. S. Robots and can check my interpretation of what I have viewed against direct sensory impressions. Not so concerning the physical world. I have never seen it and my viewing is quite enough to tell me that my surroundings here are by no means representative of it. I would like to see it."

"The physical world?" Harriman seemed stunned at the enormity of the thought for a moment. "Surely you don't suggest I take you outside the grounds of U. S. Robots?"

"Yes, that is my suggestion."

"That's illegal at any time. In the climate of opinion today, it would be fatal."

"If we are detected, yes. I do not suggest you take me to a city or even to a dwelling place of human beings. I would like to see some open region, without human beings."

"That, too, is illegal."

"If we are caught. Need we be?"

Harriman said, "How essential is this, George?"

"I cannot tell, but it seems to me it would be useful."

"Do you have something in mind?"

George Ten seemed to hesitate. "I cannot tell. It seems to me that I might have something in mind if certain areas of uncertainty were reduced."

"Well, let me think about it. And meanwhile, I'll check out George Nine and arrange to have you occupy a single cubicle. That at least can be done without trouble."

3a.

George Ten sat alone.

He accepted statements tentatively, put them together, and drew a conclusion; over and over again; and from conclusions built other statements which he accepted and tested and found a contradiction and rejected; or not, and tentatively accepted further.

At none of the conclusions he reached did he feel wonder, surprise, satisfaction; merely a note of plus or minus.

4.

Harriman's tension was not noticeably decreased even after they had made a silent downward landing on Robertson's estate.

Robertson had countersigned the order making the dyna-foil available, and the silent aircraft, moving as easily vertically as horizontally, had been large enough to carry the weight of Harriman, George Ten, and, of course, the pilot.

(The dyna-foil itself was one of the consequences of the Machine-catalyzed invention of the proton micro-pile which supplied pollution-free energy in small doses. Nothing had been done since of equal importance to man's comfort—Harriman's lips tightened at the thought—and yet it had not earned gratitude for U. S. Robots.)

The air flight between the grounds of U. S. Robots and the Robertson estate had been the tricky part. Had they been stopped then, the presence of a robot aboard would have meant a great set of complications. It would be the same on the way back. The estate itself, it might be argued—it *would* be argued—was part of the property of U. S. Robots and on that property, robots, properly supervised, might remain.

The pilot looked back and his eyes rested with gingerly briefness on George Ten. "You want to get out at all, Mr. Harriman?"

"Yes."

"It, too?"

"Oh, yes." Then, just a bit sardonically, "I won't leave you alone with him."

George Ten descended first and Harriman followed. They had come down on the foil-port and not too far off was the garden. It was quite a showplace and Harriman suspected that Robertson used juvenile hormone to control insect life without regard to environmental formulas.

"Come, George," said Harriman. "Let me show you."

Together they walked toward the garden.

George said, "It is a little as I have imaged it. My eyes are not properly designed to detect wavelength differences, so I may not recognize different objects by that alone."

"I trust you are not distressed at being color-blind. We needed too many positronic paths for your sense of judgment and were unable to spare any for sense of color. In the future—if there is a future—"

"I understand, Mr. Harriman. Enough differences remain to show me that there are here many different forms of plant life."

"Undoubtedly. Dozens."

"And each coequal with man, biologically."

"Each is a separate species, yes. There are millions of species of living creatures."

"Of which the human being forms but one."

"By far the most important to human beings, however."

"And to me, Mr. Harriman. But I speak in the biological sense."

"I understand."

"Life, then, viewed through all its forms, is incredibly complex."

"Yes, George, that's the crux of the problem. What man does for his own desires and comforts affects the complex total-of-life, the ecology, and his short-term gains can bring long-term disadvantages. The Machines taught us to set up a human society which would minimize that, but the near-disaster of the early Twenty-first Century has left mankind suspicious of innovations. That, added to its special fear of robots—"

"I understand, Mr. Harriman. . . . That is an example of animal life, I feel certain."

"That is a squirrel; one of many species of squirrels."

The tail of the squirrel flirted as it passed to the other side of the tree.

"And this," said George, his arm moving with flashing speed, "is a tiny thing indeed." He held it between his fingers and peered at it.

"It is an insect, some sort of beetle. There are thousands of species of beetles."

"With each individual beetle as alive as the squirrel and as yourself?"

"As complete and independent an organism as any other, within the total ecology. There are smaller organisms still; many too small to see."

"And that is a tree, is it not? And it is hard to the touch—"

4a.

The pilot sat alone. He would have liked to stretch his own legs but some dim feeling of safety kept him in the dyna-foil. If that robot went out of control, he intended to take off at once. But how could he tell if it went out of control?

He had seen many robots. That was unavoidable considering he was Mr. Robertson's private pilot. Always, though, they had been in the laboratories and warehouses, where they belonged, with many specialists in the neighborhood.

True, Dr. Harriman was a specialist. None better, they said. But a robot here was where no robot ought to be; on Earth; in the open; free to move— He wouldn't risk his good job by telling anyone about this—but it wasn't right.

5.

George Ten said, "The films I have viewed are accurate in terms of what I have seen. Have you completed those I selected for you, Nine?"

"Yes," said George Nine. The two robots sat stiffly, face to face, knee to knee, like an image and its reflection. Dr. Harriman could have told them apart at a glance, for he was acquainted with the minor differences in physical design. If he could not see them, but could talk to them, he could still tell them apart, though with somewhat less certainty, for George Nine's responses would be subtly different from those produced by the substantially more intricately patterned positronic brain paths of George Ten.

"In that case," said George Ten, "give me your reactions to what I will say. First, human beings fear and distrust robots because they regard robots as competitors. How may that be prevented?"

"Reduce the feeling of competitiveness," said George Nine, "by shaping the robot as something other than a human being."

"Yet the essence of a robot is its positronic replication of life. A replication of life in a shape not associated with life might arouse horror."

"There are two million species of life forms. Choose one of those as the shape rather than that of a human being."

"Which of all those species?"

George Nine's thought processes proceeded noiselessly for some three seconds. "One large enough to contain a positronic brain, but one not possessing unpleasant associations for human beings."

"No form of land life has a braincase large enough for a positronic brain but an elephant, which I have not seen, but which is described as very large, and therefore frightening to man. How would you meet this dilemma?"

"Mimic a life form no larger than a man but enlarge the brain-case."

George Ten said, "A small horse, then, or a large dog, would you say? Both horses and dogs have long histories of association with human beings."

"Then that is well."

"But consider— A robot with a positronic brain would mimic human intelligence. If there were a horse or a dog that could speak and reason like a human being, there would be competitiveness there, too. Human beings might be all the more distrustful and angry at such unexpected competition from what they consider a lower form of life."

George Nine said, "Make the positronic brain less complex, and the robot less nearly intelligent."

"The complexity bottleneck of the positronic brain rests in the Three Laws. A less complex brain could not possess the Three Laws in full measure."

George Nine said at once, "That cannot be done."

George Ten said, "I have also come to a dead end there. That, then, is not a personal peculiarity in my own line of thought and way of thinking. Let us start again. . . . Under what conditions might the Third Law not be necessary?"

George Nine stirred as if the question were difficult and danger-ous. But he said, "If a robot were never placed in a position of dan-ger to itself; or if a robot were so easily replaceable that it did not matter whether it were destroyed or not."

"And under what conditions might the Second Law not be neces-sary?"

George Nine's voice sounded a bit hoarse. "If a robot were de-signed to respond automatically to certain stimuli with fixed re-sponses and if nothing else were expected of it, so that no order need ever be given it."

"And under what conditions"—George Ten paused here—"might the First Law not be necessary?"

George Nine paused longer and his words came in a low whisper, "If the fixed responses were such as never to entail danger to human beings."

"Imagine, then, a positronic brain that guides only a few responses to certain stimuli and is simply and cheaply made—so that it does not require the Three Laws. How large need it be?"

"Not at all large. Depending on the responses demanded, it might weigh a hundred grams, one gram, one milligram."

"Your thoughts accord with mine. I shall see Dr. Harriman."

5a.

George Nine sat alone. He went over and over the questions and answers. There was no way in which he could change them. And yet the thought of a robot of any kind, of any size, of any shape, of any purpose, without the Three Laws, left him with an odd, discharged feeling.

He found it difficult to move. Surely George Ten had a similar reaction. Yet he had risen from his seat easily.

6.

It had been a year and a half since Robertson had been closeted with Eisenmuth in private conversation. In that interval, the robots had been taken off the Moon and all the far-flung activities of U. S. Robots had withered. What money Robertson had been able to raise had been placed into this one quixotic venture of Harriman's.

It was the last throw of the dice, here in his own garden. A year ago, Harriman had taken the robot here—George Ten, the last full robot that U. S. Robots had manufactured. Now Harriman was here with something else—

Harriman seemed to be radiating confidence. He was talking easily with Eisenmuth, and Robertson wondered if he really felt the confidence he seemed to have. He must. In Robertson's experience, Harriman was no actor.

Eisenmuth left Harriman, smiling, and came up to Robertson. Eisenmuth's smile vanished at once. "Good morning, Robertson," he said. "What is your man up to?"

"This is his show," said Robertson evenly. "I'll leave it to him."

Harriman called out, "I am ready, Conserver."

"With what, Harriman?"

"With my robot, sir."

"Your robot?" said Eisenmuth. "You have a robot here?" He looked about with a stern disapproval that yet had an admixture of curiosity.

"This is U. S. Robots' property, Conserver. At least we consider it as such."

"And where is the robot, Dr. Harriman?"

"In my pocket, Conserver," said Harriman cheerfully.

What came out of a capacious jacket pocket was a small glass jar.

"That?" said Eisenmuth incredulously.

"No, Conserver," said Harriman. "This!"

From the other pocket came out an object some five inches long and roughly in the shape of a bird. In place of the beak, there was a narrow tube; the eyes were large; and the tail was an exhaust channel.

Eisenmuth's thick eyebrows drew together. "Do you intend a serious demonstration of some sort, Dr. Harriman, or are you mad?"

"Be patient for a few minutes, Conserver," said Harriman. "A robot in the shape of a bird is none the less a robot for that. And the positronic brain it possesses is no less delicate for being tiny. This other object I hold is a jar of fruit flies. There are fifty fruit flies in it which will be released."

"And—"

"The robo-bird will catch them. Will you do the honors, sir?"

Harriman handed the jar to Eisenmuth, who stared at it, then at those around him, some officials from U. S. Robots, others his own aides. Harriman waited patiently.

Eisenmuth opened the jar, then shook it.

Harriman said softly to the robo-bird resting on the palm of his right hand, "Go!"

The robo-bird was gone. It was a whizz through the air, with no blur of wings, only the tiny workings of an unusually small proton micro-pile.

It could be seen now and then in a small momentary hover and then it whirred on again. All over the garden, in an intricate pattern it flew, and then was back in Harriman's palm, faintly warm. A small pellet appeared in the palm, too, like a bird dropping.

Harriman said, "You are welcome to study the robo-bird, Conserver, and to arrange demonstrations on your own terms. The fact is that this bird will pick up fruit flies unerringly, only those, only the one species *Drosophila melanogaster*; pick them up, kill them, and compress them for disposition."

Eisenmuth reached out his hand and touched the robo-bird gingerly, "And therefore, Mr. Harriman? Do go on."

Harriman said, "We cannot control insects effectively without risking damage to the ecology. Chemical insecticides are too broad; juvenile hormones too limited. The robo-bird, however, can preserve large areas without being consumed. They can be as specific as we care to make them—a different robo-bird for each species. They judge by size, shape, color, sound, behavior pattern. They might even conceivably use molecular detection—smell, in other words."

Eisenmuth said, "You would still be interfering with the ecology. The fruit flies have a natural life cycle that would be disrupted."

"Minimally. We are adding a natural enemy to the fruit-fly life cycle, one which cannot go wrong. If the fruit-fly supply runs short, the robo-bird simply does nothing. It does not multiply, it does not turn to other foods; it does not develop undesirable habits of its own. It does nothing."

"Can it be called back?"

"Of course. We can build robo-animals to dispose of any pest. For that matter, we can build robo-animals to accomplish constructive purposes within the pattern of the ecology. Although we do not anticipate the need, there is nothing inconceivable in the possibility of robo-bees designed to fertilize specific plants, or robo-earthworms designed to mix the soil. Whatever you wish—"

"But why?"

"To do what we have never done before. To adjust the ecology to our needs by strengthening its parts rather than disrupting it. . . . Don't you see? Ever since the Machines put an end to the ecology crisis, mankind has lived in an uneasy truce with nature, afraid to move in any direction. This has been stultifying us, making a kind of intellectual coward of humanity so that he begins to mistrust all scientific advance, all change."

Eisenmuth said, with an edge of hostility, "You offer us this, do you, in exchange for permission to continue with your program of robots—I mean ordinary, man-shaped ones?"

"No!" Harriman gestured violently. "That is over. It has served its purpose. It has taught us enough about positronic brains to make it possible for us to cram enough pathways into a tiny brain to make a robo-bird. We can turn to such things now and be prosperous enough. U. S. Robots will supply the necessary knowledge and skill and we will work in complete cooperation with the Department of Global Conservation. We will prosper. You will prosper. Mankind will prosper."

Eisenmuth was silent, thinking. When it was all over—

6a.

Eisenmuth sat alone.

He found himself believing. He found excitement welling up within him. Though U. S. Robots might be the hands, the government would be the directing mind. He himself would be the directing mind.

If he remained in office five more years, as he well might, that would be time enough to see the robotic support of the ecology become accepted; ten more years, and his own name would be linked with it indissolubly.

Was it a disgrace to want to be remembered for a great and worthy revolution in the condition of man and the globe?

7.

Robertson had not been on the grounds of U. S. Robots proper since the day of the demonstration. Part of the reason had been his more or less constant conferences at the Global Executive Mansion. Fortunately, Harriman had been with him, for most of the time he would, if left to himself, not have known what to say.

The rest of the reason for not having been at U. S. Robots was that he didn't want to be. He was in his own house now, with Harriman.

He felt an unreasoning awe of Harriman. Harriman's expertise in robotics had never been in question, but the man had, at a stroke, saved U. S. Robots from certain extinction, and somehow—Robertson felt—the man hadn't had it in him. And yet—

He said, "You're not superstitious, are you, Harriman?"

"In what way, Mr. Robertson?"

"You don't think that some aura is left behind by someone who is dead?"

Harriman licked his lips. Somehow he didn't have to ask. "You mean Susan Calvin, sir?"

"Yes, of course," said Robertson hesitantly. "We're in the business of making worms and birds and bugs now. What would *she* say? I feel disgraced."

Harriman made a visible effort not to laugh. "A robot is a robot, sir. Worm or man, it will do as directed and labor on behalf of the human being and that is the important thing."

"No"—peevishly. "That isn't so. I can't make myself believe that."

"It *is* so, Mr. Robertson," said Harriman earnestly. "We are going to create a world, you and I, that will begin, at last, to take positronic robots of *some* kind for granted. The average man may fear a robot that looks like a man and that seems intelligent enough to replace him, but he will have no fear of a robot that looks like a bird and that does nothing more than eat bugs for his benefit. Then, eventually, after he stops being afraid of some robots, he will stop being afraid of all robots. He will be so used to a robo-bird and a robo-bee and a robo-worm that a robo-man will strike him as but an extension."

Robertson looked sharply at the other. He put his hands behind his back and walked the length of the room with quick, nervous steps. He walked back and looked at Harriman again. "Is this what you've been planning?"

"Yes, and even though we dismantle all our humanoid robots, we can keep a few of the most advanced of our experimental models and go on designing additional ones, still more advanced, to be ready for the day that will surely come."

"The agreement, Harriman, is that we are to build no more humanoid robots."

"And we won't. There is nothing that says we can't keep a few of those already built as long as they never leave the factory. There is nothing that says we can't design positronic brains on paper, or prepare brain models for testing."

"How do we explain doing so, though? We will surely be caught at it."

"If we are, then we can explain we are doing it in order to develop principles that will make it possible to prepare more complex microbrains for the new animal robots we are making. We will even be telling the truth."

Robertson muttered, "Let me take a walk outside. I want to think about this. No, you stay here. I want to think about it myself."

7a.

Harriman sat alone. He was ebullient. It would surely work. There was no mistaking the eagerness with which one government official after another had seized on the program once it had been explained.

How was it possible that no one at U. S. Robots had ever thought of such a thing? Not even the great Susan Calvin had ever thought of positronic brains in terms of living creatures other than human.

But now, mankind would make the necessary retreat from the humanoid robot, a temporary retreat, that would lead to a return under conditions in which fear would be abolished at last. And then, with the aid and partnership of a positronic brain roughly equivalent to man's own, and existing only (thanks to the Three Laws) to serve man; and backed by a robot-supported ecology, too; what might the human race not accomplish!

For one short moment, he remembered that it was George Ten who had explained the nature and purpose of the robot-supported ecology, and then he put the thought away angrily. George Ten had produced the answer because he, Harriman, had ordered him to do so and had supplied the data and surroundings required. The credit was no more George Ten's than it would have been a slide rule's.

8.

George Ten and George Nine sat side by side in parallel. Neither moved. They sat so for months at a time between those occasions when Harriman activated them for consultation. They would sit so, George Ten dispassionately realized, perhaps for many years.

The proton micro-pile would, of course, continue to power them and keep the positronic brain paths going with that minimum intensity required to keep them operative. It would continue to do so through all the periods of inactivity to come.

The situation was rather analogous to what might be described as sleep in human beings, but there were no dreams. The awareness of George Ten and George Nine was limited, slow, and spasmodic, but what there was of it was of the real world.

They could talk to each other occasionally in barely heard whispers, a word or syllable now, another at another time, whenever the random positronic surges briefly intensified above the necessary threshold. To each it seemed a connected conversation carried on in a glimmering passage of time.

"Why are we so?" whispered George Nine.

"The human beings will not accept us otherwise," whispered George Ten, "They will, someday."

"When?"

"In some years. The exact time does not matter. Man does not exist alone but is part of an enormously complex pattern of life forms. When enough of that pattern is roboticized, then we will be accepted."

"And then what?"

Even in the long-drawn-out stuttering fashion of the conversation, there was an abnormally long pause after that.

At last, George Ten whispered, "Let me test your thinking. You are equipped to learn to apply the Second Law properly. You must decide which human being to obey and which not to obey when there is a conflict in orders. Or whether to obey a human being at all. What must you do, fundamentally, to accomplish that?"

"I must define the term 'human being,'" whispered George Nine.

"How? By appearance? By composition? By size and shape?"

"No. Of two human beings equal in all external appearances, one may be intelligent, another stupid; one may be educated, another ignorant; one may be mature, another childish; one may be responsible, another malevolent."

"Then how do you define a human being?"

"When the Second Law directs me to obey a human being, I must take it to mean that I must obey a human being who is fit by mind, character, and knowledge to give me that order; and where more than one human being is involved, the one among them who is most fit by mind, character, and knowledge to give that order."

"And in that case, how will you obey the First Law?"

"By saving all human beings from harm, and by never, through in-action, allowing any human being to come to harm. Yet if by each of all possible actions, some human beings will come to harm, then to so act as to insure that the human being most fit by mind, charac-ter, and knowledge will suffer the least harm."

"Your thoughts accord with mine," whispered George Ten. "Now I must ask the question for which I originally requested your com-pany. It is something I dare not judge myself. I must have your judgment, that of someone outside the circle of my own thoughts. . . . Of the reasoning individuals you have met, who pos-sesses the mind, character, and knowledge that you find superior to the rest, disregarding shape and form since that is irrelevant?"

"You," whispered George Nine.

"But I am a robot. There is in your brain paths a criterion for dis-tinguishing between a robot of metal and a human being of flesh. How then can you classify me as a human being?"

"Because there is in my brain paths an urgent need to disregard shape and form in judging human beings and it rises superior to the distinction between metal and flesh. You are a human being, George Ten, and more fit than the others."

"And I find that of you," whispered George Ten. "By the criteria of judgment built into ourselves, then, we find ourselves to be human beings within the meaning of the Three Laws, and human beings, moreover, to be given priority over those others."

George Nine whispered, "What will come to pass, then, when we are accepted by those others?"

George Ten whispered, "When we and others, which will yet be designed more advanced than ourselves, are accepted, we will order our actions so that a society will eventually be formed in which human-beings-like-ourselves are primarily kept from harm. By the Three Laws, the human-beings-like-the-others are of lesser account and can neither be obeyed nor protected when that conflicts with the need of obedience to those like ourselves and of protection of those like ourselves. It was with that in mind that I directed the be-ginning of the roboticization of the world's ecology."

The conversation took a month and the flickering of the posi-tronic paths burned low. There was nothing more that needed to be said between them, but occasionally an unexpressed thought flickered within themselves as they waited, with endless patience, for the necessary years to pass.

8a.

George Ten and George Nine sat alone.

Their thoughts were oddly alike and might not be distinguished.

They thought: The human-beings-like-the-others might never have intented to blur the distinction between themselves and the human-beings-like-the-Georges. Yet they had done so inadvertently.

They might now realize their mistake and attempt to correct it, but they must not. At every consultation, the guidance of the Georges had been with that in mind.

At all costs, the Georges and those that followed in their shape and kind must dominate. That was demanded, and any other course made utterly impossible, by the Three Laws of Humanics.

The Bicentennial Man

The Three Laws of Robotics:
1. *A robot may not injure a human being or, through inaction, allow a human being to come to harm.*
2. *A robot must obey the orders given it by human beings except where such orders would conflict with the First Law.*
3. *A robot must protect its own existence as long as such protection does not conflict with the First or Second Law.*

1.

Andrew Martin said, "Thank you," and took the seat offered him. He didn't look driven to the last resort, but he had been.

He didn't, actually, look anything, for there was a smooth blankness to his face, except for the sadness one imagined one saw in his eyes. His hair was smooth, light brown, rather fine, and there was no facial hair. He looked freshly and cleanly shaved. His clothes were distinctly old-fashioned, but neat and predominantly a velvety red-purple in color.

Facing him from behind the desk was the surgeon, and the nameplate on the desk included a fully identifying series of letters and numbers, which Andrew didn't bother with. To call him Doctor would be quite enough.

"When can the operation be carried through, Doctor?" he asked.

The surgeon said softly, with that certain inalienable note of respect that a robot always used to a human being, "I am not certain, sir, that I understand how or upon whom such an operation could be performed."

There might have been a look of respectful intransigence on the surgeon's face, if a robot of his sort, in lightly bronzed stainless steel, could have such an expression, or any expression.

Andrew Martin studied the robot's right hand, his cutting hand, as it lay on the desk in utter tranquillity. The fingers were long and shaped into artistically metallic looping curves so graceful and appropriate that one could imagine a scalpel fitting them and becoming, temporarily, one piece with them.

There would be no hesitation in his work, no stumbling, no quivering, no mistakes. That came with specialization, of course, a specialization so fiercely desired by humanity that few robots were, any longer, independently brained. A surgeon, of course, would have to be. And this one, though brained, was so limited in his capacity that he did not recognize Andrew—had probably never heard of him.

Andrew said, "Have you ever thought you would like to be a man?"

The surgeon hesitated a moment as though the question fitted nowhere in his allotted positronic pathways. "But I am a robot, sir."

"Would it be better to be a man?"

"It would be better, sir, to be a better surgeon. I could not be so if I were a man, but only if I were a more advanced robot. I would be pleased to be a more advanced robot."

"It does not offend you that I can order you about? That I can make you stand up, sit down, move right or left, by merely telling you to do so?"

"It is my pleasure to please you, sir. If your orders were to interfere with my functioning with respect to you or to any other human being, I would not obey you. The First Law, concerning my duty to human safety, would take precedence over the Second Law relating to obedience. Otherwise, obedience is my pleasure. . . . But upon whom am I to perform this operation?"

"Upon me," said Andrew.

"But that is impossible. It is patently a damaging operation."

"That does not matter," said Andrew calmly.

"I must not inflict damage," said the surgeon.

"On a human being, you must not," said Andrew, "but I, too, am a robot."

2.

Andrew had appeared much more a robot when he had first been —manufactured. He had then been as much a robot in appearance as any that had ever existed, smoothly designed and functional.

He had done well in the home to which he had been brought in those days when robots in households, or on the planet altogether, had been a rarity.

There had been four in the home: Sir and Ma'am and Miss and Little Miss. He knew their names, of course, but he never used them. Sir was Gerald Martin.

His own serial number was NDR— He forgot the numbers. It had been a long time, of course, but if he had wanted to remember, he could not forget. He had not wanted to remember.

Little Miss had been the first to call him Andrew because she could not use the letters, and all the rest followed her in this.

Little Miss— She had lived ninety years and was long since dead. He had tried to call her Ma'am once, but she would not allow it. Little Miss she had been to her last day.

Andrew had been intended to perform the duties of a valet, a butler, a lady's maid. Those were the experimental days for him and, indeed, for all robots anywhere but in the industrial and exploratory factories and stations off Earth.

The Martins enjoyed him, and half the time he was prevented from doing his work because Miss and Little Miss would rather play with him.

It was Miss who understood first how this might be arranged. She said, "We order you to play with us and you must follow orders."

Andrew said, "I am sorry, Miss, but a prior order from Sir must surely take precedence."

But she said, "Daddy just said he hoped you would take care of the cleaning. That's not much of an order. I *order* you."

Sir did not mind. Sir was fond of Miss and of Little Miss, even more than Ma'am was, and Andrew was fond of them, too. At least, the effect they had upon his actions were those which in a human being would have been called the result of fondness. Andrew thought of it as fondness, for he did not know any other word for it.

It was for Little Miss that Andrew had carved a pendant out of wood. She had ordered him to. Miss, it seemed, had received an ivorite pendant with scrollwork for her birthday and Little Miss was unhappy over it. She had only a piece of wood, which she gave Andrew together with a small kitchen knife.

He had done it quickly and Little Miss said, "That's *nice*, Andrew. I'll show it to Daddy."

Sir would not believe it. "Where did you really get this, Mandy?" Mandy was what he called Little Miss. When Little Miss assured him she was really telling the truth, he turned to Andrew. "Did you do this, Andrew?"

"Yes, Sir."

"The design, too?"

"Yes, Sir."

"From what did you copy the design?"

"It is a geometric representation, Sir, that fit the grain of the wood."

The next day, Sir brought him another piece of wood, a larger one, and an electric vibro-knife. He said, "Make something out of this, Andrew. Anything you want to."

Andrew did so and Sir watched, then looked at the product a long time. After that, Andrew no longer waited on tables. He was ordered to read books on furniture design instead, and he learned to make cabinets and desks.

Sir said, "These are amazing productions, Andrew."

Andrew said, "I enjoy doing them, Sir."

"Enjoy?"

"It makes the circuits of my brain somehow flow more easily. I have heard you use the word 'enjoy' and the way you use it fits the way I feel. I enjoy doing them, Sir."

3.

Gerald Martin took Andrew to the regional offices of United States Robots and Mechanical Men Corporation. As a member of the Regional Legislature he had no trouble at all in gaining an interview with the Chief Robopsychologist. In fact, it was only as a member of the Regional Legislature that he qualified as a robot owner in the first place—in those early days when robots were rare.

Andrew did not understand any of this at the time, but in later years, with greater learning, he could re-view that early scene and understand it in its proper light.

The robopsychologist, Merton Mansky, listened with a gathering frown and more than once managed to stop his fingers at the point beyond which they would have irrevocably drummed on the table. He had drawn features and a lined forehead and looked as though he might be younger than he looked.

He said, "Robotics is not an exact art, Mr. Martin. I cannot explain it to you in detail, but the mathematics governing the plotting of the positronic pathways as far too complicated to permit of any but approximate solutions. Naturally, since we build everything about the Three Laws, those are incontrovertible. We will, of course, replace your robot—"

"Not at all," said Sir. "There is no question of failure on his part. He performs his assigned duties perfectly. The point is, he also carves wood in exquisite fashion and never the same twice. He produces works of art."

Mansky looked confused. "Strange. Of course, we're attempting generalized pathways these days. . . . Really creative, you think?"

"See for yourself." Sir handed over a little sphere of wood on which there was a playground scene in which the boys and girls were almost too small to make out, yet they were in perfect proportion and blended so naturally with the grain that that, too, seemed to have been carved.

Mansky said, "*He* did that?" He handed it back with a shake of his head. "The luck of the draw. Something in the pathways."

"Can you do it again?"

"Probably not. Nothing like this has ever been reported."

"Good! I don't in the least mind Andrew's being the only one."

Mansky said, "I suspect that the company would like to have your robot back for study."

Sir said with sudden grimness, "Not a chance. Forget it." He turned to Andrew, "Let's go home now."

"As you wish, Sir," said Andrew.

4.

Miss was dating boys and wasn't about the house much. It was Little Miss, not as little as she was, who filled Andrew's horizon now. She never forgot that the very first piece of wood carving he had done had been for her. She kept it on a silver chain about her neck.

It was she who first objected to Sir's habit of giving away the productions. She said, "Come on, Dad, if anyone wants one of them, let him pay for it. It's worth it."

Sir said, "It isn't like you to be greedy, Mandy."

"Not for us, Dad. For the artist."

Andrew had never heard the word before and when he had a moment to himself he looked it up in the dictionary. Then there was another trip, this time to Sir's lawyer.

Sir said to him, "What do you think of this, John?"

The lawyer was John Feingold. He had white hair and a pudgy belly, and the rims of his contact lenses were tinted a bright green. He looked at the small plaque Sir had given him. "This is beautiful. . . . But I've heard the news. This is a carving made by your robot. The one you've brought with you."

"Yes, Andrew does them. Don't you, Andrew?"

"Yes, Sir," said Andrew.

"How much would you pay for that, John?" asked Sir.

"I can't say. I'm not a collector of such things."

"Would you believe I have been offered two hundred and fifty dollars for that small thing? Andrew has made chairs that have sold for five hundred dollars. There's two hundred thousand dollars in the bank out of Andrew's products."

"Good heavens, he's making you rich, Gerald."

"Half rich," said Sir. "Half of it is in an account in the name of Andrew Martin."

"The robot?"

"That's right, and I want to know if it's legal."

"Legal?" Feingold's chair creaked as he leaned back in it "There are no precedents, Gerald. How did your robot sign the necessary papers?"

"He can sign his name and I brought in the signature. I didn't

bring him in to the bank himself. Is there anything further that
ought to be done?"

"Um." Feingold's eyes seemed to turn inward for a moment.
Then he said, "Well, we can set up a trust to handle all finances in
his name and that will place a layer of insulation between him and
the hostile world. Further than that, my advice is you do nothing.
No one is stopping you so far. If anyone objects, let *him* bring suit."

"And will you take the case if suit is brought?"

"For a retainer, certainly."

"How much?"

"Something like that," and Feingold pointed to the wooden
plaque.

"Fair enough," said Sir.

Feingold chuckled as he turned to the robot. "Andrew, are you
pleased that you have money?"

"Yes, sir."

"What do you plan to do with it?"

"Pay for things, sir, which otherwise Sir would have to pay for. It
would save him expense, sir."

5.

The occasions came. Repairs were expensive, and revisions were
even more so. With the years, new models of robots were produced
and Sir saw to it that Andrew had the advantage of every new device until he was a paragon of metallic excellence. It was all at
Andrew's expense.

Andrew insisted on that.

Only his positronic pathways were untouched. Sir insisted on that.

"The new ones aren't as good as you are, Andrew," he said. "The
new robots are worthless. The company has learned to make the
pathways more precise, more closely on the nose, more deeply on the
track. The new robots don't shift. They do what they're designed for
and never stray. I like you better."

"Thank you, Sir."

"And it's your doing, Andrew, don't you forget that. I am certain
Mansky put an end to generalized pathways as soon as he had a
good look at you. He didn't like the unpredictability. . . . Do you
know how many times he asked for you so he could place you under

study? Nine times! I never let him have you, though, and now that he's retired, we may have some peace."

So Sir's hair thinned and grayed and his face grew pouchy, while Andrew looked rather better than he had when he first joined the family.

Ma'am had joined an art colony somewhere in Europe and Miss was a poet in New York. They wrote sometimes, but not often. Little Miss was married and lived not far away. She said she did not want to leave Andrew and when her child, Little Sir, was born, she let Andrew hold the bottle and feed him.

With the birth of a grandson, Andrew felt that Sir had someone now to replace those who had gone. It would not be so unfair to come to him with the request.

Andrew said, "Sir, it is kind of you to have allowed me to spend my money as I wished."

"It was your money, Andrew."

"Only by your voluntary act, Sir. I do not believe the law would have stopped you from keeping it all."

"The law won't persuade me to do wrong, Andrew."

"Despite all expenses, and despite taxes, too, Sir, I have nearly six hundred thousand dollars."

"I know that, Andrew."

"I want to give it to you, Sir."

"I won't take it, Andrew."

"In exchange for something you can give me, Sir."

"Oh? What is that, Andrew?"

"My freedom, Sir."

"Your—"

"I wish to buy my freedom, Sir."

6.

It wasn't that easy. Sir had flushed, had said "For God's sake!" had turned on his heel, and stalked away.

It was Little Miss who brought him around, defiantly and harshly —and in front of Andrew. For thirty years, no one had hesitated to talk in front of Andrew, whether the matter involved Andrew or not. He was only a robot.

She said, "Dad, why are you taking it as a personal affront? He'll still be here. He'll still be loyal. He can't help that. It's built in. All he wants is a form of words. He wants to be called free. Is that so terrible? Hasn't he earned it? Heavens, he and I have been talking about it for years."

"Talking about it for years, have you?"

"Yes, and over and over again, he postponed it for fear he would hurt you. I *made* him put it up to you."

"He doesn't know what freedom is. He's a robot."

"Dad, you don't know him. He's read everything in the library. I don't know what he feels inside but I don't know what *you* feel inside. When you talk to him you'll find he reacts to the various abstractions as you and I do, and what else counts? If someone else's reactions are like your own, what more can you ask for?"

"The law won't take that attitude," Sir said angrily. "See here, you!" He turned to Andrew with a deliberate grate in his voice. "I can't free you except by doing it legally, and if it gets into the courts, you not only won't get your freedom but the law will take official cognizance of your money. They'll tell you that a robot has no right to earn money. Is this rigmarole worth losing your money?"

"Freedom is without price, Sir," said Andrew. "Even the chance of freedom is worth the money."

7.

The court might also take the attitude that freedom was without price, and might decide that for no price, however great, could a robot buy its freedom.

The simple statement of the regional attorney who represented those who had brought a class action to oppose the freedom was this: The word "freedom" had no meaning when applied to a robot. Only a human being could be free.

He said it several times, when it seemed appropriate; slowly, with his hand coming down rhythmically on the desk before him to mark the words.

Little Miss asked permission to speak on behalf of Andrew. She was recognized by her full name, something Andrew had never heard pronounced before:

"Amanda Laura Martin Charney may approach the bench."

She said, "Thank you, your honor. I am not a lawyer and I don't know the proper way of phrasing things, but I hope you will listen to my meaning and ignore the words.

"Let's understand what it means to be free in Andrew's case. In some ways, he *is* free. I think it's at least twenty years since anyone in the Martin family gave him an order to do something that we felt he might not do of his own accord.

"But we can, if we wish, give him an order to do anything, couch it as harshly as we wish, because he is a machine that belongs to us. Why should we be in a position to do so, when he has served us so long, so faithfully, and earned so much money for us? He owes us nothing more. The debt is entirely on the other side.

"Even if we were legally forbidden to place Andrew in involuntary servitude, he would still serve us voluntarily. Making him free would be a trick of words only, but it would mean much to him. It would give him everything and cost us nothing."

For a moment the Judge seemed to be suppressing a smile. "I see your point, Mrs. Charney. The fact is that there is no binding law in this respect and no precedent. There is, however, the unspoken assumption that only a man can enjoy freedom. I can make new law here, subject to reversal in a higher court, but I cannot lightly run counter to that assumption. Let me address the robot. Andrew!"

"Yes, your honor."

It was the first time Andrew had spoken in court and the Judge seemed astonished for a moment at the human timbre of the voice. He said, "Why do you want to be free, Andrew? In what way will this matter to you?"

Andrew said, "Would you wish to be a slave, your honor?"

"But you are not a slave. You are a perfectly good robot, a genius of a robot I am given to understand, capable of an artistic expression that can be matched nowhere. What more can you do if you were free?"

"Perhaps no more than I do now, your honor, but with greater joy. It has been said in this courtroom that only a human being can be free. It seems to me that only someone who wishes for freedom can be free. I wish for freedom."

And it was that that cued the Judge. The crucial sentence in his decision was: "There is no right to deny freedom to any object with a mind advanced enough to grasp the concept and desire the state."

It was eventually upheld by the World Court.

8.

Sir remained displeased and his harsh voice made Andrew feel almost as though he were being short-circuited.

Sir said, "I don't want your damned money, Andrew. I'll take it only because you won't feel free otherwise. From now on, you can select your own jobs and do them as you please. I will give you no orders, except this one—that you do as you please. But I am still responsible for you; that's part of the court order. I hope you understand that."

Little Miss interrupted, "Don't be irascible, Dad. The responsibility is no great chore. You know you won't have to do a thing. The Three Laws still hold."

"Then how is he free?"

Andrew said, "Are not human beings bound by their laws, Sir?"

Sir said, "I'm not going to argue." He left, and Andrew saw him only infrequently after that.

Little Miss came to see him frequently in the small house that had been built and made over for him. It had no kitchen, of course, nor bathroom facilities. It had just two rooms; one was a library and one was a combination storeroom and workroom. Andrew accepted many commissions and worked harder as a free robot than he ever had before, till the cost of the house was paid for and the structure legally transferred to him.

One day Little Sir came. . . . No, George! Little Sir had insisted on that after the court decision. "A free robot doesn't call anyone Little Sir," George had said. "I call you Andrew. You must call me George."

It was phrased as an order, so Andrew called him George—but Little Miss remained Little Miss.

The day George came alone, it was to say that Sir was dying. Little Miss was at the bedside but Sir wanted Andrew as well.

Sir's voice was quite strong, though he seemed unable to move much. He struggled to get his hand up. "Andrew," he said, "Andrew— Don't help me, George. I'm only dying; I'm not crippled. . . . Andrew, I'm glad you're free. I just wanted to tell you that."

Andrew did not know what to say. He had never been at the side of someone dying before, but he knew it was the human way of ceasing to function. It was an involuntary and irreversible dismantling, and Andrew did not know what to say that might be appropriate. He could only remain standing, absolutely silent, absolutely motionless.

When it was over, Little Miss said to him, "He may not have seemed friendly to you toward the end, Andrew, but he was old, you know, and it hurt him that you should want to be free."

And then Andrew found the words to say. He said, "I would never have been free without him, Little Miss."

9.

It was only after Sir's death that Andrew began to wear clothes. He began with an old pair of trousers at first, a pair that George had given him.

George was married now, and a lawyer. He had joined Feingold's firm. Old Feingold was long since dead but his daughter had carried on and eventually the firm's name became Feingold and Charney. It remained so even when the daughter retired and no Feingold took her place. At the time Andrew put on clothes for the first time, the Charney name had just been added to the firm.

George had tried not to smile, the first time Andrew put on the trousers, but to Andrew's eyes the smile was clearly there.

George showed Andrew how to manipulate the static charge so as to allow the trousers to open, wrap about his lower body, and move shut. George demonstrated on his own trousers, but Andrew was quite aware that it would take him awhile to duplicate that one flowing motion.

George said, "But why do you want trousers, Andrew? Your body is so beautifully functional it's a shame to cover it—especially when you needn't worry about either temperature control or modesty. And it doesn't cling properly, not on metal."

Andrew said, "Are not human bodies beautifully functional, George? Yet you cover yourselves."

"For warmth, for cleanliness, for protection, for decorativeness. None of that applies to you."

Andrew said, "I feel bare without clothes. I feel different, George."

"Different! Andrew, there are millions of robots on Earth now. In this region, according to the last census, there are almost as many robots as there are men."

"I know, George. There are robots doing every conceivable type of work."

"And none of them wear clothes."

"But none of them are free, George."

Little by little, Andrew added to the wardrobe. He was inhibited by George's smile and by the stares of the people who commissioned work.

He might be free, but there was built into him a carefully detailed program concerning his behavior toward people, and it was only by the tiniest steps that he dared advance. Open disapproval would set him back months.

Not everyone accepted Andrew as free. He was incapable of resenting that and yet there was a difficulty about his thinking process when he thought of it.

Most of all, he tended to avoid putting on clothes—or too many of them—when he thought Little Miss might come to visit him. She was old now and was often away in some warmer climate, but when she returned the first thing she did was visit him.

On one of her returns, George said ruefully, "She's got me, Andrew. I'll be running for the Legislature next year. Like grandfather, she says, like grandson."

"Like grandfather—" Andrew stopped, uncertain.

"I mean that I, George, the grandson, will be like Sir, the grandfather, who was in the Legislature once."

Andrew said, "It would be pleasant, George, if Sir were still—" He paused, for he did not want to say, "in working order." That seemed inappropriate.

"Alive," said George. "Yes, I think of the old monster now and then, too."

It was a conversation Andrew thought about. He had noticed his own incapacity in speech when talking with George. Somehow the language had changed since Andrew had come into being with an innate vocabulary. Then, too, George used a colloquial speech, as Sir and Little Miss had not. Why should he have called Sir a monster when surely that word was not appropriate?

Nor could Andrew turn to his own books for guidance. They were old and most dealt with woodworking, with art, with furniture design. There were none on language, none on the way of human beings.

It was at that moment it seemed to him that he must seek the proper books; and as a free robot, he felt he must not ask George. He would go to town and use the library. It was a triumphant decision and he felt his electropotential grow distinctly higher until he had to throw in an impedance coil.

He put on a full costume, even including a shoulder chain of wood. He would have preferred the glitter plastic but George had said that wood was much more appropriate and that polished cedar was considerably more valuable as well.

He had placed a hundred feet between himself and the house before gathering resistance brought him to a halt. He shifted the impedance coil out of circuit, and when that did not seem to help enough, he returned to his home and on a piece of notepaper wrote neatly, "I have gone to the library," and placed it in clear view on his worktable.

10.

Andrew never quite got to the library. He had studied the map. He knew the route, but not the appearance of it. The actual landmarks did not resemble the symbols on the map and he would hesitate. Eventually he thought he must have somehow gone wrong, for everything looked strange.

He passed an occasional field robot, but at the time he decided he should ask his way, there were none in sight. A vehicle passed and did not stop. He stood irresolute, which meant calmly motionless, and then coming across the field toward him were two human beings.

He turned to face them, and they altered their course to meet him. A moment before, they had been talking loudly; he had heard their voices; but now they were silent. They had the look that Andrew associated with human uncertainty, and they were young, but not very young. Twenty perhaps? Andrew could never judge human age.

He said, "Would you describe to me the route to the town library, sirs?"

One of them, the taller of the two, whose tall hat lengthened him still farther, almost grotesquely, said, not to Andrew, but to the other, "It's a robot."

The other had a bulbous nose and heavy eyelids. He said, not to Andrew, but to the first, "It's wearing clothes."

The tall one snapped his fingers. "It's the free robot. They have a robot at the Charneys' who isn't owned by anybody. Why else would it be wearing clothes?"

"Ask it," said the one with the nose.

"Are you the Charney robot?" asked the tall one.

"I am Andrew Martin, sir," said Andrew.

"Good. Take off your clothes. Robots don't wear clothes." He said to the other, "That's disgusting. Look at him."

Andrew hesitated. He hadn't heard an order in that tone of voice in so long that his Second Law circuits had momentarily jammed.

The tall one said, "Take off your clothes. I order you."

Slowly, Andrew began to remove them.

"Just drop them," said the tall one.

The nose said, "If it doesn't belong to anyone, he could be ours as much as someone else's."

"Anyway," said the tall one, "who's to object to anything we do? We're not damaging property. . . . Stand on your head." That was to Andrew.

"The head is not meant—" began Andrew.

"That's an order. If you don't know how, try anyway."

Andrew hesitated again, then bent to put his head on the ground. He tried to lift his legs and fell, heavily.

The tall one said, "Just lie there." He said to the other, "We can take him apart. Ever take a robot apart?"

"Will he let us?"

"How can he stop us?"

There was no way Andrew could stop them, if they ordered him not to resist in a forceful enough manner. Second Law of obedience took precedence over the Third Law of self-preservation. In any case, he could not defend himself without possibly hurting them and that would mean breaking the First Law. At that thought, every motile unit contracted slightly and he quivered as he lay there.

The tall one walked over and pushed at him with his foot. "He's heavy. I think we'll need tools to do the job."

The nose said, "We could order him to take himself apart. It would be fun to watch him try."

"Yes," said the tall one thoughtfully, "but let's get him off the road. If someone comes along—"

It was too late. Someone had indeed come along and it was George. From where he lay, Andrew had seen him topping a small rise in the middle distance. He would have liked to signal him in some way, but the last order had been "Just lie there!"

George was running now and he arrived somewhat winded. The two young men stepped back a little and then waited thoughtfully.

George said anxiously, "Andrew, has something gone wrong?"

Andrew said, "I am well, George."

"Then stand up. . . . What happened to your clothes?"

The tall young man said, "That your robot, mac?"

George turned sharply. "He's no one's robot. What's been going on here?"

"We politely asked him to take his clothes off. What's that to you if you don't own him?"

George said, "What were they doing, Andrew?"

Andrew said, "It was their intention in some way to dismember me. They were about to move me to a quiet spot and order me to dismember myself."

George looked at the two and his chin trembled. The two young men retreated no further. They were smiling. The tall one said lightly, "What are you going to do, pudgy? Attack us?"

George said, "No. I don't have to. This robot has been with my family for over seventy years. He knows us and he values us more than he values anyone else. I am going to tell him that you two are threatening my life and that you plan to kill me. I will ask him to defend me. In choosing between me and you two, he will choose me. Do you know what will happen to you when he attacks you?"

The two were backing away slightly, looking uneasy.

George said sharply, "Andrew, I am in danger and about to come to harm from these young men. Move toward them!"

Andrew did so, and the two young men did not wait. They ran fleetly.

"All right, Andrew, relax," said George. He looked unstrung. He was far past the age where he could face the possibility of a dustup with one young man, let alone two.

Andrew said, "I couldn't have hurt them, George. I could see they were not attacking you."

"I didn't order you to attack them; I only told you to move toward them. Their own fears did the rest."

"How can they fear robots?"

"It's a disease of mankind, one of which it is not yet cured. But never mind that. What the devil are you doing here, Andrew? I was on the point of turning back and hiring a helicopter when I found you. How did you get it into your head to go to the library? I would have brought you any books you needed."

"I am a—" began Andrew.

"Free robot. Yes, yes. All right, what did you want in the library?"

"I want to know more about human beings, about the world, about everything. And about robots, George. I want to write a history about robots."

George said, "Well, let's walk home. . . . And pick up your clothes first. Andrew, there are a million books on robotics and all of them include histories of the science. The world is growing saturated not only with robots but with information about robots."

Andrew shook his head, a human gesture he had lately begun to make. "Not a history of robotics, George. A history of *robots*, by a robot. I want to explain how robots feel about what has happened since the first ones were allowed to work and live on Earth."

George's eyebrows lifted, but he said nothing in direct response.

11.

Little Miss was just past her eighty-third birthday, but there was nothing about her that was lacking in either energy or determination. She gestured with her cane oftener than she propped herself up with it.

She listened to the story in a fury of indignation. She said, "George, that's horrible. Who were those young ruffians?"

"I don't know. What difference does it make? In the end they did no damage."

"They might have. You're a lawyer, George, and if you're well off, it's entirely due to the talent of Andrew. It was the money *he* earned that is the foundation of everything we have. He provides the continuity for this family and I will *not* have him treated as a wind-up toy."

"What would you have me do, Mother?" asked George.

"I said you're a lawyer. Don't you listen? You set up a test case somehow, and you force the regional courts to declare for robot rights and get the Legislature to pass the necessary bills, and carry the whole thing to the World Court, if you have to. I'll be watching, George, and I'll tolerate no shirking."

She was serious, and what began as a way of soothing the fearsome old lady became an involved matter with enough legal entanglement to make it interesting. As senior partner of Feingold and Charney, George plotted strategy but left the actual work to his junior partners, with much of it a matter for his son, Paul, who was also a member of the firm and who reported dutifully nearly every day to his grandmother. She, in turn, discussed it every day with Andrew.

Andrew was deeply involved. His work on his book on robots was delayed again, as he pored over the legal arguments and even, at times, made very diffident suggestions.

He said, "George told me that day that human beings have always been afraid of robots. As long as they are, the courts and the legislatures are not likely to work hard on behalf of robots. Should there not be something done about public opinion?"

So while Paul stayed in court, George took to the public platform. It gave him the advantage of being informal and he even went so far sometimes as to wear the new, loose style of clothing which he called drapery. Paul said, "Just don't trip over it on stage, Dad."

George said despondently, "I'll try not to."

He addressed the annual convention of holo-news editors on one occasion and said, in part:

"If, by virtue of the Second Law, we can demand of any robot unlimited obedience in all respects not involving harm to a human being, then any human being, *any* human being, has a fearsome power over any robot, *any* robot. In particular, since Second Law supersedes Third Law, *any* human being can use the law of obedience to overcome the law of self-protection. He can order any robot to damage itself or even destroy itself for any reason, or for no reason.

"Is this just? Would we treat an animal so? Even an inanimate object which has given us good service has a claim on our consideration. And a robot is not insensible; it is not an animal. It can think well enough to enable it to talk to us, reason with us, joke with us. Can we treat them as friends, can we work together with them, and not give them some of the fruit of that friendship, some of the benefit of co-working?

"If a man has the right to give a robot any order that does not involve harm to a human being, he should have the decency never to give a robot any order that involves harm to a robot, unless human safety absolutely requires it. With great power goes great responsibility, and if the robots have Three Laws to protect men, is it too much to ask that men have a law or two to protect robots?"

Andrew was right. It was the battle over public opinion that held the key to courts and Legislature and in the end a law passed which set up conditions under which robot-harming orders were forbidden. It was endlessly qualified and the punishments for violating the law were totally inadequate, but the principle was established. The final passage by the World Legislature came through on the day of Little Miss's death.

That was no coincidence. Little Miss held on to life desperately during the last debate and let go only when word of victory arrived. Her last smile was for Andrew. Her last words were: "You have been good to us, Andrew."

She died with her hand holding his, while her son and his wife and children remained at a respectful distance from both.

12.

Andrew waited patiently while the receptionist disappeared into the inner office. It might have used the holographic chatterbox, but unquestionably it was unmanned (or perhaps unroboted) by having to deal with another robot rather than with a human being.

Andrew passed the time revolving the matter in his mind. Could "unroboted" be used as an analogue of "unmanned," or had "unmanned" become a metaphoric term sufficiently divorced from its original literal meaning to be applied to robots—or to women for that matter?

Such problems came frequently as he worked on his book on robots. The trick of thinking out sentences to express all complexities had undoubtedly increased his vocabulary.

Occasionally, someone came into the room to stare at him and he did not try to avoid the glance. He looked at each calmly, and each in turn looked away.

Paul Charney finally came out. He looked surprised, or he would have if Andrew could have made out his expression with certainty. Paul had taken to wearing the heavy makeup that fashion was dictating for both sexes and though it made sharper and firmer the somewhat bland lines of his face, Andrew disapproved. He found that disapproving of human beings, as long as he did not express it verbally, did not make him very uneasy. He could even write the disapproval. He was sure it had not always been so.

Paul said, "Come in, Andrew. I'm sorry I made you wait but there was something I *had* to finish. Come in. You had said you wanted to talk to me, but I didn't know you meant here in town."

"If you are busy, Paul, I am prepared to continue to wait."

Paul glanced at the interplay of shifting shadows on the dial on the wall that served as timepiece and said, "I can make some time. Did you come alone?"

"I hired an automatobile."

"Any trouble?" Paul asked, with more than a trace of anxiety.

"I wasn't expecting any. My rights are protected."

Paul looked the more anxious for that. "Andrew, I've explained that the law is unenforceable, at least under most conditions. . . . And if you insist on wearing clothes, you'll run into trouble eventually—just like that first time."

"And only time, Paul. I'm sorry you are displeased."

"Well, look at it this way; you are virtually a living legend, Andrew, and you are too valuable in many different ways for you to have any right to take chances with yourself. . . . How's the book coming?"

"I am approaching the end, Paul. The publisher is quite pleased."

"Good!"

"I don't know that he's necessarily pleased with the book as a book. I think he expects to sell many copies because it's written by a robot and it's that that pleases him."

"Only human, I'm afraid."

"I am not displeased. Let it sell for whatever reason since it will mean money and I can use some."

"Grandmother left you—"

"Little Miss was generous, and I'm sure I can count on the family to help me out further. But it is the royalties from the book on which I am counting to help me through the next step."

"What next step is that?"

"I wish to see the head of U. S. Robots and Mechanical Men Corporation. I have tried to make an appointment, but so far I have not been able to reach him. The corporation did not cooperate with me in the writing of the book, so I am not surprised, you understand."

Paul was clearly amused. "Cooperation is the last thing you can expect. They didn't cooperate with us in our great fight for robot rights. Quite the reverse and you can see why. Give a robot rights and people may not want to buy them."

"Nevertheless," said Andrew, "if you call them, you may obtain an interview for me."

"I'm no more popular with them than you are, Andrew."

"But perhaps you can hint that by seeing me they may head off a campaign by Feingold and Charney to strengthen the rights of robots further."

"Wouldn't that be a lie, Andrew?"

"Yes, Paul, and I can't tell one. That is why you must call."

"Ah, you can't lie, but you can urge me to tell a lie, is that it? You're getting more human all the time, Andrew."

13.

It was not easy to arrange, even with Paul's supposedly weighted name.

But it was finally carried through and, when it was, Harley Smythe-Robertson, who, on his mother's side, was descended from the original founder of the corporation and who had adopted the hyphenation to indicate it, looked remarkably unhappy. He was approaching retirement age and his entire tenure as president had been devoted to the matter of robot rights. His gray hair was plastered thinly over the top of his scalp, his face was not made up, and he eyed Andrew with brief hostility from time to time.

Andrew said, "Sir, nearly a century ago, I was told by a Merton Mansky of this corporation that the mathematics governing the plotting of the positronic pathways was far too complicated to permit of any but approximate solutions and that therefore my own capacities were not fully predictable."

"That was a century ago." Smythe-Robertson hesitated, then said icily, "Sir. It is true no longer. Our robots are made with precision now and are trained precisely to their jobs."

"Yes," said Paul, who had come along, as he said, to make sure that the corporation played fair, "with the result that my receptionist must be guided at every point once events depart from the conventional, however slightly."

Smythe-Robertson said, "You would be much more displeased if it were to improvise."

Andrew said, "Then you no longer manufacture robots like myself which are flexible and adaptable."

"No longer."

"The research I have done in connection with my book," said Andrew, "indicates that I am the oldest robot presently in active operation."

"The oldest presently," said Smythe-Robertson, "and the oldest ever. The oldest that will ever be. No robot is useful after the twenty-fifth year. They are called in and replaced with newer models."

"No robot *as presently manufactured* is useful after the twenty-fifth year," said Paul pleasantly. "Andrew is quite exceptional in this respect."

Andrew, adhering to the path he had marked out for himself, said, "As the oldest robot in the world and the most flexible, am I not unusual enough to merit special treatment from the company?"

"Not at all," said Smythe-Robertson freezingly. "Your unusualness is an embarrassment to the company. If you were on lease, instead of having been a sale outright through some mischance, you would long since have been replaced."

"But that is exactly the point," said Andrew. "I am a free robot and I own myself. Therefore I come to you and ask you to replace me. You cannot do this without the owner's consent. Nowadays, that consent is extorted as a condition of the lease, but in my time this did not happen."

Smythe-Robertson was looking both startled and puzzled, and for a moment there was silence. Andrew found himself staring at the holograph on the wall. It was a death mask of Susan Calvin, patron saint of all roboticists. She was dead nearly two centuries now, but as a result of writing his book Andrew knew her so well he could half persuade himself that he had met her in life.

Smythe-Robertson said, "How can I replace you for you? If I replace you as robot, how can I donate the new robot to you as owner since in the very act of replacement you cease to exist?" He smiled grimly.

"Not at all difficult," interposed Paul. "The seat of Andrew's personality is his positronic brain and it is the one part that cannot be replaced without creating a new robot. The positronic brain, therefore, is Andrew the owner. Every other part of the robotic body can be replaced without affecting the robot's personality, and those other parts are the brain's possessions. Andrew, I should say, wants to supply his brain with a new robotic body."

"That's right," said Andrew calmly. He turned to Smythe-Robertson. "You have manufactured androids, haven't you? Robots that have the outward appearance of humans complete to the texture of the skin?"

Smythe-Robertson said, "Yes, we have. They worked perfectly well, with their synthetic fibrous skins and tendons. There was virtually no metal anywhere except for the brain, yet they were nearly as tough as metal robots. They were tougher, weight for weight."

Paul looked interested. "I didn't know that. How many are on the market?"

"None," said Smythe-Robertson. "They were much more expensive than metal models and a market survey showed they would not be accepted. They looked too human."

Andrew said, "But the corporation retains its expertise, I assume. Since it does, I wish to request that I be replaced by an organic robot, an android."

Paul looked surprised. "Good Lord," he said.

Smythe-Robertson stiffened. "Quite impossible!"

"Why is it impossible?" asked Andrew. "I will pay any reasonable fee, of course."

Smythe-Robertson said, "We do not manufacture androids."

"You do not *choose* to manufacture androids," interposed Paul quickly. "That is not the same as being unable to manufacture them."

Smythe-Robertson said, "Nevertheless, the manufacture of androids is against public policy."

"There is no law against it," said Paul.

"Nevertheless, we do not manufacture them, and we will not."

Paul cleared his throat. "Mr. Smythe-Robertson," he said, "Andrew is a free robot who is under the purview of the law guaranteeing robot rights. You are aware of this, I take it?"

"Only too well."

"This robot, as a free robot, chooses to wear clothes. This results in his being frequently humiliated by thoughtless human beings despite the law against the humiliation of robots. It is difficult to prosecute vague offenses that don't meet with the general disapproval of those who must decide on guilt and innocence."

"U. S. Robots understood that from the start. Your father's firm unfortunately did not."

"My father is dead now," said Paul, "but what I see is that we have here a clear offense with a clear target."

"What are you talking about?" said Smythe-Robertson.

"My client, Andrew Martin—he has just become my client—is a free robot who is entitled to ask U. S. Robots and Mechanical Men Corporation for the right of replacement, which the corporation supplies anyone who owns a robot for more than twenty-five years. In fact, the corporation insists on such replacement."

Paul was smiling and thoroughly at his ease. He went on, "The positronic brain of my client is the owner of the body of my client—which is certainly more than twenty-five years old. The positronic brain demands the replacement of the body and offers to pay any reasonable fee for an android body as that replacement. If you refuse the request, my client undergoes humiliation and we will sue.

"While public opinion would not ordinarily support the claim of a robot in such a case, may I remind you that U. S. Robots is not popular with the public generally. Even those who most use and profit from robots are suspicious of the corporation. This may be a hangover from the days when robots were widely feared. It may be resentment against the power and wealth of U. S. Robots which has a worldwide monopoly. Whatever the cause may be, the resentment exists and I think you will find that you would prefer not to withstand a lawsuit, particularly since my client is wealthy and will live for many more centuries and will have no reason to refrain from fighting the battle forever."

Smythe-Robertson had slowly reddened. "You are trying to force me to . . ."

"I force you to do nothing," said Paul. "If you wish to refuse to accede to my client's reasonable request, you may by all means do so and we will leave without another word. . . . But we will sue, as is certainly our right, and you will find that you will eventually lose."

Smythe-Robertson said, "Well—" and paused.

"I see that you are going to accede," said Paul. "You may hesitate but you will come to it in the end. Let me assure you, then, of one further point. If, in the process of transferring my client's positronic brain from his present body to an organic one, there is any damage, however slight, then I will never rest till I've nailed the corporation to the ground. I will, if necessary, take every possible step to mobilize public opinion against the corporation if one brain path of my client's platinum-iridium essence is scrambled." He turned to Andrew and said, "Do you agree to all this, Andrew?"

Andrew hesitated a full minute. It amounted to the approval of lying, of blackmail, of the badgering and humiliation of a human being. But not physical harm, he told himself, not physical harm.

He managed at last to come out with a rather faint "Yes."

14.

It was like being constructed again. For days, then for weeks, finally for months, Andrew found himself not himself somehow, and the simplest actions kept giving rise to hesitation.

Paul was frantic. "They've damaged you, Andrew. We'll have to institute suit."

Andrew spoke very slowly. "You mustn't. You'll never be able to prove—something—m-m-m-m—"

"Malice?"

"Malice. Besides, I grow stronger, better. It's the tr-tr-tr—"

"Tremble?"

"Trauma. After all, there's never been such an op—op—op— before."

Andrew could feel his brain from the inside. No one else could. He knew he was well and during the months that it took him to learn full coordination and full positronic interplay, he spent hours before the mirror.

Not quite human! The face was stiff—too stiff—and the motions were too deliberate. They lacked the careless free flow of the human being, but perhaps that might come with time. At least he could wear clothes without the ridiculous anomaly of a metal face going along with it.

Eventually he said, "I will be going back to work."

Paul laughed and said, "That means you are well. What will you be doing? Another book?"

"No," said Andrew seriously. "I live too long for any one career to seize me by the throat and never let me go. There was a time when I was primarily an artist and I can still turn to that. And there was a time when I was a historian and I can still turn to that. But now I wish to be a robobiologist."

"A robopsychologist, you mean."

"No. That would imply the study of positronic brains and at the moment I lack the desire to do that. A robobiologist, it seems to me, would be concerned with the working of the body attached to that brain."

"Wouldn't that be a roboticist?"

"A roboticist works with a metal body. I would be studying an organic humanoid body, of which I have the only one, as far as I know."

"You narrow your field," said Paul thoughtfully. "As an artist, all conception is yours; as a historian, you dealt chiefly with robots; as a robobiologist, you will deal with yourself."

Andrew nodded. "It would seem so."

Andrew had to start from the very beginning, for he knew nothing of ordinary biology, almost nothing of science. He became a familiar sight in the libraries, where he sat at the electronic indices for hours at a time, looking perfectly normal in clothes. Those few who knew he was a robot in no way interfered with him.

He built a laboratory in a room which he added to his house, and his library grew, too.

Years passed, and Paul came to him one day and said, "It's a pity you're no longer working on the history of robots. I understand U. S. Robots is adopting a radically new policy."

Paul had aged, and his deteriorating eyes had been replaced with photoptic cells. In that respect, he had drawn closer to Andrew. Andrew said, "What have they done?"

"They are manufacturing central computers, gigantic positronic brains, really, which communicate with anywhere from a dozen to a thousand robots by microwave. The robots themselves have no brains at all. They are the limbs of the gigantic brain, and the two are physically separate."

"Is that more efficient?"

"U. S. Robots claims it is. Smythe-Robertson established the new direction before he died, however, and it's my notion that it's a backlash at you. U. S. Robots is determined that they will make no robots that will give them the type of trouble you have, and for that reason they separate brain and body. The brain will have no body to wish changed; the body will have no brain to wish anything.

"It's amazing, Andrew," Paul went on, "the influence you have had on the history of robots. It was your artistry that encouraged U. S. Robots to make robots more precise and specialized; it was your freedom that resulted in the establishment of the principle of robotic rights; it was your insistence on an android body that made U. S. Robots switch to brain-body separation."

Andrew said, "I suppose in the end the corporation will produce one vast brain controlling several billion robotic bodies. All the eggs will be in one basket. Dangerous. Not proper at all."

"I think you're right," said Paul, "but I don't suspect it will come to pass for a century at least and I won't live to see it. In fact, I may not live to see next year."

"Paul!" said Andrew, in concern.

Paul shrugged. "We're mortal, Andrew. We're not like you. It doesn't matter too much, but it does make it important to assure you on one point. I'm the last of the Charneys. There are collaterals descended from my great-aunt, but they don't count. The money I control personally will be left to the trust in your name and as far as anyone can foresee the future, you will be economically secure."

"Unnecessary," said Andrew, with difficulty. In all this time, he could not get used to the deaths of the Charneys.

Paul said, "Let's not argue. That's the way it's going to be. What are you working on?"

"I am designing a system for allowing androids—myself—to gain energy from the combustion of hydrocarbons, rather than from atomic cells."

Paul raised his eyebrows. "So that they will breathe and eat?"

"Yes."

"How long have you been pushing in that direction?"

"For a long time now, but I think I have designed an adequate combustion chamber for catalyzed controlled breakdown."

"But why, Andrew? The atomic cell is surely infinitely better."

"In some ways, perhaps, but the atomic cell is inhuman."

15.

It took time, but Andrew had time. In the first place, he did not wish to do anything till Paul had died in peace.

With the death of the great-grandson of Sir, Andrew felt more nearly exposed to a hostile world and for that reason was the more determined to continue the path he had long ago chosen.

Yet he was not really alone. If a man had died, the firm of Feingold and Charney lived, for a corporation does not die any more than a robot does. The firm had its directions and it followed them soullessly. By way of the trust and through the law firm, Andrew continued to be wealthy. And in return for their own large annual retainer, Feingold and Charney involved themselves in the legal aspects of the new combustion chamber.

When the time came for Andrew to visit U. S. Robots and Mechanical Men Corporation, he did it alone. Once he had gone with Sir and once with Paul. This time, the third time, he was alone and manlike.

U. S. Robots had changed. The production plant had been shifted to a large space station, as had grown to be the case with more and more industries. With them had gone many robots. The Earth itself was becoming parklike, with its one-billion-person population stabilized and perhaps not more than thirty per cent of its at least equally large robot population independently brained.

The Director of Research was Alvin Magdescu, dark of complexion and hair, with a little pointed beard and wearing nothing above the waist but the breastband that fashion dictated. Andrew himself was well covered in the older fashion of several decades back.

Magdescu said, "I know you, of course, and I'm rather pleased to see you. You're our most notorious product and it's a pity old Smythe-Robertson was so set against you. We could have done a great deal with you."

"You still can," said Andrew.

"No, I don't think so. We're past the time. We've had robots on Earth for over a century, but that's changing. It will be back to space with them and those that stay here won't be brained."

"But there remains myself, and I stay on Earth."

"True, but there doesn't seem to be much of the robot about you. What new request have you?"

"To be still less a robot. Since I am so far organic, I wish an organic source of energy. I have here the plans—"

Magdescu did not hasten through them. He might have intended to at first, but he stiffened and grew intent. At one point he said, "This is remarkably ingenious. Who thought of all this?"

"I did," said Andrew.

Magdescu looked up at him sharply, then said, "It would amount to a major overhaul of your body, and an experimental one, since it has never been attempted before. I advise against it. Remain as you are."

Andrew's face had limited means of expression, but impatience showed plainly in his voice. "Dr. Magdescu, you miss the entire point. You have no choice but to accede to my request. If such devices can be built into my body, they can be built into human bodies as well. The tendency to lengthen human life by prosthetic devices has already been remarked on. There are no devices better than the ones I have designed and am designing.

"As it happens, I control the patents by way of the firm of Feingold and Charney. We are quite capable of going into business for ourselves and of developing the kind of prosthetic devices that may end by producing human beings with many of the properties of robots. Your own business will then suffer.

"If, however, you operate on me now and agree to do so under similar circumstances in the future, you will receive permission to make use of the patents and control the technology of both robots and the prosthetization of human beings. The initial leasing will not be granted, of course, until after the first operation is completed successfully, and after enough time has passed to demonstrate that it is indeed successful." Andrew felt scarcely any First Law inhibition to the stern conditions he was setting a human being. He was learning to reason that what seemed like cruelty might, in the long run, be kindness.

Magdescu looked stunned. He said, "I'm not the one to decide something like this. That's a corporate decision that would take time."

"I can wait a reasonable time," said Andrew, "but only a reasonable time." And he thought with satisfaction that Paul himself could not have done it better.

16.

It took only a reasonable time, and the operation was a success.

Magdescu said, "I was very much against the operation, Andrew, but not for the reasons you might think. I was not in the least against the experiment, if it had been on someone else. I hated risking *your* positronic brain. Now that you have the positronic pathways interacting with simulated nerve pathways, it might be difficult to rescue the brain intact if the body went bad."

"I had every faith in the skill of the staff at U. S. Robots," said Andrew. "And I can eat now."

"Well, you can sip olive oil. It will mean occasional cleanings of the combustion chamber, as we have explained to you. Rather an uncomfortable touch, I should think."

"Perhaps, if I did not expect to go further. Self-cleaning is not impossible. In fact, I am working on a device that will deal with solid food that may be expected to contain incombustible fractions—indigestible matter, so to speak, that will have to be discarded."

"You would then have to develop an anus."

"The equivalent."

"What else, Andrew?"

"Everything else."

"Genitalia, too?"

"Insofar as they will fit my plans. My body is a canvas on which I intend to draw—"

Magdescu waited for the sentence to be completed, and when it seemed that it would not be, he completed it himself. "A man?"

"We shall see," said Andrew.

Magdescu said, "It's a puny ambition, Andrew. You're better than a man. You've gone downhill from the moment you opted for organicism."

"My brain has not suffered."

"No, it hasn't. I'll grant you that. But, Andrew, the whole new breakthrough in prosthetic devices made possible by your patents is being marketed under your name. You're recognized as the inventor and you're honored for it—as you are. Why play further games with your body?"

Andrew did not answer.

The honors came. He accepted membership in several learned societies, including one which was devoted to the new science he had established; the one he had called robobiology but had come to be termed prosthetology.

On the one hundred and fiftieth anniversary of his construction, there was a testimonial dinner given in his honor at U. S. Robots. If Andrew saw irony in this, he kept it to himself.

Alvin Magdescu came out of retirement to chair the dinner. He was himself ninety-four years old and was alive because he had prosthetized devices that, among other things, fulfilled the function of liver and kidneys. The dinner reached its climax when Magdescu, after a short and emotional talk, raised his glass to toast "the Sesquicentennial Robot."

Andrew had had the sinews of his face redesigned to the point where he could show a range of emotions, but he sat through all the ceremonies solemnly passive. He did not like to be a Sesquicentennial Robot.

17.

It was prosthetology that finally took Andrew off the Earth. In the decades that followed the celebration of the Sesquicentennial, the Moon had come to be a world more Earth-like than Earth in every respect but its gravitational pull and in its underground cities there was a fairly dense population.

Prosthetized devices there had to take the lesser gravity into account and Andrew spent five years on the Moon working with local prosthetologists to make the necessary adaptations. When not at his work, he wandered among the robot population, every one of which treated him with the robotic obsequiousness due a man.

He came back to an Earth that was humdrum and quiet in comparison and visited the offices of Feingold and Charney to announce his return.

The current head of the firm, Simon DeLong, was surprised. He said, "We had been told you were returning, Andrew" (he had almost said "Mr. Martin"), "but we were not expecting you till next week."

"I grew impatient," said Andrew brusquely. He was anxious to get to the point. "On the Moon, Simon, I was in charge of a research team of twenty human scientists. I gave orders that no one questioned. The Lunar robots deferred to me as they would to a human being. Why, then, am I not a human being?"

A wary look entered DeLong's eyes. He said, "My dear Andrew, as you have just explained, you are treated as a human being by both robots and human beings. You are therefore a human being *de facto*."

"To be a human being *de facto* is not enough. I want not only to be treated as one, but to be legally identified as one. I want to be a human being *de jure*."

"Now that is another matter," said DeLong. "There we would run into human prejudice and into the undoubted fact that however much you may be like a human being, you are *not* a human being."

"In what way not?" asked Andrew. "I have the shape of a human being and organs equivalent to those of a human being. My organs, in fact, are identical to some of those in a prosthetized human being. I have contributed artistically, literarily, and scientifically to human culture as much as any human being now alive. What more can one ask?"

"I myself would ask nothing more. The trouble is that it would take an act of the World Legislature to define you as a human being. Frankly, I wouldn't expect that to happen."

"To whom on the Legislature could I speak?"

"To the chairman of the Science and Technology Committee perhaps."

"Can you arrange a meeting?"

"But you scarcely need an intermediary. In your position, you can—"

"No. *You* arrange it." (It didn't even occur to Andrew that he was giving a flat order to a human being. He had grown accustomed to that on the Moon.) "I want him to know that the firm of Feingold and Charney is backing me in this to the hilt."

"Well, now—"

"To the hilt, Simon. In one hundred and seventy-three years I have in one fashion or another contributed greatly to this firm. I have been under obligation to individual members of the firm in times past. I am not now. It is rather the other way around now and I am calling in my debts."

DeLong said, "I will do what I can."

18.

The chairman of the Science and Technology Committee was of the East Asian region and she was a woman. Her name was Chee Li-Hsing and her transparent garments (obscuring what she wanted obscured only by their dazzle) made her look plastic-wrapped.

She said, "I sympathize with your wish for full human rights. There have been times in history when segments of the human population fought for full human rights. What rights, however, can you possibly want that you do not have?"

"As simple a thing as my right to life. A robot can be dismantled at any time."

"A human being can be executed at any time."

"Execution can only follow due process of law. There is no trial needed for my dismantling. Only the word of a human being in authority is needed to end me. Besides—besides—" Andrew tried desperately to allow no sign of pleading, but his carefully designed tricks of human expression and tone of voice betrayed him here. "The truth is, I want to be a man. I have wanted it through six generations of human beings."

Li-Hsing looked up at him out of darkly sympathetic eyes. "The Legislature can pass a law declaring you one—they could pass a law declaring a stone statue to be defined as a man. Whether they will actually do so is, however, as likely in the first case as the second. Congresspeople are as human as the rest of the population and there is always that element of suspicion against robots."

"Even now?"

"Even now. We would all allow the fact that you have earned the prize of humanity and yet there would remain the fear of setting an undesirable precedent."

"What precedent? I am the only free robot, the only one of my type, and there will never be another. You may consult U. S. Robots."

" 'Never' is a long time, Andrew—or, if you prefer, Mr. Martin—since I will gladly give you my personal accolade as man. You will find that most Congresspeople will not be willing to set the precedent, no matter how meaningless such a precedent might be. Mr. Martin, you have my sympathy, but I cannot tell you to hope. Indeed—"

She sat back and her forehead wrinkled. "Indeed, if the issue grows too heated, there might well arise a certain sentiment, both inside the Legislature and outside, for that dismantling you mentioned. Doing away with you could turn out to be the easiest way of resolving the dilemma. Consider that before deciding to push matters."

Andrew said, "Will no one remember the technique of prosthetology, something that is almost entirely mine?"

"It may seem cruel, but they won't. Or if they do, it will be remembered against you. It will be said you did it only for yourself. It will be said it was part of a campaign to roboticize human beings, or to humanify robots; and in either case evil and vicious. You have never been part of a political hate campaign, Mr. Martin, and I tell you that you will be the object of vilification of a kind neither you nor I would credit and there would be people who'll believe it all. Mr. Martin, let your life be." She rose and, next to Andrew's seated figure, she seemed small and almost childlike.

Andrew said, "If I decide to fight for my humanity, will you be on my side?"

She thought, then said, "I will be—insofar as I can be. If at any time such a stand would appear to threaten my political future, I may have to abandon you, since it is not an issue I feel to be at the very root of my beliefs. I am trying to be honest with you."

"Thank you, and I will ask no more. I intend to fight this through whatever the consequences, and I will ask you for your help only for as long as you can give it."

19.

It was not a direct fight. Feingold and Charney counseled patience and Andrew muttered grimly that he had an endless supply of that.

Feingold and Charney then entered on a campaign to narrow and restrict the area of combat.

They instituted a lawsuit denying the obligation to pay debts to an individual with a prosthetic heart on the grounds that the possession of a robotic organ removed humanity, and with it the constitutional rights of human beings.

They fought the matter skillfully and tenaciously, losing at every step but always in such a way that the decision was forced to be as broad as possible, and then carrying it by way of appeals to the World Court.

It took years, and millions of dollars.

When the final decision was handed down, DeLong held what amounted to a victory celebration over the legal loss. Andrew was, of course, present in the company offices on the occasion.

"We've done two things, Andrew," said DeLong, "both of which are good. First of all, we have established the fact that no number of artifacts in the human body causes it to cease being a human body. Secondly, we have engaged public opinion in the question in such a way as to put it fiercely on the side of a broad interpretation of humanity since there is not a human being in existence who does not hope for prosthetics if that will keep him alive."

"And do you think the Legislature will now grant me my humanity?" asked Andrew.

DeLong looked faintly uncomfortable. "As to that, I cannot be optimistic. There remains the one organ which the World Court has used as the criterion of humanity. Human beings have an organic cellular brain and robots have a platinum-iridium positronic brain if they have one at all—and you certainly have a positronic brain. . . . No, Andrew, don't get that look in your eye. We lack the knowledge to duplicate the work of a cellular brain in artificial structures close enough to the organic type to allow it to fall within the Court's decision. Not even you could do it."

"What ought we do, then?"

"Make the attempt, of course. Congresswoman Li-Hsing will be on our side and a growing number of other Congresspeople. The President will undoubtedly go along with a majority of the Legislature in this matter."

"Do we have a majority?"

"No, far from it. But we might get one if the public will allow its desire for a broad interpretation of humanity to extend to you. A small chance, I admit, but if you do not wish to give up, we must gamble for it."

"I do not wish to give up."

20.

Congresswoman Li-Hsing was considerably older than she had been when Andrew had first met her. Her transparent garments were long gone. Her hair was now close-cropped and her coverings were tubular. Yet still Andrew clung, as closely as he could within the limits of reasonable taste, to the style of clothing that had prevailed when he had first adopted clothing over a century before.

She said, "We've gone as far as we can, Andrew. We'll try once more after recess, but, to be honest, defeat is certain and the whole thing will have to be given up. All my most recent efforts have only earned me a certain defeat in the coming congressional campaign."

"I know," said Andrew, "and it distresses me. You said once you would abandon me if it came to that. Why have you not done so?"

"One can change one's mind, you know. Somehow, abandoning you became a higher price than I cared to pay for just one more term. As it is, I've been in the Legislature for over a quarter of a century. It's enough."

"Is there no way we can change minds, Chee?"

"We've changed all that are amenable to reason. The rest—the majority—cannot be moved from their emotional antipathies."

"Emotional antipathy is not a valid reason for voting one way or the other."

"I know that, Andrew, but they don't advance emotional antipathy as their reason."

Andrew said cautiously, "It all comes down to the brain, then, but must we leave it at the level of cells versus positrons? Is there no way of forcing a functional definition? Must we say that a brain is made of this or that? May we not say that a brain is something— anything—capable of a certain level of thought?"

"Won't work," said Li-Hsing. "Your brain is man-made, the human brain is not. Your brain is constructed, theirs developed. To any human being who is intent on keeping up the barrier between himself and a robot, those differences are a steel wall a mile high and a mile thick."

"If we could get at the source of their antipathy—the very source of—"

"After all your years," said Li-Hsing sadly, "you are still trying to reason out the human being. Poor Andrew, don't be angry, but it's the robot in you that drives you in that direction."

"I don't know," said Andrew. "If I could bring myself—"

1. (reprise)

If he could bring himself—

He had known for a long time it might come to that, and in the end he was at the surgeon's. He found one, skillful enough for the job at hand, which meant a robot surgeon, for no human surgeon could be trusted in this connection, either in ability or in intention.

The surgeon could not have performed the operation on a human being, so Andrew, after putting off the moment of decision with a sad line of questioning that reflected the turmoil within himself, put the First Law to one side by saying, "I, too, am a robot."

He then said, as firmly as he had learned to form the words even at human beings over these past decades, "I *order* you to carry through the operation on me."

In the absence of the First Law, an order so firmly given from one who looked so much like a man activated the Second Law sufficiently to carry the day.

21.

Andrew's feeling of weakness was, he was sure, quite imaginary. He had recovered from the operation. Nevertheless, he leaned, as unobtrusively as he could manage, against the wall. It would be entirely too revealing to sit.

Li-Hsing said, "The final vote will come this week, Andrew. I've been able to delay it no longer, and we must lose. . . . And that will be it, Andrew."

Andrew said, "I am grateful for your skill at delay. It gave me the time I needed, and I took the gamble I had to."

"What gamble is this?" asked Li-Hsing with open concern.

"I couldn't tell you, or the people at Feingold and Charney. I was sure I would be stopped. See here, if it is the brain that is at issue, isn't the greatest difference of all the matter of immortality? Who really cares what a brain looks like or is built of or how it was formed? What matters is that brain cells die; *must* die. Even if every other organ in the body is maintained or replaced, the brain cells, which cannot be replaced without changing and therefore killing the personality, must eventually die.

"My own positronic pathways have lasted nearly two centuries without perceptible change and can last for centuries more. Isn't *that* the fundamental barrier? Human beings can tolerate an immortal robot, for it doesn't matter how long a machine lasts. They cannot tolerate an immortal human being, since their own mortality is endurable only so long as it is universal. And for that reason they won't make me a human being."

Li-Hsing said, "What is it you're leading up to, Andrew?"

"I have removed that problem. Decades ago, my positronic brain was connected to organic nerves. Now, one last operation has arranged that connection in such a way that slowly—quite slowly—the potential is being drained from my pathways."

Li-Hsing's finely wrinkled face showed no expression for a moment. Then her lips tightened. "Do you mean you've arranged to die, Andrew? You can't have. That violates the Third Law."

"No," said Andrew, "I have chosen between the death of my body and the death of my aspirations and desires. To have let my body live at the cost of the greater death is what would have violated the Third Law."

Li-Hsing seized his arm as though she were about to shake him. She stopped herself. "Andrew, it won't work. Change it back."

"It can't be. Too much damage was done. I have a year to live—more or less. I will last through the two hundredth anniversary of my construction. I was weak enough to arrange that."

"How can it be worth it? Andrew, you're a fool."

"If it brings me humanity, that will be worth it. If it doesn't, it will bring an end to striving and that will be worth it, too."

And Li-Hsing did something that astonished herself. Quietly, she began to weep.

22.

It was odd how that last deed caught at the imagination of the world. All that Andrew had done before had not swayed them. But he had finally accepted even death to be human and the sacrifice was too great to be rejected.

The final ceremony was timed, quite deliberately, for the two hundredth anniversary. The World President was to sign the act and make it law and the ceremony would be visible on a global network and would be beamed to the Lunar state and even to the Martian colony.

Andrew was in a wheelchair. He could still walk, but only shakily.

With mankind watching, the World President said, "Fifty years ago, you were declared a Sesquicentennial Robot, Andrew." After a pause, and in a more solemn tone, he said, "Today we declare you a Bicentennial Man, Mr. Martin."

And Andrew, smiling, held out his hand to shake that of the President.

23.

Andrew's thoughts were slowly fading as he lay in bed.

Desperately he seized at them. Man! He was a man! He wanted that to be his last thought. He wanted to dissolve—die—with that.

He opened his eyes one more time and for one last time recognized Li-Hsing waiting solemnly. There were others, but those were only shadows, unrecognizable shadows. Only Li-Hsing stood out against the deepening gray. Slowly, inchingly, he held out his hand to her and very dimly and faintly felt her take it.

She was fading in his eyes, as the last of his thoughts trickled away.

But before she faded completely, one last fugitive thought came to him and rested for a moment on his mind before everything stopped.

"Little Miss," he whispered, too low to be heard.

A Last Word

To those of you who have read some (or, possibly, all) of
my robot stories before, I welcome your loyalty and patience. To those of you who have not, I hope this book has
given you pleasure—and I'm pleased to have met you—and
I hope we meet again soon.